T0366732

The World Walker

The World Walker

M. W. Albeer

Winchester, UK
Washington, USA

First published by Roundfire Books, 2014
Roundfire Books is an imprint of John Hunt Publishing Ltd., Laurel House, Station Approach,
Alresford, Hants, SO24 9JH, UK
office1@jhpbooks.net
www.johnhuntpublishing.com
www.roundfire-books.com

For distributor details and how to order please visit the 'Ordering' section on our website.

Text copyright: M. W. Albeer 2013

ISBN: 978 1 78279 490 5

A CIP catalogue record for this book is available from the British Library.

Design: Stuart Davies

Printed and bound by CPI Group (UK) Ltd, Croydon, CR0 4YY

We operate a distinctive and ethical publishing philosophy in all
areas of our business, from our global network of authors to
production and worldwide distribution.

Open

"I want to explain something to you...

You wanted to know the reason why people anger in the world in which you live?

Your world is time-constrained. It evolves slowly. If respected, that can be the most wondrous thing in all existence.

But in your world, you cannot let go of your past. It is ingrained into you, in every cell of your physical body, just waiting for a trigger, a trigger that will unleash the unbelievable.

And the unbelievable is that there are many flavours of reality, many truths. Some of those are hard to acknowledge.

Even though we started this, it is your past that holds you back, that in which we all played a part..."

Prologue

It was a dream so familiar.

She saw a dim light in the distance, fading in and out.

The endless struggle was before her, a cycle of birth and death; a reminder of the past, the present and the future.

All around were other lights that felt closer, like guiding blobs of luminosity, impossible to focus on. Then she was flying past speeding stars, across jewelled galaxies and silent emptiness until she reached it.

Before her was a nauseating void of nothingness, sucking everything in, an eye of noir, relentless and unstoppable. It tugged on her naval as if it might turn her inside out.

She heard a voice, a magical voice.

"It grows stronger…"

The pull was powerful, like a parent pulling a child by the arm. The pressure irresistible, the control overpowering. She could not escape and yet the feeling was consoling. She was floating home.

The voice spoke again.

"You choose…

Walk to freedom…

Realise that you are looking into a mirror…

Otherwise be swallowed… "

As she stared at the darkness consuming all the light around, she felt primordial panic, as if she was trying to escape, trying to fight against the unstoppable force.

Then she heard another voice speak to her. It sounded like her father. She hadn't heard that voice for so long.

"There is no reason to fight it, Elera. It is part of you."

The void was waiting. Its pull had ceased.

Then she was inside the eye of nothingness. She had dispersed, absorbed by a power beyond the world she knew. The blobs of glowing awareness returned, surrounding her, tenderly cushioning her.

The darkness faded to light and she opened her eyes.

She was on her bed and someone was beside her. She couldn't think. She still felt disparate, as if she had dissolved into the essence of the world. She could not get her bearings.

Tears began to stream, down her soft cheeks to her ears. She wept silently, unable to fathom why. The cleansing sunlight bathed her face from a window in front of her, drying her eyes. Thoughts began to spring into her mind.

A new day had arrived and with it a gripping revelation. She could no longer determine what was real and what was not, what was the past and what was the present. That uncertainty of reality had freed her somehow. Her tears were those of freedom. The unknown was now her dear friend.

The voice of her father still echoed in her ears. She stood up and walked over to the window, opening the curtains and looking out on a tranquil scene of mountains and forestland. Her body felt shaken, as if she had just travelled a long distance. She could not focus.

Then she saw something, bouncing energetically through the copse below. It was glowing, trying to get her attention. Still she struggled to focus. She saw eyes that sparkled like the stars. She felt an overpowering wave through her head. She closed her eyes.

When she opened them again, she sat up in her bed. The room was more solid. There was nobody lying next to her. Her recent memories were fading away and she stood up.

Seeing that the curtains were closed, she walked over and opened them with a hazy feeling of déjà vu. Looking out on the untouched landscape, there was no movement. The sun was shining brightly and warmed her from the inside out, the complete opposite of the dark void she had witnessed in her dream.

She looked back at her empty bed and feelings of love flooded her. She had felt him lying there next to her but she knew he was far away.

As the warming rays fell on her skin and energised her heart, she wondered if the journey she was now bound to would lead him back to her.

Chapter 1 – Universal Language

3 months later

Rekesh walked slowly through one of Ciafra's largest deserts, covering his face with a long sheet wrapped around his head. His black hair poked out through the folds, snakelike and matted.

He was determined to get to *Giza* as soon as possible, an ambition that had left him torn.

After taking an abandoned patrol boat from *Bimini*, he had reached the northern coast of Ciafra within a week. He had then ridden across the continent on horseback for three days, but he was forced to abandon his horse when it suffered from lameness due to the incorrigible terrain.

Rekesh was now on foot, somewhere in the northeastern region. He knew only to head due east to reach the Giza plateau where the ancient pyramids stood.

He kept telling himself that Elera was okay, that somehow she knew how to survive in the depths of a labyrinth that was now sealed. He fought to keep back the dreadful feeling that he would never see her again by walking faster and harder.

The hot, yellow-white sun was beating down intensely on the sand making it difficult to walk, even with thick leather-soled footwear. He decided to push past the pain and pangs of guilt that kept shooting up and down his belly.

He started to run across the desert, thinking about the moments of passion and love he had shared with Elera. Every tear he felt like shedding was turned into another determined step, and before he knew it he had been running for twenty minutes in the blazing sun. He then began to feel faint and stopped for breath.

"No, Rekesh," he spoke to himself. "There's no hope if you're dead."

He looked around for any kind of shelter and spotted a large cactus group in the distance. He quickly walked to the patch. Rekesh pulled a flask from the satchel he was carrying. It was running out of water. He drank half and rested a while behind the shade of the cactus patch.

He reflected on the moments before the pyramid entrance had collapsed. He had witnessed Elera passing through the tallest of stone doors. Then, the seabed had begun to shake.

"Elera!" Rekesh had cried out in horror as giant slabs began to slide away from the arched entryway. A flash of rumble and dust flying towards him crossed his eyes.

His memory flickered back to when he and Elera first met and the dreams they shared of exploring the world freely. They talked of sailing around the globe without fear of encountering a warship and riding without restraint across a nation on horseback.

"I want to see everything before I die," Elera had once told him. "This planet is so beautiful, I cannot think of anything better than to see as much of it as possible together."

An overwhelming wave of emotion started to well in Rekesh's heart and he decided to push on, the unbearable thought that he would never see her again wavering in and out of his mind. Ahead he could see a mountain range looming in the distance.

A slight feeling of relief swept over him, as he knew that he would reach Giza more quickly if he stayed cool. The landscape of Ciafra that he had seen so far was largely barren, with only a handful of villages clustered around the coastal perimeter.

As he walked across the remainder of the desert, he spotted a small shrew with a long nose walking alongside him. The shrew seemed to be foraging for insects but after a while of fast-paced walking, Rekesh noticed that it was still close by. Its passing companionship made Rekesh feel inherently calmer and he found himself naturally focusing on his present whereabouts and understanding that life had its plan, just as Elera always persisted. He pushed on with determination.

After a few hours, he was walking into the shade of the natural giants. They looked like giant sloping slabs as the sunlight struck their streamlined crevices.

They seemed alive somehow.

As the dry sun began to disappear behind the highest peak, Rekesh started to see smoke in the distance coming from a small forested area. He began to speed up, heading in the direction of the smoke. When he reached the edge of the forest, he could make out a small clearing and a smouldering fire through the trees. He ran to the clearing and found an elderly man, wearing a cloth wrapped around his head and loose cotton clothing. There was something unusual about the man, almost as if he were emitting a soft light.

The man glanced over at Rekesh and then signalled for him to join him on a large tree stump. Rekesh sat down next to him, a little out of breath and the man reached over with a metal beaker filled with water. Rekesh took it and nodded in appreciation, taking a large sip.

"Where are you travelling to?" the elderly man asked, turning a skinned rabbit that was spit-roasting over the fire. The sight of it somehow shocked Rekesh.

"I am heading to Giza," he answered. "How long does it take to cross this mountain range?"

"The mountains are days of travelling on foot," the man declared. "However, these mountains have many secrets." He smiled at Rekesh in a most peculiar but warm way. "I am Casar," he declared. "Do you have a name, young traveller?"

The way Casar said *young traveller* seemed to imply to Rekesh that it meant more than a simple description. He immediately felt the man knew a lot about him.

"Rekesh," he answered abruptly. "I need to get to Giza as quickly as possible. I travelled by boat to Anca Casa, but was stopped by some patrollers and they took all my belongings. Luckily, I found a horse trader but I set the horse free this morning." He paused. "I have been walking since."

Casar scratched his wiry white beard. "After this range, there is a small village where I come from. I have a horse there that you can ride. I know that you are in a most urgent situation."

3

Casar's words seemed ominous and Rekesh could not disagree with them.

"My horse should get you to Giza within a few days from the village," the old man added. "She is no ordinary mare. She has the wind inside her."

Rekesh's face seemed to lighten. "That would be a great help."

"So why are you in such a hurry, Rekesh?" Casar asked, somehow humouring him.

"You are right. I am in an urgent situation where the one person I care about more than anything is in great danger."

"Sounds serious," Casar said in an attentive manner. "So *you* are in great danger?"

The question took Rekesh aback. "No," he said solemnly with a tone of annoyance, not sure if he had understood Casar's question. "I have to get back to the Bimini Islands. But before I can I need the help of someone in Giza."

"You were in Bimini?" Casar asked with astonishment. "You don't look like a *Raiceman*."

"Hey," Rekesh said quite defensively. "How do you know what a Raiceman looks like anyway?" The annoyance had sprung to his chest all of a sudden. "And another thing, why do you think that I consider myself to be in great danger? I said it was someone I care about."

"I mean no offence," Casar said. "It is very hard these days to understand what people mean, don't you agree?"

Rekesh nodded and began to feel a little calmer.

"I am from Vassini originally," Rekesh admitted. "But I do live in Raicema most of the time."

Casar passed a wild strawberry to Rekesh and it immediately gave him a boost of cleansing energy as he ate.

"Thank you," he said. "So, if you live on the other side of this mountain, why are you here?"

"I stay here for some days at a time when I need to think and contemplate. The planet is changing so quickly, and coming here

4

reminds me that the planet is part of all of us."

Rekesh leant forward, listening with interest.

"The continent is shrinking, yet the deserts get bigger every year and have fiercer storms. Only a few hundred years ago, there were many cities on this continent that are now buried beneath the sand. I have also *seen* that storms are fiercer in the ocean. Have you seen this?"

"Yes," Rekesh answered. "When I travel, I encounter many a storm that never seems to subside."

"That is because with so much unnatural technology draining the energy of the planet, imbalances occur. The planet is becoming unstable."

Rekesh felt a pang of annoyance at the old man's warning, mainly due to his anxiety over Elera. It passed. "Well, it seems like there's not much out here. No vehicles or anything. Not even an old train line."

"Indeed, things are quite extreme. Either you find nothing or you find everything. It is almost like the tale of Lemuria, the way things have become."

"Casar, have you heard of Lemuria?" Rekesh said with surprise. His astonishment was not only at Casar's awareness of the concept but also at the striking coincidence that he should mention it now. It was because of Lemuria that Rekesh was trekking through Ciafra.

Casar nodded. "It is an old legend, maybe as old as Ciafra itself."

It was a legend that had led Rekesh to places that he did not want to go, to see things that he did not want to see.

"The land of Lemuria was supposed to have held some of the most advanced life-forms this planet has ever given home to," Casar said. "The legend has told of a nation where people had a great understanding of this planet and the universe, far more advanced than the lands that surrounded it. Of course, the idea of Lemuria could just be an ideal told to give people something to strive for. What do you think?"

Rekesh did not reply.

Casar removed the now-roasted rabbit from the fire. "It is difficult out here not to eat meat. People have gotten so used to it. Even I find it difficult, and I spend so much time here in the forest."

He cut some with a long knife and passed it to Rekesh. Both were silent for a while whilst they ate. The sun was starting to set and the firelight began to illuminate the clearing.

The meat made Rekesh feel full quickly.

"Elera, my partner, is trapped in Bimini," Rekesh confessed, clearly needing to relieve himself of the constant worry. "She believed we could find the location of Lemuria there."

Casar looked both fascinated and concerned. He had the most serious of expressions on his wrinkled face. "Many have pursued the dream of Lemuria and its magical promises. What drives her in her search?"

"She loves this planet. She thought that if she could find Lemuria, peace would somehow fall over all those who seek war. It seems that many believe the opposite but I think she is right. Also, she's a historian, so she likes to find things from the past and preserve them."

"So the soldiers have her? Is that why she is trapped?" Casar asked.

"No," Rekesh said, "actually she's trapped in a ruin."

At that statement, Casar let out a deep and mighty bellow of a laugh.

Rekesh felt a pang of anger. "It's not funny!" he tried to say seriously, but he couldn't quite.

Casar smiled. "She sounds like a very courageous woman. I am sure many things are there to protect her, in this ruin."

There was silence for a while as the sound of birds getting ready to hide in their high-up nests chirped through the air. Dusk was falling.

"Forgive me, I don't mean to sound insensitive to your dilemma, but from my perspective, the way I am communicating is particularly appropriate."

"Why?"

Casar leaned forward, his dazzling yellow eyes coming into full view. His bushy white hair poked out from his scarf. "You will see her again," he said seriously, almost echoing what Rekesh was thinking in his own mind.

Both men sat silently for several moments, chewing the meat slowly. Rekesh began to feel a little silly at his anxiety. He smiled at the old man who was looking at him softly.

"Why don't you sleep here tonight? I have a spare blanket you can use and there are some branches over there that you can make a bed out of. Tomorrow I will travel with you to my village. There is a faster way to get there than walking."

Rekesh nodded with a weak smile. He felt so tired that what Casar was suggesting seemed like the only option even though he wanted to know more. Within five minutes of building and preparing the bed, Rekesh had fallen into a deep sleep as the stars became visible through the trees above.

☼

As the early sun speckled through the sheltering leaves of tall Acacia trees, Rekesh awoke to see that Casar had already packed up the small camp. Casar was in the motion of stuffing a small sack with nuts and berries that he had gathered. "Ah, you are awake, *young traveller*!" he exclaimed as Rekesh began to get to his feet. "You were in a deep sleep. I assume you didn't dream of anything?"

"If I did, I cannot remember," Rekesh replied.

"Try to remove yourself from worry. It can only hold you back," Casar advised.

Rekesh nodded but knew it would be difficult. He quickly gathered his things.

"You mentioned a quicker way to get to your village?" he reminded Casar.

"Yes, there may be a way but we must find an open space and we need to fashion some strong rope. A few miles ahead there is an open clearing. Maybe we will find rope along the way."

Rekesh nodded and they started to walk quickly. A short while ahead, Rekesh noticed long vines hanging from tall trees.

"That's unusual," Casar remarked. "These vines are not from this forest, but they are strong enough for our need. Most fortunate."

Rekesh was about to ask what they would be needed for when Casar quickly climbed the tree and retrieved the vines. Rekesh couldn't believe the old man's agility.

"Now we have rope, we can start the *calling*!" Casar exclaimed with enthusiasm.

"The calling?"

"In this mountain range lives a very strong animal. Not many people know about it but it will help us get to the edge of the range if we call it."

"How do we do that?" Rekesh asked.

"With our minds," Casar said, pointing to his head, the pupils of his eyes widening.

Rekesh was not surprised by what Casar was implying. He had known many shamans in Vassini who had all attested to the fact that such feats of the mind were possible, though he had never witnessed such acts himself.

Rekesh grew excited at the possibility that such a feat could be true and that he might see it happen. The two men walked for less than an hour up a steep slope until they reached a large clearing. Immediately, Casar sat in the middle of the clearing and crossed his legs. He pulled some dried sage and other herbs from his sack and lit them on the rocky floor.

"Okay, before we begin, I need to make sure you are aware of something. You see, if you do not believe what I am about to tell you then the calling will not work."

Rekesh just nodded, not sure what to expect.

"Yesterday we talked, and you misunderstood me a few times, correct?"

"I guess," Rekesh said in response.

"Well if you believe what I am now going to tell you, this will never be a problem again okay?"

Rekesh suddenly felt a lot of affection towards the old man, like he knew at that moment he was genuinely trying to help him.

"Besides communicating with our voices, there is an energy that you can feel directly that tells you exactly what a person means," Casar said. "And not only a person, but an animal of any sort or even a plant."

Rekesh was not sure he believed what Casar was telling him.

"You feel it in your throat. It is there and you have always known it."

Suddenly Rekesh did feel like he was particularly aware of his throat area. It felt like it was wavering, like something was trying to connect to it.

"This area of your body is particularly sensitive to messages from beings in this universe. One way to really open up this energetic channel is to sing. Singing is the universal language."

Rekesh could not disagree with what Casar was saying.

"Now listen carefully for I am going to call the creature." He adjusted himself. "Sit as I do," he told Rekesh. "I am going to describe the animal. When I do, visualise what I am describing in your mind and breathe in the atmosphere. Imagine your voice is calling out to the creature."

Rekesh sat down and couldn't help letting a feeling of scepticism take over him. But, he was willing to try if it meant speeding up his journey to Giza.

"Imagine a beautiful falcon with black and white feathers, a gold stripe running down its forehead to its beak. This falcon is as large as a lion and as calm as the mountains. When she flies, she appears as if from nowhere, silent, a great hunter."

Rekesh concentrated hard and breathed deeply. With every breath he could feel himself becoming elated, more positive, and suddenly a clear image came to mind of the great falcon. His throat was throbbing, pulsating and he wanted to open his eyes to see. Casar started to sing softly. It was a melodic chant in a language Rekesh could not understand.

"Her eyes are bright, yellow and piercing. She soars with the wind," Casar sung, hovering his hands over the smouldering pile of herbs.

Rekesh opened his eyes and saw Casar swaying his hands in a circular fashion, almost like he was trying to mould something. Rekesh saw a flash of the falcon's eye in his mind.

"Now call her!"

Rekesh felt a sound come out of his and Casar's throats, almost involuntarily. It was a deep hum. A moment later they both heard an almighty screech from somewhere in the distance.

"Good!" Casar said. "She will soon be here."

A pang of fear suddenly struck Rekesh, but he shrugged it off and excitement quickly filled him. Within minutes the sight of the giant falcon had taken him aback.

The golden feathers of her brow illuminated her yellow eyes. The falcon was enormous, almost the same size as a horse. Casar was still singing his chant to her, dancing in a wave-like motion.

The falcon slowly descended from the sky to the clearing, and as she did Casar quickly piled berries and nuts onto the floor from his sack. She landed gracefully and gazed carefully at Rekesh and Casa, but then began to eat the food that Casar had laid out.

"Slowly walk to her left side," Casar instructed Rekesh, whilst walking to her right. He threw one end of the vine rope to Rekesh so it was draping over her back. Casar crawled underneath and tied the rope several times. Rekesh was astonished that the falcon allowed Casar to do this. The great creature seemed to be allowing herself to be harnessed, in fact, she seemed most comfortable with him.

"Hold on tightly to the rope until we are in the air, then wrap the rope around her claw so you don't swing wildly."

Before Rekesh could fully contemplate what was about to happen, the falcon flapped her giant wings and lifted off with ease, sending Casar and Rekesh swaying intensely on the ends of the rope.

Casar slowly climbed up with dexterity and wrapped the length of the rope gently around her claw and the end around his own foot, making a foothold. Rekesh found Casar's sense of balance hard to believe. He followed Casar's lead and saw that the falcon had already flown high above the highest mountain peak.

It was hard to breathe so high up. She flew elegantly over several forests, tall mountains and smaller hills. The view was breathtaking and for the time Rekesh was flying through the air he forgot that he was a human and saw the world through the eyes of a bird.

Then, the falcon started to descend. She was heading for a large forest clearing. As she leaned back to land, Rekesh lost his footing and began to swing wildly again. The great bird landed gently, fully aware of the presence of the two men, allowing Rekesh to fall softly as he could no longer hold the vine.

"At the end of this forest is my village!" Casar announced as he untied himself. He slid the rope over the giant bird's silky black feathers and stroked them for a while. She seemed to return his affection. He looked at her and gestured his gratitude.

She looked forward and then quickly flew off.

"I can't believe what just happened!" Rekesh said, a new energy flowing through him as he looked up at the creature in the sky. "And she was so tame."

"Come," Casar urged. "There is still a day for you to travel by horse to reach Giza."

Rekesh felt warmed by the man's concern over his situation and they both pushed on through the forest. Within half an hour they had arrived at a bustling village, with traders selling wheat, rice and dried meats.

"My dwelling isn't far from here," Casar said, navigating his way through the crowds.

Rekesh noticed militants on the roofs of some of the stone buildings with scarves wrapped around their faces. They were carrying guns and other sharp weapons.

Both men turned down a small alley with only a few market stalls. Next to a small wooden table with a man selling scrap metal was a polished wooden door. Casar nodded to the man behind the table and he opened the door with a key.

Inside, the place was filled with metallic gadgets and contraptions. Rekesh quickly deduced that Casar was some sort of astronomer from the large telescope sitting at the back of the room. To the left was an old barn door and the sound of horses shuffling could be heard from the other side. There were wall-hangings scattered around the room, all with strange symbols on them, some of simple geometric shapes and others with complicated patterns of stars and circles.

"Before you set off," Casar said, "I want to show you something." He went to the back of the room where there were stacks of scrolls piled up on each other. He picked up one off the top and spread it across a large table. "When I am here, I observe the stars at night," he told Rekesh, who now saw that the scroll was actually a plot of the stars. "I have observed something that is very unusual. Here…" Casar pointed to a position within the solar system that was illustrated on the map. "…This entity appears from time to time but it is not a star. It does not follow an orbit either. Take this map to Giza. It is very much connected to the journey that you are on."

Rekesh was puzzled but agreed and put the rolled-up map in a satchel.

"This entity has got closer to this planet each time I have observed it," Casar added. "It is a warning."

Then he leaned in close to Rekesh in a manner that made him feel slightly uncomfortable. He whispered to Rekesh.

"That scroll is the future," he said quite ominously. "We can change the future. It is in our hands."

Rekesh did not know what to say, so he looked around Casar's dwelling instead, unsure if he was crazy. His face seemed to be emitting the same strange light as when he had first seen him in the forest.

"What do all these symbols mean?" Rekesh asked, pointing to the wall-hangings. For a split second Casar's eyes looked like they were glowing.

"Remember I was telling you about communicating using the energy of your throat?" Casar said in response. "The way we used to call the eagle of the mountain?"

Rekesh nodded but was still in some disbelief about how that entire event had taken place.

"Well, these symbols are another universal way of communicating. Not everyone understands these symbols at face value, but deep down, we all understand what they mean. Some of these symbols are the oldest form of written language in the world and are still used today even though most people don't even realise that they mean anything significant."

Rekesh was intrigued by the concept but was eager to start travelling.

"The stars too," Casar said. "The skies speak to us."

Rekesh nodded and thanked Casar for his help. He was then led through the old door where two stallions and a mare were feeding.

"Take care of her," Casar said, patting the horse on the right.

"I will," Rekesh vowed.

"She has won races in the past," he announced, obviously proud. "Make sure she goes to a good home."

Rekesh nodded with reassurance to Casar, eager to depart. "Just one question before I go – who were those masked men on the rooftops?"

"They are spies for Raicema," he told Rekesh. "They work for the ruler of the city where your boat was taken, King Rufi of *Anca Casa*, but Rufi works for the Raiceman government."

Rekesh nodded and mounted the horse.

"Head out of this back lane and you will reach the desert. Take this…" he handed Rekesh a small compass, "…and head due east. You will reach the Giza plateau before you know it."

"Thank you for everything," he said, holding Casar's arm with gratitude. He could not quite believe that he had met such a knowledgeable and helpful individual. He held on to the horse's leather saddle and sprung over its strong, arched back.

"Her name is Firefly," Casar told Rekesh, patting his strong friend on the neck one more time.

Rekesh nodded and cantered off along the dusty path, his focus on one thing only. He was determined to reach Giza as soon as possible.

Chapter 2 – A Day in Seho

The village of *Seho*, situated on the eastern coast of the continent of *Ciafra*, was a rural community that survived in segregation from the rest of the world.

Isolated in a secluded bay, it was rare that an outsider set foot on the hot sands of the small fishing village. With only a handful of cities remaining on the shrinking continent of Ciafra, most of the land was desert. Where vegetation did still thrive, a remote village would exist there. Trees and bushes still grew in Seho, however the people of the village looked increasingly to the sea to supply them with the nourishment they needed.

On one particular morning, a village elder by the name of Javu was telling the younger villagers of Seho about the concept of *summoning* before their first school lesson. The children were sitting on an open grassed area, surrounded by dusty fields.

"I'm sure that as you all go about your lives you notice the things around you," Javu was saying. "Every day we see animals, shrubs and trees, rocks and the sand around us, the ocean and the sky."

Some of the children looked up into the bright blue sky.

"Everything you see has its place in a natural and constantly changing universe of energy. There is also energy in many things that we cannot see." Javu gazed around as if looking at things that were invisible to everyone else. "We can call upon this energy to help us in situations that we find ourselves in every day. I call this ability *summoning*."

The twenty or so young children were all sat in a circle, looking up with interest at the leathery-skinned old man, his long grey beard crisping in the hot sun.

"And it is not only humans that have been endowed with this skill. Every living being on the planet, including the planet itself, summons energy in one way or another."

"Can you show us how to summon?" one boy asked, his eyes lit up with excitement.

"You already know how," Javu told the children. "Whenever we talk or move, we are summoning energy. We are not always aware that we are doing so because we talk and move so often. But when you become aware of how you affect the world around you in terms of the energy you summon, you can achieve unbelievable things!"

Every child's eyes were fully open, excited by the notion.

"Show us, Javu!" many of them said melodically in unison.

"Well, I will have to concentrate to show you an example. It will only be simple though and something you could all easily do yourselves."

He smiled at the group of children mischievously. Standing up straight, he outstretched both of his arms with his palms facing up. He closed his eyes and began to breathe deeply and quietly. The children looked on with expectancy. There was silence for many moments.

Then, two small insects that had been buzzing around in the air began to fly around Javu's head. Javu continued to breathe in slowly and methodically, which seemed to affect both flies overhead. The heat was starting to make Javu's body radiate.

Then, with a shimmered buzz, the insects separated and landed peacefully on each of his palms. It looked like they were both cleaning themselves. The children all let out a sigh of amazement, mouths half open.

Javu opened his eyes and the insects flew away.

"I summoned energy to connect with those two insects. Through that energy I created a bond with them."

Some of the children were smiling at what they had seen.

"Of course, few people have managed to understand that summoning is not a form of evil magic. Far from it, to summon is but a simple gift that all human beings, indeed all beings, have been given."

Everyone could hear the soothing sound of waves crashing into sea in the distance.

"An agreement!" Javu exclaimed, cupping his hand around his

ear.

The heat seemed to be rising with every minute that passed, like a fire that had just started burning properly.

"In the big cities, people summon and use a tremendous amount of energy, yet they are often the most oblivious to that energy. Even though it surrounds them constantly, if someone like me told them about it, it is likely that they would laugh at me and think I was crazy. *Why* do you think someone would react like that?"

"Because they are scared?" a young girl suggested.

"Yes, exactly," Javu replied. "People can get afraid of what they do not understand. Though we are all children of the earth, of this planet, there can be great differences in the ways that we learn about it as we grow up. Some see this planet as food alone. I see it as my mother."

The children all smiled.

"It is unfortunate that some people do not learn from those who have come before them. And sometimes, it is unfortunate that some people do…" Javu's thoughts trailed off to his own concerns in life, of the suppression and greed that he had witnessed through his lifetime. "In *Raicema*, the leaders there have not learnt at all from the mistakes of the past and continue to take as much as they can from the planet."

Again, Javu's thoughts trailed off.

"Here in Ciafra and in many other places on the earth, our ancestors left us many valuable pieces of knowledge," he said after a while. "They were brave in the face of danger."

"Ancestors?" A stocky boy asked. "Like my grandmother?"

"Well, I'm sure your grandmother can teach you many good things, Gunhe, but I am talking about our ancestors from many generations ago," Javu said, smiling to himself at the thought of the boy's grandmother. Indeed, she was the best cook in the village and Javu was sure she could teach him a few delicious things.

"Our ancestors' wisdom has been passed down in many ways over time. They wanted us to know how important every single person, animal, insect, plant and rock really is."

One girl picked up a pebble from the floor and began to observe it in an adorably curious fashion.

"No matter where we are originally born, the ancestors I am talking about are the same. We all have a common root."

Some of the children looked slightly confused at how this could be so.

"The *forgotten teachings* would have begun from a very young age in the past," Javu continued. He gestured towards a small girl listening intently. "You, Nehne, would begin to learn about *dreams* at your age. You and your friends would try to understand what your dreams try to tell you when you go to sleep. And learning about dreams would help you understand how special and wondrous life really is."

Javu sat on a tree stump and wiped his brow with a cloth. The hot sun was shining down brightly. He had every child's full attention now.

"Our ancestors were often nomadic, travelling across the lands and settling on sacred sites on the earth. Many of these sites were chosen because of that which I have just been talking about – energy!"

"Like where?" One child asked.

"Well..." Javu began, "...many places in Ciafra for a start. There is an incredible river that runs down through the east. All along there you will find old buildings, placed there because of *energy*." He paused, deciding whether to continue. "Another place...is a land which is now sunken, deep down in the depths of the ocean. It is a place bigger than the entirety of Ciafra!"

A young boy interrupted. "Which place are you talking about, Javu?"

Javu smiled, aware that he was getting ahead of himself. His enthusiasm often did this to him. "There was once a very old land whose peoples were capable of phenomenal feats. The land on which they lived disappeared," he explained, his eyes wide with mystery.

"But many of the inhabitants moved to other lands and created other civilisations. That was a long time ago."

Javu paused while the young villagers drank water from their flasks. The young boy once again looked confused, although the other children seemed fascinated.

"Javu, I don't understand. Was the old place near to Ciafra? Is that why those people are our ancestors?"

The boy's question made Javu realise that he didn't actually know the answer. He had been intrigued by the concept of the submerged continent ever since he had heard the folktales as a child, but he had no proof, no tangible way of explaining it to the children.

Luckily, he was spared having to explain that nobody really had proof about the mythical continent. The boy's attention was suddenly averted.

In the distance came the sound of a ship's horn, the distinct hum of the village's fishing ship, the *Juniper*. The ship had been used to bring food into the village for as long as anybody could remember. The land surrounding Seho was becoming dryer with every year that passed, increasing the villagers' dependency on the ocean as the main source of food.

Nehne jumped up from her cross-legged position.

"The *Juniper* is back! How long will it take to get here, Javu?" Nehne started to jump up and down excitedly.

"It should be back in an hour or so, Nehne. I'm sure you will be happy to see your mother and father?"

Nehne nodded enthusiastically. "Yes. They always bring me a surprise from the ocean." She pulled a shiny oyster shell from her pocket and gave it to Javu. "Mama says that it has a pearl inside, and she will make a necklace with it when the shell opens."

Javu smiled and handed it back to her. "We should all go inside now. The sun will soon start to burn. Besides, it's time for your first school lesson."

The children and Javu started to walk from the open plane towards the sandy, dirt track that led to a group of shoreline huts.

Embedded securely in the beach was the village school. Javu and the children went inside. The school's walls were littered with maps of the earth and charts of the solar system. One wall was completely dedicated to pictures drawn by the children, of animals, the sea and several of the *Juniper* and village huts.

Javu stopped to look at a picture of a horse, painted by a girl who had now grown up and left the village. It touched a spot in his heart.

Lentu, the main village educator who was seated in a corner of the room, told the children to take their seats. He began to teach the children about Ciafran history, starting at where he had left off in a previous lesson.

Javu sat at the front of the room on an old redwood chair, his usual spot.

Lentu cleared his throat. "As we left off yesterday, only fifty years ago, the Raicemans took the people of Seho to the mainland of Ciafra and forced them to build roads and towns. They had to harvest food and work in the mines. The same thing happened to most villages along the east and northern coasts."

Most of the children seemed uninterested in the lesson about the past.

"In return for this difficult and laborious work, people were given nothing except protection." A slight tone of bitterness could be detected in Lentu's voice. "Can anyone tell me what the Raicemans told the Ciafran people that they needed protection from?"

"The Raicemans!" one boy called out, causing everyone to laugh.

"Not quite, Sele, but you are right," Lentu mused.

"From ourselves?" Nehne stood up and said enthusiastically.

"Yes, Nehne, excellent," Lentu said to his top student. "The Raicemans succeeded in convincing not only this village but countless others that their traditional ways of life were primitive and lazy. Many were promised better lives by working for the Raicemans and many did what they were told."

More children looked out of the windows with lack of interest.

"What that led to was a long war in this great nation. Those who

20

worked in the mines soon began to starve as the Raicemans began to send everything that was harvested back to Raicema. Ciafra can be a difficult place to live without food and water. It didn't take long for a rebellion to happen."

Lentu took a sip of water and referred to a map of Ciafra on the blackboard. He pointed out the area of the mines in the centre of the continent and Seho on the east coast.

"This village has been strong as have others. Many villages united and fought the Raicemans all over the mainland and drove those murderers away," Lentu said boldly. "That was the beginning of Ciafran independence and is the reason why there is now very little Raiceman military here in Ciafra. They did not count on this nation having so many fearless warriors."

Javu, sensing that some of the children were become anxious at Lentu's predisposition, spoke out to change the direction of the lesson. "Just as the seasons change, so does *power*. It is the insane few at the top who try to control people, which is the trait of any empire." Javu smiled at the children. "I am sure that there are many people in Raicema that do not agree with violence and stealing, so we should not look upon its entire people as murderers or thieves."

Lentu reflected and tugged at his growing beard, realising he had allowed his negative emotions to come through in his words. "Javu is right. No matter where you go, you find good and bad people."

He turned to Javu and began to converse, leaving the children to scribble and doodle on bits of paper. "I have heard that Raicema have opposition inside their own country from the *Makai*. Some are saying there may be a civil war..."

"Yes," Javu said stridently. "Raicema is a diverse place and was built by the hands of many people. When it comes to the struggle for power, it is never as simple as it seems..." The children were all busy talking or doodling. "But there are different ways to get a point across and some sects of the Makai are resorting to violence," Javu told Lentu. He was certainly the more knowledgeable of the two about the matter. He had travelled the globe throughout his life and seen the polarisation in attitude first hand.

"We should all consider if that is the right way to defend oneself. I myself believe in talking, not fighting. Why don't you teach the children about all the different places on the planet that the Makai exist, Lentu?"

Lentu nodded in agreement and tapped on his table to get the children's attention again. "The war here in Ciafra lasted sixteen years. One of the reasons that the war ended was because of a global uprising that still continues to this day. Most of the people that are part of this uprising would classify themselves as *'Makai'*."

Lentu began to teach the children about the different groups, organisations, communities and religious ceremonies that the word *Makai* represented. Javu knew Lentu would enjoy talking about this subject as he had grown up with many people who would categorise themselves as Makai.

"The one common belief in Makaism is that we should all have an equal say in the direction of our communities. Whilst there are still leaders, those leaders are acting on the will of the people," Lentu said.

"I don't think there has been a leadership throughout time that hasn't promised the same," Javu mused to himself.

The political topic certainly bored the children.

"Now, time for our mathematics lesson," Lentu said after he had finished talking about Makaism. "Today we will be talking about *currency*. Does anyone know what *currency* means?"

"Gold!" one boy shouted out, his eyes alight.

"Fish!" another child said in a high-pitched voice causing a few of the children to laugh.

"Yes, gold and fish are examples of a currency, especially for us here in Seho as we sometimes trade fish and gold with other villages in the surrounding area. So currency is simply that – something you can trade. For us, it is quite simple. We trade what we have for what we need. For example, melons don't grow very much in this region so when the *Juniper* goes fishing around the south-east coast, we trade fish for melons with some of the villages in that area." Lentu drew a melon and a fish on the blackboard and some arrows between them. "In Raicema, people don't trade physical things. People work for something called *creds*, which they can then use to get the food they need. People never see or touch these creds. In fact, to my understanding, they don't really exist in a physical form anywhere."

Most of the children seemed confused by the concept. Lentu continued talking about other types of currencies that existed throughout the world.

A short while later, a tall villager walked into the school and announced that the *Juniper* was landing.

The children ignored Lentu's narrative and headed out towards Seho's dusty beach to greet the fishers who had been away for five days.

The *Juniper* was a large ship made of redwood, vast in length, sleek and streamlined for fast movement through the water. At the head of the ship was a statue representing the ancient leader *Amentep*, the man that legend told had led tribes to build vast pyramidal temples to worship the stars thousands of years ago. With a gold pouch in one hand and a sceptre in the other, the statue had been a treasured talisman of the people of Seho. They believed it brought the village protection from Raicema and future empires and always provided good fortune in fishing. As the ship drew closer, Nehne, who was standing next to Javu, asked him about the statue.

"Was Amentep a fisher like my mama and papa?"

Javu smiled at the pretty child, her long dark hair tied into curled plats. "I'm not sure, Nehne. Before you were born, a large group of people who had travelled to the area to fight for the Makai lived here in this village. It was at the time Lentu was teaching us about, when many people worked in the mines. These brought with them the stories of Amentep. When the Raiceman army left, those people told the villagers that it was because Amentep was looking over the village, protecting it. A few of them actually carved that statue and so we put it on the ship to bring good luck."

"Is what those people said true, Javu?" Nehne asked him sincerely.

"There is truth in everything, Nehne."

The *Juniper* pulled ashore with grace and ease, sand spraying either side off the base as it cut the beach sharply. Immediately, the ladder slid down from the deck and Fera, Nehne's mother, was the first to descend.

The rest of the crew followed her.

"Nehne!" she said, kneeling down and hugging her daughter as she ran into her arms. Everyone gathered around and greeted each other.

Fera was a lean woman with long, tightly curled hair tied up in a bun. She wore hardy brown-cotton clothing and several necklaces made of pretty patterns of shells. She had long, slender muscles.

"Javu!" she exclaimed as she embraced him.

"Fera, it is good to see you. How was the expedition?"

"Something strange has happened near Raicema," she told Javu. "There are no patrol boats in the ocean or guards on the Bimini Islands." She looked at Javu with wide eyes.

"So you went all the way to Bimini? Quite a feat!"

"Javu, we got closer to Raicema than ever before," she said with intensity. "It was so strange. A week ago, we were out in the ocean and then we saw this boat just floating there. Then I couldn't believe my eyes! Rekesh was on that boat!"

"Rekesh?!" Javu said, most surprised.

"There were two others with him and they have come back with us."

Javu looked intrigued and glanced over at a young-looking man and woman walking towards him from the *Juniper*, led by Chief Hasu, who was dressed in a blue and green thick cotton outfit.

"Welcome back, Hasu," Javu greeted the short, rotund village leader who was waddling towards him.

Hasu looked pleased to see Javu. "My dear friend, it seems as though Bimini has been deserted by the Raicemans," he said, his bushy grey beard puffing up with the sea breeze. The man and woman behind Hasu were silent. "This is Sita and Rama. We met them near to the coast of Bimini. They were with Rekesh on an old ship. Most strange, most troubling..."

The couple looked like they were of Vassinian decent. Vassinia was Javu's homeland.

"He was distant, very cold," Hasu continued. "I questioned him but he ignored me. He only asked us to bring Sita and Rama here and then he sailed off. Neither of them has spoken a word for the entire time that we have been travelling back on the *Juniper*."

The couple held each other's arms in an affectionate way and were both smiling.

"I think that you might be able to communicate with them, Javu," Hasu said.

Javu nodded and suggested to Lentu that he take them to the school. He also asked some young villagers to gather some water-vegetables from the shore.

Fish was being unloaded from the *Juniper*, guided by Teltu, Nehne's father. Nehne, who was still hugging her mother, ran to her father as soon as she saw him. He kissed her and pulled a shiny blue-tinted crystal from his pocket, rough at one end and double-terminated at the other.

"I found this crystal near Bimini, Nehne. It was floating in the ocean. Take good care of it," he said affectionately to her as Fera came over.

"Don't forget to rinse it in salt water, Nehne, to keep it clean and pure," she advised her daughter.

"I won't forget, Mama," Nehne replied, looking carefully at the crystal. "It is beautiful, like water."

She walked with her parents towards Javu.

"No problems whilst we were away, Javu?" Teltu asked.

"Not one," he replied, looking at the large catch of fish being dragged to a small, decked area by six burly men. "You seem to have caught many more fish than usual, Teltu."

"The two from the Makai are the best fishers I have ever seen," Teltu responded humbly. "They hunt like sharks, sensing the presence of everything in the water. Also, there's plenty of fish near Bimini, much more than around here."

Javu nodded and left Teltu to his task with the other men.

All of the fish were being placed in barrels full of salt. Javu sat and watched for a while until Teltu was finished. Then he started to guide Teltu back to the village for a long chat.

As they walked away from the beach, a *Kivili* named Matree approached Javu carrying a bag of mixed fruit. He reached out his hairy arm and presented it to Javu.

"Thank you, Matree. Please take some to our visitors, Sita and Rama," he said slowly, pointing to the school in the distance. The short creature got the message and began to meander in that direction.

"Do you know that Kivilis are descendants of a former species of primate?" Javu told Teltu. "They are all over the planet. Though they are quite small they are very efficient in their environment. Most other larger primates are now dwindling in numbers all over the globe and the Kivili population continues to boom."

Teltu just nodded.

There were five Kivilis living in Seho, all belonging to the same family. Matree was the father of three children and had a life partner, Enee. Kivilis could understand basic instructions from humans and were thus often treated as pets and servants.

Javu waved at Matree in an affectionate manner.

"Though they don't speak, Kivilis communicate with each other through a form of sign language."

"I have noticed that," Teltu said.

Javu had known of Kivilis all his life and had seen them coexist with humans in a most symbiotic way.

"In many suppressive and wealthier parts of the world these creatures are often severely mistreated," Javu told Teltu. "It is a shame because they have remembered many things that we have long forgotten."

Before Teltu could respond, a small group of children came up to them.

"Come on, Matree, let's go together." A little girl ran up to him, holding his hairy hand and leading him away.

With the sun high in the sky, casting an intense heat over the village, Javu ushered Teltu into his hut to catch up about the last few weeks. They spoke for an hour and were eager to continue their conversation later that evening.

"Rekesh has changed, Javu," were the final words that Teltu spoke before he headed off to continue with his duties.

It was something that Javu already knew.

Chapter 3 – A Journey Begins

It had been a full day since the *Juniper* had returned to Seho. Every person in the village had spent the entire time since then preparing and preserving the food that had been hauled and gathered.

As was customary on the second day after the ship returned with its monthly load, the villagers began to prepare for a feast in celebration of the latest catch. This time, the feast was extra special, as it was also in honour of the two Makai warriors that had come to the village and helped with the haul.

The smell of roasted fish and freshly baked flatbread drifted in the air. Teltu was sitting with Javu in Chief Hasu's hut, where the feast was to take place. The two men had not spoken since Teltu's arrival the day before, since which time Teltu had mainly been swabbing the decks of the *Juniper* with cedar oil.

He was describing his brief meeting with Rekesh as they sipped tea on a cushioned bench made out of a fallen tree trunk.

"He was cold, Javu," Teltu sighed rubbing his sore arms. "Unlike everything that I have heard about him, he didn't speak or look at Fera or I. He only asked Hasu to take the young ones with us. Bimini was deserted. Fera was asking after Elera and he just ignored her, lost in a dream world. She was very upset for days afterwards."

"That's not like him," Javu said, frowning with concern. "He usually can't stop talking about Elera, that's why I never ask him anymore. Hurts the ear you know." He gave Teltu a cheeky smile, his beard covering his entire chest. His expression quickly turned back to one of concern. "I have no idea what he was doing out there. The last I heard, Rekesh was still living in Raicema City."

"How did you first meet him, Javu?" Teltu asked. "I have seen him a few times in the village but I never seem to get the chance to speak to him properly. I'm usually out on the *Juniper*."

"Rekesh and I were born in the same village in Vassini. Before I came to this village twenty years ago, I lived there and so did he. Of course, he was only a boy then. It was I who introduced him to Elera when he came to visit me here."

Just then Lentu entered the hut, followed by the young couple, Sita and Rama. They both wore brown-cotton outfits and the entirety of their possessions was contained within leather shoulder belts that had a number of large pouches woven into them. Each belt ran from their right shoulder diagonally across their chests.

Rama had short, wiry hair and wide brown eyes that skimmed the hut interestedly. They stood very close to each other and Sita seemed to have a constant smile on her face. She wore a long string of beads around her slender neck and had the most lacquered, shiny black hair that Javu had ever seen.

"Everybody, welcome Sita and Rama," Lentu announced to the hut. "They have had a long journey to Ciafra, and have worked hard ever since, so please don't stifle them."

He looked intently at the group of children in the corner, casting a warning to them.

"Also, they do not speak our language so use sign language or drawings to communicate with them."

Lentu led them to where Javu and Teltu were sitting.

"They speak *Hindi*," Javu stated. "I'll talk to them."

Javu asked Sita what she and Rama were doing in Bimini with Rekesh.

Sita spoke calmly and with detail to Javu.

"Mmm, it seems as though Bimini holds a road that goes under the ocean," Javu translated to Teltu.

"A road? Leading where?" Teltu asked.

Javu translated the question.

This time Rama spoke in a distressed fashion. Javu looked surprised at what he was told. The narrative went on for some time and Javu let out a large sigh of surprise as Rama finished talking.

"The road leads to an underwater pyramid!" Javu exclaimed. "Rekesh, Elera, Sita and Rama travelled underwater to the pyramid entrance. Elera entered and then the entrance collapsed. Rama says that there was so much dust that they couldn't see anything and they all had to resurface. Elera is still trapped down there for all he knows. Rama says Rekesh dove down over and over but couldn't find a way in. No wonder he was distraught."

"I had no idea that Elera was with him. I thought that she was still in Turo," Teltu said, frowning at the news. "Why didn't he tell us?"

"I have no idea, Teltu," Javu said. "Elera must still be inside the pyramid. It is a good thing that she knows so much about their structures. All that time studying and researching will come in useful now."

Teltu felt relieved that a worse fate did not seem to cross Javu's mind, yet a pit of anxiety had formed in his stomach.

Javu turned to the young Vassinian couple and asked them why they were searching for the underwater pyramid in the first place. They both replied that they did not know and that they were there to help Rekesh.

Sita asked Javu if he had known Rekesh long. Javu implied that he had known him since a child by lowering his hand to the floor. Sita smiled and said that she and Rama had not known him very long.

"I will have to tell Fera what has happened," Teltu said.

Javu nodded.

"Tomorrow, we should take a journey," Teltu suggested. "You, I, Sita and Rama should go back to Bimini and see if Elera is still there. I wish we had a faster ship, though."

Sita, seemingly sensing what Teltu was suggesting, leaned in towards Javu and began to tell him something.

"Giza," she said over and over in her narrative, the only word Teltu knew. After a while, Javu relayed what he had been told to Teltu.

"It seems as though Rekesh may be on his way to Giza as we speak."

"But why? Why would he travel all the way back to Ciafra when he knows Elera is trapped in Bimini?"

"That I don't know, Teltu."

The expression on Teltu's face turned to one of grave concern for his sister-in-law. Javu could tell he was dreading passing on the news to Fera.

"I believe Elera will be fine," Javu said in a reassuring fashion. "She has always been someone who knows what she is getting into."

"What can we do to help?" Teltu asked, chewing on a piece of flatbread.

"I know this sounds strange, but I think we should also go to Giza."

"Why?"

"Elera's teacher, Sorentius, is in Giza," Javu said to Teltu. "If anyone knows what's going on, it will be him."

"But what if Elera is in trouble?" Teltu argued. "I think we should head straight to Bimini."

"What good would we be if we don't understand how to help her? If she is still trapped down there, from what Sita and Rama have said, there is no direct way in. Sorentius will be able to help us, I am sure of it."

"Okay," Teltu agreed reluctantly. "Do you think Rekesh is going there to see Sorentius too?"

"Probably," Javu answered. "One thing that is for certain is that he will not rest until he knows Elera is safe. It may be that we will reach Giza before he leaves. I hope that is the case, for now is a time that I would very much like to see Rekesh."

Javu asked Sita and Rama if they felt strong enough for a journey across the continent, east to west. They instantly agreed without any questions.

Some teenage villagers began to bring around trays of food including many elaborate fish dishes from the *Juniper*'s latest expedition. Everyone in the village ate together that night and the feast was followed by several musical performances with drums, singing and flute-playing.

Afterwards, as everyone left Hasu's hut for their own late at night, the stars above seemed to twinkle with a strange uncertainty as if they might fade away at any moment.

Javu lay outside on a hammock for a while, just staring up into the cosmos.

Something is changing, he kept thinking to himself. *I can feel it in my belly.*

Then silence fell in his mind as he drifted into a slumber under the stars.

☼

The next day was bright and yet shrouded with fine clouds, a perfect day to begin a journey. Fera was trying to communicate with Sita on the beach, each of them drawing pictures with a stick.

"When Elera went into the pyramid..." she said, speaking slowly and drawing a triangle and stick woman in the sand, "...was she safe?"

Fera demonstrated walking into the pyramid with her fingers. Sita shook her head and drew a scribble on one side of the pyramid, indicating an explosion within the pyramid. She then held her hands up gesturing she was unsure of Elera's fate.

Fera sighed. Ever since Teltu had informed her of her sister's latest quest, she had been trying to get more information about what had happened.

The last she had heard of Elera had been three months earlier, when Elera had told her that she was travelling to Turo in southern Lizrab to meet with Kirichi and some people from the Makai sects on the continent. She had assumed she was still there. Now, she knew that her younger sister was involved in something much more dangerous than she first assumed.

Fera's thoughts went back to their childhood. Their mother and father had raised Fera and Elera in northeast Ciafra until Fera was ten and Elera was six years old. Both sisters had taken a great interest in the astronomical work of their parents, eager to learn from whomever they could about the planets, stars and moons in the solar system.

At that time, the Raiceman forces were still heavily occupying most of northern Ciafra, monitoring activity in Giza, draining local natural resources and exporting any valuable goods they could find. Many of the local people were helpless against this vast force and simply submitted to whatever fate that should befall them.

However, during Elera's fifth year, the Makai rebellion was extended to the north from southern Ciafra. Rebels flooded in, battling the Raiceman troops and encouraging the locals to defend themselves against the onslaught of murder and pillaging.

Fera and Elera's parents decided it was much too dangerous to be in high-profile astrological areas and travelled to Seho to leave the girls with their uncle in the safer fishing village. Then, their parents left to join the rebellion.

One year later, Fera and Elera heard that their parents had been killed by the Raiceman troops. Since then, Fera had remained in Seho but Elera had always remained close with the Makai warriors who would tell her of the bravery of her parents.

She had supposed that this was the reason that Elera had been attracted to Rekesh when he had first visited the village, being a strong supporter of the Makai rebellion in Raicema. She herself could not understand the appeal. But then again, she had never gotten involved with the rebellion.

She had always found the traditional fishing lifestyle of Seho more appealing, marrying Teltu, a man with a long lineage of local fishermen in his family.

As Fera pondered her thoughts, Javu approached the beach, accompanied by Rama. Sita looked up and smiled. Javu greeted Sita in Hindi and sat down next to the two women on the beach. Rama did the same.

"Fera, we will be setting off to Giza in an hour or so. Understandably you are concerned about you sister," Javu said in a comforting manner.

"Yes, I am worried," Fera said with emotion. "I had no idea she was travelling to Bimini. I don't even know if she is dead."

"She is alive, Fera," Javu said reassuringly. "Elera is trapped in an ancient place and I believe it is for good reason. There is a danger, however, that unless we help, the Raiceman forces may capture her when they return to Bimini. That is why we will be leaving soon to find out what is going on."

Rama spoke to Javu for a moment, as if reminding him of something.

"Rama tells me that something is not right on the island. After they came back up to the surface, everyone had disappeared. Let's hope that remains the case. I am certain that Sorentius will shed some light."

"Our old astronomy teacher?" asked Fera, slightly puzzled.

"Yes. He knows more than just astronomy. He has knowledge of the structures of ancient pyramids and will thus help us understand what the significance of this pyramid is."

He rose to his feet, sensing that it was time to load up the horses for their journey. Fera lowered her head with disappointment and unease. Javu knew she wanted to come along as well but wouldn't risk bringing Nehne.

"It is better you stay here with Nehne," he said. "She is growing so quickly. I will miss our conversations while I am away." He leaned close and rubbed her shoulder in a warm, affectionate manner. "Every one of us chooses our own path in the life we live. Be happy for Elera. I am sure she has not acted lightly. I just know that she will emerge safe and sound, Fera."

"I'll help you pack up your supplies," she said smiling, cheering up slightly.

Elsewhere in the village that morning, Nehne and some other children were playing with the three Kivili infants. The infants were rolling a ball back and forth with the children. One of the children, a young boy who had not played with the infants before, turned to Nehne.

"Why can't they speak, Nehne?" he asked.

"They do speak!" she said emphatically. "Only not our language."

"But I never hear them make any sound," he insisted.

The cute creatures smiled at each other with their eyes.

"That's because they speak with their minds."

At this statement the boy burst out laughing, which slightly irritated Nehne.

"It's true!" she maintained adamantly. "I have seen them when they are alone. They only use sign language when they want to talk about doing something physical, like throwing the ball."

At that she caught the ball rolled by the eldest infant. She smiled at him as he signed to her with affection.

"When they want to tell each other something important, they do that with their mind," she continued. "I think other animals are the same."

This time the boy was listening, as were the other children. One young girl seemed unnerved by what she had heard.

"How do we know what they are thinking?" she asked, timidly.

"How do you know what *I* am thinking?" Nehne asked in response.

The question took the youngster aback.

Nehne softened. "You don't need to know. They just want to play with us. Let's have fun."

With that the children and infants played heartily until Fera came over to get Nehne.

"Your father, Javu and the others are about to set off to find your Auntie Elera. Shall we go and see them off?" Fera said to Nehne, kneeling down to her level. Nehne nodded and rose to her feet.

The other children were intrigued by the activity in the village and followed Fera and Nehne along the dusty track towards the beach. The three Kivili infants also followed the children, fascinated by the sudden rush of excitement.

At the beach, Teltu was already mounted upon a stern stallion, six feet high and its muscles bulging with vigour and strength. Sita was ascended upon another, with Rama trying frantically to hoist himself up on the tall, powerful creature. Only Javu was on the ground, paying farewells to the villagers as if he might not return. He gave solemn and dutiful advice to the less aware members of the village, mainly reminding them that unity would see them through the most difficult of times.

Indeed, Javu was the sage and spiritual guide of the village and many felt uneasy with his departure.

Nehne ran up to him. "Javu, Javu!" she said, pulling on his robe. "I want to go with you and Papa. I want to see all of Ciafra and the rest of the world."

"You will, Nehne," he said gently. "But there are many dangers where we are going. There is a war happening between the Makai and Raicema, and an even bigger one that some have pledged against this planet. With all this conflict, you must use your feelings and insight to stay where it is safe. Here is safe for now."

Javu stroked her hair and urged her to bid her father a safe journey. Then he turned to Fera. "I do not know how long we shall be gone. Lentu and the others will help you take out the *Juniper* whilst Teltu is away. I intend to return here as soon as we have Elera with us."

He leaned closer, lowering his voice to a whisper. "And try to keep Hasu from making any dangerous decisions. Your uncle is susceptible to believing that all Makai warriors are trustworthy. If any should pass through the village whilst we are away, treat them with caution."

Fera knew exactly what Javu meant. One of the main reasons she had been so repelled from the Makai way of life was due to those raucous, aggressive individuals who only saw in black and white. They were unpredictable and violent at times, most coming from rogue sects or gangs.

Javu climbed upon the third horse, a less boisterous white gelding with rolled-up packages strapped to the hind, containing supplies and clothing. The first day would be easier, with some forest and mountain cover from the hot sun. The villagers waved as they set off. One villager played a small flute, a signal of a safe and successful journey.

Chapter 4 – The New Recruit

Bene, a young member of the *Raiceman Makai Organisation*, was waiting in a back street of *Raicema City* for Reo, a new recruit. Bene paced back and forth impatiently. Reo was late, a young man used to living in his own way.

"Hey man!" Reo shouted from the bottom of the street as he turned a corner.

"You're late!" Bene shouted back.

"What's up?" Reo asked as he drew closer, swinging his arms in a carefree manner.

"You're late. Don't ever be late again," Bene said, his face deadly serious.

"Hey sorry!" Reo said, seeing the annoyance in Bene's expression. "You know that I haven't been here long – and there are so many distractions in this city." He smiled mischievously but his expression quickly changed when he saw that Bene was still sombre. "What's wrong?"

"Nothing. Just be on time from now on. The leadership don't like it if you don't show on time. Somebody might be relying on you," Bene said somewhat sarcastically, mimicking something that he had heard before.

"Ok, ok, I'll be on time. So, what happens now? Do I get to meet the bosses?" Reo asked.

"Soon. First I need to tell you a few things." He took out a round yellow sweet from his pocket and popped it into his mouth. "If anyone asks you why you are here, you must say that you are against the Raiceman government. It's okay for you to tell them where you are from, but don't give anyone any spiel about your life history. Keep your answers short and sweet, okay?"

Reo nodded, thinking it strange how regimented this meeting would be. Vehicles could be heard screeching past in nearby roads and there was a constant humming sound from above.

"So I shouldn't mention anything about money? About the job

you mentioned?"

"Definitely not," Bene said adamantly. "They'll tell you what to do. There's no need to mention anything about that. And another thing, they'll expect you to know a bit about the Makai. If they ask, just tell them what I told you before, that the Makai is united across the planet against the oppressive regimes like Raicema. That a Makai government means freedom for the people."

"What about Lizrab?" Reo interjected. "You said that if I joined this Makai organisation thing that I would be able to make some money and help people back home. Should I mention that to them? You know, to show that I'm serious about helping as well as making money."

"Under no circumstances mention anything about that!" Bene said sharply, sensing the air of patriotism in Reo's voice. "Remember that the Makai here are only interested in our allegiance to overthrowing the government inside Raicema. Just keep quiet and only answer if absolutely necessary. We have to get going now."

Bene and Reo headed up to the top of the street and got into Bene's truck. The truck had mahogany interiors with cream leather seats. There was an array of technology embedded into the mahogany, from digital screens to tracking systems, all laced with flashing blue and gold lights.

"Whoa!" exclaimed Reo. "This motor is unbelievable. It must have cost a fortune. The Makai must pay pretty well, huh?"

"Just focus on your meeting with the leadership," Bene said coldly, ignoring Reo's question. He sped off towards Raicema City's premier casino, Le Grande.

Reo felt that for a fellow Lizrabian, Bene was not very understanding of his enthusiasm for new things. After all, the part of Lizrab where Reo had come from had been suppressed for generations, young children turning to drugs and crime from in their early years. He decided to probe at Bene's past.

"Why did you join the Makai?" he asked.

"I have been in this city for three years now and there is not one moment that passes that I don't miss Lizrab." He replied quietly but then suddenly realised that he was getting sentimental and quickly changed his tone. "I have always been involved. But I joined the RMO because I hate injustice and this is the best way to put things right."

This last statement was said in an awkward way and Reo couldn't help but sense that it had a hidden meaning, that Bene wasn't telling him the entire truth.

"So the RMO *do* help people?" Reo tried to confirm.

Bene was silent for a while before answering. "As far as farmers help their animals."

Reo was slightly confused by his cryptic answer and wondered why Bene had come to him in the first place. It seemed like he had deliberately sought Reo out, coming to the old squat where he had been staying late at night.

"You have been chosen for a well-paid job," Bene had said, his short black curly hair glistening from the light of the moon. Reo didn't know Bene, but had sensed that he had come to help him, to free him from the poverty he had found himself in since arriving in Raicema.

"What kind of job?" Reo had asked cautiously.

"You will be required to deliver something but I can tell you no more."

Looking over at Bene now, he noticed an arc-shaped scar on the right side of his jaw, almost hidden by his thick stubble. Sensing Reo staring at him, Bene glanced at Reo with his hazel eyes.

"Why did you choose me for this job?" Reo asked. "There were hundreds of people staying in that rundown factory building."

"The RMO are fussy about who they take on board," Bene replied callously. "You have to look a certain way, like you could fight if needs be. I know it's unjust, but most of those people were weak from hunger and would be no good for this job."

He looked over to the passenger seat and noticed that Reo tied his hair back very tightly. Despite living in malnourished circumstances,

Reo had kept himself in good physical shape, his body toned and slender.

The truck sped along a very straight road, with hundreds of similar-looking buildings close together on either side. Each one was at least forty stories high.

"You know, everybody who was living in that building had the same clouded dreams before they came here," Reo revealed, "that Raicema would bring them wealth so they could provide for their families in other places. I met people from Neoasia, Vassini, Lengard, all over. But nobody could find any work. Why is it so hard to get a job in this city if you weren't born in Raicema?"

Bene seemed uninterested but after a short silence, he turned to Reo, a small smile of sympathy appearing on his face.

"It's just the way here," he said as he sped around a sharp corner towards a long empty stretch of road, with nothing but dusty ground in surround. "The Raiceman people only want Raicema to exist, and that means making it near impossible for everyone else to survive. You can find work, but only if you're willing to be surrounded by ten thousand rads from the generators. Of course, that kind of work has a limited lifespan."

Up ahead, the road forked and the vehicle swerved down the left branch towards a remote group of giant buildings, all sporting bright lights, which seemed strange as it was still daytime. The rays of the clouded sun shone down like cone-shaped beams, casting a strange arrangement of moving shadows on the surrounding plains. Within seconds, the ultra-fast vehicle was approaching one of the buildings, a tall glistening glass structure with hundreds of vehicles parked around. It was shaped like a tall obelisk, with a gold spire coming out of the top. Written in large letters across several floors of the building were the words *Le Grande Casino*.

"This is it. Remember, try not to tell them too much."

The truck pulled up outside the casino and a valet immediately approached the window, dressed in formal attire. "Ahh, Mr Bene. How are you today, sir?"

Bene nodded.

"Please go straight to the roof terrace. They are waiting for you."

Bene and Reo got out of the truck and entered the casino though large swing doors encrusted with gold and jewels and guarded by six large bodyguards. Bene flashed a medallion he wore around his neck to one of the guards and they both passed without any quarrel.

"If you are wearing sig-lenses, take them out now," Bene ordered Reo.

"Sig-lenses? You mean those things that give you information about things you look at? I thought they were only used by the military for following orders?"

"They have come into the public domain over the past few years," Bene informed him.

"Not wearing any. Even if I could find some, you think I could afford them? Why do you ask?" Reo queried.

"The eye scanner will set off an alarm if you are wearing any," Bene explained. He led Reo through the main casino floor, where people were gambling, drinking and discussing business. Hanging from the ceiling were the most decorative chandeliers, their jewel-encrusted arms glimmering in the bright lights.

"This is Raicema City's largest casino. It's owned by Spiro Marxx, but he's hardly ever here. He's probably in another poverty-stricken area opening up another one of these."

"Who are we going to see?" Reo asked.

Bene didn't answer and walked to a back door again guarded by two muscled men wearing black suits. They seemed to recognise him and let him pass, but one of them blocked Reo with their arm.

"He's a new member," Bene said quietly and calmly. The guard removed his heavy arm from Reo's path. Beyond the door was a steel elevator door with two panels to the left. One panel was an eye scanner, the other an indentation of a hand.

"Put your hand there and look through that hole," Bene directed, pointing to the hand panel.

Reo did so and then heard a whirring mechanism. He suddenly

winced. "Damn! What just stabbed me?"

"A DNA scanner. This door won't open unless you match what's on record."

Reo looked confused. "I'm not on any record!" he declared.

"I would be surprised if you weren't on Raicema's core data bank," Bene stated. "If you've ever been to see a doctor anywhere in the world it's likely that you are on record. I know you didn't get into Raicema through conventional methods but they've got most of the globe covered."

"Unknown person," the panel blurted out suddenly. *"Authority needed."*

"Told you," Reo said.

Bene followed the procedure and the door slid open, the panel now silent. Inside the lift were thirty buttons and below them was a small hatch. Bene opened it and took off his medallion. There was a slot in the hatch and Bene inserted the medallion into it. The lift sped upwards.

"How can the RMO use Raicema's core data bank if they are against the government here?" Reo asked, confused by what he had been told.

Bene simply put his index finger up to his mouth, avoiding the camera in the corner of the lift. The lift began to slow.

As the doors opened, a ray of sunshine illuminated the inside of the lift. Reo and Bene stepped out onto a paved path and when Reo had stopped squinting from the glare, he saw three elderly men and an elderly woman ahead. They were all sitting around a semi-circular table in a large rooftop garden, and he estimated they were each about seventy years old. One of the men, sitting on the right side, signalled for Bene and Reo to approach the large, engraved mahogany table.

"So, young Reo," he said. "How are you finding it here in Raicema?"

The man wore a grey beard and a bemused look. "It is very different to Lizrab, yes?"

"Where am I going next?" Bene interjected abruptly, frowning before Reo could answer.

"We require you both to go to the south of Lizrab," one of the other elders, sitting on the left replied. "There is a very important message that we need you to deliver personally, Bene."

Reo got a very strange feeling from the man, who was clean-shaven and had the most piercing silver eyes that he had ever seen. He seemed much more authoritative than the other three elders, wearing a decorative robe with gold thread woven in mesmerising patterns all over. The man looked almost regal.

"You both may stop in your hometowns to see your families along the way," the woman elder said in a soft voice.

"When you reach the Makai base in Turo, pass on this message to Kirichi," the silver-eyed elder continued, reaching over and placing a small box on the table, a preoccupied and creepy smile curving up his narrow lips. "Only Kirichi's eye can read this lens so there is no point in trying to see what it says. It means death to anyone who tries."

The breeze from the height of the building made the surrounding plants and trees sway. Reo noticed that the male elder who was sitting in the middle said nothing but was staring intently at Bene, as if trying to tell him something.

"Who is Kirichi?" Reo asked innocently. Bene's eye twitched as he tried to control his annoyance at Reo's question.

The bearded elder laughed loudly. "He is the leader of the Makai in Lizrab. The generations of leaders throughout the Makai's history in Lizrab have culminated in Kirichi. His vision is one of peace and unity. Are you not from Lizrab?"

Reo felt a little embarrassed and wondered why Bene had not mentioned such an important figure.

"It would be interesting to get your opinion on Kirichi when you return, Reo," the woman elder added, looking at him longingly. "We are interested in the current messages he is giving to the people of Lizrab."

The silver-eyed elder called over a servant and requested drinks and food. He had a strange smirk on his face, as if very pleased with himself, and Reo felt the man's piercing eyes meet his own with a startling energy.

"My name is Master Sadana Siger," the authoritarian man stated. "I have led the Makai here in Raicema for the past nine years. How did you come to hear about the RMO, Reo?"

"I came to Raicema looking for work," Reo replied. "I met Bene recently and he told me about your company. He said there was work here."

Sadana laughed stridently. "Company?!" he cackled. "You could call the Makai that I suppose. Ha ha, I wonder what Kirichi would say if he heard that? This is an organisation, Reo, not a company. We are not the government!"

Reo glanced over a Bene, but he was looking straight down at the floor, lost deep in thought with a ferocious intensity.

"So how does this work?" Reo asked loudly, feeling a little uncomfortable. "You pay me for going into dangerous places to deliver messages to people?"

Bene shot him a serious glance.

"We may require you to do more than that," Sadana said, his composure instantly changing to be stern and serious. "As I said, firstly deliver this message to Kirichi and we shall take it from there. We will be able to get messages to you both when you are in Lizrab if needs be."

Bene looked up with an expression of concern, but quickly lowered his head again.

"There is about to be a large change in the way this nation is run, do you know that?"

Reo shook his head silently.

"Well, let's just say it was wise of you to take Bene up on his generous offer," Sadana said sarcastically. "When the smoke clears, this organisation will be the only place left that will be safe."

"And what about money?" Reo pursued, slightly chilled by

Sadana's words and ignoring Bene's warnings.

"We shall take care of your needs, Reo. First, accompany Bene on performing this task, then you shall be fully rewarded. Now, take this box and guard it with your life," he told Reo strictly, a creepy smirk forming on his wrinkled face. "Bene knows where you are going."

The last statement was said slowly with such sarcasm that it sent a chill down Reo's spine. Bene was now looking directly at Sadana. Reo walked over and took the box as the servant returned with a luxurious platter of meats, wines and fruits. He placed it directly in front of Sadana. The other two male elders bowed their heads slightly forward, whilst the lady elder seemed to be in deep contemplation. Sadana offered to nobody and ate for a while before looking up in surprise that Bene and Reo were still standing there.

"You may go now!" he said, and then returned to his indulgence.

As they left in the lift, Bene looked withdrawn and worried. Reo had never met people like this and a thousand questions were whirling around in his head. The lift sped downwards and Reo couldn't help but wonder how these supposed visionaries could justify lining an elevator with gold and jewels.

"This Spiro Marxx, you know, the guy who owns this place. Is he part of this Makai organisation?" Reo asked loudly.

Bene was silent and did not speak until they were both outside the casino. Then he took Reo to a quiet area on the way to the car pickup area.

"Spiro Marxx is part of the Makai here in Raicema. I will explain more when we are safely away from here. Everything we say is being recorded."

The truck was brought back by the valet and they got inside. Reo was about to speak, when Bene covered his mouth with his hand. He reached under their seats and produced two pin-like devices. He drove for a while, stopped near another vehicle on the edge of the Casino district and got out. The door of the vehicle had an electronic reader on it. Bene produced a thin film from his pocket and waved it in front of the reader. The door opened. Bene placed the two pins under the seats in the vehicle and closed the door. He got back into the truck and continued driving, now heading back towards the inner city.

"They always do this," he remarked. "Those things are called ticks. They can be tracked but can also record sound. It's part of that valet's job to plant those in the vehicles he handles."

"How did you open the door of that other vehicle?" Reo asked inquisitively.

"Those scanners use light patterns to lock or unlock doors. The film I have in my pocket has a very reflective surface with millions of light patterns transcribed onto it. Just by waving it in front of the scanner, the film will find a match for the light pattern."

Reo was impressed. Within a few minutes they were back in the metropolis of Raicema City. He gazed out of the side window for a while, watching the giant reflective buildings gaze back. One reached so far into the sky he imagined the shadow of it must cross half of the city.

"Is that why you wouldn't speak before? Because you were afraid of being heard?" Reo enquired in a teasing fashion.

"Let me explain something to you," Bene said shrewdly. "There are many that call themselves Makai, but there are different sects that do things differently, have different approaches to the oppressive governments that exist. The Makai here in Raicema have a very hands-on approach, you know, fight fire with fire. Tactics are everything. The Lizrabian Makai, on the other hand, fights the fire of oppression with water, or more strictly speaking, non-violence. Kirichi has maintained for many years that this is the only way to stop this cycle of empires and wars on the planet."

"Why didn't you tell me about this Kirichi person before? I felt stupid not knowing anything about him."

"It was better that way," Bene replied vaguely.

"So where are we going now?"

"Back to my place, then we are getting out of this city."

Silence fell in the vehicle as Bene sped along several wide roads. Reo noticed that there were cameras everywhere. They were on every building and every lamppost. He counted at least ten arches laden with an array of camera-like technology along every road they travelled. Before long, Bene pulled down a small lane and then down a ramp which led to an underground car park. He pulled the truck snugly in between two smaller vehicles, which both reminded Reo of large ugly insects.

"We won't be long. I just have to pick up a few things," Bene said as he closed the truck door quietly. They walked briskly to an elevator and Bene took out a strange square device with flashing lights. He placed it up to a panel next to the doors and they opened.

"Welcome home, Bene," the lift spoke in a cheerful voice.

As soon as they were inside, it sped upwards, and knew which floor to stop on. The doors opened with a gentle whir. Ahead there was a small square landing with three metallic doors. Bene held his electronic key up to the leftmost door and it opened, the lights inside coming on instantly and classical music fading in from a sound system inside.

Reo was astounded by Bene's apartment. It was laden with contraptions and computerised devices and had a magnificent view ahead of the bustling city. Reo walked slowly past the brightly lit bathroom. Inside it had a round ball, big enough for a person to sit in, glowing with an enticing ambience.

"Unfortunately we don't have time for you to try it out," Bene said in a light-hearted manner. "It's a steam ball. Very useful for sending you to sleep." He rushed into a small room to the right and began pulling clothes out of a wardrobe and stuffing them into a duffle bag. Reo wandered over to the tall window and looked out on the electric view of Raicema City. It was a montage of giant skyscrapers, all lit up like beacons combined with a fine mesh that seemed to be suspended over the city like an artificial sky. Little sparks shot of this mesh every now and again. As Reo looked out, he suddenly saw something move in the reflection of the window. It was a person! He turned around to see an aggressive-looking man lunging at him from behind a door.

"Bene!" he shouted as he was shoved violently into the window, hitting the back of his head on it. Luckily the glass did not break, though Reo felt a sharp pain at the back of his head. Bene emerged from the bedroom and upon setting eyes on the intruder, swiftly dove to the ground as the man pulled out a gun and opened fire, five bullet holes raging into the wall. Then, Bene sprung up from the floor like a tiger and with an agile movement, tackled the man to the ground, the gun clanking to the wooden floor.

"Uggh!" the man groaned as Bene managed to pin his arms behind his back. Reo got to his feet and rubbed his head.

"Who are you?" Bene barked at the man. Bene now had his knee on the back of his neck and the man looked very uncomfortable. Bene slowly applied more pressure. "Talk!"

"I was paid to kill you!" the man squeaked, now hardly able to breathe.

"By who?" Bene yelled at him, wrenching his arms up into his neck.

"I don't know!" the man cried. "The guy wouldn't let me see his face. I only met him once."

Bene released his grip. The man winced as he rolled over exhausted, unable to move his arms. Bene stood over him like a predator ready to eat its prey. He grabbed him by his neck and picked him up with one arm, his large and defined triceps tense and full of power. He pushed him against the wall and looked directly into eyes of the assassin.

"How much?" Bene demanded in a more composed manner.

"Ten thousand creds," the man said in a shamed voice looking like he was almost about to cry.

Bene dragged him with force across the apartment to the kitchen area next to the main door. He slammed him against a wall and the man cried out. "Please don't kill me!" he whined. "I've got a family, man! I was desperate."

"Who paid you?" Bene said aggressively to the cowering hit man, slapping him in the face.

"I don't know! This guy found me in a bar I usually drink in. Someone must have told him about me. He wouldn't let me see his face. He just sat there with his back to me. He just gave me a key and a photo and paid me the ten grand."

Bene seemed to believe what the man was telling him. He searched his pockets and found what looked like an exact copy of Bene's apartment key, which he then placed in his own pocket.

"Get out of here!" he said after a moment of contemplation, letting the man go and swiftly picking up the gun on the floor. He pointed it at him as he walked slowly towards the door with his hands up. The intruder opened the front door and almost ran out and into the open lift outside. Reo heard it whiz down to the bottom of the building.

"Why'd you let him go?" Reo asked, in shock at what had just occurred. "What if he tries to kill you again?"

"We're leaving now," was all Bene said in response.

Bene grabbed the bag he had packed and ushered Reo out of the apartment. As they took the lift down to the parking floor, Reo couldn't help but feel afraid that they might walk straight into another attack. However, the parking lot was silent and within a few moments they were back in the truck and heading out onto the wide roads of Raicema City.

"Why was that guy trying to kill you?" Reo asked after they had driven down a couple of streets.

Bene was silent, deep in thought about what had just occurred.

Up ahead, the road joined a wider one with eight lanes. Bene was quiet as he studied the eight possible routes that could be chosen out of the city. The truck sped up significantly as it latched onto the automatic vehicle route, otherwise known as the *autoway*.

"*Vehicle latched*," the dashboard of the truck blurted out in a woman's voice.

"I couldn't believe it when that guy jumped out," Reo said, more to himself than Bene.

"Someone doesn't want me to make it to Lizrab."

"But who?" Reo asked. "Do you believe what that guy said? That he doesn't know who hired him?"

"It doesn't matter. You can't trust anybody in this city."

"Not even the RMO?" Reo asked, though he already knew the answer.

"The Raiceman Makai track everything that their members do, to keep control. If one of their members goes against their orders, it can mean that it's a threat to their way of doing things. That is why you cannot trust such people."

Reo felt like Bene was being much more honest with him.

"So are we actually going to Lizrab?" he asked.

"Yes, Reo," Bene said. "It is not a coincidence that I have been chosen to deliver this message. The Makai here are no different than the government here. Take Spiro Marxx as an example. He used to work for the government. I wouldn't be surprised if he still did."

"In that place I was living, I heard some people talking about Makai warriors. Is that different to the Makai here?" Reo asked.

"It depends. Most of those warriors travelled from Neoasia. The Makai there follow a different principle and believe in defending yourself physically if you are attacked. They have many ancient techniques of self-defence and they are willing to die to stop those who may invade their homelands."

The vehicle was now travelling so fast that all Reo could see was a string of lights. They were driving automatically along a route at high speed and Bene had no control.

"Many warriors now reside in Lizrab and Ciafra and have caused a large revolution against Raicema over the past thirty years," Bene continued. "Kirichi has been forced to compromise on his stance, otherwise there would have been a civil war a long time ago."

He went silent for a while as Reo tried to take it all in and rested his hands by his sides, the controls rendered useless. He glanced in the wind mirror and his eyes widened as he suddenly noticed something.

"We are being followed," he said slowly.

Reo looked back over his seat and could see a low-lying, black car with oversized wheels and a pointed front latched onto the autoway. The windows were completely black and Reo couldn't see who was in the car.

"This stretch ends soon. We've got to lose them."

"Who are they?" Reo asked, looking at Bene.

"Don't know," Bene replied, gripping the steering ball tightly, ready to regain control of the vehicle. Up ahead as the autoway ended, the road dipped down into a giant slope, eight lanes splitting off into four different directions.

"De-latchment imminent," the dashboard said.

As soon as the vehicle detached, Bene put it into overdrive, the fastest possible speed. He swerved into the far right lane, weaving in and out of slower-moving vehicles.

"Cool it, Bene! You're going to kill us!" Reo yelped, gripping his seat. Vehicles were being passed so quickly they appeared just a blur of colours to Reo. He looked through the back window, seeing that the black vehicle was not far behind, also driving manically between vehicles, some forced to veer sharply into other lanes.

"They've got a much faster motor than us, so you should be praying this thing manages to lose them!"

Bene steered sharply to the left, into the lane heading due west towards Tyrona.

"We're going in the wrong direction!" Reo attempted to make Bene aware as they approached the exit.

"Just wait..." he said, slowing the truck slightly, allowing the black vehicle to get right behind them. Then, at the last moment, he pulled right suddenly, the truck bumping violently over metal rims in the road, used to separate out the lanes. The black vehicle tried to follow but almost crashed into a barrier just after the rims, so carried on in the westbound lane.

Bene steadied the vehicle. "Whew! We lost them," he sighed, the truck now safely on the southbound lane towards the border.

"Who were they?" Reo asked, still gripping the seat with white knuckles.

"If I had to bet, I'd probably put my money on Sadana being behind it. The main thing is that we lost them," Bene reiterated.

"Do you think he hired that guy in your apartment too?" Reo asked, a little confused. "But why would he give you a job to do and then have you killed?"

Bene smiled at Reo in a coy way, and then looked back seriously to the road ahead. "That's the thing about life, Reo. The spider often helps you into its web."

Reo looked out ahead, seeing nothing but open plains, a giant flow of vehicles streaming across like the fastest ants. The sun was starting to set in the distance, casting a reddish glow across streaky clouds.

"Get comfortable for a while," Bene advised. "We'll have to ditch this truck when we reach the port and then it gets less and less cosy from there."

Reo leaned back, wondering what he had allowed himself to get involved with as the line of electric ants blurred into a winding snake of red lights.

Chapter 5 – To Start a War

Jen King waited patiently outside of the *Raiceman Defence Head Quarters* in the central zone of Raicema City. 'The Beehive', as the zone was known, was a technological marvel with every metre of ground space utilised by the transport system or a multi-story skyscraper.

At six and a half feet, King was a large man with an intimidating appearance, his closely shaven head sweating slightly from the midday heat.

"Hey King!" a short, well-dressed man called out to him from behind the steel barrier that surrounded the defence building. "Good luck on your next mission."

The man quickly scurried off towards a boarding dock for the transport system, which mainly consisted of self-regulating, self-policing hover trains that operated at super-fast speeds. The trains had gone through a multitude of tests throughout the last century, resulting in many fatal crashes. Out of the twenty thousand hover trains in operation, now only the odd one would crash every year. The public of the central zones had no choice over the form of transport, however, as all non-governmental vehicles were banned from Raicema City's business and central residential zones.

King had been instructed to wait outside the Defence HQ in full view of the bustling public to place fear in any Makai rebels that were watching the building. With heavy, lean muscle on every bone of his body, his appearance was almost inhuman. Besides, he had a reputation of being indestructible. To some he was a celebrity and to others he was an omen to the dominance of Raicema over anyone who would oppose them. He had not gained such a reputation lightly, having proven his superior physical strength on many an occasion. He rubbed his head as Amaru Ramone, a young assassin originally from Neoasia, walked out of the large, electronically controlled sliding doors of HQ.

"President Tyrone is on his way here," he stated as he walked up to King who just grunted in response, uninterested by the news. There was only one person he would listen to in this insane empire, the president's brother, Seth Tyrone.

"Do you know where General Seth plans to take us next?" Amaru asked King, knowing full well of their close relationship.

King turned his head slightly towards Amaru, still not looking at him fully. "We will be travelling to Lizrab."

"You know, I never really understood why General Seth leads the battle on the ground whilst his brother just sits in an office all day," Amaru said in a rebellious fashion, yanking the wings of his black leather jacket as if it didn't fit properly.

"Each to their own," replied King. "Jeth is a greedy man; he owns this country, yet he will not stop until he owns this entire planet. Seth, much like the rest of us, just follows."

"But if they are brothers, why is Jeth the owner of the empire?"

"He was controllable by his father."

At that point, Seth came out of the building, followed by six guards. His straight hair was slicked back and his dark green eyes scanned the area as he walked. Each of the guards carried a large black gun and had several more strapped to their shoulder belts.

"We will wait for my brother to get here," he announced.

King nodded. All nine men piled into a mobile unit used to monitor flying activity over Raicema. Recently, some of the test flying machines on the Lizrabian border had been taken by Makai rebels, each with the capability to destroy a small village. The Raiceman government were the only known people on the planet to have developed such machines, powered by the fusion of a substance known as Omniadd, which was crystalline in structure. However, it had been discovered through countless tragedies that the fusion did not work in radioactive environments. As it currently stood, there were only a handful of locations that were radiation free.

"I don't know why we're even bothering tracking these damn things," a stocky guard said as he began to operate one of the computer terminals. "They'll just explode if they try and take 'em up."

"Each one of those machines has a valuable reactor inside it. It is imperative that the enemy do not put such technology to their own use," Seth scolded him with a stony stare.

"I was reading this article about old flying machines in the library," Amaru began to say. "And apparently it was possible to run them on oil in the past..."

"I don't know why you waste your time reading such crap," Seth cut him off mockingly. "There's no proof of those old myths. Besides, even if it were true, this planet is as dry as desert when it comes to oil. You know the law, all oil is reserved for city reactors."

Amaru lowered his head, wishing he had never mentioned it.

"We have mapped one of the machines!" one of the guards declared, working on a complex touch screen with a virtual map displayed on a metallic panel. "It is grounded on the south-west zone."

Seth sat at the back of the unit, frantically searching through a huge library of virtual files through a screen console. "Do not lose tracking," he ordered.

King and Amaru were both seated at the entrance of the unit, both in deep thought.

Suddenly, Seth jumped up. "Ahh, I have found it." He plugged a portable device into the console and it blinked for a moment whilst the file transferred. He passed another similar device to one of the guards who wasn't doing anything. "Take this and plug it into the sequence stream of the education system. It will 'inspire' people in that zone to inform us when they spot the stolen machine."

The guard saluted his leader and ran out of the unit and into the building outside.

One of the younger guards was no older than sixteen and had not been with the unit long. "Why would people volunteer to turn in the Makai?" he asked naively. "Most believe that they are heroes and the rest are afraid of them."

"Don't you know about the system my brother built?" Seth laughed with amusement. "We can use the broadcast stream to alter brain patterns and thoughts. Why do you think we spend so much every year giving the education system away for free? The public love us for it and we get our point across, if you understand what I mean?" He laughed again. The young guard just looked even more confused and began mumbling to himself.

Before long, the other guard returned to the mobile unit. "All done, General Tyrone," he reported with enthusiasm.

"Good," he replied. "Keep that sequence with you. If we haven't got all of the machines back by sunset, I want you to stream it nationwide into the entertainment system as well." Seth walked outside and signalled for Jen King to follow. "My brother will be here within the hour. As I told you earlier, we will be travelling to Aradonas in southern Lizrab. My brother intends to finally get rid of Kirichi and command the base in the region. He believes the sects here in Raicema and in Neoasia will lack leadership and deactivate over the next year when we accomplish this."

King just nodded, a look of detachment on his face. "Until then I will patrol one of the institutes," he suggested.

"Make sure you are back soon," Seth said sternly, raising an eyebrow.

Jen King walked along the mobile unit tracks, used only by the government, until he reached a boarding unit. The units existed as connection elevators between the hover trains and building entrances. He pushed a call button and a whoosh could be heard. Suddenly it appeared and its doors opened.

"*Where to?*" the unit asked.

"Reik Institute," King stated.

"*You will require a purple-route hover train from platform D in this building,*" the boarding unit announced back, speeding upwards and then leftwards. The doors opened and a busy platform appeared before him, with workers, tourists and families bustling on and off the trains that were hovering up and down to the platform.

The city was a multicultural haven, people flooding into Raicema City every year with the promise of highly paid jobs and an ever-expanding array of entertainment choice.

King looked around carefully. He was accustomed to doing so on every patrol he was assigned. He remembered a time on a similar platform when a rebel had tried to blow up a train that had a government officer on. King had run onto the train and quickly disarmed the man, yet before he could be taken into custody, he had been executed by the train's automatic weaponry system.

A group of children ran past and boarded the waiting train. It hovered downwards and then was gone in a flash of speed. The next train hovered down from above. King couldn't help but feel how dangerous life was in Raicema City. He often wondered what life would be like elsewhere. He had only travelled within Raicema and Lizrab, fighting rebels for as long as he could remember. He had heard of other more natural places elsewhere and every so often he had mental flashes of places that were not in Raicema or Lizrab. He wished very much to travel to those places; in fact he often felt a strong yearning to.

King boarded the next train and within ten seconds he had arrived at the entrance to the Reik Institute. This particular centre for academic learning was the most advanced in the fields of astrology, cosmology and planetary studies. These subjects had always fascinated King and he would often make excuses to enable him to visit the centre and talk with its students. The institute was made of a deep blue stone, sculpted beautifully into large domed rooms leading off from a grand entrance hall. A giant crystal globe hung from the rafters of the hall, creating a spectacle of dancing light on the reflective floor, which had a giant image of a star engraved into it.

Toji, a young boy of outstanding rational intellect noticed King's arrival and rushed towards him. "Hello, Jen!" he shouted from across the main entrance hall.

A small smile appeared on Jen King's face. He greeted Toji with a pat on the back.

"Jen, I have been learning about the universe," Toji said enthusiastically. "I think that this planet is much older than all the education systems are saying. I found a book at home that my grandfather owns. I was trying to find out about the things it talks about here, but there isn't any information."

Jen King wasn't surprised and felt sympathy for Toji. He knew personally that Raicema had been feeding the public a distorted version of history for centuries now. All he knew was that Raicema was, and as far as he knew always had been, the dominant and most advanced human force on the planet.

"Do the people you work for know something different?" Toji asked.

"You know I can't answer that question, Toji. All I can tell you is Raicema is the supreme force on this planet, so we must follow their rule."

"But I don't think Raicema has always been here," Toji remarked. "My grandfather's book talks about previous empires in this land and in other lands."

King put his hand over Toji's mouth to stop him talking. He had witnessed many killed by the military over lesser unpatriotic words. "Be careful what you say, Toji. Don't you know everything we say is recorded?"

"Sorry, Jen," Toji said sheepishly. King smiled weakly.

"Where are you going to next?" Toji asked energetically.

"Lizrab," King replied. "Looks like I'll be there for weeks."

"Do you have to fight again? Against the Makai?"

"I always have to fight, Toji. It is my job in this world. I kill who they tell me to, when they want me to," King said coldly.

"But, Jen, I know you hate to kill. I saw you place an insect from your arm to safety once. You only kill other humans because you are forced to."

Toji's words were too much for King to think about. "Nobody is forced to do anything. I chose this." He dismissed the youngster's comment. "I have to go now. I have something to do before I leave." He ruffled Toji's hair and walked to into the map room of the institute.

The night before, King had experienced an unusual dream. He was walking up a steep mountain, every step getting more difficult, the top always seemed in reach but he never quite got there. In the dream, he was following an animal that was running with ease up the rocky terrain. King remembered how realistic the dream was and that he was out of breath, in desperation to keep up with the animal and reach the top. Towards the end of the dream, King remembered seeing another person at the top of the mountain shouting something, a warning. He had turned around to look behind him and then he woke up. King wanted to know if the place in his dream really existed. He walked to the back of the map room to the large map of the planet. He saw the vast land of Neoasia to the west and Lengard even further westwards. Ciafra was southeast and Lizrab was directly to the south. Each of the major landmasses had mountains, but King was specifically looking for an especially massive mountain, one that reached high into the sky. The two biggest mountains on the map were in northern Lizrab and in central Neoasia.

In the corner of the map room was a fitted desk with semi-circular drawers. King walked over and opened a drawer labelled *'Terrain maps of Lizrab'*. He rolled up a small map from inside and placed it in his black leather shoulder belt. This would come in useful if he decided to take in some of the sights of the Lizrabian land. He then headed out of the map room. King wondered what the education systems were teaching the youngsters these days and decided to have a look at one of the learning centres. He had heard a lot about these from Seth and other officials. They had raved on about how they would unify Raicema and bring order to uneducated extremists, yet King had never had the desire to use one. He walked into one of the smaller learning centres. Some young students were wearing head units and visors, whilst others were looking collectively at a large bowl-like dip in the floor. Inside, scenes of historic battles between the Raiceman army and the Lengardians could be seen to be taking place as if watching it in real life from above. A voice played from the bowl.

"...the Lengardians in 178 AA, aimed to overthrow the growing Raiceman army in an attempt to capture Tyrona. Here we see the Lengardians being aided in their onslaught by the Imperialist army of western Neoasia. This was the first of a series of bloody battles that would last for thirty-four years..."

Suddenly, King heard a crackling in his ear and then the voice of Seth Tyrone could be heard.

"All report to HQ immediately," the embedded speaker said. All defence workers had such a device implanted in their eardrum and it had irritated King since he was first trained for these military operations many years ago. On this mission, he thought, he would do some exploring for himself for a change.

There were no trumpets playing as President Jeth Tyrone arrived into Raicema City. Usually, the arrival of the president to the beehive would spark a buzz, with crowds gathering and a regal fanfare arranged beforehand. This time, however, Jeth wanted his plans kept as quiet as possible. He was travelling in a black, standard government vehicle used to carry military troops. As the vehicle reached the inner city gate, which was used for strict outside access control, four heavily armed robotic units approached, all hovering slightly above the ground and shining lights and cameras at the vehicle.

"Legitimacy investigation in progress..." one of the devices resonated. "If you are a Raiceman government member, please connect your key to this pad..." the unit continued. A small pad was ejected from the device and held in front of the vehicle. The driver climbed out and placed a silver medallion in a slot on the pad.

"Reading and evaluating..." echoed the robotic unit. "Governmental *key confirmed. Prepare for eye and DNA scanning…"*

All four units moved the vehicle and shone large round cameras inside. The driver pushed a button and the windows slid open. The guards and Jeth all had their eyes scanned by the cameras and a blood sample taken. The driver then quickly closed the windows.

"Legitimacy confirmed. Welcome to Raicema City," resonated the first robotic unit. The vehicle drove on into the transport system. Soon after, it reached another gateway and the driver pushed a button on the vehicle's control panel, opening a gate to a tunnel ahead. They travelled through the direct government route to the centre, and within a few moments another gate opened and Defence HQ could be seen in the distance, towering above the other buildings.

As Jeth and his guards arrived at HQ, a large section of the road leading up to the entrance dipped into the ground and the vehicle drove into a private chamber beneath the building. Seth, Amaru and the six guards were waiting. Jeth stepped out of the vehicle wearing a black, shimmering, thick cotton suit. A thick black metal plate covered his chest and neck and he wore a jewel-encrusted shoulder belt with strong black boots. "My brother, we are about to embark on a great legacy," he said, embracing Seth. Amaru and the guards all stood to attention. Jeth turned to them and puffed out his chest. "Soon we will join the might of the Raiceman forces and invade the south of Lizrab. The sole purpose of this invasion is to bring peace to our beloved land by commandeering the Makai base in Turo. Many of you will have faced the Makai warriors in their homeland before, and the fact you are still standing here before me is the reason you are considered to be among Raicema's elite. The terrain where we will travel is harsh, with vast forests and hills providing protection to the enemy. Yet we have a secret weapon that I have been developing in Tyrona."

He signalled to one of his sentries who climbed into the vehicle and appeared again carrying a small spherical device the size of an orange. He held it up so the men could see.

"This device…" said Jeth Tyrone menacingly, pointing to it in the sentry's hand "…is powered in the same way we intend to power the future flying machines, through the fusion of Omniadd. This, however, can cause much more damage than a flying machine." He grinned sadistically. "Each one of these devices has the capability to destroy a small town, so they will be invaluable in our onslaught of the Makai."

As he gleamed menacingly at the onlooking guards, a lift door opened and Jen King walked into the chamber, showing no interest in the fact Jeth was standing before him.

"Well, well," Jeth said sarcastically. "Our star attraction!"

King ignored Jeth's comments and fell in line with the other seven men.

After a moment of composure, Jeth continued with his motivational speech. "Each of you will command important units in the field. You will be looked upon as leaders by the others, their guidance and instruction is your responsibility. You will all be accompanying my brother and me on the warships down towards Aradonas. The majority of the troops will travel over land but each of you must select five hundred men to tutor with the new weapons on the ships."

He turned to Seth, almost stamping his feet in a march-like manner. "You have a battalion nearby?" he asked.

Seth nodded, rolling his eyes as if it was a ridiculous question.

King stepped forward, taking Jeth somewhat aback. Ever since their father, Guyo Tyrone, had brought King into the royal palace when the Tyrone heirs were only children, Jeth had always had a dislike of him. He had avoided King throughout his life, letting his father and his brother mould him into one of Raicema's strongest soldiers.

"I wish to travel over the land," King demanded.

"You shall do no such thing!" Jeth stated back forcefully, the tension in his voice immediately present. "I have commanded that you travel by warship and train the men."

"I only take orders from General Seth," King said coldly to Jeth.

Jeth began to fume at this comment, his face getting red and flustered with irritation.

"You will travel by warship," Seth ordered to King, intervening to support his brother.

King stepped back, his face sour with disappointment. He had been looking forward to creating his own excursions into the natural Lizrabian land, exploring and sightseeing before the inevitable killing and maiming began.

"You are scared of me, aren't you?" King said slowly and quietly to Jeth, grinning slightly.

Jeth's expression changed from one of annoyance to one of astonishment at King's nerve. He tried to speak, but stuttered as he opened his mouth, flummoxed at the mighty soldier's awareness of his fear. Then, embarrassed, he rashly pulled out a gun and pointed it at King's arm. Without hesitating he pulled the trigger. The shot hit the top of King's forearm. The blow did not cause any reaction, except that King looked down slowly at his bleeding arm, looked back up at Jeth and laughed in his face, showing his defiance. He turned away to leave the underground chamber, shaking his head in pity. Jeth, hand trembling, raised his gun and aimed for King's head. As he was about to pull the trigger, Seth stepped quietly next to his brother and took the gun from him quickly.

"No," he whispered. "We need him."

Again, a look of anger swelled onto Jeth's face as King made his way outside to gain another taste of freedom before he would be decreed into more bloodshed.

"That dirty Ciafran!" Jeth seethed. "I curse the day Father ever brought him home. I don't give a damn how strong he is, one day he'll get what's coming to him!"

The other men pretended not to be listening and all looked down at the floor. Jeth composed himself and stroked one side of his parted brown hair. "Now go," he said to his line of leaders. "And bring pride upon Raicema."

The men all saluted their president and then departed for the war vessels. After they had left the chamber, only the two brothers and Jeth's sentries remained.

Seth took his brother to one side. "You have heard of what happened in Bimini?" he said.

"You mean the evacuation?" Jeth responded. "I know of it but not the reason why. I have ordered an investigation. Do you know something I don't?"

"All of the men have disappeared. I haven't been able to contact anyone down there."

"Most worrying," Jeth muttered to himself, pulling on his beak-like nose.

"I have also taken some readings from the area and the radiation in the atmosphere has increased tenfold."

"I better send a specialist then," Jeth decided. "So we are completely open from Bimini?"

"We can divert some troops as we travel south," Seth suggested, to which Jeth nodded and hurried his brother towards the vehicle, eager to put his plan into action.

Outside, Jen was having his wound tended to by a medical officer.

"If you carry on like this, you'll end up dead," the woman said sternly to him.

Jen said nothing, his mind wandering to thoughts of being completely alone, free from people telling him what to do. It often felt like something in his stomach wanted to burst out with uncontrollable rage, decimating everything around him and leaving him in peace. He fought back the feeling and smiled weakly at the officer as she finished binding his arm. He walked towards a line of mobile units, all destined for the east port. As he stepped into one of the vehicles, he breathed out deeply, imagining his life had escaped into the air, floating away to freedom.

Chapter 6 – The Secret of the Bimini Islands

The islands of Bimini, situated fifty suns from the southeast coast of Raicema, were a unique formation of irregular-shaped land masses surrounded by the purest turquoise waters. The region was comprised of two main islands, North and South Bimini. Whilst the south was the more populated land mass hosting pretty beaches and military buildings, the north was home to an intricate mangrove forest that was shrouded in mystery. Within the forest, there were elaborate waterways and to the west were megalithic, polygonal stones that had been paved into the seabed.

Sealed beneath the depths of the Bimini Islands, Elera walked slowly down a dark tunnel, feeling her way along an enormous wall. It felt rough and sediment crumbled away in her hands. She was breathing loudly and found this helped to calm her. Her body was weak and she estimated that it must have been two days since she had eaten the last of her supplies. She noticed that pangs of anxiety suddenly ran through her midriff now and again.

Elera had been in the underwater pyramid for what seemed like an eternity. She had spent a long period of time in a colossal chamber she had entered by crawling along a narrow shaft from the pyramid's entrance. Inside, Elera had found the chamber illuminated by glowing stone and the greenest of algae. Every wall had seemed like a dead end until a few hours ago when she found a stone slab at the back of the chamber that could easily be lifted from the floor. Only the faintest breeze of air had given away its passage.

She had been following the tunnel ever since, remembering to keep a positive outlook on the situation. After all, she had found out about the pyramid only by following the things that came to her naturally. The events that had led to her now being a sun under the ocean were remarkable to say the least.

It had all started three years earlier when the Makai leaders in Raicema City had begun to actively disagree with Kirichi's leadership of the Makai in southern Lizrab. Kirichi had always taken the standpoint of non-violence, encouraging education and knowledge of truth and reality. He had embraced the Neoasian pilgrims who travelled to settle in Lizrab and the population was getting larger and larger every year. Sadana Siger and his followers had argued for many years that the spiritual, submissive approach of Kirichi was undermining any future authority of the Makai on the planet. They were adamant that Kirichi should stand down as a leader of the people. The meeting had been called and Elera, being tutored by Kirichi since a young age, had agreed to his request for her to accompany him. Kirichi for the first time in his life was to travel to Raicema to meet with Sadana.

Elera had travelled to the border and met Kirichi's entourage to escort them to an outer region of Raicema City. Upon their meeting, Elera knew that Kirichi was aware of something that she was not. Many fearless guardians had accompanied him, all with the sole focus of his protection. It was during this journey, from the border to the small monastery where the meeting was to take place, that Elera first realised the power of the Lemurian myth.

One of the guardians, Taraka, originally from a western region of Neoasia, had begun to tell Elera about the village he came from.

"It is a very patient place. Many have told me that to outsiders it seems as though no human progress is made due to the simple way of life, yet those cannot really see that the most potent of advancements are constantly being made."

"Such as what?" she had asked Taraka.

"Such as the cultivation of sacred human gifts. Anything to do with harmony between mind and body or mind and matter is of primary learning importance. It reminds me of the legend of Lemuria, the way things are going."

"I have heard of Lemuria," Elera had said, with interest, "but the stories about it always seem so farfetched and one is never the same as the other."

"Lemuria did exist," Taraka had claimed. "Maybe it still does exist. It is not just a physical place, but a spiritual place as well. It is the place that makes people see that they are interconnected; that they are the same as one another."

Elera was fascinated by Taraka's account and as he went on he spoke of more utopian qualities of the mythical place, such as harmonic communication between all beings that dwelled there, the flourishing of love for all things and a level of evolution that seemed impossible.

"Where have you heard of all of these stories?" she had asked him.

"The stories are passed down to each generation. I was told about Lemuria when I was a child. It is said that many civilisations that exist on the planet today are descendants of the Lemurians. Of course, most people probably haven't even heard the stories, never mind believing that there once was such a place."

Later that day, when the group had arrived at the meeting place, a terrifying situation had occurred. An assassin, completely camou-flaged in a black outfit and with their face completely covered, appeared as if from nowhere and charged into the derelict building where all the leaders were congregating. The assassin withdrew a blade, but before they had a chance to attack, Taraka had slashed the assailant across the waist with his sword, felling them to the ground with a spray of blood. The intruder then made a swift exit, hotly pursued by some of the guardians.

"Seems like I was needed after all!" Taraka had said, placing his sword back in its sheath. "Kirichi was warned that there might be attempts on his life. You know, he didn't want any guardians to come!"

Elera had understood at that moment that it was her place in life to try and change things. She wanted to put an end to the desper-ation. She had felt deeply for the assassin. What would drive someone to such an act of hatred?

Elera's thoughts were stirred back to the present by a rumbling up ahead, yet there was still no light to be seen with only darkness prevailing in the musty tunnel. She decided to follow the vibrations.

As she walked for what seemed like hours with the pulses getting stronger and stronger, her mind wandered back to the events of the meeting three years earlier.

After the shock of the assassination attempt, the meeting had begun with all guardians now extra alert in the large room.

"We insist that the time has come for you to relinquish your leadership of the sects in Lizrab," Sadana had said quite forcefully. "There is confusion and a lack of direction. We in Raicema think it is best for the Makai leadership to be centralised to Raicema City, where we have a more direct understanding of the needs of the Makai people as a whole. Furthermore, the Makai people of Neoasia are becoming more and more distant from the Raiceman Makai, despite talks with leaders in Neoasia. It is down to your influence that such segregation is occurring."

"I have never asked to be a leader, yet people turn to me for guidance. While ever they turn to me, I will guide," Kirichi had replied quite calmly. "I agree there is segregation, but I believe this to be due to selfishness amongst some of the leaders."

The statement had infuriated Sadana, a sly snarl creeping onto his face. "You dare talk of selfishness?!" he retaliated. "When you only bless your own family with power and respect!"

Kirichi had not replied to this question. Instead, he had called Elera towards him and asked her to introduce herself. She had stepped forward nervously, the eyes of some of the most influential Makai leaders upon her. Kirichi had nodded to her encouragingly.

"My name is Elera Advaya. I was brought up in Ciafra, and Kirichi has been my teacher since I first met him when I was a child. He has requested my presence here today."

"What has this girl got to do with anything, Kirichi?" another elder had asked him.

"Hiding behind your students now, Kirichi?" Sadana had added sarcastically.

"This woman..." Kirichi began, speaking a little louder "...will take my place as leader of the Makai in Lizrab when I leave this physical realm."

The statement had silenced the room, save for gasps of disbelief. Elera herself was stunned at his intention.

"The problems we have faced in the past years have come from trying to progress the simple concepts of unity and peace into that of a nation or worldwide leadership and control of the people," he continued. "This has arisen solely from the influence of current Makai leaders in Raicema and Neoasia."

The statement enraged most of the leaders who stood up in reprisal.

"How dare you?" said one.

"What impertinence!" remarked another, waving her hands wildly in the air.

The outbursts had not swayed Kirichi, who continued his speech. "I would also like to warn everyone here, that the pursuit of power through the destructive methods of the distant past can only end in suffering."

With this statement, Kirichi had sent a piercing glance to Sadana.

"The Makai should be a basis of love and universal faith. It is not a replacement for the current empire that is trying to rule us all. I shall not stand down from my rightful place in Lizrab, nor shall any future leader there. May the force of love be with you all."

With no more words, Kirichi had left the meeting quickly, Elera and the guardians travelling back to Lizrab with him. Kirichi had known what the leaders had wanted, but they never knew that he was as determined as he had always been to reduce the suffering on the planet through his continued guidance. Kirichi had advised Elera not to dwell on her intended role or fear such responsibility. However, Elera couldn't help but feel daunted by the future. On their journey back to Lizrab, where Elera had lived since she was a young teen, Kirichi discussed her future plans.

"I think that the time may be coming for you to leave Lizrab for the meanwhile," he had said, somewhat sharply. "You are a skilled astrologer and historian and I do not want your views to be corrupted by all of this political nonsense."

"But Turo is my home now," Elera had protested. "Where would I go?"

"Well, even though there is much wrong with Raicema, it is also a place where many great minds culminate."

"You are not implying that I move to Raicema?!" Elera had asked with repulsion, aghast at the thought.

"You see, this is what I was afraid of. You have already judged a place that you have never been to."

After months of contemplation back in Turo, Elera had eventually come to the same conclusion as Kirichi. She moved to Raicema, where she had found that Kirichi was right and there were many interesting and knowledgeable people living in the beehive-like metropolis of Raicema City. The strangest thing was that some of the greatest developments of her life had occurred there; she had been reunited with Rekesh and had learnt more and more about the myth of Lemuria. Her life had been a happy one in Raicema City, waking up next to Rekesh every day and meeting many like-minded people.

Now, she wondered if she would ever get out of the pyramid to see Rekesh or the places she loved again.

Up ahead, a crack of light could be seen and as she approached it, she realised it was another stone slab above her head. She pushed up hard, but it was so heavy that she soon grew tired, already feeling weak and frail. The vibrations were very strong now. Elera could feel them pulsating through her body. She noticed that the crack of light got a little bit bigger with every vibration, indicating that the slab was moving. She positioned herself carefully and pushed up on the slab in time with the rhythm of each pulse. The slab moved bit by bit, more light streaming down through the widening cracks onto Elera's face. With one final push, the slab began to hover upwards, much to Elera's surprise. She saw it rise high into the air above her and linger there mysteriously. She climbed out of the square hole to find a most remarkable location before her.

She was inside a pyramid-shaped room, light and airy, though there was no sign of any light source. The walls were immaculate and lacked the algae that the other chamber had been covered in, yet the stone seemed to emit the same comprehensive light. In the centre of the room was a long metallic rod hanging from the top point in the ceiling. Attached to the end of this rod was a pair of sculpted, cupped hands made from the same metal. They shone with a reddish, gold colour. Upon the metal hands rested a crystal orb of unbelievable purity. Looking around, the rest of the sloping room seemed to be empty.

As Elera got closer to the sphere, she felt more and more at ease, entering into an increasingly calm state of being. The ball was labyrinthine and sophisticated, with thousands of tiny hollow channels running spherically within it. As she moved from one position to another, she noticed a holographic image of what looked like three pyramids appear in the sphere, one immediately behind the other and increasing in size. The crystal was mesmerising and Elera almost lost herself completely, examining the images and intricate channels. She reached out to touch the metallic hands and immediately pulled away in pain. They were intensely hot, although they looked cool. Elera decided to look around the room to see if there were any other passageways, but she found nothing, all of the walls completely sealed and airtight. She wondered how there was any air getting into the room, seeing as no algae was growing and yet she could breathe perfectly well. As she looked up to where the stone slab had floated, she noticed a small tunnel at the top, directly next to where the slab was hanging in the air.

She walked back over to the crystal orb, again becoming mesmerised by it. She touched it with caution and was surprised to find it ice cold. She wondered why the hands were so scorching hot. Then, she got the overwhelming feeling that the sphere was trying to tell her something. Elera carefully picked up the immaculate ball in her hands and looked deeply into it. Suddenly a blinding white light shot out of the orb towards her forehead.

The next thing she knew, she was transported to a place that she had never seen before. She could smell the pungent fragrance in the air and feel the immense humidity. There was a gathering of several people, all tall and slender, crowding around something and she was stood behind them.

The place was beautiful, with the most luscious foliage she had ever seen, growing high into the sky with shiny glowing buildings spread all around. The trees seemed different, tall and all-encompassing as if they were a great family that protected the landscape. Each building was made of shimmering stone, each with intricately carved decorations on the surface. Every one was carefully built within a group of trees so that it could only be seen from ground level. In most cases the buildings, oval in shape and modest in size, had been built around the trunks of the widest trees and almost merged into them.

Moving closer to the group of people, she couldn't quite see what they were looking at and edged closer towards the congregation. Through one of the tall people's legs, she saw a creature, like no other she had ever set eyes on. It was small and frail with the silkiest of light brown fur and a face that looked like a combination of every animal in existence. It was beautiful, with eyes like stars and radiating a presence of pure love. It stood up on its four legs, almost resembling a foal, tail shining brightly, with fur that seemed to continually fluctuate between feathery and glowing orange energy. The sight was dazzling and surreal, the people silent, looking at the creature with love and care.

"*Baala Aova*," one of the tall humans said softly in an accent that Elera couldn't relate to.

The surroundings looked like nowhere she had ever seen or heard about on the planet, like a dream world. She felt the presence of something else close by. The feeling of a mother watching over its child. Then all of a sudden, the vision was over and Elera was back in the pyramid holding the crystal sphere. She dropped it back into the hands with a startled gasp.

The crystal started glowing and specs of energy like miniature fireflies could be seen whizzing around the internal channels. Elera could feel heat radiating from the hands and she started to panic a little, looking around for a way out of the room. She rushed back to the hole that she had entered the chamber through as the hands and rod started to shimmer a little more, the sphere now glowing intently and the temperature of the room climbing rapidly. The vibrations pulsating through the room had grown much stronger and the chamber was almost shaking. Elera felt panicked and breathed deeply, thinking what to do.

She almost climbed back down the hole but stopped herself when she once again felt like the crystal was trying to tell her something. She suddenly realised that her own anxiousness was causing the overwhelming tremors and the temperature of the room to increase. She sat on the edge of the hole, breathing deeply and feeling like she might pass out. Then the vibrations began to subside.

After a moment of composure, she got to her feet and walked over to the crystal ball in a daze. She picked it up again, feeling a lot calmer. The vibrations had now stopped completely and the temperature of the room had dropped.

How can this be? she thought, a little scared at how she was affecting her surroundings. Orb in hand, she looked up at the slab that was hovering in the air.

I need to get up there.

Instantly, the stone slab magically floated back down to the floor, sealing the hole again.

It can't be! Intrigued, she swiftly walked over and stood upon it, thinking as hard as she could that she wanted the slab to rise. At first there was no reaction, but then the slab rose back up again and Elera fought to keep her balance whilst holding the sphere as it moved upwards.

As the stone slab stopped smoothly, Elera was brought to the entrance of the tunnel. It was short and narrow, with just enough space to crawl along. The channels in the crystal were still vibrant with energy, but the overall brightness of it had dimmed. Elera ducked down and began to crawl along the tunnel, hoping it would lead to a way out of the pyramid. She kept thinking about the vision she had seen, of what seemed like another world, another time. Ahead the tunnel skewed upwards into a diagonal shaft and Elera struggled to put the crystal in her small satchel to ensure it wouldn't get damaged. Even there, its light still penetrated, lighting up her satchel like the moon.

She crawled her way up the shaft, pushing outwards with her arms and legs so she wouldn't slide back down. Her mind drifted away with the effort, to thoughts of Rekesh and her time with him.

Their relationship had been full of ups and downs, of agreements and disagreements, kindness and sadness. But she always missed him when they weren't together. Though feeling slightly claustrophobic, her thoughts spurred her on with more determination and before long she had reached the end of the shaft, coming out into a small cavity. It was just big enough to stand and with the light from the crystal still illuminating everything, she could see an inscription on one of the cavity walls. It was some form of hieroglyphics, though Elera had never seen these symbols before. They looked quite similar to hieroglyphs that she had studied in Ciafra and Lizrab, yet they made no sense to her.

Above, another thin shaft went vertically upwards and as she looked around, she saw another of similar width running horizontally along. She decided to go down the flat tunnel, perspiration running from her brow. It was no more than a crawl space, her satchel casting a ghostly glow on the airtight cracks between the slabs that surrounded her. She edged her way along, scraping her knees and elbows and feeling like the tunnel was almost narrowing.

At the end, the shaft was sealed with another stone slab, but on closer inspection, Elera saw that two handles had been carved into the stone. She used them to push against it, finding it hard to find leverage in the small space. She felt the door opening with a scraping noise and pushed harder, breathing loudly with the exertion. As the opening widened enough to allow her to squeeze through, she was astounded to find that it led to a great chamber, at least five time her height. The satchel cast light on thousands of ancient objects that had been stored in the room; golden statues and furniture, stone blocks with carved inscriptions and numerous other decorative items made from gold and jewels.

She stood upright, stretching and amazed at the decorative roof above, engraved with a circular pattern and covered in gold. The chamber was hot and musty and Elera presumed it must have been many millennia since it was last opened. Her heart fluttered with excitement. She walked over to the largest stone block in the centre of the chamber and tried to read the carvings. They were written in a hieroglyphic language foreign to Elera but some of the symbols looked familiar. She spent a while trying to make sense of the monument.

"Four were built...the spirit lives in each..." was all that Elera could decipher from the twelve lines of hieroglyphs. She moved around the chamber, observing everything in detail. There were mirrors coated in gold and statues reminiscent of those found in the Giza pyramids. There were many smaller sculptures made of jade and onyx, some of lions and jackals, others of people. She pondered the meaning of *"Four were built"*.

Could this mean four pyramids?

She took out the crystal sphere. The room illuminated brightly, causing anything shiny to glow fantastically. She looked into it and saw the image of the three pyramids again as she moved a little. As she continued to rotate it in her hand, the image changed to that of four pyramids, each slightly different in shape and size. She decided to look around some more and in the brighter light, she noticed a familiar-looking tablet resting on an oesophagus at the back of the room. It was written in a *Naqada* structure, a language pattern that Elera had studied and knew well. She had seen many tablets of this form in excavations she had done at the Great Pyramid of Giza in her youth. She found it easy to translate the tablet's meaning.

"The gods have bequeathed our king with four monuments to which our benevolent king will bestow further monuments in honour of this gift.

We pledge our everlasting commitment to serve the gods.

In this monument to which our testament stands, the god of water has claimed it for his own and it will be duly swallowed. To the north, in the land of colossal mountains is the third monument and the fourth has been witnessed by the gods only.

Our benevolent king wishes out of his munificence to remain only in the first monument, in our homeland, where the great lion and the great dragon watch over us."

Elera realised that the tablet must have been created at a time when the Bimini pyramid was in the process of sinking into the sea. She was surprised that the tablet indicated there were four scattered pyramids of antiquity in the world. She deduced that the Great Pyramid of Giza was the first of this four and her current location the second. After examining the chamber for a few moments more, Elera began to feel very faint and a sudden desperation to breathe fresh air enveloped her. She searched for another hidden door or tunnel but finding none, she decided to backtrack and continue up the vertical shaft that she had reached before. She crawled back along the tight tunnel that had led to the chamber, wincing as she brushed her grazed knees again on the rough stone. She reached the cavity junction and with sweat pouring from her brow and body, she shimmied her way up the stuffy vertical shaft, stopping in mid-air every so often to breathe heavily. She felt like she was near the top of the pyramid as the air was heavy and her head drowsy with the pressure. Her body felt lighter, as if it were being invaded by something ethereal.

Before long, she had reached the top, which came out at another cavity, this one slightly larger but with no further tunnels or shafts. It was perfectly pyramidal of shape, the walls glowing just like in the chamber where she had found the crystal orb, the strangest of stones, like no other she had seen. She realised that she was at the top of the pyramid, in its capstone.

Elera began to feel concerned again. She was certain there would be a way out, but she felt very tired and was finding it hard to breathe. The orb next to her was speaking. It was singing to her. Then, she noticed something about the walls. They were flickering slightly, and Elera was sure she could see the deep waves of the ocean moving beyond. For a moment she thought she may be dreaming and that she would wake up in her bed in Turo.

What is this capstone made of? she questioned, coming back to the reality of her entrapment. Elera had no idea, but she felt mild vibrations again, in time with her increasing unease. She unbuckled her satchel and removed the crystal ball. Its intricate innards were alive with activity once again, and as she looked up, she was dazed at what she saw. The walls were now transparent, and the ocean was directly in front of her, so close that she could reach out and touch it. She remembered the entrance to the pyramid, which had mysteriously collapsed. Before that had happened, she was fascinated that the water was held away in a similar sense, as if an invisible wall was holding the vast ocean back.

The entrance must have been made from the same material as this capstone, she thought. Elera sat motionless for many moments, amazed at the sight around her. It was as if she was floating in the middle of the ocean and she could see beautifully unusual creatures swimming by now and again. She observed a red batwing crab crawling up the wall, a giant loggerhead turtle cutting through the water with delicate grace and a slender dusky shark, calmly stalking a school of smaller fish. She reached out and her hand went straight through the wall into the water. She pulled it back. It was wet and salty. She laughed out loud with relief, amazed at the pyramid and its incredible structure. A wave of euphoria passed through her body and she almost felt like crying at how she would have never believed such a sight only a few days earlier.

She stood to her feet and prepared herself, holding the crystal tight and making sure her clothing was secured tightly. Then she jumped straight through the wall.

Chapter 7 – An Unlikely Friend

As Elera passed through the wall of the capstone, she took a large breath but was not prepared for the immense pressure of the deep ocean. It hit her like a heavy weight, pressing down on every part of her body. The surface looked much higher than before and she began to panic that she would run out of oxygen before she could reach the air above. She swam as hard as she could, holding on tightly to the crystal orb. With every movement of her body, Elera grew more and more tired and before long, she was making little progress, hardly gaining any distance. She began to feel faint and within a minute she had stopped moving and tried to accept calmly that she would never reach the top.

This is the end, she thought.

As she began to lose consciousness, a miraculous thing happened. A spotted dolphin, whirling and waving through the water, appeared before Elera and began to nudge her with its rubbery nose. She felt it pushing in the small of her back. Almost unconscious, the orb slipped out of her hands into the ocean. As her mind drifted into a dark abyss, she felt a surge of speed bringing her back to life as the dolphin reached the surface. It propelled Elera with vigour up into the air.

Elera gasped instinctively and the dolphin blew out a spew of water through its blowhole. The splash of landing back in the water from the air stirred Elera into consciousness and she spluttered for a while trying to catch her breath. Her vision came back into focus just in time to see the dolphin swimming away.

She looked around for the crystal sphere. It suddenly emerged from the ocean not far away and hovered gently over the surface of water. Elera was in awe of the entity, which she immediately stopped seeing as an object and now saw as a being. After breathing heavily for a while, Elera swam over and placed her hand slowly on its smooth, curved surface. It allowed her to place it into her satchel for safekeeping.

She looked around again, kicking slowly with her legs to keep afloat. She could see the shoreline of Bimini in the distance, perhaps three suns away.

It will take a while for me to reach there in my current condition, she thought, widening her arms and legs so that she floated easily in the water. Her body felt immensely tired and malnourished. She had a strong fluttering sensation in her midriff. She began to swim slowly in the direction of the island, but then she heard a faint humming noise from behind. Looking back, she saw a motorboat speeding towards the island. She waved her arms and called out to get the driver's attention.

"Hey!" she shouted, spluttering a little in the process. "Over here!"

The boat did not change direction at first but after a few more attempts at drawing attention to herself, Elera saw it heading towards her. The driver was a woman, wearing a black waterproof suit and with dark curly black hair tied back in a tight bob. She looked quite young and had a serious expression on her face. She slowed the boat until it stopped and she reached down to Elera, a slight grin appearing on her face.

"Need a lift?" she asked casually, offering her hand to Elera over the side of the boat. Elera did not hesitate to take it and the woman's strength surprised her, pulling her into the boat with relative ease.

"Thank you," Elera said weakly, lying back on a padded seat and unable to move easily. She placed her satchel at her side in the slick boat, which was painted white and red on the outside with grey interiors. Elera noticed a shoulder belt filled with gadgets and knives, lying haphazardly on the seat next to her. The boat roared back into action as it sped up towards the island.

"What were you doing in the ocean?" the woman asked nonchalantly, glancing back at Elera whilst steering. Elera thought for a moment about her response, used to being a tactician in answering questions.

This woman could work for the Raiceman government, she thought.

Quickly, she decided to answer entirely truthfully, realising the truth was nothing to be ashamed of.

"There is an old ruin under this ocean," she stated calmly. "I have been trapped down there for about a week, maybe two. I have only just found a way out."

The woman looked back at Elera with surprise and scepticism, veering off to the right slightly. She quickly manoeuvred the boat back towards the island, the trees of which could now be seen quite clearly.

"I have been looking for a place that has been lost for a long time," Elera continued in a dazed manner. "This island holds many links to that place."

The woman was quiet for a moment and then she slowed the boat to a gentle trawl. She turned to Elera. "So are you some sort of explorer?"

"Sort of."

"Do you know why the power went out on this island?" she asked intently. "Did you have something to do with that?"

"Who are you?" Elera asked in return, growing a little suspicious.

"I might ask you the same thing," she replied. "My name is Sula and I work for Tyrona. I'm here to find out why every guard and soldier that is supposed to be here has suddenly disappeared off the island."

This news made Elera very cautious. "I don't know where the guards have gone," she said truthfully. "I admit that I and my friends were involved in a power cut on the island, but that was only so we could get past the patrol boats on the coast. There were thousands of guards here then."

Sula's eyes were firmly locked on Elera's, suspiciously trying to work out if she was telling the truth. Her expression was one of inkling and deep thought. She finally smiled mischievously. "In that case, you can help me work out where the hell everybody's gone!" she said humorously. Her statement eased Elera's concern slightly.

Sula put the boat into its fastest speed and within a few minutes they were cruising up to South Bimini's rich shore, deep brown and cream sparkles majestically smoothed into a serene beach. Sula stopped the boat and threw a small anchor over the side. She grabbed her shoulder belt and jumped into the water, which came up to her chest.

"Come on!" she said. "You look like you could do with something to eat."

Elera put on her satchel and slowly lowered herself into the water. As they walked onto the beach, Elera felt relieved that her feet were touching solid earth after so long under the ocean.

Ahead was a small beach forest. Elera walked over, sat down and slowly pulled a few pieces of fruit from a shrub. As she ate, Sula walked over and sat beside her. She offered her some dried fish from a pouch in her shoulder belt. Elera took it and thanked her.

"So where are you from? Raicema?" Sula asked.

"I lived in Raicema once," Elera replied, feeling rejuvenated by the fruit. "I am an astrologer. I used to live in Raicema City."

"And where do you live now?" she asked as Elera chewed off a small piece of meat.

"All over," Elera admitted honestly. "This past year I have been travelling to many places studying ancient sites and structures..."

"To find this magical lost place you are looking for?" Sula interrupted a little sarcastically.

"Yes," Elera said defensively. "It is a place that we all have a connection with. It is a root for us all."

Sula looked uninterested in Elera's depiction and quickly changed the subject. "So how'd you cut the power here?"

"It wasn't me who did that. Some friends of mine managed to get into the reactor at the other end of the island and shut it down. The commotion caused all the guards out in boats to come back to the island. That was how I was able to get out there to find the pyramid."

Sula began to look around at the desolate shore, scanning for movement but finding none.

"Find anything in there?" she asked Elera after a while.

"No," Elera lied, still not fully trusting of Sula's intentions.

Sula seemed to accept her answer, again apparently uninterested. She began to look into the beach forest, trying to work out where it led. She got to her feet. "I'm going to try and find the military base here. This island isn't so big so it shouldn't take long. You should stay here. I'm going back to Raicema once I've finished my investigation here and I can take you with me if you want?" Sula offered, her voice sounding genuine. "If I was you, I'd stop wasting time getting trapped in old ruins that nobody cares about. You'd be much better off just getting on with your life."

Elera just nodded, unsure of what to say. She dare not mention that she had any affiliation with the Makai and that permanently moving back to Raicema was the last thing on her mind.

"I'll wait for you here," Elera said, continuing to eat the orange-coloured fruit from the shrub. Sula headed into the forest and within moments she had disappeared within its interplay of shadows and light. Elera wondered about the woman.

She works for the government, but in what facet?

She was unsure if she should even wait around for her, as now would be a good time to get away in the boat. But then Elera remembered how she was feeling whilst trapped in the pyramid and how trusting her instincts had always brought her to safety. She believed that this woman had come along at a time when she really needed her. With this in mind, Elera decided that she would build a fire on the beach and wait for Sula. She knew that as it got darker on Bimini, it would get cold quite quickly. Having a warm fire ready and waiting was a smart move.

It didn't take Elera long to gather a stack of deadwood and she used a tinderbox in her satchel to get the fire going. Then she sat by it and took out the crystal ball, laying it gently in the dusty sand.

The sun was still shining brightly but there were a number of large clouds that blocked its rays intermittently and during these periods, the temperature dropped as the wind pummelled the island. Elera's matted hair swayed in the breeze. She felt eager to dive into a pool of water and thoroughly cleanse herself. Looking at the spherical crystal, she tried to get the effigy of the four pyramids to appear again but to no avail. It was no longer alive and energetic as it had been below in its underwater home. She began to doubt if taking it was a good idea, but then she remembered that she probably wouldn't have escaped the pyramid without it. She also remembered how it floated out of the water.

Her mind began to recollect how she had found herself on Bimini in the first place. It had started with a dream, a dream she had experienced over and over. It was of a giant eye somewhere in space, dragging her towards it. After having this dream for weeks she had experienced a most vivid, realistic dream in which she had met an old lady. She could never quite make out the face of the lady but she remembered every word that was spoken between them.

"I want to tell you a story, Elera," the lady had said, her clothing old and in rags. *"There was once a young woman who lived with her parents. This young lady had everything she needed: food, shelter and the support of her elders. But she was unhappy. One day, this young lady wished so hard that her life would change. And one day, she woke up and found herself to be someone else, a woman who was married with three children. Looking back, it was only an instant yet the time that had lapsed was ten years. Unfortunately for her, she could not remember anything that had happened in between and longed to go back in time and live with her parents again. When her children came to her, she felt like they were strangers though they seemed to know her very well. The same was true of her husband."*

"What happened to her?" Elera had asked.

"The woman spent months with her new family and eventually she grew to love them all very dearly. But then, the woman went to sleep one night, and when she awoke she was once again living with her parents and it was ten years earlier. She was a young woman again. From that day, she understood something fundamental about life."

"What?"

"That reality can change very quickly, so make the most of what you are

currently living."

After that dream, Elera had begun to experience the most extra-ordinary coincidences. She would meet someone randomly, bump into them on a frequent basis and then be helped by the person to achieve something. She had met a teacher who seemed to turn up every time Elera went shopping for food in the markets of Raicema City. It had turned out that the teacher was an avid traveller and had sailed around the globe. She had told Elera about the island of Bimini and the stones that led under the ocean. She was also a strong believer that Lemuria once existed on the planet and was certain that Bimini had a strong link to it. The meeting had been a tremendously uplifting experience.

After that, occurrence after occurrence would encourage her to visit Bimini, including an offer from the learning institute where she worked to visit the islands on a three-week holiday. In the end, after conversing with Kirichi, she had decided to leave Raicema City and travel on her own terms.

Now, looking around the tranquil beach, she saw a small line of huts at one end. She got to her feet and took her boots off. She ran barefoot to the huts and saw that they were all locked. They were painted white and each had a small window. She peered into one, seeing row upon row of logs. The smoke was rising high from the fire further up the beach and Elera quickly looked into the other two huts.

"Wha—??" she blurted out whilst looking into the last one. It was full of explosives. The sight made her heart skip a beat.

She headed back to the fire, remembering that she had left the crystal ball lying in the sand and wondering what the explosives were intended for. As she arrived back, she noticed the orb had come alive and little fireflies of light were shooting around the compli-cated mass of inner channels like an electric racecourse. The image of the four pyramids had appeared again and this time she saw that they were not only all different sizes but slightly different shapes.

One pyramid was clearly the Great Pyramid of Giza and another smaller one looked very similar to the underwater pyramid from which she had just escaped. The other two were like no pyramid that Elera had visited or heard about. One looked twice the size of the Great Pyramid of Giza but had grooves running down its sides and the other was smaller but with staggered, stepped slopes. As she tried to study the increasingly clear detail, she heard a rustling in the trees behind her and saw Sula emerge from the undergrowth.

She quickly placed the crystal sphere into her satchel.

"Not a damn thing back there," Sula huffed, looking deflated. "Might as well call it a day. It took me ages to get over to this island. I don't know, the jobs I get!"

"What do you need to do?" Elera asked her, still unsure what task she had been assigned.

"I have to get the island's core computer system running again. It just disappeared off the grid. That's how they were alerted to the fact that everyone's vanished into thin air!"

Elera couldn't understand it. She, Rekesh and the others had only shut down one small power station to cause a diversion.

Surely that wasn't enough to cause everyone to leave, she thought.

"How many power stations are there on this island?" Elera asked Sula.

"I think nine," she pondered, "not including the backup station on the northern island."

"And all of those are down?"

"Did you not hear what I said?" Sula said in a comical manner. "Nobody is here. Every power station is down, not been run by anyone. No wonder they are stressing to high heaven in Tyrona. I don't usually get jobs like this, you know, critical ones but with the war and all—"

Elera didn't want to hear any more about the Raiceman government's pathetic excuses for invading other lands so she quickly interrupted Sula. "—So what kind of jobs do you usually do?"

"Well it's funny you should ask," Sula said with a smile. "I research old buildings."

"Really?" Elera said with surprise, to which Sula nodded.

"Nothing like where you've been recently. I'm not that crazy! But I mainly investigate derelict buildings in lots of different nations. Sometimes the buildings are so old, they're like ruins. I have to record if anyone lives there and recover any artefacts. The oldest building I ever explored was five hundred years old! Can you believe that? Almost as old as Raicema itself."

A great feeling of sympathy for Sula promptly filled Elera's heart. She was clearly unaware that human civilisation dated at least many millennia before the birth of the Raiceman Empire. Sula opened a flask and began to drink from it.

"Sula, I have a strong reason to believe that the ruin in the ocean over there is over ten thousand years old."

"What?!" Sula said, spluttering with disbelief at Elera's statement. "I think you've got it wrong, babe. It's probably some early Raiceman temple that was built on an island that sank. After all, people were primitive animals ten thousand years ago."

Elera realised that it would take a lot of explaining to clear the clouds of misinformation hanging over Sula's head.

"Okay," Elera began seriously. "I will tell you what I know but it might take a while."

Elera told Sula about all the evidence she had amassed over her years of study proving that not only were there scores of previous empires in the past, but that many of these empires reigned over the planet for much longer than Raicema. She talked until it got dark and Sula provided a tasty meal of beans, baked potatoes and salted fish that she had stowed on her boat.

Sula was silent and wide-eyed as she listened to Elera's account. She told Sula of her strong belief that there was a large part of human history that was completely lost and that she was looking for it. "I can't believe it!" Sula said many times during the evening. However, Elera got the distinct feeling that all the pieces of information that had never really made sense to Sula were beginning to fit together into a bigger picture in her mind.

"My God!" she blurted out suddenly. "Once I visited this place in Ciafra where there were all these old ruins. Must have been six years ago now. It was like nothing I'd ever seen before. I recorded everything, took sketches, took pictures and wrote a hundred-page report. I thought I'd discovered something incredible but when I got back to Tyrona and submitted the report, I was branded a traitor because I'd suggested it was older than the empire. After that I always got sent to bigger towns and cities where the buildings were only a few hundred years old. I almost forgot about it until now."

"Well, I'm not surprised they tried to discredit you," Elera said with sympathy. "Have you seen how much they invest in their so-called learning system? It's everywhere. They want everyone to think Raicema is the be all and end all of the world."

Sula entered a state of deliberation as she absorbed everything that they had discussed.

"The really sad thing is that as far as I know, it has always been like this, with an empire suppressing knowledge to the masses," Elera continued. "That's why I'm looking for Lemuria. I believe that was the place where the first empire was born. I want to know why and what we were all like before."

Sula seemed indifferent but Elera understood it was difficult to accept that one has been methodically lied to for most of one's life.

"I think I want to go to sleep now," Sula said after a while.

Elera agreed and wished Sula a good night's sleep, hoping that when they awoke in the morning, Sula would feel freer and more in control of her life. As Elera went to sleep under the stars with three warm blankets on top of her, she knew that meeting Sula was not a coincidence and that somehow they would become good friends.

Chapter 8 – The Professor and the Plateau

The tallest pyramid in the Giza plateau stood over four hundred feet high, each giant stone used in its structure weighing at least two tonnes. The grandeur of the pyramid had bewildered visitors to the area for as long as could be remembered. Two smaller pyramids were not far away, forming the well-known trio the Giza plateau was famous for.

Rekesh rode ferociously across the vast desert that encompassed the upland ahead. His horse had been a true warrior, pressing on with little rest through the intense heat of east Ciafra. In the distance, the triad could be seen, the glimmer of the sun running down the edge of the farthest megalith.

The smallest of the pyramids had been fully infiltrated during Raicema's second century of rule and had been converted into the largest astrological observatory on the planet. The Raicemans had abandoned full control of the giant observatory two hundred years later when a major earthquake caused half of the pyramid to collapse, killing most of the astronomers inside. Since then, Raicema had given sovereignty of Giza back to the Ciafran government but kept a watchful eye on the activity in the pyramids and on the astronomers in the area.

As Rekesh arrived at the Great Pyramid from across the vast range of desert sand-dunes, he was greeted by a group of young children. He slowed his horse and dismounted, tying its reins to a nearby tree.

"I am looking for Professor Sorentius," Rekesh said to the children. "I have travelled a long way to see him. Do you know where I can find him?"

One of the older children stepped forward and pointed to a small opening in the distance at the western corner of the Great Pyramid.

"Professor Sorentius is in the lower west chamber," said the tall child. "It is a map room, where they plot the movement of the stars."

Rekesh nodded and walked slowly to the entrance, weak and

weary from the long journey. He was surprised at his fatigue as he had prided himself at being able to fight past such adverse conditions. This time, however, his concern and fear over Elera's fate had drained him both mentally and physically. A sharp pang of guilt struck his chest.

I will reach you soon, Elera, he vowed to himself.

The entrance to the lower west chamber had been dug out years earlier. It had now been reinforced by massive wooden blocks, and Rekesh assumed huge stone slabs must have covered this entrance previously. In the distance, he could see the other two smaller pyramids, the smallest with a giant dome built on the side that had collapsed.

Inside the chamber, two women and three men were working. The women and one of the men were plotting points on a large map on the floor, talking amongst themselves and laughing. The other two men were reinforcing some of the walls in the chamber with wooden struts and seemed to be straining under the effort.

The man working on the map looked up and smiled. Rekesh guessed that he was about sixty years old. He had black hair with silver streaks, round spectacles and wore a small shirt and tan shorts. He immediately got up and walked over to the entrance where Rekesh was standing.

"Hello," said the man. "I am Professor Sorentius."

Rekesh breathed a slight sigh of relief. "I have been travelling for days to reach you, Professor. I am Rekesh, Elera Advaya's partner. She is in danger and I need your help."

Sorentius looked behind him at the two women who were now climbing to their feet and walking towards them.

"This is Doctor Selina Rudh," he said, introducing a blonde, fair woman. "And this is Professor Tifu Osaba," he continued, gesturing to a tall woman with a beautiful golden complexion and dark brown curly hair. Sorentius removed his spectacles and wiped the lenses with a dark cotton cloth. "What has Elera got herself into this time?" he said grinning, a clear look of amusement on his face.

Rekesh couldn't help feeling a little annoyed at Sorentius' lax attitude. He decided to shrug off his annoyance and waste no more time. "A few weeks ago, we travelled to Bimini to explore an ancient path that led under the ocean. After three days, we were able to trace the path along and then dive down to its ending. We found an underwater pyramid."

Sorentius' eyes grew wider and a look of concern now spread over his face. "Go on..." he said.

"Elera found an entrance to the pyramid and entered. I followed, as did two others that were with us. Inside there was no ocean water. It was incredible. Something was keeping the ocean out. There were stone doors that were sealed but Elera opened them. I don't know how. The next thing I knew, the pyramid entrance was collapsing. Somehow Sita, Rama and I were not harmed. We were thrown back into the ocean and within a few minutes we were at the surface but Elera is still trapped in there. I tried to go back but the ocean turned grey with dust."

Sorentius scratched his head, contemplating what he had heard.

"I remembered Elera saying that she had studied with you about pyramids and so I travelled here for your help," Rekesh continued. "I remember Elera telling me about how most pyramids have underground tunnels and labyrinths and I thought you might know of another way into the pyramid. I feel bad travelling so far away from her to get help but I couldn't think of anyone else."

"How did you explore Bimini when Raicema have troops all over the island and shores?" asked Tifu.

"We managed to distract the Raiceman troops away from the shore by shutting down one of their power reactors," Rekesh explained quietly with a little reservation.

Sorentius was still in deep thought. "Who found out about the path? Was it Elera?" he asked suddenly.

"Yes," Rekesh answered. "She visited Turo a few months before and then she suggested that we go there. We planned it for a while."

"And did she bring anything back from Lizrab?" the professor

91

pressed on.

"Not that I know of," Rekesh replied. "Why? Do you think that's how she opened the doors?"

"It's a possibility, but it makes things more difficult if that is the case. You see, this pyramid we are standing in is over ten thousand years old and it has been very difficult to get inside. There are many others on the planet that are younger, copies if you like, notably the two other pyramids outside. But we have found scriptures within this pyramid that indicate that there are older ones out there, pyramids that are more advanced in their structure. These were built by people that knew many things that we do not now. For example, there are many inner stones in this building that fit together so perfectly, it is almost as if they have been melted together. I know of no technique to melt stone on such a level. Whoever these people were, they came from a civilisation that we know very little about."

"Lemuria?" Rekesh probed. "Elera has been talking about it for years now."

"Possibly," Sorentius remarked. "Unfortunately we have only been able to explore certain areas of this pyramid, so we have little idea of how it was designed as a whole or how it correlates to other structures on the planet."

"That's right," Selina said. "Many things about this monument are a mystery. I have been studying the structure of this pyramid and it is perfectly constructed and placed to receive the maximum amount of sunlight in this area. In fact, many scriptures indicate that this pyramid was once called the *Sun Pyramid* or sometimes the *Pyramid of Fire*. At one time, it is likely that this pyramid was covered with some kind of massive panel – stone slabs that may have somehow powered the pyramid by channelling the energy from the sunlight. We are convinced that a long time ago, these stone slabs were stolen by looters."

"So what can we do for Elera?" Rekesh pressed on impatiently, directing his question to all three scientists.

"I would like you to tell me more about what Elera told you

before embarking on your trip to Bimini," Sorentius answered. "Let us go to my office in the observatory. It is not far from here. Did you travel by horse?"

"Yes. He's outside."

"Good. Then let us waste no more time," he said reassuringly, gesturing goodbye to Selina and Tifu who went back to their map-plotting exercise. Rekesh and Sorentius walked outside, the sun still shining brightly. Rekesh ran back to his horse and rode it over to the side of the Great Pyramid where Sorentius was mounting his grey mare.

"Over there," he said, pointing to the smallest pyramid with its spherical observatory in the far distance.

Sorentius rode off and Rekesh quickly followed. The sand spewed up with every fleeting step of the horse's hooves, and a feeling of relief began to pass through Rekesh's body. The dry air flying by seemed to blow all of his worries away.

The plateau was a combination of sand and rubble, huge blocks of stone often protruding out of the sand. As Rekesh rode past the second of the pyramids, he noticed that it had been positioned on a hill, giving the impression it was bigger than the Great Pyramid from certain vantage points. Behind it was a vast, barren desert. Rekesh had heard from the old Makai legends that huge cities had once surrounded these ancient pyramids. Raicema had tried hard to dispel that legend, instead insisting that only primitive villages had ever surrounded the great structures.

As Rekesh approached the observatory, he saw that the left side of it was completely caved in, now just a huge pile of giant stone rubble. The right side, however, had a variety of metallic gadgets affixed to it; large dishes laden with glistening crystals, giant metal sheets and other climbing structures. There were two entrances on the remaining intact corners, both quite grand.

"Head to the eastern corner," Sorentius shouted from his horse, as they approached. The two men halted their horses and tied them to a nearby tree. "This is called the entrance of Menkaure, named after the tomb of the king that it originally led to. Of course, that tomb was raided long before anybody can remember and is now used as another star-plotting room. Quite useful as well, as there are shafts which point directly at specific stars."

Sorentius and Rekesh entered through Menkaure's entrance, which immediately led into a vast hallway with a set of huge stone steps going deep into the depths of the pyramid.

"The Raicemans dug out this hallway two centuries ago and built that stairway down to the lower chambers," Sorentius commented to Rekesh as they walked past the stairway to a small room at the back of the hall. "They were convinced that the tunnels of the pyramids here in the plateau went deep into the earth."

Sorentius opened a large wooden door and gestured for Rekesh to sit on a stone bench in his office, which was quite bare apart from a huge bookshelf running along two of its walls.

"Now, let's try and get to the bottom of this dilemma," Sorentius said, sitting down in a large leather chair and striking up a pipe to puff on. "You said that Elera visited Turo before embarking on this journey?"

"Yes," reiterated Rekesh. "She went to visit her old teacher – Kirichi – and when she returned to Raicema she told me about an old pyramid that was under the ocean. She was quite adamant to find it. We planned for a month how to get past the Raiceman guards near Bimini and once we had arranged it all, we set off and located the pyramid. It was right where Elera said it would be, at the end of an underwater stone road."

"How did you follow the road? I presume it went to quite a depth."

"The path was very windy and it did go very deep, down to about six hundred feet. We tried anchoring ourselves along at first with breathing tanks, but the pressure was too much and as we got deeper our breathing tanks stopped working. Needless to say we didn't get too far that way but then we noticed something unusual about the stones. They were covered in a luminous algae and the deeper down we got, the more of it covered the stones, sometimes to the point that you could see nothing but a green mass where a stone was."

He paused for breath.

"Not only was this algae illuminating the way but it was actually producing a lot of oxygen. So we went back to the island and created a pod out of an old boat. Then using nothing but that pod over our bodies and a few grappling hooks and anchors, we dragged our way along the path. The oxygen from the algae floated up into the pod and we made it all the way along without any breathing tanks or anything!"

"Mmm. Quite remarkable."

"Yes," Rekesh agreed. "And the further along we got, the easier it was to walk, almost like we were being pulled towards something. After a few hour of walking, we reached it."

"And the pyramid? What did it look like?" Sorentius enquired with enthusiasm.

"Huge, with a slight glow to it. It was bigger than this one but not as big as the Great Pyramid. And I just can't understand how the water was kept out of the main entrance. It was as if an invisible barrier was holding the water at bay. You could put your hand or arm into the wall of water and it would come out wet. But all that collapsed when Elera opened the door." He sighed. "I went back, but it was sealed."

Sorentius stood up and went over to a bookshelf. He picked up an old dusty stack of ancient pages.

"These scrolls were found in a chamber in the Great Pyramid. They are made of papyrus and are all very fragile. Both I and Elera have studied it in great detail."

He placed the stack on the desk in front of Rekesh.

"Inside it talks of many things," Sorentius continued. "The most interesting being the description of a power source within the Great Pyramid and the existence of other similar pyramids all over this planet. If you open the last page in the book, you will see a depiction of a chamber with fifty-four holes in the wall. This, I believe, is the central chamber that contains the power source."

"What power source? What does it do?" Rekesh asked, opening the book to the last page, slightly confused.

"A power source that controls things in the pyramid, like opening other chambers and many other things we might not understand, such as invisible fields that keep water at bay, for example. We also have reason to believe that underneath the Great Pyramid is a very deep system of tunnels and catacombs that may spread over a large region of the Giza plateau or beyond."

Sorentius pointed to the last page.

"This central room is also a map room of sorts. It is conceivable that a similar underground system exists under the Bimini pyramid."

"So there is another way in?" Rekesh tried to confirm, observing the drawings.

"Not sure," said Sorentius, shaking his head. "I'm pretty sure that finding the central chamber in that book would give us a greater insight into how the pyramids were designed. Nobody has ever found the chamber. But if we could, we might understand the pyramids better and learn of a way to get into the Bimini pyramid."

Sorentius puffed on his pipe and seemed to be contemplating whether to keep talking. After a while of serious contemplation, a wry smile formed on the wrinkled face of the professor.

"You have impeccable timing as I have been planning the deepest exploration of the Great Pyramid to date for some time now. The Ciafran government don't know but Selina and I found a chamber that has not been explored. There are several tunnels that go deep underground. I was planning to start the expedition next week, but seeing as though you are here…"

Rekesh was both excited and frustrated by the news. "Well, I had hoped that you would know how Elera opened the entrance. I thought that she might have had a key or something…"

Sorentius thought to himself for a while. "Even if there was a 'key' as you say for that strange entrance, it would do no good now. You have already said it is sealed. The only hope for getting back in is to understand the tunnel system."

Rekesh had heard enough and rose to his feet, ready to begin the exploration.

"Wait, Rekesh. Slow down," Sorentius advised, holding his hands up. "You have had a long journey and it is better to start tomorrow. It will be dark soon. Get some rest and we shall begin early."

Rekesh was almost going to argue against this advice, when he realised how physically drained he really was. He felt as if he hadn't slept for a week. He knew getting some rest was the right thing to do. He nodded in acceptance at Sorentius' advice.

"Good. I shall show you to our camp."

Sorentius got to his feet and put his hand on Rekesh's shoulder.

"Elera will be fine. Trust me, she has been in deeper pickles than this." With that he chuckled to himself and Rekesh got to his feet. They made their way out of the pyramid into the warm air of the plateau. In the distance Rekesh could see a large group of tall tents, next to what looked like an enormous metal box. It was quite an eyesore.

"What's that metal thing over there?"

"Oh that," Sorentius said in an irritated fashion. "That is a giant casing that covers the Great Lion."

"Great Lion?"

"Yes. The two oldest structures on this plateau are the Great Pyramid and the Great Lion. Unfortunately, it is forbidden to explore it and that casing has been around it for decades."

Sorentius leaned towards Rekesh's ear to speak quietly.

"It's Raicema's doing," he whispered. "And the western corner of this pyramid didn't collapse by accident either."

Rekesh was intrigued to hear more, but then several locals walked by and Sorentius quickly changed the subject and guided Rekesh to their horses.

"I'll meet you over there," the professor said, jumping onto his horse with agility and cantering off. Rekesh followed slowly, the epic surroundings quite hard to take in. The sun looked enormous and he began to think how little he knew about the planet and the things that were upon it. Thinking of Elera was the only thing that made any sense. He trotted along in the dry heat, wishing that she were there with him.

As the warm glow of the sun started to hide behind the scattered palm trees of Giza, Javu and Teltu arrived at the edge of the plateau, followed closely by Sita and Rama. The journey had been long and tiring and Javu hoped that Rekesh was there. He could feel an air of excitement, almost like a period of great change was upon them.

"We should arrive before sunset," Javu shouted back to Sita in Hindi, who was leading the stallion that she and Rama sat upon. Listening to the gentle patter of the horse's hooves against the sand was almost transcendental.

As they rode along, Teltu began to think about Fera and Nehne back at home. His wife had always been very intuitive and he was sure the same intuition was present in Elera. That alone he was sure, would guide her to safety. Teltu was still confused about why Elera had ventured into an old ruin in the first place, however.

"Javu," Teltu started to ask, "what did Elera hope to find out when she went to Bimini?"

"I know she was looking for information about the location of Lemuria. I do not know specifically what she was looking for. We will find out more soon."

Teltu had heard of the legends of Lemuria, many of them describing a peaceful culture. He was sceptical, however, that these legends were purely inventions to give hope to struggling communities. A wave of frustration passed through him at his lack of understanding about how the societies of the world had come to be as they were.

"Javu," he started again, "what do you know about what the

world was like before Raicema controlled everything?"

Javu smiled at Teltu's question. "Before Raicema there were many other empires with exactly the same intentions as those who currently hold power, namely the pursuit of even more power. A story has been passed down for many generations in my family that this planet was almost completely destroyed on more than one occasion because of such a pursuit. It is the common trait in the empires that have come and gone. At those times many brave souls fought against the repression and violence and somehow saved this planet. So to answer your question, Teltu, I don't think the world has changed very much for a long time."

"Why doesn't anybody have any details about the previous empires, though? This world seems to have no history!" Teltu exclaimed. Javu could sense the dissatisfaction in his voice.

"Recorded history in books and the Raiceman computer systems only go back to the birth of Raicema. There is more, much more, but all the public knowledge was destroyed a long time ago here in Ciafra and in Raicema. You are not alone in your frustration, Teltu. Elera believes that finding Lemuria would help us understand a lot more about who we are and the history that we all share. I am sure there are many who know the entire history of the planet," Javu reassured him. "The truth can never be destroyed. It is just there, floating in the air, with us at all times."

"But what do *you* know?" Teltu pressed, growing impatient.

"Patience is important in gaining knowledge, Teltu," Javu remarked in response. "I tell you what I know in the moment it is right to tell you."

The statement calmed Teltu who looked embarrassed by his impatience. He looked out over the plateau and saw three points in the far distance.

"I see the pyramids!" he said, pointing to the slowly emerging triangular shapes.

Javu nodded, his head held high and long wiry beard wrapping around his face and neck with the movement of the air. Sita and

Rama rode slowly behind, in awe of the dusty land and its monuments. As they got closer a beautiful image could be seen of the large glowing sun hovering between the Great Pyramid and its neighbour. Within the hour, they had arrived. It was almost dark. Children ran up to the visitors and started asking all sorts of questions. Javu dismounted and approached the children, followed closely by the others.

"Have any of you children seen a man called Rekesh? He has black hair and a short beard, much shorter than this one," Javu asked gleefully, tugging on his beard.

"A man called Rekesh arrived today and he went to the camp with the professor," an older child said, dutifully.

Javu breathed a sigh of relief.

"Can you take us to the camp, friends?" Javu asked, politely.

The children all nodded with enthusiasm and the four began to walk with the children behind the pyramids and towards the group of large tents that had been erected on a hilly dune. The ominous shadow of the great metal box looked creepy in the fading light.

"Were you worried about missing him?" Teltu asked Javu, sand tickling their ankles as it sprayed up whilst they walked.

"Rekesh has a lot of passion within him," Javu said, quite seriously. "He can become very headstrong and aggressive when he becomes afraid. He has been like that since he was a child, like corn that explodes when it becomes too hot. My concern is primarily for Elera. Rekesh could put her life in danger if he gets into that frame of mind. It is better that we are here to support them both."

"So you think Elera is okay?"

"I am sure of it, Teltu. She is a very intuitive woman, like all the women in your life," he said with a wink. "She will be safe wherever she ventures."

After a while, the group arrived at a group of red tents, thick carpets laid down all around. The smell of sweet tea and fragrant rice wafted through the air from the largest tent. A herd of camels rested close by.

"I will find the professor!" one of the children announced, disappearing into the large tent. After a moment, he reappeared with Sorentius, guiding him firmly by the hand.

"Slow down, Mahed," he said, taken aback slightly by the child's enthusiasm. He peered up at Javu with instant recognition.

"My, my. Javu of Seho. How have you been?" He greeted him, holding Javu's hand with warmth. "I suppose you are here for the same reason that young Rekesh is?"

"Indeed," Javu said, smiling. "I am well, Sorentius. Is Rekesh with you now?"

"Yes. He is inside eating. Please join us."

Everyone went inside and were greeted by an array of large, round trays filled with rice, vegetable stews and breads. Many people were sitting eating, most astrologers or construction workers. They mainly ate with their hands from the ornate metal trays, but some used spoons to take stew from one tray and mix it with the rice in another.

Sorentius led Javu and the others to a section at the back of the tent, where Rekesh was eating alone, solemn-faced. A thick candle burned away in the corner. Javu approached slowly.

"Rekesh?" he said softly, stirring him from his thoughts.

Rekesh looked up, his eyes lighting at the sight of Javu. He rose to his feet and embraced the shorter elder with affection.

"How did you know I was here?"

"Don't you recognise your two friends behind me?" Javu replied, alluding to Sita and Rama who waved at Rekesh as they entered the area. He held him by the shoulders and looking up intently into his eyes. "I am aware of Elera's *situation*." Javu raised his eyebrows.

"Well, it's not easy, Javu. I don't really know what's happened to her."

"That may be so, but there are many situations in life when faith is the only way forward. Why did you come here?"

The direct question took him back a little and before he could muster an answer, the others moved into the private area. Rekesh looked over Javu's shoulder and was pleased to see Teltu, Sita and Rama. He hugged them all warmly.

"We should all eat!" Sorentius said as he bounded in, to which everyone agreed. Javu sat on the floor and poured himself some tea. He sat looking at Rekesh for a while as he was eating with the others, all sharing from a raised tray filled with rice and vegetable pastries.

"You have come in good time, Javu," Rekesh said, smiling weakly. "Tomorrow we are to explore the depths of the Great Pyramid."

"And what do you hope to find down there?" Javu asked, directing his question to both Rekesh and Sorentius.

"We are trying to find the control room. It is the epicentre of the pyramid," Sorentius explained. "If we can find it, we will understand a great deal about the structure and tunnel system that is deep under the plateau."

"Are there not dangers in going inside?" Teltu asked, a little wary. "I have heard from Fera and Elera that some of the tunnels are very narrow."

"It is true," Sorentius said. "But I know as much about the layout as anyone in Giza and we recently found a new route that has been unexplored. In fact, we have known about it for over a year now but the government have blocked any proposed explorations."

"So what is so different, this time?" Javu asked.

"Oh, nothing," Sorentius said with a glint in his eye. "But someone's life is at risk and it just happens that King Rufi needs all his men this week for a royal visit from Neoasia. It should be easier to undertake the exploration without being noticed."

Everyone ate in silence for a while, the flickering from the candle making the light sway against the carpet and tent wall-hangings.

"Why did you come here, Rekesh?" Javu asked again, having not received an answer the first time he had asked.

"I am here to help Elera," Rekesh replied defensively.

"What has urged you to come here?" Javu probed further.

"Elera spoke about Giza many times," Rekesh said a little more aggressively.

"And you have come to the conclusion that the Giza pyramid is much the same as the one in Bimini?" Javu continued, the others now all attentive that he was alluding to something that they were not aware of.

"That's what I'm hoping," Rekesh responded firmly.

"It's likely, Javu," Sorentius added, supporting Rekesh's answer.

"I only ask because I often feel like such structures are better off undisturbed."

There was silence at the warning.

"Well, if we are to make such a dangerous journey in the morning, we should all rest peacefully tonight," Javu said after a while, looking at Sita and Rama who were eating slowly.

"Yes, I suddenly feel very tired," Rekesh said, getting to his feet. He wished everyone goodnight and left for the bed tents.

"Me too," Teltu said following Rekesh. Shortly after, Sita and Rama both got to their feet and headed in the same direction.

"Tell me, Sorentius," Javu began. "Is the Bimini pyramid sealed now that the entrance has collapsed?"

Sorentius stared down for a while.

"I don't know. I had an inkling that there were other pyramids of similar age in existence but today is the first that I have heard of the one in Bimini. It is likely that there are multiple routes in but the fact it is underwater is not a good sign. Many of the underground chambers and tunnels may have collapsed. To be honest, I am quite concerned about Elera's welfare."

Javu smiled empathetically at the long-nosed professor. "I have a strong feeling that she is safe and my senses do not usually deceive me."

The two men sipped tea together and Sorentius puffed away on his pipe. After a while, Sorentius looked up seriously and gazed at Javu through his round spectacles.

"Things are changing here, Javu," Sorentius revealed. "Our research is becoming more restricted and it is my view that it is only happening because we are finally getting somewhere in understanding why the pyramid was built here."

"What is your belief on the matter?" Javu asked quite indifferently.

Sorentius paused for a moment before answering. "That this land is not only special to this planet, but to our solar system and the universe as a whole."

Javu rocked slightly in his seated position and waited for Sorentius to elaborate.

"I believe that the Great Pyramid is much more that a tomb or observatory. I believe it is a beacon, a marker in the universe."

"A marker for what?"

"That I do not know, but I have spent many years plotting the movement of the stars in relation to positioning of the Great Pyramid and its inner shafts. There are so many correlations that it cannot be a coincidence."

"And the Ciafran government know of your findings?"

"Yes," Sorentius said, sour-faced. "I made the mistake of submitting a lengthy report as justification for more funding but instead of support, they banned any further explorations of the pyramid."

"Mmm, sounds like your theory is correct then," Javu mused, to which they both laughed. "Unfortunately, it probably means that your actions are being monitored more closely than before. The time may be coming for you to move on from Giza."

A look of disappointment spread across the wrinkled face of the professor but then he smiled. "I have been thinking the same thing, but not before I find the control room."

"Let's get some sleep then," Javu said. "It seems like tomorrow will be a very eye-opening day."

Chapter 9 – Giza Secrets

"So what exactly are we looking for in here, again?" Teltu asked Javu as they slowly walked through a dark shaft of the Great Pyramid. He held his torch higher to try and illuminate the way, as the distant glow of the torches from ahead went out of sight.

"Each pyramid has a way of bringing itself to life, shall we say. Sorentius and Rekesh are looking for a way to bring this pyramid to life."

"But how will that help Elera? She's so far away in Bimini."

"Sorentius thinks that the pyramid Elera is trapped in was built by the same people who built this one. If we know how this one works, we will have a better understanding about how the one at Bimini works."

The group had risen at sunrise to make headway into the gigantic pyramid. Some of the tunnels had been excavated in recent times and others by unknown explorers of the past. The group were now reaching the end of the last-known shaft, reaching deep into the heart of the pyramid, a hundred feet under the surface. Teltu was silent for a while as they continued along, the large irregular cut blocks of stone fitting tightly together like a jigsaw puzzle. It was hot and musty and the air felt thick as it entered the lungs.

"Why were you questioning Rekesh so much last night?" Teltu asked Javu, trying to understand what Javu was concerned about. He turned to Teltu wide-eyed.

"I was merely making sure that Rekesh has his wits about him. What people often forget is that there was once a time when we all knew a lot more than they do now, Teltu. And have you ever heard the expression 'knowledge is power'? Well, my questions are intended only to remind people of that. There are many who would use the secrets of this pyramid and every other ancient structure on the planet to further their quests for power."

"And you think that is what Rekesh is doing?" Teltu asked with horror. "He's not here to help Elera?"

"I have no doubt he wishes to help Elera," Javu clarified.

Teltu was confused by what Javu was saying.

"What are pyramids used for, Javu?" Teltu asked, after a while. "I know that they are used for astronomy here."

"Okay, Teltu," Javu said, smiling mischievously. "I will tell you my own theory, but you may find it hard to believe. Firstly, let me tell you something that most people do not know. You may have been told of pyramids on many parts of this planet such as here in Ciafra, in Lizrab and in some parts of Neoasia. As Elera found, there are some under the ocean as well, which at one time were also on the surface. But what many are not aware is that there are pyramids on other planets as well!"

"Are there?" Teltu asked in disbelief, his eyes glazing over.

"Yes. Of course, nobody that you or I know has ever physically visited one, but it is knowledge that has been passed down by word of mouth for thousands of years. Kirichi told me and his benefactor told him."

"Was Kirichi your teacher, Javu?"

"Indeed, a long time ago he was," Javu said, thinking back. "He has taught many and led many to freedom. I now tell you what I know to help you be free too, Teltu.

"So," Javu continued. "Why are the pyramids here? Well, before I can answer that question, you should know that the number three and its various representations is a very sacred number that it is an insight into the way many things work in our physical life. The pyramids are very special because each side has three lines that connect together, a very special meaning."

Teltu was slightly confused and had no idea what this had to do with the purpose of the pyramid. He decided to stay quiet for the meanwhile.

"The pyramids hold very special energy because of their shape. I am certain that you shall see what I mean as we discover more about this pyramid. They can also channel energy in various ways because of it."

Before Teltu could ask anything else, a lot of shouting could be heard up ahead.

"Hurry!" Javu said as they sped along the shaft. As it started to become more illuminated they saw that it opened out into a large chamber with a tall ceiling and larger irregular stone slabs. It was cooler in the chamber and Rekesh and Rama were shouting at each other in Hindi.

"What are they arguing about?" Teltu asked Javu.

"Rama says he feels a bad presence here, negative energy. He wants Rekesh to turn back, but Rekesh is adamant to continue on," Javu translated. He walked over to Rama and held his shoulder softly. He instantly calmed down, clearly anxious about the enclosed environment. Sita also comforted Rama, but she was uneasy as well. She told Javu that the chamber was a tomb and that it should not be disturbed.

"There is a door over here. Nobody has ever been able to open it," Sorentius said, walking over to a wall and ignoring the young couple's apprehension. Faint lines could be seen, outlining a doorway. "This chamber was only discovered last year and very few people have been down here."

"And the control chamber is through there?" Rekesh asked. "That holds the power source?"

"According to the tablets and scriptures we have found, yes. It should lead to the centre."

"How do we get through?" Teltu interjected, also starting to feel an uneasy sensation.

"I don't know," Sorentius said. "As I said, nobody has ever got further into the pyramid than this chamber. However, there are a few small shafts that run along the tunnel we just came down. We should investigate everything."

All fell quiet for a while.

"What does this inscription say here?" Teltu asked, looking at the wall with a door-shaped groove faintly visible and some symbols imprinted into the stone.

"Oh that," Sorentius said. "We have interpreted it to mean *guardian of gold*. It is likely that the chambers ahead hold many gold artefacts."

Javu's eyes had lit up at the statement and he leaned against one of the ancient walls, stroking his beard and entering a state of contemplation. Everyone else looked around in a cautious manner.

"How deep down are we?" Teltu asked Sorentius inquisitively.

"We are about a hundred feet below ground level," Sorentius told him. "Actually, most of the well-known chambers are above ground level within the pyramid. We are now underneath the visible pyramid that you see from outside."

"How deep down do you think these chambers go?"

"I'm not sure but I'd expect at least another fifty feet."

As he said this, Javu suddenly let out a long, deep sigh that startled everyone to attention.

"Professor Sorentius," Javu said quite deeply, in such a tone that it sounded quite humorous. "Can you please translate the inscription again?"

Though taken aback by the request, Sorentius complied with it and began to read the inscription on the sealed wall again.

"No, I'm sure the translation is accur—" he began to say before stopping mid-statement. "—what's that?"

Looking closely at one of the hieroglyphs, Sorentius saw something that he hadn't noticed before. There were a few faint lines attached to one of the symbols that changed the meaning of it.

"I didn't notice this before," He said, tracing the lines with his finger. "The glyph for *gold* might actually mean something else."

"And what would that be?" Javu probed him. Sorentius was thinking hard for a while before finally voicing his conclusion.

"I think it means *star fire*."

"So that inscription more accurately means *guardian of star fire*?"

"Yes," Sorentius confirmed.

"What's star fire?" Teltu asked before Rekesh, who was thinking the same thing, had a chance to.

"It's a mythical substance that is supposed to be the 'nectar of the gods' according to many old scriptures," Sorentius explained. "Also known as monatomic gold."

"It is also known in many cultures around the world as a magical matter that can turn any other substance to gold," Javu added knowingly.

Teltu smiled at the fantastic explanations and had a closer look at the inscription, though he had no clue about what each of the shapes meant.

"So is that a clue to how we can get through that doorway?" Rekesh asked them both.

"Stand aside," Javu replied calmly as he approached the doorway. Everyone moved away behind him. He closed his eyes and held his left arm up, palm outstretched towards the stone wall. He began to chant something lightly and quietly, his mouth moving quickly. Everyone looked at each other in confusion at what Javu was doing. His eyes firmly shut, Javu seemed to be singing a melody in the strangest of manners, his entire body pulsating slightly.

It was a surreal sight.

The next thing that happened made everyone gasp with disbelief. The wall started to rumble gently and then more strongly. Sita and Rama held each other tightly, whilst Teltu, looking around for somebody to hold and seeing only Rekesh, decided to back away from the wall towards the other end of the shaft. Javu was still chanting and seemed to be in some sort of trance. The wall continued to shake and then a large crack began to appear in the stone door. The whole chamber was shaking now and dust started to fly down from the roof.

"Stop it, Javu!" Sorentius appealed. "Or the whole tunnel will collapse!"

Javu was not listening, still fully absorbed in his practice. The door vibrated violently within the wall before beginning to crumble. Within seconds, a hole could be seen in the stone door and chunks of rock crashed down near Javu's feet. Then, the rumbling started to decrease, getting less and less. Javu opened his eyes and the whole chamber was peaceful again, only the odd fragment rolling down from the crumbly door with an echoed clatter.

"How did you...? What did you...?" Teltu began, stumbling his words in shock. There was silence for many moments. The small stones rolling down from the newly formed hole almost sounded like running water.

"I did not know you were a magician, Javu!" Rekesh said, walking towards the door and surveying the wreckage.

"That I am not, Rekesh," Javu replied, smiling at the remark.

Rekesh started to pry rubble from the door, making the hole bigger. "If we can clear some of this cracked stone away, we might be able to crawl through," he said, breathing hard with effort.

Teltu and Rama began to help move the stone. The hole was soon as big as a person's head.

"Let me see what's in there," Sorentius said enthusiastically, ushering the three labourers to the side and peering through the hole. "Mmm, too dark to see from this side."

Rekesh, Rama and Teltu continued to move rubble until the hole was big enough to climb through. The skin on their hands was rough from the effort.

"Let me go first!" Sorentius said excitedly like a young child when they had finished. He squeezed his body through the hole slowly, being given a push Rekesh to help him to the other side.

"Wow," the others heard him say. "This doorway is almost as thick as it is wide! Can someone pass me a torch?"

Rekesh carefully passed through a lit torch. As Sorentius turned around with it, he let out a high-pitched scream. Staring right at him was a human-sized granite statue with big oval eyes and an intricately carved unique headdress.

"What is it?" Rekesh said, starting to climb through.

"A statue, guarding the entrance," Sorentius stated.

Everyone took turns climbing through the hole and reaching the other side, their first sight was the ominous statue glaring at them.

Javu crawled through last and upon seeing the statue, let out a loud laugh. "I was counting on you!" he said to the statue, chuckling.

Behind the statue was another long shaft-like tunnel. Sorentius began to inspect the ominous figure. "Marvellous," he said, rubbing his spectacles. "Perfectly preserved. Untouched for thousands of years!"

Rama noticed a small hole in the statue's belly and pointed it out to Javu. He just nodded to Rama, smiling widely.

"Javu. What did you do?" Rekesh asked, still amazed and confused about what had happened a short while ago.

"You see that this statue has a hole in its navel?" Javu began, pointing to the small hole as they reached the statue. "Out of this hole comes great energy, enough to break through the wall in front."

"But how did you know it was there? And how did you release this 'energy'?" Sorentius asked with disbelief in his voice.

"I have known of the concept of star fire since I was a boy. Some people say it is the nectar of the gods, others say it is the blood of the gods but the reality is much simpler in my opinion. Star fire is a type of gold that is quite rare, which is probably where you initially translated the inscription as *guardian of gold*."

"Indeed," Sorentius agreed. "The symbols for gold and star fire are very similar."

"Well, this special type of gold is powerful in many ways. One of its uses is to channel an intense form of energy."

Everyone was intrigued at how much Javu knew, especially Sorentius. He gleamed, seeing the anticipation on the faces of Sorentius, Rekesh and Teltu.

"This statue actually had some star fire inside it."

"But how did you know that?" Sorentius asked bewildered, the veins in his temples bulging slightly at his frustration. "And how did you make it break the wall when you were stood on the other side?!"

"It is possible to interact with energy in physical objects using the mind," he said, tapping the side of his head lightly. "I released the energy from this statue using this method. In the past, this ability was commonplace."

Sorentius laughed out loud with sarcasm and disbelief. "Are you saying that the people who built this pyramid could control things with their mind? And that you are capable of the same feat?"

Javu beamed and nodded, not dismayed by Sorentius' scepticism.

"I don't believe it!" Sorentius blurted out pompously. "In the past thirty years I have found no evidence of such ability."

"How do you suppose I released the energy from this statue? I have heard of such guardians before in sacred temples. They are there for those who possess the knowledge to use them. That is why I knew it was highly probable that similar means were used to protect this temple. After all, this pyramid was not built for the average person, was it, Professor? It is for royalty."

Sorentius nodded weakly, still finding it hard to accept Javu's explanation.

"Why isn't what you say common knowledge?" Teltu asked, becoming more intrigued. "How do you know about all this?"

"Only trusted individuals are told about the ancient's ability by someone who knows. Besides, even if it were common knowledge that such ability could exist for every human, the current empire would always suppress the bearers of such knowledge. Such has happened continually throughout history. Entire nations have been wiped out because of such knowledge. The reason for such secrecy is to protect this knowledge."

"And you are able to perform such feats of the mind?" Rekesh asked for affirmation.

"With practice and reflection anyone could," Javu said, still smiling light-heartedly. "Those who were taught from a young age about how to train their minds in the past could perform feats we are incapable of comprehending. I have meagre ability compared to those of the past."

Teltu was deep in thought and scratched his short, wiry beard.

"The energy from this statue has now dissipated. In fact, I am certain that if we could look inside this statue we would now find a solid piece of pure gold in place of the star fire," Javu told everyone.

"What does star fire look like?" Teltu asked.

"It is a fine white glowing powder. I once was fortunate enough to see some in Vassini. It is quite an incredible substance."

"Let's press on," Rekesh urged, wanting to reach the control room.

The group walked slowly down the tunnel, which seemed to be built at a diagonal slant going deeper into the pyramid. The group stayed close together as they walked.

"Javu, you were telling me about pyramids on other planets before..." Teltu began.

"Indeed, Teltu. They exist."

"But how did they get there? Who built them?"

"I don't believe they were built in a conventional sense, Teltu," Javu explained.

"You mean they have always been there?" he asked, puzzled.

Before Javu could answer, Sorentius let out an excited yelp.

"This is it!" he said loudly, shining the torch on what looked like a dead end. "The scriptures were true!"

The tunnel had ended at another stone wall, some hieroglyphs intricately etched into it. Javu did not recognise the symbols nor understand them.

"Behind this wall is the control room," Sorentius stated to the group. "We shall discover the secrets of the pyramid if we can get inside."

"What do the hieroglyphs say?" Javu asked Sorentius. "Can you translate them?"

Sorentius nodded and began to read the inscriptions. The others surveyed the eerie surroundings. The shaft was cold and stale, the air musty with a smell of death.

"These hieroglyphs are different to the others. They are much more intricate in their structure. I understand this symbol here," Sorentius said as he pointed to a symbol on the wall. "It means *light from the sun."*

He continued to study the symbols carefully, scanning along the wall closely with his lit torch.

"Ahh, I understand this one too!" he announced. "It means *appeasement*, usually used to describe some kind of offering."

"Can you understand any more?" Javu pressed, sensing the uneasiness of some people in the group. Again, Sorentius examined the inscriptions.

"This one…" he said, pointing to a symbol towards the end of the carvings "…could mean *divine* or *forbidden* but I am not really sure. I don't understand any of the other glyphs. Elera is the real expert on ancient writings. She learnt over ten forms in great detail."

Elera's name being mentioned seemed to remind Rekesh of the urgency of the situation.

"So what do you think it's saying?" he asked Sorentius, a little impatience resonating in his tone.

"Not sure. But I think to get past this wall we need to know something about its structure, and it is somehow related to the sun."

Sorentius went back to the wall and began examining it methodically. After a while of searching around with dim lights, Teltu let out a cry of excitement.

"Look!" he said, bending down towards the floor in an awkward position. "A small shaft! It's no bigger than my finger in width but it goes all the way up to the sky."

The group each took it in turns to look up through the well-concealed shaft and see a point of daylight.

"How did you find it?" Rekesh asked Teltu.

"I saw a small dot of light on the floor."

"Maybe we are supposed to use the light from this shaft somehow."

Teltu, Javu and Sorentius all agreed. Sorentius began to read the hieroglyphs again for more clues. Rama was kneeling on the floor, examining something carefully. He looked up at Javu and waved at him to come over. He pointed to the floor and said something in

Hindi. Javu knelt too and began to observe what Rama was showing him.

"Mmm, yes, very difficult to notice," Javu commented.

"What is it?" Sorentius asked.

"Rama has discovered a small groove here in the floor. It runs up to the wall."

Javu produced a small cloth from his robe and began to remove dust from the groove, following it along away from the wall. It curved to the left towards the spot where the shaft focused the light. Covered in tightly packed crushed stone and dust was a circular-shaped furrow, the size of a large coin. Javu unblocked the furrow with his nimble fingers.

"I think the offering is supposed to go in this rut to channel the sunlight," Javu said, growing more exited with every word. "Sorentius, have you ever excavated anything that would fit this groove?"

Sorentius closely inspected the furrow, but then shook his head in disappointment. "We have never found anything that size and shape."

Rekesh breathed out a loud sigh of frustration. "We must think!" he stated anxiously.

The saddened emotion could be heard in his voice. His face dropped with deep contemplation and he began to pace back and forth.

"Didn't you say that you were certain some gold had now been produced in the statue? Maybe that's what we need?" Teltu suggested.

Everyone travelled back up the tunnel to the granite statue at the suggestion. Using the flashlights they had, they examined the statue carefully. It wasn't long before Sorentius discovered a small rectangular outline at the back of the statue.

"Look! I think this part comes out," he said, trying to dislodge something using a small sharp tool he had. Everyone looked on as Sorentius slowly pulled out a stone drawer and inside was a solid gold disk that fitted perfectly into a mould in the drawer. He took it out carefully. It shone like with brilliant lustre, like no gold any of them had ever seen before.

"I've never seen anything like it!" Teltu exclaimed, staring in wonder at the deep-yellow gold disk, which had a circular pattern on one side, matching a pattern in the mould of the black granite drawer.

"This gold was only formed recently," Javu said. "Let's try it in the rut down there."

They all walked back down to the sealed wall and Sorentius placed the gold disk into the circular-shaped furrow. It fitted perfectly. Immediately the gold disk was illuminated, glowing with radiance and a strong glare.

"Remarkable!" Sorentius gasped in awe.

"The light is getting brighter," Javu said, bending down and looking up the shaft again, quickly pulling back with a wince. "Soon the sun should align with the shaft. When it does, I think that something will happen."

They waited for a while in anticipation and soon enough the sun found its place over the shaft. The group knew when it had happened, for from the gold furrow suddenly shot a beam of light up to the roof of the tunnel, where they were amazed to see another hidden furrow illuminated. The thin channels along the floor were now shining brightly.

Sita immediately took Javu's cloth and proceeded with the help of Rama to unblock the top furrow. Everyone was surprised to see that it had a layer of crystalline in it. As soon as the pair ceased to obstruct the beam's path, it struck the upper furrow and immediately filled the tunnel with a blinding light. There was a rumbling sound and a perfectly straight crack appeared at the top of the wall. Then the wall began to sink into the floor, revealing the summit of a grand chamber beyond. Sorentius gasped as the wall lowered further, divulging a variety of stone statues and golden objects. The chamber was surprisingly bright, multiple shafts reflecting the sun's light using golden spheres on the floor of the chamber beyond. As the wall sank to its limit, it suddenly changed direction and began to rise up again.

"Quickly!" Rekesh shouted above the echoing rumble. "Everyone move quickly!"

Everybody hurried across into the magnificent chamber, that itself was shaped like a pyramid. The wall rose up and closed, leaving the group trapped inside. Everyone immediately began to look around, the grand architectural structure astounding everyone. The golden spheres were the size of a human's head, and with the midday sun shining brightly down the shafts, they gave a wondrous yellow glow, enlightening everything in the chamber.

"Look!" Sorentius wheezed, trying to catch his breath and staring in disbelief at the back wall. "The fifty-four holes as described in the ancient scriptures!"

The group all moved over to the back wall, which was at a perfect diagonal.

"There are stones in the holes," Teltu exclaimed looking carefully at each one. "Rubies, emeralds and other gemstones."

"This is indeed a remarkable place," Sorentius said solemnly, still in a daze and with a few tears in his eyes. "These stones must be used to control the pyramid."

Each hole was the size of a finger in diameter and polished inside as if hollowed out to a smooth precision. The stones reflected light off their shiny enclosure giving an overall multicoloured glowing panel effect. Four holes were distinctly separate, the other fifty were arranged in a five-by-ten grid.

"They're so colourful," Teltu commented to Sorentius. "How are they used?"

"I don't know," Sorentius admitted. "The scriptures that we found in a hidden tomb last year only tell of the existence of this room and describe these fifty-four holes. I don't know what they were used for."

Rekesh had walked over to the holes and was examining each

one carefully.

"What is the significance of the number fifty-four?" Javu asked himself out loud. "Does it have some special meaning in Giza?"

Everybody thought for a while about what the number could mean.

"How about the number of chambers?" Teltu suggested.

"It could be," Sorentius pondered out loud. "But I only know of the six main chambers and this control chamber."

Again everybody gave the matter some thought. Sita made a suggestion to Javu in Hindi.

"Sita is suggesting that the top four holes may be separate to the fifty below," Javu translated, smiling at Sita.

"Mmm," Sorentius mused in deep thought. "But what could the four represent?"

"What about the four elements? Earth, air, water and fire?" Javu suggested. "That is what the number four usually represents."

Sorentius thought carefully for many moments and then his face lightened as if he had discovered a revelation within his mind. "It could be! This pyramid was once known as the pyramid of fire after all."

Rekesh was engrossed in his examination of the holes and their stones and paid no attention to Sorentius' new line of thought. The others were all listening, however, and Teltu suddenly let out a sigh of excitement.

"I've just had a thought!" he said enthused. "What if each stone is a switch of sorts that opens a passage in this pyramid?"

The others all agreed, including Sita and Rama who both nodded as Javu translated Teltu's theory.

Oblivious to the conversation, Rekesh continued his inspections. A stone slab in the middle of the room had mysteriously slid down into the shiny, smooth floor. Rama was the first to notice and attracted the others' attention. As they walked over to the new opening, they were astounded when a giant, multicoloured crystal suddenly rose up out of the hole. It was the size of a large person, with a single sharp termination and an intricate catacomb of internal channels, all glistening brightly from the reflected light. Then a remarkable thing happened. The room began to fill with the brightest white light as the giant crystal began to glow. It became so bright that everyone had to close their eyes and shield themselves from it with their hands. All they could hear was a faint vibration. The light was blinding and the crystal was streaming light upwards into a small shaft at the pinnacle of the pyramid-shaped room. The shaft ran directly upwards and came out at the very top of the Great Pyramid.

Outside, two children were playing, drawing pictures in the dusty sand. Their attention was suddenly averted when they saw a beam of brilliant white light shoot directly up and out of the Great Pyramid and into the sky. The children let out a sigh of awe. The workers around the Giza plateau all stopped what they were doing as they caught sight of the spectacle. The beam had gone into the stratosphere and through it, its furthest point looking like a bright star, far away. It continued for a few moments before stopping completely. Some workers blinked hard repeatedly to make sure that they were not hallucinating.

Back inside the pyramid, the control chamber started to dim and within a minute had ceased to be filled with blinding light. The vibrations subsided and the crystal stopped glowing. The group were in astonishment at the occurrence, indeed Teltu was in such surprise that he sat on the floor, braced with his arms cradling his head.

"What happened?" Sorentius said in a daze, flapping his eyelids.

"How did you do that, Rekesh?" Javu asked, walking over to the holes where Rekesh was standing. "Did Elera tell you something about this pyramid?"

"No!" Rekesh said defensively. "I just touched one of the stones."

"Where did that light come from?" Teltu asked, finally getting to his feet. The others all looked at each other, themselves quite confused.

"It seems like the pyramid released some sort of light through this crystal here," Sorentius said, tapping the crystal with his fingernail and looking up at the vertical shaft in the room's pinnacle. "It was directed up there."

"I couldn't see anything for a while," Teltu said, rubbing his eyes.

"Which one did you touch?" Sorentius asked Rekesh, walking over to the panel. Rekesh pointed out one of the holes in the lower fifty arrangement, which had a bluish-coloured stone inside. Sorentius reached out and touched it and then Rama, who had wandered to the opposite side of the room, immediately began to shout something in Hindi. As the others walked over to him, they saw that another stone slab had slid away from the floor, revealing a giant opening with an immaculate staircase leading deeper down into the pyramid.

"Looks like that one does more than just one thing," Sorentius said to Rekesh, who just nodded sheepishly.

"Should we go down there?" Teltu asked with a little caution.

"Before we do, I want to have a look around and see what some of these stones do. I may not get another chance," Sorentius told him. He turned back to the panel and as he was about to touch another of the stones, Javu called out to him.

"Be careful, Sorentius. I can feel great power here."

Sorentius nodded and gently reached out into the first of the four holes of the upper arrangement, touching an icy cold red gemstone. He felt a fizzling sensation on his fingertip as he made contact with it. Then the giant crystal began to glow again.

"Oh no!" Teltu yelped, covering his eyes once more but this time there was no blinding light. Instead, a strange, ethereal image began to present itself above the crystal; an unearthly hologram. It was of the Giza plateau and beyond. There were scores of pyramids depicted in the three-dimensional image. It also showed a vast tunnel system that connected each of the pyramids.

"Incredible!" Sorentius exclaimed, mesmerised by the effigy. Everyone gathered around to take a closer look.

"Look, there is the Great Pyramid," Javu said, pointing out the largest pyramid in the centre of the hologram. "And it looks like you were right, Professor; the tunnel system goes deep into the earth."

"Where is that?" Teltu asked, pointing out a long chamber that was at the deepest point on the image.

"I have no idea," Sorentius replied with fascination. "That chamber is five times as deep as anyone would have thought the chambers go. It looks like it exists under the entirety of the Giza plateau! It must be four suns down in the earth."

"It almost looks like the Great Pyramid is built upon an upside-down pyramid of equal size," Javu said, noticing that the chambers below ground level almost reflected those within the Great Pyramid, as did the tunnels depicted on the map.

"Incredible!" was all Sorentius could say.

"Do you think there is a map like this for Bimini?" Rekesh asked with a tone of impatience in his voice.

"Let me have a look," Sorentius replied, observing the stones in the holes again. "I could try and touch the second stone in this set of four. Maybe each correlates to a different pyramid?"

"Go ahead," Rekesh said as everyone looked on with bated breath.

Sorentius put his finger in the second hole which contained a dark-blue stone and the hologram changed to a different map, this time of a single pyramid surrounded by mountains.

"No, that's not it," Rekesh said getting frustrated. "It should be surrounded by islands."

"No, wait!" Javu said to Sorentius as he was about to experiment with the other stones. "Remember that the Bimini pyramid might not have always been underwater. This could be what it once looked like."

The insight quelled Rekesh's anxiety and he began to study the image carefully.

"I think you're right, Javu!" he suddenly blurted out. "The peaks of these mountains correlate to the islands in that area."

"And look," Teltu pointed out some lines on the image. "It looks like there is a tunnel system there too, but they run up into the mountains from that pyramid instead of underground."

"That means those tunnels might still exist on some of the islands?!" Rekesh said with hope. "Elera might have found a way out."

"Or we could find a way in?" Javu suggested, implying he would be willing to travel to Bimini.

Rekesh felt warmed by the encouragement and felt increasingly confident that Elera was safe. The release of his concern crashed in his stomach like a great wave.

"It seems that there is a tunnel here from this cavern at the top of that peak," Javu pointed out, looking carefully at the map. "Do you know where that cavern is?"

"Not sure but it's probably on the south island."

"So can we get out of here now?" Teltu asked, feeling a little suffocated in the enclosure. Sita and Rama seemed to be feeling the same way.

"We should see what the other stones do first," Sorentius said sternly. Before anyone could respond, a minor vibration could be felt in the floor and then a much stronger tremor. Sita toppled to the floor from the force.

"It's coming from above," Javu said as another vibration juddered through the floor.

"Let's get out of here!" Teltu said, a little panicked.

"Let me just take a photograph of this panel," Sorentius said, taking out a small pen-like device and pointing it at the stones. "And also the crystal."

"Let's head down that stairway," Javu suggested as the professor took a few pictures. Rekesh, also eager to leave, did not hesitate to go down the staircase. The others followed, lighting torches as they went. Only Sorentius lingered as he took a last look at the amazing room, which was now becoming less illuminated. Minor tremors could be felt as the group headed down the stairway, which led to a long, wide, dark and musty tunnel. They walked along in silence, all mulling over the spectacles they had witnessed and listening out with fright as the surroundings groaned with the eerie trembling from above.

An hour passed.

"Maybe we should turn back and have a look at that map again," Teltu said, feeling panicked once more. His suggestion was met with silence.

After a long period of walking, the tunnel started to incline.

After another few hours, light could be seen up ahead, streaming in from cracks between giant stone blocks. Shouting could be heard in the distance.

"Dead end," Teltu stated.

"No," Sorentius corrected. "We are at the edge of the pyramid. These blocks are the outer stones. They are much smaller than the ones inside."

"What's all the commotion outside?" Rekesh pondered out loud.

"This one is loose," Teltu said, eyeing the biggest of the blocks that rocked slightly when he shoved it. Teltu, Rekesh and Rama pushed with all their might until the block seemed to tip and then fall neatly into a groove, revealing a small crack, big enough to squeeze through.

"Amazing!" Sorentius said. "There is no way you could move that block from the other side."

Rama, the first through, was greeted by warm sunlight bathing his face and the easing dry air of the Giza plateau. In the distance, he saw swarms of soldiers around the encampment and also noticed smoke was rising from a number of places around the plateau.

Sorentius was the last to reach the outside and he quickly noticed something about the pyramid.

"We are not at the Great Pyramid now," he said as he observed his surroundings. "That must have been a connecting tunnel to the Chephren pyramid."

"Look! Soldiers!" Teltu said with a little fear as he spotted them in the distance. There were also hundreds of men dressed in black attire in support of the soldiers.

"It's King Rufi's men," Sorentius stated, looking carefully at the surrounded camp through a small pair of binoculars. "They've come much earlier than I thought. We need to leave the plateau immediately."

"What do they want?" Teltu asked quietly.

"Probably what we've just been exploring."

Everyone walked slowly around the giant blocks that rose high above, to a spot on a nearby dune where they could more clearly observe how the area had been occupied.

"I thought you said that an invasion was unlikely," Rekesh whispered to Sorentius.

"Something must have changed."

Down at the encampment, the soldiers were leading all of the researchers and astrologers into trucks, and it could be seen from this viewpoint that parts of the Great Pyramid and the observatory were smouldering from the explosions they had felt underground before.

"Where are they taking everyone?"

"Probably to Anca Casa," Sorentius hypothesised. "Rufi must be feeling the political pressure to lock down the site. We can't go down there or we'll be forced to leave too."

"I want to head back to Bimini," Rekesh stated. "I just need to get my horse."

"I will come with you," Javu said to Rekesh. He turned to Teltu. "I understand if you want to go back to Seho."

"No, I'm coming too. Fera told me not to come back until I know that Elera is safe."

Rekesh did not even have to ask Sita and Rama for they were already on their feet and standing by his side.

"I need to remain here for the meanwhile," Sorentius declared, "until I know what's going on here, but as it currently stands, maybe not for much longer."

"But where will you go?" Javu asked the professor, his deep-set features eminent in the sun light.

"I have a laboratory that only I, Selina and Tifu know about. It's over there on the other side of the plateau. I doubt anyone will find me there. Actually I'm hoping Selina and Tifu were thinking the same thing."

"Well, be careful," Javu said warmly, to which Sorentius nodded with a smile.

As the professor prepared to split from the group and sneak around the rubble of the plateau to get to his secret lab, Rekesh remembered something.

"Sorentius, before you go, I have something for you. A while ago I met a stargazer named Casar."

"I have not heard of him," Sorentius interjected boyishly.

"Nevertheless, he asked me pass this on to someone here."

Rekesh pulled the scroll out of his satchel and gave it to Sorentius. He opened it and looked at the chart of the sky, which outlined all the major constellations, and had a diagram of a trajectory scribbled on it. After a while, a serious expression spread across the professor's face and he looked up at Rekesh.

"When did he discover this?"

"He said it appears now and again but he thinks it's getting closer."

"I will take a look as soon as I can," Sorentius said, starting to walk away towards a giant group of boulders. "Have a safe journey and tell Elera from me to be more careful when you see her. Go that way around the pyramid and I think you'll be able to retrieve your horses unnoticed."

The five set off to discretely gather their horses. They stayed close to the perimeter of the pyramid and got a better view of the scene at the encampment. Even more soldiers were there now and it seemed like a perfect opportunity to get across, without being noticed, to the Great Pyramid where the horses were tied. As they ducked down and shimmied across an open part of the plateau, they saw that most of the soldiers were building a tall metal fence around the nearby observatory and encampment.

Before long they had reached their horses and within a few minutes had quietly slipped away, heading due north, the promise of the sun straight ahead, guiding them. Suddenly, they heard a horse galloping behind them and looking back they saw Sorentius, frantically trying to signal to them to stop. They halted and dismounted, now on the edge of the plateau, surprised to see Sorentius in such a fluster.

"Wait!" he shouted as he approached, slowing his horse to a canter. "I must warn you of what I have heard."

He dismounted as the horse came to a stop with an unexpected agility. Everyone could see a look of fear in Sorentius' eyes.

"I overheard two soldiers speaking as I was on the way to my lab. It seems that there are plans for Giza to be destroyed!"

"What?!" Javu and Teltu said aghast, almost in unison.

"Everything we have discovered will be lost!" Sorentius said with distress. "We must stop this from happening."

"But why would they want to? Who wants to?" Rekesh asked.

"I don't know, but the strangest thing is I heard them mention *that thing in the sky*. That sky chart you just gave me? It's unbelievable because the trajectory that your friend has outlined mirrors several points in the cosmos that the pyramids are linked with here. The ancient Pharaohs certainly believed that the pyramids were connected to the stars."

"What are you saying?" Teltu asked in bewilderment.

"Well, I'm not sure what it is, but if it's real and this trajectory is accurate, whatever it is will eventually reach this planet."

Rama was listening to Sorentius carefully, trying to understand. He now more than ever wanted to learn the Raiceman language, a language that he and Sita had avoided by living in Vassini most of their lives. He asked Rekesh in Hindi to translate, which he did in some detail. Rama and Sita conversed for a moment and then spoke to Javu.

"Sita tells me that in the town she and Rama are from, it is taught from an early age that two things can be far apart but in essence still be the same thing and behave in the same way. She gives me an example of a holy woman who took a cup of water from a nearby lake, brought it to the village and then turned it red with a dye. When the villagers went up to the lake, it too had turned red."

"What does this have to do with anything?" Sorentius asked impatiently.

"Maybe Sita is trying to tell us what the entity is," Javu said sternly.

"And what is that?" Sorentius asked.

"Part of this plateau. If something has been summoned or attracted here as you seem to be implying, it must be part of something that is already here."

Sorentius seemed confused at Javu's explanation.

"Be careful who you talk to about this," Javu warned Sorentius, leaning in closely to his ear. "If I were you I'd think about how long you really need to remain here in Giza."

Sorentius nodded in acknowledgement of the warning and then leaned in closer to Javu. "I will be careful. There is something else I wanted to tell you. I had a look at the photograph I took of the fifty-four-hole panel. It seems that one of the four upper stones is missing, the first one. I wanted to ask you if you could remember if every hole had a stone in when we entered the chamber?"

"I'm not sure," Javu whispered back.

"Me neither," Sorentius admitted.

"Hey, we have to get going," Rekesh said impatiently.

With that, Sorentius mounted his horse and turned back in the direction of the Giza plateau.

"I hope to see you all soon," he said as he rode off.

Everyone else headed northwards towards the shore, cantering along at a steady pace.

"Has all this got anything to do with what you were telling me before?" Teltu asked Javu as their horses rode side by side, like two rocking chairs. "You know, about pyramids on other planets?"

"I am unsure, Teltu. But I have a strong feeling that we have only just begun to pull the mountain from under the sand."

The sun was strong, but somehow less bright than usual, a hazy flow of uneasiness dousing its rays. As they rode forth, Rama looked back at the pyramid and was sure for just a moment that it moved before his eyes. He blinked and it looked as solid and monumental as ever. He shook his head, hoping the road ahead would bring more clarity.

Chapter 10 – The Movement

Lizrab was a land of many conflicts. Other nations avoided trading with the great continent due its diverse and largely uninhabitable terrain, along with fear spread politically about the land's history of rebellion. The southern areas of the continent were home to a mixture of thick jungles and dry plains. Positioned in the centre was the only remaining city recognised by the international community, *Calegra*, the birthplace of Reo Fernandez.

Bene and Reo had travelled by ship for four days, finally reaching the port town of *Realiss* on the east coast. Since their departure from Raicema City, Reo had anticipated his return home to Calegra with great enthusiasm, yet he had been surprised at Bene's lack of eagerness for the journey. Either that or he was greatly uneasy, Reo thought. As they walked down the ramp from the heavily populated ship, the hot sun instantly hit their faces, making it hard to see clearly. The heat was dry and the smell of salt could be tasted in the air.

"Ahh," Reo sighed, "to be back here makes me feel right at home and we are still to get to the bustling favelas of Calegra!"

"Do not forget that we are not here to bask in our homecomings, Reo," Bene said rather sharply. "We have an important message to deliver."

The two walked to the town's market, fisherman selling their catches in a variety of creative ways; fresh, roasted, seared, in barrels and in crates. Also in the market was the horse trader, a man whose occupation was common throughout the world. As electronic vehicles were expensive and hard to come by, horses had been bred extensively and reared for transport for as long as anyone could remember. The horse trader would trade any valuable items for the horse and again trade a horse back for items when a traveller could not keep it any longer. Indeed, the horse trader had seen more horses come and go than leaves in the wind.

"What do we have to trade?" Reo asked, rummaging in his

woven sack for something of value. "I'm low on gold."

"Do not concern yourself," Bene replied, as they approached the trader. "I have something that shall get us two strong horses and a good supply of water."

Bene greeted the man in the Lizrabian language, a common language that was understood throughout the continent. He then produced a large cubed-shaped block of metal, infused with crystalline channels. It was the rechargeable power source of a Raiceman land-vehicle. The man took it and examined it carefully. He offered a horse for it. Bene told him his price; two horses and several flasks of water. After a while of bickering and mumbling, the man finally gave in and guided the two travellers to a barn close by. He led two small horses out and threw Bene two hide-flasks filled with water.

"This won't be enough," Reo said to Bene as he handed him a flask. "We have at least a day until we reach Calegra and the horses will get thirsty in this heat. Maybe we should stay here until dusk."

"No!" Bene said firmly, mounting a horse. "We are on a tight schedule. You *do* want to spend some time in Calegra don't you? Otherwise we will be travelling nonstop."

Reo reluctantly agreed and mounted his horse.

"Let us go by a river I know," he suggested to Bene. "It will only take an hour more that way."

The men set off along a grassy path that headed due west. The horses were quite old and trotted at a steady pace. The surroundings were green and plentiful, with bushy trees and shrubs stretching to the vision's end. Soon this beautiful scenery would disappear, however, and huge dirt tracks with half-built houses would litter the view. For hundreds of years the poor had travelled to Calegra in search of work. Dense populations now caused a scarceness of resources in the area. Indeed, there was something amazing and horrifying about the city, its close-knit communities working together to lift the repression of poverty, yet such crowded societies only led to crime waves and exploitation. The surrounding regions were much the same and the city seemed to expand as every year went by.

"Do you think anyone followed us to Lizrab?" Reo asked Bene, still haunted by the men he'd seen stalking them in Raicema City.

"More than you know," was all he got in response.

The pair travelled for hours before stopping near a river to refill their flasks and let the horses drink their fill. The hot sun was beating down with a sleepy heat.

"How do you intend to travel to the south in only three days?" Reo enquired, wiping the sweat from his brow with the back of his hand. "The land train was halted six years ago and these horses cannot possibly achieve that!"

Bene just grinned and said nothing. Then he took a large gulp of water and took off his cotton shirt, revealing his deeply tanned, ripped body with a scar near his left ribs. "Not only shall we get there in three days, but we shall spend two of them in Calegra," he said cunningly, his grin widening.

"I don't see how it's possible," Reo repeated, dismissing Bene's claim. The sun seemed hotter than ever as midday approached.

"The heat in Lizrab is like nowhere else, huh, Bene?" Reo said, changing the subject.

"You're right about that!" Bene replied, sweat pouring from his face.

"Say, how come that piece of metal was so valuable to the horse trader? There are few Raiceman vehicles out here," Reo enquired.

"That power cube has crystals in it that store energy. They can be used to power other things like electric lights and many types of motor. Some hold more energy than others. The crystals in that one had a pretty big capacity."

"Is that how the Raicemans power all of their technology?"

"Almost all. Some power stations still just burn things and directly channel the power out, but using cubes is more stable and quicker to channel the power. I heard that Raicema have been developing a new type of cube that would be a thousand times as powerful as any available today."

"Say, Bene, how do you know so much about all this?" Reo enquired enthusiastically.

"I just picked it up from a lot of people that I worked with. Before I went to Raicema, I used to fix up old vehicles so I learnt a lot that way."

"What did you do with them after you fixed them?"

"I used to transport them. Raicema produces masses of vehicles every year but they are very strict about allowing the vehicles to cross any borders. They tend to only make it across if they are broken. So there is a big demand in Lizrab for fixed-up vehicles as you can't get them otherwise."

"So how'd you end up joining the Makai?"

"Enough talk now," Bene said sharply. "We must be on our way."

Both men got back on their horses and continued on their journey to Calegra. It took the rest of the day to navigate to the red plains, on the edge of the great city. The red plains were so called because they were laden with copper and had a rustic red soil because of it. Little grew there and many said that the soil was red because of the amount of blood that had been spilt on the plains. Countless battles over the city had been fought for centuries on the plains, most recently with Raicema over its mining facilities.

"These plains are what Raicema wanted so badly at one time," Bene commented. "Before they used crystals they used copper for channelling power around Raicema. Now they're more interested in a different type of mine."

Reo listened but said nothing, his eyes glazing over slightly as he approached his home city. Dotted all around were the sites of abandoned copper mines, the grubby pumps and train tracks fallen into disrepair. In some cases, old carriages had been tipped over by bored youths.

"You can see the favelas from here," Reo said to Bene, as they crossed the plains at a trot, side by side.

Over seven million people lived in shantytowns in Calegra,

mostly made of scrap metal and other waste, all sculpted together to make dwellings. The other million people lived in stone-built houses and most were merchants or weapons traders. There was also a large organised narcotics industry in Calegra and many of the higher-ranking gang members lived in houses amongst the richer members of society.

"Hey, Bene!" Reo said loudly, bringing his horse closer to Bene's. "I still don't really understand very much about this Makai thing. I know it's some sort of cult or something in Raicema but I have never heard of the Makai in Calegra. To be honest, I've never really heard if it at all before I met you."

"Not even in the south?" Bene asked, surprised.

"I've never been there."

"Okay, Reo," Bene said, rolling his eyes. "I'll try to explain it all to you. Let's start with Makaism, which is a fairly new religion that was started about three hundred years ago. There are different sects of it now, but the main belief is that life is a cycle of death and birth. This central belief comes from many ancient religions that are now forbidden in Raicema and in some other parts of the world."

"What ancient religions?" Reo asked.

"I'm not really sure. Some of the elders may be able to tell you, if you are interested. Anyway, some sects of the Makai people believe in non-violence like Kirichi, and others believe in self-defence as a merit to being reborn as a more fortunate being."

Bene took a swig of water from his flask, the leather hot in his hand as the sun began to set in the west.

"Since the religion was formed, a political movement has occurred within Raicema, Neoasia and some parts of Lizrab, trying to create societies based on the religion. This is where Kirichi's standpoint is slightly different as he believes that this will only lead to another empire if this ambition is successful, when he thinks there shouldn't be any empires at all."

"So, most people in the south follow Kirichi?" Reo asked.

"Yes, but a lot are still willing to defend their homes against attacks and invasions. However, most Makai here in Lizrab all want the same thing, to live in peace and harmony with the land."

"And what about Sadana back in Raicema City. He looks like he enjoys the city life!" Reo exclaimed, still a little confused.

"Sadana thinks that the Makai should be the definitive source of law and order on this planet. He doesn't have a problem with using force to achieve his vision either."

The two were now approaching some dirt tracks with some shed-like dwellings on either side. Children in rags were playing with stones on the floor, with wild, matted hair and a dazzled look in their eyes. Some people came out of their dwellings as they heard the trotting of the horse's hooves clacking against stones in the ground.

"So, what do you think about this message that we are supposed to deliver? What's it all about?" Reo asked as they passed through the shanty village.

Bene smiled coyly and glanced at Reo.

"Question after question!" he sighed loudly and slightly sarcastically. "I am not sure, but I'd imagine it's some sort of warning."

He sped up to a canter and rode ahead of Reo quickly.

"And before you ask," he shouted back, "I don't know what that warning is!"

Reo rode into the centre of the city slowly and with great observation. He spent time viewing the house where he and his eight siblings had been brought up during his childhood, now a split dwelling for four families. He reminisced over the streets where as a youth, he and his friends had been drawn into the underworld of selling drugs, and the times they spent talking about their plans to leave the city for the prosperous land of Raicema, where they thought everybody was taken care of and everything was clean and safe. It was an illusion that Reo wondered if his friends had ever awakened to.

It was now dark and every crude house had a lantern outside, made from old animal-skins and tree saps. This was the time when Reo truly thought that Calegra was beautiful, as if a lantern had been lit for every person who had ever lived and died. To look out upon the city from raised ground at this time was to see a million specs of light, as if the ground were glowing with fireflies.

There was little electrical power in Calegra and the wealthier zones of the city quickly consumed what was available. Reo was now approaching such a zone, the region where one of his brothers and Bene would definitely be. Flashing lights could be seen and the sound of vehicle engines could be heard in the surround of an excess of drinking establishments, drugs houses, brothels and rundown diners. This was the place you could spend your living, if you had one. As Reo travelled through the outskirts of the zone, more known for its surrounding markets and trading houses, he saw that the streets were alive with shoppers, looking for a bargain, haggling with the traders and eyeing the vast variety of goods on offer. Many traders flocked here to sell the region's most popular export, copper goods and knick-knacks, moulded and crafted from the mines of the red plain.

"Have you seen a man called Bene Mattero?" Reo asked a local trader, who was selling what seemed to be a collection of copper cooking utensils. "He would have ridden past on a black and white horse."

"No," the trader replied in a gruff voice. "Try in the tavern down the next street. That's the only place I know that'll let you use its yard for your horse."

Reo rode down to the tavern, yellow and green lights flashing outside with hundreds of animal-skin lanterns hanging from its thin metal roof. The tavern had a dirt track that wound around to a small yard, where seven horses were tied to wooden stumps. Reo dismounted and tied his horse to a stump next to Bene's horse. He looked up at the sky filled with stars. He walked back up the track and into the tavern. The roar of laughter of four men sitting at an old painted copper table immediately flooded into his ears. The men were all drinking *Sovre*, a hallucinogenic drink made from a combination of sugar cane, tree saps and water. A young waiter came over to Reo, who was standing in the doorway trying to spot Bene.

"Whadaya want?" he said quite bluntly, in a slang dialect.

Reo spotted Bene at the back of the tavern, talking to another man.

"I'll have a bodi," Reo requested and the young waiter held out his hand for payment. The usual currency in Calegra was bits, which was literally small bits of gold. The amount you would receive would depend on the weight you gave. A rougher place like this didn't bother to actually weigh the gold bits but preferred to use an estimation process. More exclusive establishments, however, had a fairer way of pricing. Reo searched his pouch and found a tiny crumb of gold, enough for a medium-sized bodi. He gave it to the waiter, who walked away in disgust. He quickly returned with the smallest of drinks, to which Reo nodded without complaint. He walked over to where Bene was sitting and pulled up a wooden stool. Bene was somewhat surprised by Reo's presence at the table as he glanced up from his conversation.

"Ahh, Reo," he exclaimed, slurring slightly. "You found me."

Reo nodded, looking over at the man Bene had been talking to. He was young with black hair, longer at the back than at the front. He had a grimy look, with rough stubble and clothing.

"This is a friend of mine," Bene said, gesturing towards the man. "His name is Raoul and he has been part of the Makai since he was this high." He lowered his hand to the floor in a drunken fashion, smiling slightly. "We have been here for most of the evening drinking bodi. I see you too have one. A fascinating drink, the bodi..." Bene slurred uncontrollably, swaying a bit, "...it is found naturally in some jungles here in Lizrab, you know, much tastier than this mass-produced swill. Ever since those damn Raicemans occupied this city, things just ain't natural."

He took a few deep breaths, trying to compose himself.

"Raoul here cannot understand the Raiceman language as he lived in the south most of his life," Bene informed Reo.

Reo greeted Raoul in Lizrabian. The three drank and talked for hours about the state of the planet and the different views of the regions. Raoul explained how he had been brought up amongst warriors, who were ready to fight to defend the planet if Raicema tried to attack. He talked of previous invasion attempts ten and twenty years ago and their failure to succeed in the dense jungles of the south. After a while, Raoul said he had to go and Bene and Reo followed him outside on their way to collect the horses.

They said their farewells and then Reo turned to Bene. "Tomorrow, I want to find my brother!" he stated, walking down the dirt track aggressively, probably due to the litre of bodi in his body. "When I left, he was in trouble with some local gangs. I told him to lay low but I need to make sure he's okay."

"Tomorrow, Reo," Bene said, burping and dismissing the subject. "Let's get some rest tonight. We shall stay with some people I know."

They mounted the horses and rode out of the bustling zone, which seemed busier than before even though it was the middle of the night. They travelled towards some of the wealthier stone houses in the *Cohen Zone*, named after the Raiceman family that had once founded a vast trading business within the city.

"The house is just along here," Bene said, as they trotted along a cobbled road, the clapping of hooves on the rounded stones echoing along. Some of the houses had vehicles outside whilst others had an assortment of unusual plants and colourful flowers displayed on their windowsills and front gardens. They arrived at a large house made of brown stone, square in appearance with a selection of shrubbery resting on the flat roof. The moon was shining brightly and there was a slight crispness to the air, the cold snap of the dead of night. Bene dismounted and lightly rapped on the door. After a moment, a tall woman answered and upon seeing Bene, immediately ushered the two men into the house.

"Bene, it is good to see you!" she said with affection, giving him a firm hug. "I shall get Pedro to take care of the horses."

She guided them through the hallway into a large living area with leather chairs and a sturdy wooden table. She asked them to sit and disappeared into another room. She soon returned with some hot water, brew mixture, fruit and flat breads. She prepared a hot brew of berries and herbs and served it to the three of them in shiny, white oval cups.

"Well, Bene. You have been in Raicema for a long time," she said. "It has been more than three years since I saw you last. I am glad you came here tonight. Tell me, who is your friend?"

She gazed at Reo with an expression of interest, she herself about forty years of age with round hazel eyes, wavy brown hair and a slender face.

"His name is Reo Fernandez. He is a local of Calegra that I recruited in Raicema City. Quite a young one, huh, Karina?" There was a tone of guilt in his voice.

Karina smiled at Reo and then turned more seriously to Bene.

"You are aware that the Raiceman forces are on their way here as we speak?"

"That is what I am counting on to get us to the south in a couple of days," Bene replied calmly.

Reo frowned at this news. He was not aware that he was about to get caught up in a war zone.

"Wait just a minute!" he blurted out, keen to elevate his concerns. "I didn't really know about this Makai stuff until you dragged me into this, Bene. I only wanted a job. But now you're saying we're going to get involved with the Raiceman military as well. Are you trying to get us both killed?"

Bene said nothing, but Karina leaned over to Reo.

"Don't worry, Reo," she said in a kind voice. "I know a lot of this must be new to you. How old are you? Maybe seventeen? It's not surprising that you don't know about the movement here in Lizrab. Let's face it, they don't want the kids to know. But this war has been going on for hundreds of years. Who do you think has been holding Raicema off from completely dominating this planet?"

Reo was silent, in disbelief at what he had gotten himself

involved in.

"Many brave souls have died over the years," she continued. "And not just here in Lizrab but in Ciafra, Neoasia and Raicema too."

Bene leaned over and touched Reo on the hand to get his attention.

"Reo," he said firmly. "Our trip will be dangerous but for good reason. It is no coincidence that Sadana has sent me here with this message at the same time Raicema plan to invade. I have worked for many years to gain his trust, but unfortunately he has recently discovered my secret. You saw those men that were following us in Raicema. This world is dangerous and we have to do what is best for everyone."

Reo was now totally confused and blinking repeatedly, thinking hard about what Bene could possibly be talking about. He took a large gulp of his brew. "I don't really understand. I thought that we were delivering this message as part of our job, you know, working for the RMO?"

"That's what you want Sadana to think," Karina interjected. "Really you are here to help bring down the Raiceman government as part of the movement."

Reo thought hard for a while, trying to remember all the things Bene had told him over the past few days. "But wouldn't Sadana be on our side if that's what we were helping to do? He wants the same thing right? After all, he is part of the Makai isn't he?"

Karina and Bene looked at each other with slight sadness, partially due to Reo's naivety and innocence.

"Sadana isn't Makai!" Karina stated fervently, shocking Reo somewhat. "He only uses the name in Raicema to attract people who detest the government. He has no intention of unifying the so-called 'Makai' there with the sects in other locations on the planet."

"But he was talking with such leadership, like he was part of it all and there were those other leaders with him," Reo insisted. "Are you sure he isn't part of this Makai thing?"

"Definitely not!" Karina reaffirmed. "He was born in Raicema and is a very good actor. Only Bene and a few of us that he has been sending messages to over the years really know Sadana's true intention and that is not to help people live in peace on this planet. It is to control them, no different than what the Raiceman government try to do."

"You said Sadana discovered your secret. What secret?" Reo continued, turning his questioning to Bene.

"Sadana originally hired me to recruit desperate individuals into the RMO. He believed I was one of them when he first met me, believing I came from a similar background to you here in Calegra. But recently he discovered the truth," Bene said. He took multiple sips of his brew, almost losing himself watching the herbal leaves swirling around in his cup. "I was born in the south. My father's name was Juhi Mattero. Have you heard that name?"

Reo shook his head.

"Not surprising, I guess, since you have never even heard of the Makai. Well, Juhi Mattero was the original leader of the Makai in Raicema. Sadana had him killed nine years ago. Can you guess why?"

Again Reo shook his head.

"Juhi Mattero is the only son of Kirichi, a man who stands for the same principle of peace and unity. But for Sadana, that meant letting go of his vision of power and control and so he murdered him."

Reo was speechless.

"You mean, you are Kirichi's grandson?" he finally said after several moments.

Bene nodded and leaned his head back against the hard wood.

"How could you stand in the same room as your father's killer and do nothing?" Reo asked in disbelief, himself feeling anger and frustration at the man who had bossed them both about recently. Bene said nothing, clearly holding back his feelings but Karina offered a quick explanation.

"It would be suicide if he even breathed on Sadana," she said.

"He is very connected to the Raiceman government."

"So why'd you include me in all this?" Reo asked, suddenly feeling a pang of anxiety. "How can I possibly help you? You don't need me."

"I needed you because I knew I could trust you. If I didn't pick a recruit myself to take with me, Sadana would have sent me with someone who could have killed me and my grandfather, and it is imperative that he is protected at all times."

Reo was still confused and even though it was late and both Bene and Karina were fighting to keep their eyes open, he pressed on. "So why didn't they just kill us before? You know, when we were at the top of the casino. I mean, they tried to kill you when we went to your apartment."

"Some of those elders have no idea of what Sadana is planning, of how involved he is with Raicema and his vicious nature. They all believe Juhi's death was the work of the Raicemans and they appointed him as leader. He could never kill us in front of them."

Bene paused for a minute, searching his thoughts.

"Besides, he is waiting for something before he shows his true colours. He is planning something big."

"But I don't understand why he'd give you something to deliver and then send a guy to your apartment to kill you?" Reo questioned.

"I don't think Sadana paid that guy," Bene said. "I think that was the Raiceman government. Sadana wants me here, so I have to watch what is going to happen."

The last statement seemed to put Bene in a melancholic mood. Reo picked up a crunchy, red fruit and bit into its watery flesh. He contemplated everything that he had heard. He had to admit, it all sounded somewhat exciting, if not also quite terrifying. The knowledge that there were so many people out there moving against such oppression was a great comfort and his new feeling of hope was soothing.

"What is going to happen, Bene?" Reo asked after a while. "What does that message say?"

Bene leaned in close to both Reo and Karina.

"It is only for my grandfather's eyes but no doubt it is a declaration of war. The Raiceman military may be running the war but its people like Sadana that are directing it."

Reo could not believe the level of conspiracy that Bene was alluding to.

"So, what are you planning, Bene? How can we stop them?" Reo asked, unsure of what should be done next.

"We shall stay in Calegra for the next two days. You may do what you wish during that time," Bene told him. "Then, on the third day, a huge Raiceman military unit will travel through Calegra, picking up supplies whilst they head south. We will disguise ourselves as soldiers and travel towards Aradonas with them. That is where there are over thirty thousand Makai warriors situated and where Kirichi is based in a jungle close by. Because they will be travelling in fast land-vehicles, it should only take a day to reach Aradonas. We should then get as far away from the fighting as possible and find my grandfather as soon as we can."

Reo was relieved to hear the last statement. "So we won't get caught up in the fighting?" he asked fearfully, trying to gain reassurance.

"After we have talked to my grandfather, we must do what we can to help defend Lizrab," was all Bene said in reply.

Karina rose to her feet and gathered the remaining food together. As she left the room carrying the trays, Bene leaned close to Reo to whisper something.

"There is another reason I wanted you to come with me, Reo, but I don't want to talk about it in front of Karina."

"Will you tell me later?" Reo whispered back.

"Yes."

Karina came back in the room and sat down again, lighting up a cigarette. The smell of the smoke was strong, like burning leaves that were slightly damp. A young man entered the room with curly black hair and worn boots. He sat down silently against a wall. "If it's okay with you, Bene, we'll keep the horses here for whoever needs them. Pedro will take care of them."

Bene just nodded. Reo began to think about what Karina and Pedro did there in such a large house.

"I suppose you are wondering what it is Pedro and I do here?" she said quite psychically as she breathed smoke through her nostrils.

"Well, I was wondering," Reo admitted.

"We run a safe-house for Makai warriors," she declared. "It is our job to make sure that people like yourself and Bene have somewhere to stay and get what they need when they are in Calegra."

Reo was quite flattered to be thought of as a warrior, whether or not the description was at all accurate.

"There are safe houses like this one all over the world. Sometimes we host large meetings and it gets pretty full," she continued, while Pedro grinned from his seated position, checking his fingernails. "You're lucky. You both get a room to yourselves this time."

"And nobody knows about this place?"

"Only those who are willing to die for freedom!" she stated boldly. Then she laughed and stubbed out her cigarette in a terra-cotta dish. "Follow me, we have talked enough tonight. I'll show you to your rooms."

She walked out into the hallway and they both followed. Karina led them up some stone stairs, lit by candles burning brightly on an overlooking ledge that ran all the way up. At the top was a hall with several doorways. At the end were two dark rooms, each with several hard mattresses on the floor. She wished them goodnight, yawning herself slightly.

After she had gone back down the stairs, Reo turned to a waning Bene. "So, why *did* you bring me along?" he asked quietly.

"Karina would never understand why, just as Sadana would never understand why Karina does what she does," Bene trailed off, avoiding the question.

"What wouldn't she understand? Why did you pick me?" Reo pressed, raising his voice slightly.

"Shhhh!" Bene scolded him. "It is just who you are, that is all. The same as my father."

Then he stumbled into his room as Reo tried to get him to elaborate. But it was too late. Bene had closed the door and within minutes he was asleep, mainly due to the large dose of alcoholic fluids he had consumed earlier. Reo walked into his room and closed the door. He lay awake for several hours, pondering Bene's words and the imminent conflict in the south. He felt nervous, but he was sure he felt that way because he finally had a chance to prove that he could do something good with his life.

Chapter 11 – Rivalry at Sea

If Jen King ever witnessed a beautiful moment when least expected, it was aboard the *Stryder* war vessel as it was just becoming dusk. The sky had turned ember red, illuminating everything metallic on board with a magenta glow. The entire vessel looked like it had been heated in a giant oven and it surprised King that even the ugliest four-barrel cannons looked pretty in the warming light, like they might melt at any moment. The men roamed freely about the decks, their two hours of free time almost over. Next there would be the never-ending task of servicing weapons, assembling, crating, polishing and oiling to name a few of the regimented tasks involved. King often wondered if some of the men developed friendships with the pieces of intricate metal, based on the amount of time they spent with them.

Another two days until I can put my feet on land again, King thought to himself over and over. He was sure he'd spent half of his life floating on the seas. Though it could be calming looking out at an endless stretch of ocean, he much preferred the grounded feeling he got by living on the earth. Amaru, who was close by, approached King and stood next to him as he was gazing out at the sunset.

"You think we'll have any success this time?" he asked nonchalantly, crossing his legs and leaning on the metal barrier with his forearms.

"Doubt it," King replied with little interest. "As you can see, I lack the motivation to conquer, yet I am sure those that we will face will have great motivation to defend. I am sure all the men feel similarly, especially since it is becoming clearer by the day that the government don't care if we are killed in the line of fire. With everyone against you, it's simply a nightmare to fight such a campaign."

King's reflection surprised Amaru and he quickly slipped away in search of less serious conversation, leaving King alone with the imminent darkness of night. He walked over to a small, decked area at the bow, mainly used for operational planning on warm days. There were a few wooden benches and King often came here to escape the harshness of his metal surroundings. For as long as he could remember he'd been travelling on vessels such as this and though they now felt like a second home, there was something cold and empty about them, as if every person who had every walked aboard left their sorrow wandering about on the decks.

King was surprised to see three tea-candles left on one of the benches. He searched his pockets for some matches and upon finding some, decided to light the candles. He sat and stared into the soothing, flickering orange flames dancing in the subtle breeze. The air was warm, one of the things that King looked forward to on his travels to the southern regions. Raicema City was often blustery and chilling at this time of year and there was something innate within King that longed for bright, hot sunshine to beat down upon him. He noticed the flames of the candles had attracted a multitude of insects towards the bench on which he was sitting; black beetles, flying moths and strange little dragonflies. The moths hovered danger-ously close to the flames and it took King aback when one caught alight and dove crashing to the floor. He noticed that a black beetle was walking slowly to one of the candles and as it reached the metal casing and tried to step up, it was jolted out by what must have been an intense heat to the small creature.

Doesn't it know that it's dangerous? King questioned himself, astounded that the beetle repeated its attempts to climb up onto the hot molten wax, the flame intensely alluring to it. Finally, after four more attempts, it jumped forward, catching on fire and then submerging into the wax, perfectly preserved. The scene gave King an eerie feeling and he was about the blow out the candles when he looked up and saw hundreds of insects floating down towards them. He decided to leave them alight. Though he didn't understand why all of these creatures wanted to join with the bright flames, he decided that it must be what they all truly desired.

He rose to his feet, ready to head back to his quarters for the night. As he walked along the deck, he noticed a shadowy character lurking behind some containers. The man jumped out confrontationally.

"You wait there, King!" the man said in a hostile, deep voice, greasy brown hair stuck to his face. Then, five other men appeared from their hiding places, all aggressive in approach.

"What do you want?" King said to the first aggressor, retracting into a defensive stance.

"We want you to show more respect," the man growled as three of the men grabbed King from behind. The greasy man pulled back and hit King heavily in the stomach with his fist, forcing the air out of him. The remaining two produced blunt metal objects and were about to beat King with them, when a bubble of rage exploded inside him and with a single blow to each of the muggers, he crumpled three of them to the floor. The others gained a look of terror on their face but as they turned to run, King kicked the greasy man's legs, felling him whilst throwing the other two overboard with an intense shove. They both screamed as they hit the water with a splash. King grabbed the initiator by the collar of his uniform and raised him up against a metal tank, slamming him so hard that the metal dented with the force.

"Urrrh!!" the man moaned, slumping down in pain.

"What the hell do you want?" King barked with ferocity at the man, causing him to wince even more.

"I'm sorry," he begged, his voice now high-pitched. "I had to do it."

"Why?" King bellowed, rage pulsating through his veins. "I don't even know you!"

He pushed on the man's throat and he began to choke, his face turning a strange shade of blue with the force.

"President Tyrone told us to!" the man croaked, spluttering and gasping for air. King released his grip on the man, pushing him to the ground. He marched quickly along the deck, fully intent on confronting the cowardly leader. He passed many soldiers who all asked him where he was going, ignoring some and pushing others out of his way. Memories of his adolescence came to mind as he entered the ship's elevator.

"Operations," he barked into the controls, remembering Jeth's many attempts to sabotage King throughout his life in Raicema. The lift sped upwards and opened its doors at the end of a well-decorated hallway. All along were large cabins used for navigation and planning.

One particular memory had stuck in King's mind. Whilst training to be a soldier along with Seth under the guidance of his father, Guido, there had been a severe injury to one of Guido's closest aides. The aide had been attacked and robbed of several valuable items which had been in his family for several generations. An antique pistol, a stopwatch and a gold ring were amongst the items stolen. The entire fleet of troops had been interrogated about the crime, but nobody had admitted to it. Then, in the middle of the night, King was awoken by Guido along with several aides, holding the stopwatch and ring in his hand. They had found them hidden in a pile of King's clothes.

"I'll give you one opportunity only. Where is the pistol?" Guido had asked King forcefully.

"I don't know. I have never seen those things in my life," King had replied sincerely.

King had been punished severely for the framed crime and he sometimes thought that this one event had altered the path of his life. After several incarcerations and beatings, King had been forced to work as a member of the cleaning staff for several years, treated as a worthless animal by most of the troops. It was only when Guido died that Seth recruited King back into the military where he had been ever since. It was then that King found out the true identity of the criminal who had robbed the aide. One day whilst discussing an upcoming mission with Seth in the president's office, he noticed a small, old-looking pistol hidden on the top of a line of books at the back of the room. When Seth left the office, he inspected the pistol and found it to match the description that the aide had given all those years ago. It was then that he knew that not only was Jeth Tyrone a cowardly thief but also that he despised King and wanted him to suffer.

Now, approaching the large double redwood doors that led to Jeth's extravagant office, King took a deep breath, knowing that Jeth was capable of sickening acts. He pushed the doors open and Jeth was waiting, sitting behind an oval table with a gun pointed straight at King.

"It's a shame you cannot accept the gifts that I send to you gracefully," Jeth said sarcastically, aiming at King's head. He got to his feet cautiously, approaching with small shuffling movements.

"Why do you hate me so much?" King asked Jeth, the man who had never expressed a kind intention to anyone.

"It's quite simple," Jeth said with spite in his voice. "My father always thought you were something special, a golden child. I remember the day he brought you back to my home, thinking that he had made the greatest discovery in the world. I told him then that you were just a filthy Ciafran, but he didn't listen to me. I couldn't believe he treated you like one of his own children and expected us to treat you like a brother."

King listened with dismay, though he could not understand why he was surprised at Jeth's malice as he had accepted it long ago.

"You never treated me like a brother!" King made it clear to Jeth. "You ignored me for as long as I can remember."

"Why would I even give eye-contact to a sickening, dirty Ciafran like you?" Jeth said with chilling conviction. "You are not a Raiceman. You are not from my blood. You are not even fit to represent Raicema in warfare, regardless of what my brother thinks."

The statement infuriated King.

"What do you know about warfare?" King questioned Jeth, raising his voice angrily. "All you do is dream up sick ways to hurt people. It's soldiers like Seth and I that have to witness the pain and death. You speak of warfare like it's only a game. People die because of your decisions and you say that I am unfit!"

"People die because they are inferior," Jeth declared, cocking back the lever of his pistol. "People must be controlled, otherwise there would be anarchy like in this godforsaken nation that we are heading towards."

"Why are they inferior? Just because you say so? What makes your opinion so special?" King fired back. "It is only because your father inherited power that you have too! You would be nobody otherwise. And at least your father used to fight the wars he started!"

King's words caused an expression of wickedness to spread across Jeth's face, his eyes focusing on something distant, and his face screwing up with bitterness. He pointed the gun directly at King's face and in a moment that seemed to stretch on supernaturally, King heard a piercing bang as the pistol was fired and the bullet left the gun. Before King knew what was happening, he found himself on the floor, sure he would soon feel the burning pain of the bullet. As he felt nothing, he looked up, surprised that Seth was standing over him with a look of annoyance focused squarely on his brother.

"What are you doing, you maniac?!" Seth spewed, marching quickly over to his brother and yanking the pistol out of his hand. King was checking himself for wounds and was surprised to find he was completely unharmed, pushed out of the line of fire by Seth.

"Your precious soldier is nothing more than a traitor!" Jeth stated in a whiny manner, shrill and hysterical. "He cannot be trusted! He will be the downfall of Raicema!"

"Leave!" Seth ordered King, who quickly got to his feet, hesitating slightly before walking through the office doors. A deep feeling of sadness filled him. He felt worthless and for a moment became disoriented looking for the way back towards the cabins. Fatigued, he walked back slowly to the dormitories.

"What the hell are you playing at?" Seth barked at Jeth, walking over to the office doors and making sure they were closed. "Have you lost your mind?"

Jeth slumped back into his leather chair, sulking like a moody child.

"It's that damn Ciafran!" he snarled, retreating into deep thought.

"You know that we need him," Seth said, walking over to his brother's desk. "I told you to stay out of his way."

"We don't need him!" Jeth argued defiantly. "I don't believe all that hocus pocus crap."

Seth leaned over the desk so that his face was right in front of Jeth's. "Do you think father would have brought a Ciafran child into our home for no good reason? Think about it; you know that his strength is not natural."

Jeth said nothing. The gloom of his silence had permeated the air creating a tainted ambience. Even Seth felt slightly fearful looking into the expressionless face of Jeth Tyrone. His eyes glazed over, lost in a calculated mindset of planning and scheming. Seth knew that deep in his brother's mind, the greatest of resentments was festering into the consuming seed of pure hatred.

"Stay out of his way," Seth told his brother, turning to leave. "He is the centrepiece of the efforts on the ground."

"Until Lizrab falls then…" Jeth said under his breath.

Chapter 12 – The Shores of the Past

Vassini was a giant region near Neoasia with a long history of spiritual practice and autonomy amongst the people. Only in the past hundred years had the region begun to experience warfare on its lands. There were many areas where people had been undisturbed for hundreds and thousands of years.

Sita was fourteen years of age when she was betrothed to Rama, the youngest son of a carpenter in the mountainous village of *Kimrit*. She was the youngest of seven children. Each had left the Vassinian village for bigger towns where more work was available. Sita had been alone with her parents since the age of nine, helping them with their farming duties and occupation of jewellery making. The necklaces that she and her parents made were used all over the region for spiritual practice and good luck.

Both Sita and Rama's families were village advisors of sorts, giving remedies for ailments and advice for the troubled. They were both taught from an early age about the Vassinian ethos of energy flows and the intricate ties between body and mind.

When the Raiceman troops invaded a nearby town when Sita and Rama were both sixteen, Rama decided to join the local Makai warriors who were defending the town. Because of this, Rama was outcast, his actions going against the strict provincial standpoint of non-violence. Sita was betrothed to another, but quickly escaped to join Rama and the Makai. Neither of them had seen their parents since they had left Kimrit, instead turning to the Makai communities they had lived with over the past ten years.

Now, both in each other's arms, they bobbed on a small vessel like a bottle in the water, looking out on the distant silhouette of Bimini island. It was late dusk and an amazing event was occurring. At the top of the single mast on the boat, a phenomenal fire-like energy was burning away brightly. Javu was sitting on a rickety old wooden chair on the deck looking up at the sight, whilst Teltu navigated the vessel and Rekesh dived repeatedly into the ocean to see if he could spot the aura of the pyramid. Every so often he would come back up with a huff, tell Teltu to steer the boat in a different direction and then dive down again.

"Have you seen this spectacle?" Javu shouted to Teltu at the rear of the boat.

"What spectacle?" he replied.

"Come and see."

Teltu locked the rudder and walked towards the main deck where Javu was smiling and humming.

"Look, up there. It's known as *Elm's fire*."

"Whoa!" Teltu exclaimed as he caught sight of the magical blaze.

"The fascinating thing is that it is doing no damage to the mast. Though it is known as a fire and looks like a fire, it is actually not," Javu explained. "It is in effect, a sort of plasma."

"But how is it lingering there if it is not burning away on the mast?" Teltu asked.

"Nobody knows why it appears, Teltu, but it is a presence of energy that has an awareness of its surroundings somehow. There are other energy forms that have similar awareness like lightning balls and wisp lanterns."

"Amazing," Teltu said candidly. "It's like magic."

"Some say they are from other worlds."

Sita and Rama both came over and stood beside Javu's chair observing the Elm's fire. Then they heard a shout in the distance as Rekesh came back up to the surface.

"Whoops!" Teltu said sheepishly, running back to the rudder. "We've gone a bit too far out and left him behind."

Javu turned to the young Vassinian couple and began to converse with them in Hindi. He asked them about their home.

Rekesh was climbing over the side of the boat, dressed in a navy jumpsuit and carrying a small air tank on his back. He pushed himself off the wooden decking, water dripping all over it. His long black, knotted hair wound into a twist, snaking around his neck.

"Wondered where you were all going for a while..." he said,

slightly more jovially that before.

"Did you find anything?" Javu asked, turning away from Sita and Rama.

"No. Not a thing. I was sure that the pyramid was close by to this stretch of ocean."

"I think we should head for the island," Javu said, looking towards it. "We should look for a cavern there."

Rekesh just nodded in agreement and Teltu walked over to the rudder to steer the ship to the island. Sita and Rama had both walked over, smiling and talking to each other softly. The Elm's fire had now disappeared without a trace from the mast.

As the boat approached the isle, the trees swaying in the breeze looked like a dark mass writhing and twisting. The boat landed on a short beach, with giant smooth rocks embedded into the sand.

"This is close to the road," Rekesh said, recognising the beach. "And not far from here is a military base. We should be careful because there were thousands of troops here before. That's why we had to cut the power of a station in the forest just over there to create a diversion."

"It seems very quiet now," Javu said, climbing over the side carefully and lowering himself into the water up to his knees. "Oooh, the water is freezing!"

Rekesh picked up a few bags and jumped over the side with agility, landing in the water with a splash. The others all gathered some supplies and followed. They waded out to the beach and Teltu immediately began to gather dry wood to build a fire. Sita and Rama joined him.

"We should wait until the morning to start looking," Javu said to Rekesh, who was unpacking a canvas tent from a large bag.

"I think you're right," he agreed reluctantly, letting out a huge sigh. "It's getting dark now and the pyramid is deep so we will probably have to spend quite a while searching for a tunnel in. We need as much light as possible."

The tent had been sprawled over the beach, a light tan colour with the faint moonlight reflecting on its waxed surface.

"Besides, I'm starting to have more faith that Elera is safe," he said, cheering himself up a little and pushing the canvas up with two wooden poles. "Just being here, closer to her makes me feel better."

Javu smiled at Rekesh's newfound optimism. He helped him secure the large tent near some trees that were growing at a unique angle, bent over slightly from a previous tropical gust. The air was now picking up force and some of the smaller bags containing food and bedding began to roll along the beach. Teltu ran after them, his long shirt blowing in the wind, and weighed them down with some heavy stones. Sita and Rama emerged from the dark forest carrying armfuls of loose wood. They began to set up a fire and within a few minutes it was ablaze wildly, whilst Teltu returned with more wood and a variety of fruits.

"Some really nice fruit grows on this island," he said cheerfully, making a small stockpile near the fire. The island was now shrouded in darkness and only the light from the fire cast a warm glow on the immediate surroundings of the simple camp. Javu began to roast some vegetables that he had brought with him over the fire and lit some candles that he found in the bottom of his bag. Everyone began to settle around the fire.

"Did I ever tell you about the time that Kirichi and I met Albedor the peasant?" Javu asked everyone.

Both Teltu and Rekesh shook their heads.

"Well, whilst we were walking in a wood outside Aradonas, we met a homeless peasant who lived under a fallen tree. On that particular day, we saw the peasant discover a small leather pouch, hidden in the grass. Inside the pouch were a number of valuable gemstones, enough to supply Albedor with food and shelter for a long time. However, Albedor immediately noticed that the pouch was engraved with the initials of an affluent merchant that lived in Aradonas."

Javu paused as he turned the sticks that skewed the vegetables.

"Albedor decided that he would return the pouch to the merchant and he asked Kirichi and I to show him the way. We walked with him to the merchant's house and we all went inside. When Albedor returned the pouch, the merchant thanked him but offered no reward for his honest nature or good deed. Instead, he asked us all to leave as he was entertaining an important customer. Well, we left and invited Albedor back to the monastery in Turo where he now resides to this day. However, two weeks later we all heard a wonderful story. It seems that the important customer that the merchant was entertaining was a wealthy widow who was intending to have a fine necklace made out of the gemstones. But when she overheard that a homeless peasant had honestly returned such a valuable find, she decided to give much of her wealth to those who were homeless instead."

Javu smiled to himself at the remembrance.

"And of course, if Albedor hadn't decided to hand back the pouch, he would have not spoken to Kirichi, who gave him a home in the monastery."

"Remarkable," Teltu said wide-eyed whilst crunching on a few nuts.

"And that's not the end of the story!" Javu continued with enthusiasm. "The widow used most of her money to set up sanctuaries on the borders of Aradonas. One day, a group of nomadic travellers stayed overnight at one of the sanctuaries. They had travelled all over the world and rarely stayed in one place for longer than a few days. When they heard of how the sanctuaries had been started, they decided to remain in Lizrab and dedicate their time to creating more and more sanctuaries for those in need. Now in Lizrab, there are over two hundred places that you can stay if you are in need. And all of that was started with one honest act from someone who was homeless."

Even though Sita and Rama could not fully understand, they were both still listening intently and each tried to translate to the other parts of the story. Javu nodded at the accuracy of their translations.

"And what happened to Albedor?" Teltu asked as Javu handed him one of the hot vegetable sticks.

"He is happy in Turo. He now spends most of his time venturing out to help others that are in a similar situation to what he once was."

Rekesh had been listening but seemed distant, lost in his own thoughts. "Why is there so much poverty on this planet?" he asked melancholically, almost to himself.

"Do you really need to ask that question, Rekesh?" Teltu said, himself sure of the reason. "It's down to greedy empires like Raicema that take more than they ever need, leaving so little for everyone else."

"How did it start?" Rekesh continued to speak to himself, ignoring Teltu's response.

"How some end up in unfortunate circumstances whilst others seem to live in the cradle of luxury is indeed troublesome," Javu said, rubbing his wiry beard. "In my view, poverty begins when there is widespread fear of something, like a war or a disease. Then there is an instinctive feeling to run away in oneself. And when that happens in mass, there is an imbalance. Of course, the cause of such an exodus could be the threat of an empire as you say, Teltu."

Sita seemed to understand and began to converse with Javu in Hindi. After a few minutes of talking, whilst the others ate, Javu translated for Teltu.

"Sita tells me of the recent wars in Vassini. The views of people have split between those who wish to fight to defend their homes and families and those who continue to believe in non-violence no matter what. This too has caused poverty in Vassini as people from one view are less likely to help someone with another view. So in Vassini there is a struggle occurring between the two viewpoints."

"I think you are right, Teltu," Rekesh said suddenly, his tone a little aggressive. "Greedy governments like Raicema are to blame. If they didn't want so much, there would be enough for everyone!"

Silence fell on the group and Javu felt an overwhelming urge to change the subject.

"Tell us of your endeavours over the past year, Rekesh. It has been a long while since you last came to Seho."

"There is not much to tell," he replied, slumping back onto his side and supporting his head with his hand. "I am still trying to change things in Raicema with the Makai. The main thing is trying to make people aware that they are being controlled. The Raicemans are very good at manipulating people into thinking they have a good life, but I have seen it time and time again; the day comes when the person realises that there is something very important missing from their lives."

"And that would be?"

"Freedom. They decide they want to find out for themselves what life is about, what is outside the pretty prison that they are contained within and then they realise, they realise that if they leave, they can never come back. You're either with them or against them. I have seen countless amounts of people put in horrendous situations just for questioning the way it all works. Those that are more careful turn to the Makai. That's mainly what I have been doing, helping people turn."

"And does that help them?" Javu asked reservedly.

"It helps most. They find a new purpose to their life, the fight for freedom. But some go the other way, become fearful of leaving their fake life behind and they panic. Those are the dangerous ones because they become the same as those that control them, desperate to preserve that way of life."

"It must be hard for you and Elera as you spend so much of your time in Raicema," Teltu commented. "I know she travels a lot."

"It is difficult sometimes," Rekesh sighed. "We used to spend much more time together until she learnt about this forgotten civilisation. But I guess any historian would be fascinated by that."

"But it's much more than that, Rekesh," Javu stated. "The history that Elera is trying to uncover is important for us all, so we can further understand ourselves. She knows that and I think that is what is motivating her."

Rekesh was silent, contemplating his heavy thoughts under the cast of the warm firelight. The breeze had dropped to a whisper, stroking the faces of everyone now and then.

"I feel so different when she is not around," he said finally, almost speaking to himself. "Like I am lost, wading aimlessly through an ocean. When I am with her I feel like I have a purpose, a reason for existing."

An image of indifference drew itself across Javu's face but it quickly turned to concern over Rekesh's dependency on Elera. Javu knew how it had developed. Though he was sure Rekesh truly loved Elera, he also knew that growing up alone had rooted a seed of loneliness deep within him.

"I think I'm going to sleep now," Teltu announced, moving into a more sheltered part of the large tent, whilst Sita and Rama went for a walk along the beach, seemingly sensing that Javu wanted to talk to Rekesh alone. With the faint crackle of dry wood as the only intermission to the peaceful sound of the nearby waves, Javu decided to bring up the painful subject of Rekesh's parents.

"Do you think about them much?" he asked quietly.

"Who?" Rekesh asked aloofly.

"Your parents."

A stony look froze Rekesh's face for a while. "No," he said without any emotion. Javu had started this conversation many times before; when Rekesh was only a boy, a teenager and now a grown man. It had been tragic that Rekesh had witnessed his parents' death at such a young age but what was more upsetting for Javu was how Rekesh had blocked out all emotion on the subject, dismissing it as unimportant, projecting a false strength from his hidden suffering. The conversations always ended on the same dismissive point; it was in the past. It would take a great deal to make Rekesh realise the events of his childhood were still very much in the present.

"I think about them," Javu said warmly. "They were very kind people."

The words seemed to bore Rekesh, who simply stared out into the darkness hiding the vast ocean.

"They had great love for you and each other," he continued. "Do you remember them?"

"Of course I do!" Rekesh exploded uncontrollably, immediately trying to calm himself by taking a few deep breaths. "I mean, I can remember us all together in Vassini, sitting and eating together. Then the Raicemans came and everything is a blur after that. I only remember travelling constantly and staying with distant relatives and family friends. Afterwards, those people were all I had left. They told me a lot about them, but I was never listening. They are gone and it must be accepted."

It was paradoxical to Javu that his last statement was so true and yet he had not accepted it at all.

"Talking about them is not intended to bring them back, but it may help us in our current lives," he said softly, offering Rekesh another skewer of vegetables. He declined and there was silence for a few moments.

"I am afraid, Javu," he said openly after a while. "Not for myself, but for others. It is as if a dark cloud has followed me ever since then. I cannot tell the difference between my imagination and my instinct any more. Everywhere I go, I think that I am there to prevent something, prevent more deaths."

"We cannot be responsible for everything, Rekesh," Javu consoled him. "It is important to keep your feet on the ground when you experience fear or it can take you away. Just remember that you have experienced some of the most beautiful things in life as well, such as the love you have for Elera. Focus on that. Even though your parents are gone, that does not mean to say that the love that you had between you is also gone. That is still there, here with us now."

Rekesh smiled weakly.

Javu felt as though they had conversed enough and wished Rekesh a good night's sleep. All were resting peacefully a short while later, except for Rekesh, who looked out into the sea of darkness hoping that Elera was safe. His last thought before finally falling asleep was one of her running towards him, and every drop of fear evaporated at that beautiful sight.

Chapter 13 – The Bearer of the Jade Mask

"Rekesh? Rekesh?" a soft and soothing voice whispered.

The world was blurred, new and vivid, an unrecognisable flourishing of colours coming in and out of focus. For a moment, the feeling was that of safety and relief, of waking up after the worst of nightmares. A warm hand touched his face, a dream of unexplainable wonderment.

"I knew you'd be waiting here," the voice continued, slowly stirring Rekesh from his slumbering. He shot upright suddenly and the greatest surge of emotion crashed through him with the recognition of the voice that was speaking to him. He turned around and saw Elera sitting next to him, smiling. There was nobody else around and for a moment Rekesh thought he might be dreaming. After a few seconds of dazed realisation, he flung his arms around her and kissed her face and neck passionately.

"I can't believe it!" he stuttered, blinking hard a number of times to make sure she was real. "How did you get here?"

Elera giggled, invoking a similar reaction in Rekesh, though he was sure it was the immense relief that had an underlying joviality to it.

"Well, it's quite unbelievable, so I will tell you later, but I am safe as you can see."

Again Rekesh embraced her and then stared devotedly into her eyes. "I am never leaving you alone again!" he said firmly, again causing Elera to giggle slightly. He rubbed her arms, once again to affirm that she was solid.

"The others all went to have a look around. They told me you have been halfway across Ciafra and back. It seems like an eternity since I last saw you."

Rekesh nodded in agreement. "I thought you might be..." he began to say, a tear forming in his eye. Elera put her finger to his lips to stop the words. She smiled affectionately and then embraced him. They stayed in each other's arms for many moments. After a while, she drew him to arm's length and could see that his torment was slowly drifting away.

"I'm sorry for venturing in ahead of you," she said to him sincerely. "The entrance seemed so safe and then before I knew it I was thrown and I had been sealed inside."

"No, it was my fault for not pulling you out," Rekesh said with a genuine guilt in his voice.

"Well, it doesn't matter now," Elera said definitively. "We are both safe and here together now. There is so much I have to tell you."

A light wind rose and fell like a wave in the sea with a crisp essence of sea kelp riding upon it. The waves played like a euphoric harmony on the ears of the two lovers, who again embraced passionately before sitting and facing each other in a more relaxed position.

"The island has been deserted," she continued. "I met somebody here who helped me get back to the island. I don't know where she's gone. Shall we go and have a look around to see if we can find Javu and the others?"

They got to their feet just as everyone was walking back across the beach. Rekesh was still in disbelief, as if he was living in an entirely different world. Everyone looked happy and full of vigour.

"Can you believe it that Elera found *us*?" Teltu said, as he got closer. "Funny, huh, after we searched through the Great Pyramid and all for a way to get her out."

Rekesh, still reeling, just nodded.

"It would be good to let Fera know you are safe. She is sick with worry."

Elera agreed with Teltu and gestured for everyone to sit down. Though it was only early morning, the sand was already warm from the giant disc of molten orange hovering above the sea.

"I am touched that you all came here to rescue me," she said to everyone, but her eyes lingered on Rekesh for a few extra moments. "I have discovered some extraordinary things inside the pyramid."

"So did we!" Teltu said excitedly.

"The capstone was made of a material that I could walk through. Can you believe it? That is how I got out."

"When?" asked Rekesh. "How long were you trapped?"

"Well, I'm not sure how long I was down there but it seemed like a long time. I have been out for a week now. I must have been underground for at least two weeks because I ate all the food I had with me and I didn't eat for a long time after that. I managed to find a passage and not long after I found a way out. While it was a little scary, I saw the most beautiful things down there."

"Like what?" Teltu asked. "We saw some pretty incredible things in the Giza pyramid too!"

"I found strange chambers, one with something valuable inside; a crystal sphere. I still have it with me. Then, I got to the top of the pyramid and found it was made of walls you could see through. I just sat there, looking out at the beauty of the ocean. I was compelled to walk through it and I did! The next thing I knew, I was in the ocean!"

Rekesh had a slight look of disbelief on his face, though he was listening attentively.

"Everyone sit. I will show you what I have found."

Elera sat cross-legged on the fine sand and took the crystal sphere out of her leather satchel, placing it on the sand in front of her. Everyone sat in a circle around it, mesmerised by the interaction of the morning sunlight with its complicated innards.

"If you move slightly around you will see an image of four pyramids inside."

Everyone looked carefully into the orb, trying to see what Elera was describing.

"I don't see anything," Teltu said, moving his head around in a circular motion.

"Neither do I," Rekesh concurred, crouching on his knees to get closer to the ball but still holding Elera gently by the arm.

"Do you see them, Javu?" Elera asked, herself seeing the four pyramids in clear detail, all visible in three dimensions as if she were looking down into a miniature version of the planet.

Javu shook his head, staring carefully into the sphere.

"Well I can see them," Elera stated, slightly flustered. "And I found a chamber in the pyramid with tablets that spoke of them. I think the Naqada wrote them. It seems that the first pyramid of the four is the great pyramid of Giza and it seems that as I expected it was built long before the others there. I think the Naqada somehow inherited the use of both the Great Pyramid and the Bimini pyramid. The king at the time only used the Great Pyramid of Giza to show his benevolence to Ra."

"Ra?" Teltu asked, not aware of the term.

"It is what the Naqada and those that came after them called the Sun God. This was their most important deity."

A beautiful range of clouds had formed over the ocean, almost looking like a great white mountain range.

"The second pyramid," she continued, "is the Bimini pyramid itself. The image I can see looks just like it too. I don't know why it sank but I think this orb was created a long time before that happened."

Sita and Rama were sitting next to each other, each with an arm around the other's waist. They looked like two small children hugging each other with such affection. The gentle breeze made the trees rustle with a papery resonance.

"The tablet described the third pyramid as being *to the north*, which must mean it is located in Raicema or Lizrab. I've got a strong feeling that each of the pyramids I can see in this crystal were built at a similar time."

"I do not see pyramids," Javu said slowly, concentrating on something within the crystal orb. "But I see an image of a statue, stood at the edge of a pool or lagoon of some sort." His eyes were glazed over and he seemed to be focused on a point beyond where the orb was lying.

"Then the crystal is trying to tell you something," Elera said.

"I feel as though it is on this island," Javu said, now straining like he was being blinded by what he was seeing. "But the image is fading."

Suddenly, a sharp image of the foal that she had seen in the vision below popped into her mind. It melted her.

"The foal was beautiful..." Elera said softly, trailing off into her own thoughts. Then she saw the statue. She did not see it in the crystal orb, but in a strange glare that the orb was giving off in its interaction with the morning sunlight. It was at the edge of a pool like Javu had said. It almost felt like she knew where it was, though as a cloud passed over the sun, she lost the vision and the feeling of familiarity disappeared.

"I saw it," she said to Javu. "I saw the statue."

Everyone else was confused, having not seen a statue, foal or any pyramids.

"What do you mean? What are you talking about?" Teltu said in a baffled manner, his voice at an elevated pitch.

Everyone sat in silence for a while, thinking about the strange events that had taken place. It actually made Teltu feel a little nauseous thinking about the origins of a structure such as a pyramid. Such a construct fundamentally confused his view of reality. For him, life was as simple as loving the people around him and the environment that was naturally there. The trees and sea, sun and crisp sea air was all he desired. But a deep intrigue had formed within and only talking would satisfy it.

"So what did you find in Giza?" she asked them all, just as Teltu was about to volunteer the information anyway.

"We found the control room!" Teltu said ardently, speaking quite quickly and assuming Elera would know what he meant. "And there was this statue that was the guardian of the entrance and a tunnel that connected two of the pyramids together."

Elera's eyes lit up at the news yet she was not surprised but almost gratified at such a find.

"What was in the control room?" she asked. "Did you find the fifty-four holes?"

"Yes, and technology like you wouldn't believe," Rekesh told her, carrying on from Teltu's description. "It was like some sort of ancient computer. There were ghostly maps of the plateau and of here. In fact, the plan today was to find a cavern we saw which has a tunnel to the pyramid but thankfully we don't need to now." The last statement was said in a joyous tone and it warmed Elera's heart.

"Maps of the pyramid here?" Elera pondered out load.

"Well, we thought so," Javu said with a smile.

"That must mean that Dr Ardale's theory was true," she said.

"What theory?" Teltu asked.

"Dr Ardale?" Rekesh said, the person unbeknownst to him.

"He was a researcher in Raicema City," Elera explained. "Unfortunately, he disappeared under mysterious circumstances one day but I think we all know what that means."

"You mean he uncovered the truth and Raicema shut him up?" Rekesh clarified bluntly.

Elera just nodded.

"Well, he had a theory that the tunnel system of the Giza plateau went much deeper that anyone could possibly imagine. He proposed that the tunnel system might even connect major land masses on the earth."

"You mean that the Giza pyramid and the one here might actually be connected underground?" Teltu asked.

Again Elera nodded.

"Well I wouldn't like to go down that tunnel," Teltu said, to which Sita and Rama seemed to understand and shook their heads avidly.

"Well maybe instead," Elera said with a smile, "we could search the island whilst it's empty. We might find the statue that Javu and I just saw in the orb."

Javu raised his eyebrows with indifference.

"I've got a strong feeling that it is important."

As she said this, a figure emerged from a small forest nearby and upon spotting Elera, began to move towards them.

"Hey!" Sula shouted. "I've been looking all over for you."

Elera quickly got to her feet followed swiftly by the others.

"There's not a breathing soul on this island," she said, baffled. "I found the base but it was deserted."

Rekesh was looking carefully at Sula's face. Something seemed familiar.

"Everyone, this is Sula," Elera announced. "She found me in the water exactly when I needed her. She brought me back to the island." Elera smiled with gratitude at the well-dressed woman, her wetsuit new and accessorised with many useful pieces of equipment. She introduced Sula to each person individually. Everyone except Rekesh commended Sula for her help. Whilst the others were talking, he suddenly realised where he had seen her before.

"I know you!" Rekesh said to Sula, quite openly. "I met you two years ago in Raicema City during a defence arts pupillage."

Sula looked slightly uncomfortable as Rekesh recalled their meeting.

"I remember you because you were sitting next to Yangjam Satori throughout his seminars. We met briefly during some of the discussions. "

"So you are Makai then?" Elera asked, confused. "I thought you said you worked for Raicema?"

Sula shuffled her feet as she thought about her reply. Javu had an informed grin on his face and before Sula could muster an answer, he clarified what was going on.

"So Yangjam works for Raicema?" he muttered to himself, somewhat taking Elera by surprise. "No wonder Raicema have done nothing to suppress the Makai in Neoasia. With Yangjam on their side, there is no need. I half-expected as much from the old toad."

Elera looked horrified at the news.

"It can't be!" she said in disbelief, looking at Sula. "Is it true? Tell me, Sula. "

Sula gave a half-hearted smile. "Yes it's true. He has been working with Raicema for as long as I've worked for the government. In fact, when I used to work in an office in the palace, I heard President Tyrone speak to him quite frequently. I even saw him there a few times. A few of us were told to accompany him wherever he went, as both a guide and informant."

"Who is Yangjam?" Teltu interrupted, who had been silent until now.

"He is one of the most prominent leaders in Neoasia," Rekesh explained. "He is a descendant of one of the oldest Makai families on the planet. I too cannot believe that he is affiliated with Raicema. He has taught defence arts against such oppression for years."

"And you've even got the same name as him," Javu said to Rekesh in a teasing fashion, not really surprised by the revelation of conspiracy. Elera, however, seemed disturbed by the entire concept. There was a silence of disappointment amongst everyone for a while.

"It's not the end of the world," Sula finally said, breaking the quiet.

"Well, let's head into the mangrove," Elera said to everyone, shrugging off her disappointment with the leaders of the world. "The pool we *saw* should be in there."

"What pool? What are you looking for?" Sula asked Elera, who was hesitant to tell her, unsure if she could be trusted.

"There is a statue I have to find. It could be of great historical importance," Elera said, somewhat reservedly.

"Are you still pursuing *that* even though you ended up in the middle of the ocean?" Sula asked, rolling her eyes. "As I said before, you should leave the past behind and start living, girl. You don't even get paid for your kind of exploring!"

Elera just smiled at Sula's brash form of concern.

"I have to find it, Sula. I just know it. You don't have to come with us."

"No, I will," Sula said rolling her eyes. "In a strange way, I sort of feel responsible for you now."

The group set off, Teltu walking ahead with an exuberant

fearlessness, followed in pairs by Sita and Rama, Elera and Rekesh and Sula and Javu. The ground was dry and sandy, yet there were little bogs scattered around inside the forest.

"What keeps one working for an empire such as Raicema?" Javu asked Sula in an unbiased manner as they walked along. "Do the military campaigns not disturb you?"

"It just sort of happened as a matter of course for me," Sula said indifferently. "Everyone in Raicema is the same. It's easy to build your own little world to live in, and separate yourself from everyone else. Also, I don't really feel like there is much choice. There is no way I could travel this freely around the world if I didn't work for them. As for the military, I don't really get involved but on a personal note, no, I don't agree with the reasons behind most of the invasions."

"Do you have family in Raicema?"

"No. I live there alone. Well, that is when I am actually in Raicema City. Somehow I prefer to keep moving."

"I understand the feeling," Javu related.

"I think it's because I don't want to stop and think about what I am involved in," Sula revealed unexpectedly. "I mean, what's the point unless you can actually change it, right?"

"Oh, but you can always change your life, my dear," Javu commented, somewhat stirring Sula from her indifference. "Anytime you want. And you'd be surprised at the effect that has on so many others."

The words sent Sula into a state of deep contemplation. Javu just smiled as they kept on walking.

After a while, Teltu suddenly shouted back to everyone. "Hey, there's a lake up ahead." He was pointing to a lagoon, connected to the large system of waterways by small creeks branching off in several directions. The surrounding trees went deep into the pools of water. A wide range of aquatic life wove in and out of their thick roots.

There was no statue in sight.

"This is not the place I *saw*," Elera said. "And there wasn't a tree growing out of the middle." The tree had long drooping branches of leaves almost touching the water.

"No, it's not the pool I saw either," Javu agreed. "It was much smaller. Mmm, let's have a look around."

Everyone took a look around the lagoon, still as a mirror with giant lily pads and reeds growing out of it. Small insects seamlessly glided upon the water like miniature rowing boats.

"Wow, that tree is huge," Teltu commented, looking at the giant weeping branches towering over the lake. Birds and rodents scampered in the surround of the tranquil pool, darting in and out of bushes and branches. The undergrowth was so dense all around it felt like they had all reach a dead end.

"It looks like the path ends here," Rekesh said. "Maybe we should turn back and head in a different direction."

As he said this, Sita quite mysteriously began to swim across the lagoon towards the tree trunk. She dived down for a long while, causing Rekesh to push Rama lightly on the shoulder with concern, indicating that he should go after her. She came up taking a long gasp of air. Then she started shouting something in Hindi, her words causing a look of intrigue to spread across Rama's face.

"Sita is saying that the trunk of the tree is very wide and goes right to the bottom of the water. There is a large hole in the trunk. She says it is a passageway," Javu translated.

Sita had dived under the water again. After a while, she resurfaced once more and made her way to the edge, her lacquered black hair glistening in the warming sun. She began to converse with Rama as she got out of the lagoon and Javu understood every word.

"Apparently the trunk of the tree is dry and seems to go deep underground. It is completely hollow."

"Just look at the roots," Teltu said, observing twisting mass entwined around the great trunk, which was as wide as several people. "They must go very deep."

"Shall we go down the trunk?" Javu asked Elera adventurously, a twinkle of excitement in his eyes.

"I think we should," she said with confidence.

Though there were a few doubts amongst the group, everyone waded into the water and swam along to the tree. They all hugged it in circle whilst Elera dived down and investigated.

"It's true!" she said, coming up with her fine black hair whipping back. "Just swim down for a little while and pull yourself into the opening. You might have to use your arms and legs to lower yourself down the trunk. Rekesh, why don't you go first?"

Rekesh nodded and dived down with agility, quickly reaching the hole in the trunk and pulling himself inside. As he left the water, he felt a slight pull as some kind of force held the water back. He immediately pushed outwards with his arms and legs against the wide trunk, which was slightly illuminated with a dim green glow and echoed the sound of his breath. He began to lower himself down slowly and as he did, he saw Javu come through the hole and immediately begin to fall down. Rekesh pushed harder against the trunk as Javu's weight landed on the back of his neck with a thud.

"Spread yourself out!" Rekesh spluttered, straining to support Javu. He tried but his success was thwarted as Teltu fell directly on top of them as he passed through the hole.

"Whoaah!" he wailed as he landed on Javu, causing all three of them to fall freely down into darkness. They wailed in unison, causing an eerie echo. After a second or two of this plummet, their weight was caught one after another by the shaft sloping to a diagonal incline, causing them to slide down it at a spectacular speed. Before they knew it, they had reached the end of the slide, which culminated at the junction of a very muddy tunnel. They each landed in the soft mud. The thick roots of the tree weaved every-where like a family of giant snakes.

"Where are we?" Teltu croaked, struggling to see in the dark atmosphere.

"We must be under the island," Rekesh said as they heard somebody else sliding down the long winding trunk. Sula emerged with a bump into the soft dirt, followed shortly afterwards by Sita, Rama and lastly Elera.

"Quite a ride, mmm?" Javu said with joviality, beginning to get to his feet with mud all over his clothes.

"It is not completely dark," Elera noted, herself sopping wet. "Where is the light coming from?"

"We should try to follow this tunnel along," Rekesh urged. Everyone agreed and began to move slowly along the tunnel, dodging in and out of the rough, meandering roots. Elera noticed that the dirt was silty, just like that in the entrance of the underwater pyramid. After a short while the tunnel began to open out into a large cave, the roof sealed yet shining with glowing blue algae covering large ridges and stalactites.

"The light is coming from these algae!" Sula said in astonishment, moving around slowly.

"Just like the Bimini road," Rekesh said.

"This place is enormous," Teltu added, scanning the shiny cavern that almost looked like its surface was made of water. Small dark green clusters of seaweed-like plants gathered on the ground, some with spongy heads to collect moisture. Rekesh walked to the other side of the cave in search of an onwards path whilst Elera seemed much more interested in some blackened sticks she had found in the silt.

"What have you found, Elera?" Javu asked, walking over to her as he noticed her concentration.

"People have been here before," she declared, holding up one of the sticks that resembled half-charred firewood. "This place must lead somewhere."

"This must be one of the tunnels we saw on that map," Teltu suggested.

"Over here," Rekesh hollered, now almost out of sight at the other end of the glistening cave. Everyone walked over to find Rekesh at the entrance of a junction of two tunnels, almost perpendicular to each other.

"Which way?" Teltu questioned.

"Does anyone have a compass?" Elera asked, to which Sula produced an elaborate piece of Raiceman equipment, complete with lit-up computerised display.

"This tunnel heads due east," she said, gesturing towards the rightmost tunnel, "and this one heads almost north".

"The pyramid is east of the island. This tunnel could lead to the pyramid in some way," Elera suggested.

"You want to go back to the pyramid?" Rekesh asked with some apprehension.

"I think we should follow this tunnel and see where it leads," Elera decided. Everyone agreed and headed along the passageway, which too had the same illuminating algae along its surface. Before long, however, they had reached a dead end, rubble and a large boulder blocking the way.

"There is not even a draft coming through," Rekesh said, moving his hand all around the blockage. "It is tightly sealed."

"Then let us take the other route," Javu said, ushering everyone back towards the other tunnel. They walked back and headed north. Before long, relief spread amongst the group as a light breeze could be felt wavering down the mine-like passage.

"So when you are sent to investigate old buildings, what do you usually have to report about them?" Elera asked Sula as they walked along in semi-darkness.

"The ruins sometimes contain artefacts that the government are interested in. To tell you the truth, I think they sell most of them to Lengard. So I guess on one hand you could call me a treasure hunter. More recently they've been sending me to different places to gather information on what is going on there. Then I report back. They want to know what people think about Raicema in those places or what people produce there. It's a dangerous job. That's why I've had to learn ways of defending myself."

"Did you ever go to Lizrab?"

"Not yet."

Elera thought of the beautiful architectural achievements and wildlife that was allowed to roam freely about the cities of southern Lizrab.

"Do you enjoy living in Raicema? For the time that I lived there I often felt quite trapped," Elera said honestly. "I guess if you prefer travelling around then you mustn't like living there very much?"

Sula glanced at the shorter woman with her fine, wavy hair cascading down her neck. Looking into her light brown eyes, she saw specks of purple and though feeling slightly anxious about talking about her home, an overwhelming sense of confession came over her.

"I really don't like living there," she replied truthfully. "I have lived in both Tyrona and Raicema City and both places are so controlled and automated that there is sometimes no need to go outside during the day. I deliberately live in an older part of the city. Not sure if you noticed whilst you were there, but most of the sectors of Raicema City are now fully *auto-piped*."

"Auto-piped?"

"Yes. All the newer buildings have an auto-pipe, for deliveries of food, clothes, even furniture. The pipes are all linked up to the city mainframe system and are powered by the underground reactors. You can order whatever you like through the system and it will be delivered through an auto-pipe. There's hardly any reason for the modern-day Raiceman to leave their apartment."

"Well, the government wants it like that," Elera said boldly. "I saw the mainframe system when I was there. It's scary how people can't live without using it."

"Tell me about it," Sula sighed. "Everything's on there – your creds and work files, your access keys to the city sectors, your entire history. I'm sure that if the system ever closed down, Raicema would just stand still."

"People work through that system too, don't they?"

"Only a tiny fraction of people don't," Sula informed her wryly whilst pulling a small yet complicated gadget out of her bag. "Even

I do. This thing connects to it, though I can't seem to get a signal here."

They walked on in silence for a while, Elera dismayed by the automation that Sula had described. It reassured her own reasons for searching for such a different way of living, whether it still existed or not. Undeniably, she saw Lemuria as the complete opposite of Raicema, where there were no laws, no rules nor boundaries.

"It's incredible how technology has advanced but I'm not the sort of person who likes it to consume my life," Sula continued. "That's why I prefer the work I do as I get to see the real world."

Elera smiled at her newfound friend in harmony at the sentiment. Ahead, Elera could see that the tunnel was opening out and no level of imagination could have prepared anyone in the group for the panorama that was about to emerge.

Above, the clear cloudless sky could be seen peering down on the most colossal cavern. Standing at the bottom, the cavern stretched upwards at an incline for its entire boundary, like a naturally formed coliseum with thousands of trees and plants as its audience. In effect, the surfaces of the cavern looked like furry green carpet from where everyone was standing, the merging of the sky and slopes making it hard to tell where green ended and blue began. The mysterious lower banks of the circular valley were cloaked in darkness from the forests that climbed high up into the sky. Step by step, they walked deeper into the centre.

Before them was a human-shaped statue sitting peacefully at the heart of the natural coliseum, its pose one of a seated yogi praying with its entire body for some unknown purpose. The statue was incredible in its intricacy, the facial features smooth and beautifully curved, a greenish light glimmering from its surface. The carved stone looked delicate and rare, a subtle blend of lime green and ocean blue with a misty opaqueness. Certain parts of the stone looked more translucent than others, yet it was almost as though an ocean was moving within, constantly changing the way light reflected from the statue.

Everyone walked slowly into the middle of the cavern towards the statue, past a few larger trees that grew at ground level. The scene, though beautiful, seemed so wild and isolated that it gave Rekesh a shiver down his spine. For a moment, a childhood fear that some unknown monster might jump out and startle him raced through his body.

"It's made from jade," Sula said, taken by the immense beauty that was before her. It was the statue's face that had stunned everyone into silence. They were all sure that if one were to describe the most serene and virtuous-looking human face, this would be it, however the face was like no human any of them had ever seen.

"It looks so beautiful, so unusual," Sula said calmly.

"Why did that crystal orb want us to find this?" Teltu asked Elera, hands on hips though his eyes never diverted from the statue's tranquil face. It was as if was enchanted, drawing the undivided attention of everyone around it.

"I think it will tell us something," she replied, herself bewitched by the elegance of the jade sculpture.

"Whoever made this was very talented," Sula added.

The trees at the base of the cavern were unique, swaying as though alive with a dexterous intrigue. In fact, the entire area seemed alive in the way that the light danced from one spot to another, energised leaves skimming the ground like ballerinas, though there was little breeze.

Though Rekesh was fighting it, he felt compelled to stare deep into the androgynous, wide-eyed green face before him. He saw something move, like a ripple in a pond. He entered a trance-like state and munificently fell to his knees. It was as if the world was fading away and he was dreaming lucidly, his eyes fixed and unable to move away from what was happening before him. He was now somewhere else on the island.

An elderly man was before him, dying and walking crookedly from the weight of his illness. He was in a part of the mangrove forest and the elderly man was looking at an archaic map and muttering to himself as he strained to take each step. His clothes were tattered and the weak veins of his arms could be seen bulging out as if they were infected.

He came to a clearing that contained a single, tranquil pool of water. The man's eyes lit up and widened as if he were about to die.

Rekesh felt an unearthly presence close by but could not see anything around him except the man and the pool. Then, Rekesh felt an icy cold sensation descend on the clearing. A primordial fear paralysed him to the spot as the man before him looked straight past with terror at whatever was behind him. Rekesh wanted to turn but could not. He heard a slithering in his ear, the poisonous sound of something imminently fatal.

The man took a step backwards and plummeted into the pool, lying there motionless. Rekesh was certain he was dead but then the man's fingers began to move, followed by his arms and legs. The man rose up and Rekesh saw his face. It had changed. He looked younger and vibrant. His muscles held a lean and slender shape and his skin looked as plump as a young child's. He slowly walked out of the water looking at his hands and his face in the reflection of the pool. Then he dropped to his knees and stared at the sky, praying with gratitude in an unknown language.

The horrifying presence seemed to have disappeared. The man before him continued to stare at his reflection, in disbelief at his youthful appearance.

But then, in a petrifying moment, the man's reflection changed. Staring back at the man from the water was what could only be described as a dragon man. The face was terrifying, scaly with a ring of horns around a hairless head. The sight sent a shiver like no other down Rekesh's being.

In that moment, the vision was over. Rekesh looked up from his kneeling position and immediately everyone looked at him, as if the statue had released them all from its enchantment.

"It was so clear," he said in a bewildered state, almost talking to himself, "…the Devil himself."

Elera was the first to kneel by Rekesh rubbing his shoulders affectionately and trying to get him to look at her.

"What did you *see*?" she asked with a tender tone, stroking his face.

"A man, he was old and ill. He found a pool in the forest. He was cured, just by bathing in the water. He looked so much younger."

He paused, jolted by what he had just experienced.

"But there was something else," he began, mumbling somewhat. "Something horrible…"

Javu seemed disturbed by the words Rekesh was relaying.

"The pool…" he garbled. "…It could heal him. But that face…" He was speaking as though in a deep trance, clearly affected by what he had seen. "That awful face reflecting back at him."

Everyone was now concerned by Rekesh's words.

"I felt his despair," he said. "I thought what he was thinking. I felt what he was feeling. But he was poisoned. He was being watched…"

"Did you see the statue, Rekesh?" Javu asked, feeling that something was very familiar to him about Rekesh's narrative.

"There was no statue, only a pool," he said, looking at the statue before him. "And things seemed different, like it was a different time altogether."

"Do you mean to say you've just seen into the past?" Teltu asked with doubt.

"I don't know," Rekesh said weakly. "Everything just seemed to fade away and then I was somewhere else, just observing."

"I have had a similar experience recently," Elera told everyone, "when I found the crystal orb. I had the most lifelike of visions. These crystal structures must invoke them, they are trying to tell us something."

"And you say this pool you envisioned could heal him? Make him younger?" Sula asked Rekesh. "Like a fountain of youth?"

"Yes, but…" Rekesh said chillingly, "it was a trap. There was a horrible being close by. A dragon man."

"A healing hole?" Elera suggested to Javu. "A dragon man?"

Javu took in a short gasp of air as he realised what they could have stumbled upon.

"I cannot believe it!" he said, now deliberately trying not to look at the statue. "We have found the bearer of the jade mask! I was sure that the tale was only an ingenious invention, created to make people see the misfortune of seeking power."

Everyone was surprised that Javu knew anything at all about what they had found.

"What is it?" Teltu said, sensing Javu's seriousness.

"It is a story that my uncle told me when I was only a young boy. The bearer of the jade mask was a beautiful being that held immense power. The bearer always wore an unattractive mask made from jade upon its face. One day, the bearer of the jade mask was kidnapped, stolen from the land in which it was born – the motherland of this earth."

Lemuria, Elera thought.

"The thief knew the value of the mask and its bearer and intended to inherit the incredible powers that the bearer possessed. What the thief had been told was that the bearer of the jade mask covered its face for a reason."

"What reason?" Elera asked.

"The bearer's eyes were capable of imprisoning souls and draining power from all around. That is why the bearer's face was covered at all times."

"Whoa!" Teltu said, afraid to even glance at the statue. Its presence now seemed ominous.

"The bearer, still wearing its mask, was taken to a sacred pool. This pool too had great power, capable of healing and restoring life. It was there that a *ritual of power* took place, there where the mask was removed."

Everyone was listening with bated breath, keeping one eye on the entrancing statue besides them.

"When the mask was taken away from its true owner, it warped the space in which it occupied. It was used to open doors that should not be open. It was used to reach into other realms of existence, and what emerged was similar to what Rekesh has mentioned, a being that looked like a dragon."

Everyone was both captivated and horrified by the tale.

"It was never made clear to me that the bearer wasn't human, but now I see that the owner is actually this statue."

"So where is its mask?" Teltu asked.

"If the story is to be believed, it is still with the people who performed the ritual."

"In my vision," Rekesh started to say, somewhat stirred from his knelt position, "I did not see the statue. I only saw that frightening face."

"Do you think the pool is here? On this island?" Sula asked with interest.

Everyone thought for a while, the intrigue of such a powerful location playing on their minds.

"I think we should try to find it," Elera said. "One thing has led to another, the pyramid, the crystal orb and now this statue. Maybe the pool will show us something too. I think that Lemuria knows I am looking for it and it is trying to help me."

Javu did not argue with Elera. He simply nodded, acknowledging her intuition, though Rekesh felt dismayed at the notion.

"I will help you find it," Sula said. "I cannot find out what I came here to, and a magical healing pool sounds much more interesting!"

"Isn't it the same lake where we were before? Where the hollow tree was?" Teltu suggested.

"No," Rekesh interposed, somewhat fixated on the task. "I saw a smaller single pool of water. It wasn't really a lake and there wasn't a tree there."

"Besides, none of us look any younger," Teltu said jovially.

Everyone laughed as he said this, especially as his gaze fell on Javu, who rolled his eyes in a most comical manner.

"We should tread carefully. So let us not be blinded by the temptation of such a notion."

It was midday and even the speckles of sunlight reaching through the trees quickly got the skin feeling hot. The jade statue seemed to be lightening in its opaqueness.

"About Lemuria?" Teltu asked Elera, trying to understand the term he had heard broadly before. "Is it a place? How can it know that you are looking for it?"

Elera smiled fondly at her brother-in-law. The way he asked questions was endearing, always with the slightest hint of jubilance.

"Lemuria is a place I heard about a few years ago. It is described in many folktales as a motherland that once existed on this planet. Some people, however, see it purely as a way of life that previously existed in a time when we all had a different form. So to answer your question, Teltu, I don't truly know what Lemuria is. But I am trying to find out."

"But you said you think it knows that you are looking for it."

"That's true, but I am unsure of what I am looking for. All I know is that recently, it seems like something has been reaching out to me. It led me here to Bimini and who knows where next, but it feels like I am supposed to find it, whatever it is."

She paused for a moment, contemplating her own words.

"Of course, it is astounding to me that at this moment there are now seven of us looking for it," she continued, chuckling to herself. "I do not expect you all to continue with me but I am happy we are all here together now."

"Well, water that makes you look younger sounds like a good enough reason to continue!" Sula said jovially, causing a frown to spread upon Javu's brow.

"Let us move swiftly then," he said.

They began to take a look around the clearing for clues to the whereabouts of the pool. Beginning to spread out, they all witnessed a very strange occurrence. The statue, now glowing a bright turquoise colour, swiftly became a very faint shade of light green, looking very much like slightly tinted glass. Then, in a bizarre moment, it became completely transparent and suddenly disappeared from everyone's sight. Teltu immediately ran over to see if it was still there.

"It's gone!" he said astounded, waving his arm through the space where the statue had clearly stood. Everyone had to check to convince themselves that they weren't hallucinating.

"This place is eerie," Teltu said feeling flustered by all the mystery.

He backed away from the space that the statue recently occupied.

"What is it with all these statues with strange powers, like that one in Giza," Teltu said to Javu, his voice a little shaky. "Remember what you were telling me, Javu? About statues storing energy and guarding sacred places. "

"Indeed, Teltu, though I have never witnessed an object disappear like that before."

"It *is* powerful!" Teltu admitted with fervour, starting to believe the story that Javu had told them.

No sooner had he said that than there was a shout of excitement from Sita, who had made her way towards the back of the giant gorge and was pointing to something. Everyone rushed over to see what it was she was so excited about. Imprinted deeply into the grassy earth were unusual hoof-prints, puzzling in their formation as they were filled with water, yet the earth surrounding them was as dry as dust. Algae had formed at the edges of the hoof-prints, which ran from where the statue had been standing towards the back of the gorge. As everyone followed the trail, they all heard the faint sound of an animal grazing. However, every time they looked around in the direction of the sound, there was nothing there.

"Did you hear that?" Elera asked the group. They all agreed and with each movement they made, once again they heard the subtle steps of something and the sound of grass being gently ripped from the earth. Each person believed they could hear where the sound was coming from. They all headed in a different direction, spreading out like a star.

Elera walked slowly and silently, believing that she would see some kind of doe or a buck at any moment. The direction of the sound seemed to change every moment causing her to feel slightly unbalanced. She stood still and closed her eyes, listening carefully to how the sound of the grazing moved. She heard it to her left, then to her right and then quite clearly straight in front of her, like the grass was being pulled out from the ground right in front of her feet.

She felt the breath of something on her chest, near her heart. It was warm and comforting. She sensed a peaceful energy surround her.

She opened her eyes and was greeted by the sight of what looked like a great white horse with a silver mane, grazing at her feet, its black eyes looking up at her like two spheres of pure visceral liquid. Her breath stopped for a moment as the beautiful creature raised its head, its hooves standing in pools of water.

"*You have come looking for me.*" A whisper sounded through the air like a wave rising. Elera was frozen in that moment; everything else had faded into nothingness and a silent feeling of wellbeing drained every desire from her body. She thought that she asked a question, but even before the sentence finished playing out in her mind, the whisper answered, vast oceans rising and falling within the celestial eyes of the majestic horse before her.

"*It is beyond the world you know. If you continue, you will have to make difficult choices.*"

A misty light seemed to be radiating from the creature, almost as if it were smouldering. Elera could see this energy touching her and within a moment it had surrounded her, blurring her view of the cavern.

"*What you are seeking holds many bridges and some of these bridges are one way only.*"

The words shook her and the world around her seemed to melt away leaving only herself and the magnificent horse. An ethereal energy was alive around them, like a blanket of dancing light. She felt compelled to close her eyes, yet she still saw the light.

"I will help protect you, Elera."

Once again she felt the warm breath of the equine being on her chest, followed by a strange sensation in her heart, like it had burst open and was now connected to the universe. The sensation lasted for several moments before leaving her in a tranquil state.

She felt her eyes open, and the sight of Teltu searching for the sound of the grazing stirred her into a drowsy awareness. She could see the backdrop of the rising cavern and felt the earth beneath her feet. She looked around for the horse, but it was nowhere to be seen.

Chapter 14 – Water Guardian

"Where has it gone?" Elera heard herself say out loud, feeling dazed.

"What?" Teltu asked, standing nearby.

"The horse!" Elera stated, looking on the floor and seeing the hoof-prints where the horse had been standing directly in front of her. "Look, its prints are right here where it was standing!"

Teltu came over to her. "So which way did it go?"

Elera did not answer the question, accepting something was going on that she didn't understand. For a moment, she thought that she may have imagined her encounter with the animal. She began to think that the hoof-prints were already there before, but an overpowering sensation that she had gained something very valuable stopped her from drawing that conclusion. She felt different, as if somebody had told her something incredibly profound and moving, something life-changing. She knew at that moment that she had just experienced something unearthly. Everyone came over to where she was standing, almost sensing that she had found the creature whose prints were everywhere. She felt a little dizzy and like there was a ball of disquiet in her chest.

"Did you find anything?" Rekesh asked her, observing her dazed expression. "I noticed that there is an opening in that cliff over there. We could see if it leads anywhere."

Elera did not speak, thinking deeply about the words that had been whispered to her. They seemed familiar, like she had dreamt them many times before. Though unsure of their meaning, a great sense of determination was flowing through her body, for she now knew that her search for Lemuria was not just a series of emotions spurring her on. There was something deeper occurring. Her head felt light, as if it might float off her neck at any moment.

"Endless eyes…" she said, almost in a trance.

"What?"

"The horse," she said softly. "Like no other animal I have ever met. As if it were pure water moulded into the image of a horse."

Everybody was quite confused by the words coming out of Elera's soft lips. They all looked around to see if they could spot the creature.

"So where is it?" Sula asked, scanning the perimeter of the cavern slopes.

Nobody except Javu seemed to hone in on how monumental the encounter had been for Elera.

"You say its eyes were endless?"

"Yes, like I might fall into them and be lost forever. Endless oceans."

"I think it is best for us to leave now," Javu said. "I think we have spent enough time on this island and the time may have come for us to move on."

Though Rekesh seemed to instantly agree with Javu's words of caution, Elera quite adamantly blurted out a forceful objection.

"I will not leave this island!" she said firmly, a profound sense of purpose welling inside her. "I am here for a reason and won't leave until I know more about Lemuria. I can feel so strongly inside me that this island is part of it all."

Though they could not fully understand what Elera was trying to convey, her conviction was enough persuade them to accompany her on her search. They all walked towards the enclave that Rekesh had found. It was quite high up on a steep face of the gorge, the trees in surround growing out diagonally from patches of soil on the array of ledges that it held.

"Wait here. I'll go and take a look."

Rekesh climbed the gorge with ease, jumping from ledge to ledge and swinging around the trunks of trees for support. Slipping a few times, he reached the opening of the cave, which was surprisingly wide. It went deep into the rock at a steep incline.

"There is way of passage," he shouted from the edge. "Can you all make it up?"

Everyone began to slowly climb up the gorge.

"Some of the footholds are quite soft!" he yelled down from

above. "Watch your step!"

Elera, followed by the others, shimmied along the narrow ledges using the sturdy tree trunks as resting places along the way. As they got higher, it could be seen that most of the circular gorge was formed as a series of grated echelons, like giant steps climbing high up into the sky.

"Whoa, I'm feeling a little dizzy," Teltu said as he reached the entrance of the enclave, the last of the group to do so.

"It's very dark," Sula said peering into the darkness of the cave. "And it looks very steep."

"It will be fine," Rekesh reassured her. "There isn't much choice anyway. We have to get back to the top of the island to get back to the ship."

The group lit every electric light they had including Sula's compass. It was barely enough to see the path ahead as they ventured up the dark cave slope.

"Elera, can I ask you something?" Sula said softly.

"Of course. What is it?"

"I don't understand how that statue just disappeared. Even if it is part of this old civilisation that you are looking for, I don't see how it's possible to make something disappear like that. Is that why you're looking for this place Lemuria? So you can find out how such things are possible?"

Elera smiled at the question, though in the darkness Sula did not see her expression of endearment. "Well yes, though I am not trying to find out how to make things disappear. You have seen many of the ancient structures on this planet. Raicema can't explain when or how they were built and some of them are so perfectly positioned and constructed that it would be impossible to recreate them now. But I'm not interested in how, more in why. I really think these people knew something important that has been long forgotten and I really think rediscovering it can only help this planet."

Sula was silent as she took in what Elera was philosophising. The incline was getting steeper and more slippery and Rama had to be stopped by Javu and Teltu from falling down the slope. Glimmering rock could be seen in the faint light available, like great sheets of ice. The slope became so abruptly vertical that everyone had to stop climbing suddenly.

"Where to now?" Teltu said, breathing heavily. The air was cool, a faint breeze wafting from above.

Rekesh took the brightest of the lights from Rama and stretched upward to see what was above. "There is a ledge. We need to help each other get up."

He immediately began pushing Sita, Elera and then Sula up, where they grasped the edge of the ledge and pulled themselves up.

"Hey, along there is light," Elera said, spurring everyone to climb up. The men helped each other up onto the ledge. Everyone quickly proceeded through the narrow cave towards the light which was coming from outside. As they emerged, they were all amazed to find that the entryway was part of a forged opening in the trunk of a large tree. There were a few symbols inscribed into the inner trunk, a marker for something.

"This is amazing!" Javu said, upon seeing what was now apparent, a discreet tunnel to where the cavern had been located. As they all walked out of a narrow crack in the trunk, they found themselves back at ground level, surrounded by a forested area. Ahead was a small pool of water, as still as a sleeping horse.

"This is it!" Rekesh said. "This is what I saw before, this exact place!"

The place had a holy atmosphere, as though the air was charged with an ethereal power. The rigid trees in surround felt like royal guards protecting the sacred area, still as the earth itself, not a wisp of wind flowing through the air. The ambience could almost be visualised, a ubiquitous cloud of pure light encompassing the vicinity.

"Look!" Teltu blurted out suddenly, pointing at something.

Astoundingly, the jade statue was reappearing. It looked ghostly as first, a hazed green silhouette visible just above a grassy patch behind the pool. It gradually faded in, more aqua green weaving through the statue as it solidified in front of everyone's eyes.

"It's back!" Sula said, a little frightened.

"It must have been guiding us here," Elera said taking a few steps forward. She walked very slowly towards the statue. Its face was so tranquil, just like the pool it stood before. She walked around and stood in front of the jade figure. Compelled, she touched her forehead to the forehead of the statue. She was not expecting what happened next. She felt electricity in her eyes and then in an instant she was somewhere else.

A wave of nausea flashed through her midriff. The pool was still in sight, though everything else was completely different. There were more trees and everyone else had disappeared. The grass around her was tall and large. Unusual insects that she had never seen before crawled amongst the blades. Bewildered, she began to walk towards the pool until the sound of rapid galloping startled her. She looked around and in the distance saw men on horseback riding towards her in a fury. A pathway appeared leading up to the pool. She jumped for cover behind a tree, watching the men go straight past her. There were three of them, two quite large, wearing thick cotton robes and tall headdresses whilst the third was young, a boy no older than fifteen. Tied to his horse by a metal chain around its neck, was the beautiful white and silver horse Elera had recently encountered. Upon spotting the pool, the boy dismounted, his plaited black hair twisted into strange bundles upon his head. He unhooked the chain from his own grey horse and began to drag the great white horse towards the pool.

It did not fight and though Elera was aware that she was watching an event that had already occurred, she was startled when she saw the horse's endless eyes glance over at her. Then the boy yanked the great creature into the pool to which it submerged quickly up to its neck.

Elera heard more galloping and looking back down the path saw two more horses pulling a cart. The driver was yelling at the horses and they sped past her. Sitting silently on the cart was the jade statue, though it looked different for it had an unpleasant bulky mask on its face, made from the same turquoise jade. She gripped the rough trunk of the tree with suspense.

As the cart came to a stop near to the pool, the two burly men and the driver began to hoist the heavy statue onto the ground, and they dragged it to the edge of the pool. The young boy began to direct them in a language that Elera could not understand. They lined the statue up so it was facing the horse that was submerged silently in the pool.

Elera could see the long, slender face of the phenomenal creature looking straight at the statue being placed before it.

The young boy walked over to the statue and placed his hand on the mask, looking at it carefully for a while before taking it from the statue, all four of them gasping in surprise at the beautiful face uncovered before them. A strange light shot out of the eyes of the statue, surrounding the pool and horse within. All four men covered their eyes from the glare. An immense flow of energy was occurring. The white horse had now completely disappeared from the pool.

The men spoke to each other and Elera recognised that certain sounds in their conversation had a resemblance to the way some words were said in the Lizrabian language. She noticed as the boy lifted up the mask to observe its reaction to the light that he had a number of jagged patterns embroidered into his lightweight outfit. As Elera moved carefully around the tree she was hiding behind, she began to see something slimy, scaly and unearthly emerging from the pool. It looked like the top of a bald greyish head. A river of fear ran through her, especially as the men began to speak to each other in panic. The world began to fade and blur.

When Elera's vision came back into focus, the environment looked even more different. The four men had gone and the vegetation and flora around was wildly uncultivated, as neither human nor animal had ever touched the land. It reminded her of that first vision she had experienced in the depths of the pyramid.

There was no statue in sight but the pool was there, still as clear and tranquil as before.

Trees rose so high into the sky that they seemed endless and the grass was as tall as most regular trees. She immediately felt a sweltering heat like she had never experienced. It was silent, and then the same sound of an animal grazing that she had heard before seeing the silvery white horse in the gorge.

She looked around with an excited pining to see the creature again. She was not disappointed as it walked slowly towards her through the feral undergrowth, its body moving poetically and gracefully with every step. It stopped at the pool that was between them and drank from the tranquil water. As its mouth touched the pool, light seemed to radiate out from it, like it was a giant round lantern. The horse's eyes lit up in the way that the glare of the sun hits the ocean. It raised its head and took several slow steps forwards, once again extending its head toward her heart.

At that moment, Elera could feel for the first time her own intrinsic nature, the way in which every drop of water in her body seemed to wave in unison. Her thoughts were carried to one place after another like she was riding on a great ocean. She felt how she was driven by this nature, the elemental need to be connected to the things that she loved and cherished. That was what was motivating her to search for a better life. That was what made her who she was. Everything looked different, more vibrant, more joined together.

"You know me," a voice said, one that sounded like it was coming from inside her. "I am here to help you, Elera."

Elera had a great feeling that she could not speak, but also that she did not need to. It was like she could convey what she wanted to through her thoughts to the beautiful creature that had its head in her chest.

"You have seen me in your dreams, yet you find it hard to remember."

"What happened to you?" Elera felt herself ask, referring to the scene she had previously witnessed.

"I am everywhere, yet here I am trapped in your world, just like you."

"Where are we?" she pondered. "*When* are we?"

"*It is hard for you to see. We are somewhere else, somewhere where they can't touch us.*"

"Who were those people? What did they do to you?"

"*Who reduced me from everything, until I would be in a cage, a beautiful cage? They are afraid to face the truth and so lock it away. Does it matter I hear? For I remain as one. It is undeniable, unchangeable and the truth that is inescapable. They only fear that which is ugly within themselves.*"

Elera got a direct feeling that the horse in front of her was very old, almost as though it had lived forever.

"What about Lemuria? Is it here?"

"*You are tracing your roots, but step carefully. Death stalks you at every turn. It too is inescapable.*"

In a strange moment that felt like she had lost consciousness, Elera was dropped once again near to the pool, this time the friendly faces of her companions looked down at her on the forest floor. The statue was there without its mask, peering out across the tranquil water.

"You disappeared!" Teltu was saying, pointing at her with a finger shaking so hard she thought he might collapse at any moment.

"Just like before. But this time the statue took you with it!" Rekesh told her, himself shaken to the core.

Elera said nothing, looking only at the beautiful statue, now knowing it was more powerful than she had ever imagined.

"Where did you go, Elera?" Javu asked her gently, helping her get to her feet.

"I saw how the statue's mask was taken. I saw the ritual you spoke of. The horse I met, I think it is imprisoned in this statue. It is some sort of spirit being. And something else emerged, something grotesque."

Everyone, including Javu was confused by the words.

"I saw the past. I was there. I was really there!"

As she said this, everyone noticed that Elera's satchel, which was lying on the floor nearby, started to glow. She slowly got to her feet and walked over to it. As she took out the crystal sphere inside, everyone could see that it had come to life and was shining vibrantly. To their astonishment, the orb began to rise up in the air from Elera's hands as if it had a life of its own. Teltu's jaw dropped with disbelief as it floated smoothly down onto the still water of the pool. It glided gently into the middle before sinking down into its depths, illuminating the entirety of the water. Then, an image appeared.

It was of a mountain range, tall and vast with rocky highlands. The sun shone brightly down on a deep concave valley covered in dense jungle. In the middle of the jungle was a pyramid and from the top of it Elera immediately recognised it as the one that was now on the Bimini seabed. The mountains in surround were colossal and Elera spotted a pathway leading up to the pyramid through the jungle and rising up into the mountains. It was the Bimini road of another time, an incredible jigsaw-like pattern embedded into the forest floor. As she began to wonder how such a colossal land had largely submerged beneath the ocean, the image faded.

"Is this Lemuria?"

Elera walked down to the pool and knelt at its edge. She leaned over and saw the crystal sphere glowing in the distance, falling down the pool, which looked like a bottomless well. She watched it fall deeper and deeper until she could no longer see its glow.

"It is going home, Elera," she heard Javu say as she felt Rekesh's strong hands on her shoulders, keeping her from falling into the pool.

"If you fall in, I might have to dive in after you," Rekesh warned her in a warm tone as she got to her feet.

Before anybody had a chance to contemplate what they had just witnessed, a loud bleeping noise blurted out from Sula's shoulder belt.

"Hey!" she said, pulling a small electronic device out and holding it up to the sky. "I got a signal." She read a message that had flashed up on the device and then put it back in her shoulder belt.

"It's started!" she said.

"What has?" Rekesh asked.

"The invasion in Lizrab," Sula stated simply, as if everyone already knew.

"What?!" Elera and Javu said in unison with horror. "When?!"

"Now," Sula said. "The Tyrones have been planning it for months."

The news was quite a shock to both Javu and Elera, who had both prayed for such devastating incursions to end.

"We have to go to Lizrab," Elera said without hesitation.

"Yes, we must leave as soon as we can," Javu agreed. "It is vital that Turo is protected and we must do what we can to help. The Tyrones have kept things very close to their chest this time."

"The land troops will be at Calegra within the hour," Sula updated everyone, reading from her device.

"Then it won't be long before they reach the south," Javu added, turning to Elera. "I think the time has come for us to leave."

Elera agreed, nodding slowly. Sita and Rama, who had been standing together on the other side of the pool, walked over to Rekesh and stood beside him and Elera.

"Was that Bimini before?" Teltu asked, still staring at the pool.

"I don't think it was known as Bimini then," Javu said.

"Well, I feel quite confused," Sula stated brashly. "What, with things disappearing in front of my eyes and all these fantastic stories."

Teltu seemed a little apprehensive too.

"I am worried about Fera and Nehne," Teltu said. "I want to go with you but it sounds like you may be gone for quite a while. I think I need to go back to Ciafra."

"I am going to Ciafra now too," Sula declared to everyone. "That is the next place I am supposed to go after here."

"Really, Sula? Why do they want you to go to Ciafra?" Elera asked with some concern.

"Okay, I'll tell you but you cannot mention my name to anyone, okay?"

Everyone agreed not to cite her name, though none of them could think of a scenario where they would want to.

"Well, as you probably know, Raicema has been looking for an energy source for its vehicles and machines for years now. President Tyrone has got it in his brain that both Lizrab and Ciafra have abundant supplies of energy that can be used by Raicema. Besides trying to restrain the Makai in Lizrab, he is trying to locate these sources to achieve his vision."

"What vision?"

"To create flying machines all over the world."

"But there isn't an energy source like that in Lizrab or Ciafra," Elera protested. "The people in both of those lands survive with very little, hardly any machinery."

"That's all I know. I'm supposed to travel around Ciafra and see if I can find any evidence of these energy sources."

"Sula, do you know what you are looking for?" Javu asked her. "Oil? Coal?"

"No. They've already mapped all oil and coal left on the planet and from what I have heard, that's already reserved for the city reactors. This source is stored in some sort of crystal rock and apparently there is no need to burn it. But as I said, that's all I know."

Teltu was thinking deeply whilst Sula was talking.

"Sula, I have a favour to ask," he said softly. "I want to go with Elera to Lizrab but I need to let my wife and daughter know that we are all safe. Could you pass through Seho on the northwest coast when you reach Ciafra and let them know that we are all safe?"

Sula agreed to the request.

"My wife is called Fera. Tell her what is happening and where we are going. You are most welcome to stay in Seho too."

An air of sadness fell as the group realised that the time had come for everyone to move on.

"I hope that I will see you again, Sula," Elera said affectionately to her newly found friend. "I hope that you will be happy on your travels."

Sula wished everyone farewell before getting out her compass and disappearing into the jungle, heading back in the direction of her boat.

"Well, I guess we should also be going," Rekesh said, beginning to walk in a similar direction. "We have quite a walk to navigate our way through the mangrove."

"What just happened with that crystal ball?" Teltu asked, stopping everyone in their tracks. "How did that picture appear?"

"It was a memory of long ago," Elera said.

"Let's talk about it on our travels," Javu suggested, his mannerisms a little agitated. "We need to get to Turo."

"Why don't you all head back to the beach where you were camped. I will see you there in a while," Elera said, to Rekesh's consternation. Javu, understanding that Elera wasn't ready to leave the statue behind yet, ushered everyone to begin their journey back to the beach where they had landed. After they were out of sight, Elera approached the statue.

"Great horse. Will you appear in front of me again?"

As soon as she had asked this question, the statue began to fade away until it was almost transparent. Then, as it disappeared, the same sound of an animal grazing could be heard from behind her. She turned around to the sight of the deeply incessant eyes of the white and silver horse, standing within arm's reach in front of her.

"How can I help you be free?" she asked the creature, feeling a deep sense of love for it. She felt love radiating back.

"We are both in a bubble, yet you are in a much smaller one than I. If you continue your search, your bubble will burst and you will be free. Step carefully, Elera. What you see around you is only a fraction of what exists. I am here to protect you and help you protect yourself. Follow your intuition. Trust yourself. May the force of love be with you, always."

Then the horse was gone, as if Elera had blinked and in that moment everything had changed. Her vision was fuzzy and there was electricity all around. She felt light, like she was floating and for a moment she thought she felt the air beneath her feet.

Thoughts of Turo and its people flooded her mind. A sense of urgency followed and her perception returned to normal. She turned in the direction the others had gone. As she walked rapidly to catch up, Elera suddenly had the strange sensation that she had just dreamt her entire experience on the island but this feeling quickly evaporated as she methodically recounted the events in order. Everything she had visualised seemed as fresh as a morning breeze.

With the flutter of playful birds overhead, Elera looked deeply into the heart of the undergrowth, sure that she could see wavering light emanating from every leaf, branch and flower. She smiled, the thought of going home overshadowing the threat of war that loomed over the ocean.

Chapter 15 – Retreat

"They say you can judge a man by the company he keeps. Those who he surrounds himself with can tell you his true agenda. A man with love embraces those around him and helps them. But a man who is insane surrounds himself with those that he does not care about."

"So what kind of people do you surround yourself with, Bene?"

"Soon it will be with those I love. But for a long time it has been with those I have no love for."

"So I guess that makes you insane then?" Reo joked.

Bene just shrugged off the muse, a weak smile curling on this face. It was the third day since Bene and Reo's arrival in Calegra and both men were waiting patiently in a small eatery in one of the downtown zones. The Raiceman troops were going to be passing through the central zones of Calegra shortly and Reo had been strongly briefed on how to get onto one of the vehicles heading towards the south.

"So, did you find your brother?" Bene asked.

"Yes. I found him last night," he replied, somewhat dejectedly.

Reo had found his brother, Teto, living with a group of drug dealers in the Cohen Zone, not far from where he and Bene had been staying. He had travelled all over Calegra for two days trying to find him, asking on the streets and venturing into notorious neighbourhoods for any leads he could find. It had been a young boy who had been used as a runner by Teto's gang that had finally informed him of where his brother lived. Reo had been shocked to see the amount of weight his brother had lost. He looked haggard and drained, not the young athletic man Reo remembered him as.

"He's not doing well," Reo admitted to Bene, looking down at the black, metal table. "He got caught up in dealing, living with these four guys who've got plans to take over all the drugs in Calegra."

Bene laughed, bemused. "I've heard that many times," he said, rolling his eyes and composing himself. "It's sad though. Most kids don't have much choice but to deal or steal in cities like this."

"I tried to convince him to leave, but he just won't listen!" Reo continued.

Reo had told Tito of the movement and its cause to free people repressed by governments like Raicema.

"Those fools!" Teto had laughed sarcastically. "With those dreamers, you're just food for the military to eat up."

Despite his best efforts to make Teto see that at least that would be a better, more honourable life, Reo felt he had already been corrupted by dreams of wealth and power and had decided to leave him to the life he had chosen.

"I'll go back for him when we get back to Calegra," Reo said to Bene, who said nothing in reply. Instead he changed the subject.

"So, are you ready to do what I told you to do?"

The roar of vehicle engines could be heard in the distance, thunderous like a wave of bad weather.

"I'm ready," Reo replied. "But how can you be sure they'll stop here?"

"Trust me," Bene said. "I know."

Within minutes a huge military unit consisting of forty large land-vehicles was passing through the dirt track outside, the thin metal walls vibrating with the cutting motion of the speedy cavalcade.

Bene leaned close to Reo to whisper. "I heard word before we met here that a huge rebellion has formed at the edge of the city. There is a battle taking place on the red plains as we speak."

Reo started to feel slightly anxious at this news.

"How many soldiers has Raicema sent to Lizrab?" he asked Bene quietly.

"Over a hundred thousand," Bene replied. "The Tyrones fully intend to crush the rebellion here in Lizrab, but once they reach the south, their sophisticated technology will not help them. Aradonas is surrounded by some of the thickest jungles in the world."

Suddenly, two large armoured vehicles pulled up outside the

eatery and eight Raiceman troops emerged and barged in, crashing the door against the wall and bending its hinges. Each was dressed in black and grey metallic armour, with traditional square-cut helmet. Each man carried a large shoulder belt loaded with firearms and blades.

"Load these sacks with food!" barked one soldier to the owner of the eatery, shoving large woven sacks in her face, almost toppling her over.

The others started helping themselves to anything they found amusing including cups, candles and stools. Some vandalised a shrine dedicated to the sun, to which an elderly man tried to intervene and was punched violently in the face. Reo was shocked to see this and felt a sudden pang of anger swell in his body. Bene glared at him, a sign to not get distracted and start moving. They both slipped out of the eatery when the troops were being handed sacks full of food and quickly dropped to the floor, rolling underneath one of the vehicles.

"Hold on to the fuel ducts," Bene said, grabbing two and hoisting himself up into the underlying machinery. He twisted himself into a stable position.

Reo followed suit and lifted himself up, hooking his feet around a thick iron pipe and holding on tightly. Within seconds, the soldiers were out and the vehicle was moving at speed. Reo dare not look down for fear of falling off.

"They'll stop soon," Bene said loudly over the noisy, intrusive engine. Sure enough, the vehicle stopped moments later outside another eatery and the troops got out again, repeating their routine of pillaging.

"Move!" Bene said forcefully.

The two rolled out from under the vehicle and hopped inside. Bene opened a metal trunk with a key he had in his hand. He grabbed two uniforms and two helmets and pushed Reo out of the vehicle, towards a small alley filled with rubble. They laid low until they heard the vehicles drive off.

"Great. Phase one complete," Bene said. "Now for phase two!"

They walked down the alley, reaching another part of the zone with shops and traders trying to carry on as normal, though Reo noticed that everyone was on edge, looking around shiftily for signs of hostility.

"We need to get to the main square in this zone. The troops will have set that up as a temporary base whilst they hunt around the perimeter for insurgents."

They carried on walking though the busy district, passing numerous crowds and gatherings. Bene hid the uniforms carefully, knowing that many within Calegra would happily attack any man sporting one of the grey and black outfits.

"Say, Bene," Reo said as they walked hurriedly along. "How come you know all this about the Raicemans? You know, where they'll be and what they'll do."

"I told you before," Bene whispered into Reo's ear. "I used to work for the government of Raicema."

He pressed swiftly on, guiding Reo down another alley, close to the main square.

"Now go over there and change into this," he said to Reo, handing him the uniform and pointing to a concealed alcove.

"I thought you worked for the RMO? You worked for the government too?" Reo asked Bene as he tried to pull on the uniform.

"Same thing," Reo replied simply.

The suit was heavy, padded and had many useful devices attached to it including an electric light, wire cutters and other gadgetry. There was also a small pistol in the inside pouch. The suit was slightly big for Reo, but he could walk plausibly in it, even if with a little drag. The helmet was heavy and covered his entire head except for a small part of his face, where his lips, nose and eyes were. He heard a crackling in the helmet.

"What's that noise I can hear?" he said to Bene through the T-shaped opening, seeing that he had now changed into the other Raiceman uniform.

"It's the communication line. Orders are given through it. It will be useful for knowing what is being planned."

Bene pushed a button on the inside of Reo's helmet and a voice could be heard, penetrating everything that Reo could hear.

"*All non-scouting troops return to base...*" was all that was being said, over and over.

"We're lucky we're not real soldiers," Bene said. "Otherwise, we'd have one of those voices in our head all the time. Let's go!"

He urged Reo along and they soon reached the main square, where over sixty vehicles were stationed, soldiers patrolling the perimeter and interrogating anybody who walked by. Reo and Bene walked straight through it all and sat down quietly in a large vehicle, designed for carrying many people. There were already three soldiers sitting patiently in the vehicle. Bene had told Reo about these carriers and how they were used to carry troops over long distances. Chances were that they'd be leaving soon for Aradonas.

"When does the general's battalion arrive?" one of the soldiers asked his comrade.

"He's not coming here," replied the other soldier. "I think he's heading to the south by ship with the president. Got loads of cool shit to blow those damn Makai to kingdom come!"

Reo began to get nervous that one of the soldiers might try to speak to him but then he saw that Bene was pretending to be asleep and decided to do the same thing. After a while, the vehicle filled up with soldiers.

"Look at those two!" he heard one soldier say, laughing as he got in. "They've probably been in a brothel all morning!"

The next thing Reo knew, the vehicle was moving, travelling for hours over bumpy terrain, the other soldiers amusing themselves by spinning stories of their escapades in Raicema and beyond. Every now and again, Bene would nudge Reo and whisper to him the distance they were from Aradonas; three hundred suns, two hundred, then one hundred. Reo thought of his brother a lot during the journey and of the dangerous people that he had associated his life with. He tried to think of ways that he could convince his brother to leave Calegra. It had been much simpler for his other siblings. They had travelled to Raicema ten years earlier to work in the north of the country where there were many industrial regions. Reo and Teto had never wanted to follow. Ploughing the government lands or working in dire factories never appealed to either of them.

The vehicle started jittering more as the territory changed to more hilly land. The carrier only had small square windows. Reo attempted to look out of one and saw beautiful forests, spreading over a range of valleys. There was a river in the distance and more carriers could be seen travelling besides it.

"You been to Lizrab before?" a soldier asked Reo, somewhat startling him from his scenic escape.

"No," he lied, speaking in a disguised voice.

"I've been here before," the soldier said solemnly. "Gets pretty rough once we reach the jungle. You don't know where the bastards are coming from. Watch your back. Even your fellow comrades get jumpy and shoot each other by mistake."

Reo felt sad listening to the soldier's account.

"I once saw my friend killed right in front of me," he continued. "He opened fire on a Makai but didn't realise a soldier was right behind him. After my friend took a shot, the soldier's reflex was to shoot back. All three of them died in front of my eyes."

The soldier's eyes glazed over and he looked to the metal floor of the carrier.

"I hope I get to die in the comfort of my own bed."

Reo didn't want to enter into conversation with the man, so he shook his head, acknowledging the tragedy and then pretended to go back to sleep. After a while, he actually did doze off. He awoke to the sound of a crash, the vehicle jolting violently.

The fighting had begun. Gunshots, explosions and shouting could be heard outside and the men were hurriedly piling out of the vehicle. Bene pulled Reo by the neck to the back of the carrier, where they ducked down behind some seats.

"Listen!" Bene said quickly. "When they all disappear into the jungle, we need to drive this carrier nearer to Aradonas. I know the way to Turo from there."

"But the driver's still in the cab," Reo said anxiously as an explosion echoed in his ear.

"We'll lie low here for a minute and then one of us will have to dispose of him."

"No!" Reo protested in horror. "I never agreed to kill anybody."

Bene rolled his eyes, waiting for a few moments. Then he got out of the vehicle and entered the driver's cabin. Reo heard a thud and then Bene appeared in the doorway.

"Come on!" he said urgently.

As Reo walked outside he saw fire streaming in a distant part of the thick forest. He noticed the driver, lying unconscious near the cab.

"Don't worry," Bene said sarcastically. "I didn't kill him."

"So much for non-violence," Reo said staring at the unconscious man curled up on the floor.

The two quickly got into the cab and Bene started the engine, which made a tinkering sound and then let out a roar as it spurred into action. He pushed a lever and the vehicle sped up. They drove rapidly through the jungle whilst twigs, leaves and insects piled onto the windshield. As they got further, the jungle got denser and denser. Eventually, Bene couldn't even see where he was going. Leaves and foliage were piling up so thickly against the glass shield that soon it turned completely green. Reo knew the vehicle was moving, but he could not tell by looking out. He actually felt safe for the first time in a while, as if Bene and he were embedded deep inside a jungle hideaway.

"How long has it been since you've seen your grandfather?" he asked Bene, who was haphazardly trying to steer by looking through the smallest of window space.

"It's been about three years," Bene said, opening his side window and trying to remove some of the foliage by hand.

"Did he send you away to Raicema? You know, to take the place of your father as Makai leader?"

Bene was silent, thinking deeply. Reo sensed that he was contemplating whether or not to talk about the matter. He turned to look at Reo, inspecting his face for a sign that he could trust him. As he was about to speak, the vehicle came to a sudden halt and Bene and Reo were both thrown against the windshield with shuddering force.

"Uhh," Bene groaned, pushing himself back into his seat. "It's a good thing that this glass is so thick."

Reo too adjusted himself but noticed that there was a subtle difference in the feeling of the vehicle.

"It feels like the vehicle is tipping," he said, detecting fine movements in balance and hearing a slight creaking sound. The two opened the cab door and were shocked to see that the driver's cab was leaning over a vertical drop, a small ravine running down at the bottom of a giant gorge.

"I thought you said we were heading for Aradonas!" Reo raved uncontrollably in a panic. The cab moved forward slightly.

"Look, don't move!" Bene said firmly. "These vines are holding the carrier on the edge."

The long vines were wrapped around the drivers cab and were caught on trees in the nearby jungle behind them. Leaves, shrubbery and vines were intertwined into the wheels and crevices of the carrier, which now looked like a heavily camouflaged bunker.

"We have to climb over the top, away from this drop," Reo suggested, suddenly getting his nerve back.

In the far distance, the faint noise of explosions could be heard. Reo began to climb up onto the roof of the driver's cab, slightly rocking the vehicle.

"Quickly, weigh down the other end!" Bene urged, as the vehicle began to tip further into the canyon.

Reo carefully walked along the cab, made a small hop onto the main carrier roof and stopped at the end, arms outstretched almost boyishly. Bene followed and when he reached Reo, they both carefully clambered down. Reo breathed a sigh of relief as his feet touched the ground. Bene smiled at him. All around was dense jungle. There were no paths and Reo got a little dizzy staring into the green and yellow mass.

"Do you know where we are?" Reo asked quite naively.

"No," clarified Bene, "but we were heading due south in the right direction. Last time I went to Aradonas, I flew there so this ravine wasn't a problem."

"How?" Reo asked, amazed at his statement. "Even the Raicemans don't fly aircrafts. That much I do know!"

"In Turo we have flyers that don't use electric power. They glide like birds and can hold up to three people," Bene explained. "I will show you one when we reach there."

"So how are we going to cross this cliff?" Reo pondered to himself out loud, looking around for possible ways. Bene ventured to the jungle's edge looking around for a while. Reo tried to look inside the carrier for any useful equipment.

The canyon was at least the length of five people, far too big to jump. The rock face looked light and sandy, with little plants growing outwards and vines hanging down over the edge.

"Hey, look what I found!" Reo announced, holding up a substantial length of thick rope. Bene emerged from the forest carrying some thick vines.

"We need to make two strong swing ropes. We can attach our helmets to them and swing over to the other side."

Reo didn't like the sound of this plan but couldn't think of another way, so they both went to work intertwining the vines and the rope to make two reinforced lengths. They tied them strongly to the helmets making two crude grappling ropes. Bene swung the helmet forcefully to the other side, whilst tugging it towards two trees. It snagged in between two branches. He tugged hard and it would not move.

"Okay," he said, "Wish me luck!"

With that he jumped into the ravine holding on tightly to the rope. He bounced on it for a second and then it swung to the furthest face. He slowly climbed up to safety on the other side.

"Your turn!" he shouted over as he got to his feet. "Throw it over. Oh, and don't look down."

Reo checked his rope several times before throwing it over. Bene helped and made sure it was firmly lodged between two tree trunks. Reo felt like he was falling to his death as he jumped, but the strong pull as the length was reached brought him back to life.

"Crazy!" he exclaimed as he climbed up, Bene's thick Raiceman boots directly in front of him.

"We should dispose of these uniforms," Bene said, taking his suit off. He removed the useful gadgets and took the shoulder belt with him, putting things in its pouches. Everything else he threw into the canyon. Reo did the same.

They walked for hours through the jungle, seeing birds with every colour of the rainbow on their feathers. The heat was moist and sweltering. Large beads of water ran down their faces and off their arms like rain off glass.

"You know, I always wanted to go to the north of Lizrab," Reo said in a ramble as they plodded along. "My father used to tell me stories of long-lost forgotten cities. Who knows if there are even people still living there?"

"Impossible," Bene said firmly. "If you think these jungles are hard to navigate, then you haven't seen anything compared to the northern land. I once tried to fly there, but where there aren't the densest jungles there are the tallest mountains I have ever seen. There is no way anybody could be living around there."

They continued along until the jungle seemed to clear slightly, with more space between each tree and a little light streaming in through the treetop gaps. Ahead they saw a river, its banks littered with tiny snakes.

"I know this river!" Bene exclaimed almost jogging towards it. "It runs from the east coast until Aradonas. We should follow this for a while."

Reo just nodded in agreement, himself totally lost. They travelled alongside the river which was now running southwesterly, until they came to a bridge made of large logs. The trees overhead had thick leaves dripping with moisture. Reo's clothes were drenched because of the humidity.

"We are close to the fort," Bene said, wiping the heavy liquid from his arms. "Much of it is underground but the main entry way is due south of this bridge. From there we can get to Turo where my grandfather will be."

They carried on through the jungle, which seemed to get thicker with each step. Above, Reo continually heard rustling and strange noises to which Bene told him to quicken his pace.

"This part of the jungle is not only home to the Turonian people. There are many poisonous snakes and wild cats living in these trees."

They sped up their movement to a jog and before long reached a crowded part of the jungle where the trees seemed to grow only a finger's width apart.

"Mmm. It looks like those trees are growing in a giant circle," Reo commented to Bene, looking at the arrangement which was at least a sun wide.

"It is the gate to the fort!" Bene said, suddenly recognising the formation. "Each of these trees was once planted here on purpose, to blend in with the rest of the jungle."

The gate was broad and looked like it hosted a large town. Each tree was tall enough to hide its top and the entire set of trees was an overwhelming sight. Bene approached one of the trees and rapped on it loudly with a large stick he found on the floor. Nothing happened.

"They are being cautious because of the invasion," he said to Reo. Bene then began to shout his name though the small gap of two trees. Again, there was no reply or sound of movement.

"There are usually hundreds of people within this circle. They should be able to hear us from any part of the gate. It seems as though we will have to walk around until we hear someone on the other side."

They walked around the giant circle for a while until they reached the other side. Reo tried to imagine what the gate must look like from the sky; like an enormous ring of green. Bene stopped as he heard shuffling on the other side.

"Hello?" he said loudly. "It's me, Bene Mattero. Who's there?"

They heard a sound like somebody clearing their throat and then a rustling of leaves on the floor.

"It's Puzo," a young voice said quietly from the other side. "Who are you? Are you a Raiceman soldier?"

"No, Puzo. It's Bene Mattero. I remember you from when you were only a little baby. Find one of the adults and tell them I am here."

"I can't," said the voice. "Nobody is here. Everyone has gone to Aradonas to see the big ships arriving."

Bene and Reo looked at each other in astonishment.

"Only me and my friends are here to guard the gate," the high-pitched voice continued. "I can't let you in until the adults get back."

"I guess we'll have to wait," Reo said acceptingly to Bene, crouching down in a seated position on the leafy floor. Bene frowned with agitation at Reo's comment and turned back to the narrow gap.

"I am the grandson of Kirichi Mattero. You must know of me," Bene appealed to the youngster. "I have important things to tell him."

"No, sorry!" Puzo said firmly. "Master Kirichi couldn't possibly travel all the way here to recognise you. You'll have to wait out there."

Reo smiled to himself at this young child being so adamant.

"Quite feisty, huh?" he said playfully, resting his head against one of the giant trees. Bene just nodded in a huff and sat beside him.

They waited for hours until dusk, a streak of red spreading through the sky like it had been scorched. Then, as they were both almost asleep, a swishing sound could be heard as multiple gliders skimmed and floated above the gate before descending downwards.

"They're back!" Bene said, stirring from his slumbered position. They both got to their feet and within minutes faint talking could be heard on the other side of the tightly packed trees. Then heavier footsteps approached and stopped, a small silence following.

"State your business!" a familiar voice said loudly and deeply.

"Gaho, its Bene!" said, recognising the voice.

Gaho peered through the tiny gap of two of the trees and instantly identified him.

"Who's that with you?" Gaho enquired to Bene, spotting Reo standing sheepishly behind him.

"His name is Reo Fernandez."

"Are you sure he can be trusted?" Gaho asked bluntly.

"Yes," Bene said adamantly. "Trust me."

Gaho grunted slightly and then walked away. Reo peered at Bene blankly and then tried to look through a gap between two trees. All he could see were more leaves on the ground, shimmering with a rustic glow as the sun was setting. Then, a slight creaking sound could be heard and one of the trees not too far away, suddenly came crashing down, making the ground tremble and the leaves all around jump wildly into the air.

"Whoahh!" Reo exclaimed, jolted by the crash.

As they walked to the newly formed opening, Reo was astonished to see that the tree had a one-way hinge engineered into it so it could be pushed over and then stand back upright again. The hinge looked very intricate, made from a strong metal. There were ropes anchored along the fallen tree hooked up to a small pulley system, evidently for hoisting the tree back up. Inside, the gate was nothing more than a giant circle of trees, leaves scattered throughout the grand round space.

"It is good to see you, Gaho," Bene said, hugging his friend.

"And you too, Bene," Gaho said, deep voiced in reply.

Reo stepped forward to offer his hand in friendship to Gaho, but he ignored him, instead walking towards to centre of the gate.

"Follow me," he said bluntly, urgency present in his tone.

Bene and Reo followed quietly, sensing great apprehension and worry amongst the seven men that had returned from the coast. In the middle of the gate was a slightly raised patch of ground, covered in leaves. One of the men brushed some aside with his foot, revealing a wooden trap door.

"Go on, Puzo," Gaho said to a young girl, somewhat surprising Reo. "You go first."

Puzo was quite muscular and carried a collection of contraptions on her back, ranging from small tools to ropes and electric torches. She opened the hatch and started to climb down the ladder. Gaho ushered Bene and Reo to follow. Peering down the long shaft, Reo could see that it led to a barely lit passageway. They climbed down, followed by Gaho and his men. Five or six children stayed behind to supervise the gate.

"You know, the gate is usually a village," Puzo said to Reo as he reached the bottom. "It is usually filled with huts and tents, but every time there is an attack, we have to pack everything up and spread out."

They all walked along the passageway, dim electric lights lining the rough walls.

"Have there been a lot of attacks that you can remember?" Reo asked Puzo, guessing the girl was about ten years old.

"There have been lots of small ones, every year that I can remember, but nothing like this. The elders all say that even the leaders of Raicema have come this time."

"Hurry up along there!" Gaho's voice echoed from the back. Everyone quickened their pace and within minutes the group had reached the end of the tunnel. There was a long ladder and Reo was stunned by what he saw at the top of it as he reached the surface. His head popped out at the base of a large square, bustling with people busy and paying no attention to his presence. There were easily seven hundred people occupying the square, some standing and

M. W. Albeer

dealing in everyday needs such as groceries, clothing and oils, others trading complicated-looking metallic objects and household goods from long tables. All around in the distance were high walls, some made of stone, others logs, the view behind impossible to see from his vantage point. Reo clambered out, dusting the dust and grime off his worn clothes. The others quickly ascended to the surface as well.

"This is Turo," Bene quickly introduced the place to Reo. "This part is the market region, where the people of Turo do their trading."

There were beautiful buildings all around, made mainly from wood with different intricate carvings of animals and landscapes in the outer walls, each looking like a work of art. Each building had a pointy wooden roof, the slats winding around to the pinnacle and stained, deep and rich colour. The roofs reminded Reo of a collection magician's hats, delicately balancing on the sculptured buildings. Some of them had hanging trays made of bark, laden with the most vibrant range of coloured flowers that Reo had ever seen. In fact, colour was racing to Reo's eyes like he had never experienced before. The ground felt like it was glowing with a cherry brown, the scattered, interspersed trees vivid greens and many of the buildings decorated with chalky vibrant paints.

"Do people live in these houses?" Reo asked Bene, as the last of the men climbed out of the hole.

"They do not," Gaho interjected, somewhat defensively. "These buildings are only used for trading and entertaining. They belong to everybody. Most people live in the monastery or in the surrounding villages of Turo."

Reo just nodded, pleased that his question had even been acknowledged by Gaho.

"We are going to the monastery now," Puzo informed Reo, smiling warmly at him. Gaho grunted and signalled for everyone to follow him. Reo, Bene and Puzo stayed at the back, away from his disgruntled mood.

"You'll have to excuse Gaho," Puzo said quietly and quite responsibly. "He doesn't trust outsiders very much."

They all travelled through the market region, past tall statues of strange characters, powerful and watchful, one a cross between a hawk and a man. They travelled over many quaint, carved bridges that stood over ponds and small lakes, and past a group of children playing an unusual game with round discs and a circular mat. The entire group of mini-towns and villages that made up Turo was enchanting as if created through a common unity of style and interest, though each part was imaginatively unique. Reo felt both the peace and excitement that could be drawn from the decorative and influential structures and arrangements, yet he couldn't help but feel as though he was left out of it all, like he couldn't really relate to life within the heart of the Makai civilisation. Maybe it was him, he thought, always focusing on money and the niceties he never had. Maybe that had left him with a lack of appreciation for the belief that seemed to seep out of every entity in Turo.

"Over there is *Meska*, the field of cures," Puzo pointed out as the group moved into a more open area, stretching far and wide with hilly plains. "It is used to grow all of the medicinal plants that are used by the monks."

Meska was an enormous field that stretched towards a small surrounding forest. Ahead were hilly paths and all around animals roamed freely including horses, cattle and small lizards.

The monastery was breathtaking in a multitude of ways. Its structure was tall yet unimposing, an old, intricate round building with long floral pillars and a dome made from the most artistic wooden arrangement of slats and carvings. The entire roof looked like a giant wooden flower. The stone had been painted light blue and from certain positions as the group walked around the grand construction, it seemed as though it merged seamlessly into the clear sky. There were many open windows around the monastery and some people were looking out to see who was approaching.

"This place was built over five hundred years ago," Bene told Reo as they approached a giant stone staircase, as wide as the monastery itself. Some of the steps were crumbling at the edges and pretty flowers grew out of the cracks.

At the top, a man in a long orange robe had appeared, accompanied by five others wearing similar attire. Without even asking, Reo knew the man was Kirichi. His long white beard flowed down to his belly, contrasting with his deeply tanned skin. His face was long and defined. He had an overwhelming presence even from the distant standpoint Reo was observing from. Many people in and around the monastery simply stood still at being in his company.

Led by Gaho, Bene and Reo climbed the stairs slowly. Reo was a little out of breath as they reached the top.

"Welcome home, my grandson," Kirichi said enthusiastically to Bene, embracing him affectionately. He held his face and looked into his eyes, one corner of his mouth rising into a happy grin.

"You had a safe journey?" he asked Bene, who was much less enthused than his grandfather.

"Yes," Bene stammered slightly. "Well sort of. We actually got here by disguising ourselves as Raiceman soldiers."

Kirichi burst out in a deep laugh, resonating in the surrounds of the monastery. His followers joined in and chuckled to themselves.

"So very dangerous then?" he said, his bushy white eyebrows raising up and down mischievously. "And who is your friend?"

Kirichi looked with intrigue directly at Reo, who suddenly felt nervous, shuffling his feet and looking around.

"This is Reo Fernandez. He is a Calegran whom I discovered in Raicema City."

Kirichi walked over to Reo slowly and placed both of his hands on Reo's shoulders. "Welcome!" he said sincerely. "I am sure you have been learning a lot since your arrival in the south. Things are very unstable here, but in that bring great stability, so have no fear, Reo."

Reo was surprised at Kirichi's words, mainly because it was as if he knew what Reo was thinking. He just nodded in acknowledgement.

"Come," Kirichi said loudly, walking towards the monastery entrance. "Let us all go inside and talk about our experiences. Bene, I am sure you have many things to tell me."

They walked through the great arch which was ribbed with decorations and flowerpots. Inside, the monastery was light and airy with large open spaces and people congregating on the floors and raised ledges. There were intricate colourful woven rugs and carpets placed randomly on the ground and many people sat peacefully upon them meditating in unusual poses.

As they walked along the main halls, Reo was fascinated by the peaceful energy of the place, an instant calming effect overcoming all of his concerns.

"Did you live here as a child?" Reo asked Bene.

"For a while," he replied. "There are giant sleeping areas that are open to anybody but there are also many villages that surround the monastery. I lived in a small village to the west of here for most of my childhood."

"And is everybody from this region part of the Makai?"

"The entirety of the south follows the true Makai ethos," Bene elucidated. "Aradonas is the main city. This region is very old and sacred to the Makai people. That is why they make it so difficult to reach my grandfather and the monastery. I am sure that you will hear all about it soon."

The party had now reached a round open area, with a flowerbed and pond in the middle of the floor. There were large carpets all around and oval cushions scattered everywhere. The area looked like it could easily hold several hundred people. They all walked to the centre of it and Kirichi sat cross-legged upon a cushion next to the pond.

As everyone else sat down, Reo noticed a domed skylight, providing sunshine for the pond and flowerbed. Two men approached carrying trays of fresh vegetables and pickled nuts.

"So, Reo," Kirichi said loudly. "What do you know about the

Makai?"

The question threw Reo off his guard and he began to panic. Bene had warned him when they first met that he would be asked this question, but he didn't expect that it would be from Kirichi.

"Well," he said, his voice shaking a bit. "You don't like the way Raicema do things..."

The statement made Kirichi bellow out the deepest of laughs, ripples forming on the pond from the force coming out of his mouth.

"You are right, though I think most people on this planet would agree with that statement." He chuckled. "But what do you know about our history?"

Again Reo was stumped and looked at Bene for help, who simply looked away uninterested.

"I don't know much..." he admitted weakly.

"That is fine because I will tell you," Kirichi said reassuringly, picking up a crisp piece of green pepper and crunching on it. "After all, you are now in a country where most people live as Makai."

Reo just nodded, picking up a pickled nut.

"The Makai began as a spiritual movement about seven hundred years ago. At the time, this planet was suffering from the aftermath of a devastating war that had unleashed a plague amongst everything that was living. Plants were dying, animals were already dead and only humans that lived in very natural surroundings survived well. At that time there were two rival empires that were at war with each other, both pursuing power and control of the planet. Whilst it is uncertain yet widely debated where these two empires were based, one thing that is certain is that collectively, they almost destroyed the planet with their sophisticated weaponry."

Kirichi paused for a moment, as if trying to remember a speech that he had given many times before.

"The Makai seems to have risen simultaneously in mass in two regions of the planet after the destruction, here in Lizrab and also in Neoasia. This was probably because these two regions are amongst the most natural and diverse in the world. These sects raised the hopes of the people and created more unity. So, our origins are down to much debate. Some say the Makai was formed in Neoasia, some say here in Lizrab. What is recorded is the union of the two sects about five hundred years ago, when the Makai became a political movement as well as a spiritual one. At that time one could say that Makaism became a religion."

Reo was listening with interest along with the others, although Reo was sure they must have heard the story many times before.

"Now, that's enough about that for now. I would like to know about your journey here? What compelled you to return?" Kirichi said to Bene, also glancing at Reo.

Bene was stirred from his melancholic slumber at the question.

"Sadana sent me here with a message for you," Bene said, getting straight to the point. "I have been watching him for three years now and nothing!"

A tone of bitterness could be detected in his voice.

"He never slips up. I failed to expose him to the other elders. He found out about me. That's why he sent me here with a message, to taunt me for failing."

Kirichi smiled weakly as if he already knew what Bene was telling him.

"Bene, my child," Kirichi said soothingly. "You have tried very hard to get justice for the death of your father but I believe the time has come for you to follow another path."

Bene was silent, seemingly in disagreement.

"Sadana is intent on forming another empire," Kirichi continued. "And only a unified people can stop that!"

"I can't just give up on him," Bene mumbled, more to himself than anybody else.

"So what do you think the message is?" Reo interrupted, a burst of enthusiasm running through him. "Bene said that a sig-lens can be created to kill. I don't think you should use it just in case."

"Do not worry, Reo," Kirichi said affectionately. "Sadana would not kill me in such a way. It would be of little use to him if I was murdered like my son. What he really desires is for there to be doubt amongst the people about my intentions towards them. Death by sig-lens would not create this. In fact, it would probably have the opposite effect."

"So Sadana wants to take your place?"

"He wants entire control," Kirichi clarified. "Firstly, of the two billion followers of the Makai on this planet, and then everyone else! Do you have the lens, Bene?"

Bene opened a small pouch and handed Kirichi a shiny black box that looked like it was made of turtle shell. Kirichi opened it and inside was a single lens, the size of an iris with tiny red rings around the rim. Everyone huddled over to look at it.

"Is it dangerous, Bene?" one monk asked, obviously a little worried.

"It's hard to tell by just looking at it," Bene said. "It certainly is to someone because of those red rings, but there's no easy way to tell who the poison rings have been programmed for. Probably everyone except my grandfather."

"There is no need to worry," Kirichi said adamantly, picking up the lens by his fingers. He placed it on his right eye to the gasps of all present. A small line of text whizzed across his eyes. What Kirichi saw next did little more than fill him with a grief he had felt many times before.

A scene played out in front of Kirichi's eyes, as if happening in the great vestibule of the monastery, the virtual scene augmented with the reality around him. His son, Juhi Mattero was speaking to somebody with urgency. No words could be heard and the image of Juhi brought a tear to Kirichi's eye. Then, something hit Juhi in the stomach and he fell to the floor in pain, clutching his wound and praying. Kirichi knew that this was a film of the moment that Juhi died. After a while, a peaceful look came over Juhi's face and he was still, lying on his side in silence. Sadana appeared in view, carrying a gun and grinning sadistically. Then he looked directly at the camera and held something up to it. It was a rounded stone.

Overwhelmed by the images, Kirichi removed the lens and threw it into the pond, where it crackled and smoked upon touching the water.

"Kirichi, what is wrong?" one of his followers asked him, clearly surprised by his actions.

Kirichi breathed rhythmically, trying to gain composure.

"It is an upsetting message, one of true hate."

"What did it tell you?" Bene asked his grandfather.

"Nothing that we didn't already know. Sadana must be removed from power if this world is to be safe."

There was silence as everybody realised Kirichi was not willing to discuss the matter any further. After a few moments had passed, he changed the subject, addressing Reo.

"Do you know why it is forbidden for the Makai to use firearms, Reo?" he asked him.

Reo shook his head.

"The reason why the Makai do not use pistols or any other weapon that has a mechanical component is that we believe that the use of this sort of weapon can only lead to warfare. Long ago, our ancestors gave strict guidelines on what was an acceptable means of defence should one decide that a physical altercation was the only available option. Here in Lizrab, the *giban* or short sword has been adopted as the traditional means of defence. In Neoasia, the body itself was deemed as the only necessary tool one needs in physical defence. Of course, against the advanced weaponry of empires such as Raicema and Lengard, these approaches can often be quite useless. However, it still remains, the *warrior's way*."

Reo was fascinated by the brave and dangerous way of life that Kirichi was describing of the Makai warriors. He wondered how they had managed to survive the attacks of Raicema with such an approach.

"Unfortunately, Reo, there are those who believe that the Makai should fight fire with fire and in Raicema, the Makai that you have witnessed yourself, have no such ethos of violence as an absolute last resort. Many of those under the influence of Sadana Siger carry guns and other hideous weapons as if they are companions that can grant an easy path through life. That is the path of fear, not the path of the warrior."

"Guns are no better than a giban in Lizrab anyway!" one stocky follower said, listening in to the discussion. "The jungle makes sure of that!"

Kirichi paid no attention to the comment. Instead, he rose to his feet, his followers mimicking his movements.

"It is time to sleep. Tomorrow morning we shall travel to the retreat as I have been advised. Bene, Reo, I wish you both to accompany me."

Though Bene agreed with his grandfather and Reo followed suit, in actual fact Reo was wide awake and wanted to hear more and more about the customs and ways of the Makai to which he had only recently been introduced. Kirichi must have sensed this somehow as he smiled compassionately at Reo.

"Tomorrow you will understand a great deal more, Reo," he reassured him, also looking at Bene. "There is much to learn for you both."

With that final statement, the group walked to another part of the monastery, with large chambers full of piled mattresses. Reo saw that darkness had fallen outside and realised what a long day it had been. They had travelled all the way from Calegra to Turo. The stars seemed much brighter than he had seen them before. As they reached the room in which they would be staying, Kirichi bade them both a good night's sleep and said that they would be setting off as soon as the sun rose.

Reo found it hard to go to sleep. He couldn't see to find a comfortable position on the hard mattress, his mind full of thoughts and questions. Finally, the thought of gliding above the vast jungles of Lizrab seemed to calm him enough to allow him to drift off into a restful slumber.

When Reo awoke, the first thing on his mind was the vivid

memory of a dream he had had. Though he could not remember the setting, he could remember every detail of what he was doing. Reo recalled that he had been walking for a long time, on a journey of immense length. Then he had been approached by some sort of wild animal, a large cat with brown fur. The cat had been slowly biting his hand with its sharp fangs, not hard enough to draw blood, but enough to cause deep marks on the surface of his skin. Reo was so convinced that this had actually happened that he examined his hand carefully for the marks. He was sure he could still feel the points where the cat's teeth had been. He then remembered walking side by side with the cat somewhere, a feeling of strong friendship within. As he struggled to remember more, he realised that his recollection of the overall dream was slipping from him and after a few minutes, he couldn't even remember what the cat looked like anymore.

He shook off his thoughts, stirred out of bed by the clanging of what sounded like metal objects outside the dormitory room. He remembered that he would be going on a journey with Bene and Kirichi today and a childlike excitement filled his body. He quickly got dressed and noticed Bene was already up, his bedding folded neatly on the mattress he had been sleeping on. Reo tidied his own bed and then headed out into the hallway outside, light streaming in and causing every speck of dust in the air to be visible, all floating about in a magical way.

The clanging was coming from somewhere outside and he followed the sound, along the hallway past a number of dorms, down a wide staircase and through a florally decorated stone archway.

Outside in a large pasture, several Makai monks were taking part in competitive exercise, using long wooden blocks in a friendly sort of combat. From what Reo could gather, the aim of the activity was to knock your opponent's block out of their hands, by either using your own block or your feet. Both hands were kept on the block at all times, which looked like a half-cut square log. Many of the monks moved with incredible agility, twisting and jumping as part of their defence. Whilst Reo was captivated watching the monks, Kirichi and Bene approached him.

"They have been heavily influenced by our Neoasian brothers and sisters," Kirichi stated, shaking his head in seeming disagreement.

"Well, it seems as though you are very safe here with all these skilled guardians," Reo commented.

"Nevertheless, I have been advised to relocate temporarily to an even safer place and we shall set off very shortly. Did you sleep well, Reo?"

Reo nodded, not mentioning the vivid dream he had had.

"Good. I shall come back and get you both in a few moments."

Kirichi headed back into the monastery, leaving Bene and Reo observing the competing monks in the morning sun.

"Those blocks represent a giban," Bene informed Reo, pulling out a strange sword from a sheath on his back. "Here, have a look at mine."

Bene handed the sword to Reo, which was roughly the same length as the blocks the monks were using. The sword had a round handle, bound in a silky rope and had a wide blade which inclined sharply from one side at its end, with a slot-like handle set into the blade for the other hand. Reo was surprised at the weight of the short sword, and he strained slightly to stop it falling to the floor.

"Put your right hand on the handle and your left in that slot in the blade. By holding it that way, it is easy to defend yourself and manoeuvre around."

Reo once again glanced over at the monks who were training, trying to imagine them moving with a giban instead of a block. Bene took the sword from Reo and put it back in his sheath.

"If we had more time, we could have got one forged for you here. These swords are also used for farming, so a lot are made throughout the year. This one belonged to my father," Bene explained. The same distant grief mirrored in his eyes. "I had to leave it here whilst I was in Raicema."

"This retreat that we are going to," Reo began, changing the subject, "is it a long way from here?"

"It will only take us a few hours on foot," Bene said, sensing that Reo had been shaken by their risky journey to Turo. "But it is in the safest part of the jungle, some of it so thick that hardly any light gets through."

Before Reo could ask any more questions, Kirichi swiftly returned carrying a substantially sized satchel.

"Well, let us set off! There is a gate to the east of the monastery that leads out towards the retreat. Do you both have everything you need?"

After gathering a few of their belongings, the three set off along a path that went around the back of the monastery and through several fields, all surrounded by deep undergrowth. They walked for a while before arriving at a wall made out of tall, wide tree trunks. There were several men guarding a pointed gate also made of the wide logs. They smiled with affection as they let Kirichi and the two young men through.

Kirichi and his two companions immediately walked out into an untouched expansion of jungle flora. The rise in temperature could instantly be felt and Reo wondered why it was so much cooler within the walls of Turo. The gate closed behind them with a heavy thud as they headed through the maze of trees and bushes ahead.

As they walked, Kirichi strode ahead with an enthusiasm like Reo had never seen before. The sound of a hundred hummingbirds danced through the humid air and Kirichi hummed with them before beginning to speak.

"I want to explain to you two important terms that are central to Makai belief, Reo," he said, not looking back and continuing to walk straight ahead at a swift pace, "the concept of *Affero* and *Ambitio*."

Reo had not heard either term before.

"I can only describe it like this. Somewhere in space there is Affero, a source of pure untainted energy. All it does is give out this energy. It expands out so quickly that it is unimaginable for us. It never takes energy in, just gives it out."

The trees overhead hid the bright morning sunlight.

"At the opposite end of space there is Ambitio, a source of pure unadulterated power. All it does is consume and take energy into itself. It is an ominous black hole sucking everything into it. It never gives out energy. Indeed, not even light can escape its vast power."

Both Bene and Reo were listening like small children to the white-haired elder in front of them.

"Now we, as unique beings, are capable of behaving like Ambitio or Affero. We can become mini black holes and suck energy in or we can become sources of energy that we can give out to others. Indeed, there are times when we all behave in either way. The important thing is to maintain a balance, just like a balance is needed between these two great extreme forces in space."

Reo was silent, captivated by the concept and way that Kirichi thought of things in terms of energy, whilst Bene felt grounded by the talk which he had heard many times during his childhood.

"The universe as we know it could not possibly exist without these two great forces."

Many thoughts came into Bene's mind and he contemplated whether to bring up a certain topic of conversation that had been concerning him for a long time. The gentle rustling of leaves overhead spurred him on.

"There is something that Sadana told me that has been worrying me," he said finally to them both, causing Kirichi's head to turn slightly even though he was quite a distance ahead. As he adjusted his heavy pack laden with bedding, Reo also turned with interest to Bene.

"At one time Sadana trusted me. It took a long time for me to gain his confidence, for me to fully disguise who I was, but once I did he let me into his confidence."

By this point, Kirichi had picked up on the seriousness of the conversation and had stopped, allowing the two to catch up with him. He fell back silently behind them.

"Sadana has a manuscript in his possession. It gives predictions of the future, written long ago. He never spoke of where it came from but I think it might be from Lizrab."

The pace had quickened, mirroring the anticipation that could now be felt radiating from Bene's words.

"The manuscript talks about the world coming to an end."

"What?" Reo responded, aghast at the idea.

"It speaks of a time in which great catastrophes will happen on this planet and when 'a great truth' will be revealed. Sadana wants this time to come as soon as possible for some reason. He actually told me that he wants such destruction to happen! That's when I truly realised what a dangerous person he is."

Bene glanced back at Kirichi and was dismayed to find his grandfather's expression devoid of emotion. He half-expected the mention of Sadana's negative intentions to stir some fire within. In fact, Kirichi was listening with the most distant of blank expressions, almost indicating he wasn't listening at all.

"That was all he ever confided in me but there's more. About a year ago, I had the opportunity to look at the manuscript. There were translations written all over it."

"So what did they say?" Reo urged, waving his hand in an attempt to speed Bene up in his account.

"They said that during this prophesised period of time, humans would discover hidden capabilities within themselves and that one individual would emerge to prove that such feats are possible."

"What kind of feats?"

"Acts of the mind, to what I understand. You know, being able to move things by just thinking about it for example," Bene replied.

"It also said that special objects existed on this planet that were capable of showing people the way too. I found out that Sadana is searching for these objects and for this person who is prophesised to emerge."

"But why?" Reo asked.

"Sadana wants to prevent the masses from believing that they are capable of such feats. He believes that his entire reason for existing is to hide such knowledge from people. Can you imagine how rapidly the world would change if you realised that you were that powerful? Tyranny would be a thing of the past if everyone really believed that. Also, he thinks that if he can find this person before they realise who they are, he can learn from them how to harness such power. I guess that's why he's also searching for the objects that the manuscript mentioned."

The account was followed by a prolonged silence and Bene could see a slight look of doubt on Reo's face.

"The manuscript foretold that at the time of its creation, the true abilities of humans were being forgotten, yet they would return radically in one human in the future to lead people in a great war. That could be the war that is happening right now!"

Kirichi, who had been patiently listening until now, broke his silence with a startling point. "I think that the prophecy that you are describing is in fact only *part* of a very old scripture. Our culture has known since its beginning that humans are capable of many more magical feats than they have displayed in recent times. This prophecy holds some truth but is incomplete."

"I have seen the manuscript!" Bene declared, somewhat defensively. "It was written in the same symbolic language as those scriptures in the caves near Aradonas."

"I do not doubt the authenticity of the text that you speak of. Indeed, I know of another part of the prophecy that Sadana clearly does not."

"And what is that?"

"The person and objects you speak of are not the only factor in changing the world's culture of control over the physical. Throughout the years many have displayed such acts of the mind as you have described and yet there has been no worldly shift in ethos. The display of such ability can only have a widespread effect if everyone who witnesses it knows that *they too* are capable of it. And to give such confidence to each person requires everyone to know about our collective past, our shared origin."

"And what is that origin?" Bene probed, now slightly more receptive.

"It is an *awakening* that occurred, an event that thrust every one of us into the reality that we all live. The proof of that event is also needed to fulfil the prophecy you speak of. It is the age-old question of *where do we come from?* Until that is answered, we cannot move forward. And the answer is likely to be incomprehensible to most."

There was silence as they walked along, the extraordinary topic of conversation creating a buzz in the atmosphere of the jungle.

"Of course, not everyone needs proof," he continued more jovially. "Some just accept that there is more to life than the material world. But the majority need reassurance."

They pressed on for an hour, reflecting on the words that had been spoken. The jungle was now a multitude of magnificent colours; luminous yellows, strikingly bright greens and extravagant pinks. The overall size of the leaves around was starting to decrease slightly, yet there were many more of them creating a fractal effect that appeared three dimensional and projected outwards. Reo often thought he was hallucinating as he would reach out to touch a leaf that he believed was at arm's length only to discover it was several strides away.

"So have you seen the manuscript before?" Bene asked his grand-father calmly after a good while of silent walking.

"Yes," he answered. "The script you speak of was stolen from your father about ten years ago. Luckily, he only had half of it with him in Raicema."

The mention of Juhi sent a wave of pain through Bene, yet he persevered and let it pass though him like a tremor in the earth.

"Where is the other half?"

"It is where we are going," Kirichi said reassuringly, with a compassionate tone. "When we get there, I will show it to you."

They walked in silence for another hour before reaching a less dense area of the jungle, the ground slightly sandier and less flying insects buzzing around. Ahead, there was a slope and Reo was surprised at how steep it was as they approached the edge.

"Whoa!" he said, as the ground beneath him started to slide a little.

"At the bottom of this incline is a cave. We must travel through it to reach the retreat."

The three tried their best to slowly walk down the steep slope, but grasping onto the odd branch was not enough to stop the sandy soil from causing all of them to lose their balance and career down the hill at a rapid pace. They all rolled down like apples toppling from a tree.

Luckily, nobody was harmed as they came to a stop where the slope levelled out. Reo jumped up and shook all the soil off his clothes. Looking around, he saw that they were at the bottom of a large ditch and Reo could see the entrance to the cave Kirichi had mentioned.

"Quite an adventure, um?" Kirichi said cheerfully, brushing dirt out of his long beard.

Reo just smiled as they headed towards the cave. It was quite narrow but Reo could see that it was slightly illuminated by natural light which indicated it wasn't very long. Indeed, it only took them a few minutes to navigate their way through the winding rock formations and reach an entrance that came out to a large clearing. Ahead, was a large wooden structure, completely surrounded by thick jungle.

"We are here," Kirichi declared, gesturing to the building, which had four wooden towers built onto four giant trees, all connected by bridges. There was a tall outer wall made from logs bound with thick rope.

"It is a very simple place. I often come here to be in silence with the jungle."

Kirichi led Bene and Reo towards a small door in the wall, which surprisingly to Reo was unlocked. Inside, the retreat was little more than it looked from the outside, a few simple staircases led up to two of the towers and everywhere else was simply the jungle floor, cleared of its more bushy shrubs. The place reminded Reo of a giant natural garden with an elaborate treehouse.

"Anyone is free to come here. We have no guards here," Kirichi mentioned, surprising Reo somewhat as he had expected there to be more people.

"This place is deemed a very spiritual location and as such should be completely open to everyone, even those who may wish to harm us."

Reo noticed a minor look of scepticism on Bene's face as his grandfather spoke the words.

"Let me show you the other half of the prophecy," Kirichi said to his grandson, beginning to walk up one of the staircases, which creaked with every step. He opened the door in the leftmost tower and inside was a simple office, with a few pieces of furniture, a bookcase and a thickly woven rug on the floor. A desk with intricate carvings of animals sat in the middle of the room, which had open windows with muslin stretched across them.

"This is it!" Kirichi said, picking up a thin, flat piece of thick parchment from his bookcase that had writing engraved into it. He handed it to Bene.

"You can read this, Bene."

Bene seemed to struggle to interpret the language at first, but then he seemed to understand the message that was imprinted in front of him.

"The Great Masters know that one day, all will remember that we were imprisoned by the great deceivers. The one who brings them back to the truth can only free them from the illusion if all remember our shared origin. Without that remembrance, we are all lost. With it, we are all free."

"That's all it says," Bene said after doing his best to translate and looking at his grandfather for endorsement. "Who are the great deceivers?"

"They are the *children of Ambitio*," Kirichi said, which didn't really mean anything to Bene or Reo.

"This doesn't say much more than the other half," Bene said, a little disappointed at what his grandfather had shown him.

"Oh, but it does. Those words tell us much more than Sadana knows."

At this statement, Kirichi let out a good-humoured laugh that echoed around the small office.

"I don't really understand," Reo, who had been listening quietly, said. "What does it mean – *our shared origin*?"

"This scripture is describing an event that is beyond what has been recorded in history. The origin is when we all realised why we are here and what we are all capable of. If we cannot remember the origin, we cannot progress. That is what the scripture is saying. Humans can only go so far physically, building giant structures and taking more and more from the planet. After that there is nowhere to go without realising who we are."

Reo still didn't fully understand, yet he decided to accept what Kirichi was telling him, sure he would realise later what it was all about.

"And the *one* that was described," Bene said. "Why does that person need everyone to remember this origin?"

"Without it, people would never truly accept the amazing things that this person would show them. Make no mistake, Bene, many have existed over the years of human existence that have tried to open eyes of the people to that which is so clear yet still so shielded from us. Our world is not all that exists and we have no limits. It is because of people like Sadana, who deliberately hide the truth, that we are all prevented from understanding this. Now, things could be different."

"Why?" Bene and Reo asked in unison.

"Because this planet is dying," Kirichi stated shockingly. "It will soon be time for humans to realise that they can change that, otherwise the cycle will begin again, and we will have learnt nothing!"

Chapter 16 – A Troubled Arrival

On the southern coast of Lizrab, the Raiceman military had arrived in full force. Solid metal boats and giant crates full of weaponry lined the shore. As the men poured out of their vessels and into the warm sea, the sky overhead rumbled with the threat of rain.

Jen King walked calmly along the beach of shingles, carrying his small sack of belongings over his shoulder. Up ahead the smell of roasted meat was drifting on the breeze, catching the senses of every soldier who was climbing off their boat. The earlier groups had set up encampments bordering the jungle, using military equipment combined with long solid branches to make an imposing line of strong shelters. King could hear the sound of several commanders barking at their battalions, ordering them to create the most impenetrable base camp possible.

There was a sense of fear in the air of an impending attack. The memory of ten years earlier was clear in the minds of some of the veterans. In the last invasion many had been killed before they even took a step onto the shores of a land they barely knew.

King had thought hard many times about why Raicema could never succeed in battle in such a land. Even with more advanced technology and a greater number of troops, there was much more unity within the Makai opposition. King knew that they never lost heart and he believed that it was simply because the resistance had much more passion and cause to defend their homes.

How can one truly be passionate about imposing the will of another? King thought.

A young boy stirred him from his deliberation, maybe sixteen years of age, addressing him in a formal manner.

"Commander King." The young boy saluted, trying to deepen his voice. "Your battalion is ready, sir. We are based a short walk into the forest. The men await your orders, sir."

"Good," King said, unenthused. "I shall join you shortly. Carry on, soldier."

The young soldier saluted again and quickly hurried back into the jungle. King knew how he must be feeling, slightly nervous yet excited and eager to prove his worth. But the harsh reality was soon to come. The numbing pain had not yet arrived and King decided to make the most of this more productive preparation period. He walked along the beach, the shells and stones crunching under his heavy boots, the air slightly cool and the sky awash with streaked clouds.

All around the soldiers buzzed about like worker bees in a hive, wearing only the trousers of their strict black uniform and netted vests. The ominous presence of the three war vessels could be seen looming on the ocean in the distance.

King began to think about the unfair way that Raicema's military operations were run, with the leading officials always protected and secure whilst the minion masses were placed in the firing line. It somehow seemed ironic that no matter how many soldiers were killed in battle those at the top would always survive to plan yet another war.

Maybe if they took more of an active part, they wouldn't be so eager the plan more and more, King thought. Of course, the one exception to that was Seth Tyrone. He enjoyed taking an active role in warfare and was always enthusiastic about it. King had never understood this about Seth and had vague memories as a youth of looking up to him for his strength and leadership. He vividly remembered Seth being much more aggressive and bloodthirsty than his brother as a youth. That had driven him to fight, unlike Jeth who had preferred to stay behind the scenes.

War is just a game to him, King thought, instantly feeling hot under the collar at the idea of Raicema's president.

All along the beach, long motor boats were arriving, each carting a hundred soldiers and a mountain of supplies. Other wider boats carried only giant metal containers, filled with weapons and armour. The sight of Raicema's military might against the backdrop of this serene natural location gave King a flourish of chills that ran from the back of his head down to the base of his spine. He had a sudden feeling of dread deep in his gut that he desperately didn't want to be involved in the impending invasion. He was bewildered by this strong feeling as he had been in similar situations before without such sensitivity. For a moment he had seen something differently, as if the most beautiful thing in the world was about to be destroyed. He felt a sincere urge to protect whatever it was he just saw.

Once again, King was disturbed from his thoughts by the voice of the young soldier.

"Commander King," the boy said. "The troops are waiting, sir."

King welled with frustration.

"Let them wait!" he bellowed at the boy, causing him to topple over onto the shells and stones. Many soldiers stopped what they were doing, looking over in King's direction. Then they carried on with their orders. King bent over and offered his hand to the boy. He refused to take it and rose to his feet quickly, his face flushed with embarrassment. He saluted King vigorously and stood to attention, just staring into the air.

"Relax, soldier," King said more softly, breathing out a sigh. "There is no need to rush what is already a doomed objective."

The boy was surprised at King's comment and released the tension in his shoulders.

"Why are you here?" King asked the boy. "Are you that eager to die?"

"I am here to protect my nation, sir," the boy said, reciting the line as if he were a robot.

"Protect it from what? Nobody is attacking Raicema."

The boy's eyes wavered as he tried to think of an answer. "I..." he began, stuttering a little. "...I came here because my family needs money. The army pays more than working in a factory up north so I thought I'd enrol. They said coming to Lizrab would be a good training opportunity for me."

King shook his head with pity for the boy.

"They are paying for your life," he said, placing his large hand on the boy's narrow shoulder. "You shouldn't have come here."

The boy began to look upset, as if he was fighting back tears by swallowing repeatedly.

King smiled weakly at him. "Okay, soldier. Show me where the battalion are camped."

The boy led King along the beach towards an opening into the jungle, a thousand boot footprints shaping a path. Luminous green floss silk trees lined the path, their bottle-shaped trunks wide in girth and studded with large prickles. Some of the trees had pink-tipped cream flowers growing on their horizontal leaflets. King noticed large butterflies feeding from these flowers which led him to observe that the trees had camouflaged green pods. He wondered what was inside.

After a short trek, the boy pointed out a circle of tents that had been hidden in branches and large olive-coloured leaves. There were ten men standing to attention and another two were busy trying to get a fire started. When they saw King approaching, they all quickly stood to attention and the group saluted him in unison.

"Stand at ease, boys," he said to them. "I may have been placed in charge of you all but as far as I'm concerned, it's every man for himself once the fighting begins."

Some of the men looked uncomfortable at King's words. Then they dispersed and went about their duties including securing a perimeter with complicated laser equipment, digging a pit to store explosives in and unpacking some supplies for that evening's meal. A crackle came through in King's helmet that was resting loosely between his shoulder blades. He pulled it onto his head and heard Seth's voice.

"King, pay attention. You will have a difficult mission that will begin tonight. In a northwesterly direction from your current position, we have estimated that there is a large stronghold, possibly containing up to two hundred of the enemy. Your mission is to infiltrate this group and determine the location of Kirichi. Most of the troops have been deployed to Aradonas where there is a large resistance. I will focus my efforts on capturing Aradonas until you report back."

There was another crackle and then silence, leaving a heavy emptiness in King's stomach. He felt the overpowering urge to run far away. After a moment of blankness, he decided to forget about the mission by helping some of the others set up the camp perimeter.

A few hours passed and the men were ready to eat, a large pot of stew hanging over the open fire they had built. It was getting dark and the blue lasers surrounding them reminded everyone of home. One of the men had a small computerised device on his lap as he began to eat.

"The ground is secure," he said whilst looking at the screen that gave him information on movement in proximity.

King suddenly began to feel quite nauseous and a wave of anxiety passed through him as he remembered the mission and that he would have to tell the men that they would not be having a peaceful night. The anxiety was quickly quashed, however, when one of the men said something very strange.

"What is that glimmer of light over there in the trees?"

Unexpectedly, a swishing sound was heard followed by a loud groan and one of the men who was standing slumped forward, revealing a knife lodged in his back. The next thing everyone knew, there were scores of men emerging, jumping down from the trees in the surrounding jungle, dressed in dark attire and carrying a multitude of sharp instruments.

"Quick!" one of the soldiers shouted. "Open fire!"

Several of the men grabbed guns and began shooting in the direction of the hard-to-see assassins. The gunfire created bright flashes in the foliage and loud sirens began to sound from the laser equipment around them. Shouting could be heard far and wide and then the sound of heavy gunfire and explosions emanated from the beach where they had landed.

"They're attacking the entire beach!" another of the soldiers said in fear as the screams of the warriors charging towards them pierced their ears. A long-haired warrior ran towards the young soldier that had led King to the camp. The boy was frozen with terror, his gun loosely by his side. King jumped out and tackled the man to the floor, followed swiftly by a sharp blow to his head which caused the man to crumple into a heap. The young boy was trembling and King grabbed him by his sleeve.

"Come on! We have to get out of here."

They ran quickly, going deep into the jungle away from the beach. The sound of screaming and more explosions could be heard, intermixed with the sirens of Raiceman equipment.

It has begun, King thought, running even faster, though he could hardly see where he was going in the limited light of dusk. He looked back and saw that the boy had fallen behind, breathing heavily and hobbling. King ran back and began to drag him to which the boy began to whine and lose his balance.

"You must move if you want to live! Trust me, there are many of them and they know this land better than anyone."

The words seemed to spur the boy on and he managed to keep up. Before long they were totally lost, masses of thick foliage surrounding them and the only light coming from the small electric torches on their helmets.

A sharp sound swished through the air and then King felt a prickly pain in his shoulder. He looked down to see a small blade lodged in the shoulder pad of his uniform. He reacted quickly, pulling the young boy to the jungle floor and switching off their helmet lights. He shoved him and they crawled amongst the thick shrubbery to the trunk of a tree. King ripped his sleeve off and saw the knife had gone halfway into his shoulder muscle. He pulled the knife out and the boy winced at the sight of blood flowing down his arm. They heard footsteps approaching. The young soldier began to withdraw his pistol but King quickly grabbed it from him, seeing tears in the boy's eyes.

"Wait!" he whispered.

Whoever was close by seemed to be listening carefully and after several moments they heard two men speaking quietly. King held his hand over the young boy's mouth as he had begun to breathe heavily. After a few moments, they heard the men heading off in a different direction.

They heard a loud explosion in the distance followed by a chorus of screams. The speckles of sky that could be seen through the trees glowed orange. More gunfire, but then the terrible sounds seemed to fade away.

"We should climb this tree," King suggested. "It is not safe on the ground."

They could no longer hear the sound of shouting or gunfire, the melody of millions of insects the only sound audible. King looked up at the broad trunk and thick branches and urged the boy to climb up.

"Quickly!"

They came to rest on a giant knot halfway up the trunk, five huge branches protruding and crossing over each other forming a strong platform.

"We must wait here until morning," King instructed, completely disregarding Seth's earlier orders. The boy said nothing, just shaking whilst deep in thought and shock. King began to feel surges of guilt for leaving the others behind and pondered his new urge for desertion. He had never felt this way before. He had always stood by those who were his comrades, but now he could think of nothing but escape from the violence. For the first time in his life, he wished with all his willpower that he would awake in the morning unharmed.

Chapter 17 – The Watching of the Wings

The blue abyss of the ocean held secret upon secret. Beneath the surface, an intricate alliance existed beyond any city or nation, species after species connected in essential and elaborate ways. Large red snappers cut gracefully through the dense water, looking out for smaller fish to sustain them. One exception to their diet however, was a very small fish. The fluorescent green and pink cleaner-wrasse mischievously darted in and out of the snapper's mouth like a playful child. The snapper's made no attempt to eat the wrasse for it provided them with the great service of teeth cleaning. In return, the snapper provided predator protection for the tiny cleaners.

Rekesh was watching and he often observed the actions of sea dwellers when he ventured below fishing. He had learnt over the years that by following the unwritten laws of the sea, it would adopt you into its watery web and provide you with what was needed. The first time Rekesh went underwater fishing when he was a child, he had not learnt to follow these laws and thus never caught any fish. It had taken quite a while for him to learn to glide like he himself had fins. Then the fish came to him. Swimming besides him were three snapper that he had caught in a net.

One more, he thought, gliding towards a small school with subtle movements of his feet. He untied the net and swiftly captured one more fish in it. Then he rose quickly to the surface, taking in a large gasp of air as the water sprayed up.

Not far away, Elera and Teltu were steering the small ship that had made the journey from Bimini along the eastern coastline of Lizrab to their eventual destination in the south. Somehow they had managed to completely avoid any military vessels on their voyage, something that Rekesh was very grateful for. He swam quickly to catch up with the ship and pulled himself and his catch up onto the deck with the aid of a thick rope that dangled over the side.

"Mmm, snapper," Teltu said, eyeing the four large red fish.

"Are you hungry already?" Elera asked mockingly, knowing full well that Teltu had eaten several bowls of oatmeal just a few hours earlier.

"I'm always hungry!" Teltu declared, laughing. "It's the sea air!"

Rekesh placed the fish in a wide bucket of seawater for the meanwhile.

"I have heard that in Raicema you can buy meat and fish that never lived, meat that is grown. Is this true?" Teltu asked, directing his question at Rekesh and Elera who had both lived in Raicema.

"Yes, it's true," Elera said, somewhat dishearteningly. "There are farms where blocks of meat are grown in giant containers. I once visited one. It isn't pretty. Also they add all sorts of chemicals to it."

"So that's why it tastes so nice?" Rekesh said jokingly, having eaten quite a bit of the readily available meat whilst he had lived in Raicema.

"Well I've never tried any but from what I know, the chemicals that are added are meant to be addictive to keep people eating it. Also you'd think that because they grow it that means that no animals are killed. That's not the case. Millions are slaughtered every year after being experimented on with the chemicals they use."

Rekesh was silent, unaware of the reality of the meat farms.

Javu, who had been below decks in the small hold where the group had been sleeping, appeared and began to smell the air.

"We are close!" he said, excitedly. It was approaching midday and the sun was sweltering. The sea breeze gave a reprieve from the pounding heat. In the distance a faint outline of land could be seen.

"How long has it been since you last came to Lizrab, Javu?" Elera asked him, knowing of his fondness for the land.

"Oh, not too long," he said. "Maybe five years."

"You have travelled a lot. I hope that when I get to your age I've been to half the places that you have," Teltu stated ineptly.

"I am sure when you are my age you will have seen many great places," Javu said jovially. "You are about to see one very shortly."

"How will we get to Kirichi?" Elera asked. "It could be dangerous to travel from Realiss inland."

"I want to remind you all of what is around us," Javu said avidly. "The four basic things that enable all things to flourish and travel; the land around us, the water we are floating on, the air that we are breathing and the fire that is keeping us warm."

He gestured towards the bright, yellow sun.

"What does all this have to do with getting to Turo?" Rekesh asked impatiently.

"I will tell you, Rekesh!" Javu said wildly and with a hint of derision. "The way the elements interact with each other can be very valuable on our journey. You will *see!*"

Everybody was quite confused by Javu's ramblings, his archaic way of speaking often creating more questions than answering them.

"Teltu, head towards that tall cliff edge over there," he said, pointing towards a line of cliffs behind them that all varied in height along the shore.

After turning the small ship around, with Sita and Rama still asleep below decks, they headed south, staying close to the shore and trying to shelter from the blazing sun.

"Look out for a small forest, with large yellow fruit growing. When you see that, stop sailing."

Javu walked over to where Elera was standing, gazing out over the deck towards the passing shore. She had a look of nostalgia on her face, combined with an expression of sadness.

"Everything will be fine," Javu reassured her, sensing her fear of imminent war.

Before long, the ship had arrived at the base of the tall cliff Javu had pointed out. There was a tight crack down the centre of the face, just wide enough for the ship to navigate through. The ship creaked noisily as if the timbers were being stretched after decades of stillness.

"That's it. Go down there."

Teltu breathed in sharply, only to feel the hot air scorching the inside of his nostrils. The rocky shoreline threatened the bobbing ship with every wave that made contact with it as it slowly passed through the narrow gorge, a winding river ahead. Beyond were small patches of land, one of which hosted an enclosed collection of bushy trees.

"Is this it?" Teltu asked, looking out across the small forest and spotting yellow fruits.

"Looks like it," Rekesh said, unsure himself. The ship had stopped creaking now upon the calmer waters of the river.

"This is it!" Javu declared with eagerness. "I need to get to that forest. Teltu, pull in as close as you can."

Teltu navigated the ship with great skill to the bank of the thicket, allowing Javu to climb down its crude wooden ladder to the forest. He quickly ventured towards a spot that he seemed very familiar with and the group soon noticed that it was a dug out pit, quite shallow with trees all around. After gathering a few pieces of dry wood, he quickly lit a fire in the pit, adding more and more dead wood to it until it was blazing fiercely.

Then he ran back over to the river.

"Throw me down a container," he shouted up.

Elera threw him down a small bucket. He promptly filled it with water and walked back over to the pit which was now heavily smouldering.

"This pit has a small moat around its edge," he shouted, filling it with water from the bucket.

Everyone watched peacefully as steam began to rise out of the pit. Then, they heard a rumbling and the entire pit began to sink into the ground. By this time Javu was already standing at its edge. The pit continued to sink deep into the earth until a thud was heard and then the sound of gushing water.

"This deep well is now filling up with water that is connected to the canal you are floating on," Javu informed everyone. "It will take a while to fill up."

As the water continued to gush into the newly formed well, they all noticed the water level of the canal was lowering. After a while, it was drained entirely, the ship now not visible from ground level on which Javu was still standing. He walked over to the edge of the canal. The ship was floating on a much narrower channel, only slightly wider than the ship itself and entrenched in the bottom of the larger canal. The water in the sea beyond the cliff face was kept out by a solid wall that had risen up, built out of irregular-shaped blocks that seemed to be completely airtight. At the bottom of the new canyon, the narrow channel of water ran along it for some way before turning into a cave that was now clearly visible.

"I can't believe it!" Teltu was shouting up from the ship's deck, causing quite a substantial echo. "How are you going to get down here?"

"There is a stone staircase over there," Javu said loudly, pointing to a newly uncovered set of steps near to the dam wall. He walked over slowly and proceeded down to the bottom of the canyon, counting exactly one hundred and ninety-three steps until his feet touched the silty stones, some of which had slimy algae spread all over it. He walked over to where the ship was floating and climbed the ladder to the deck.

"Have you done this before?" Elera asked Javu as he clambered over the starboard barrier.

"Kirichi and I once took this route," he explained to Elera. "Quite magnificent, how the elements have been used to create such sophisticated technology."

"How did that well fill up with all the water from this canal?" Teltu asked with bewilderment, scratching his head. "I didn't even know it was man-made. I thought it was a river."

"That well has two circular stone rings around the pit that are tightly bound to it. The fire and steam causes the outer ring to separate, allowing the inner ring and pit to sink down the well shaft and the water to fill it from here. The really amazing thing is what will happen later when we are gone."

"What?" Teltu asked enthusiastically, whilst the others listened eagerly as well.

"I will tell you once we set off. We do not have very much time. Navigate down this channel and into that cave."

Teltu started up the engine of the small ship again and it began to move slowly along, sometimes banging into the sides of the channel.

"Careful!" Rekesh warned him as they made the turn into the mysterious cave, where the channel continued along past many shiny rock formations. The cave was narrow and looked naturally formed. Rekesh held his breath as the ship just avoided several jagged rocks protruding from the walls of the cave. Before long, however, another opening could be seen and the ship soon came out to a similar canyon-like canal with the channel embedded in its centre.

"Ah, we are safe now," Javu said with a hint of relief. "We just wait here now."

Teltu raised his eyebrows, trying to remind Javu of his promise to unveil the workings of this unusual tunnel.

"Oh, yes, well now the water will come back and fill up the cave and the canyons. We will be raised up and the river ahead leads directly to Turo."

"But how will it fill up again?"

"After a while, the inner ring separates from the pit because of the pressure of the deep water in the well. When this happens, both pieces float up slowly and allow the water to escape back into the canal. Later the two rings and the pit join back together because of a combination of the cold water and air. Then it will be ready to use again. The well and pit are made of a special stone that expands and contracts with heat and pressure. So you see, the elements can be used to great effect."

Teltu was impressed, but Rekesh seemed much less enthused, his years of living in Raicema City numbing his interest about technology. The canal slowly filled up with water, causing the ship to cascade from side to side. Elera noticed another dam wall ahead that sank down in harmony with the speed of the water pouring in. Soon, the ship was floating along what now looked like a perfectly natural river, at which point both Sita and Rama emerged from the deck below, surprised at their luscious surroundings.

"Lizrab...?" Rama asked Elera.

She nodded and asked Javu how long it would take before they reached Turo.

"Not long. It is only a sun from here," he replied.

The ship floated along the river peacefully for a while, past beautiful jungle trees with brightly coloured birds sitting in them. Sita observed several deer-like creatures living in the forest, along with lizards and scaly-skinned anteaters. Light poured onto the ship from the gap in the tree line above, yet looking deep into the jungle only revealed shadows.

"Did you hear that?" Rekesh said suddenly, his head turning quickly at a distant sound.

"What?" Teltu asked, trying to listen out.

"I heard gunfire and explosions."

The sound of heavy blasts got louder and louder as the ship advanced towards Turo. The river began to wind more, like a giant snake slipping through the grass.

"Most of the fighting will be in Aradonas, but we must be careful around Turo as well. The Raicemans will no doubt be attacking many locations at the same time."

After a few moments, the smell of burning could be caught every so often in the air. Everyone could sense the fighting was close by. Javu began to scan the river banks, looking for something.

"How far is Turo from Aradonas?" Teltu asked with concern as the whistle of a falling rocket was heard in the distance before the imminent bang that sounded like a short burst of thunder.

"They are several suns apart."

"What can we do when we get there?"

"We can help the people stay calm. Things will get much more dangerous if fear takes its grip on everyone? Indeed, we must encourage just the opposite."

"And what is that?"

"To embrace what has been given to us, even in such a traumatic time as this."

Teltu was slightly mystified by Javu's words, though they did fill him with an inner confidence to boldly progress. The danger seemed to intensify the beauty of the forests that surrounded him.

"Over there!" Javu said, spotting a small creek running off the river. "We must go down there."

"The ship will never make it," Teltu declared.

"We do not need to go far down it, just enough to reach a mere where we can leave the ship out of sight."

Teltu steered the ship carefully down the slim waterway, Rama and Rekesh having to disembark and push from the banks every now and then. A short way down, a concealed mere could be seen with several smaller boats moored on its banks.

"This is it! Turo is not far from here."

After anchoring the ship near one of the mere's banks, everyone gathered their belongings and headed into the nearby jungle, led by Javu. Elera seemed somewhat disoriented at first having only travelled to Turo over land before, but when she noticed a series of clearings leading to one of the town's great walls, she quickly gained her bearings.

"We are near the monastery," she told Rekesh as they approached a large log gate. "I can't believe we have never been here together. This place is like a home to me. It's a shame that we had to come here whilst Lizrab is under attack. It is usually a very peaceful place."

Rekesh nodded, himself feeling saddened that most of Lizrab was now a war zone. The gate opened slowly after Javu explained who he was to the guards on the other side. Everyone plodded along a footpath past some fields and several endearing dwellings with thatched roofs and stunning plants growing all around them. The fields dipped into a shallow valley and at the bottom, the monastery could be seen beyond the main part of the town.

"It seems very quiet," Elera mentioned, used to seeing the fields full of people tending to the crops and land.

As they got closer to the monastery a few monks appeared. One in particular looked quite distressed, yet a pleased expression appeared upon his round face when he spotted Javu.

"Hello, my friend," he greeted Javu warmly. "You have arrived at a difficult time I'm afraid. We have just heard that Aradonas is under heavy attack and many of our people have been killed during the fighting. There are many here who are afraid for the town."

Looking around, only a few small children could be seen playing in the fields.

"It seems as though they have brought every soldier possible from Raicema. There has never been an invasion this big. We have heard that there has been the biggest battle in the history of Lizrab on the red plains in Calegra. They attacked there first to stop people coming down here to help defend Aradonas. Almost every person has left Turo to help in Aradonas, even many monks and women have gone and put themselves in great danger to help defend the city."

There was silence for many moments as the gravity of the situation sank upon everyone's shoulders. Elera realised that the nature of the warrior had presented itself in everyone in this time of intrusion.

"I will go to Aradonas now!" Rekesh declared fierily. "We must do everything we can to stop the Raicemans from taking over."

Elera felt an incredible urge to protest at Rekesh's rapid statement, but the profound sense of determination in his voice somehow prevented her from speaking. Rama placed his hand on Rekesh's shoulder and pledged his allegiance to him in Hindi.

"Where is Kirichi?" Javu intervened, also feeling the instinctive need to protect. "We are here to help but first I wish to speak with him. Is he here?"

"He went with his grandson to the retreat," the other monk said. "It will be harder for the Raicemans to find him there. It is better for the people here to know that he is safe."

"Let us not waste any time," Rekesh said authoritatively. "Rama and I will join the warriors in Aradonas. Teltu, you take Elera, Javu and Sita to where Kirichi is."

"I don't know where I'm going," Teltu protested, a little shaken by the fast pace of decision-making.

"I'm sure Javu and Elera know the way."

There was silence for a few moments whilst they digested the plan.

"Rekesh," Elera began, feeling a little emotional. "Promise me that you will run if you are in danger. Sometimes battles are not meant to be fought."

"I promise," he tried to reassure with affection. "I hate to be separated from you again but I really think I can help."

"Come back to Turo as soon as you can. I have a feeling that this town will not be touched by the Raicemans."

Rekesh nodded and he and Rama were led by one of the monks to gather some supplies before they set off with some of the other Makai warriors.

"Let us, too, gather a few things and then we will head to the retreat," Javu said. "There is something that we may be able to do to help Aradonas but it will take the greatest of strength of all of us and we will need Kirichi's help."

Once again, the mystery of Javu's words left everyone baffled, yet there was no time to ponder because the constant sounds of explosions in the distance continued to interrupt their thoughts. Sita began filling up some of the leather flasks with water from a nearby well, whilst Teltu was given a sack full of fruits and bread by another of the monks. Elera and Rekesh faced each other, as did Sita and Rama. Both couples embraced, though it was Elera this time that did not want to let Rekesh go. He pulled away slowly. Sita and Rama held each other's faces with love in their eyes. Then, without Rekesh and Rama, Elera and Sita set off along the same path that they had recently arrived by, Javu and Teltu plodding behind.

Rekesh and Rama were led to a large armoury filled with gibans, spears and thick leather suits. They were given one of each by two stern-looking men, clearly distressed by recent events. The two men spoke Lizrabian, which neither Rekesh nor Rama could understand. Rekesh also had some difficulty communicating with Rama as he was by no means fluent in Hindi, only remembering a small subset of the language from his childhood in Vassini. Rama, however, would speak to Rekesh as if he could understand every single word.

They quickly set off through the town in a perpendicular direction to Elera and the others. They walked across a large open field where stood several bird-shaped gliders, the wings made out of stretched hide and strong flexible branches. The field was particular windy, being at the base of a steeper valley. The two Turian men began to fiddle with the base of the gliders, elevating them up onto a small rocking base. They gestured for Rekesh and Rama to each sit on the back of one of the gliders and the two men began to rock the gliders back and forth with their feet, in time with the sweeping wind that travelled down the valley. After a while of this, the gliders began to rise up and down as the air lifted the wings from beneath, and suddenly the gliders shot along the valley with a force that Rekesh was not expecting. They swept along with the wind like a leaf. Rekesh held on tightly to the man sitting in front of him, the view of the entirety of Turo coming in sight.

The town was surrounded by large walls made of inventive combinations of tall trees and great logs. To the south of the town was a steep cliff and the sea stretching into the distance beyond. The gliders quickly soared over thick jungle, and from the sky Rekesh could see certain parts of it smoking as explosions on the ground caused fire to pour into the atmosphere. In the far distance, he could see the vast city of Aradonas along the coastline and out to sea, several monstrous vessels all spawning hundreds of smaller boats heading towards the coast. The giant war vessels were repeatedly firing missiles directly into the city and from Rekesh's perspective, the vessels looked like great whales made out of shimmering grey metal.

The city was smouldering in some of its outer parts. Rekesh realised how far these vessels could shoot. As that thought entered his mind, he saw with horror a great silvery object flying in the sky at a much-too-familiar trajectory.

It's heading straight towards us! he thought with panic.

The object flew just over head. It was a metal sphere and in a surreal moment, time seemed to stand still. Then Rekesh saw a spark of blinding light followed by a dark and purple swell of electricity. Then there was an intense and loud crack followed by a powerful explosion. The glider flew backwards like a delicate moth from the force. The next thing Rekesh felt was a heavy blow to his back and head as the glider hit a tree and then fell to the floor, dragging Rekesh through the tree branches and to the floor whilst his companion was thrown further away. Rekesh felt the wing of the glider break as he landed heavily with a thud on top of it. He winced at a pain in his side, caused by a long and deep graze from his fall through the trees. He was relieved to discover that he could move his arms and legs without any pain. Nothing was broken.

He heard shouting not far away. Raiceman soldiers were coming to finish off their wounded prey. He got to his feet with a little dizziness, the floor feeling like it was swaying beneath him. He headed towards bushy undergrowth where several small trees were amalgamated into an enclosure.

Hearing gunshots in the near distance, he crawled under the bushy dwelling, finding a den lined with old fur inside. In the darkness of the shelter, he could see the soldiers appear though gaps in the closely entangled branches, but after quickly scanning the area, they swiftly moved on. Rekesh heard them mention that troops would be following them to invade Turo. He began to pray that Elera and everyone would be safe travelling in such a dangerous environment. Looking around, he noticed the abode was very clean, moving his thoughts to what sort of animal lived there.

His wondering was given clarity fairly swiftly, for as he was about to crawl back out of the enclosure, he was prevented from doing so by the appearance of the dwelling's inhabitant, a spotted jaguar. It was sturdy of build and majestic in its presence. Its fur look slightly wet as if it had just been swimming. It walked calmly around Rekesh, who rocked back down to the earth and hugged his knees, sniffing him and now and again showing its frighteningly sharp teeth. Though it was dark within the undergrowth, the jaguar's wide yellow eyes and patterned fur were vivid and piercing.

Rekesh dared not move, aware that a cat of this size could kill him with one bite to the head and that he was sitting in the middle of its home. The cat circled him for many moments, seemingly getting more aggravated by the second. Rekesh began to feel very faint and the habitat quickly became surreal, the sound of the jaguar's rough purring interspersed with the odd growl sending mixed signals about its mood. He felt like they were almost having a strange conversation, until the growling became much louder and aggressive.

Rekesh contemplated his next move, unsure if the jaguar would allow him to crawl out of the shelter. He also remembered that his giban was in easy reach to his side. He was sure that he could quickly draw it and strike a fatal blow before the hefty cat could attack. Though both of these options seemed like Rekesh's greatest chance of survival, he felt compelled to succumb to sitting in the exact position he was in, as if a heavy weight were stopping him move any part of his body.

He shifted his eyes and saw the jaguar was ready to pounce, yet for a reason he could not explain, he did not feel panicked. He closed his eyes and prayed that the huge cat would realise he was not a threat, though he heard repeated hostile growls. He then heard a swift movement, like an arrow shooting through the air and he was sure this was it; he braced himself for death.

For the most majestic of moments, Rekesh felt the blood in his body travel to every cell, the tension he had held dispersing into a warm happiness, but instead of the feeling of sharp teeth piercing his skin, his face was kissed by a tickling sensation, which must have been the cat's whiskers brushing past his face.

He opened his eyes to see the great creature lying comfortably on the floor. The sight almost caused him to burst out laughing, but deep confusion quickly took over the joy of the spectacle, his mouth dropping wide open in astonishment. The black irregular-shaped spots tickled the jaguar's gold fur and the entire scene looked unreal. He blinked several times, sure he was hallucinating from the fall, that he'd imagined the jaguar. He slowly looked around the den and it did not seem to bother the creature. Rekesh then had an overwhelming urge to get out of the dwelling.

After crawling out with his eyes averted from the jaguar's, Rekesh looked around to see if there was anyone lurking in the density of the woodland. He saw no one, yet in the distance, he heard footsteps, slow and heavy. He decided to hide behind a thick tree and see who was coming. Through the trees, he could see the silhouette of a man of heavy build, walking in a slow and fevered manner. As the man got closer, Rekesh could see that he was wearing a white cotton vest and part of a Raiceman uniform. He wore black trousers, boots and a shoulder strap. The man's short black hair and wide jaw structure gave Rekesh a pang of recognition, and he noticed that his bronze skin was pulsing with drops of humidity. He was sure he knew this man.

"Hey!" Rekesh shouted at him, exposing himself from behind the tree. The man looked over instantly with both a startled and hostile look. He began to walk in Rekesh's direction and a rush of adrenaline caused Rekesh to feel a little anxious. As the man got closer, he drew his giban instinctively and took a defensive stance.

For some reason, the appearance of the brawny man caused surges of anger to throb around Rekesh's body, making him grip the giban so tightly his knuckles turned white. Rekesh realised where he had seen the man before.

In Raicema, news flashes were constantly used to spread propaganda to the inhabitants of its two great cities. One of these news flashes had been to commemorate the achievements of the military in other nations, including successful invasions and occupations. The man that now stood before Rekesh in the humid jungle was one of the men given accolade for being an exceptional ground fighter and leader, enabling many strongholds to be defeated.

Rekesh now knew why his anger was quickly turning to rage in his body, knowing this man had probably killed countless people.

"What are you doing here?" Rekesh asked him aggressively.

Jen King, who was looking carefully at Rekesh threateningly holding his short sword as if ready to strike, had a feeling of apprehension within.

"I came here with the Raiceman forces," King declared honestly.

"Yeah, to kill everyone!" Rekesh barked in anger.

"I don't want to kill anyone," King protested.

"I don't believe you!" Rekesh fired back. "I know who you are. You are famous in Raicema for killing people!"

King felt a guilty pang of remorse at the statement, knowing it was all too true.

"What has it got to do with you anyway?" King said in a defensive manner. "I was just passing through here. Move aside and let me pass."

"No!" Rekesh griped. "I will not allow you to murder any more innocent people. Leave Lizrab now or this will be the last place you will ever lay your eyes upon."

King did not take kindly to the threat, feeling a rage welling inside of him, pulsing with a poisoned seed. He took a step towards Rekesh, intending to push his way past but was shocked when Rekesh swiftly and accurately swung his short sword towards his face, drawing blood with a shallow cut to the cheek.

"The next one will be fatal."

The next thing King felt was an explosion of wrath in his belly and chest. He wrapped his large hand around Rekesh's neck with a swift movement and lifted him up against the tree he was stood against. Rekesh felt air beneath his feet as he was hoisted up with force. The pressure of the choke caused Rekesh to drop his giban and he placed both of his hands on King's sweaty, muscular forearm. He struggled to get free, his face turning a pale shade of blue from the pressure and seeing nothing but a void in King's eyes. He felt an intense regret at attacking the man and was sure he was going to pass out any moment. As he began to fade, an adrenalin rush of urgency shot through him.

Somehow, he managed to lift his knee and force it into King's ribs, causing him to wince and drop Rekesh to the floor. After quickly catching his breath, he scrambled quickly for his giban and rose to his feet only to see King's large fist hurling towards his face. He dodged it just in time and spun around clockwise, allowing his giban to fan out, just catching King across the midriff. Blood trickled out of a light gash and King fell backwards. He quickly got to his feet and then something unexplainable happened.

Rekesh suddenly could not move. He felt as though he were frozen by a cold fear of something. A flash of something horrible entered his mind, something unearthly. He could see the overwhelming power swelling through King's body and could do nothing but allow him to deliver a colossal blow to the head. Rekesh crumpled to the floor, instantly unconscious.

King's rage subsided unusually quickly and was replaced by regret. He decided to flee, shaken and anxious about the conflict that had just occurred.

In the distance he heard explosions and he swiftly walked in the opposite direction to the invasive sounds. The jungle grew denser and he found himself in a clearing with the trees overhead all culminating into a giant roof of green leaves. He heard something move to his right and he met the fiery gaze of the jaguar that lived there.

It arched its back and its black spots seemed to move around over its golden fur in a dreamlike moment. It locked its shoulders, ready to pounce, but King stood deathly still.

It growled loudly at him and King felt his heart rate increase rapidly. His temples were throbbing and the heat seemed to be unbearable. He looked into the big cat's eyes and it growled again, showing its enormous and powerful-looking two front fangs. It had large, distinctive yellow eyes that faded to light green towards the pupils.

King took a small step and the jaguar roared primordially causing his stomach to flip. Panic shot around his body. The cat began to creep forwards towards him and King's mind went blank, completely at the mercy of the dominant creature, unwilling and unable to fight it.

Then, just behind the muscular animal, King saw a shadow move, the shadow of a human. Expecting to see a soldier or Makai warrior any second, King was taken aback when a flock of birds suddenly flew out of a nearby tree and for a split second he thought he saw a woman walking very slowly in the distance.

The jaguar took another look at the worn-down soldier in front of him and it lowered its growling top lip, covering its deadly teeth. Then after one last glance it promptly fled, running into the jungle at an incredible speed.

After a few moments, King headed towards the area where he thought he'd seen the woman, but there was nobody there. Then he heard a whisper.

"Keep moving."

He turned around in a daze but there was nobody around. He got an innate feeling to press on into the jungle away from the fighting.

Before long he'd been walking for hours and the twilight seemed to fill the forest with a presence that King couldn't quite comprehend. It was the first time in his life that not even a single thought entered his mind. He felt like an empty shell but it felt good, as if all the bad things in his life were draining out of him with every footstep.

Looking into the undergrowth ahead, King was lost and disoriented. However, he also felt like a six-tonne boulder was being gradually lifted from his back with every step that he took. He had an inner determination to find a new life, to feel inspired instead of disheartened.

Ahead, there was a small creek and he followed it along for a while before coming to an area where the trees grew tall and closely together, with barely a human's width of space between them. He squeezed through a gap between two wide trunks, scraping his back and arms on the tough bark. Then he heard something above, a fluttering sound. He looked up and saw a shadow move out of sight. He looked around but saw nothing.

A shot of anxiety struck his heart and he began to move more quickly through the closely interwoven trees, scraping his arms and shoulders more severely. Speckles of blood formed on his scrapes. The trees ahead looked like they were all sprouting from the same origin and before long he was walking only on the hard bark of thick roots. He heard the flutter again.

He looked up to see something flying above his head. It was so large that it shocked King to witness it. He couldn't make out anything distinct, only the silhouette of a huge creature with a wide wingspan. It was easily the same size as himself. It soared high before coming to rest somewhere high up in the trees.

Then he felt the most peculiar of sensations below his neck. It was as if a whole region of muscles in his upper back were pulsating uncontrollably.

Fear took over and he moved as quickly as he could through the labyrinth of tree trunks ahead, praying that whatever it was sitting up there would leave him alone. He heard the whisper again.

"Keep moving."

The trunks were getting closer and closer, like a hidden door gradually getting farther out of reach. After a while, he couldn't even fit an arm through the gaps between trunks. He suddenly felt quite afraid. There was no way out except to turn back.

King was about to turn around but then he noticed something above. There were small hollows in the trunks above him, which looked like they had been carved out across from each other at a considerable height. He gathered his strength and started to climb the tree.

It was wide but had thick bark that could be used for grips. He climbed halfway before he started to get a strange sensation in his belly, like a giant hand was coming out to grab the tree and propel him up. Somehow, he almost leaped up the tree in three quick movements to reach the edge of the unusually shaped enclave.

It was like half an egg, and Jen was surprised to see a large hole in the middle of the trunk. He turned around and the opposite tree had the same shape carved into it and it also had a hole in its trunk. Jen stood upright, which he could only just do, and stepped towards the hole. It was big enough to fit through and peering up and down the trunk only revealed darkness.

Then he heard the sound again. He glanced down the gap between the two trunks and saw something moving towards him. He saw its wings spread and glanced at its face, the face of something almost human.

Raw primordial fear shot around his body like he'd been injected with a hundred needles and he quickly dived into the hole in the trunk. As he fell vertically, his mind swirled around and around, with nothing but darkness surrounding him.

Chapter 18 – The Protectors

Elera arrived at the retreat north of Turo, after walking a winding and confusing route through the tropical forestland. Javu was by her side and he felt excited at being reunited with Kirichi, a man who had imparted many valuable pieces of knowledge to him over the years.

Teltu and Sita, who were not far behind, drew their breath in awe as they walked through the gate of the wooden structure and into a beautifully kept natural garden. The sun was shining brightly on the wooden walls and walkways, causing the heavily varnished timber to glimmer.

"Ammi!" Elera shouted out as she spotted Kirichi sitting towards the back of the retreat, an affectionate Lizrabian word for *father*.

"Filia!" he replied with equal affection, the word for *daughter*.

She ran over to him and they embraced, the others following slowly behind.

"When did you arrive?" he asked, peering at the vibrant young woman standing before him.

"Not long ago," she said, looking around at the familiar environment. "I have so much to tell you."

A great smile formed on his face as he saw his old friend Javu walking slowly towards him with palms open.

"Javu, I am very happy to see you," he said, holding both of his arms in an endearing way.

"And I you."

They embraced for a while, saying nothing.

"How did you come to be here with Elera?" Kirichi asked him.

"It is a long story. I will let Elera tell you," Javu said, smiling calmly and turning to Teltu and Sita who were standing quietly behind him.

"Please meet Teltu, a good friend of mine from Seho," he said gesturing to the young fisherman. He beamed at Kirichi whilst shaking his hand.

"And this is Sita who is from Vassini."

Sita bowed her head gently in greeting Kirichi, who reached out for her hand and held it for a few moments. Sita felt her hand tingling whilst in the warm palm of the white-haired old leader.

"Are you here alone?" Elera asked Kirichi who was dressed in a loose yellow cotton robe.

"No, my grandson and his companion are here with me."

He gestured towards an area on the ground that had a series of logs arranged in a circle, a pleasant seating area in the attractive, flowered gardens of the retreat. Everyone took a seat on one of the logs. As Kirichi sat down, Elera began about to tell him about the past few months.

"A lot has happened, Ammi. I feel as though my life has changed so much. After I left here, it was like information was coming to me from every direction, like one thing would naturally lead me to the next."

"It is good," Kirichi declared. "You are speaking to the planet and it is speaking back."

"But I'm starting to experience things that I don't understand," she confessed. "Things that are making me feel afraid."

"Afraid of what?" Teltu asked in a caring manner.

"Of the unknown," Elera replied softly.

"It is normal," Kirichi said in a simple fashion.

Overhead, two brightly coloured birds danced around each other in the air, chirping with excitement.

"And what of your strong young man? When will I meet him?" Kirichi asked, more to himself than Elera.

"Rekesh is here in Lizrab," Elera told him, sensing that Kirichi already knew that. "But when he heard of the attack on Aradonas, he left to help defend it with some of the men from Turo."

Kirichi simply raised his eyebrows at this news, his indifference clouding his view on the matter.

"Well, it will be nice to meet him," Kirichi said spiritedly. "Javu has also mentioned Rekesh to me many times before. He has lived for many years in Raicema, yes?"

Elera nodded.

"And how has your time been in Raicema recently?"

"Good and bad," Elera told him. "There is a lot of interest in history and even though it can be difficult to find an accurate version of it, the people there have used a lot of technology to their advantage. There are computer systems that you can use to access lots of hidden records about the past that the government try to hide from people. Of course, the very same technology is used to enslave people."

"Are you talking about the reactors?" Teltu asked.

"That is just the beginning. People can't live without technology in Raicema. They can't eat or move without it. But as I said, people are using the systems to find out more information about what Raicema is doing to them. I used such a method to find out that Bimini has been guarded for years because it has always been deemed an area of immense energy. Not surprising seeing as though there is a giant pyramid close by."

"Why? What significance does that have?" Teltu asked, remembering Javu having mentioned something about the structure of pyramids.

"Pyramids are perfect structures to channel energy out of. Think about how all the sides gradually reach one point at the top. That is where the energy is the most concentrated."

"Well, this is all getting too scientific for me," Kirichi joked, laughing to himself.

"Don't you remember what Sula said?" she pressed Teltu. "She told us that Raicema are trying to take over lands that have some sort of energy that can be harnessed, like here in Lizrab. Well, I think the people who hold power over others have always known about the places where there is abundant energy. They just choose to keep it secret."

Kirichi just nodded, seemingly already aware whilst Teltu was in deep thought.

"So you entered the pyramid?" Kirichi asked, with interest.

"Well, yes and I sort of got trapped down there."

Kirichi let out a mighty laugh at this news, somewhat surprising both Elera and Teltu.

"Your inquisitive nature is most amusing," Kirichi chuckled. "You were the same when you were just a little girl, trying to go down rabbit holes and getting stuck. Bah ha ha...."

He leaned back in another fit of laughter. Elera also saw the funny side of her experience. Indeed, it was quite a haphazard act to venture into underwater ruins.

"Well, it was an eye-opening experience. I found out that the Lemurians may have built four original pyramids on the planet. The first is the Great Pyramid of Giza. The second is the underwater pyramid at Bimini and the third is somewhere in Cibola."

Elera paused for a moment as she recalled the unbelievable vision she had experienced under the depths of the ocean.

"In the centre of the pyramid was a room, empty except for a pair of metal hands holding this perfect crystal orb. When I touched it, I was transported to another world. It was beautiful, the plants and trees so uncultivated and natural. I saw this creature. It looked like a foal. Everyone was just staring at it, in love with it."

Her thoughts trailed off as she realised her story was quite incredible.

"I found a way out and made it back onto the island. Then I met Rekesh and everyone else some days later."

She smiled at her three companions with affection.

"The crystal orb I found seemed to hold a lot of knowledge about the island. It showed us an image of a statue and we set off to find it."

"The bearer of the jade mask!" Javu added jarringly, causing Kirichi's eyes to light up.

"That statue was eerie," Teltu commented. "It disappeared, right before my eyes!"

Kirichi leaned forward slightly, his interest greatly stirred.

"What did the statue show you?" he asked Elera specifically, who for some reason felt invaded by the question and did not reply.

After a few moments of silence, which confused everyone else, Kirichi retracted his question subtly. "Maybe nothing."

"Do you really think there is another pyramid in Cibola?" Teltu asked out loud.

"Most likely," Kirichi said with surety. "It is a greatly unexplored region, partly due to its landscape. It would take great perseverance to navigate through the mountains and jungles of Cibola, let alone build such a structure there. Having said that, it is well-known that many lost cities lie in that region, uninhabited for centuries. Many of my ancestors came from that region."

Elera seemed more enthused with each word Kirichi spoke.

"In fact, I have visited one such city in my lifetime, the *City of the Old Mountain*. There are still communities living there. Javu, do you remember when we once flew to the north? The old mountain was the tallest one far in the distance?"

"I remember," Javu said, recalling the long journey on the glider.

Rustling could be heard outside the retreat and Teltu immediately got to his feet defensively.

"Do not worry," Kirichi said to him, chuckling. "It is only Bene and Reo returning from their gatherings."

Sure enough, the large gate of the retreat swung open and the two men appeared, both wearing loose cotton slacks and their shirts tied around their waists. They were each carrying a large sack and both men looked lean and muscular, Reo's long black hair loosely draped over his back and shoulders.

"Hello," Bene said, surprised to see so many people with his grandfather. They both put their sacks on the ground and hastily put their shirts back on, clearly bashful of their raw appearance.

"They are very shy!" Kirichi said jovially, letting out a great laugh. Javu joined him. The two approached the group and introductions were made. Though Reo didn't recognise any of the visitors, Bene was sure that he had seen Javu before.

"Have I met you before?" he asked him.

"Only when you were this high!" Javu said laughing and holding his hand towards the floor. Kirichi laughed as well, the two feeding off each other like hearty brothers. "I spent a lot of time here in Lizrab with your grandfather when I was younger. I remember you and your father very well."

The mention of Juhi cast a dark cloud over Bene, who just nodded silently and managed a wry smile.

"You had a very close relationship," Javu commented kindly. "I see much of him in you."

The words seemed to perk Bene up a bit, his spiked short brown hair reflecting the sunlight like the spines on a hedgehog.

"Reo and I will make a fire. We have gathered a lot. Good thing, huh?" he said to his grandfather, who nodded with warmth.

Teltu got to his feet to help, eager to contribute. The three of them disappeared outside to gather firewood, leaving Javu talking to Sita about Vassini and the places that they had both visited there.

Kirichi suggested that Elera and he take a stroll together in the nearby jungle to have a chat. This surprised Elera as Kirichi was rarely secretive and enjoyed being open. She wondered what it was that he wanted to discuss in private.

They walked out of the retreat towards a spacious forested area, great buttress trees widely spread out, their roots protruding from the earth as they expanded. They both sat upon a sturdy buttress root.

"You saw the horse of water, didn't you?" Kirichi said to her quite directly, taking her aback.

"I...yes, I did," she said, surprisingly shaken and knowing exactly what Kirichi meant. However, she felt violated by the question, like her most intimate feelings were being revealed.

"It is not uncommon for you to feel defensive," Kirichi explained with reassurance. "Whilst what has happened to you is quite remarkable, it is also very absorbing. You must understand, Elera, that you will not be the same again."

She knew that it was true. She had felt different ever since her encounter, as if her body and mind had been enriched in some way.

"How do you know about the horse?" she asked him.

"I too have met the creature," he informed her. "It will only make itself known to you if it wants to give you something. What did you receive?"

"Nothing," Elera said quickly and protectively.

"Elera", Kirichi said softly. "I know how you feel. You have a well of love inside you for this planet. You are scared that if you make a wrong move, everything is going to crumble around you. But I can tell you now that no such fate will befall you. Life is much simpler than you think. What you have seen is no more special than the ground that we are standing on."

The words calmed Elera and she felt silly for a moment.

"I saw the past," Elera said after a while. "Well, at least I think I did. I saw some men performing some sort of magical ritual and then that great horse was imprisoned in a jade statue."

"Imprisoned?" Kirichi said in a strange manner, like he might burst out laughing at any moment. "*Aova* is not imprisoned. We are more imprisoned."

"But I saw these strange men!" Elera insisted, now confused at whether she had dreamed the entire affair.

"No doubt you did," Kirichi said more calmly. "What you saw is Aova trying to tell you something."

"Aova? Is that the horse's name?"

Kirichi nodded with a smile, almost as if Elera's question were absurd.

After contemplating her visions, she decided to tell Kirichi about them in more detail.

"It showed me how the jade mask was taken from the statue."

"It showed you?"

"Yes. The others said I disappeared."

"Then it *did* give you a gift," Kirichi declared. "It took you to its world and gave you a gift!"

"But I wasn't given anything," Elera protested, becoming irritated for some reason.

"You don't feel any different?"

"I do," she admitted. "But I don't know why."

"Let me tell you some things, Elera," Kirichi said, positioning himself on the root more comfortably. "I too have met the horse of water, yet very few people on this planet have. The reason for the innate caution you possess at discussing this creature is down to who you are and what you represent."

"What do you mean?"

"Both you and I have energy within us that has been born out of water. This is not the water that you drink, but an all-pervasive essence of water that exists everywhere. We have connected with it to the extent that a representation of the pure essence of water has contacted us."

Elera was astounded by what Kirichi was implying.

"Are you saying that the horse I encountered was some sort of elemental spirit form?"

"Sort of," Kirichi said, frowning due to his inability to describe the being. "The horse and the pool that it protects for that matter, represent water. It would be a mistake to simply call this manifestation a spirit and equally wrong to call it a deity. Instead, I refer to such manifestations as *protectors*."

"Manifestations? You mean there are others?"

"There are four *pure protectors* that I am aware of. You and I are extremely fortunate to have met the one that we did, which will probably be the only one we will ever meet."

"How did you meet Aova?" Elera asked.

"I met her whilst I was dreaming."

"Her?" Elera asked, not sensing any sort of gender when she had encountered the creature. "Aova is a she?"

"Yes. Water is intrinsically female, just as fire is essentially male."

"How could you meet her in a dream?" Elera asked, a bit daunted by Kirichi's explanations.

"Not in a dream. I met her whilst *dreaming* which is different. That is when one visits the *Dream World*."

"The Dream World?"

"It is the place where one can gain valuable knowledge, but also where many other worlds join together. It is like a meeting place for the different realms of existence."

Elera was finding it hard to believe that what Kirichi was saying could be a real possibility.

"Everyone ventures into the Dream World, but few remember their time there," Kirichi continued. "It has taken many years for me to remember my time in that world and one of the most vivid memories is my encounter with Aova. She likes to dwell there, observing the visitors rediscovering all those things they forget on a daily basis. To tell you the truth, I think it amuses her."

Kirichi chuckled at the thought and Elera felt like joining in, though so felt excluded from the sentiment.

"One night, I awoke on a strange beach, completely naked! The sand was so fine that it felt like powder between my toes. In front of me was the stillest of oceans with not a wave, not a sound coming from it. Then in the distance, walking towards me from across this vast ocean, I saw her. That time seemed like forever but eventually, she reached the sand where I was standing."

Kirichi paused, a glint in his eye.

"Aova likes to take the form of a horse because every horse has an essence of water flowing within it." He made a waving movement with his arm like the gentle flow of water in a river. "Unlike you, however, Aova did not show me anything. She only gave me her gift."

"What was it?" Elera asked.

"Just by looking into her eyes I received it. Just as she was able to walk to me over the water in that world, after that day I too could walk upon the water."

"It's not possible," Elera objected.

"Not only is it possible, but I realised I already knew how. Aova's gift to me was one of memory, a memory of long ago. She gave me the key to unlock the seemingly impossible within myself."

"Show me," Elera said excitedly, feeling like she had just been let in on the world's greatest secret.

"Be calm, Elera. I will demonstrate to you in good time. Before that, however, we should establish which gift Aova made to you."

"There are other gifts?"

"Yes. And the possibilities are endless."

"Ammi, I'm finding it very hard to believe all of this. Are you telling me this to teach me some philosophical lesson?"

"I know it is a lot to take in, Elera, but I tell you the truth, not my belief. So, tell me how you feel different since your met her."

"I remember feeling like I understood how water is driving me in my life, and since that I have felt a longing, but I don't feel physically different. I don't feel like I have any special abilities."

"Okay, let us go to a small river that runs near here," Kirichi said, getting to his feet. They began to walk in a northerly direction, past some mushroom stools and bushy shrubs.

Before long they reached the river Kirichi had spoken of. He immediately took off his woven sandals and placed them by the river bank, the water fairly deep, though shallow enough to see the pebbles at the bottom.

"I will show you."

He took a gentle step onto the water and where his sole connected with the running surface, a dip occurred, as if there were some invisible force underneath his foot. Then he moved his entire weight onto his foot and Elera held her mouth in wonder as Kirichi balanced there on the surface of the running water, not sinking in any way. He took a step with the other foot and another dip formed. He looked back and smiled at Elera with a good-humoured glance. Then he slowly walked to the other side of the river.

"Now you try," he said to Elera from the other side of the narrow river. "It is only a few steps."

Elera took off her tan leather boots and took a cautious step towards the river. She mimicked Kirichi, placing one foot on the surface of the river, its rapid movement wetting her foot with a tickling stroke. For a moment, she thought she felt something firm underneath her foot but as she put her entire weight onto it, she gasped as she plummeted down to the bottom of the river. As she emerged, soaking wet, Kirichi was in hysterics.

"Well, it seems she did not give you that gift!" he laughed with gusto.

She climbed out of the river to the side where Kirichi was standing, her clothes sticking to her slender body.

"You knew that I would fall in didn't you?" she accused Kirichi, irritated.

He just smiled in response, his signature glint of mischievousness shining brightly in his eyes. She sat down on a broken tree stump, sopping wet. He sat beside her, both of them looking ahead at the pool of water.

"It may take time for you to know," Kirichi said softly whilst examining the soles of his feet.

"So you are saying that the horse I met was a protector? A protector of what?"

"Of us!" Kirichi said dramatically. "Of everything. The universe!"

The statement hit a raw feeling and Elera felt something click inside her brain. She realised she too wanted to protect. She wanted to protect all those around her and everything she touched.

She stood up suddenly, realising that she felt different because she felt more complete, as if a bridge had been built between her body and mind, one that would allow magical things to happen.

"I feel powerful!" she declared, to which Kirichi let out a cheeky chuckle. He had to breathe deeply to compose himself.

"I don't mean to laugh at you, my dear, but it is so funny."

"What is?"

"Your enthusiasm. You are very young. Don't get me wrong, that's not a bad thing. It is indeed wonderful that you are exploring the boundaries of your body and mind. I am sure that meeting Aova has had a profound impact on you. What you will soon discover is that however amazing new knowledge is, it also brings with it a weight of responsibility. You question yourself, you question in what vein are your actions; selfish or compassionate? Vengeful or forgiving? Hateful or loving?

"But then you realise the startling fact. You can always change and you are testing yourself constantly. You are testing your knowledge, you are testing your progression. Before long you begin to ask yourself something. You ask why is it you put yourself through so many difficult challenges all the while knowing you don't need to do so, like a time loop unable to unwind.

"Then you come to the ultimate question. Who did this to me? Who put me in such an unbreakable cycle? Well it doesn't matter because you already know that you can change it!"

Kirichi burst out laughing, staring at Elera's bewildered face, eyes glazed over from the trail of thought just expounded to her. Kirichi was on the floor now, holding his belly and rolling around like a madman, almost convulsing with laughter.

Elera suddenly began to feel like she might be going crazy herself. She wondered if she had imagined recent events like it was a fairy-tale dream. But she couldn't accept it. The horse was so real, its eyes were so real. She could still smell the mustiness of the Bimini pyramid. She remembered the feeling of the water touching her face as she passed through the translucent wall of the capstone at the top.

The only thing she knew to be certain was that a different world had opened up before her, and it was one without boundaries.

Chapter 19 – The Battle of Aradonas

In a forest outside Aradonas, Rekesh was stirred into consciousness by the dappled sunlight shining through the web of leaves and branches high above. His head was throbbing and for a few moments he couldn't remember why he was lying of the jungle floor in such an exposed way.

As the scenes of his encounter with Jen King came back to him, he tried to sit upright but was immediately met with an intense dizziness. He fell back down, staring up at the trees and noticing the same jaguar-patterned butterflies flapping around above him. The sun's position had moved, indicating that several hours had passed by.

For several minutes, Rekesh thought about what he should do next. Aradonas could be destroyed by now, he thought, growing frustrated at the turn of events that had transpired. After toying with the idea of heading back to Turo, he decided that the best thing to do would be to head towards Aradonas. He would help to defend it, he thought, no matter how far along the invasion had come.

He breathed deeply for a while and then slowly got to his feet, surprised to see his giban lying untouched on the floor. He picked it up and headed southwards, in the direction he had been flying before he crashed. As he walked over dense fallen leaves and vines, he wondered what had happened to Rama, who couldn't have landed far away.

A strange blankness then took over his thoughts. The only explanation to which Rekesh could muster was that his fight with Jen King had caused some sort of concussion. He walked mindlessly for a while before noticing that the forested area was coming to an end, the steep drops of the Aradonas cliffs up ahead. He headed to the edge of the forest where a series of ledges stepped down to the beach area. As he looked out he could not believe the sight before him.

From the ledge on which he was crouched, he could see the full attempt that Raicema had mustered to take over Aradonas. There were several lines of boats formed in the ocean, each firing rockets from their decks into the city at different ranges. On the beach, thousands of Makai warriors were battling the Raiceman troops, using only hand weapons.

Every moment, gunshots could be heard as the soldiers fired upon their opponents. There were dead bodies lying everywhere from both sides. Fire could be seen rising from within the city, both buildings and trees ablaze wildly. At the border of the city itself, the fighting continued, a wall of fire lit by the Makai to keep the onslaught at bay. From what Rekesh could tell, there weren't any troops actually inside the city yet, a realisation that both astounded him and urged him to take action immediately. He got to his feet and began to run down the bank side, jumping over rocks and dodging the twisting trees that were hiding him from view. As he reached another ledge covered by a small bushy copse, he spotted one of the giant war vessels in the distance moving in a strange way.

The light from the sun was reflecting off something on top of the vessel. It was moving, something long and round. Rekesh quickly realised that it was a heavy cannon and he began to shout down at the beach to warn the warriors and tell them to run. In doing this, he caught the attention of several soldiers who began to open fire in his direction. One bullet would have hit him had he not slipped back whilst staring at the cannon looming in the distance.

The next thing he heard was a loud bang followed by a strange whistling sound. Then the trees of the copse shook violently from the force of the explosion that had landed on the beach. The sound was terrifying, like the roar of a colossal lion. When the trees stopped shaking, Rekesh got to his feet and the sight of the beach caused him to convulse with distress. There were dead bodies everywhere and those left standing had stopped fighting. The soldiers looked on in shock that their own vessels would be so careless with their lives. Every warrior was in despair at the level of fatal violence that surrounded them.

Rekesh quickly kept moving, down the bank until he reached the forested edge of the beach surrounding the base of the cliff. His mind was racing with the anticipation of combat, and sporadic flashbacks played through his thoughts. They were mainly of his time with Elera. He felt no fear, yet a concern had gripped him, a concern about death. He ran through the sandy forest, which was thick with palm trees and small ponds scattered about. About halfway through, he spotted a warrior lying on the floor, not moving.

He knelt next to him, a man with a thick brown beard and long matted hair. There was blood on his chest, the result of a gunshot wound. Rekesh could see his sternum rising and falling, his breathing rhythm was irregular and troublesome. He knew the man was close to death and the same concern gripped him. The man opened his eyes and glared at him, trying to open his mouth to say something.

"Friend, there is no honour in killing," the man whispered to Rekesh in the Lizrabian language. Then, he sunk into the earth with complete release from his pain.

Rekesh did not allow himself to dwell, continuing on through the beach forest. He now knew what he had to do. The thought that had been formulating in his mind since he had heard that Raicema was attacking had now taken root. *The only way to end this is to go to the top,* he thought. He would take one life to save many. The forest ahead was thinning and the mesmerising motion of the ocean could be seen in the distance.

The gunfire had resumed, ringing out piercingly all around. He knelt to the floor, trying to keep a low profile. Crawling along like a cat stalking its prey, he used every shrub and tree as a barrier, stopping and observing who was around him regularly. There were two men scuffling close by, a warrior and a soldier who had lost his gun. Rekesh almost lost himself watching them, struggling against each other as if they were doing the most bizarre of dances.

The soldier pinned the warrior to the floor and drew a knife. An instinctive loyalty pumped through Rekesh's body and he swiftly ran over to the soldier and hit him heavily across the head with the handle of his giban. He fell to the floor unconscious, leaving the warrior to quickly hurry to where his comrades were fighting in a large group.

Rekesh spotted a line of Raiceman boats wedged into the sand close by. He ran over to one and pushed it into the ocean, jumping in flat on his stomach so nobody could see him. He allowed the boat to float randomly for a while until he was quite a way from the shore.

Missiles flew through the air above towards Aradonas, sounding like screeching animals in the sky. When the sound of gunfire from the beach was faint, he started up the boat's engine and steered it towards one of the two giant war vessels. He kept his head down, though he felt safer being in the boat than on land as everyone's focus was towards the city. The vessel was quite a way out and as Rekesh got closer he noticed how desolate it seemed.

The war vessel's sheer size lost any sense of unity or coordination for those on board. The small boat he was steering seemed like an insect compared to a great pike. He switched off the engine and floated slowly towards the enormous metallic sternpost at the rear, where there was a ramp coming down from within. He slipped over the side of the boat and lowered himself into the water, diving under and swimming towards the ramp.

From beneath the ocean, he could see how deep down the hull went into the water. From what he could tell, it was the same depth as a twenty-story building. There was line upon line of portholes and Rekesh thought it looked like a brightly lit underwater city.

As he reached the ramp, he rose to the surface, only allowing his head to appear. He listened carefully and hearing no one around, he crept up the ramp, which was lined with boat after boat for its entire length. He had to hide in one of the stationed boats, as he heard several men heading down the ramp. He covered himself with a plastic sheet.

"We need to stack these boats," one of the men said in a gruff voice. "We need to make way for the *wide load* later. You two should just about do it by nightfall."

"Do you think that the general will really deploy it?" another man asked.

"If it goes on at this rate, then who knows?" the third man said.

"Those damn Makai just don't know when to quit!" the gruff man said. "Even with those crappy weapons, they'll carry on till the end. Geez, if they only knew the powerful shit we got on board here. Jeth Tyrone isn't leaving here until Aradonas is burnt to the ground. I heard him speaking to the commander from the *Stryder*."

The last statement was said with pride.

Rekesh realised that the leaders of Raicema must be aboard the other ship. He was simply on a carrier vessel that held all their equipment.

"I thought that the Tyrones wanted to take over Aradonas, not destroy it," one of the men said with a slight tone of sympathy in his voice.

"The Tyrones are only interested in the region," the gruff man informed him. "There is some sort of special rock that they want to mine in southern Lizrab. Think they've found a way to make it into fuel for the flying machines they've been creating back in Raicema."

The gruff man laughed nervously to change the subject, sensing he may have shared too much with what Rekesh gathered were two much younger men.

"Anyways, once they set off the *wide load*, the job will be half done for them already. The power of that thing will wipe out half a city! That's why you guys are gonna have to break your backs to make way for it. It's got to be done at night so nobody sees it in the ocean."

Rekesh could hear the two men begin their task further up the ramp.

I should warn the city, he thought, changing tactic. He could come back to the other vessel later to carry out his original plan. He stealthily got out of the stationed boat and crawled quietly amongst the line of them until he was back at the base of the ramp. Before he climbed back in the water, he looked back to observe the two men who were lifting their third boat onto another, looking around glumly at scores left that they would have to get through. The men couldn't have been more that eighteen and Rekesh wondered as he submerged beneath the water how many of the soldiers on the beach were the same age. The thought invoked a deep feeling of dread, like it was inevitable that a tragedy would happen.

He managed to make his way back into the boat and navigate across to a secluded part of the beach. By this time the sky was turning red and the men had stopped fighting, as if they had mutually agreed that it was time to eat. Rekesh rested against a tree trunk, looking in the direction of the retreat. His head was spinning and he prayed that he would see Elera again.

Before long he had fallen asleep and was only woken by the rusting of the trees. It was now dark.

The seashore of Aradonas was an eerie sight as night fell onto its landscape. The beach was littered with candles, lit by the male and female monks of the Aradonas monastery.

As if the working day were over, every living Raiceman soldier had returned to their floating metal home, leaving a relatively calm period upon the sea and land.

Rekesh waited for a while in the surrounding forest for an opportunity to head into the city. The time had come and he stepped onto the beach, walking with arms open towards the blaze of fire torches that had been like a beacon to the warriors to fight on. Several men were standing guard there, all looking distraught and tired.

"I am one of you," Rekesh said loudly, hoping that the men spoke not only Lizrabian, a language he did not know fluently.

They let him approach, analysing him carefully.

"Who are you?" said one burly man with short matted hair and a face covered with stubble.

"My name is Rekesh Satori and I have come to help you," he said boldly, causing some of the men to don a look of suspicion.

"You are Makai?" another man asked him with caution.

"Yes. I am originally from Vassini. Do you know Elera Advaya? I travelled here with her and some others to see Kirichi and help you in your cause."

"We have heard of Elera," the burly man said. "Do you know Master Kirichi?"

"I have never met him," Rekesh said honestly. "But Elera has been close to him for many years."

The men all talked to each other in Lizrabian for a few moments, their eyes falling on Rekesh every so often indicating they were talking about him.

"What do you want?"

"I want to warn you of what the Raicemans plan to do tonight. Can you take me to your leaders?"

Again the men had a quick discussion before the burly man nodded and indicated for Rekesh to follow him. Behind the line of fire was the main gate into Aradonas, beautifully carved out of a white chalky stone with a short wall running from either side around the boundaries of the city. Beyond were fascinating pathways, made of blocks of similar stone cut in irregular shapes yet fitting tightly together on the floor. All around were grand but low buildings, a minimum of ten trees surrounding each one. Rekesh remembered how the city looked like it was interspersed with a forest from above.

The city seemed to be laid out in a circular fashion, pathways branching off into several directions like a star in numerous places. The burly man led Rekesh though the city past the monastery, which again was a low building, round in shape with several carved overhangs and a flat roof. Four men were following Rekesh and he couldn't help but feel that he was still being suspected of foul play. Past the monastery were several well-kept gardens, filled with flowers and fruit trees and in the distance, another low building but much greater in width and painted an eggshell colour. The building had at least two hundred floral pillars around its perimeter holding up a shallow domed roof.

"The elders of Aradonas are inside," the man told Rekesh. As they approached the building, he stopped and turned to him, looking down at his giban hanging from his side.

"Leave your giban here," he requested. Rekesh acquiesced and dropped his short sword to the floor, holding out his hands in a gesture of openness.

"Come," the man said, leading him into the building, which was entirely empty except for a chamber that had a large semicircular table in the centre. Several men and women sat around it. The burly man began to converse with them in Lizrabian, looking back at Rekesh every now and then. He could only make out a few of the words. They listened carefully before one woman spoke slowly.

"You want to help us against the Raiceman army?" she asked in a croaky voice.

"Yes," Rekesh said firmly. "I know what they are planning tonight."

"Tell us what you know," one of the younger men said, his face covered with a thick brown beard.

"I snuck aboard one of their war vessels and overheard a plot to destroy Aradonas tonight using a powerful explosive. I think they are going to float it out to the shore. I heard one man talk about how it could wipe out the entire city."

"I doubt it," an older man, with a shrivelled face and small eyes, said. "They want to take this city for their own, not destroy it!"

"That's not why they are here," Rekesh protested. "Raicema had been running out of a power source for years now. The Raicemans know that there is energy that can be harnessed here in Lizrab. I heard them talking about mining special rocks."

"The *wisdom rocks*," one of the women elders said to herself.

"Those rocks are sacred," the older man said, still protesting. "There would be no benefit to mining them."

"Apparently, they have found a way to use them," Rekesh told him. "Regardless, their intention is to destroy Aradonas. We have to intercept that bomb. They could be sending it out right now!"

The elders talked amongst themselves for several minutes. Then, the younger elder called for the men who had led Rekesh there to come over. He whispered something to them.

"Thank you for your information," he told Rekesh. "We will take care of it."

"How can I help?" Rekesh asked, eager to participate.

"You cannot," the man said bluntly. "Why don't you stay here in the city tonight?"

Again he whispered something to the burly man, who quickly walked towards Rekesh and ushered him out of the building, the look on his face telling him not to ask any more questions. As they left, Rekesh heard the elders talking intensely amongst themselves, clearly arguing about what should be done.

Outside, the burly man handed Rekesh his giban and pointed down one of the pathways. "You can stay at Bagvir's house tonight," he said matter-of-factly, beginning to walk easterly. "It is this way."

"I want to help you against the Raicemans," Rekesh declared again, trying to keep up with the quick pace. The man said nothing and again the other men followed behind, keeping a watch on his movements. They walked for a while before coming to a small house with a lantern hanging outside. The burly man knocked on the rickety wooden door loudly. It opened and a tall thin cleanly shaven man appeared. He greeted them all in Lizrabian, to which the burly man began to converse with him.

"This is Bagvir," he said, turning to Rekesh. "You will stay with him tonight."

As Rekesh walked through the door, Bagvir smiled at him and was then warned something in Lizrabian by the burly man, which Rekesh knew was a warning not to let him leave.

"Welcome..." Bagvir said as the others left in quite a hurry. "Me...no speak good..."

He tried to think of the words he was trying to say, clearly only speaking Lizrabian fluently. Rekesh smiled at him, holding up his hand in a gesture to Bagvir not to worry. He nodded in appreciation mumbling something to himself in Lizrabian.

"You sleep..." he said, pointing towards a room at the back.

Though it was the last thing Rekesh wanted to do, he humoured Bagvir by agreeing and following him into the simple yet comfortable room with layers of padding on the floor for a bed and a stone fireplace in the corner. He then disappeared, returning quickly with a beaker of water and some bread and fruit. Rekesh thanked him and then Bagvir closed the door, fully expecting him to be lodging there for the night.

Rekesh did not know what to make of it. On one hand he appreciated the hospitality of the people of Aradonas in such trying times but on the other hand he couldn't help but feel as though he was being kept out of the way. He sat down on the padding to think about what he should do, eating the soft pink berries and crunchy mellow bread.

A lot has happened today, he thought remembering that the day started out fishing in the ocean. He felt an urge to be in the water once again. He wondered for a while how Elera and the others were, though he knew they would be safe in Kirichi's company. Though he had never met him, the stories that had heard about him made it impossible not to respect or admire the man for his ethos and support of others. He was sure that he would keep Elera out of harm's way.

After a while had passed, he wondered if Bagvir had gone to sleep. He opened the door to his room quietly, peeking out and seeing the door across the way closed. He took a few steps out of the room but was surprised to find Bagvir sitting at a table to his right, reading a dusted book by candlelight.

The moment he spotted Rekesh he began to say something in a pleading way in Lizrabian. Rekesh quickly retreated back into the room, bidding the man goodnight in an attempt to avoid offence. He closed the door and look around with his back to it, noticing only one window that was sealed. He walked over to the fireplace and looked up, relieved to see a wide enough chimneybreast for him to climb up.

He ducked down and positioned himself in the well-used

fireplace, crushing the delicate charcoal beneath his feet. Taking careful steps onto protruding stones inside, he push himself up being careful not to make any noise. The chimney was sooty and Rekesh could feel the silt covering his arms and hair with every movement he made. He quickly got to the top of the stack and had to remove a circular disk to make way for him to get onto the roof. As he emerged under the night sky, the stars greeted him with a brilliant twinkling. He replaced the stack top and saw a tree was overhanging onto the roof.

He positioned himself and jumped carefully onto one of the branches, but the force of his body impacting caused it to crack and break off the tree. Rekesh tumbled down to the ground with a thud. He heard Bagvir mumbling something from within the house so he quickly got to his feet and began to run in the direction of the city gate. He dared not look back as he ran past house after house until he could see the smoke from the wall of fire near the beach. As he approached, he noticed there were fewer men standing guard than before. It made it easier for him to sneak past them onto the beach. He got down on his belly and crawled slowly out of sight, keeping within tall reeds and behind trees until he was in a more open part of the coast. He looked out and saw the ominous presence of the two war vessels in the darkness, like the eyes of a great monster.

Rekesh began to think about what he should do, wanting to get aboard the rightmost vessel to carry out his plan of sabotaging the Raiceman leadership, however he quickly grew concerned about the thousands of soldiers that would now be aboard. His thoughts only lasted for a few moments because he then heard shouting in the distance, coming from the direction of the leftmost vessel, the one that Rekesh had been aboard earlier. The shouting was in Lizrabian and a moment of panic gripped him as he realised in an instant of premonition what was about to happen.

In a moment that seemed to stretch on for eternity, Rekesh saw a bright white flash come from the leftmost war vessel, followed immediately by an almighty explosion that sounded like a million lions roaring at the top of their voices.

The force of it, though a sun or more away, physically lifted Rekesh off his feet and into the air in a sweeping motion. He landed violently on a bush some way behind him and was then bombarded by a wave of sand flying through the air at great speed. Trying to sit up and with a terrible ringing in his ears, he looked on in horror as a giant wave had risen up into the air, a thousand pieces of the carrier vessel riding upon it. Debris was suspended in the air as if it were being held up by something and the rightmost vessel had seemed to move some way out into the distance from the force. It had rotated and was alive with the electric lights of everyone on board scurrying around.

A moment of remorse flowed through Rekesh's body as he realised that his warning had not been serious enough. The sentiment was short-lived as the great wave came crashing down on the shores of Aradonas. Rekesh felt the water hit him so hard in the face that he lost consciousness for a few moments, and he awoke shortly after tangled in debris and vegetation with the sound of shouting all around. The wall of fire had been extinguished and as Rekesh woozily got to his feet, he saw boats being launched from the one remaining war vessel.

The city behind him had also come to life, the sound of the warriors all awakening from their short rest. The clanging of metal objects could be heard followed by the rallying cries of the warrior leaders preparing their men for battle.

As the remnants of the explosion coated the star-lit sky in red, grey and orange streaks, Rekesh realised that this time he would have to join in the battle directly, as the swarm of boats loomed closer to the shore and the footsteps of a thousand men rumbled the ground of Lizrab behind him.

Chapter 20 – A Balance

"Did you hear that?"

At the retreat, it was dark and a roaring fire was ablaze upon a stone pedestal. Bene and Teltu were hard at work roasting plenty of vegetable skewers that they had spent a few hours preparing. A mushroom and nut stew was bubbling away in an iron pan positioned near to the fire, the smell of which was making everyone's stomach rumble.

"It sounded like an explosion," Elera reiterated. There was currently only the sound of bushes rustling and the odd grasshopper now and then.

It seemed that nobody else had heard the explosion.

"I want to talk to you all about something," Kirichi said to everyone, looking at each person in turn. The noise of the fire crackling was a perfect accompaniment to his mellow voice. Everyone turned their attention to the wise old man, his golden skin and deep-set brown eyes contrasting with his long white hair and beard.

"It seems quite remarkable that you have all culminated here at the same time. It is a time when, whether you realise it or not, the planet desperately needs all of our help."

He now had everyone's full attention.

"The place that we are all sitting is a sacred place. For over ten thousand years this place has attracted people to help them understand their journey in the life they are living. Just sitting in this retreat can give a person clarity about where they should be heading.

"I myself have received invaluable knowledge from this planet and beyond by simply dwelling here. So it seems fitting that this should be the place where you all discover that you are closely connected to one another."

Teltu and Reo seemed confused, whilst Bene had a look of doubt upon his face as if he had heard it all before.

"Elera has begun a great journey and you all have a part to play.

What she is looking for is much more than an understanding of the past. Whether she knows it or not, things on this planet are going to change dramatically."

"Are you talking about the prophecy?" Bene asked his grandfather.

"For those who are unaware," Kirichi began in response, "the prophecy Bene is referring to was written down a very long time ago by people who used to dwell on this land. When I was young I learnt that the prophecy was known about for as long as the Makai had existed in Lizrab.

"It speaks of a change within humans due to a greater understanding of our shared origins. Whilst I believe that this prophecy has an underlying truth to it, it is not what I am talking about in this instance."

Bene now had a look a sheer confusion, and anticipation could be seen forming on the faces of everyone around.

"When I talk of things changing dramatically, I am referring specifically to this planet. Many are unaware of the sheer power that this planet holds. It has the power to change itself if provoked."

"What is provoking the planet?" Reo asked with interest.

"The energy that this planet holds is being drained in measures that have never occurred before. Just like you and I need energy, so does the planet to sustain itself. In the past one thousand years, many humans on this earth have begun to drain the earth's most sacred energy, the energy of the wisdom rocks. These rocks are like the planet's memory of how to maintain itself. They are its brain, its essence."

The fire was crackling away, as if it were applauding Kirichi's narrative.

"Unfortunately," Kirichi continued, "there are some on this planet who only wish to destroy it. And I think they are getting closer to achieving their ambition."

Everyone was silent for a while and then Teltu remembered what Sorentius had said in Giza.

"Has this got something to do with that thing in the sky? When we were in Giza, Sorentius said there was something in space that he hadn't seen before."

"You are very intuitive, Teltu," Kirichi complimented him with a smile. "But let us not dwell on that. What is important is that we help to conserve the wisdom rocks. That is all the protection that this planet needs."

"And how can we do that?" Javu asked.

"Continue the journey to find Lemuria," he declared. "The knowledge of the planet is locked within the myth of Lemuria. Elera, you have always been drawn to learning about history. Well, this is the most precious of history that one can ever discover for it will show us how we are all connected."

"I am confused," Reo said loudly, not keeping up with the pace of Kirichi's explanations. "What are wisdom rocks?"

"They are extraordinary crystal formations that hold a special kind of energy. That energy could have come from many places. Humans in the past have contributed energy to the wisdom rocks, as do many creatures and plants all over the planet. Everything that happens gets recorded in these rocks; an energy form that we as people cannot appreciate unless we open ourselves up to it. But now, this sacred energy is being sapped as the empires of this world have discovered its material value."

"That's why Raicema are invading Lizrab!?" Reo said, more to himself than anyone else.

"Yes. They discovered recently that this land has a number of energetic hotspots due to the wisdom rocks being close to the surface. We are sitting on one such location right now!"

Everyone was silent, trying to take in everything that Kirichi had said.

"It is a good time to eat!" he declared, signalling Bene to serve the roasted food. For a long while, everyone ate in silence with only a twig crackling in the fire or a light rustle of the trees around making a sound. After some time had passed, Bene was the first to finish eating and the one to break the silence, which almost felt like it had taken on the form of a blanket.

"You said we are all connected. Why?"

"Since you like prophecies, Bene, I have another one for you." Kirichi replied jovially. "This one, however, is not written down.

"It has been said that to understand where we all come from, an equal balance is needed. That balance is represented by those of you who are here tonight."

"What do you mean?"

"Each of you is different in terms of what drives you. It is what makes up your spirit, your existence. Those differences create a balance."

He paused for a moment.

"Take Javu for instance," he said looking at his old friend. "He is like the air, like the wind. He is good to talk to, a good person to turn to if you need advice."

"How is that like the wind?" Teltu asked, confused.

"Sshhh," Elera told him and prompting Kirichi to continue.

"Teltu, too. I feel like you are from the air," he told him. "Unlike Elera and I, who have the spirit of water flowing within us both."

He turned to his right and looked carefully at the silent Sita, who had not uttered a word and could not understand many that had been spoken, yet she sat peacefully.

"My new friend, Sita. She is like water too."

Sita was unstirred from her stillness.

"What about me?" Reo asked boyishly.

"Fire!" Kirichi said immediately, causing Javu and Elera to laugh. "So much energy!"

"And I?" Bene asked more serenely.

"You are like the earth, my grandson. Strong yet impatient."

Bene wasn't sure whether to feel complimented or offended by his grandfather's analysis of him.

"But how is that a balance, Kirichi?" Javu asked him, trying to understand the insight. "There are two of Air, three of Water and only one of Fire and Earth."

"Firstly, I am not included in the particular balance that I am speaking of. Secondly, there are two elements missing," he replied simply.

"Rekesh and Rama!" Elera announced, feeling awake by the conversation.

"Indeed," Kirichi said enthusiasm. "Elera, what would you say Rekesh's nature is like?"

"I would say he is somewhat like Bene," Elera said glancing at Bene, who looked down with a little uncharacteristic shyness. "Very strong, mostly calm but sometimes explosive."

"Sounds just like the earth," Javu said cordially. He then asked Sita in Hindi about Rama's temperament and as she spoke slowly Javu laughed at her response.

"She says Rama is a constant flame. Full of energy and quite the opposite of herself."

"Then once they join you, you will have the balance," Kirichi affirmed.

His words relieved Elera of her concern for Rekesh's welfare, for it seemed destined that they would be reunited again.

"And what are we supposed to do with this balance?" Bene asked dubiously.

"That I do not know. But I suggest you all follow Elera on her journey to rediscover Lemuria. You may find out then!"

Again, there was silence for a while as everyone contemplated their future. The sky was now so full of stars that it was mesmerising to look up, above looking like a sparkling and speckled blue dome. The moon was also clearly visible, several craters positioned like a face on the luminous crescent.

"I don't understand why I am like air and Elera is like water," Teltu reiterated his bewilderment from earlier, ending the hush.

"You would understand if you could see what I can," Kirichi said. "It is down to how you are energetically. For example, if you got to know young Reo here, you would agree that the energy inside him is constantly ablaze and it actually looks like that."

"You can see it?" Elera asked him, herself trying to look at the young Calegran.

"Not really with your eyes. It is more a feeling that you can sort of visualise. Our energy looks like waves and at times it can be hard to see because it can also be still."

Everyone was now trying to look at each other in attempt to visualise the energy, causing Kirichi to let out a deep laugh from within his belly, which jiggled a little.

"*Seeing* energy will come naturally," he told everyone. "It is easier to see it when you are dreaming."

"So what does air look like?" Teltu said.

"You cannot see air. You can only feel it."

"And earth?" Bene asked.

"It appears to be sizzling or pulsing," Kirichi replied, surprised at the level of enthusiasm for the topic.

The retreat had become slightly cooler, yet there was still a humidity in the air. The group was in contemplation at what they had discussed and they ate the last of the food in silence.

"So, I hope you are all willing to continue the journey into Cibola and beyond," Kirichi said, changing the subject. "It is important that you set off as soon as possible, early tomorrow morning."

His direction surprised many who were sitting around the fire, especially Reo and Elera who were both just settling into their environment.

"Why so soon?" Elera asked him, a tone of protest in her voice. "I thought we needed to wait for Rekesh and Rama anyway."

"They can join you later. The time is right for you to continue. The Raicemans will soon go beyond Aradonas and reach this area. It will not be safe for any of you to be around then."

"I won't leave you here alone," Bene said protectively. "I am not sure I should be leaving Lizrab at all. I have been away so long."

"And you will return again," Kirichi reassured him. "I will be safe here. You can be sure of that. It is time for you to go on a great adventure, Bene. After all, that is what life is all about."

With those final words, Kirichi got to his feet and began to head towards the simple wooden steps that led up to his office.

"I will see you all in the morning," he said, before climbing the stairs and disappearing into the cabin. Everyone who was left looked at each other carefully, except Javu who had the widest of smiles across his face.

"Why are you smiling?" Teltu asked him.

"Because it feels right. I wondered why events had turned out as they had but now it all makes sense. I am sure that each of the pyramids that we have seen and are looking for are also on energetic hotspots. That is why they have so much power that we don't understand."

Elera nodded, thinking the same thing.

"Where do we start in finding the third?" she asked.

"Let us get some sleep," Javu said to everyone. "Maybe it will come to us during the night."

Javu, Elera and Sita all headed to one of the three cabins that held several simple beds, bidding the other three goodnight. Bene, Reo and Teltu stayed up for several hours, keeping the fire burning brightly and trying to make sense of what the old leader had told them. After talking about it until they could bear no more, they all fell asleep outside, a million stars watching them from above.

☼

"Do not be afraid, Elera. One can never really lose another."

A misty presence hovered in the air for a few moments, surrounded by the stillness of serenity. Her eyes felt heavy, as though each lash had transformed into a strand of stone. Blind, she could only hear, only smell. Lilac, jasmine and vanilla pierced the air. The combination was sharp yet soft, strong yet mellow.

"Life is like a snake eating itself. The coil of unfolding worlds is before you, Elera. You just need to open your eyes."

Her mouth opened but she could not breathe for there was no need to. The abyss of solitude had stopped every cell, every flow.

"What am I afraid of?" she felt herself ask.

"There is really nothing to be afraid of. Accept it to strengthen your will. One can never really lose another."

Energy began to flood in, a wash of dreaminess and drifting to nowhere. Her eyes began to feel lighter, like a particle at a time was being lifted from the weight. An orange light could be seen, blurred and shielded.

Elera woke up slowly on a hard mattress in the Turian retreat. She glanced over at Sita fast asleep on the mattress next to her. Light shone through the cracks in the wooden room, spotlighting in streaks on the floor.

She sat up feeling mindless and woozy. The feeling was soon replaced with a cramp of anxiety as she thought of Rekesh and his unknown whereabouts. She felt guilty for letting him go into such a dangerous environment.

Standing up slowly, she noticed that her mind felt like it was buzzing a little, like it was fading in and out of her head. Shrugging the sensation off, she opened the hut door to be greeted by bright, hot sunshine.

Kirichi was sitting by himself next to the charred remains of the previous night's fire, the shade of a tree nearby protecting him from the blinding rays. Sitting on one of the logs, his forearms were resting on his thighs and his hands on his knees. His eyes were closed.

"How did you sleep, Filia?" He greeted her as she walked down the wooden stairs towards him.

"Strangely," she told him, sitting on a log opposite, the sun shining directly on to her golden-brown skin. He opened his eyes widely and smiled.

"Did you go dreaming?" he asked with an amused tone to his voice.

"I had an odd dream in which somebody was speaking to me.

They kept telling me not to be afraid."

"She likes you a lot," Kirichi said positively.

"Who?"

"Aova."

"Aova? You think she is speaking to me in my dreams?"

"I still want to know what gift she gave you," Kirichi said, ignoring her question. "Have you remembered yet?"

"I am sure I didn't receive anything, Ammi," Elera restated. "Or if I did, I certainly can't remember it."

"Never mind," Kirichi said, standing up and walking towards the sacks of food that had been gathered. "You cannot rush such things."

"Ammi, you said yesterday that you met Aova in the *Dream World*. What is it like?"

"It is different for every person who ventures there," Kirichi told her, gathering some nuts and berries in his cupped hands. "And that is mainly because you yourself help create it. You can only know by going there yourself. The funny thing is, most people *do* go there on a nightly basis but they cannot remember their visits."

Elera didn't have the energy to ask how one could remember that world for she was too preoccupied with the concern that was growing inside her.

"I wonder what is going on in Aradonas," she said, a glumness coating her stomach. "Do you think the Raicemans have reached Turo?"

"Can you not hear?" Kirichi said with a tenor of optimism. "The fighting has stopped."

"I can't hear anything."

"Exactly. Where there is silence, there is no violence."

He laughed out loud at his unintentional rhyme, bringing his handfuls of food towards a bronze plate that rested on the pedestal of stone.

"Very early this morning, as dawn broke, the explosions and gunfire stopped and there has been silence ever since. That means the war is over!"

"What if they took over the city?" Elera said a little panicked.

"They could not have," Kirichi said resolutely. "If they had, there would not be silence. There would be more gunfire as they progressed towards Turo."

Kirichi's words put Elera's imagination at rest and she calmed herself whilst eating some berries and nuts with him. A door above opened as Javu, Teltu, Reo and Bene all emerged from another of the huts.

"Good morning!" Javu said cheerily, almost picking up on the more upbeat atmosphere. "What a nice day to begin our journey!"

Teltu, who was walking behind Javu, did not seem to reciprocate, his face solemn and tired.

"Are you okay, Teltu?" Elera asked him, noticing his gloomy disposition.

"It's nothing," he said slowly. "I've got a headache, that's all. I get them sometimes. We all woke up out here last night and crawled up the stairs. I'm probably just tired."

"Let me massage your head for you," she suggested. He walked over and sat down on the floor in front of her and she began to rub his scalp with her fingertips.

"How often do you get these headaches, Teltu?" Kirichi asked him, sitting with agility on the floor next to him. Javu, Bene and Reo all were silent, taking a seat on the surrounding logs. Reo looked like he was still half-asleep.

"Now and again. Maybe once every few months."

"Then you are not as susceptible as some," Kirichi said informatively. "Many get headaches every day because of their sensitivity to the planets around us."

"The planets?"

"Indeed. The seven planets around us can have a great effect on our body and mind, especially when they align in certain ways. One of these effects is to cause a strange type of headache like you are experiencing now. Unfortunately, Elera, no amount of massage is likely to ease the pain that Teltu is going through."

"Do you know a way to ease the pain?" Elera asked Kirichi, intrigued by his theory.

"Well, it depends on which planet is primarily responsible for the headache. Each planet corresponds to a colour in the spectrum of light, and there are gemstones that can be used to alleviate the effect. I know that at the moment, the planet Neptune has aligned with us and the sun, so we would need a blue gemstone to help ease your pain."

Kirichi got to his feet and walked over to the stairway to his office. He ascended and disappeared into the wooden shack for a moment or two, before reappearing with something shiny and blue in his hand.

"It is better if the sun is shining brightly," he said, moving with a certain grace towards where Teltu was sitting. "It will make the cure more effective. Now lie down on your back."

Teltu did as he was told, resting his head on a raised mound. Kirichi placed the gemstone upon his forehead and it lit up, casting a blue glimmer as the sun's rays fell upon it.

"Now rest here for a while," he said. Then he walked towards Javu and sat beside him. "Elera and I were talking about dreams before."

"That's strange," Javu said. "Because I had a wonderful dream last night. I dreamt that I saw my son again and that he was safe."

Kirichi raised his eyebrows with interest.

"You rarely speak of your son, Javu," Teltu said from his horizontal position.

"That is because there is little positive to say. He is gone and it is unlikely that I will ever see him again."

"What happened to him?" Bene asked.

"He was taken from me when he was a child," Javu said quite openly. "He was a very special child. I don't know where he is now."

Kirichi, for some unknown reason, was beaming.

"I think that you should prepare to leave," Kirichi said to everyone. "I don't mean to rush you out but I think the timing is very good to begin your journey."

Though everyone except Elera was unsure, they all agreed to gather their things and be ready in a few hours to leave. It actually took less than that for the group to be ready to set off. Everyone gathered by the gate of the retreat to say their farewells to Kirichi. Teltu seemed to be much more alert and happy, having rested outside for a while.

The sun was so hot that the skin burned within a minute in the midday heat.

"Phew, it's a good thing we've got Bene and Reo to help us carry the water," Elera said, wiping a drop of perspiration from her short nose. "Are you sure there are lots of rivers and lakes in Cibola?"

"There will always be water wherever you go," Kirichi said jovially to Elera, who did not find his musing funny.

"And you will tell Rekesh and Rama about the route that we are taking?"

"Yes, Elera. I will make sure they find you safely," he reassured her.

"What route *are* we taking?" Teltu asked, unsure about what had been discussed.

"We will walk westwards on foot from here towards Turo and then towards the town of Cuzco which borders Cibola. There we can hopefully get some horses to take us towards the old mountain," Javu explained to him. "After that, who knows?"

Teltu nodded, though Javu was certain he still was unsure about where they were going. Bene, who had been packing a number of supplies into a large satchel, turned to his grandfather with concern.

"I do not think that you should stay here alone," he told him. "There could still be many soldiers wandering around. What would you do if they found this place?"

"Bene," Kirichi said softly, placing his hand on his grandson's shoulders. "You will have to learn to let go. I will be fine here and even if a soldier did stumble into this retreat, I would welcome him or her with open arms. It is touching that you care for my welfare, but I have not lived to be this old because I fear every little thing that could possibly happen."

Bene seemed satisfied with the wise elder's words, so he hugged his grandfather and began to load up several barrels of water bound with rope onto his shoulders.

"Let's get going," Javu suggested, spurring the three young men out into the forest. He bid farewell to Kirichi before following them. Elera hugged and kissed her mentor, Sita standing by quietly.

"Listen carefully to Sita," he told her. "Whilst you are like a river, she is like a lake. Sometimes it is good to be like a lake."

They both said their final farewells to him and then joined the others outside. They set off immediately in the direction of Turo, unaware that someone was watching them walk into the jungle from afar.

Chapter 21 – Facing the Past

Jen King was hiding behind a large tree, tired and hungry from wandering all night with no clue as to where he was headed. He looked up at the large wooden structure before him. The group of people were now moving into the forest.

He did not want another confrontation with anyone, so he stayed in his kneeling position, waiting patiently until the group had disappeared completely from view. He then got to his feet with a wince, for his knees and calves were aching from the constant walk. His black trousers were ripped down the left leg and his heavy boots felt like the greatest of hindrances. He began to walk in an incoherent manner towards the wooden structure of the retreat, hoping to find food and water.

On this short walk, King reflected on how he had fallen down the trunk of the strange tree in the forest. How he had peered upwards and seen the strange creature that proceeded to follow him.

What was that? he thought to himself. *I am confused, lost in a dream world.*

He opened the gate and was greeted by a feeling of relief as he saw a bag of berries and nuts over by a stone pedestal. He hobbled over and began to stuff his mouth with handfuls of the mixture, crunching the nuts and soft fruit with a ravenous appetite. He looked around but saw nobody. He noticed that the door of a hut above was slightly ajar, invitingly so.

After he had eaten all he could, he began to feel much better and the sun also began to feel like it was giving him energy. He decided to climb the stairs and see what was beyond the door above. The stairs creaked under his heavy footsteps and he pushed the door cautiously open as he reached the top.

Inside, Kirichi was waiting calmly. He was sitting in a small wooden chair and smiled as the tattered soldier entered. King instantly felt a feeling of safety and a look of mystification slowly spread across his face.

"Jen King, you have finally made it here," Kirichi said in a bemused voice.

King was taken aback and for a moment he looked as though he was about to leave.

"How do you—?" King began to say.

"Do you know where you come from?" Kirichi looked at King who was in a stunned silence and starting to sag. "Why don't you sit down?" he suggested, speaking slowly to the large man.

King kneeled to the floor, his eye level now at the same height as Kirichi's, his wide calf spread underneath his ripped trouser leg.

"You are probably wondering how I know your name? Well, you may be aware that you are not originally from Raicema."

"I was born in Ciafra," King declared, somewhat defensively.

"Though you lived in Ciafra for much of your childhood, you were not born there."

Jen King grew weaker. He almost needed to rest his weight on his hands, besieged by how the long-haired man knew so much about him.

"A friend of mine, Javu of Seho, found you when you were a small baby. Do you remember Javu?"

King shook his head.

"Javu raised you like his own son. You were taken away when you were ten years old," Kirichi continued. "Guido Tyrone and his army travelled to Seho and took you from Javu. They took you to Raicema. I remember very well the days that followed. Javu visited me here. He was distraught and it took a long time for him to accept that you wouldn't be coming back."

King was confused and had no memory of the event that the old man if front of him was recalling.

"There was quite a commotion when you were found as many said that you were the reincarnation of a brave Vassinian warrior from the past. At that time, Raicema had heavily invaded Vassini and people had prayed for such a warrior to come and save them. In fact, it is because of that rumour that Raicema sought you out."

"You are wrong. I kill people for Raicema. I am not brave at all," King said depletedly, after a few moments of silence.

"You have been manipulated, Jen, like so many others."

King fell back, perplexed by what he was being told. The floor of the hut shook at his weight.

"Why don't I remember?" he asked, growing frustrated, as there was something so familiar about the story being told to him.

"The Raicemans have ways to make one forget their origins," Kirichi said clearly. "In fact, they are experts at it. They would have wanted you to forget where you came from more than anyone. There are many out there that still believe that you are the re-embodiment of that brave warrior and would have wanted to help you connect to your past. I am sure that if Raicema had let you discover that, you would have been sitting before me a lot sooner."

Kirichi paused.

"You have been cut off from the world."

The confusion became too much for King. "You lie, old man. There is nothing special about me. There is nothing to discover. I am here because Raicema wants to destroy this land, wants to wage war. That's all I have become, a weapon of war!"

Kirichi's expression changed to concern. He knew that Jen was a dangerous individual, brainwashed to react with violence. Kirichi fought back the wave of anger he suddenly felt for the Tyrones, breathing deeply and realising that Jen's anger was somewhat contagious.

"I myself have no view on the matter," Kirichi said, distancing himself from the sensitive issue. "The fact *is* that you have been manipulated."

King sat quietly, breathing heavily as though overcome by some sort of illness. He began to sweat a little, though not from the heat.

"I haven't even introduced myself. My name is Kirichi," he said, changing tack. "No doubt you have heard my name said countless times in a negative fashion."

"All I know is they want you dead," King said coldly.

"Quite," Kirichi replied with a lifted tone. "However, I am sure you are becoming aware that those that wish death will only receive it in return."

There was silence for a moment.

"How did you know who I was?" King asked with puzzlement, changing the subject.

"I am a strong believer in *temporality*," Kirichi explained. "Have you heard of this subject?"

King shook his head.

"It is the subject of how certain events will happen at certain times to create meaningful results," Kirichi described cryptically. "Quite the opposite of coincidences. I believe you are here at this moment because you will make an important progression in your life by being here now.

"Indeed, you seem lost and what a 'coincidence' that I can point you in the right direction! But is it also just luck that the person who raised you recently occupied the same space that you are now occupying? Here in the same place that you have stumbled across in the middle of this vast jungle?"

King was perplexed, yet he was listening carefully.

"The man who brought you up as a child, who can tell you what you have long forgotten was one of those people who just left this retreat."

It took a few minutes for Jen King to fully realise the significance of what the wise man was saying. Not only did it seem that his frustrating lack of memory from his early life had been deliberately hindered, it actually seemed possible to alleviate the loss through the father figure that Kirichi was telling him about.

"Javu is not far away!" the wise Turian said. "And to answer your question, I was almost sure that you were Jen King when you walked through my door because this morning Javu mentioned that he had dreamt about his son and he said he was happy that you were safe. I knew you were close when he told me that."

"Are you saying that this man is nearby?"

Kirichi smiled widely whilst nodding. "And he is your father."

King immediately got to his feet and began to head out of the door.

"Wait!" Kirichi said to him. "Before you go, I wish to tell you a few things that will help you from this point onwards."

King slowly moved back into the doorway.

"Firstly, head west from here until you reach large wooden walls and then head northwest. Hopefully you will catch up with Javu quite quickly.

"Secondly, Jen King, it is important to remember the past but not hold on to it. I know you must have seen many horrific things during your life but that does not mean that you will not see many beautiful things in the future."

Kirichi thought he almost saw the troubled soldier's eyes well with tears, but he shrugged off any sentiment, nodded with an air of appreciation and then swiftly exited, his heavy steps sounding like logs falling as he walked down the stairs. Kirichi could feel the torment of the broken soldier. One thing that he had said, however, had stuck like a recording in Kirichi's mind.

"All I know is they want you dead."

The statement rang through Kirichi's head over and over, as if Jen King were there speaking the words in repetition.

It is a sign, Kirichi thought to himself, before opening a drawer in his desk and searching for something. He became frantic in his search, throwing papers on the floor and carved wooden items on the desk. Eventually, he found what he was looking for – a small dark blue crystal, jagged and hung upon a simple woven thread. He held it up, looking at it ominously. Hardly any light shone through it, though there was plenty in the room. Then he leaned back in his wooden chair and closed his eyes, waiting patiently for an encounter that he knew was inevitable.

A few hours passed and on the borders of Cuzco, the clouds had cleared and the sun was shining brightly once again. King had hobbled as quickly as he could in the direction that Kirichi had described to him and recently he had seen a glimpse of Javu and his party around every turn in the forest. As the forest opened up into wide plain land, King got his first good look at the six people all walking with determination towards a set of mountains in the distance.

"Wait!" King shouted, out of breath from the unbearable midday heat.

There was no response from anyone, still too far away to hear his weak calls. He winced as he pushed his pace to a jog, causing shooting pains to run up and down his left leg. With the sun beating down on his head and a final push, he got close enough for them to hear, collapsing on the ground in a heap.

"Wait!"

Everyone looked back with caution, but Javu took a few steps towards the exhausted soldier.

"What do you want?" he asked boldly as he drew closer to King, who was struggling to get to his feet.

"I..." King spluttered. "I... spoke with the man in the wooden fort – Kirichi. He said that you knew me."

Javu looked at King and an expression of disbelief spread across Javu's face as he realised who could be stood before him.

"Jen?" he asked with shock, moving closer to him to examine his features. King nodded and there was silence for a while as a mystified Javu looked at him carefully, trying to recognise the resemblances to the boy he once knew. He noticed a worn leather band around King's neck, and an uncontrollable smile formed on Javu's wrinkled face.

"There were many years when I feared you were dead," he said quietly whilst the others all looked on with confusion in the distance.

"Why is Javu speaking to that soldier?" Teltu asked Elera.

A clear look of suspicion was painted on Bene's face as he stared at the muscular loner.

"Not sure," she replied, as they all sat down on the dusty floor, clearly dehydrated from the dry sunshine. Javu was walking back towards them. King still knelt on the ground in the distance.

"I need to speak with this man," he told them as they looked on with interest. "Why don't you all head into the shade and make something to eat. When I am finished, I will find you and we will continue our journey."

Everyone agreed to Javu's suggestion, especially Reo who was eager to fill his belly.

"Who is he, Javu?" Elera asked as he was about to walk back. Javu did not answer, just smiled, and then swiftly headed towards where King was waiting patiently. The man looked broken and desperate, his large structure shrinking from the weight of his uncertainties. Javu felt pangs of guilt and sadness as he got closer.

"Now, let us find a quiet area and I will tell you everything that I can."

As they walked to a shaded area behind a large boulder, Javu's guilt quickly turned to joy as he realised the forces at play that had brought them together again.

"Do you remember me?" he asked King, moving his face from side to side slightly.

King shook his head though he had a perplexed expression on his face, as if he were experiencing a deja vu.

"Tell me about your life. From as early as you can remember."

King's expression changed to one of embarrassment at the old man's frank probing. He was silent for many moments.

"The first thing I remember is Tyrona," he said finally, shifting his position against the boulder. "I remember living in a large dormitory with many other children. I was the oldest."

"Do you remember anything before that? Anything from another place?"

King thought hard and searched his memories.

"I sometimes get these images in my mind of mountains. I often feel like they are located somewhere that I know…"

"Ahh," Javu said loudly with delight. "So you remember

Sarmaldha!"

"Sarmaldha?"

"Yes, Sarmaldha. That is the place that you were born."

King's eyes widened.

"Is it true that you brought me up?" he asked Javu, feeling slightly calmer and more comfortable.

"Yes it is true, I did. Do you know where Sarmaldha is?"

"No."

"It is a small village at the base of a great mountain range in Vassini. That is where we are both from. When I was forty-two years old, I was walking through a small forest near the mountains when I came across the sound of a baby laughing. I followed the sound and I found you, lying in a small basket next to a brook. You were laughing at a monkey that was swinging in a tree above you. I waited by the brook until it went dark, expecting your mother or father to return for you but when nobody came, I decided to take you back to the village with me."

King was listening like he was in a dream, his eyes dilated and unmoving.

"I went back to the brook with you every day for ten weeks but nobody came. From then on it was just you and I."

"The Tyrones always told me I was from Ciafra," King said, more to himself than to Javu.

"That is where they stole you from," Javu explained. "When you were no more than a few years old, some men came looking for you. We were not safe in Vassini anymore so we travelled to Ciafra. We lived in Seho until you were ten years old but then they tracked you down."

King was finding it hard to take in what Javu was saying, mainly as he couldn't recall any of these events.

"Why can't I remember what you are saying?"

Javu leaned close to King and touched him lightly on his grazed forearm. King almost jumped at the tenderness.

"You have to understand that you have been indoctrinated with a different past than is real. The Raicemans have many ways to make one forget about where they come from and at such an early age, it would have been easy for them to erase your entire past from your memories."

King was starting to get frustrated and agitated at what Javu was telling him.

"Why would they do this to me?" King asked with anger.

"They have done it to many," Javu said softly, trying to calm the irate soldier. "Twenty years ago, the Raicemans were very enthusiastic about creating their new 'breed' of soldiers from an early age. They scouted out physically strong children and then turned them into fighting machines. You were of great interest to them because you have a remarkable physical strength. When you were six years old, you were capable of lifting boulders that grown men could only struggle with. Besides this, Guido was very superstitious and he had heard the stories about you."

"What stories?" King asked, calming down somewhat.

"One of the villagers in Sarmaldha, a respected wise woman named Vidya, was convinced that you were the re-embodiment of a very famous Vassinian leader. Before long, the entire village and beyond were convinced of what Vidya believed and word travelled quickly."

"But why would Guido be superstitious about that?"

"This famous Vassinian leader, *Sai Rinpoche*, had brought an end to violence in Vassini in the last millennium. At that time, the Raiceman Empire was at war with Vassini and had heavily occupied the lands for its resources.

"Sai not only managed to end the fighting but he also convinced many of the soldiers to lead more peaceful lives. Because of this, Raicema was set back for hundreds of years in its aim of dominating the globe. When Guido heard that you could be Sai's reincarnation, he made it a priority for you to be captured in fear that you would suppress Raicema once again.

"Many said that your strength was a testament to Sai, who was known to have incredible powers when he was alive. Sai was known as the last king of Vassini, and so the villagers and I named you Jen King."

The ground rumbling in the distance diverted King's attention and he shot upright, alarmed that a battle would ensue.

"Not to worry," Javu reassured him. "It is only a herd of elephants."

As King observed the large grey creatures passing by with a charismatic elegance, he wondered how Javu knew without looking. He felt like a small child, who had so much to learn and sat back down to the dusty ground.

"I wish you were more familiar to me," King admitted, inspecting some of his wounds.

"It will come with time, Jen," Javu said reassuringly. "What caused you to run?"

"I have been feeling strange for a while now, like I'm wasting my life. If I think about it carefully, I have felt like this my whole life. It was always the men who relied on me that kept me fighting."

Javu nodded, encouraging King to continue.

"I was in the jungle and it began again, violence and death. I couldn't be part of it anymore. I had to run."

"There is no shame in it, Jen," Javu said sincerely, though King seemed unconvinced, hanging his head in dishonour. "The time has come for you to follow a different path. You have already taken the first steps. It will become easier and easier from now on."

"What am I supposed to do?" King asked, beginning to feel fearful.

"You can travel with me if you like. We are about to undertake a long journey. I can tell you many things along the way and we can become reacquainted with one another."

Suddenly, an overwhelming feeling of disloyalty and disgrace filled King's entire being, starting at his stomach. It quickly became crushing to the point that he found it hard to breathe. A great sadness gripped his heart and again he felt compelled to run. He rose to his feet.

"I...can't," he said weakly before limping back in the direction that he had come from. Javu almost called out to him, but then realised that he needed time to break out of the prison that Raicema had placed around him. He too rose to his feet, watching King disappear into the jungle in the distance. He headed in the opposite direction.

King did not make it far into the deep vegetation of the jungle before he once again felt weak, this time a feeling of gloominess forcing him to the ground. He felt a strong urge to cry, yet his eyes were as dry as dust. The emotional pain throbbed through his body like nothing he had felt before.

Out of the corner of his eye, he was sure he saw something moving. He looked around swiftly but nothing was there. He dropped his head but once again, at the edge of his vision, he saw the movement of something. He saw nothing when he looked around.

I am going crazy, he thought to himself, feeling increasingly paranoid and anxious. Once again, whatever it was darted around when King was not looking directly at it.

King covered his head with his arms and lay on the floor, hoping whatever was out there would leave him alone.

He heard a voice.

"Sai..." it whispered in his eye, causing the hairs to prick up along his neck and spine.

"Don't you know who you are?"

The voice had a strange and echoed resonance to it.

"You are powerful. Much more powerful than them."

The words were disturbing to King and he suddenly felt very frightened, unable to look up and not wanting to either.

"I have been waiting for you."

King then felt a most unusual sensation, as if someone had lifted him up from an invisible string in his back. He opened his eyes to see the air beneath him and he struggled to turn over. What he saw when he finally managed to turn his head was so overwhelming that it paralysed every cell in his body.

Staring down at him with its hand open was what could only be described as a wavering vision of something that looked vaguely human. It had a mainly human face and body, but its bones seemed to be elongated, and King instantly realised it was the same unknown creature that had been following him before.

Its eyes were coming into focus. They were large and silver with what seemed to be rough greyish skin around them.

"I have been waiting for you. I have been watching you. You are powerful."

He felt an intense heat around his neck and a painful sensation in his back.

"You know me. You have always known me, Sai."

The last thing King experienced before losing consciousness was the wings of the creature spreading upwards and touching each other as an overpowering metallic vibration waved through his body.

Chapter 22 – The Death of Jeth

On the borders of Aradonas a tired group of tired Makai warriors were sitting together on the beach. Rekesh was amongst them. The battle had been long and gruelling, beginning shortly after the explosion that had rocked the coast.

It had seemed like every Raiceman soldier available had been dispatched in a final attempt to claim the city. The boats had arrived in their hundreds, each with fifty soldiers aboard. There were only five warriors per boatload and the toll had been high on both sides.

Everyone had fought with a ferocity that seemed to have been cast upon both sides. It was an intensity born out of survival and fear. In the end, the warriors were left standing. The darkness of night had been a major hindrance to those firing bullets, yet an aid to those carrying a sword.

Rekesh felt a disturbance within. The recent memory of running countless men through with his giban had spread a deep-rooted anxiety through his body. He felt a powerful energy was still present within, the same energy that had carried him through battle. It was a sickening feeling. He stood up and began to walk towards the water.

"Hey, where are you going?" one of his comrades shouted to him as his feet touched the wet sway. He dived in, the sharp impact of the water against his face cleansing his hot angst. He swam with an energy that he was unaware he possessed, only coming to the surface now and again for a short breath of air.

Before long he was a long way from the shore and he floated motionless in the ocean for a while, staring out at the remaining war vessel that now seemed like a giant ghost ship.

There can't be many left on board, he thought. *It's time to end this.*

He began swimming again towards the vessel, a strange tingling sensation coming over him. It was the feeling of being on the edge of a cliff and he was just about to jump off.

He dived deeply, pushing hard with his legs to fight the pressure, wanting the light to disappear and for darkness to surround him. He stayed under for what he thought must be the longest he had ever achieved and when he resurfaced, the vessel was right in front of him. He swam straight to a metal ladder, the pull of his wet clothes a challenge as he emerged from the water to climb it. Looking up, the ladder was curved into a convex, creating the illusion that it led straight to the sky.

As he climbed, he heard voices from above. They were all panicked and argumentative.

"What do you want me to do about it?" one man was shouting loudly.

"Get it fixed, soldier!" another was barking. "That sentry cannon is the only powerful piece of weaponry we have left now that the *Valkcry's* gone under."

"There's no point!" the man wined loudly. "We've lost. We've lost."

The sound of the man being slapped heavy across the face resonated down to where Rekesh stood on the ladder, followed by a thud as he hit the deck.

"We have not lost until every man on this ship is dead! Now get to your feet and fix that damn cannon!"

As everyone hurried about their business, Rekesh slowly climbed to the top and peered over the barrier. The immediate vicinity was empty so he hopped over and ran to the nearest door in front of him. Inside, a circular metal ladder led down to the engine rooms. He climbed down, the roar of the furnaces and machinery sounding like the depths of hell. At the bottom, there were several metal passageways.

After a few moments' contemplation, he took one and it led into a long hold with hundreds of metal barrels stacked on top of each other. At the end of the hold was another door, and beyond several storage rooms all full of guns and boxes of ammunition.

Rekesh heard voices coming down the passageway so he ran onto one of the storage rooms and noticed a door at the back – a small bathroom. He closed the door behind him, standing silently still.

"I'm sure there's somebody down here," he heard a man with a coarse voice say in the distance beyond the layers of metal. "There's water on the deck where someone has climbed up."

A feeling of panic crept up Rekesh's neck and he contemplated grabbing a gun and laying in wait. However, upon discovering there was a vent above his head, he decided to climb up instead. It was dingy and laden with dust, but he managed to cover his face with his top and close the vent just in time, as he heard men rooting around in the storage room below. He lay still for several moments until they moved on, then he began to crawl along the duct until it reached a vertical incline.

The smell of metal and dust reminded Rekesh of hard work and he pushed with effort using his forearms and knees to shimmy up until the duct forked horizontally. He took the right fork and before long he had arrived at another vent. Through its zigzagged wire, he could see a room below that looked like an office.

It was empty and maps and papers lay strewn over several desks, along with several computer terminals lined across one side. A crackle could be heard coming out of one of the machines. He pressed on for a while until he came to another vent.

Below, two men were talking but Rekesh couldn't quite see their faces because of his vantage point.

"It is serious, brother," one of the men was saying in a controlled manner. "The *Valkcry* held most of our technology. It was a mistake to send the remainder of the men out during the night. Very few have come back."

The man walked across to a porthole towards the back of the room and Rekesh caught a glimpse of his face. It was Seth Tyrone, instantly recognisable by his exceptionally bony jaw and deep-set eyes. A twinge of excitement raced around Rekesh's body as he realised he was suspended above the two primary leaders of Raicema.

"What about our troops in Calegra?" Jeth Tyrone asked his

brother.

"Again, heavy losses. Only two battalions left."

There was silence as both men thought about their next move.

"And what about Lengard?"

"There is no response."

"Damn!" Jeth exploded, banging his fists on what sounded like a desk. "It's Kirichi's doing! With him still around, the people will keep going. We've got to get rid of him."

"But we don't know where he is," Seth replied.

"You will find him personally," Jeth ordered antagonistically. "Get the rest of the men and put an end to this, Seth!"

"We've got a bigger problem than hunting down Kirichi," Seth told his brother. "King's gone missing."

"So what?" Jeth balked. "Let's hope he's rotting in the sea somewhere."

"Think, Jeth!" Seth said frustrated. "If he finds out where he is from, he may turn against us. If he does then that's the end of Raicema."

"You sound just like Father," Jeth replied sarcastically. "So superstitious! There is nothing special about Jen King and the next time I see him, I'll prove it. I can't believe you stopped me from shooting him. If you hadn't, you'd have nothing to worry about, would you?"

There was silence as Seth began to rethink his reasoning.

"Get the men together," Jeth said with authority. "I don't want you to come back here until the old man is dead. I will contact Lengard."

Rekesh heard Seth leave the office and the president of Raicema let out a loud sigh. Then he heard him walk over and open what sounded like a heavy drawer. He took something out and swiftly left the office.

Rekesh decided to press on along the duct and before long he had come to another vent, this time over an extravagant-looking suite, with intricate wooden panelling on the walls and expensive-looking furniture. From his current viewpoint, he could see an armchair, a highly polished coffee table and the corner of a magnificent walnut desk.

He waited for some time before hearing a door slide open and then Jeth Tyrone emerged in full view beneath him, completely unaware of his presence. He walked over to the walnut desk, now out of sight. Rekesh heard a sharp beep.

"Connect me to Westway's office," Jeth said.

"*One moment, Mr President,*" a speaker resonated back from below.

There was silence for a while.

"*Lengard Central Defence,*" someone spoke in a sharp accent.

"Who am I speaking to? This is President Jeth Tyrone. I wish to speak with Lord Westway."

"You are through to central defence. We are currently in a state of national emergency. Lord Westway and King Constynce were both assassinated in an attack on the palace early this morning."

Jeth expressed his concerns, though Rekesh couldn't help but feel that he wasn't being entirely genuine to the speaker.

"Who is in command?"

"General Redwood. He is leading the national security initiative."

"I wish to speak with him."

"*It is not possible, sir. All military personnel are bound under a state of national emergency.*"

He then heard another beep as Jeth disconnected the call.

"Connect me to the following line – X666XENO3424," Jeth said to the speaker.

"*One moment, Mr President,*" the speaker said in a Raiceman accent.

There was silence for a while and then a crackle.

"Hello," a familiar voice crackled through the speaker.

"It is done," Jeth said definitively.

"Good," the voice said. Rekesh had heard the voice before but he couldn't quite place where.

"It will not be long before the declaration is made."

"And when will I be called?" Jeth asked, anxiety in his voice.

"Soon."

The line disconnected and there was a beep. Jeth got up from the desk and moved over to the armchair. He was now sitting directly beneath the vent Rekesh was looking through.

Jeth looked worried, like he had done something he was regretting. As he sat there contemplating, he heard a scraping sound in the vent duct above his head. He rushed over to his desk and opened a small drawer in its centre, taking out an antique-looking pistol and checking that it was loaded. He pointed up towards the duct, his hand shaking.

"Who's there?" he stated loudly intending to sound powerful, though his trembling voice gave the opposite impression. "I will shoot!"

"Wait!" a voice echoed from the vent, causing Jeth to fall back into his chair with terror and drop the gun to the floor.

Rekesh emerged from the duct, dropping to the floor with agility. He was dusty and took a defensive stance as he landed, knowing that the Raiceman leader had a gun. He saw it on the floor and quickly drew his giban. Jeth reached down to pick up the gun, but as he pointed it in the direction of the intruder, Rekesh knocked it out of his hand with a swift swipe of his short sword. The gun clunked to the floor.

"What do you want?" Jeth asked, clutching the arms of his padded chair with tension. The question took Rekesh by surprise. He hadn't thought about how to describe why he was there in the luxury cabin of the Raiceman war vessel.

"I want you to leave Lizrab and never come back," Rekesh stated forcefully after a while.

"Ha!" Jeth snarled mockingly. "Another do-gooder. For a moment there I thought you were an assassin."

Jeth seemed to be less frightened now.

"The problem that *you* have is that you are living in a dream world! If it weren't for Raicema, there would be no progression. Who do you think supplies all those primitive villages and towns with the means to develop? It is only when they rebel that they end up with nothing, just like they started out with."

"Most people don't want much," Rekesh protested firmly. "They just want to be left alone."

"Most people don't even know what they want," Jeth fired back. "And if it wasn't for all those small-time leaders rallying people together to keep hold of the small morsel of power that they have, Raicema would have made their lives better already."

Jeth's eyes shiftily glanced down at the gun on the thick pile carpeting.

"You're totally deluded. I know about you. You've had everything you've ever wanted since the moment you were born. You have no idea what it feels like to come from a place where you only take what you need."

Silence fell between the two for several moments as both thought about their next move. Rekesh had thought it would be so easy to swiftly dispatch of the Raiceman leader and had gone over it hundreds of times in his mind whilst in battle on the shores of Aradonas. Now, however, he was having second thoughts, thinking of ways to spare the man whilst guaranteeing the safety of everyone else.

"Get up from there!" Rekesh ordered.

"Or what?" Jeth balked with arrogance. "You are no more capable of killing me with that pitiful sword than I am able to stop my pursuit of liberation on this godforsaken planet."

"Liberation?" Rekesh blurted out loud, being drawn into a further argument. "You call murder and robbery liberation! You encourage that of your men and care nothing for them either. I am sick of corrupt leaders who do nothing but spread death yet talk of liberation."

Jeth was silent for a second before a creepy smile appeared across his face. "I am talking about the liberation of myself," he said chillingly. "You think there is some golden pinnacle that civilisation can reach? Well, you are living a fantasy. Raicema has hidden the harsh truth from our people about this 'wonderful' past that the Makai go on and on about. You think you are excluded from obeying authority?"

Jeth almost cackled at the thought.

"You think there was a time when people were more peaceful? All that existed was survival and the same is true today – survival, and obeying those above you. Why else would you be here pointing that sword at me right now?"

Rekesh didn't want to listen to what the Raiceman leader was saying, yet he felt hypnotised and weakened. The man in front of him was cunningly challenging his entire belief system.

"The empires of the past were giants compared to what you see today," he continued creepily and with a dark inspiration. "Only a thousand years ago there were over a hundred nations. Now the landmasses are vast and without structure. Back then the nations fought, just like now. And back then people killed for survival, just like now."

"So why are you telling me this?" Rekesh said, pointing his sword firmly at Jeth's neck.

"All of Raicema's technological might is based on that of the previous empires," he continued, ignoring Rekesh's question. "But they drained this planet to the extent that we are starved, unable to progress without sacrificing the more primitive populations."

"I don't care about the past," Rekesh stated clearly. "All I know is that you are killing the future. All you do is order people to kill others."

"And you think the answer is to do the same?" Jeth quizzed Rekesh, his eyes widening madly. "Kill me? The truth is, I am starting to think you can!"

Rekesh was weakening from Jeth's words and the Raiceman leader was fully aware of it.

"You have a lot of guts to sneak in here like this. You have signed your own death warrant by doing so," the creepy-eyed leader continued. "But I am willing to give you another chance. You should join me and let us focus on the order we must bring to the wastelands. I could use someone like you."

"Those wastelands are people's homes," Rekesh said, growing angrier. "It's people like you that create the wastelands. You are no different, no more visionary than the fools that came before you. You act like you have a divine right to control everyone."

"And you know what makes me know that?" Jeth toyed with Rekesh, hissing and scraping his voice. "I am willing to do whatever is necessary to keep order and I was born to do so. If you kill me, you too are dead. Serve me and I will make your life a thousand times better."

"You are crazy," Rekesh said, disturbed by Jeth's offer. Once again the leader glanced down at the loaded gun on the floor with shiftiness.

"Who were you speaking to earlier?" Rekesh demanded. "Did you arrange those assassinations in Lengard?"

"So, you are sneakier than I thought," Jeth said sarcastically. "Let's just put it this way. The people you follow care no more about this planet that you are so eager to protect than I do. You think you are a 'warrior'? Ha, what a joke!"

Rekesh had had enough and brought the edge of the blade closer to Jeth's throat, confused about what to do. Jeth slid off his chair and bent to his knees, kneeling on the floor. He was looking down. Then he looked up with a sick grin.

"Go ahead. Do it!" he said forcefully and disturbingly.

Rekesh began to withdraw his blade, a glint of light sliding across Jeth's neck. A vision of blood on the floor flashed through Rekesh's mind and he stepped back, disturbed and repentant.

"You can't do it," Jeth ridiculed, whilst Rekesh dropped his sword slightly, a cold perspiration and light-headedness overcoming him. Jeth moved his arm slowly down near his ankle, then suddenly lunged for the gun on the floor. As he brought it up to point it at Rekesh, something seemed to propel Rekesh forward.

The two struck each other and the breath was forced out of both of them from the impact. They were both suspended there for only a moment, though it seemed like hours. Then Jeth let out a low breathless sigh and slumped backwards in his chair, Rekesh's giban lodged deeply in his chest. He looked at it in disbelief and then began to stare past Rekesh with horrified eyes.

Rekesh slowly looked at his hands, which were lightly splattered with Jeth's blood, and began to feel faint.

Jeth Tyrone let out one last expiration and then his body slumped into silence. Rekesh felt a strange ringing sensation around his head and an intense pain in his belly. Then he fell to his knees, the depths of darkness swallowing him.

Chapter 23 – Raicema Falling

On the borders of Cuzco, it was late in the afternoon.

Javu had earlier located Elera, Sita and Teltu. They were all now eating roasted vegetables under the shelter of a tall tree. A small fire was dying out but the group had saved some food for later, which lay on a large leaf on the floor.

"Bene and Reo should be back soon," Elera said to Javu. The two men had gone in search of more supplies. As if called, they appeared in view carrying armfuls of fruits and dug-up roots. Reo had a dead rabbit over his shoulder. Sita gasped a little at the sight of it.

"This should make a nice stew," Reo said happily as he dropped the rabbit's body to the floor.

"So you are a hunter, Reo?" Javu asked whilst eating some pieces of roasted cassava root. "Mmm, this is sweet."

"I know how," Reo replied.

"Was it necessary for you to kill that animal, Reo?" Elera asked him indifferently.

"Well, I think so," Reo responded, quite sure of himself. "I mean, I could probably have survived on the vegetables we had, but I don't think I get the same kind of energy from them as I get from meat."

"Mmm, that's interesting," she said, feeling a little uncomfortable at the sight of the lifeless animal on the floor. "Because, there is much less life force in that body than in the vegetables we are eating."

The statement seemed to shock Reo, who realised his assumption could be wrong and that Elera seemed to know more about the subject than he did.

"So who was that man?" Elera asked Javu, changing the subject.

Javu had not talked about his rendezvous with the mysterious stranger yet. He had just smiled but had said nothing when asked about it.

"He is my son," Javu stated calmly, causing Teltu to splutter his food a little.

"Your son?!" Elera and Teltu said in unison, looking at each other with confusion.

"Not by blood, but in every other way I am that man's father. His name is Jen."

There was silence for a moment.

"I heard you once had a child," Elera said with disbelief. "I don't know why, but I just assumed he'd died."

"In some ways he has. The Raicemans took him away when he was ten years old."

"But why?" Teltu asked staggered by the subject, one that Javu never talked about.

"Because he has a special gift and the Raiceman military wanted to exploit that. It doesn't matter now. What remains is that he has found me again."

Everyone could tell that Javu did not want to discuss it further, so they all sat quietly reflecting on where they had come from and where they were going.

After a while, Elera turned to Teltu and broke the silence.

"Did your headache go away?" she asked thoughtfully.

"Yes," Teltu said happily. "Since we set off the pain has gone. Kirichi is a great man."

"Mmm, I wonder how that gemstone works. I wasn't aware that each of the seven planets represents a different colour," Elera pondered.

"Got no idea," Teltu commented. "But Kirichi did say that the stone wouldn't work every time. He said it depends on the alignment of the planets and moon."

"I studied planetary alignments as a child when Fera and I lived with our parents near Giza. I always remember my parents being interested in the subject and when I got a bit older, I was taught all about it by a man that had studied with my mother and father."

"Professor Sorentius?"

"Yes. He really got me interested in the relationship between some of the ancient buildings on this planet and their relationships to the planets and stars."

Teltu was thinking about something related to the topic.

"When we were in Giza, Javu told me that there are pyramids on other planets," Teltu said. "Do you think that's true, Elera?"

"It could be," she deliberated, turning towards Javu. "But no evidence has been found to suggest that. Why do you think that Javu?"

Javu looked up from his food with a mischievous smile.

"I have seen them," Javu stated.

"How?" Elera said with an astonished intrigue.

"I have seen them whilst dreaming," he said simply.

"But if you dreamt it then it wasn't real," Teltu said feeling a little duped.

"Wait, Teltu. Kirichi was telling me something about this yesterday," Elera said, surprised that Javu knew about it too. "He said that there is a *world* that you can visit whilst you sleep."

"Indeed," Javu confirmed. "To the layman it may seem like a fantasy, but to those who are aware, it is a *portal* with endless possibilities including being able to travel anywhere you want in the entire universe!"

Both of them were rocked by Javu's words, almost afraid of the concept.

Bene and Reo, who had been eating silently, now looked up with interest at the conversation. Sita was sitting quietly as usual, pondering her own thoughts.

"Can anyone do this?" Bene asked Javu.

"As I said, only those that are fully aware that the dream world exists will be able to move around and explore it. One of the greatest challenges for anyone is coming to the realisation that the dream world is real and not just a figment of your imagination."

"And you saw pyramids on other planets this way?" Elera asked again, drawing the conversation back to its origin.

"Only on the moon. I cannot remember very much of what I saw. That is another challenge of visiting the dream world. Remembering what you experienced when you wake in this reality is quite difficult. However, I do remember being astounded by the aura of the place and its towering structure."

"Are you saying you were actually on the moon?" Teltu asked with scepticism.

"I am saying I visited it through the dream world," Javu clarified. "That is all. To be there physically is another matter completely."

Now everyone was confused and the conversation quickly faded away.

The anticipation to push forward on their journey was growing in everyone at the same time.

"It's time to get going," Bene declared with leadership.

Everyone gathered their things. Reo picked up the dead rabbit and tied it to his bag of belongings. Before long they were all walking at a steady pace towards the mountain range in the distance. As they walked, Elera couldn't help but feel a little anxious about going to sleep that night, nervous about what she might see or where she may end up. She wondered where Kirichi travelled to every night and began to think that she had forgotten a large part of her life.

As these thoughts entered her mind, they were suddenly pushed out by an overwhelming sensation that Kirichi was in danger. She imagined soldiers entering the retreat and climbing the stairs. She saw the face of one of them so clearly, a long scar under his right eye.

My imagination is going wild, she thought to herself as she pressed on with the others into the mountains.

Though Elera concluded that her vision was her own imagination, in fact, Seth Tyrone and his band of soldiers had landed on a small beach at the edge of the Turian jungle, near to the retreat.

The sky had become grey, wholly shrouded with the sadness of death. The heat could still be felt yet it made everyone shifty-eyed and delirious.

Following his five front men and occasionally barking out orders to change direction through the maze-like undergrowth, Seth pushed the men deep into the heart of the rainforest. The long ant-like line of soldiers behind Seth were all horrified by the dead bodies surrounding them, partially fearful that they would be led to a similar fate by their leader, but mainly shocked at seeing comrades they once knew lying lifeless. Every soldier strove to keep their eyes forward, but it was impossible not to look, impossible not to think about what had occurred.

"I have been thinking," Seth said quietly to Brigadier Gangel as they walked. "If we fall back for a few days, we could wait for more troops from Tyrona to reach here from the west. We only have five hundred men left."

Gangel just nodded at Seth's plan. The Brigadier was a cold man, known for his ruthlessness and often serving as Seth's second in command. He had a partially bald head from burns he had received in battle and a large L-shaped scar under his right eye.

They marched for a long time, often in what seemed like circles. The heavy thick uniforms of the soldiers felt like wet suits as they plodded on, the moist heat weighing them down even more. Every brow was dripping under their square-shaped helmets. After some time they came to a small river and followed it along into the darkness as the trees became denser overhead.

Seth had a small tracking device in his hand and was scrutinising its display.

"He is not far from here!" Seth declared to himself, trying to locate Jen King.

Seth marched ahead quickly, spurring the men on. Before long they had reached the entrance to a cave at the bottom of a great ditch.

"We are close now, I can feel it!" Seth said loudly, walking in a crouched position through the cave as if he were a hunter, stalking his prey.

The horde plodded on, the cave cooling them somewhat, until one of the front men called out with relief as he reached the other side.

"Ahead, sir. It's a wooden fortress!"

A devilish glint entered Seth's eye as he spotted the stronghold and realised he might be able to fulfil his brother's wishes.

"What primitive imbeciles to have built their fortress out of wood!" Seth exclaimed to his front-runners with glee as they approached. "One small fire and it will be gone."

Suddenly, Seth's tracking device began to bleep.

"King is close by," Seth said to Gangel. "Take the men and kill everyone inside. Make sure you find Kirichi. Then I want you to burn this place to the ground and wait for me here. I will go ahead."

Gangel nodded and with thirty men following him, he pushed on the gate of the fort, surprised to find it open. Seth headed off in a westerly direction in pursuit of his prized fighter.

"Abandoned!" Gangel said with disappointment as he walked into the silent gardens of the retreat. The men began to slowly walk around, their guns at the ready. Two of them walked over to the stone pedestal and upon observing the charred ashes of a fire and a bag of berries and nuts, they alerted their leader.

"Sir, someone has been here recently."

Gangel came over and then began looking above at the tower huts. Upon noticing that one of the doors was ajar, he signalled for the men to be quiet, withdrew his pistol and began to climb the wooden stairs, every man following him.

He kicked the door violently and it swung open, startling Kirichi from a gentle slumber in his chair.

"Whaa!" he said, surprised to see the heavily built brigadier and ten men huddled in the small space behind him. "I was expecting you earlier."

The statement cast a look of bafflement on Gangel's face but it was quickly replaced with antagonism.

"You are Kirichi, leader of the Makai?" he half asked, half declared.

"Indeed I am," Kirichi said in a bemused tone. "And you are from Raicema I presume?"

"I am a Raiceman and your executioner," Gangel bellowed with intimidation. "You have rallied your rebellion for too long. Now it all ends for you."

"It shall do you no good to murder me like you have others," Kirichi said, standing up sternly with his hands behind his back.

"With you dead, the Raicemans shall take their rightful role as leaders of this world!" Gangel said, repeating something he had heard countless times before.

"You are all fools!" Kirichi said loudly, laughing at Gangel and his men.

They all began to edge slowly around their commander.

"You believe that all that exists is purely physical and thus you crave more and more of the physical. You have let Ambitio, the great deceiver dupe you!"

Gangel and the soldiers looked confused, but Gangel's expression quickly changed back to one of aggression.

"You think I care about your philosophical concepts, old man? You are the main reason of rebellion against Raicema and nothing will stop me from ending your life. I have been ordered to do so!"

The brigadier withdrew his pistol from its holster.

Once again Kirichi burst out laughing, this time much more wildly. "Ambitio is not a concept!" he boomed with authority. "Ambitio is the artisan and its creations are an illusion designed as a trial for us all. You have indeed been *ordered*. You have been ordered into minions under Ambitio's pyramid of illusion."

Gangel was clearly not impressed and became more and more frustrated that Kirichi was so composed. He aimed his pistol towards the old man's forehead.

"Is this the way you brainwash the people of Lizrab? With fairy tales?" Gangel sneered, his followers all sniggering along.

At this question, the widest of smiles spread across Kirichi's face and he closed his eyes.

"If you do not seek the truth, then you seek only death!" Kirichi whispered in a creepy voice that seemed to become from beyond him.

Then, to the astounding shock of everyone present, Kirichi's body began to fade away, until he had disappeared completely.

"What?! What is this?!" Gangel stammered, feeling unnerved. He re-pointed his pistol at the place where Kirichi had stood. "You think you can fool me, old man, with your childish illusions?"

An eerie moment of silence fell, followed by an overwhelming feeling of anticipation, like the air was swelling with thickness. Then Gangel heard the most terrifying of screams from one of the soldiers behind him and quickly turned to see the young boy's face as white as a sheet, his finger pointing and trembling violently at something on the back wall.

All the men gasped in horror as a giant snake's head began to emerge from the wall, eyes burning with a misty energy.

The whole unit screamed and ran from the tower, Gangel himself pushing his followers out of the way aggressively to escape the terrifying sight. It was a moment of pure terror for all and something innate had taken over. Not one of the men could fight the uncontrollable urge to flee.

Some of the soldiers were pushed over the narrow walkways in the frenzy of the panic. As Gangel approached the stairway, he looked back and was hit with a shockwave of fear as he saw a mammoth, partially translucent snake towering above everything in sight. The sky had turned red and the clouds were black.

"It's the end of the world!!" one soldier was screaming frantically behind Gangel and in a scuffle he got pushed down the wooden steps, injuring his arms and legs in the fall. Then there was the most terrorising scream that vibrated through the entirety of Gangel's body and left him paralysed in fright at the bottom of the stairwell. Soldiers passed him without a second look, fleeing towards the jungle. Gangel stared, eyes widening as the snake seemed to grow larger and larger and denser and denser until its scales could be seen clearly. The sky turned the colour of blood and he began to feel like his entire body was being poisoned. His heart beat so fast that he lost breath. His chest palpitated irregularly and Gangel resigned himself to death as the head of the surreal snake in the sky turned to face him.

As he looked into its reptilian eyes, laced with gold and glowing red, he began to feel a heavy pain in his chest, like his heart was about to stop. The last thing he saw before everything turned to darkness was Kirichi on one of the walkways above, holding his hands high in the sky and looking up with reverence.

"It will eat us all! Run!!" was all Seth heard through his headset as he looked up at the glowing sky. It was so bright it changed the colour of every leaf and flower in the forest. He had reached a thinner part of the jungle and was about to give up and turn back to find out what had occurred.

"Will somebody respond!" Seth said again into his headset. "What is going on over there?"

Then his tracker beeped and he spotted King, lying on the floor in the distance.

At first he thought he was dead when he saw the dried blood on his arms and neck, but then he noticed King was breathing faintly. He knelt beside him and prodded.

"Go away!" King said weakly, his fragility somewhat shocking Seth.

"It is me, Seth."

"Make it go away. It is haunting me!" King griped, refusing to look around him.

"Not you as well!?" Seth said callously, wondering what was happening to everyone in this strange land. "Get up, man, you are being a fool!"

King continued to cover his head with his arms, refusing to look up or move. Seth knelt down with more sensitivity and touched King on the shoulder.

"King, there is nothing here."

King began to look up slowly and seeing only Seth, he gradually got to his feet.

"Where have you been?" Seth asked him. "Our entire army is almost wiped out."

"I can't do it anymore," he confessed, lowering his head in shame. "I can't kill anyone anymore."

The statement seemed make Seth slightly angry, but he relented and continued to converse about the matter.

"King, if we don't all stick together there will be more and more death," he said firmly. "You running off has cost us lives. If we don't fight death, then it will surely come to us."

"No," King said defiantly. "We bring it on ourselves, coming to nations where we have no place. Even you don't know why we are here."

"I know exactly why we are here," Seth said aggressively, raising his voice. "We are here to liberate this land!"

"You sound just like your brother," King said with pity.

"Who the hell are you to talk about me and my brother, soldier?" Seth barked, growing angrier by the second. "Despite your differences, we are both your leaders and don't you forget it! You are lucky to be part of one of the greatest nations on this planet."

"I cannot trust you anymore. You told me I was an orphan. You said that I didn't have any family and that your father found me during a trip to Ciafra."

"It is that way. You have no family."

"You are a liar!" King roared, an overwhelming energy raging through his body. "I met my father and I am starting to remember him."

A strange piercing sound emanated from the sky, resonating through their bodies, making them both wince.

"Whomever you think you met has clearly played you for a fool," Seth said more calmly, trying not to aggravate King any further. "You would have nothing if it wasn't for Raicema and the pity of my father. Haven't I always treated you well? And this is how you repay me – with treason!"

The words struck a chord in King and he fell silent, thinking of his past and the comradeship that he and Seth had shared during difficult times.

After many moments of silence, Seth breathed out loudly. "I am willing to overlook what has happened and won't mention it to Jeth," he told King. "Now come on. Something strange is happening here. We must retreat at once."

At that moment, a crackle came through Seth's headset and before the caller could speak, Seth barked at them. "What took you so long?! What is going on over there?"

"Uh, General Tyrone?"

"Yes!" Seth said with impatience.

"I am sorry to have to tell you this, sir, but we just found President Tyrone. He is dead, sir. Someone has killed him."

Seth's face turned to stone and his eyes glazed over. Then he looked at King lying weakly on the floor and the words of his father whispered through his mind. "Watch that boy closely, Seth. When he falls, so will Raicema."

Chapter 24 – Cuzco

It was late evening at the border of the town of Cuzco. Javu led his party through lush asparagus-green fields. Bright yellow butterflies floated above their heads. After walking for hours, everybody's legs hurt, the long hike new to most of them.

In front of them loomed a series of great mountains, the closest not more than a few suns ahead. Cuzco itself was a farming town, its location at the base of a mountain giving the surrounding soil a nutritious and fertile quality. The fields were full of a stout, feathery plant arranged in long rows.

"Ow!" Teltu yelped as he brushed against one of the plants, which had bell-shaped, greenish-yellow flowers. "They look like feathers, but they are prickly!"

Javu chuckled to himself as he, Teltu and Sita paced on ahead. Behind, Elera, Bene and Reo chatted whilst they walked at a slower pace through the fields. They were talking about the prophecy that Bene had discovered whilst living in Raicema.

"I am sure that there is nothing sinister behind it," Elera said to Bene, referring to his grandfather's secrecy about the subject.

"But he told me that he and my father knew about it for a long time," Bene argued. "It was only because my father died that I knew that such a prophecy existed. And about something so prominent to where I come from."

His voice trailed off with disappointment, like a scolded child.

"Maybe Kirichi was trying to protect you from something," Elera suggested, thinking about what Bene had told her. "It seems that there is much speculation about what it means. Maybe he didn't want you placing all your hope in such a prediction."

"What? That someone out there can help us all change? Can help bring peace to this planet?" he questioned, unsure why anyone would be against such a notion. "That seems like something that we *should* put our hope into."

He paused for a moment.

"It seems that you feel the same, Elera. Otherwise why would you be looking for Lemuria?"

Elera had to think for several moments before she could articulate an answer.

"The difference, Bene, is that the prophecy you have described puts hope in one person to save us all from the evils of this world, whilst what I am trying to prove is that we are all capable of saving ourselves."

"And how do you intend to do that?" Bene asked her, accepting the point.

"That I really don't know, but I feel so strongly that we will discover a way by finding out more about the past."

"Well my grandfather seems to believe in you," Bene commented with a hint of resentment. "He seemed positive that your journey has a meaningful purpose."

Elera fell silent, contemplating the deeper confidence that Kirichi had in her. She was slightly concerned about how she could tell Bene that she was intended to succeed Kirichi in Turo after he was gone. She herself felt a little frustration at how the Makai leader had kept his grandson in the dark about such matters.

Reo, who had been trailing behind listening to the conversation, felt excited to be part of such a journey filled with mystery. His life now was so different to what it once was. He had preoccupied every moment of every day with making enough money to keep off the dangerous streets of Calegra. He pondered about the people that he had previously associated himself with, only interested in taking drugs to escape from the woes in their life. He felt inspired by the people that surrounded him now.

"When I lived in Calegra, I always thought that everyone lived in the same way, crowded and fighting to get through each day," Reo said suddenly, changing the flow of conversation. "I can't believe that so close to where I am from, there are people that live in such a free way. Just look here, no pollution or people shouting. Amazing!"

"I have never been to Calegra," Elera said. "But I have heard that it is overpopulated. In Ciafra, where I am from, there are very few cities left. People seem to have spread out into smaller communities and are a lot freer now that Ciafra isn't occupied."

"When was it occupied?" Reo asked her.

"About twenty years ago," Elera informed him. "The Raicemans had a large presence in western Ciafra but many Makai warriors came from Neoasia and Vassini and there was a lot of fighting. I think they decided to leave anyway when they found that there were very few fuel sources left."

"Yeah, and ever since they've had their sights set on Lizrab," Bene commented with bitterness.

"So I guess there are not many vehicles in Ciafra, then?" Reo asked, half ignoring Bene's comment.

"There are hardly any," Elera said. "People mainly get around by horse or by the sea."

"In Calegra, only the rich people own vehicles," Reo told her. "Everyone else uses the horse traders."

"It's great how so many people all over the planet have adopted that approach," Elera remarked. "There are even traders in the more remote areas of Raicema. If you think about it, you have to have a lot of trust for that to work. You have to trust that you will receive healthy animals and trust that people will continue to give them to other traders to keep the cycle going."

They all thought about it for a while as they reached the edge of the town, where several people were out in empty fields ploughing the ground, each with a small plough attached to their feet. As the farmers walked over the fields, they too turned over the earth and the dozens of men, women and children all doing this in unison made the work look like a cheerful dance.

Running along the edge of the town was a thick wall made from the same sort of irregular blocks that Elera had seen countless times before, all fitting together tightly like a honeycomb. Built alongside the walls were long-running buildings with small windows, all covered with wooden shutters. A small wooden canopy ran along the top of each of the terraces, with lanterns hanging along their length. As they walked past, they noticed how the walls extended into the town, creating a number of pathways, all with similar terraced houses running alongside. Elera thought how much the town must look like a maze from above.

Further into the town was a circus with a number of trees and flowers planted all around. There were several benches and the group all sat down upon them, resting from the long journey from the Turian region.

"Do you think we will find a place to stay?" Teltu asked Javu, looking around. "There aren't many people around."

"If not we may have to set up a camp on the edge of the town."

As Javu said this, a young girl walked around the corner of one of the pathways, carrying a small grey puppy. When she saw the six strangers sitting in the circus, she quickly rushed over to them and began speaking in a language that nobody seemed to understand.

"She must be speaking a local dialect," Elera said to the others.

"I wonder if she speaks Lizrabian," Bene said, crouching down so he could speak to her at eye level. She did not understand the words that Bene spoke to her.

"Maybe she speaks *Quechua*?" Elera suggested, herself kneeling down and stroking the puppy. "Yaw! Ayllu?"

"Napaykullayki!" the girl replied, clearly understanding Elera's words.

"She understands!" Teltu exclaimed. "Speak to her more, Elera."

"I am not fluent in Quechua," she told him. "I only know a few words."

Elera did not have to speak any more, however, as the girl turned away to leave.

"Kaypi," the girl said to everyone, gesturing that she wanted them to follow her.

Bene suggested they did, so everyone gathered their things and followed the pretty girl through the streets of Cuzco. Before long they came to a house that was part of a row. The girl took Elera by the hand and led her inside, where a middle-aged man and woman were sitting at a wooden table preparing some vegetables and bread. When they saw the girl and Elera enter, they slowly got to their feet and offered a warm-hearted greeting that Elera did not understand. The girl told her parents something and the man went outside, bringing everyone into the small dwelling.

The couple found a place for them all to sit, continually offering welcoming words and gestures.

"Thank you," Reo said gratefully as the man prepared a woven cushion on the floor for him to sit upon. Then the couple began to boil water on a stone fireplace at the back of the room, leaving the young girl and the puppy sitting on the floor with the guests.

"Pay sunqulla," Elera said to the woman as she brought a clay mug of tea to Elera. The woman understood and smiled at the words of thanks, which Elera knew she probably didn't pronounce correctly.

"Can you ask them where we can stay? Is there an inn?" Teltu asked Elera.

"I am sure there is not," she told him. "I will try."

She attempted a number of words that she thought might get her question across but neither the parents nor the girl understood. Finally she put her hands together and rested her head on them making a sleeping gesture and then pulled out a small piece of gold from her bag. The parents seemed shocked at what she was implying and quickly made a number of gestures of reassurance. The man took Elera's hand and placed the gold back into her bag. He then gave her the warmest of smiles and gestured that she should remain in their house.

"I think they want us to stay here," Elera told everyone. The parents went back to work preparing the meal as they had been before but they added many more vegetables, fully intending to feed and house their new visitors.

"Pay sunqulla," was all Elera could say, to which the young girl laughed over and over.

Chapter 25 – Call of the Dragon

In Turo it was dusk. The two guards at the main gate sat peacefully, chatting about the recent battles in Aradonas. Suddenly, there was a large rapping outside that sounded like a large stick being run along the logs of the gate.

"Hello, let me in," a voice said from outside. "I am here to see Kirichi."

The guards opened the gate with caution but they let the man pass when they saw his clothing and recognised his face from the day before.

Rekesh's clothes were slightly tattered with shredded parts tied into knots on his sleeves and waist.

"Is Kirichi here?" he asked the guards.

"He is here," one replied. "But he only just returned and is very tired. He is resting in the monastery."

Rekesh began to walk quickly down the valley towards the town as the guards closed the gate. His mind was swirling with a multitude of thoughts as it had been since he left the Raiceman war vessel with blood on his hands. He felt exhausted and heavily anxious, like all his internal organs could cease functioning at any minute. His only thought of comfort was catching up to Elera and holding her close. He was sure the warmth of her body could heal any negativity dwelling inside him.

Rekesh almost began to run down the hill, a false sense of urgency coming over him. His neck felt so hot and no matter how many buttons he undid on his shirt, it made no difference.

As he got closer to the town, he could see the great orange sun beginning to dip into the ocean, casting a sparkling stream of amber across the sea. In the surrounding fields, people sat talking and eating. The monastery came into view as he began to walk through the streets of the outskirts, and after a brisk walk he arrived at its steps. Several monks sat quietly at the front, stirred from their thoughts by Rekesh's presence.

"Hello," one greeted him. "You have returned."

"Yes. I was told Kirichi is here."

"He is resting so I will have to check if he is strong enough to speak with you."

Just then, thoughts of Rama popped into Rekesh's head. He felt ashamed that he hadn't been more concerned about his welfare.

"Do you know if my friend is okay?" he asked the monks. "I left here for Aradonas along with two of the villagers a few days ago."

"Your friend came back here with the others yesterday. He is fine."

The news came as a great relief to Rekesh.

"He is staying with a family in the town. Maybe you can go and see him tomorrow."

Rekesh agreed, more eager to speak with Kirichi. The monk led Rekesh into the monastery through some hallways towards a room with a strong wooden door. He told Rekesh to wait whilst he entered quietly. After a short while, he returned with a smile.

"He wishes to see you."

Rekesh entered the room. Kirichi was resting, and he began to sit up slightly in his wooden bed. The monk departed, leaving the door slightly ajar.

"Ah, so you are the famous Rekesh?" Kirichi said cordially, his movements depicting that he was frail and old.

Rekesh was taken aback by the question and was unsure how to respond. "It is nice to meet you finally," he said approaching the side of the rigid bed.

"Likewise, Rekesh," Kirichi said. "Elera has spoken of you many times."

The words filled Rekesh with instant calmness.

"And I have heard much about you," Rekesh reciprocated, a little surprised at Kirichi's current condition, having heard so much about his vibrancy.

"Are you okay? Are you unwell?"

"I am recovering from a bad deed that I felt compelled to

perform," Kirichi confessed. "Indeed, one that could have been a mistake and ended my life. I am sure that I will get better soon."

Rekesh nodded, feeling remarkably similar to how Kirichi was describing. "I came here to find out where Elera and Javu are," he said, hoping that they were close by.

"They are on their way to Cibola," Kirichi told him. "They left early yesterday so they should be close to the mountains by now."

Rekesh thought about whether he should set off as soon as possible to try and catch up with them, but looking outside revealed darkness – something that Rekesh did not want to be surrounded with when alone in the jungles of Lizrab.

"You should stay the night in Turo," Kirichi advised, picking up on Rekesh's indecision. "A strong young man like you will easily catch up with them. I am sure they have stopped travelling for the night as well. There are a number of rooms here in the monastery where you can stay."

Rekesh agreed and thanked him. He was about to bid the old leader goodnight when Kirichi asked a question that threw him completely off guard.

"So, you are a friend of Sadana Siger?"

"Um..." Rekesh stuttered. "I know him, yes."

"I assumed so because the Makai community in Raicema is closely knit. How long have you known him?"

"For a few years," Rekesh told the old Turian, who had both of his arms over the covers in quite a symmetrical manner.

"I see," Kirichi said sombrely. "And what do you think of him?"

"He seems determined," was all Rekesh could say.

"Indeed," Kirichi agreed. "Are you aware of the history between the Matteros and the Sigers?"

Rekesh shook his head weakly, not sure he wanted to hear it.

"You should be aware," Kirichi said as if he were reading Rekesh's mind. "Both tribes were present at the inception of the Makai faith in Lizrab, several hundred years ago. At some point along the way, the Matteros settled in southern Lizrab whilst the

Sigers established communities in the Calegra region. Sadana is the last in the line of Sigers and feels that it is his birthright to rule. Indeed, many others believe so too."

Kirichi sat up, leaning as close as he could to Rekesh.

"And you would be surprised at how many of those *others* know each other."

Kirichi paused for a moment.

"Unfortunately, there has been competition throughout history between the two tribes because of their different approaches to leadership. For example, my approach is one of guidance only whereas Sadana's is one of decree. It has been like that for as long as the two tribes have existed. In fact, within the Raiceman Makai communities, there are actually laws that one must abide by. You may be aware of such laws?"

"Yes, but they are not like the laws of the Raiceman government. They are only suggested, not enforced."

"I disagree," Kirichi contested, sensing Rekesh's defensive stance. "If one does not abide by the laws, then one is condemned by the community. I believe this approach only damages the overall community."

"But without such rules, there would definitely be anarchy."

"Wrong," Kirichi said firmly. "There would only be anarchy if the community expects anarchy."

Silence fell between the two as they both realised their differing opinions could quickly cause a heated discussion.

"It is late and we are both tired. Now is not the time to delve deeper into such subjects."

Rekesh turned to leave and as he did, Kirichi left him with one chilling warning. "I only mention it because the approach of the Sigers is open to deliberate corruption and manipulation," he told him directly. "You know that Sadana murdered my son, don't you?"

Rekesh said nothing, surprised at the challenge. He shook his head weakly and then bid Kirichi goodnight. He left the monastery room with an overwhelming fatigue hanging over his head.

Kirichi lay back and breathed out deeply, quickly falling into a deep sleep. The monk returned and made sure the door was firmly closed before leading Rekesh to another room where a bed was made for him.

Lying awake in the comfortable bed, Rekesh's mind raced about Kirichi's questioning. He drifted into a surreal sleep, like his thoughts had created a vacuum that he was being pulled deeper and deeper into.

☼

Rekesh had slept through the entire morning and awoke as the midday sun beamed through the window. His body ached from the previous day's events and though he had slept deeply for a long period, he still felt fatigued and troubled. He slowly got out of bed and dressed, scenes of the battle on the beach racing through his mind. He could still smell the sweat, taste the blood. He looked at his giban, which was lying on the floor and he felt repulsed by it. Regardless, he picked it up and hung it over his shoulder.

Heading through the monastery, he found that it was silent and empty.

Outside, Kirichi, Rama and several monks were all sitting around a table in the sunshine playing a game of *patolli*. The table itself was inscribed with the patolli playing board, which looked like a large X with a number of grooved-out spaces snaking around the inner edge of the shape. It looked like an unusually shaped racetrack.

There were a number of different coloured pieces on the board, all in different positions and one of the monks was shaking something in his hand. After a moment or two of this, he threw four grains of flat rice onto the table. Two of them landed with black marks facing up and the other two landed plain side up.

"Ooh, you were close," another monk said to the monk that had just thrown, who moved one of his pieces two spaces.

"Good afternoon, Rekesh." Kirichi greeted him from the table, looking much more youthful and energetic than the night before. "I trust that you slept well."

"Very deeply," Rekesh commented with a weak smile, approaching Rama and rubbing him on the shoulder. "I am glad to see you, Rama."

Rama patted Rekesh on the hand, comforting him, yet his attention was squarely on the game.

"Will you join us?" Kirichi invited Rekesh to the game. "Do you know patolli?"

"I think I'll pass," Rekesh declined politely. "I intended to wake much earlier and set off. Now we will have to make up the time."

"If you wait for an hour, Jaho will be back with a group of horses. You can take two and you'll reach Cuzco in no time."

The offer seemed like a much better idea to Rekesh than trying to make up time on foot so he accepted and pulled up a chair to the patolli table.

"So how do you play?"

"Here are six pebbles," one of the monks said, handing him six smooth and rounded blue pebbles. "You need to get one when it's your throw to enter a pebble onto the board. Then it's a case of getting as high rolls as you can to get around the board. If you finish the race before everyone else, then you win."

"But beware of the *danger spaces*," another chubby monk warned him, pointing out a selection of spaces in the middle of the X. "If someone lands on the space you are on, your piece has to go back to the beginning and you have to give one of your *assets* to the person who got you out."

"Assets?"

"Yes. You can use anything you like as an asset," the chubby monk said, reaching for his small collection of objects. "I am using an apple, a belt and this gemstone. I have already won one asset from Kirichi."

"And the winner gets all the assets when all their pieces have finished going around the board," another said.

Rekesh only had his giban and a shell he had found on the beach as collateral, so he placed them both on the edge of the table. The game continued and when it was Rekesh's time to throw the rice, he managed to get a roll of one on the first go.

"Mmm, lucky," one of the monks said jovially, pointing to the board. "So you put one of your pieces on that space."

Another round went by and one of the monks lost a piece and so gave a small vial of oil to the monk that had got him out. Rekesh's turn came again and this time he threw the rice with no black marks showing.

"Nothing," he said in a deflated manner.

"No, you got five," the chubby monk told him. "All plain means five. You are lucky."

Rekesh moved his piece five spaces along one leg of the X. The captivating game continued and everyone got lost in it.

Eventually, Rekesh, Kirichi and the chubby monk were all close to completing. Rekesh had lost his shell, yet he hadn't managed to win anything. It was Kirichi's turn and he rolled three, moving exactly onto a danger space where Rekesh's penultimate piece was placed.

"I guess that means that this giban is yours," he said to Kirichi holding it out to him. Kirichi took it somewhat reluctantly. Another few rounds occurred and again Rekesh found himself in a similar position, with the same piece vulnerable on a danger space. Kirichi rolled once again and came up with the exact number to land on Rekesh's piece again.

"I don't have any more assets," Rekesh said to Kirichi.

"Well you have to offer something," the chubby monk said. "There is still a chance you may get it back if you complete the game."

"What's that around your neck?" another monk asked him, spotting a thin thread.

"I can't bet that," Rekesh said defensively. "It doesn't belong to me."

"If you show me what is around your neck," Kirichi said strangely, "I will accept that as payment."

Rekesh reluctantly reached down into his shirt and produced a strange-looking, sharply cut red crystal stone bound tightly to a thin length of leather. It shone eerily, like there was a dim flame within threatening to explode outwards.

"You are right. It does not belong to you," Kirichi stated upon seeing the stone. "Where did you get that, Rekesh?"

"It was a gift. I am only looking after it."

"You are wrong," Kirichi said quite forcefully. "It is not a gift, but a burden."

Feeling shaken, Rekesh put the stone away and after a few moments of awkward silence, the game continued. After a few rounds, Kirichi got his last piece to the finishing space and won the game. Everyone handed over their remaining assets.

"Kirichi always wins," the chubby monk said with a childish tone, but then laughed off his disappointment. The monks got to their feet and headed back into the monastery to continue with their daily routine, leaving Rekesh, Kirichi and Rama sitting around the patolli table. Kirichi looked at Rekesh carefully, as if trying to read him.

"What do you know about the stone that is around your neck?" Kirichi asked him after a while.

"Not much," Rekesh said sincerely. "As I said, I am just looking after it for someone."

Kirichi was about to ask Rekesh something else but then he seemed to change his mind and decided to alter the subject. "Jaho will be here soon. Do you know the way to Cibola?"

Rekesh shook his head. He felt awkward around the Lizrabian leader, almost afraid that he was trying to read his mind.

Kirichi spent a while describing the way to Cuzco and beyond, anticipating that Elera and party would be on their way to the old mountain by now. Whilst he was describing landmarks to look out for, the sound of several horses trotting could be heard coming down the valley. Before long, a group of eight horses came into sight, ridden by three men.

"Ah, Jaho." Kirichi greeted one of the men as he pulled the horses up outside the monastery. The man had oily semi-long black hair and short, thick stubble. Some of the monks came out of the monastery upon hearing the arrival.

"This is Rekesh and Rama," said Kirichi, "whom I was telling you about."

Jaho got down from his horse as did the other two men. He walked over and shook both of their hands firmly.

"I heard you helped fight off the Raicemans on Aradonas beach," he said directly to Rekesh. "Thank you for your help."

The appreciation came as a slight surprise to Rekesh. He was led to believe that the sentiment of non-violence was much stronger in Turo. Nevertheless, it lifted some of the remorse Rekesh was feeling from the brutality he had participated in.

"I have just come from Aradonas. The Raiceman ships have left and the funerals have begun for the dead. This was one of the largest assaults they have unleashed on us for decades, but I have a feeling that they will not be coming back anytime soon."

Rekesh nodded with a smile, glad that the invasion was over.

"So you are to travel to Cibola with Elera and Bene?"

"Bene?" Rekesh asked, with a hint of suspicion in his voice.

"Bene Mattero. He is Kirichi's grandson. He has only just returned from Raicema."

The news was a revelation to Rekesh. He knew exactly whom Jaho was talking about, yet he had never known that Bene was related to Kirichi.

"Do you know of him?" Jaho asked.

"Yes. I have met him many times in Raicema City. He seemed very involved with the Makai there."

"Only to find out what that bastard Sadana is plotting," Jaho said with resentment, gritting his teeth. "You know he murdered Bene's father for power?"

Rekesh did not want to get drawn into a political discussion. "We really need to get going as we have a long way to travel."

Jaho nodded and led him to two horses at the back of the quiet group.

"You can have these two," he told him. "They are originally from the mountains, so they'll run like the wind. Shouldn't take you more than a day to catch up."

The estimate gave Rekesh a feeling of relief and he ushered Rama to get on his horse.

"Before you go," Kirichi said, stepping forward, "I want to share something with you that may help you in dangerous situations." He looked specifically at Rekesh like a father about to impart some wisdom to their child. "Sometimes things get out of our control and we invite into our lives entities which we cannot handle," Kirichi said, now being deadly serious. "If that ever happens to you, remember that there are many things out there that can help you.

"The one that I want to tell you about is known by many as *the angel*. The angel is a very special manifestation of the cleansing force that exists in the universe. It comes to help us when we are most in need but one must truly wish for it with their entire being. Remember that if you ever feel that you are lost, deeply wish for the angel to come to you and it will help you break free of the place where you are trapped."

Rekesh didn't really understand what Kirichi was implying, unsure if he was speaking metaphorically or not. "Are you saying that there is something out there, a being that you can call upon?"

"Not a being but a force, Rekesh," Kirichi told him. "Really, it is present in all of us already, but calling upon the angel can help us realise this and manifest it in our lives at that moment, which in turn can help us break free if we have become trapped."

Rekesh wasn't sure if he could believe what Kirichi was saying.

"It is the cleanser. Its sole existence is based on cleansing the bad energies that exist and encouraging forgiveness amongst us."

"It is good to know that such a force exists," Rekesh said.

"Indeed," Kirichi agreed. "However, for those who plummet into the realms of dangerous and power-hungry energies, an encounter with the angel can be so overwhelming that their physical bodies cannot handle it."

"Are you implying that someone would die?" Rekesh asked with a dreadful feeling in his stomach.

Kirichi said nothing, his silence confirming Rekesh's conclusion. Then he smiled at both of them and laughed a little. "Since I have made you aware of the cleansing force, it is unlikely that you will ever reach such a position." He tried to reassure Rekesh, who had a worried expression on his face. "Remember the force is already innate within us."

Then Kirichi leaned close into Rekesh and whispered into his ear. "But if you want my advice, I wouldn't carry that stone around for much longer."

Rekesh didn't know what to say so he mounted his horse and Rama quickly followed. They waved to the monks and Jaho as they rode out of the town up towards the valley.

Seeing the red stone had left Kirichi with a concerned feeling in his chest, partly due to memories about his son, Juhi.

Within a moment the two young men were out of sight.

Once outside the gates of Turo, Rekesh led the way on his horse, allowing it to trot gently though the foliage. Then suddenly, both horses sped up, as if they knew that time had to be made up. They were fluid, cantering through the forest like they knew it intimately. All Rekesh and Rama saw was a blur of brown and green as the trees and leaves zipped past, a low branch occasionally shocking them from their dreamlike ride with a feathered slap in the face.

As they travelled through the depths of the Lizrabian jungle, the humid air rushed over their faces and washed away every possibility of thinking. It was in this state, that Rekesh noticed something very strange happening to the stone around his neck.

Beneath his shirt, an ominous red glow was radiating outwards, surrounding his entire body. It felt like it was floating, not resting against his chest like before. A vice of panic gripped him for a moment. Then he heard a terrifying voice that sounded like the rise of a thundercloud.

"I want to be free," it echoed eerily in his ear.

The voice was not loud, yet the words that had been spoken seemed to resonate on and on through Rekesh's body like a shock wave. He looked around for Rama, but the blur of the ride had now turned into a swirling haze and he could make out nothing beyond his own body and the horse's muscular back and mane. He was being consumed, wrapped in a bubble of melting vapour. Then a hand shot through the mist and yanked him hard from his horse. He fell hard onto the solid floor of the forest, bashing his knee into a tree trunk. He heard his horse bucking and screeching and he tried to gain his bearings in a daze.

Rama slowly came into focus, holding the reins of the one remaining horse – Rekesh's had bolted. Rama spoke frantically in Hindi, so quickly that Rekesh could not understand one word. The words seemed incomprehensible as all Rekesh could think about was the angel that Kirichi had described and how he desperately wanted it to protect him. The stone around his neck had stopped glowing and was resting against his chest again. After a moment of composure, he took it off and contemplated throwing it deep into the forest. Rama's horse bucked wildly as the stone came into sight and it took all of Rama's might to control it. Rekesh quickly put the stone back around his neck and out of sight. Again, Rama was speaking to him in a frantic manner, almost with an angry tone. Fatigue set in once more and after a few moments of sitting and letting calm restore itself, both men climbed upon the one horse they had left and rode off at a much slower pace.

Several hours passed and Rekesh and Rama realised that they were lost in a mountainous region somewhere near Cuzco. The horse was getting tired, stopping every now and again and jerking its head in frustration.

"We'll have to stop here," Rekesh said, more to himself than to Rama. He dismounted and Rama followed suit. They both looked around from the pathway, high up on the side of a rocky mountain with little shelter.

Out in the distance, all that could be seen was other mountains. Rekesh scanned up and down the landscape and spotted a small forest further down the slope. He pointed it out to Rama and they began to walk down, leading the horse by its reins. After slipping a few times on numerous crumbling mountain ledges, the trio made it down to the copse. Within the shadows of the forestland, Rama gasped as he saw a reddish light penetrating from underneath Rekesh's shirt. The tired horse jolted away from Rekesh's grasp and began to buck and then rear wildly, screeching in fear as the light got brighter and brighter. It then bolted with urgency into the thicket, out of sight.

"What's happening?" Rekesh shouted as the red light began to enshroud him.

The light disappeared and Rekesh was alone in the forest. He looked around frantically, yet Rama was nowhere to be seen.

A feeling of desperation gripped him. He felt totally lost and without hope.

Somehow, he was deeper in the forest and he began to run in the direction he thought he must have come from. Eventually, he found the edge of the copse, yet he didn't recognise it. Darkness had fallen in an instant. Looking up to try and find his bearings by the silhouette of the mountainous slopes, he was horrified to discover that no such silhouette existed. At that moment, Rekesh thought he might be hallucinating yet no matter how many times he opened and closed his eyes, he was still at the edge of that unfamiliar forest. Then he heard something petrifying.

A sound radiated from somewhere above, so metallic and screeching that it made Rekesh sick to his stomach.

Looking up, he saw stars, yet they were strange – unusually close and in patterns that appeared alien. He noticed one of the stars was moving bizarrely, shining in a dim, unnerving manner. It began to get closer and as much as Rekesh wanted to look away he couldn't. He was frozen to the spot, his eyes glued on the unknown entity. It glowed red and grey in a fusion of surrealism. Waves of catastrophic emotion crashed around his body as the full horror emerged.

The entity had a face, the face of something primeval.

Rekesh needed no other confirmation that he had found himself present in a nightmare beyond that which he had known imaginable. Before him, getting closer and closer, was what could only be described as a dragon. Its giant snout oozing a red mist and its gigantic body looking like a planet made of molten metal and fire. Its eyes were that of a reptile, completely silver with long vertical slits that seemed to suck everything into them.

Rekesh felt the air beneath his feet as he was lifted up in the air. He felt so fearful that he couldn't think nor breathe. He was being pulled towards the nightmare in front of him.

He felt himself losing consciousness with the sensation that his insides could take no more. The screeching sound got louder and louder until it was unbearable and overpowering. He wanted to think of the angel but he couldn't. He felt something consume him and his last thoughts were of Elera as he plummeted into the realms of unconsciousness.

Chapter 26 – Journey to the Old Mountain

It was the afternoon in Cuzco. Everyone had slept late and had to be awakened by their host family. They all guessed it was the mountain air that had sent them all into such a deep sleep.

Now all packed and ready to continue their journey, Elera was bidding farewell to the kind and welcoming family.

"Dyuspagrasunki amigu's," Elera said to them on the porch of their house, trying to say *thank you kind friends*, and knowing that she was saying it wrong. Nevertheless, the couple and young girl seemed to understand and appeared appreciative. Elera took out a small gemstone from her shirt pocket. It was a piece of garnet she had found in Seho. She gave it to the young girl as a gift. The girl showed it to her parents with delight.

The group set off, Teltu and Reo bounding ahead with a great deal of energy whilst the other four walked at a more leisurely pace through the town in the direction of the mountain range in the distance.

"I guess we should head for the old mountain," Elera said to Javu, whilst Bene and Sita brought up the rear of the party.

"Yes, but it would take us several days to reach there on foot. We need to find some transport. There are no horse traders in Cuzco. I guess as the people are able to grow food quite easily they have no need to travel long distances."

"I don't even know how to ask anyone where we could find some horses," Elera said with a sigh.

"I am sure something will come up," Javu said positively.

The group reached the edge of the town and headed towards a rough path that led down into a valley. The further down they walked, the more hardy the ground and plants became and eventually, the shadow of a great mountain ahead began to block the light from the sun, dropping the temperature considerably.

"We need to walk around this mountain and then in between the two behind," Javu told everyone. "After that the old mountain should come into view."

They walked for hours on gravelled ground, winding around the mountain path. The land dipped and rose steeply like a wave. Looking up was humbling, the view of the endless heap reaching far into the sky. Clouds cloaked the tops of the mountains.

Bene looked back at Cuzco every so often, seeing it getting smaller and smaller in the distance.

"It's starting to level out a bit," Reo shouted back from up ahead as the land began to get smoother and less hilly. The edge of another mountain was starting to show as they walked further inwards, across some plains in an easterly direction.

"I still think we should have waited in Cuzco for Rekesh and Rama," Elera said to Javu with concern. It was a topic that they had already discussed earlier.

"Don't worry. They will be directed if they reach Cuzco, but I've just got a feeling they are going in a different direction anyway. When we reach the old mountain, there is a village where we can wait."

Elera nodded, feeling more at ease as the pace quickened.

Eventually, the group were able to change to a more northerly direction as they reached the most eastern edge of the mountain. Before them was a sight of godly proportions. Nobody had realised how high up they all were.

Ahead, they could now see an immense valley of ridges, with two enormous brown and green peaks beyond.

"We need to travel down this valley and between those two mountains," Javu told them. The instruction was met with sighs of disbelief.

"It will take forever," Reo said dejectedly, estimating that the distance to reach the edge of the two mountains alone was probably twenty suns.

"After that, the old mountain will become visible to the west," Javu continued, ignoring Reo's whining. "We will then have a steep climb ahead to reach the city of the old mountain as Kirichi described."

"It looks pretty desolate," Bene commented. "What if we run out of food?"

"The planet will provide all we need," Javu said, moving onwards, leaving the others in doubt. They quickly followed and began to climb down a steep slope, which had a variety of tough plants growing along it. Reo speedily caught up with Javu who was leading the way, eager to speak to him.

"Javu, how come you are so trusting that we will find food along the way?" Reo asked him. "People don't think like you where I am from. Everyone is always worried about how they will afford food."

"I guess that living directly on the planet has helped me trust the planet more, but it is not the main reason that I believe in such natural provision. I have always found that if one focuses more on what one already has rather that what one doesn't, life has an uncanny way of providing you with what you need."

Javu paused for a moment.

"I think that is true regardless of where one is living."

"But in Calegra people have to buy food," Reo contested. "There is no way they could *find* food."

"But in that case a way would be provided to those people for them to pay for the food, one way or another."

"But how?" Reo asked, unsure and sceptical. "There are so many poor people living in Calegra and neither food nor money simply drops out of the sky for them. Are you saying that it is their fault that they cannot feed their families?"

Javu could sense the defensive tone in Reo's voice, aware that he must have experienced a great struggle to support his family whilst he was growing up.

"I do not fault anyone for not having the minimum, Reo," Javu made clear. "But are you saying to me that the people in Calegra do not help each other?"

"Some do. Others don't care."

"Well that is a burden that we all have to carry. Just as we cannot control what empires like Raicema decide to do, we cannot control those people. What we can do, however, is be grateful for what we do have, whether that be the food that grows or the kind people around us. That in itself helps everyone."

Reo was still unsure but he walked along mulling it over.

Ahead, the path was becoming slightly rocky with multiple sharp dips along the surface. A scraping sound was heard above, followed by a few pebbles and some dirt falling down in front of the group. Looking up, they spotted a white llama, its fur thick and tightly curled. It looked at them all for a moment before walking away in a parallel direction above.

"Follow it," Javu said quickly, clambering down the pathway. The others followed in pursuit and kept an eye on where the llama was going. It carefully navigated the bumpy terrain until the ground seemed to level off above.

"It seems flatter up there," Reo said. "It's gone out of sight."

He quickly began climbing upwards at a rapid pace until he was on the same level as the llama had been.

"Hey, there's a farm over there," he shouted down to the others, who immediately followed the route that Reo had taken.

Indeed, there was a small wooden building in the distance with scores of llamas wandering around the nearby land.

"Can we ride them?" Elera asked Javu as they walked towards the farm, the long necks of the llamas all turning to look at the group heading towards them.

"These animals have been used to carrying things since people came to this land," he told her, an amused look in his eye. "We will have to see if the farmer is willing to spare some."

As they reached the simple set of barns, one of which resembled a crooked bungalow with a tightly packed straw roof, Javu signalled for everyone to stop. A middle-aged man with short spiky hair and rough skin could be seen through the bungalow window sitting at a large wooden table.

"I think only I should go in and talk to the farmer," Javu told everyone. "We have little to offer, yet if we do not overwhelm him, maybe he will let us borrow the llamas."

Everyone agreed, though they were all confused as to how Javu was going to communicate with the farmer. Javu knocked lightly on the door and entered, leaving the others standing outside sheepishly.

Many of the surrounding llamas seemed intrigued by the visitors and began to slowly come over to the barn area.

One particularly large llama walked over to Teltu and looked him directly in the eyes. With the llama's long neck, its head was exactly at the same level as Teltu's.

"Hello?" Teltu said in a friendly tone.

The llama paused for a second and then it drew back and spit in Teltu's face, causing everyone to burst out laughing.

"I think it likes you, Teltu," Elera teased him, as he wiped his face with a cloth from his satchel. More llamas were now in close proximity, trying to assess their new visitors. They had a mix of brown and white woolly fur. They all had large tassel-like tails that they would shake now and again. Two llamas in the distance seemed to be playing quite roughly, wrestling each other with their necks.

"Are you sure we can ride these animals?" Teltu asked Elera, becoming more nervous as he thought about the notion. Before Elera could answer, Javu emerged from the small bungalow barn carrying a large sack and with a wide smile on his face.

"The farmer will allow us to take six llamas as far as the city of the old mountain," he announced. "He was also kind enough to provide us with this dried cereal for them should we reach areas where there is little vegetation for them to graze on."

The expressions on the faces of the group ranged from excitement to immense concern.

"Javu, I am not sure these animals are safe to ride," Teltu protested, observing the two llamas which were neck-wrestling aggressively.

"They are very friendly creatures," Javu informed him. "We will all be fine, plus they have much better feet for the mountains than we do. You will soon get acquainted with one, Teltu."

He walked over to Teltu with a hint of mischievousness lifting his eyebrows.

"We each have to choose our own to ride."

After a few moments of apprehension, everyone began to approach a llama with the intention of forming a stable bond with it. Sita was the first to gently sit upon the back of a brown llama. Javu and Elera had soon after managed to sit upon one of the creatures. Elera was surprised that how under the soft woolly fur, the llama's back was strong and muscular.

"Come on boys!" Javu said humorously to Bene, Reo and Teltu, who were all finding it difficult to get a llama to stand still. "All of the llamas have been trained by the farmer so it is not the first time they have been ridden."

After several more attempts, everyone was finally sitting upon a llama and they came together into a pack quite instinctively.

It was a bit bumpy at first, but everyone quickly gained their balance as they rode along a ridge away from the farm, cascading downwards in a snaking pattern.

"Javu, can I ask you something?" Reo said, trying to keep his llama level with Javu's as they rode down the winding path.

"Anytime, Reo," he replied genuinely.

"Is it okay to kill?" he asked, clearly troubled by the question. "I mean, in certain cases, if someone is attacking you like when Raicema attacked Calegra or if you need to hunt for food?"

"Both of those cases are quite different," Javu commented. "However, my simple opinion to your question is that it is damaging to everything around us to be wasteful. When I say wasteful, I mean wasteful of the energy that we are connected to."

There was a pause as the llamas walked over a particularly rocky part of the path.

"So in your first example of an attack, it would be a great waste of human energy to allow a massacre to take place, so I think defending yourself in that case is a good idea."

Again he paused.

"As for your second example of hunting, I think it is even more important not to be wasteful. If one was starving and there are no alternatives, hunting might seem like the only option were you not to waste your own energy, however, there are many other sources of energy. We are fortunate that we are constantly presented with so many other options."

"But you eat meat," Reo said shrewdly, finding it hard to understand his viewpoint. "And you have alternatives so why not take them instead."

"I eat the meat that is offered to me but I never request in any way for animals to be killed for meat. As I said, I do not believe in being wasteful."

There was silence for a few moments and Javu could tell Reo was trying to come up with a counter argument.

"Reo, it is down to ourselves to determine what is right and wrong. We can only share our views with one another but we cannot tell each other how to think and feel. Forcing someone to be like you also wastes energy."

The words seemed to put Reo at ease. He began to ponder why Javu thought of everything in terms of energy. He wished that he could be like Javu, instinctive and trusting of his own decisions.

"Sometimes it is not good to think too much," Javu said jovially as they reached less bumpy terrain, the majesty of the U-shaped valley before them. "Thinking can be confusing!"

Javu then burst out laughing, the deep sound echoing all the way down the valley and beyond.

Sometime later, Elera and the group had successfully begun to travel between the two giant mountains at the bottom of the valley. It had taken several hours of navigating their way down on the boisterous llamas. The mountains seemed immense, awash with a variety of different terrains visible in the distance. The group was currently travelling through a flatter patch of land covered with cacti. In the not-too-distant future, Elera could see that they would be navigating through thick forest as the ground began to ascend upwards.

"This land is very diverse," Elera commented to Javu, who was riding by her side.

"Mmm," he agreed. "I feel like I have a special connection to this place, even though I have never travelled here on foot before. Maybe it is because I originally come from a mountainous region similar to this."

Javu then retreated in his own contemplation, leaving Elera looking around in awe at her surroundings.

Memories of Javu's childhood in Vassini came flooding back to him. He had felt the same sense of magnitude from the mountains near to his hometown. Just looking around invoked a sense of nostalgia within.

Javu's uncle, who was a sage in the village of Sarmaldha, had raised him. The sacred village was well known in Vassini as a centre of mystical practice and many of the locals in the region had a great range of superstitions indoctrinated into their way of thinking. Javu had found out first hand at a very young age that some of these superstitions were well-founded.

When Javu was no more than four years old, both of his parents mysteriously died of an unknown illness. Talk immediately spread throughout Sarmaldha that the couple had fallen victim to an evil curse. At the time, Javu could not fully understand the circumstances of his parents' deaths, but when he was a little older, his uncle Actesh Rusmeli informed him that their deaths were an act of vengeance against him by a powerful man who lived in a nearby mountain.

The sorcerer *Vuktar* had been banished from the village years earlier upon suspicion that he was responsible for the death of many animals in the area. A thin and crooked man, Vuktar had dedicated his life to the practice of *summoning,* as had the Rusmeli family for many generations. Actesh had told his nephew all about the practice and its dangers as soon as he had deemed him old enough.

"The act of summoning is one of power, make no mistake about it, Sinidev," Actesh had told his doting nephew, who was then only known by his birth name, Sinidev Rusmeli. "One can summon for the good, yet it is much easier to summon for the bad."

"How do you summon, Uncle?" the young Javu had asked eagerly.

"Before I tell you, I must make sure you are fully aware of the risks involved with practicing. If you conjure energy in this manner, there is always a risk that the energy will overwhelm the summoner. In some cases it can even possess them.

"That is why you should only use the skills I will teach you when you are in great need of help. For you, it will be easy to become complacent as you come from a long line of summoners and you will learn quickly."

Javu had not taken his uncle's warning very seriously back then, however, with age he had discovered that his uncle was right and Javu had often found himself in many dangerous situations.

"The secret lies in vibrations," Actesh had told him. "Just like we can understand each other in the way we speak, energy responds to specific vibrations, in some cases, very complicated ones.

"Words are a very powerful tool in summoning. Both the choice of words and *how* they are spoken is vital. But it is not the only way.

"The most powerful summons do not need any words at all. Sometimes where you are located can make a vast difference too. Take for example our village. We are located in a special place on the planet where certain kinds of vibration are particularly prominent and a summoner can use these to his advantage. Indeed, my grandfather once summoned one of the most powerful energy forms possible due to the location of Sarmaldha. Have you heard of *Respiro*?"

Javu had not heard the name before back then, but it was a name that he would never forget.

"Respiro is a *protector* which has a great affinity with Sarmaldha.

Let me say that my grandfather was no ordinary man after his encounter. The things he could do defied the imagination!"

Javu had learnt a great deal from his wise uncle and before long was practising the art of summoning, achieving tiny feats at first like conjuring a small breeze to lift a leaf off of the ground or blow out a candle. Actesh kept a close eye on his nephew and when he was ten years old he told him more about the sorcerer Vuktar.

"He has gone too far and has been consumed by power. When that happens, one tends to surround themselves with powerful things and Vutkar has done exactly that. One day I will tell you of one of the most powerful objects in the world which Vuktar holds in his possession."

Javu had begged his uncle to tell him about it but every time Actesh had refused, citing that one must have great integrity to even know about the object. Javu remembered waiting for what seemed like an eternity for his uncle to decide that he was ready to know about Vuktar's most valued possession.

Then, one evening as the young Javu was sitting to the dinner table with a steaming bowl of spiced lentils in front of him, Actesh let him know about much more than Javu was expecting.

"Before I can tell you of Vuktar's possession, I have to explain about the most powerful act that any summoner can perform. It is the act of being a *medium,* in which you allow energy to pass through yourself in order to direct it somewhere else, more specifically, to store it somewhere. It is both a useful and dangerous ability to acquire, Sinidev, so exercise extreme caution now that you are aware of it."

"But what would I store, Uncle?" the young Javu had asked.

"The only valuable thing that can be stored; *knowledge.* However, many other things can be stored which leads me onto the object that Vuktar will not let out of his sight, that which he has in his possession and that which he is possessed by."

His uncle had paused with eyes wide.

"What he possesses is known as the *air stone.* Stored within it is a very destructive energy, that which Vuktar has been trying to unleash for the past ten years. Powerful sorcerers of the past managed to capture the essence of death in this stone using methods that are thankfully lost today. It is this stone that has caused the death of your parents, Sinidev, and it is my own failing that they are still not alive today."

Javu had felt his uncle's anguish at that moment and had promised himself that he would never hold his uncle accountable for his parents' demise.

As time went on, the more he learnt of the air stone and of Vuktar only drove Javu further in his desire the learn and protect people from such destructive energies that existed in the world.

Now, as he and the others rode through the dense, steep forests of Cibola, his childhood was so fresh in his mind that it could have just happened yesterday.

The forest was clearing ahead and a narrow bridge could be seen made of rope and small planks. It appeared as if by magic over a narrow gorge, making everyone realise how high up they already were. They stopped to assess the situation.

"I'm a little concerned about taking the llamas over that bridge," Elera said out loud as they moved closer to it, thinking that it looked old and rickety.

After a while, they decided to send the llamas across separately and as soon as they had reached the other side safely, everyone followed on foot. Whilst walking across, Reo could feel the bridge swaying and he kept looking anxiously at the large knots that held the ropes to the planks, half expecting one to start coming undone at any moment.

The ravine below seemed like a thousand suns away and Reo had to force himself not to look down. After everyone had made it safely across, they rounded up the llamas and continued to ascend upwards, the terrain now much more open, with bushy plants scattered around.

"Why doesn't anyone live here?" Reo asked, amazed at how

desolate it had been since they left Cuzco.

"There have been many wars in this region," Bene told him, trying to speed up his llama so he was climbing alongside Reo. "Not in recent history, but my father and my grandfather always used to tell us about them when we were children."

"It's true, Reo," Elera said knowingly. "Maybe two thousand years ago, this region was alive with civilisation. There were a number of different empires ranging from southern Lizrab all the way into the depths of Cibola and the most well-known of these was called the *Maeya*. At some point in the past, there was an invasion from across the sea and before long this region became uninhabited. Nobody is really sure of what happened after that."

"They say that the Maeya are the ancestors of the Lizrabian Makai," Bene added, Reo listening with interest. "I think that after the Maeya disappeared from Cibola, the lower lands started getting much more populated. That's when cities like Aradonas and Calegra started forming. People stopped living in the mountains so much."

They continued upwards for several hours, the land becoming much more sparse and open and the two great mountains beginning to spread apart. After a while, it began to level and the enormity of the terrain quickly became apparent. Before them was flat land, stretching for suns and suns into the distance. Beyond, more great mountains were partially visible.

"It so different up here," Bene commented. "The land is so dry."

"Let us press on," Javu said, the llamas picking up speed over the even ground. "If you look carefully, you can see the old mountain over there in the distance." He pointed to a peak that could barely be seen, surrounded by scores of other mountains.

"How can you be sure that is the old mountain?" Reo asked, a hint of whining in his voice. "There are so many."

"I know it by its shape. You too will notice the difference when we get closer."

The flat plains ahead contrasted greatly to the view behind. Looking back revealed the rich, deep and uneven landscape of the valley of which they had just navigated through. The llamas were walking playfully now, coming together more and travelling in a close pack.

"Elera, you lived in Raicema for a while, right?" Bene asked her as they travelled side by side.

"Yes. In Raicema City mainly."

"How come I never saw you there? That is where I lived."

"I tried to keep to myself. To be honest, the only reason I went there was to learn from the talented academics who live there. Even though the government there try to keep the general public in the dark about the long and varied past of human beings, they still endorse the research of a selected group of people. They even pay a lot of money for them to do it. I spent most of my time in the company of those people."

Bene was facing forward, concentrating on where he was going. He looked like he had become lost in his own thoughts. Elera glanced at him with intrigue.

"Kirichi told me you were living there. To be honest, he told me to stay away from you. He said that you were in a dangerous situation," she admitted, causing him to look at her pensively.

"I was there to get justice for my father's death, but I failed," he said in a wallowing fashion. "I could not prove the guilt of the perpetrator."

"Sadana?" she said, invoking a twinge of anger in Bene's gut.

There was silence for a few moments, everyone else quiet as the sky as the dust flew up from the hooves of the llamas.

"I remember first seeing you about three years ago," he said after a while, glancing at her face, her skin smooth like silk and the colour of rich honey. "After my father's death, I wanted to challenge Sadana's leadership in Raicema directly. As Juhi's son, I had the right to do so, but my grandfather stopped me. Then I heard that he had agreed to a meeting with Sadana and I couldn't believe it."

Bene paused for a moment, glancing over at her again.

"It was at that meeting that I saw you for the first time."

Elera was thinking hard, trying to remember Bene.

"I don't remember seeing you there," she admitted, feeling a little embarrassed at the admission. Then a horrendous thought crossed her mind and the expression on Bene's face confirmed what she had just realised.

"You were that assassin!" she blurted out in disbelief, shocking everyone else as well. "I always thought that it was an attempt on Kirichi's life, but you were going for Sadana."

Bene nodded, holding his stomach as if his scar had started hurting.

"After that, I vowed that I would take his life in a different way, by shaming him for what he had done. But I failed there too."

"What did you hope to achieve, Bene?" Elera asked, somewhat annoyed at Bene who was hanging his head. "Even if you'd have killed Sadana, do you think that would have helped things in Raicema? The problem is that people are so afraid of change. That's why they rely on monsters like Sadana and the Tyrones to keep things stable for them. Until the people change, corrupt leader after corrupt leader will always take advantage of that weakness."

Javu smiled at Elera's strength and wisdom, realising why Kirichi had chosen her as his successor. She leant over to Bene and rubbed his hand comfortingly.

"I know what it is like to lose your family. It is easy to become angry but will that really help anything?"

Bene knew what Elera was saying was significant, yet the burning for vengeance within was keeping his vendetta very much alive. He tried not to think about it, focusing on where they were heading.

Ahead in the distance, the glimmer of a lake could be seen reflecting the early evening sun. As they got closer, everyone realised that the lake was enormous. It was easily fifty suns wide and stretched all the way to the mountains in the far distance.

"Unbelievable!" Teltu declared. "I have never seen a lake this big. It's almost like an ocean."

"What are those over there?" Reo asked out loud, pointing to something in the lake in the distance.

"They look like islands," Elera said, squinting in the warm evening light.

"Mmm, it will be dark before long," Javu said, stroking his long beard. "There may be villages on those islands. Maybe we can find a place to stay the night. It will take us at least another day of travelling to reach the old mountain."

Everyone agreed and began to make their way to the edge of the lake, where there were bountiful bunches of reeds growing from the shallows. Further along, they could see large groups of llamas drinking from the lake and grazing on patches of grassland that were scattered around. The mountains in the distance seemed pious, some of the tallest they had seen with large snow-capped peaks.

"Maybe it's time to let the llamas go," Elera suggested. "It seems like this is a native place for them."

"But how will we get to the old mountain tomorrow?" Reo asked.

"I'm sure a way will present itself," Javu said reassuringly, agreeing with Elera's suggestion.

The llamas were let loose and they instinctively headed to the large groups further up the shore of the lake.

"So how do we get across the lake to those islands?" Teltu said to himself out loud.

The sight of a long narrow boat coming into view quickly answered his question. It was heading towards them from across the lake. The boat travelled slowly and took a while to reach the shore. Inside, there were two women and a man, dressed in coloured, chequered manila shawls and heavy leather boots. The women wore plain polleras under their shawls and the man wore a round brown hat.

Elera greeted them in Quechua, which they all seemed to understand. One of the women responded, yet Elera did not understand what she said.

"I think they want us to go with them," Javu said to Elera.

She was unsure, but as they began to gesture for everyone to get in the boat, she knew that Javu was right. The boat was big enough to hold the three islanders and the six of them, made out of a skilled use of thick reeds, woven in a meticulous and accomplished design.

"This boat is made of Totora reeds," Javu told them, whilst their three hosts rowed quietly in the direction of the islands. "Quite remarkable, mmm?"

As they got closer to the set of islands, everyone was astounded to discover that they too were made out of Totora reed structures.

The base of the island was made of thick woven stacks with the houses and fences beautifully created out of the one resource that grew plentifully in the giant lake. There were even lookout towers crafted out of the reeds on a few of the islands.

"That's how they must have seen us," Reo declared, amazed by the towers and houses on the island's villages. The long boat pulled up to a small jetty and the three islanders helped everyone out and onto the floating island.

"It feels strange walking on an island made of reeds," Teltu commented in an amused fashion. "It almost feels like the island is moving."

"It probably is, Teltu," Javu said.

One of the women gestured for the group to follow her towards a fairly large reed house. Inside, there was a woven table and chairs and a several flat bundles on the floor, with layers of pile creating mattresses. The woman said something in a friendly way and then disappeared outside, leaving them wondering what was going on.

"I think she has gone to get the leader of the village," Javu said. "And it seems that we may be sleeping here tonight."

Sure enough, the woman returned with two other men, one of whom was covered in an intricately woven shawl, indicating that he was someone of high importance.

The man was quite old with wispy white hair and deeply tanned skin. He smiled at the six of them and began to say something in a language that Elera did not recognise. To everyone's astonishment,

Javu began to converse with the man in the unknown language, holding his hand with affection and glancing back at the group every now and again. After a while of this, he turned to them with a smile.

"This is Tepeu, the advisor of the people who live on the reed islands. He has told me that he has been expecting our arrival for a while now and that the villages are preparing dinner for us."

Javu continued conversing with Tepeu, leaving the others speechless. After a while Tepeu and the others left, leaving everyone to settle in.

"What language were you speaking, Javu?" Elera asked him, a little embarrassed that she did not know.

"It is Uru, the language of the Uros people. Though these people living here now are only descendants of the Uros, certain sages and advisors such as Tepeu have made it their business to keep the language alive."

"How do you know how to speak it?" Bene asked him, intrigued.

To this question, Javu just smiled in a mischievous fashion indicating he was unprepared to answer. This only confused everyone even more, to which Javu let out a loud laugh at the expressions of bewilderment. "You all look like cattle! Bah ha ha..." Javu teased them all.

Sita was quietly sitting on one of the mattresses, looking for a change of clothes in her bag.

"Let's all freshen up a bit," Elera suggested, spotting a beautifully made wooden screen which she intended to change behind.

After half an hour, Tepeu returned and led everyone to a boat where they took a short journey across to another island. There was a much larger building there, made with a wooden frame but also mainly constructed of the Totoro reeds.

Inside, there were scores of people sitting around a large wooden table and a banquet of delicious-looking food had been laid out in honour of the six visitors. Large artistically painted clay vessels held steaming hot tea with delicate pink flowers floating in them. There were platters of a white potato-like vegetable, the steam from them streaming upwards in waves and a tray of unusual-looking fish in the middle of the table. There were also bowls of a fine brown grain interspersed with tiny white rings.

Everyone sat to the table and some of the villages began to serve plates to everyone. Tepeu sat next to Javu and was seemingly explaining what each of the dishes was. After listening with interest, Javu made the translation.

"This is a traditional dish of the Uros," Javu told everyone, pointing to the fish and grain that was on everyone's plate. "It is catfish and quinoa. This white vegetable here is actually the root of the Totora reed. Tepeu tells me it is very nutritious and gives one strong health."

Everyone began to eat and silence fell as they enjoyed each mouthful of the tasty food.

"What is this tea made of, Javu?" Reo asked him, sipping the fragrant yet bitter beverage.

Javu relayed the question to Tepeu. "The tea is made from the flower of the Totoro plant," Javu translated.

"They really make use of the Totoro in every way possible, don't they?" Reo commented, to which everyone nodded in agreement.

"As we were discussing before, Reo," Javu said, "the view that I and these people share is that it is not positive to waste anything."

Everyone ate and drank peacefully and quietly for a while, some of the younger villagers whispering to each other about the strange visitors to their village.

Outside, Sita could see that the sun was starting to set, causing the reeds to look like they were on fire in the evening light. It reminded her of Rama. As if sensing this, Tepeu said something to Javu in a vibrant and enthused manner. Javu then turned to Sita and translated what Tepeu had said in Hindi, to which Sita smiled widely and helped herself to more Totoro-flower tea.

"What is it, Javu?" Teltu asked with curiosity.

"Tepeu here is an astrologer of sorts and he told me that the stars have said that eight strangers would come to the lake when the moon was full. Well, the moon is full tonight. Hopefully that means Rekesh and Rama are on their way here."

The prediction gave Elera a boost of faith and contentment and she nodded in agreement. "I think we should wait here until they arrive. Kirichi said he would guide them towards us. I am sure they are both safe."

After everyone had finished eating, several young women began to play a number of wooden instruments including small windpipes, panpipes and wooden blocks that were used to make an interesting beat. As the music played on, everyone began to feel at home in the small village that floated on the magnificent lake high in the sky.

Chapter 27 – The Struggle

The water has come. It surrounds me and has swallowed me whole. Do I exist? Have I survived?

Hazed thoughts drifted into awareness, followed by the overwhelming urgency to breathe.

With the surge of freedom propelling him, Rekesh emerged from the darkness, his vision blurred, his ears ringing. He gasped like a fish. Water washed over him. He tried to see. He tried to look ahead but the lights were dim. Slowly, his focus returned and he was staring at stars in the sky, though this time they were familiar. He was surrounded by coldness, floating in wetness, a soft breeze tickling his face every so often.

He moved his gaze and saw the comforting sight of the round moon, its creamy healing light filling him with excitement. He sat up and found himself in a shallow part of a huge lake, the outline of mountains in complete circumference around him.

Someone was shouting something. Someone was calling his name. He looked around but saw nobody.

Something felt hot against his chest. He looked down and saw the glowing red stone around his neck, its light wavering. A jolt of panic shot through him as he saw the dragon in his mind's eye.

Rekesh quickly removed the pendant and after holding it in his hand for several moments, he turned and threw it as hard as he could into the depths of the lake. He saw it sink downwards, its light completely diminishing as it became lost in the deep abyss below. He heard his name being called again. It was a familiar voice. It was Rama's voice.

He pulled himself out of the lake and waded to the shore, trying to see through the darkness. Rekesh couldn't see Rama anywhere so he closed his eyes and followed the direction of the sound. After taking a few steps he opened his eyes and began to see the faint silhouette of his friend walking towards him. He called out to alert him to where he was standing. Rama reached him quickly.

"I am so glad to see you," Rekesh said, hugging his friend and getting him wet with his sopping clothes. Rama looked like he was in shock and just stared wildly at Rekesh. They began to walk aimlessly around the lake in a trance-like state, neither able of discussing nor fully aware of how they had arrived in such a location. Kirichi's words echoed through Rekesh's mind over and over. *'Where did you get that stone? It does not belong to you.'*

After walking for some time, they saw lights on the lake in the distance. Instinctively and without discussion, Rama leapt into the water and began to swim in the direction of the lights. His mind empty and somewhat dazed, Rekesh blindly followed, the water flowing over his face giving him a sense of peace and inner clarity. The horrible images of his nightmare had dissolved, leaving only an innate drive to push forward towards an existence without fear of such things. This moment of calm reflection lasted only a second, however, as questions began to formulate in his mind about his own sanity. His doubt invoked several feelings of anxiety within.

On one hand if what I experienced was an illusion, I am going slowly mad as I cannot remember how I got here, Rekesh thought as he swam. *On the other hand, if it was real...*

After what seemed like an eternity of swimming through the lake, Rekesh began to see that the light was coming from the windows of houses on an island.

All of a sudden, shouting could be heard from above and in a moment of panic, Rekesh thought the same unthinkable dragon had returned. His heart pounded with fear.

He was relieved to find that it was a young man sitting in a lookout tower. The man had spotted the two of them and was alerting several other people on the island, all of whom were running across to a strangely shaped jetty nearby. One man was shouting something at them both, trying to get their attention. As they swam over, the people all helped to get them onto the soft and springy surface.

Rekesh and Rama both lay there on their backs, breathing

heavily from the long swim. The people began to chat amongst themselves in a speculative manner, though neither Rekesh nor Rama could understand one word that was being said. Then, in the distance, Rekesh heard a familiar voice.

"What's going on?" the soft voice of a young woman was asking.

Rekesh sat up, elated to see Elera heading towards him. Sita was close behind and they both embraced their respective partners, equally surprised at the state they were in.

"What happened?" Elera was asking Rekesh, rubbing his wet shoulders. "Did you get caught in the fighting? How did you get here?"

"So much has happened, Elera," Rekesh blurted out, emotions rising from within. "I don't even know how we got here."

Javu, Teltu, Bene and Reo had now arrived at the scene and every villager was talking, amazed that Tepeu's prediction had come true and eight visitors had arrived on the night of the full moon. Teltu and Bene helped Rekesh and Rama to their feet and led them to the dining house where everyone had eaten earlier. As they walked over the tightly packed reeds, they could hear the whispers of the villagers, clearly excited by the new arrivals.

Sometime later, after eating some of the wholesome food that the villagers had prepared, Rekesh and Rama had both regained their strength. Tepeu and the eight visitors sat around the dining table, sipping tea and discussing what had happened. All the other villagers had retired for the night, though many of the children were eager to stay up, fascinated by the strangers that had come to their remote village.

"After I got separated from Rama, I ended up near Aradonas," Rekesh told everyone, deliberately leaving out his encounter with Jen King. "I found out that the Raicemans were going to destroy Aradonas late that night so I warned the city. Their plan failed and one of their ships was destroyed instead. Then they came in hordes. So many are dead because of the battle that resulted."

Javu translated for Tepeu in Uros.

"I managed to get back to Turo, where I was glad to find Rama had already made his way back. In the morning we set off to catch up with you."

Rama, who had been listening quietly, turned to Javu and told him something quite hesitantly.

"Rama says that you set off this morning," Javu said with surprise. "How can it be that you have reached us here from Turo within a day?"

"That I don't know. We got lost around Cuzco and we ended up here."

Javu could tell Rekesh wasn't speaking the entire truth and his suspicions were confirmed when Rama described to him the red stone and its strange mist. Rama was clearly distressed recounting what he had seen and its effect on the horses. Javu decided not to announce to everyone what Rama had just told him.

Instead, he turned to Tepeu and started to converse with him over the meaning of the eight of them being together, building on what Kirichi had envisioned earlier. Javu translated their conversation.

"I was asking Tepeu about what he thinks the meaning is behind the eight of us being here like he predicted. He has told me that he thinks it has something to do with the 'Third Gate'."

"Third Gate?" Elera immediately jumped in. "Is that related to the fact we are looking for the third Lemurian pyramid?"

"Well, Tepeu has not mentioned a pyramid but he said the Third Gate is a sort of myth that has never been seen in living memory. It is supposed to look like two mountainous peaks, side by side. Tepeu says this gate is supposed to be protected by some kind of magic that has sealed whatever is beyond."

"Maybe the third pyramid is beyond," Elera suggested with enthusiasm. "Can you ask him why it is called the Third Gate and where is it supposed to be located?"

Javu again conversed with Tepeu for some time, his wiry eyebrows rising up and down every now and then.

"Tepeu says that it has always been called that and he does not know the reason, though he suspects it is because it is a location where three different worlds join together, a place where worldly boundaries can be crossed."

They were all fascinated by the old man's theory.

"To get to it will be a great feat as it is past the jungles of Vilcabamba," Javu continued, "which is one of the largest jungles beyond the old mountain. We must reach there first.

An interesting thing that he just told me was that nobody he has ever heard of has ever ventured past the Vilcabamba jungles. He says that this is because of respect of a *'very powerful spirit'* as he puts it. This spirit is known as the protector of the gate. He warns us to be humble and respectful if we intend to venture past Vilcabamba."

Elera had already made her mind up. She intended to follow the clues that continually presented themselves, sure that the third pyramid was near the gate that was being described.

"Can you ask Tepeu what else he knows about the gate?" Elera suggested to Javu. "Who is supposed to have built it? Where does the myth come from?"

Javu relayed Elera's questions and was unsurprised by his response.

"Tepeu says that the myth has been passed down by word of mouth for many generations. Many civilisations have come and gone to this region, however, he speaks of the *'great sorcerers'* that had a raw affinity to the planet and performed incredible feats. He believes that these sorcerers built the gate and other similar structures on the planet."

"I guess that fits in with what we already know," Teltu commented, who had been listening quietly.

Tepeu said one more thing to Javu to which Javu nodded knowingly.

"He also believes that these sorcerers of the past, were able to cross into other worlds of existence at locations such as the gate."

This last statement sent everyone into deep contemplation and there was silence for a while. After some time, everyone decided that it was time to get a good night's sleep, with the intention of setting off first thing in the morning for the old mountain. Javu opted to stay up for a while longer, however. He was eager to talk to his newly found friend, Tepeu.

In fact, as the dead of night fell over Cibola, Javu and Tepeu stayed up into the early hours talking of the past and the future. They talked about the strange things that people they knew were experiencing and how the planet was finding ways of protecting itself. They talked of how the past was presenting itself in many forms despite coordinated attempts to cover it up. They talked of the legacy and consequences existing in the world from the old sorcerers' mythical doings and its relation to the state that the earth was currently in.

Before they finally retired for the night, they both agreed that a struggle was occurring, one that was as archaic as the beginning of the universe itself. It was the struggle between power and freedom. It was a struggle that would soon come to a head.

Neither man could foresee what the outcome of this struggle would be.

Chapter 28 – City of the Old Mountain

The sun was perched over the tallest of mountains, like a great yellow eye sitting on top of a pyramid. The light streamed down upon the earth and water, dazzling and soothing all those under its path.

The reed islands had left a soft spot in everyone's hearts.

The warmth of the people who lived upon the lake had particularly touched Elera. To know that despite the wars that had been so close by over the ages, a unique and historical village was still living happily was a great comfort to her.

Reo had been in his element whilst surrounded by the friendly villagers. In fact, he was feeling homesick already.

"Can't we just stay there for a little while longer?" he whined to Elera as they made their way along a dusty path away from the lake.

"There are many more beautiful places to discover, Reo," Elera answered with sensitivity, understanding how he felt.

Reo drooped his head like a moody teenager as they walked further and further away. Eventually there was nothing to see except the driest of ground, luckily scattered with a few hardy plants.

"Oh yeah. This is much better," Reo moaned sarcastically to himself. Nobody paid any attention to him as the hot sun sweltered across the land. The air was blurred because of the heat rising from the baked ground.

"So the old mountain is this way?" Rekesh asked Javu at the rear of the party. Javu simply nodded, focusing directly ahead on the range of mountains in the distance.

Teltu was several strides in front of them, thinking about his daughter and wife. He hoped that Sula had safely reach Seho.

Streaked clouds were dispersing across the sky, the white-yellow glare of the sun almost radiating a sound of dryness. There was little other sound than the footsteps of the eight travellers walking over the dusty ground.

Sita and Rama, who were walking merrily in front, held hands affectionately while Bene walked behind, deep in thought. He had been both troubled and amazed throughout his life by the inner strength of his grandfather. He always seemed to have the ability to forgive those who had sought out to harm him. He pondered over and over on his own ability to forgive. He found that his emotions always came back to his strong desire for vengeance. He realised that something so negative had happened to him that vengeance was the only antidote. He dropped back to fall in line with Elera and Reo, who were now talking quite enthusiastically about the four ancient pyramids.

"I still don't understand who built them," Reo was saying as Bene reached his side.

"Nobody really knows," Elera replied. "The Great Pyramid of Giza is the only known ancient pyramid in the world. There is a lot of debate amongst scholars as to when that was built. Traditionally, historians have believed that it was built about seven thousand years ago along with the other pyramids and structures in the region. Raicema have tried to contest that, proposing that the entire Giza region was only built about a thousand years ago, which is ridiculous.

"Some historians, however, believe that certain structures like the Great Pyramid have been around a lot longer, maybe twenty thousand years or more. They were built in a way that was aware of the energies around the stars, the moon and us. That is very different than the way that most humans approach architecture today."

She paused for a moment, thinking about that magical underwater place where she had walked alone.

"The pyramid at Bimini was even more incredible, Reo, and I'm sure that it was built by the same civilisation that created the Great Pyramid of Giza."

"The Lemurians?" Reo asked.

"Well that's the name we are giving to the civilisation that built them. If we can find the third structure as described on the tablet I found, we may learn more."

Bene who had been half-heartedly listening wanted to change the subject. "Elera, what do you expect to find from this expedition you are leading us on? My grandfather seemed to think it was a good idea to travel here, that we all have a purpose to fulfil?"

Elera smiled to herself as they began to walk into more rocky terrain, the ground now rife with sandy stones protruding prominently out of the ground.

"We are going on a journey back in time," Elera stated jovially. "We are facing the past in order to help the future." She looked up at the trees, looked up at the sky. "The reason I was in Bimini and the reason I am here now in this beautiful place is exactly the same. I intend to expose to the world that there is a way free of violence."

Bene was somewhat sceptical. His own view was that strong leadership was needed to bring people together in a unified way and that sometimes required the involvement of violent acts. He failed to see how delving into the past could help to find a way that was against what he considered to be human nature.

"Regardless of what we find, surely the only important thing is the present," he stated matter-of-factly. "Even if you can prove that a civilisation existed twenty thousand years ago, what good will it do?"

"It is not about proving the existence of Lemuria," Elera replied firmly. "But about showing people that there was and *is* another way to live that is freer that the way civilisations have developed today. What I feel is that Lemuria is not just a place or civilisation that once existed, but it is also a way of life. And I feel that it is one that can help people find happiness. And what else is life about but love and happiness?"

Bene's expression was still laden with cynicism. He just smiled weakly at Elera's vision and said no more. This was mainly due to his thoughts being stirred back to his own doubts about himself and his own intentions towards others.

"I don't really understand," Reo said to Elera. "What do you think we'll find?"

"Every myth about Lemuria, no matter how different in detail, all come to the same conclusion; we should be happy with what we already have and stop craving more and more. I think that what we will find in Lemuria will show us that we actually have a lot more already than we actually realise. I think that by finding Lemuria, we will find that which has been lost within ourselves."

"Like what?" Reo persisted, growing more fascinated, whilst Bene pondered on his own misgivings.

"Well one ability I know exists is having the ability to move things with our mind and that includes ourselves. Just imagine that. If we could show the world that all humans are capable of such feats, what a difference that would make!"

She smiled with confidence that such a notion was possible.

"All the squabbling and competition over trying to find comfortable ways to travel and having to make money to be able to do so, it would be a thing of the past!"

Elera was indeed painting an illustrious picture of utopia for Reo. His eyes widened with her visions.

"What else?" he asked.

"It's endless, Reo. Anything that you can imagine to be possible was at one time possible in Lemuria."

Reo was unsure if Lemuria actually existed or if Elera was using the concept to achieve her aspirations. He found that he had a deeply rooted seed of doubt.

The group walked on for many suns, stopping now and again in the shade of the odd tree to cool off and rest.

"How long will it take us to reach the old mountain?" Teltu asked Javu as they all sat in the shade of an old tree.

"At least all of today and part of tomorrow I would think. To be honest, I only know of what Kirichi has told us so I am not entirely sure."

"And Vilcabamba beyond?" Reo reminded everyone, remembering what Tepeu had said about the Third Gate.

"Indeed," Javu agreed. "We may be travelling for a good while yet."

They rested for another hour before resuming their journey.

By nightfall, they had only reached a more complicated set of mountains, with no clear way to identify the old mountain that Kirichi had spoken of and that Javu had seen once before.

Every mountain looked quite similar, covered in lush vegetation like mounds of fresh green broccoli. They pitched a camp near to a small stream and spent the night outside in the wilderness.

The next morning everyone set off again with renewed energy, trekking with enthusiasm through the green, mountainous and humid terrain, yet again by the time darkness fell, everyone felt completely lost and the group set up a camp once more.

The same thing happened for the next three days and nights.

Finally in the morning of the fifth day since leaving the lake, as everyone was starting to lose hope that they would ever reach the old mountain, Javu let out a shout of relief.

"This is it!" he rejoiced, looking at an oddly shaped mountain directly ahead. "I remember the shape of the peak."

It had been difficult to keep fresh over the past four days due to the humid nature of the environment. Everyone longed for a place to bathe properly and rest in comfort, driving the group to climb up the mountain quicker than any other.

By the end of the day, they were close to the summit. There was a circular range of mountains in surround like the most grand and natural wall protecting the old mountain. The brown and grey rock faces were streaked with small groups of forests growing in peculiar places, making them look like moss-covered stones from the distance.

As they climbed higher, the primal paths got steeper and harder to keep a footing on. Looking around, Elera felt like they were in the centre of the planet, with nothing but nature in view. She began to doubt that any civilisation could possibly live this far from the cities of Lizrab but as she saw an old-looking statue hidden in the bushes, her uncertainty was lifted. They continued to climb until they reached what looked like naturally formed steps. As they ascended, the sight that came into vision was truly astounding.

They had reached an elevated ledge and below there was a flat mountain ridge with rows and rows of stone houses arranged in an organised way, all on different levels. In the background was the main peak of the old mountain, with a smaller peak to the left. There were a number of large, well-kept lawns, some of which were fenced and held llamas and horses.

Every house had a straw roof and smoke was flowing out of chimneys protruding from several of the buildings. The entire plateau looked like a small city, perfectly integrated with the mountainous environment, a number of ridged walls running down the sides of the town.

There were many people getting on with their daily activities throughout the entire citadel. Some carried large pots of grains and vegetables, farming the lawns and feeding the animals. Groups of people sat in various communal areas such as a wide opening at the back of the city that looked like an open school. It was amazing to see the entire metropolis in action from such a vantage point.

"Can you believe that this exists up here?!" Rekesh said, astounded by the settlement. "A thousand people could live up here easily!"

Reo was already making his way down some beautifully crafted stone steps towards the citadel, whilst the others simply stood there, trying to take in the unexpected view. They soon followed him down, eager to meet the people of the old mountain.

As they followed the steps downwards, passing several human-sized statues, they were greeted by several of the townspeople who were trying to communicate with Reo, though he was simply smiling silently in his inability to understand what was being said.

Once again, Elera did not understand the language yet Javu half-expectedly began to converse with the people. They were wearing

beautifully woven thick garments that seemed to take their inspiration from the natural environment, some dyed a range of greens,
and others blue and white like the sky.

"They welcome us and want us to meet the elders of the city,"
Javu translated.

As they walked further down several levels of stairs towards the
centre of the citadel, Elera was baffled that Javu knew so many of the
native languages of Cibola, trying to work out when he could have
possibly learnt them all. She was about to ask him about it, when
they arrived at a stone pathway next to a row of large houses. The
stonework was irregular yet airtight in its construction, reminding
her of the pyramid at Bimini. In the middle of the row was a circular-
shaped building and an elderly man and woman appeared from its
tall doorway, smiling and holding out their hands to greet the eight
visitors.

Javu began to converse and the pair seemed pleased at what he
was saying, whilst several other townspeople ushered everyone else
into the building. It was surprisingly grand inside. The stone walls
were lined with intricate paintings of the Cibola landscapes and of
the city, with rows of strong wooden tables and hundreds of elabo-
rately woven cushions on the floor and chairs. As Javu and the elders
followed, everyone took a seat as the woman began to address them
all in a loud and enthusiastic manner.

As she was speaking, trays of tea were brought around and the
group all suddenly began to feel very tired, the long journey finally
catching up with them. Javu listened carefully to every word that the
woman elder was saying before turning to everyone to explain.

"Popol and Itzel welcome us to the city of the old mountain,
known here as *Machu Picchu*. They are the oldest living natives of
this city and the advisors of the people who live here."

Popol was quite a rotund fellow and had a permanent grin on his
face, whilst Itzel was quite slim and looked fairly nimble. They both
wore hundreds of colourful, woven wristbands that went all the way
up to their elbows.

"Itzel has said to you all that we are welcome to stay as long as we wish and that a house is being prepared for each of us in honour of our arrival."

Teltu and Reo raised their eyebrows to each other with pleasant surprise, happy that they would have some measure of luxury after sleeping next to each other in small tents for the past four nights.

"I have mentioned that we are on a journey to find the Third Gate," Javu continued. "After we have rested, they will both help us on our journey. There is much that we can learn from this city. It has existed here for millennia, through times of peace and times of war. Itzel mentions that it was predicted that we were coming and that it is of great fortune to ourselves and the city that there are eight of us."

Elera's thoughts were drawn to Kirichi's initial emphasis on this number of people. It led to her being filled with the same raw contentment that she had experienced often. It was an overwhelming trust that there was a natural order to the unfolding series of events.

A banquet was prepared and they ate heartily with several of the townspeople. Shortly after, they were led to their accommodation for the night.

Everyone slept soundly in the comfort of a soft, warm bed. The houses were endearing, cosy in their appearance and earthy in their feel. The stone walls felt like cherished friends in the candlelight and the straw roofs created an air of warmth. The stars sparkled brightly through the windows in the dark of night with the cool waning moonlight casting its ethereal light upon the mountain.

As dawn broke, the bright sun flooded in through the windows of the houses. The energy of the city was electrifying, buzzing with the news of the eight travellers. As each of them emerged from their generous accommodation, they were greeted by large crowds of people.

Reo felt baffled by it all. Being treated like a celebrity was an unusual feeling, especially as he had become accustomed to keeping his head down in large crowds.

"Intihuatana!" Itzel announced to them all as she appeared from the crowd with Popol directly behind her.

"What does it mean?" Reo asked Javu, feeling a little nervous from all the attention.

"It means 'sacred stone of the sun'," Javu told everyone. "I think she wants to show us something."

Rekesh immediately began to feel anxious as the horrible vision he had experienced came back to him. He had forgotten it completely until now.

Itzel gestured for them all to follow her and they obliged, trailing her through the town from the *Popular* district where they had stayed to the *Sacred* district, where there were several temples all made out of dry-wall.

The buildings of the area looked slightly older and were constructed on a much grander scale. Several lone trees grew on small lawns around the temples.

A large crowd followed slowly behind and eventually they reached the edge of the district and an elevated clearing, in the centre of which was a multi-tiered stone that looked like an old sundial. The central pillar wasn't very high and as the eight of them gathered around it, they noticed something quite unusual. The sun was shining directly on the top of the central pillar and there was no shadow cast anywhere on the lower tiers of the stone.

Itzel said something to Javu that greatly surprised him.

"Itzel says that a shadow never forms on this stone, regardless of where the sun is positioned in the sky."

She continued talking for some time, pointing to the sky and ground every now and again.

"The *Intihuatana* is a wisdom rock like Kirichi was telling us about before," Javu explained. "It goes deep into the mountain and is the oldest structure in the city, created by the old sorcerers to store the energy of the sun. Itzel says it has been here for as long as humans have had love in their lives. I'm not sure what she means by that."

"You mean there are wisdom rocks here too?" Elera asked Javu, who relayed the question to the elders. Popol responded with great enthusiasm.

"Popol says that Cibola has one of the greatest concentrations of such rock in its mountains and forests but it is rare that the rock is exposed as it is here."

Itzel began to speak again, moving over to the pillar and touching it affectionately.

"Itzel says that if one touches their forehead to this stone and they are of pure heart, a vision will appear of the *spirit world*. She says this will help us in our journey. The spirits will guide us."

Rekesh was immediately reluctant and started to back away from the stone slightly.

Javu began to converse with the two elders in detail about the stone. After he had finished, he turned to the other seven. "I will not be touching my forehead to this stone," Javu told them firmly, without further explanation. "However, one of you should do as Itzel says."

Elera immediately stepped forward, causing many people in the crowd to let out a gasp as the hot sun streamed down.

"Wait, Elera," Teltu said, holding her lightly by the shoulder. "Remember what happened in Bimini."

She smiled at him and placed her hand on his. "Don't worry, Teltu, I am not going anywhere." She reassured him, walking forward slowly and kneeling upon the lower tier of the stone. It was surprisingly cool. She leant forward as everyone looked on in anticipation.

As her forehead touched the rough stone she felt a tingling at the point of contact. A strange sensation spread around her body, as if she were being filled up with air, making her lighter and lighter. Then a wave-like feeling fell over her, starting from the very top of her head and travelling down through her eyes and teeth, neck and chest. As it passed through her stomach she felt a little nauseous. She could feel a pressure on the top of her head, as if something were pushing her down.

A bizarre darkness seemed to enshroud her vision. She tried to pull her head away but found she could not, her forehead glued to the stone. The darkness quickly passed, however, replaced by a hazy creamy light and a sudden feeling of weightlessness.

Now there was no desire to pull away from the pillar because it had dispersed without her realising it, and before her was what could only be described as an ocean of light, stretching endlessly all around. She was floating and looking down. Her body looked different, like it was made out of a billion streams of light, constantly interweaving into each other.

Before her, a group of hazy-looking humans emerged. They all had the same appearance of being made of light. As they floated more closely towards her, she could see the trail of illumination they had left. It almost reminded her of all the fast cars in Raicema City as they sped along the autoways.

As the group of beings came into clear view, Elera could see that they looked like natives from the Cibola region, based on their features and same woven dress that the people of the old mountain still wore.

Elera heard them speak to her, yet it was completely different than being spoken to in a particular language. It was as if she simply understood what it was they were transmitting to her. She could still feel. It was the most effective communication that she had ever experienced. She did not know how to respond but it did not matter, for she only wanted to listen.

She felt that the beings were reaching into her deepest fears and desires.

"Do not be afraid, Elera. One can never lose another."

She had heard the message before, in her dreams. It had upset her then.

"There is really nothing to be afraid of. Death exists in your world, but

not here."

She realised at that moment that she had a deeply set, inner fear of losing the people whom she loved. She imagined not being able to see them again. It wasn't a trail of thoughts that were going through her head. It was more like a series of visions.

"Life is endless, so how can you lose another?"

The question rang through her brain like a strange melodious song. The group seemed to be glowing, almost spreading out into the ocean of light. She suddenly realised what had upset her so much in the past. It wasn't the fear of loss as much as the knowledge that death existed in the first place that caused her pain. Deep down she knew that death was not really the truth and that such an illusion drove so many to acts of hate greatly disturbed her.

"The time draws near when the universal force of power will dominate everything. Power in your world is nothing more than the drive to escape death, but the consuming nature of this energy affects the entire universe and all realms of existence. Freedom is realising that death doesn't really exist. You wish to help many by seeking the truths of the past but you should ponder how you could help to awaken the truth in each being... Only with a strong seed can the cycle possibly be broken. You and those like you are that seed."

Then the beings of light dispersed completely from view and darkness returned for a moment before she felt the sensation of something pressing against her forehead. It was the Intihuatana stone.

Elera was back in the city of the old mountain. She looked around and saw everyone looking on in anticipation.

"Did I disappear this time?" she asked Teltu. "I felt like I went somewhere else."

"No, you've been there the entire time, silently," he told her.

She got to her feet and explained to Javu what she had been told. She recounted every message, though she knew the words were her own interpretation only. She felt frustrated at how to convey that which had been crystal clear to her.

"I was told that there is a universal force of power that gets stronger as more and more people act selfishly because of their fear of death," she said finally. "If we don't do something, it will dominate everything."

Javu translated the messages to the elders, who were eager to talk about Elera's vision. They immediately began to discuss it amongst themselves.

Elera started to feel a little dizzy and as she took a few steps forward, Bene noticed that her legs were giving way and he managed to catch her in his arms as she passed out, falling forward. Rekesh immediately ran over as Bene laid her on soft ground. He knelt down and began to stroke her face and hair.

"Elera, wake up," Rekesh said, his voice a little panicked. He held her head in his hands and tried to revive her.

Itzel stepped forward and ushered everyone back, saying something to Javu.

"It is overwhelming to reach into the spirit world," Javu told them. "She will be fine. She just needs some air."

Sure enough, within a few moments Elera came around, looking up at several faces peering down at her.

"What did she mean the force of power will dominate everything?" Teltu asked Javu whilst Bene and Rekesh helped Elera to her feet.

"Ima sumaq anka!" Popol exclaimed.

"Popol says the Great Eagle is watching us," Javu translated. "It is the way that many in Lizrab have traditionally described an incredible force in the universe. It is said that if one could glimpse this force, it would look like a great eagle soaring through the universe. I do not think that this is the same force that Elera is trying to convey."

"What's that got to do with the Third Gate and with the pyramids we are looking for?" Teltu asked, not understanding the relevance.

"I don't know," Javu admitted. "But it seems as though Elera has touched on something much more significant than finding out about the old sorcerers of Lemuria."

Both Itzel and Popol began to converse with Javu, a slightly more urgent tone in their voice.

"They say it is time for us to leave,"

"Have we outstayed our welcome?" Reo asked, confused at what was going on.

"Not at all, Reo. It is just that they believe we are on a tremendous path of knowledge. We will need every moment of inspiration and that will be more gratifying if we travel on foot. It is a good time to leave as we have a long journey ahead."

Everyone spent a short while gathering their things and packing up all the offerings of food the townspeople brought to them. Then they gathered by the carved steps between the two peaks of the old mountain, at the other end of the city to that which they had arrived, ready to set off by foot.

"Can't we take some of the horses or llamas from here?" Reo asked.

"The elders have already explained that we must go on foot, Reo," Javu scolded him. "Did you not listen before? We must respect their traditions and views."

Reo dropped his head in shame but quickly perked up as the group set off up the stairway between the small and large peaks.

"Qhalilla karu puriy!" Popol and Itzel said in unison, followed by a recitation by the crowd behind them. And with that farewell, they set off down the other side of the old mountain, the undergrowth of the unknown stretching far beyond.

Chapter 29 – The Third Gate

The journey of the eight companions over the next week was both gruelling and testing.

Immediately after leaving the city of the old mountain, the group headed north along the *Kiteni* river, dense jungles in surround and mountains in every direction. The environment not only felt overwhelming but also intimidating at times. The sound of unknown creatures crying out to each other was never far away and it unnerved many in the group as they camped at night.

Most of the time it was cloyingly humid. However, as the group scaled the mountains of the northern Cibola region after a few days of travel, relief was granted by the cooler air of the mountaintops.

Seven days after setting off from Machu Picchu, after climbing and descending mountainsides and trekking and weaving through the undergrowth, the group came to an unusual jungle forest towards the top of a mountain. The clouds were so low that the moist mist made it difficult to see what was ahead.

"It's like a forest in the clouds!" Teltu exclaimed, not seeing more than a few trees ahead.

After an hour of navigating through the cloud forest, they were surprised to find a small and abandoned settlement in a clearing, comprised of a few small stone structures, all now interwoven with trees and vines.

"It could be an old settlement of the Maeya," Elera suggested.

After resting for a while and taking a closer look around the ruins, they continued on, starting to descend once again back into deeper forestry. They reached the bottom and exhaustion set in, almost simultaneously in every person.

"Let's set up camp here," Rekesh suggested, finding a more open spot where there was less likelihood of being bitten by crawling creatures in the night.

Everyone agreed and all were sound asleep as darkness fell.

That night, Sita had a fantastic dream. She was floating in the sky, the forests and mountains beneath her. In the darkness the forests rustled in the shadows and the mountains rose like waves. She floated over two, then four, then six before coming to a flat, calm piece of land. It was a vast plain.

In the distance was something great, something huge. Floating as high as she was, the thing in the far distance seemed to be at eye level. The next thing she knew, she was there, next to it.

It was a mountain so strange that it looked unreal, like it was made of dim light, glowing faintly and pulsing, as if it were breathing. Sita immediately felt at ease with it, like it understood her.

Then, she woke up.

A small fire was already alight outside and the sun was just starting to break, coming over the mountains high above. A large pan of tea was brewing over the fire, watched carefully by an alert Bene, always the first to rise.

"Come and have some tea," Bene said to Sita as she emerged from her tent. Rama was still fast asleep.

"The others are sleeping like kittens."

Sita sat beside Bene and sipped from the beaker she was given.

"Mountain..." Sita said. She had started to learn a few Raiceman words over the past week.

"Yes, I know. Feel like we're in the middle of nowhere, huh?"

They sat quietly for a while before Elera and Javu awoke, the sun now shining brightly down through the trees overhead.

"Good morning, everyone!" Javu said jovially, like he always did. "I trust you all slept well."

Sita immediately began to converse about her dream, whilst Elera sat beside Bene and helped him brew more tea. Javu seemed very interested in what Sita was telling him and he kept asking her questions about things she had noticed in the dream.

"It seems that we are heading in the right direction," Javu said to Bene and Elera, "though it may a few more days yet before we reach the Third Gate."

"What makes you say that?" Elera asked him.

"Sita had a realistic dream that she was floating over the mountains of this region. She said she saw a strange mountain in the direction that we are heading. She said it felt like it was alive."

"But we've seen so many mountains in Cibola? Maybe she just dreamed about one of those," Bene said, unsure they should plan their route on such a hunch.

"As Kirichi said when we were at the retreat, sometimes when we sleep, we actually cross over into the dream world where we can still see everything around us. I think Sita may have seen the Third Gate whilst she was *dreaming*. If what she has told me is accurate, we have another six mountains to get past before we reach a large plain. After that, I think we will find the gate!"

"I didn't really understand what grandfather was saying about that," Bene mentioned as he stoked the fire. "What's the difference between having a dream and *dreaming*?"

"Well," Javu said, in a jolly manner, "the difference lies in whether you are aware that you are in a dream or not. The more real and lucid it is, the more you can control it. That is the main difference, whether you can control yourself in the dream."

"But how can there possibly be another world that you go to when you go to sleep?" Bene questioned further. "I think that there could be different types of dreams but if I'm sleeping in my bed, I'm there all night. I don't disappear to another world."

"Maybe not physically, but part of you may go travelling."

"What part?"

"The part that is aware, Bene, your energy body. That is the same part that lives forever."

At this statement, Elera was stirred into speech.

"When I had the vision at the Intihuatana stone, I was told the same thing, that life is endless," she said, somehow sure of the fact herself.

"But how do you know that?" Bene said with more emotion in his voice. "How do you know that we aren't just physical and that's it?"

"Because I know things that I couldn't possibly know if I was only physical."

Javu smiled at Elera's conviction.

"Such as?" Bene asked.

"Well, let me ask you a question instead. If you were only physical, why would you seek vengeance for your father's death?"

The unexpected question shook Bene.

"If he is fully gone, who are you trying get justice for? Yourself? Kirichi? No. You know that he is watching somewhere, don't you, Bene?"

Bene couldn't answer the question, partly because of being confronted over his sole aim over the past three years and partly because deep down, he knew that she was right. He couldn't quite put his finger on it but somehow he knew that his father still existed in some form somewhere.

Quiet fell amongst the four, but the silence was soon broken by the loud yawning of Reo waking up from his slumber, which in turn woke up Rekesh, Rama and Teltu.

As everyone came around to the new day, they began to pack up ready to set off once again. The group spent a period of time food-gathering in the imminent area, where there was a small variety of fruit trees and fungi growing. With everyone's sacks full, they set off uphill, through the densest jungles yet.

After several hours of climbing the great hill before them, they reached the top and were astounded to find that the forest cleared rapidly, revealing more heath and the remains of a big stone building. It was made of large, reddish stones used like bricks to build the outer walls and rooms. There was no roof visible. As they got closer, they saw that the building had been derelict for some time, large mounds of moss growing in between each stone brick.

"What do you think this was?" Reo asked Elera.

"Mmm. It's quite large so it could have been some sort of palace in the region."

After resting for a short while, they pressed on, walking across the more open heath land, several mountains visible before them.

"I can *see* no more than five mountains ahead," Javu said, pleased that his interpretation of Sita's dream seemed to be correct.

"Well, five's plenty," Rekesh said morosely, to which everyone agreed.

It took a further four days for the group to reach the end of the mountain range ahead and indeed, they scaled around five mountains before coming to more open ground, by which time most were seriously questioning why they had willingly decided to undertake such a journey.

Only Elera and Javu were more energetic than usual.

"Why did we come to this godforsaken place?" Reo whined as they plodded along desolate grasslands. "There isn't a soul in sight!"

"*Do* be quiet, Reo," Elera said to him abruptly. "Sometimes it is good to be silent."

"But that's all there is out here – silence!" he retaliated dramatically. "And now look, only flat land for as far as you can see. Will it never end?"

Though Reo's complaining was highly irritating, as time went on everyone couldn't help but think along similar lines.

After two more days of walking across the great plain, they saw something in the distance. It was an odd-looking mountain in front of a larger mountain range. Nobody could quite understand why the mountain looked so strange.

"Great. More mountains!" Reo said sarcastically, for which Javu yanked his ear comically.

As they got closer, the mountain became more and more surreal, almost like it had been realistically carved onto a giant canvas in front of them. Its rocks emitted a shimmering light that was still and unmoving and Elera was the first to notice that the imminent rock face was actually a great flat wall. Carefully engraved into the wall was a three-dimensional image of a steep mountainous incline. From a distance it had fitted in perfectly with the views of mountains behind it.

"That giant stone wall!" she exclaimed to everyone, so excited that she found it hard to catch her breath. "This must be the Third Gate!"

Everyone rushed over to the wall, intrigued by its presence. It looked like it was made out of one enormous piece of stone and bewilderment quickly set in amongst the group.

"What's behind it?" Rekesh asked.

"Why would someone put it here?" Teltu added, scratching his head.

"Never mind that," Reo said, now alive with excitement. "*How* did they put it here? I mean, look it at. You can't even see the top!"

The wall stretched far and ran circularly in opposite directions until it met a mountainside at either end. It took several hours of walking for the group to confirm that this was the case.

"Well there is no way in," Reo said defeated as they got back to the middle of the wall. "Not one door along its entire length!"

Elera was looking around the base of the wall, searching for something.

"What are you looking for?" Bene asked her.

"An inscription," she told him. "Not that I am expecting to be able to read it if I can find one, but there are usually inscriptions in the near vicinity of megalithic structures like this."

Everyone began to search the surrounding area at the base of the wall, trying to help Elera find an inscription. After a few moments, Sita called out. She was next to an odd-shaped pinnacle rock that was some way away from the wall.

It was about double the size of Sita in height. As Elera reached where she was standing, she saw that a tablet had been embedded into the pinnacle. There was an inscription carved into the tablet that looked like some form of hieroglyphics.

"This is the same language as what I saw in Bimini," Elera said. "I can only understand some of the symbols here."

She began to study the inscription carefully. Meanwhile, Javu was thinking to himself that something seemed to be missing.

"If this is the Third Gate, then where are the two peaks?" he said out loud. "Remember that Tepeu said that the gate looked like two peaks."

"Well, from what I can gather, this tablet doesn't say anything about two peaks," Elera said, still deciphering the hieroglyphs. "All I can make out is the symbol for the sun and a phrase that roughly translates to *Great Spirit*."

"Tepeu said the people don't venture this way because of a powerful spirit that protects the gate?" Bene reminded them.

"So this is the gate then?" Teltu asked.

"I think so," Elera said, looking around. Then she noticed something in the far distance. On top of the last mountain they had navigated around was a strange-shaped peak, though from so far away she couldn't see if it looked bizarre because of the reason that she was hoping.

"Has anyone got a spyglass?"

Bene pulled out a slim metal telescope from his satchel and handed it to Elera.

"Raiceman?" Rekesh commented upon seeing it.

Elera aimed the telescope at the peak in the distance and a huge smile spread across her face as she focused in on it. "The two peaks are over there!" she said, pointing in the direction they had travelled from. They all took turns to have a look through Bene's telescope.

"I can't believe this!" Reo said with fire. "We've walked all the way here and now we have to go all the way back!"

"Why?" Teltu asked him.

"Because the gate is over there."

"No, Reo," Elera told him. "The gate is here. It is this wall."

Reo didn't quite understand but he felt relieved.

"Do you see the way the sun moves in the sky?" she said to him, pointing out its trajectory. "We will have to wait until tomorrow now but at some point the sun will go in between those two peaks. I am sure that when that happens it might be possible to open the gate."

"How?"

"I'm not sure yet. It's just an intuition I have. We will just have to wait and see."

The group set up a camp directly outside the wall and prepared a meal out of the last of their supplies. They could only have a small fire for the plains were quite bare, with little dry wood around, and nobody wanted to venture into the mountains.

After everyone had eaten, they all fell asleep under the wide blanket of stars above, clearer than they had ever seen them before.

The morning came quickly and everybody felt unusually well-rested. Each person had slept undisturbed throughout the night. The sun was rising from the east and the group estimated it would reach the twin peaks within an hour.

"Where did you live in Raicema City?" Rekesh asked Bene, who was sitting on the floor next to him.

"I lived in the east zone for a long time, near to all the casinos."

"I know it well. I lived in one of the central zones but I used to go out to the east regularly."

"So you are a defence-arts teacher?" Bene asked him, having heard of Rekesh whilst in Raicema.

"Used to be," Rekesh said solemnly. "I originally trained under Master Yangjam Satori when I was younger. I lived in Neoasia for a while learning the way of the warrior. When I moved to Raicema, I opened a small school there. But after a while, I had to close it."

"Why?"

"Because the government started cracking down on the defence arts. They made it illegal to teach. The funny thing was, I was teaching Raiceman nationals as well as Makai. After that I just took contract work, teaching the rebels out in the east. That's why I used to go out there quite a lot."

"So you met Sadana Siger?" Bene asked directly.

"A few times. He commissioned me to train the new recruits, though to be honest, none of them seemed very interested in learning about the arts."

"That's because Sadana reels in people with the promise of money. That's all they usually care about."

They continued to talk about the political landscape in Raicema and the different sects of the Makai that existed around the world. Before long, the sun has reached the twin peaks. Looking through Bene's telescope, Elera could see the sun had almost passed the rightmost peak.

Everyone sat quietly, in anticipation of whether Elera's prediction would be true.

As the sun passed directly in between the two peaks, a brilliant beam of light shot horizontally outwards across the vast plain, right above their heads. It focused on a point on the great stonewall just out of view.

"We need to get up there and see what it's focusing on before the sun passes through!" Elera said.

Rekesh quickly put her up on his shoulders and she stood upright, leaning on the wall, just below the beam.

"There is a small hole here," she said. "This gate needs a key of some sort!"

As she said it, the beam faded away as the sun passed behind the leftmost peak in the far distance. Rekesh held up his hands and helped Elera back down to the floor.

"You would never know that hole was there," she commented, looking up at where the beam had been focused.

"So what kind of key do we need?" Reo asked.

"I'm not sure. I may have to read the tablet again."

Elera reread the hieroglyphs on the tablet, looking for clues about what the key might be, but to no avail.

"I just can't understand any of these symbols," she said dejectedly. "Like this one here. It seems pretty important as it is larger than all the others but it doesn't make any sense. It almost reminds me of an old Maeya drawing of a serpent but this one has feathers and the sun in its mouth."

Javu's eyes widened at what Elera was describing to him. "It looks like we have missed something when that beam hit the wall," he said to them all. "It looks like we will have to wait until tomorrow and look more carefully then."

Elera wasn't quite sure what Javu was getting at but she didn't have any other suggestions so she agreed.

"We should probably separate to search for food," Rekesh said. "Let's leave the camp here and meet back later."

"I saw a forest high up in that direction," Reo said, pointing to where one end of the wall joined with a cliff face.

"Okay, half of us go that way and the rest the other way," Teltu suggested.

Later, with a fresh supply of food and wood that had been brought back to the camp mainly from the forest Reo had seen, everyone sat around a fire, staring up at the ominous wall that seemed so alien.

"Someone went to a lot of effort to build this thing," Reo said. "Maybe we should just follow the trail from the forest we went to?" Bene suggested as everyone ate nuts and fruit. "But it did seem to get very steep."

"We are here for a reason," was all Javu said in response.

As the sun approached the peaks the next morning, everyone got into ready positions. Elera was already on Rekesh's shoulders. The sun passed directly in between the two peaks and the same brilliant, concentrated beam of sunlight shot outwards, hitting the wall in exactly the same place as before.

"Quickly, take me over there," Elera said to Rekesh. As he was about to move, an immense rumbling beneath them interrupted him.

"Whooaa!" Rama and Teltu wailed in unison as they were thrown backwards.

A fissure appeared in the ground, slithering from the edge of the colossal stone wall directly outwards to where the group was standing.

Everyone jumped out of the way as the ground shook, large stones spraying up from the depths of the dusty earth.

Both Sita and Reo screamed as the world around them quaked.

A perfectly straight crack appeared at the base of the wall and grew vertically upwards, looking like a beam of light.

The sun's rays streamed down with an unnatural, dazzling and sweltering wave of heat. Energy was coming from beyond the wall too, and for a moment the world seemed to be melting.

The fissure grew longer and wider, with everyone feeling delirious at the unreal sight of the wall splitting in two. Elera just stared at the shining wall whilst on Rekesh's shoulders, its top reaching far into the sky, moving like it was alive.

The others were also mesmerised, lying on the floor in awe, overcome by the godly sight. The wall split apart with a remarkable grace, a giant gap in the floor leading down into a new opening.

Javu was the first to get to his feet as the spectacle subsided, smiling uncontrollably, like he might burst out with joyous laughter at any second, whilst Reo had a slightly different look on his face, one of bewilderment and confusion. A stern grasp of the shoulder by Bene soon brought him to his feet.

"How did it open?" Elera said to herself in astonishment, turning to face everyone.

Everyone shrugged their shoulders in bewilderment.

"Whoever made this wall knew something that we don't!" Bene said, looking up at the endless height of it and the opening that had formed. "This cannot have been built by humans. No single stone I have ever seen has been so tall or remarkable."

"Never mind the height!" Teltu said brashly. "How did it split apart so perfectly?"

"Maybe it is better not to ask these sorts of questions at the moment," Javu chuckled. "We are all clearly baffled enough for now. I suggest we follow the trail."

Elera agreed, urging everyone down the sloping canyon in the floor. The ground was hot, as if heated from underneath. Steam shot out from tiny pockets in the rubble. As they walked deeper down they were shielded from the radiant sun.

"Look, a stairway!" Teltu exclaimed as they approached the gap in the wall. Passing through the gap was like travelling down a tunnel and with the darkness came a musty, earthy smell.

As they passed through, they saw that the stairway wound around a small mountain that the wall had concealed. The stairway was made of large slabs, smooth and deep brown. There seemed to be a vast space beyond. They all walked carefully around the mountain, taking many strides per step.

Sita whispered in Javu's ear.

"This is the mountain that Sita *saw* whilst dreaming."

The lighting was unusual. It was a vivid mix of sunlight and giant shadows. The rock face of the mountain almost looked like the face of an elderly woman.

Everyone was silent with expectancy and Elera couldn't help but wonder if this was the beginning or the end of her journey. As they reached the other side of the mountain, they were all surprised to find a great forest in front of them and a valley running up to the colossal mountain range beyond.

The trees were tall and bushy and grew close together. The group were high up and could see far ahead over the forest.

"That's certainly a lot of trees!" Teltu said jovially.

Rekesh looked back up at the mountain they had just traversed around. For a split second he thought the mountain moved. A pang of fear struck his heart.

Elera was scanning the treetops like an eagle, silent and crouching down. The others simply stared out at the crunchy, green vastness. The nearest mountains in the distance were so far away that they looked like small stones.

"We could be walking through that for months," Reo complained, sitting on the floor and rubbing his sore feet.

"Ssh!" Elera whispered, trying methodically to look for

something. After a moment, she let out a short gasp.

"There!" she said, pointing at a remote spot in the mass of greenery. "Look! A shiny point, just coming out of the treetops."

Everyone tried hard to see what Elera had seen.

"I see it!" Teltu announced. "If you move around a bit, the glare of the sun catches on it."

They could all now see the shiny pinnacle in the distance, hidden well in the depths of the forest. Javu, who had been lagging behind and was only just coming down the stairway, instantly spotted what they were all looking at.

"What is it?" Bene asked, trying to get a closer look with his small metallic scope.

Small stones could be heard being forced out of the way as Elera began to run down the remainder of the stairway towards the forest.

"Only one way to find out!" she shouted back with a smile, eager to reach the bottom first.

Chapter 30 – Forest of the Breathing Mountain

Elera and her followers had reached the bottom of the archaic stairwell of the Third Gate. The breathing mountain was now towering high above them.

Ahead was a dense forest. Trees of unknown species littered the pathways. Looking ahead from ground level only gave the impression of true overgrowth, the sun darkened by the thorough shading of the mass of leaves overhead.

"Mmm," Rekesh pondered out loud. "So bright, yet so dark. There may be dangerous creatures living in there."

Elera began to venture in to the forest, paying no attention and brushing aside long heavy branches with her hands.

"If we respect them, then they will respect us," she could be heard murmuring as she disappeared into the darkness.

Rekesh and Bene strode ahead quickly whilst the others trailed behind.

Teltu was deep in thought, mainly about his reasons for being in the lost land that they now found themselves in.

"Javu, I want to understand about this element aspect to ourselves?" Teltu asked his old friend and finding it hard to grasp the concept. "You know, this balance that we are all supposed to represent. I mean, how can I be air, whilst Elera is water?"

"Well, Teltu, it is quite simple," Javu said, stroking his long beard. "We all have an *elemental* aspect to ourselves. When we have talked of you being like one element or Elera being like another, it simply means that the spirit form of ourselves behaves like that element. And when I say spirit form, I only mean the part that does not die. It is the part of ourselves that is indestructible, everlasting energy."

There were incredible sounds coming from the forest, like a melody composed of animal cries, bird songs and the rustling of the trees.

"You are air because you are free like the wind, not afraid to move, not afraid to communicate. Me too," he said, raising his eyebrows and pointing to himself. Teltu let out a small chuckle as Javu's childlike mannerisms.

"Of course, it is not only our spirit that has an elemental aspect. Our bodies do too."

"Do you think I look like the wind?" Teltu asked, confused.

"Ba hah ha hah..." Javu blurted out. After he had composed himself, he tried to describe to Teltu what he meant. "The physical world is a native creation of the perfect harmony of the elements," he explained. "Each body has varying degrees of each element and will most of the time be more heavily influenced by one specific element."

Teltu looked puzzled and had an expression that made Javu want to burst out laughing again.

"Here's an example. You see how Rekesh looks very much like a lion?" Javu pointed ahead to Rekesh who had a serious expression on his face, his long black hair and short thick beard indeed reminding Teltu of a lion. "He has a face like a lion, right?"

"I guess."

"Well, when I say that I don't mean an actual lion, but you know what I mean. He reminds one of a lion more than any other creature you know. And the lion is the principle creature of fire, in fact one of the oldest creatures on this planet."

Javu paused for a moment.

"So Rekesh is influenced by fire?"

"Well, his body has taken after that element, however his *spirit energy* may behave more like another element. Having said that, Teltu, I would say that he is quite a fiery character. Would you agree?"

Teltu agreed somewhat. "So you are saying that a person's body might take after one element and their spirit after another?"

"It is possible. Sometimes the dominating element may be the same and in that case, watch out!"

Javu's eyes widened as he said that and he spread his arms out. "Someone of pure fire would be a lot to take," he said, deliberately looking over his shoulder at Reo and giving Teltu a sly grin. "But let me finish telling you about how the elements affect the way we look."

He paused for a moment, thinking how to phrase his next description.

"For air, a creature of influence is one that is no longer around today so I cannot describe it easily. Maybe if a dragon still existed in this world, you would *see* what I mean."

"Dragon?" Teltu asked with a little fear.

"Yes, Teltu. Dragons once roamed this planet in their millions." Once again he paused.

"For the earth, a creature of influence is a *kivili*, a being that is in perfect harmony with the ground and trees. You have seen Matree and Enee yes? They exist without damaging anything in Seho."

Javu smiled as Teltu could do nothing but agree.

"And for water, a creature is a horse, strong and fluid. Of course, we are all an intricate mix of these four roots anyway so there are only hints of a dominant element in any human today. In fact, throughout life one continually sees beautiful and terrifying combinations of the elements influencing the bodies of humans and animals. And each of those combinations is completely unique!"

It was an eye-opening subject for Teltu. He wasn't sure if Javu was speaking literally or not but he had to admit, he had met many people who reminded him of lions, horses, dragons and kivilis.

"How do you know so much, Javu?" Reo, who had been half following the conversation, asked from behind.

"We all know this, Reo," was all Javu said in response.

Everyone walked on in silence for some time. They would all stop now and again, admiring beautiful flowers that were larger than anyone had ever seen before. Some small birds fluttered above in a playful manner, chirping at the visitors walking through their home.

Elera had stopped ahead, looking at a small creature that seemed to be blind with a long snout. It was foraging for insects. This gave everyone a chance to regroup before they set off again.

"Let me tell you a story," Javu said to Teltu, Sita and Rama, who were all now bringing up the rear of the party. "It's about a spirit that lives on a lagoon in a forest in Vassini, *the Wisp*, as it has come to be known. Many people in a village close to where I used to live saw this creature. It only came out at night, skimming the water of the lagoon with a peculiar, green glow."

Javu translated in Hindi for Sita and Rama.

"To look at, the Wisp held the appearance of a giant, glowing butterfly. Many were afraid of it, and there were many rumours that the Wisp would kill humans if it found them alone around the lagoon."

Once again, Javu translated the story as he told it.

"One night, a young girl called Koe ventured out to the lagoon by herself. She came across the Wisp, gliding the surface of the water as if it was dancing. Koe called out to the Wisp, unafraid and with friendliness. It began to glide towards her."

The forest ahead was beginning to open up slightly, creating a more open feeling amongst the group, yet there was still little light getting through the heavily overgrown branches above.

"As the Wisp got closer, Koe saw that it had two bright wings of burning energy that were hazy to the view. As it reached her, it disappeared from sight completely."

Smiling as they walked, Javu played upon the look of suspense on Teltu's face, translating and then walking silently for many moments.

"Then what?" Teltu said, frenetically lingering on the anticipation, which made Javu chuckle.

"Koe called out to the Wisp again, shouting out that she wanted to be its friend and that she was approaching with peace. After a moment, it appeared again across the other side of the lagoon, though this time it seemed much more solid and colourful, glowing less but now with beautiful swirling patterns on its wings."

Up ahead, an illuminated clearing could be seen. Elera had almost reached the spacious area as Javu continued with the fable.

"The Wisp stopped directly in front of her and for the first time Koe could clearly see the splendour of it, a large creature with the face of a young deer, wide-eyed and with the body of a giant butterfly. It floated above the water, looking directly at her.

"She asked the Wisp why everyone else only saw it as a glowing light. The Wisp explained that it did not exist in physical form anymore and that it had decided to manifest itself to communicate with Koe because of her kind and friendly nature."

A purring sound could be heard nearby, the sound of a large cat.

"The Wisp told her that it lived between two worlds," Javu continued, undeterred. "At night it returned to the physical world where humans observed it as a glowing light but during the day it dwelled in the *dream world*."

"Like what Kirichi told us about?" Teltu asked.

"Yes, and Koa asked the Wisp about that mysterious place.

"What was the world of dreams and why did the Wisp return to the physical world? The Wisp told her that this particular lagoon was a special place where it was easy to cross over between the two worlds. It stayed there to protect it. Then it offered to show her the dream world."

The story was interrupted by an enthusiastic yelp by Reo in the clearing ahead. "Hey, everyone! Come and see this, it's amazing!"

As those at the back hurried to reach the clearing, they saw Elera, Rekesh and Bene all huddled around a small golden statue, rooted into the ground. Its palms were outstretched in a welcoming way and its face had a wide, cheerful smile upon it. All around the statue was the most intricately carved stone artwork depicting scenes of a large town. Elera examined the chronicle that the carving was depicting.

"I think the city in the scene is what we are looking for. Look here, there is a pyramid in the background," she said, pointing to one part of the artwork.

"Let's continue on," Rekesh suggested. "We must be close."

Almost immediately, Teltu was pestering Javu to continue the story about the Wisp and the dream world.

"Well, the Wisp took Koe to the dream world and the strange thing was that she recognised it," he said. "She had been there before yet her memory of it seemed weak. When she went back to the village, she told everyone about the dream world and the Wisp, but most would not believe her.

"The next night when she went back to the lagoon, the Wisp told her that it would never been seen again after that night. When Koe asked it why, it told her that the lagoon had now found a new protector in Koe. Then it disappeared and was never seen again."

The ending was unsatisfactory to Teltu.

"But what happened to Koe?" he asked.

Javu paused for a few moments as they walked along. "Koe took her new responsibility very seriously, visiting the lagoon every night and often sleeping on its banks. Then one night, Koe mysteriously disappeared too. People talked, saying that the Wisp had taken her away."

A blinding stream of light spilled down from a gap in the treetops above.

"The truth was that she had herself become a wisp, one able to live in-between the two worlds."

Teltu, Sita and Rama were all fascinated by the story.

"Is that possible?" Teltu questioned. "That a being can exist in more than one world?"

"Oh yes," Javu said without doubt. "And I think that such an existence sheds light on many of the mysteries in our world."

Up ahead, grey buildings could be seen through the trees. The walls of the buildings were similar to those that the group had seen before.

"The blocks of stone are in the same irregular Maeyan style," Elera commented.

As they walked past the first few buildings, the trees spread out more and opened onto a paved courtyard, with a number of large buildings in surround. Much of the stone was covered in moss and looked smooth.

"Let's go this way," Elera said, gesturing towards what looked like a human-made path through more dense forest ahead. The trees lined up perfectly on either side and at the bottom of the path there was a small lake and a waterfall falling from a tall dam above. It seemed to be a dead end.

"Do we climb up there?" Bene asked Elera.

She looked back and was surprised to see that through a gap in the trees there was now a perfect view of the mountain they had travelled from. It looked like a sleeping woman, curled up. She could see it breathing and began to get the odd feeling it was going to move at any moment.

"The mountain is alive, breathing and watching over this place," Elera said.

"Looks like a dead end this way," Reo said, observing a large crag behind the waterfall. "Maybe there is a way around it?"

Elera noticed something unusual about the waterfall as her eyes fell on it again. There was a glowing light coming from behind it.

"Did you see that?" she said quietly, but nobody heard her.

She felt compelled to find out what the source of the light was and without thinking she began to wade through the lake without saying a word.

The waterfall flooded down into the lake with a purifying power, and as she stepped through it, getting soaked from head to foot, she felt a strange tingling in her body. There was an opening in a rock face in front of her. She walked into it, entering a tunnel of sorts. The same light was in the distance and she followed it.

Eventually a different light could be seen. It was that of the sun shining in the sky. She emerged from the tunnel, astounded at what was before her.

Chapter 31 – Ixon

Elera was looking out at a grand pyramid. It stood in the middle of a lost metropolis that stretched far into the forest. There were four smaller pyramidal buildings marking the boundaries of the ancient city and the sight was one that Elera had only dreamed of.

The central pyramid was covered heavily in moss. It seemed to be made of a translucent stone. The mammoth blocks that made up its structure looked like great slabs of marble-like crystal.

There were at least two hundred steps leading up to the entrance of the pyramid and its top was barely visible, covered by the bushy tops of giant trees growing around it.

There were a number of smaller buildings made out of a more common limestone and every one had elaborate carvings of animals and people in their walls and pediments.

On each of the corner pyramids, there was a statue of the feathered serpent that she had seen on the tablet outside the gate.

She looked around to see if Javu and the others had followed her, but she saw or heard nothing from the tunnel.

She decided to explore, eager to have a look around the lost and undisturbed city. Though it was empty, it did not feel lonely. In fact, there was an exciting energy in the air.

Elera wondered when the last time was that somebody lived there. She had a look inside some of the smaller structures, some of which looked like storage buildings and others, which seemed to be family dwellings. She estimated that a few thousand people could have once lived in the forgotten city.

As she made her way over to the central pyramid's great stairway, she heard a rustling behind her and turned around to see Javu and Bene approaching, looking confused and disoriented.

"Can you believe this?" Elera said with raw enthusiasm. "Look at this place!"

Both men were strangely silent.

"Where are the others?" she asked them.

"They went through the waterfall before us," Bene said weakly. "But when we came out the other side, they were nowhere to be seen."

"It's true, Elera," Javu said. "The tunnel we passed through was no ordinary passageway."

After a brief moment of concern, Elera remembered the unexplainable events that occurred at Bimini and how everything had led to this point.

"Well, I am sure they are all safe somewhere," she said confidently, unafraid of their fate. "I was about to climb these stairs. Will you come with me?"

Both of them nodded and they slowly began to ascend, taking one step at a time. After they had climbed halfway up, they were at an equal height to the statues on top of the four corner pyramids. It was strange, as if those four feathered serpents might jump off at any moment. Javu seemed quite relaxed in his current position.

"What do you think this place was?" Bene asked, looking down on all the buildings and statues across from them.

"I think it was a religious city," Elera suggested. "A holy place. But I don't think anybody has lived here for a very long time. It maybe four or five thousand years since anyone has dwelled here."

"How can you tell?"

"Because of the amount of moss growing on the buildings. Look, it's even growing on this main pyramid up to where we are standing. This is a sacred temple and it has been a long time since it has been maintained."

"How old do you think this pyramid is?"

"This pyramid is definitely pre-Maeyan because of the stone that has been used. Those other four corner pyramids may have been built later than this one."

She paused, looking out at the magical view.

"The way it has been constructed is reminiscent of the Bimini and Giza Great Pyramids, using megalithic blocks instead of smaller ones."

"Do you think this is the third pyramid that you are looking for?" Bene asked.

"Let's go inside. I'm sure we will find out more."

They continued to climb the stairway until they had reached a wide terrace at the top with a tall doorway ahead. It had intricate pillars on both sides and a pediment above with the same image of a feathered serpent carved into it. The doorway was open but only darkness within.

"I'm not so sure I want to go in there," Bene said somewhat reservedly. "Why are there dragons everywhere?"

"It is Respiro," Javu said mysteriously.

"Have you got a torch?" Elera asked him, to which he pulled out a sleek silver, electric torch from his bag. She took it and switched it on, not hesitating to step into the darkness of the ancient pyramid.

Javu and Bene followed. As they passed through the threshold of the great doorway with the narrow beam of the torchlight falling on giant paved stones, they all jumped as a large slab fell down from behind them. It crashed to the floor with a heavy thud and rumbled the very space on which they were standing.

Bene, Elera and Javu were now trapped in the monumental structure. A feeling of apprehension entered Elera, but it quickly passed.

"He has chosen us to learn," Javu said eerily, causing Bene to pulsate with an unknown fear from within. They moved slowly into the hallway before them, the tall walls towering above and another doorway ahead.

They continued onwards into a spacious chamber and Elera instinctively knew that they had reached an important part of the pyramid. There was a strange interplay of light, though the chamber was totally sealed. As they walked forward, the light got brighter though not one of them could distinguish its source.

It was as if the light was everywhere, coming out of every atom in the air. There was an unknown haziness that made it hard to see clearly.

Javu walked slowly towards the centre of the chamber and out of nowhere he was approached by a round entity of hazy bluish light, which instantly filled him with a feeling of joy and peace. As Bene and Elera walked over to where Javu was standing, the aura filled them with the same feelings.

The three of them all suddenly felt as though they were floating through a dream, the pyramid fading away around them. Instantly, they found themselves somewhere else with an all-encapsulating feeling of weightlessness. There was no sensation of having to breathe. In fact Bene could not feel any part of his physical body.

A scene emerged before them, of an eerie darkness and a terrifying rumbling. Bene was filled with an intense fear, one that seemed to come from an area where his stomach should have been. It froze his ability to see, hear or perceive.

This rumbling continued for what seemed like an eternity before the scene changed to one of an endless ocean, deep and dark.

A million human-sized entities of light hovered above the murky sea and the great fear Bene had sensed had vanished in an instant, now replaced by an overwhelming feeling of love.

Bene sensed the beings were pushing something away collectively. He did not know how, but he intuited that the beings were all fundamentally the same yet they had differing qualities. This intuition was aided by a perception of colour amongst the beings, which varied in depth and brightness.

Then, in what could only be felt as a cumulative build-up of love, light shot out of every being and joined into a swirling auric beam that seemed to penetrate something above, yet no matter how hard Bene struggled to look up, he could not.

He felt as if there was someone at either side of him, also observing the spectacle. Then the scene began to fade away, a tunnel of metallic light enclosing itself around him. He sensed an encompassing loneliness, and felt despair of being weightless and without form.

The next thing he knew, he was falling down the twisting and turning tunnel. As he tumbled along, he felt the loneliness break away from him piece by piece like chalk from a cliff. The end came quicker than expected and once again a scene was before him.

It was a gigantic forest like no other, trees endless in height and number. Sitting on the forest floor was a human.

Bene felt himself move toward the person, a sense of release coming over him. Bene instantly knew whom it was sitting before him. "Father?" he felt himself ask, though no words came out.

Juhi turned around to face his son and Bene felt completeness like no other, coupled with joy. Juhi signalled towards something in the forest, a being that was walking in the distance. Bene could only see the silhouette of the entity, which looked like that of a young pony. He strained to see further and looked at his father, who smiled and waved gently. Then everything seemed to swirl away, like it was being sucked into a vacuum.

The next thing Bene knew, he was waking up on the floor of the chamber, which was now pitch black with darkness. He felt an overwhelming surge of emotion and he began to weep in the darkness. He felt clarity, a sensation of being newly born. He was open and defenceless.

"Bene?"

He heard Elera's voice call out from the shadows. Then there was a shuffling and she appeared in the darkness, pointing the torch at him. She walked over to and placed her arm around him. He was unsure if he'd somehow dreamt the entire thing and a great feeling of homesickness came over him.

"Did you see the ocean?" she asked him, herself coming around.

"I...saw my father," he mumbled.

There was a light groan from somewhere in the darkness and Elera shone the light in that direction.

It was Javu, coming around from a similar experience. "Where did the light go?" he said, somewhat incoherently. Elera walked over to him and helped him sit up.

After a moment of composure, she began to search the chamber for a way out. "Hey, there's a door over here," she said, finding a narrow opening in a corner.

After a few moments, the two men had regrouped and both got to their feet.

"You were both there?" Bene asked. "I felt you next to me."

"Yes. Where was that?" Elera pondered. "All those beings. What were they?"

Javu did not say anything, still groggy. They went through the new opening, which led to a winding stone staircase, wide enough only for the slimmest of people.

They slowly made their way up the staircase. After counting seventy steps, they reached a dead end. Elera looked around using the torch and noticed a slab in the ceiling above. It was similar to what she had seen in the Bimini pyramid.

"I think I can push it up," she said, sweating in the hot, musty atmosphere. After a few attempts, Bene squeezed past her to try. With all the effort he could muster, he pushed the slab upwards, revealing another chamber, this one aglow with a light that seemed to be dormant in the walls.

It was still difficult to see and as they clambered up into the chamber, Elera shone the torch upon the walls to reveal a number of intricate carvings and inscriptions. Excitedly, she sprang to her feet and rushed over to them, trying to understand as much as she could.

After some time, Elera had finished looking at the walls of the chamber and Javu had fully come around.

"I cannot understand everything here, but there is a painting on this wall that describes what we all saw," Elera told them, pointing to a painting that spanned an entire wall. "Look at the ocean here and all of the beings we saw."

The painting was so similar to what the three of them had seen that Bene thought he was there again. Just like in the vision, whatever it was that was being collectively pushed away was not visible. Only the spectacular beam of light running to the top of the wall and into the painted sky was shown.

"There are some symbols here," Elera said, crouching down near the painting. "They read *fire from above...the spirits...the end...*" she translated. "I can't make out anymore."

"What about those symbols over there?" Bene asked, pointing to another wall.

"I can't understand anything written there," she said, starting to feel shaky. "I think we should find a way out."

"Let's go back the way we came," Javu suggested. "I have a feeling that this place knows we want to leave."

They followed the trail back through the depths of the archaic structure, down the staircase, through the main chamber and along the hallway. The main entrance that had closed before was now open, bright sunlight shining in from the outside. The three of them made their way outside.

The rays of the sun falling onto their faces was like taking a warm bath, soothing and relaxing. Elera looked down from their high vantage point and saw someone sitting on the ground.

"Look!" she said. "There is someone down there."

From so high up, they couldn't tell who it was but the person seemed to be sitting cross-legged under a tree in the middle of the city.

Believing it was one of their group, they began to descend the stairway back down to ground level. About halfway down, they quickly realised it was an elderly man, with a narrow nose and long bushy white hair. He was cleanly shaven and dressed in a simple brown poncho. He had a wide, square jaw and sat with his eyes closed. As they got to the bottom of the staircase and made their way over to him, he opened his eyes.

Elera greeted him in Quechua but there was no response.

"Maybe he speaks Uru," Elera suggested to Javu. "Can you speak to him?"

Javu spoke a few words of Uru to the man but again there was no response.

"I wonder if other people live here as well," Elera said, not sure how to speak to the man.

Then they were all surprised at the words that came out of the man's mouth.

"Nobody lives here," the man said in a deep voice. "Not any human anyway."

"You can speak the Raiceman language?" Elera exclaimed with surprise.

"I am a *brujo*. Do you know what that is?" he questioned them in response.

"You are a sorcerer?" Javu said, having heard the term before.

The brujo said nothing but they could tell that his silence was tantamount to confirmation.

"As a brujo, language is no longer a barrier for me."

Both Elera and Bene were not sure how to interpret the old man's words.

"So you have been inside the *Temple of the Air*?" he asked, glancing up at the colossal pyramid.

"Is that what it is known as?" Elera asked.

"It was known as something similar. It is a place where one receives the knowledge of this planet."

"Is that true of all the temples?" Elera asked the brujo, her knowledge surprising him. He smiled.

"Each of the temples has an affinity to the *essence*." He said the word in an elongated way. "It is because of the rocks on which they were built."

"Wisdom rocks!" Elera said to Javu.

"Can you tell us about the spirits we saw?" Bene asked the brujo whose long white hair touched the grassy floor around him. "Hovering over an ocean. There is a picture of it in there."

The brujo's dark skin was aged but his body looked supple and agile. All around the dry ground was alive with insects and Bene wondered why they were not crawling all over him.

"First you should know about the essence!" the brujo stated, wide-eyed and looking directly at Bene. "The essence is that which connects us all, yet we cannot view it with our eyes, hear it with our ears or even feel it with our skin."

The three of them had all heard of a similar, universal connection before. Indeed, it was one of the primary teachings of Makaism.

"We are all sure that it is there, human and plant alike," the brujo said, an expression of glee and fascination upon his boned face. "It waits patiently, breathlessly for our kind wishes."

He paused, looking around at everything.

"Those who wish to learn about the essence will also learn about the *spirits*."

"How can one learn about the essence?" Bene asked, stepping forward.

"By *seeing* it!" the old man replied.

Bene felt like he was being trapped in a conundrum.

"And how does one *see*?" Bene probed.

"By knowing!" he said in such a dramatic fashion. "One shall *see*, by becoming knowledgeable."

Though the words made little sense, Bene, Elera and Javu all understood quite clearly what the wise sage was implying.

"As for the spirits, they too are everywhere. Everything you lay your eyes upon has a spirit."

Bene let out a little snigger at this last statement. He found it comical to think that his clothes or his bag had a spirit. He bent down a picked up a pebble from the floor.

"Are you saying that even this pebble has a spirit?"

"Most definitely!" the brujo said. "And you should exercise caution in your respect of such objects. The pebble that you hold in your hand is the key to a very powerful spirit!"

The way that the old sage spoke about it made the matter seem deadly serious.

"Put the pebble on the floor, Bene," Elera said. He quickly accommodated her wishes.

Javu sat on the ground slowly in close proximity, as did the others for a few moments of contemplation.

"What is your name?" Elera asked inquisitively. "I am Elera and this is Bene and Javu".

"You may greet me as Huito if you like."

"We would very much like to learn more from you about this land and its history, Huito."

"What would you like to know?"

"The temple that we came from, how old is it?"

"It is of little importance how old the building is for what is contained within is and will always be timeless."

"The light we saw?" Bene enquired.

Huito smiled in an amused fashion. "There are many places of the land that hold a special connection to the essence. These places will show you their secrets just as the spirits will tell you theirs."

"I saw a light that seemed to be everywhere and then there was a light that was sort of round and about the size of a human," Bene elaborated.

Huito looked intrigued by this information and stroked the side of his face. "The round light was a spirit. It is one that is used to living in the world that we live. It is a protector. I am surprised that it presented itself to you!"

There was silence for a few moments, a silence like none of them had ever heard before. It was a void in the moment.

"That is a most rare occurrence," Huito said, unclear if he was referring to the spirit or the silence. "The *essence*, it has a special affinity with this particular location. That is why the temple was originally built here."

Elera's eyes widened and she began to understand the relationship between the pyramids. In Bimini she had too experienced the same all-encompassing light and had witnessed visions whilst inside. She realised that the locations on which the pyramids had been built had all been carefully chosen based on their energetic properties.

"We saw a scene of darkness. It was an endless ocean with millions of spirits," she stated, adjusting her position to sit on a soft mound of dry earth.

Huito thought for a while before speaking. "The vision was one of long ago," he said eventually.

Then he closed his eyes and fell asleep promptly against the tree he was sitting, leaving Elera astounded and staring in surprise at the other two.

"Should we wake him?" Bene asked.

"Let's rest as well," Javu suggested. "We will find the others later. We should speak to Huito again when he wakes up."

A few hours later, Huito awoke from his sudden nap.

He immediately resumed the conversation from where he left off, startling the three into focused attention.

"It was a vision of a great happening," he declared. "One in which boundaries were broken."

After hours of sitting quietly, Bene felt quite groggy by the words coming out of Huito's thin lips.

"We should first focus our attention on *the essence*. We could not exist without the essence."

"Why? How does it work?" Bene asked with naivety.

Huito let out a high-pitched laugh, amused at Bene's question. "I will pretend that you did not ask that question. Let me ask you one instead. Have heard of the eye of darkness?"

"Ambitio…" Elera said quietly to herself. She could relate Huito's description to the Makai concept of a negative force in the universe. She had also dreamt of such an entity.

Bene had heard of a similar concept from his grandfather. "Are you talking about *Affero and Ambitio*? Pure light and darkness? Freedom and Power?" he asked.

"The essence is not the same," Huito said. "Without the essence, neither Affero as you call it nor Ambitio could possibly exist."

Huito paused for several moments as he stretched his arms upwards with agility.

"The *forces of antiquity*, as I call them, came from the essence. The eye of darkness, is driven totally by consumption. It is the source of true power in the universe. Like the essence, you cannot view, hear or feel it, but it is there, deep within each of us. Unlike the essence, it is a force of energy. The essence is both nothing and everything, completely indescribable. It is you, it is me, it is everything that exists."

Everyone was listening carefully to the old man.

"However, this concept you just mentioned, Affero, was it?" Huito said to Bene. "Pure light as you say, freedom, the opposite of Ambitio. This is as close to the essence as we can possibly get as physical human beings. In fact, in the pyramid before you, the light you saw that was everywhere was that of Affero, or the Great Eagle as it is known to me."

"So what was that round light?" Bene asked.

There was silence for a while whilst Huito decided whether to speak or not.

"The pyramid here was built as homage to the essence and Affero, and specifically to one of its children."

"Children?" Bene retorted, perplexed.

"Are you talking about the protectors?" Elera asked, instantly thinking of Aova and what Kirichi has told her.

"You are very aware, senorita," Huito complimented her. "Indeed, the round light you saw in the temple was that of *Respiro*, the protector. It is incredibly extraordinary that a human should come into contact with him."

Javu was filled with an overwhelming excitement and nostalgia.

"Him? Is Respiro male?" Elera asked with zest, stunning Bene into silence – he was not aware of what Huito and Elera were talking about.

"Yes, senorita. Air is intrinsically male, just as earth is essentially female."

The statement made Bene blush for some reason.

"So Respiro is the elemental protector of air," she pondered to herself out loud. "I wonder what he looks like?"

"Respiro can take many forms, yet some are so vile that they should never be wished upon."

Elera felt slightly frightened by the brujo's words.

"There are statue's everywhere here in the city of his most likely form."

"The feathered serpent?"

Huito nodded.

"Is that true of all the protectors? That they have many forms?"

"Yes."

Javu, who had been thinking deeply about something, adjusted his position before he spoke. "Huito, I have heard of *the essence* before but I have always heard it referred to as *aether*, after some sort of ethereal consciousness that binds us all."

"It is another archaic way of referring to the essence," Huito confirmed. "There are scriptures written in another era, at the same time that the pyramid behind us was built. The word *aether* is used in those scriptures."

"Please tell us," Elera said eagerly, almost pleading. "I am quite adept at reading ancient languages but I couldn't understand the language written within the chambers of the temple."

"Only a trusted few are taught the language of the *Leiruyi*. I am fortunate to have been taught from a young age how to translate the intricate symbols."

"Leiruyi? I have never heard of that," Elera said, confounded.

"It is the language of the great sorcerers," Huito told them. "They built this temple and many others all over the planet and beyond."

"The Lemurians!" Bene exclaimed to Elera, realising what Huito was talking about.

"The Leiruyi's connection to the essence was so profound that they were capable of incredible feats that people today would not believe. They were able to walk between worlds and harness the true power of creation. They have even transcended time itself!"

Elera couldn't believe that this mysterious man was now talking about the capabilities that she had long suspected were possible. She almost felt like she wanted to cry with relief, the relief that her most intimate feelings were not just a creation of her mind but real to someone else too.

"The word *aether* is fitting to that which the great sorcerers wrote," Huito said, looking at Javu. "They have avowed a period to come that is most fitting to this word. The translation is exactly this word that you mentioned. Its meaning is: that which exists yet is only space."

"A prophecy?" Bene tried to confirm.

"Yes, Bene. But knowing the future has little benefit to one's life," Huito warned, seeming to instinctively know that Bene could be overly interested in such foresights.

"What does the prophecy say?"

"It is not just a prophecy but a source of great knowledge."

He paused for a moment, closing his eyes. It was almost like he was praying for an answer.

"I will tell you what the great sorcerers wrote," he said finally.

Everyone listened with bated breath.

"The essence created pure light and the elements; fire, earth, water and air," Huito recited. "From these elements, countless spirits were born. The planets and the stars were born out of complex combinations of the elements and life formed by the constant interplay of the different energy types.

"The crux of this creation was that it required the seed of power to succeed and power was born and the eye of darkness slowly began to gain a stronger hold over every spirit in the universe.

"What started out as a seed grew into a force that was soon to be out of control."

"The battle between Affero and Ambitio had begun," Javu elaborated.

Huito looked up into the vividly blue sky. "Ambitio shielded the spirits from a full view of reality," he continued, adopting the terminology. "It split existence into two different worlds; the physical world and the spirit world, when before this there was only one world."

All three of them were listening like small children, fully absorbed in something that sounded so real yet so distant.

"Affero – pure light, responded by creating the dream world as a bridge between these two worlds and by creating the elemental protectors, its *first children*."

Huito paused as the shriek of an eagle overhead could be heard.

"Every spirit was banished to the physical world by Ambitio. Indeed, everything we see and hear around us, everything we feel is rooted in the *force of Ambitio*. In that respect, we are all living in an illusion. But let us not dwell on that for the moment."

Huito paused once again.

"At some point, as beings had evolved in the physical world through the aid and support of Affero, a breakthrough was made and we learnt to hold onto awareness about the spirit world as well. As humans, we learnt to use the dream world to gain important messages from the spirits in the spirit world, all of which had one fundamental aim."

Huito looked at all three of them directly in the eye. "An aim to liberate us from the physical limitations that had been placed on us."

Elera felt the most aggrieved at what they were hearing.

"This is where the people of Leiruyi come into the story," he continued. "The great sorcerers had learnt of the force of Ambitio through dreaming. Whilst many were then able to break many of the barriers of the physical world through this knowledge, some were not prepared for the overwhelming force of Ambitio and they were possessed by its power.

"Whilst the Leiruyi created many of the great spiritual centres on the planet, they also created many demons."

Elera, still upset by what she was hearing, became distant in her expression. "I refuse to believe that the physical world is based only on power," she said desolately. "I know that beautiful things exist here. Are you saying Ambitio created all of that as well? If so, there are wonderful things about this illusion that we are living in too."

"As I said, we should not dwell on such matters," Huito reiterated. "Now, where was I? Oh, yes, the Leiruyi. Many of the great sorcerers were duped by Ambitio and began to seek out the protectors with the aspiration of harnessing their power. The scene that you saw in the temple was the culmination of this effort by them and Ambitio."

Huito was now being sternly serious.

"Whilst it is not written what occurred, so unspeakable that to talk of it was forbidden, what resulted is very clearly described in the scriptures. Many spirits were actually able to cross over from the spirit world to the physical world to help every being push away the threat to their existence that had been created by Ambitio."

Everyone was in awe of the tale.

"I never saw what it was that the spirits were pushing away," Bene stated.

Both Elera and Javu nodded in agreement that they had not seen the threat either.

"That is because the Great Eagle did not want you to see it for your own protection. Now where was I? Oh yes, the spirits.

"Because of this event, the physical world both progressed and was set back. While many began to understand that there was more than one world of reality, some had been so overwhelmed with the fear of what they had witnessed that a divide happened and humanity began to fight each other over vastly differing opinion."

Huito's eyes were now wide with compassion.

"Fear became the new tool of Ambitio to keep most in their prisons. What we have seen since for as long as most are aware is a history of competition and domination."

Huito was silent, indicating that he had finished talking.

"What about the *era* you mentioned?" Bene asked eagerly.

"The era to come is a time when those newly created on this earth will be free of any influence. They will be the direct children of the essence, just as Affero once was."

"But didn't you say that creation needs the seed of power?" Elera questioned him.

"That is the conundrum of the prophecy. It is to be accepted without proof, without logical understanding."

Though Javu, Bene and Elera all felt like they had learnt a tremendous amount from the old brujo, they couldn't help but feel a little confused and sceptical about his explanation of the past and reality.

Javu felt deep down like he could relate to most of what had been said. There was silence for many moments.

"How do you get to the spirit world from the physical world?" Bene asked Huito. This fundamental question was something he had always wanted to know.

The old man smiled in response. "The spirit world can be observed through dreaming in the dream world, but to actually go there, I only know of one way."

"Yes?" Bene prompted him.

"One must leave the physical world for good. It is a one-way journey."

"You mean die?" Bene asked.

"Yes, but do not be so afraid, Bene. Death would only be of your physical form. Your energy, your spirit persists."

Bene seemed shaken by the topic and the vision that he had seen of his father came to mind. He was split between the grief of never being able to stand next to him again with the newfound optimism that he still existed in some form somewhere.

"Do the scriptures say anything else?" Elera asked Huito, leaving Bene in a reflective silence. "Do they speak about the other pyramids?"

Huito leaned closely to Elera with fascination. He looked deep into her eyes as if trying to read her. "Why do you seek the old temples?" he asked her with a hint of suspicion. "What are you searching for?"

"I am only looking for a way to stop the fear and violence on this planet," she said boldly. "I believe I can do that by proving to people that Lemuria exists. To me it is a place where, as you said, people had a stronger connection to the essence." She sighed, feeling a little deflated at the brujo's explanation of reality. "But with every step I make it seems to get more and more complicated."

"I beg to differ," Huito said. "I believe things are getting much simpler for you. However, I think you do not really know why you are seeking the old temples. But I think that I do!"

All of them were taken aback by the brujo's surety.

"The protector revealed himself to you because he wants to help you," he said mysteriously. "He wants to help you too become a protector."

"A protector of what?" Javu asked.

"Of many things," Huito responded. "This planet, the dream world and most of all a protector against the constant onslaught of Ambitio."

"When you say that this force of power is constantly trying to control us, what do you mean exactly?" Bene said, a little daunted by the concept.

"It is simple," Huito said. "By its very nature Ambitio wants to consume everything. It controls by making beings behave like it, a black hole sucking, consuming everything around. Ambitio, the eye of darkness, is no longer connected to the essence, the source of creation. In a way, it is its own creator. Affero, the Great Eagle, on the other hand, is as connected to the essence as any force or being could hope to be."

He glanced over at Elera.

"All of the greedy empires that have existed through time have all been fuelled by Ambitio's illusions of power and control. The separateness they feel from others is due to them being cut off from the essence."

"And the protectors?" she probed.

"The elemental protectors are here to shield us. However, more and more beings are succumbing to the force of power instead of believing in the essence. The essence binds us all as one."

Huito scratched his head in a most peculiar way.

"Affero is an antidote to Ambitio but it is not the cure. Ambitio can never touch those who open themselves up completely to the essence. That is the essential job of a protector, to help as many as possible break free of Ambitio's illusions and connect to the essence."

Bene was slowly beginning to gain an understanding, but was still confused at how they could help this impossible situation.

"But how can we help?" Bene asked. It was a question Elera too was asking herself.

"You are already helping," Huito said vaguely, closing his eyes again.

With so much to take in, everyone was overcome with a sudden fatigue. They agreed to spend the night in the forgotten city and make their way to find the others first thing in the morning. Bene and Javu found a quiet place to settle for the night, but Elera still had many questions and stayed near Huito for a while.

As the old brujo sat with his eyes closed, Elera tapped him on the shoulder.

"Yes, senorita?" Huito responded.

"I just wanted to ask you a few things. How come you know about this city? I mean, it has clearly been empty for a long time."

"I come from a small tribe of people to the north of here. Since our origins, we have known of *Ixon*, this sacred city. Sometimes we visit here but it belongs to Respiro and we respect that."

"How is it possible that you can speak the Raiceman language? Have you been to Raicema?"

"The reason I can speak to you in such a language is the same reason your friend can speak to others in their languages. You should ask your friend why."

"Javu?"

Huito was silent, again indicating he wished to speak no more.

"I think I will go to sleep now," she said to him, her mind incapable of thinking one more thought.

Chapter 32 – Sinidev Rusmeli

Javu could not sleep.

He was lying under a tall tree, staring up at the stars in the sky. Memories of his childhood were flooding back, so realistic it felt like he was reliving them.

He could hear voices in his head, urging him to remember.

When Javu reached thirteen years of age he had become quite adept at summoning. He often playfully performed mischievous acts on the people of Sarmaldha, both for his own amusement and to dish out his own form of justice from time to time.

Javu was a brave child. His uncle had encouraged him to test his abilities through a number of death-defying challenges. Actesh once took Javu to a forest high in the mountains where they camped for three days. On the third day, a great elephant had appeared at the edge of the forest. Javu was challenged to ride the elephant to the top of the mountain. He was able to attract the creature towards him and the dark grey elephant even helped Javu up onto its back. Together they had traversed the mountain and the young summoner had returned safely to his uncle.

Over time, he had learnt to summon many creatures of the sky and villagers would stare in wonder and whisper at how Javu was always surrounded by so many birds and flying insects. Many villagers felt uneasy at the young boy's command of various creatures and Javu would often revel in seeing a flock of birds suddenly surround an unsuspecting person.

The general conclusion was that Sinidev Rusmeli was a strange child with magical powers, just like the rest of his family.

"Sinidev," Actesh approached the adolescent Javu one day. "You are a strong-willed boy who will soon become a man. I am now sure that you cannot be easily swayed by the temptations of power. For this reason, I wish to teach you something that you must only use in times of need."

Javu had not realised then that the days ahead would soon be filled with uncertainty and change.

"Remember that I once told you about my grandfather and his encounter with a creature known as Respiro. Well, I wasn't entirely honest with you when I said I didn't know what he looked like. I too have encountered this creature."

Actesh leaned in close to his nephew with a serious expression, as though great responsibility was linked to what he was about to say.

"You too *will* have an encounter with him."

The words had scared Javu, but he had continued to listen as his uncle revealed the secret about the mythical being.

"Respiro will come when you want understanding. You must wish for it with the utmost sincerity, as though your very existence depended on it. You come from a long line of people who have a connection to this creature, Sinidev. Your parents, myself, your grandfather, my grandfather were all capable of making contact."

"What do you mean wish for understanding?" the young Javu asked.

"I mean that you must seek the reason for your existence. When that happens, something will always come to help us, but specifically in *our case*, the feathered serpent will present himself."

"Why us?"

"It's just who we are. We have an affinity to *air* and Respiro is an *ally* of *air*."

Javu had not understood, but it didn't matter to him. The fact that who he was now had meaning, and had purpose, was all he was interested in.

"As you have already seen in your short life, it is not only a gift but also a burden to have such an affinity. You are both a wonder and a target, just as your parents were."

A while later, whilst Javu had been playing outside, Actesh approached him carrying a large plate of bright red watermelon.

"Do you know who we are, Sinidev?"

The young Javu had not answered.

"We are not the fearful or the ignorant. We are not demi-gods nor ghosts," Actesh had said. "We exist ourselves as both gods and demons."

The statement had petrified the young Javu, who never wanted to think of himself as a demon. The cold watermelon had helped settle him in that moment.

That was the only time his uncle mentioned such a subject.

Sometime afterwards, Actesh said something that made Javu feel less afraid.

"I am moving towards an equilibrium, Sinidev. Soon, I will not fear or misunderstand, I will not desire and crave neither. I will be powerless and free of control."

A few months later, Actesh Rusmeli passed away peacefully in his sleep.

Javu had grieved alone.

Living in the same house that he had shared with his uncle for so long was both painful and a help to him. He would sit in his uncle's study, wanting to read so many of the books that Actesh so often recommended, but unable to.

It took time.

A while later, whilst sorting through some of Actesh's belongings, Javu had found a note addressed to him. It said two things, both of which greatly moved the young Master Rusmeli.

"I leave the house entirely in your possession, Sinidev," the note read, *"though I know that you do not intend to stay. Wherever you go, know that your parents and I are watching over you."*

At the bottom there was smaller writing.

"I know that you have thought of vengeance every day since they died. If you choose to face such a challenge, remember all the skills that I have taught you. It's endless, nephew. Life will always overcome death."

Javu had never divulged to his uncle that he had considered leaving Sarmaldha nor that the deaths of his parents had weighed on his mind, yet his uncle seemed to know everything about him.

Some time passed and the young summoner had spent much of

it in his uncle's house. Then one day, Javu wandered out of the village towards the great mountains that ran like a backbone between Vassini and Neoasia. He rambled for days higher and higher into the desolate roof of the world.

Javu's general ambition was reach the area where the feared sorcerer Vuktar was allegedly hiding. He was the man who was allegedly responsible for his parents' death. He now felt no remorse or anger to Vuktar, but he felt that facing him was a barrier he needed to dissolve.

The young Javu trekked for days, following the guidance of a number of birds in the sky that seemed to be guiding him.

After being out in the mountains for a week, the young man began to feel faint and delirious. He was finding it hard to find food in such a bleak environment.

Javu had soon found himself at a junction in which the only way to pass was across a deathly ledge which looked extremely unstable, like it might crumble away with the faintest of footsteps.

It was at this point that the young Javu had begun to question what he was doing up in the middle of the colossal mountain range. Did he want vengeance for the deaths of his parents? Did he want peace? He just didn't know.

He sat upon a rock and contemplated whether to turn back. During this meditation, many birds and insects began to flock to the area around where Javu was sitting and his chain of thoughts had merged into the meaning of his existence and soon after the meaning of existence in general.

Without realising it, he had sat for hours pondering what he should be doing with his life. He suddenly had a sensation, so clear a feeling that it was unmistakable. It was as if all emotions had been flushed from his body and his mind went completely blank. He could only observe, only pick up on every little sound and movement around him.

It was then that the event happened that had changed Javu's life forever. A great round light had appeared in front of him. It was a fading light, as though two worlds were merging together.

It got brighter and brighter until Javu's vision seemed to change completely.

I can see. The thought went through his head. It almost felt like the first thought that he had ever had, a feeling of being born.

Then the form had appeared before him. It was a being of incredible presence, and the atmosphere seemed to be stagnant in suspense.

A magnificent creature manifested from the light – white, blue and yellow-feathered with a long, snaking body. It floated in front of Javu, yet it had no wings. Its eyes were round and clear, bright green like a kiwi fruit and its split tongue darted in and out of its rounded snout in a rhythmic motion. Javu had instantly felt a deep-set love for the creature.

The voice that Javu had heard then sounded like the whisper of the wind in his ear.

"I can see. I can see you, Javu."

The feathered serpent had hovered in front of him, seemingly waiting for something.

A long while of disbelief passed before Javu finally managed to speak. "Why did you call me *Javu*?"

"Javu means happiness inside, something which you have in abundance."

Javu stared at the piercing eyes of the dragon-like being in front of him. Once again, his mind went black and he couldn't even remember what he had just been talking about. After what seemed like hours of just staring at the incredible serpent, he finally asked another question. "Should I seek out Vuktar?"

"In human terms, you have the same lineage as the sorcerer of the mountain. That lineage has been entrusted with the protection of one of the stones of power."

Javu's vision of the great creature seemed to waver at that moment.

"Your parents were protectors of the stone. Vuktar came last in the

lineage and it drove him to be consumed by power. Now, Vuktar does not exist anymore. He has become a vessel for power, nothing more."

Javu had begun to understand at that point why he was there in the midst of the enormous mountain range.

Before he could say a word, Respiro confirmed it. *"The stone of the air should be in your possession."*

Javu had always felt the innate desire to protect something and at that moment he realised that he should start with the sacred object in question.

"You should seek him out. The stone has undergone a transformation."

"What transformation?" the young Javu had asked.

"It is channelling consuming power, not freedom. If such sorcery continues, the negative forces of this world and those connected to it will grow strong enough to dominate everything. Already, one of the demons of the underworld has been unleashed in this world. Morbis is more a reality now than she has ever been."

A strange melody could be heard. Javu could not place it but he soon realised that it was coming from everywhere. The air around him was resonating to a tune.

"Can I take the stone from him?" Javu asked after another period of blankness. The thought had sprung into his mind.

"It will be difficult, for Vuktar has great power surging through him. If you pass this challenge, you shall never be the same again. You are not far now, brave summoner. I will be with you."

At that moment, Respiro had strongly reminded the young Javu of his uncle. Then, without warning, the great serpent vanished instantly as if he were never there.

It had left the young summoner in doubt of his sanity.

After some time trying to accept what had just occurred, Javu continued across the crumbly ledge ahead. Shards broke off with every subtle movement. He made it safely across to a more open natural platform but Javu could see a sheer drop ahead, and across the way there was a dingy cave. Javu knew Vuktar was living in that cave.

The young man pondered how to get across the narrow gorge, which was a width of at least ten long strides.

I cannot jump that far, Javu thought.

Then he heard the whisper in his ear again. *"You are weightless,"* was all it said.

An eagle above soaring through the air suddenly gave Javu a flash of spontaneous inspiration and uncontrollably, he took a run up and jumped blindly at the cave across the ravine.

The sensation he had was one of suspension. His body felt fluffy and he glided across the gorge at will. He kicked his legs and waved his arms as if he were swimming through the air before realising his mind was taking him where he wanted. He floated calmly down to the other side like a bird descending from flight.

A wave of great excitement wafted through him. He couldn't make sense of what he had just achieved. He felt slightly dizzy. Before he could think about it in any detail, he heard a voice resonating from inside the cave.

It was a language Javu didn't know, but before he tried to listen more carefully to what was being said, he heard the whisper of the wind again. *"You understand. It is the language of the ancient sorcerers."*

Suddenly and strangely, the young Javu could then understand every word resonating out of the cave before him. The voice was chanting in a focused and meticulous way.

"Rise... Fall... Cut..." The voice was repeating over and over in the strange language. The chanting sounded frightening and Javu had known instinctively that the words were being used to conjure negative energy.

Venturing into the cave, Javu laid his eyes for the first time on the man who had been feared for so long by the people of Sarmaldha.

Vuktar did not stand up straight. His back was crooked and his scraggy hair was wildly wrapped around his droopy aged skin.

He was just standing there, looking down into his cupped hands and chanting over and over.

Then, he looked up to see the adolescent boy in front of him. Javu was just standing there, staring at him.

"Who are you? What do you want?"

Vuktar had spoken in a raspy voice. However, the words Javu heard in his head did not match the words that he knew were coming out of the sorcerer's mouth. It was as if his mind was translating an underlying melody to the words being spoken. Vuktar repeated the question, this time in a more aggressive manner.

Naturally and with equal surprise, Javu opened his mouth and spoke to the decrepit sorcerer in the same archaic language.

"I have come for the stone." He spoke the words, but they didn't seem to come from himself.

Vuktar cackled at the young Javu, amused that such words were coming from his high-pitched voice.

"My name is Sinidev Rusmeli and that stone should be with me."

It was at this point that Vuktar had become very angry. It was a sudden transformation and he began to chant ferociously into his cupped hands, where Javu was sure the stone was hidden.

The sorcerer's face contorted and began to take a different shape, looking much like a scrawny bird with intense eyes. A grey aura surrounded him, making him look bigger and his shape different. It was almost if he was sprouting wings.

He chanted loudly.

Then, a great gust of wind appeared from nowhere, blowing through the cave at speed. Javu was thrown violently against one of the cave walls, forcing the air out of his lungs.

Vuktar was moving his hands and arms in a dipping motion walking forward towards Javu, the winds vibrating up and down with an eerie howl. He felt himself being pushed up towards the roof of the cave and he hit his head heavily, slumping down in pain. A trickle of blood ran down from his head, across his cheek.

Javu's head was throbbing so hard it made his entire body shake. He could see the rotten, yellow teeth of the vicious sorcerer as he chanted aggressively. He could see the stone for the first time. It was in Vuktar's hand, giving off a strange grey mist.

Then Javu had felt like he was choking, like every drop of oxygen in his body was being sucked out by some unknown presence penetrating his body, infecting him like a virus.

As the young Javu had struggled to take a breath of air and with his head pounding from the onslaught, he wished and prayed that he could be free of control, free of manipulation.

Javu was willing at that moment to forget everything that he had learnt about summoning in exchange for a simple, peaceful life.

As he stopped resisting the onslaught, he looked up and saw Respiro appear behind Vuktar, its body curling around majestically as it rose up to the height of the cave. The cave seemed to waver in a convex of energy.

Vuktar saw the young Javu's eyes fall weakly behind him and as he slowly looked back, the feathered serpent struck the wicked sorcerer directly on the top of the head.

Then darkness fell as the young Javu lost consciousness.

Javu finally fell asleep under the Ixonian tree after vividly reliving the memories of his childhood. However, one phrase had resonated through his head over and over before he had at last dozed off as dawn was starting to break.

"The stone and I are one. That is why I cannot take it."

Chapter 33 – The World Walker Prophecy

Dawn had broken over Ixon.

Elera was already awake, talking with Huito whilst eating bright green berries and drinking streaming hot tea.

"Mmm, this tastes strange but nice," she said, sipping the hot brew slowly. "It tastes like seaweed."

Huito smiled as he mixed around dark green leaves in his shiny metal bowl full of water.

"What kind of metal is that?" Elera asked him.

"It is silver. There is a lot of it close by."

Elera wanted to ask Huito about the geography of the area.

"Huito, you said yesterday that the temple was built on special rocks. Can you tell me more about them? I mean, why would the Leiyuri value these rocks?"

"They are capable of channelling energy from other worlds."

"Other worlds?"

"Yes. That is why many people have visions when near to rocks like this."

It reminded Elera of the same belief up in the city of the old mountain. "When we were in Machu Picchu before, I touched my head to the Intihuatana stone and I think I saw the spirit world. It was a vision, like you said."

"The Intihuatana is made of the very same rock on which the temple over there is built."

The sky overhead was bright blue and three birds chased each other in playful way, chirping away to a happy tune.

"The *wisdom rocks* or *Omniadd crystals* as they are known when purified, are both the oldest and most powerful material entities on this planet. Some people would kill to get their hands on these rocks. The reason they are connected to multiple worlds is due to their strong affinity with the essence, the *fabric energy* of the universe."

Huito's account reminded Elera of why she had trekked for weeks across Cibola.

"Huito, I have felt determined since I was young age to try and stop the suffering that happens in this world. How can I show the world that there is more to life that wealth, such as the people who would kill for these rocks?"

Huito said nothing.

"I am sure that if all people knew that life was endless, the wars and fighting would stop," Elera said after a while.

"Start with yourself. The fears you have make you doubt that the essence exists and when one doubts, we are allowing power to control us. We lose our connection to that which you describe as endless. Letting go of fear is the first step."

"So how can I let go of my fears? In some way, my fears are what are driving me through life."

"That is not so, Elera," Huito reassured her. "What is driving you is the hope that you will one day be free of your fears, and that is the essence trying to help you."

He paused.

"If you can realise that, you will already start to break free."

Aova came to mind for Elera. She had thought about her a lot through the night. It was strange. She almost felt like the great horse was some kind of motherly figure, there to protect her.

"I guess I've got to figure out where to head next," Elera said after a while. "I want to learn more about the Leiruyi, or the Lemurians as I have come to know them."

"Well you are here now at the temple of Air in Ixon," he said. "And you have told me that you already visited the Temple of Water in Bimini and the Temple of Fire in Giza, so it seems that the only remaining Leiruyi temple for you to visit is the *Temple of Earth*."

"I want to," Elera agreed. "But I have no idea where the fourth pyramid is."

Huito stood up with agility. He stretched his arms upwards like he was waking up from a long sleep. "I know where there is a description of its location," Huito said simply.

"Really?" Elera said with surprise, looking up at him. "Where?"

"It is written on a tablet in the temple here," he said with a smile. "Shall we go and read it together?"

Elera enthusiastically got to her feet and the two of them made their way over to the Ixonian pyramid and began to climb the steps of the monument. Huito paused every few steps, which gave Elera the chance to see every new tree that came into sight.

After reaching the top and walking through the entrance, Elera was expecting it to close as it had before. She cautiously walked under the great slab of stone that hung over the doorway. Nothing happened.

Huito knew exactly where he was going, pushing something lightly on the rightmost wall of the main chamber, which opened a secret door. It scrolled upwards with a scraping noise.

The door led to a staircase, which wound downwards into a hot and musty chamber.

"The last emperor of Ixon is buried here," he told her, pointing to a sarcophagus at the back of the chamber, made of a shiny black crystal-like stone. He made his way over to an oval tablet which was hanging on the wall, unknown symbols written upon it, still crisply carved and undisturbed.

"It reads: *The temple of earth remains in our homeland. The gate is located on an island of warmth, which is in the midst of the frozen.*"

He looked up at Elera.

"That's all it says about that. It also reads: *Our people will preserve our ways for the future, when those are born that can walk between worlds.*"

"What does it mean?" Elera asked herself, trying to interpret the translation.

"It means the old sorcerers still exist somewhere and they are waiting."

"Waiting for what?"

"They are waiting for the prophecy to come true!"

"What prophecy?" Elera asked.

"It is said that those *will* come who can create a bridge between this world and other worlds."

Huito paused as he rubbed his belly.

"Why would the old sorcerers want this you ask? Well there are good reasons and bad reasons."

Elera was speechless, unable to do anything except listen.

"Long ago, the Leiruyi made a great mistake and misused their connection to the eye of darkness to create something horribly powerful."

Huito rubbed his belly again.

The chamber in which they were standing now seemed eerie and attentive, as if it were listening to every word being said.

"Existing on this planet right now are entities known to the original people of this city as *fatums*. They are the absolute opposite of the protectors, demons of the underworlds."

Huito paused for a moment.

"They exist to control, to dominate, to destroy."

Elera's face was frozen. Her entire body was frozen.

"These demons are the loyal children of Ambitio, the ceaseless eye of darkness and bearer of unrelenting power."

He paused, unsure if he should tell Elera more about the matter.

"Here we are safe, so I can tell you what I know."

There was a rumbling from below. It came from the depths of the earth and the vibration terrified Elera for a moment.

"There are four known fatums," Huito continued unaffected. He held his hands tightly together. "*Diabolus*, the destroyer of the earth, is a stalker. He waits patiently to strike and though he looks human, he is far from it. He is only a messenger of Ambitio, completely without any free will. The eye of darkness consumed any freedom he had a long time ago."

Elera could not believe what she was hearing. She didn't want to believe it.

"*Ignis*, the dragon of death, is a giant like no other. This being of fire is driven only by revenge."

The room had somehow got lighter. An all-pervasive light was around like it was trying to protect them.

"Revenge over what?" Elera asked finally, after she felt her heart speed up slightly.

"Revenge for the death of her child."

Elera was spellbound by what Huito was telling her and wanted to know more. She had heard similar mythologies before in the more remote communities she had visited over the years, but nothing like this.

"Then there is *Murdrak*, the water dragon. He is sleeping," Huito continued. "But one day, he will wake up!"

He said this so dramatically that it made Elera jump a little, something that Huito seemed to find quite amusing. A vision of the pool in Bimini where she had seen such a horrible creature lurking beneath the depths came to mind. She had no time to contemplate further as Huito had moved on.

"And *Morbis*, the owl woman, is a most cunning creature," he said after composing himself. "She is very clever, capable of duping even the most cautious of individuals, a master of manipulation."

Huito glanced back at the symbols he had been reading.

"So these are the bad reasons to create a bridge between worlds," he said in such a comical way that it made Elera giggle a little. "These manifestations of death were unleashed on the planet once before through such ability by the old sorcerers. The event that you all had a vision of here was the culmination of such a malevolent bridge between worlds being formed."

"I thought you said what occurred was not described?" Elera asked, trying to gain clarity.

"Indeed it was not. I have gained this knowledge by other means."

"How?" Elera asked.

"By dwelling in the dream world. The spirits and the old sorcerers have told me of the fatums. Luckily, I have never encountered any of them nor do I intend to."

Elera felt a chill go down her spine.

"However, as I said, there are good reasons for world walkers to exist. Those reasons are exactly the same as your reasons for helping those who suffer. You only want people to be free. You want this planet to be free."

The words made Elera feel calm.

"But what about the fatums?" she asked after a while. "How did they cross over? What happened? I mean, where do they come from?"

So many questions had flooded Elera's mind.

"These creatures dwelled in the realms of Ambitio until the old sorcerers summoned them forth. And why would they want to do this?"

Elera did not have an answer. She had always been incapable of understanding why someone would want to rain terror and destruction over the planet and its inhabitants.

"Well, it is because they too are slaves of power." Huito looked slightly poignant at his allegation. "The old sorcerers managed to contain their earthly manifestations. That is why I was asking you what you were looking for in your search of the old temples." He looked down, clearly burdened by knowing that such entities existed.

Elera was starting to feel slightly afraid that the pyramid in which she was standing might have something to do with the horrific beings that Huito had described.

"Many have come, bewitched by Ambitio, in an attempt to unleash the fatums upon the world once again," he said ominously.

"Well I wish no such thing. How did the old sorcerers contain them?" Elera asked.

"By binding them to sacred stones. These stones are forged from the same rocks that have a special affinity to the essence."

The old brujo looked at his hands as if reading them like an open book.

"At one time, each of these crystal stones was kept in a separate temple in different corners of the planet. Indeed, the *air stone* was once kept here."

Elera had the odd sensation that she was being reminded of something that she had somehow forgotten. It was a feeling of de ja vu, coupled with a euphoria that she had lived forever.

"It became too dangerous several thousand years ago when the whereabouts of the stones reached unpredictable warmongers," Huito continued. "They believed they could use them to quash their enemies. Because of this, the stones were removed and have been handed down to trustworthy beings ever since."

"Is that safe?" Elera asked.

"The fatums thrive on pure fear and hatred. That is why the bearers of the stones must be kind and brave individuals, not unlike you, Elera. You cannot easily be swayed by power."

Huito looked around him, but he seemed to be looking beyond the walls in surround.

"If the prophecy comes true, there will be no more secrets. The fatums and the protectors will become known to everyone!"

Elera spent some time examining the scriptures before they both made their way back out to the city of Ixon. She was confused and felt tired from trying to make sense of what she had been told by Huito.

Javu and Bene were now awake and were standing at the bottom of the pyramid.

"Hey!" Bene shouted as he saw them walking down the stairs. "We thought you'd left!"

"We should really find the others," Javu said as they reached the bottom. Elera agreed.

Huito seemed pleased that he had met the three travellers and he wished them luck and wisdom on their journey ahead.

"I hope that we will see you again, Huito," Elera said to him as they prepared to leave.

"I will be here," Huito said, before going back to his favourite spot under the tree. Then he looked at Bene. "Can I speak with you, son?" he said strangely.

Being referred to in this way made Bene feel uneasy but he reciprocated and sat beside the old brujo.

"When you have overcome the anger within, come back here and seek me out. There is much I wish to show you."

Bene didn't know what to say.

"Your father is watching you."

Bene was left speechless by the words and just nodded weakly at the silver-eyed elder. He got to his feet, a little light-headed and almost feeling like he was in a dream.

The three of them headed back to the tunnel from which they had entered Ixon. Elera looked back at the great city, excited to have discovered such a magical location.

As they passed back through the dark tunnel, they emerged underneath the same waterfall. They materialized from behind it, astounded to find Rekesh, Teltu, Reo, Sita and Rama all camping around the small lake.

"Look!" Reo almost screamed as he spotted them. "They're there!"

Rekesh ran over to Elera and held her firmly by the arms, checking if she was real.

"Where did you go?" he asked quite frantically. "You disappeared!"

"What do you mean?" Bene said, stepping in. "We went through the tunnel behind the waterfall."

"There is no tunnel behind there," Reo protested. "We all went in many times and all we found was a dead end."

It took an hour of talking to convince them all that Elera, Javu and Bene had indeed passed through a tunnel to the magical city of Ixon. However, Rekesh would not allow her to go back into the cave in case she did not return.

Elera described everything that she had seen and heard. She talked about the essence, the forces of Affero and Ambitio and the spirit and dream worlds. She described the elemental protectors and the fatums.

"Aova is a protector and so is Respiro, the feathered serpent."

"I don't like the sound of these fatum things," Reo said timidly, shifting his eyes from side to side in an amusing, twitchy way. The forest in surround came alive with the noise of a multitude of animals, seemingly all in agreement.

"We have to protect this planet from Ambitio," Elera said to them all, feeling clearer about her purpose and ignoring Reo's trepidation. "And Lemuria, the Leiruyi can show us how. After all, they were able to contain the fatums."

"I am not sure, Elera," Javu said. He had not spoken much since they left Ixon. "It was the Leiruyi that unleashed such demons on this planet in the first place if we are to believe Huito's account."

"One thing I am certain of, Javu, is that there is good and bad in every situation," Elera countered. "Even if it is true that these fatums exist, I am sure there is an equal if not greater presence of love in this world."

She continued to tell them all about the world walker prophecy and about the fourth pyramid, the Temple of the Earth, and where its gate was supposed to be located.

"An island surrounded by a land that is frozen?" Teltu pondered to himself. "Sounds like *Isis*."

"Isis? You mean the northern lands?" Rekesh tried to clarify. "The sea is deadly up there."

"We would need a strong ship to get there," Bene stated with energy. "Yes, it is far to the north."

Reo stepped forward, clearly unsettled by what he was hearing. He took in a deep breath as if about to confess something.

"Hold on a minute," he said. "We have been trekking through jungles and mountains for God knows how long. I have slept with beetles, eaten weird slimy mushrooms and worn the soles off my feet."

He paused for a second, thinking hard.

"I'm not even sure how I wound up on this expedition. Bene railroaded me into coming to Lizrab, but I never thought I'd end up in the middle of nowhere listening to tales of monsters and invisible forces that try to control us. And now, you want to continue this madness out into the freezing cold?"

His expression was one of total bewilderment at the reasoning behind such a notion.

"Well, good luck! I'm heading back to Calegra."

Everyone was silent for a while as they thought of a response to Reo's dissatisfaction.

Surprisingly, it was Teltu who spoke first.

"I too miss my home, Reo. I have a wife and a daughter whom I wish I could see right now. But whether we believe it or not, Elera is right and something has to be done to stop all those who try to control us. It was only a few years ago that Raicema were killing thousands of people in Ciafra and they just did the same in Lizrab too. No matter what is driving them in their onslaught, if there is a possibility that we can change things then we should do everything we can to help."

Bringing the subject back to the very real wars in recent times seemed to shake Reo and his expression changed to one of concern.

"Remember what Kirichi said?" Teltu continued. "We all have a part in this. It is not a coincidence. And if it's true and we are all supposed to be protectors of this planet, then I think that is something that we can't walk away from."

There was silence for a while as everyone pondered the significance of Teltu's words.

"Reo, I'll understand if you don't want to come with us," Elera told him. "We will have to head back towards Turo anyway, so think about it. But you should know this, the fire you have inside has kept me going in times when I wanted to give up."

The words seemed to mean something to Reo. He had always thought of Elera as the solid, motivating person in the group, yet deep down, he wanted to be that person. He began to realise how much he'd been complaining. However, he still couldn't shake the yearning to escape back to Calegra.

"Okay. Let's see," he said.

They gathered their things and prepared to set off on the long journey back to Lizrab.

Sometime later, with the others striding ahead through the forest, Elera and Javu walked more slowly behind.

"You know, Javu, it's been puzzling me for a while now how you can speak so many languages. I mean, I know you haven't been to some of these regions before so how would you know how to speak Uru or the language of Machu Picchu? But I think I've worked it out. You have met Respiro, haven't you? Not in Ixon but another time before?"

"Yes I have," he told her.

"And now you can speak and understand any language?"

"Yes, but is wise to keep such abilities to yourself," Javu said knowingly. "Otherwise, you may be taken advantage of."

"What is it like?" Elera asked. "Being able to understand anyone?"

"It only confirms what I already knew," he said simply. "We are all the same."

Rekesh and the others were quite far ahead now and Elera wanted to talk about something else that had been bothering her. "I was also thinking that before, when the gate opened, that there was no way that anyone could reach that slot without the help of somebody else."

Javu smiled a little. "What are you implying, Elera?" he said in a light-hearted way.

"Well, it seems that if someone could somehow get up there themselves and put a key in."

Javu just smiled at Elera's deduction and she smiled too, at his acknowledgement.

"So what's it like to fly?"

Javu did not answer and Elera got the impression he didn't want to give the ability any special importance.

"I was looking for proof of such abilities and it turns out the proof was with me all along."

Javu smiled affectionately at Elera. They walked in silence for a while.

"Kirichi said that I have received a gift from Aova," Elera said, breaking the silence, "but I have no idea what it could be."

"I am sure you will find out when it is needed," he reassured her.

"I hope so," she said. "Knowing that *they* are out there certainly makes me think we need all the help we can get."

Javu nodded with a wry smile.

"I think I'll catch up with Rekesh. I haven't spoken to him much recently."

With that she ran on ahead, leaving Javu walking at a more leisurely pace.

As she got out of sight, Javu lifted his shirt a little, revealing a brown leather pouch strapped to his body. He opened it and took something out, a shiny grey crystal, smoky and perfectly circular. It was the air stone.

He held it in his hand looking at it lying in his palm, its reflected light hypnotising.

He quickly put it away.

Then his thoughts went out to his son.

Chapter 34 – The Cracks Appear

There was light everywhere.

Only one question existed as the first in a long line of stepping stones.

"How can I protect myself from them?" he felt himself ask.

The question lingered in the air like a cloud unwilling to disperse.

"You should disappear for a while," a voice responded. *"Be invisible."*

The voice was that of a woman. The words resonated through his mind, a beautiful voice so soothing.

"Be invisible," it repeated melodically. *"You are surrounded by light."*

Then silence fell and tranquillity was everywhere. He had joined the light. All memory was lost and he was free. He wished that moment could last forever, but it didn't.

Jen King opened his tired eyes to a single beam of light focused through the porthole of his cabin. He was aboard the *Stryder* war vessel and an awful weight was beginning to form in his stomach.

He felt groggy and his hearing focused on clanking from above, the sound of the daily slog of thousands of men ready to serve their leaders.

Jen sat up and looked out of the window, seeing nothing but ocean. He reflected on how his life had changed in such a short space of time. Seth Tyrone was the first person to come to mind.

The leader that he had once considered a friend and ally was now a shell of his former self in Jen's opinion. In fact, Jen had begun to think of the man as a great barrier in his life.

He's sitting over there in his fat leather chair whilst I'm stuck out here on this floating prison. He heard the thought go through his head. He looked out again across the ocean, the horizon between the sea and sky looking like an electric blue line.

He slowly got up and fought against the weight holding him down. He stared out of the porthole for several moments before getting dressed, ready to face an everlasting list of boring tasks. He heard heavy pounding on the metal door of his cabin.

"Come on you lazy bums! Wake up and get moving!" the brigadier bellowed from outside in the hallway. Jen had to take a deep breath before opening the weighty door to face the drone and dregs of the ship on which he was trapped.

As Jen's morning was just beginning out in the ocean, over on the west coast of Raicema, the Tyrona Royal Palace was buzzing with urgent activity.

In the month that had passed since the death of his brother, Seth Tyrone had slowly fallen into a downward spiral of bitterness and anger.

Upon returning to Raicema after the failed mission to capture Aradonas, Seth had been consistently dogged with political and civil problems. His main predicament was restoring Raicema's much-damaged international relationship with the nation of *Lengard*, which was using the death of their king as a lynchpin in the conflict.

"I am not a politician!" Seth had protested to his advisors. "Why do we even need a new figurehead? We have enough technology to rule without question."

The hard line approach had not sat well with various senior figures in the Raiceman elite. After a while and much persuasion, Seth resigned himself to the fact he would have to replace his brother in rulership. The moment that the new presidency was announced, Seth faced the greatest internal rebellion for centuries within Raicema.

"With news leaking out that President Tyrone was assassinated by a Makai warrior, factions in Tyrona and Raicema City have methodically created strongholds in all of our major cities," Seth's aide had told him.

The metropolis cities of Raicema were becoming divided and segregated. The law and order that had existed previously was now undermined by the unwritten laws of rebellion. Those who had previously kept secret their allegiance to Makaism now stepped forward with pride and unity. Many did not know who to support, unsure who would emerge victorious in the struggle for power.

Now, sitting in his brother's chair in the presidential office of Tyrona Palace, Seth was surrounded by aides and advisors.

"President Tyrone, I have the information you requested," one aide said who had just come in.

"Well? What of these allegations from Lengard?"

"It seems that approximately five hundred men were dispatched to a small fishing village in western Neoasia four weeks ago, about four days before the attack on the palace of Lengard. The village is well known in the region as a Makai port."

"Who gave the order?" Seth asked in disbelief, totally unaware of such a deployment of troops.

"President Tyrone did, sir."

Seth could not believe it. His brother had truly kept him in the dark about the military support that was being given to the Neoasian Makai.

"Raiceman troops were spotted on the shores of Lengard before the attack."

"Is Lengard aware that my brother sent troops to Neoasia?"

"I don't know, sir." the aide admitted.

"Well find out!" Seth boomed, a desperate anxiety rising inside him. He thought to himself for a while, trying to decide what action to take.

"We must sever all ties with Yangjam," he said, more to himself than to anyone else. He looked up.

"Make sure all traces of communication between Raicema and Yangjam Satori are destroyed as a matter of urgency."

Several of the aides scurried off to undertake the task assigned. The few that remained had another pressing issue to discuss.

"The results of the poll are in, President Tyrone," one said. "It appears that the primary loss of confidence in the government stems from lack of action over the death of President Tyrone, sir."

"So the people want revenge!" Seth deciphered, anger glowing in his eyes. "I have thought everyday of how to punish those responsible. What have you found out about the perpetrators?"

"Well, we have identified the assassin as a Rekesh Satori, a former inhabitant of Raicema City originally from Vassini."

"Satori?!" Seth barked with disbelief.

"We have no clue as to the motive for the assassination, but our sources lead us to believe that he and several of his supporters are currently residing in south Lizrab. This is a photograph of him taken by a security camera on the *Stryder*, twenty-seven minutes before President Tyrone was fatally wounded."

The aide placed a large, blown-up picture of Rekesh on the desk in front of Seth, who glared at it, seething.

"Unfortunately, Satori is not registered on our DNA database so we cannot trace his exact location."

"I want you to distribute this picture amongst every soldier who was in Lizrab and see if anyone has any more information about this criminal."

The two aides hurried away to carry out the order, leaving only one who had a large map in his hand. He laid it on the table in front of the new president.

"I need advice on our power distribution, sir. This is a map of all of our power stations," the young man explained. He pointed out each marking on the landscape.

"We have started to lose power in these three stations on the west coast, mainly because of dwindling fuel supplies in the region. We cannot transport fuel from the east because of a Makai stronghold on the main Autoroute just here."

The aide pointed out the places of difficultly on the map and Seth began to rub his head in anguish.

"I want a deployment of troops to clear the Autoroute," he told the young aide, getting to his feet. "Now I don't want to be disturbed for a while."

Seth left his office and did not return for some time. When he did come back, it was full once again, every advisor armed with a multitude of information to report back to the new president.

"So, who's first?" he asked, sitting back down in the chair of national power.

Two aides stepped forward.

"President Tyrone, we have sent an alert out to all soldiers with the picture of the assassin and it seems only one soldier has recognised him."

"And who is that?"

"Jen King, sir."

"Send for him immediately," Seth ordered, bewildered at how this could be true. "He is stationed on the *Stryder*. Have one of the new flying machines pick him up."

The two aides ran off and two more stepped forward.

"President Tyrone, we have heard from the government of Lengard," one aide said quite urgently with a letter in his hand. The letter was sealed with the letters *RNL*.

"We have received an official declaration with a number of demands."

The words seemed to be infuriating Seth, who gripped the desk tightly until his knuckles turned white.

"Read it to me."

The aide broke the seal and unrolled the thick, embossed paper.

"The Royal Nation of Lengard requests that the following demands be met by President Tyrone of Raicema," the aide read, *"in response to the alleged involvement of Raicema on the attack of the Royal Palace of Lengard which claimed the life of fifty-eight subjects including Honourable Lord Westway and our beloved King Constynce:*

Firstly, a military response is expected against the core perpetrators.

If this demand is not met, Lengard will have no choice but to assume a full alliance between the perpetrators and Raicema, which in turn could lead to our own military action.

Secondly, a public apology is demanded of the new president for any association with the perpetrators. This is to quell public dissention over the death of our king.

Please respond declaring your intentions forthwith to the Royal Council in Phoenicia.

Yours sincerely,

Adalade Redbuck

Chief Council Aide of the Royal Nation of Lengard."

Seth thought carefully about the implications of the declaration.

"They expect us to invade Neoasia," one of the aides elaborated.

"I know that, idiot!" Seth almost exploded.

He stood up and began to pace backwards and forwards around the desk, both aides feeling a great deal of anxiety over the entire affair.

"We must prepare a convoy to Neoasia and appeal to the emperor," he said out loud to himself, after contemplating for a while. "We could lose every man we have in a war with the Neoasian Makai. Only with the support of the Central Neoasian military can we have any chance of resolving this."

He paced around the office some more.

"Also, a stronger allegiance with the Neoasian government will make Lengard think twice about threatening me like this. Send an official statement of intent to visit the emperor."

The aides were nodding in agreement, though it was purely by default as neither of them could come up with a solution for the predicament that Raicema was in. What was certain, however, was that any sort of conflict with Lengard would be devastating for the nation. Its sheer size and military capability dwarfed that of Raicema's. As Seth was dismissing them both, another aide entered.

"Jen King has been collected, sir. He is estimated to arrive one hour from now."

"Good," Seth said. "I need to visit our research facility. I will be back in the hour."

Seth promptly left the office, leaving several advisors waiting anxiously for his return. An hour passed and the office grew more populated with those bearing information and needing decisions.

As Seth walked back into the office, he was greeted with scores of faces all wanting his attention.

"Jen King has arrived, sir," one aide announced to him from the doorway.

"Send him in," Seth demanded. "Everyone else leave."

Everyone left the office as Jen was brought in, accompanied by two guards. He looked deflated and less muscular than when Seth had last seen him, a shadow of his previous physical appearance. Though still strong-looking, he was on the whole a lot slimmer and his hair had grown from short and shaven into a black tangled mess, covering his ears and forehead. Seth was almost toppled over by his much-changed appearance, having not seen him since their return from Lizrab.

"You have really let yourself go, King," Seth said in disbelief.

Jen said nothing. Indeed, he had let himself go. He no longer lifted heavy weights every day to maintain muscle mass. He was eating much less and spending great lengths of time contemplating his life and future.

Jen's meeting with Javu a month earlier had cemented his uncertainty about where his life was going. However, he now *was* certain that he did not want to be part of the Raiceman military.

"So, you know this man?" Seth asked, walking over to his desk and throwing down the picture of Rekesh.

"I only met him once," Jen said quietly.

"You met him?"

"We fought in Lizrab," Jen recalled. "He would not let me pass."

"Why didn't you kill him?" Seth asked coldly.

Jen didn't answer, hanging his head in shame, though deep down he was thankful that he had not.

"This man is responsible for my brother's death. Vengeance is required. As you know this man, you will be the one who will deliver this vengeance."

Jen looked up with disdain in his eyes.

"I refuse," Jen said weakly but with determination.

Fury flashed across Seth's eyes at the disloyalty. "If you do not, then you will be considered a traitor and dealt with accordingly," Seth declared sternly. He looked at Jen menacingly but then in a moment of concern, he relaxed his voice and spoke with more affection towards him.

"I do not mean to be harsh with you, King. However, you are losing your strength and we are in difficult times. I need someone like you to set an example that Raicema will not be defeated."

Again, Jen said nothing. The sentiment of pride and patriotism that he once shared was now a distant memory. Indeed, he felt the opposite, like there was nothing to fight for.

"I am planning a trip to Neoasia in the near future and I want you to accompany me, but I need the old Jen King back, the Jen King that strikes fear into the hearts of men," Seth continued with gusto. "I will find out where my brother's killer is hiding and we will deal with him on the way."

An overwhelming weight began to descend on Jen's shoulders and a great feeling of helplessness nested itself in his gut. He nodded weakly at the man who controlled his life and he was greeted with a strong grasp of the shoulder.

"Good. Now it looks like you need to build up your strength. Why don't you head back to Raicema City for a while? I know you are not so fond of Tyrona. I'll let you know when we will depart. It shouldn't be for a few days yet."

Dejected, Jen agreed and left the presidential office. However, the prospect of being in Raicema City for a few days had lifted his spirits somewhat. He had hated living on the *Stryder* over the past month and was sure he'd been placed there as punishment.

The hallway ahead was lined with guards holding heavy guns, all eyeing Jen suspiciously as he walked along it.

Maybe I'm just tired, Jen thought to himself, trying to re-justify his lack of drive. *I haven't really slept properly for a while now.*

Indeed, Jen's nights had been disruptive to say the least, with a mixture of insomnia and strange dreams keeping him awake and exhausted.

He had dreamt of his childhood every night since his meeting with Javu, yet he was finding it hard to differentiate real memories from his imagination. He tried to stop thinking about it and focus on who he would visit when he got to Raicema City.

As he left Tyrona Palace and was escorted outside where a vehicle was waiting, a strange feeling came over him as he looked back at it, like this was the last time he'd ever lay eyes on it.

Chapter 35 – The Makai meeting

A long line up of strongly built vehicles was approaching *Le Grande Casino* in Raicema City.

Each of the cars was exactly the same, bodied in chrome and with bull bars at the front and back. They pulled up one after another at a side entrance to the casino like a row of giant silver insects.

A number of men emerged from the first vehicle, all dressed similarly in baggy trousers and long straight black shirts with stiff collars. Each man had a most serious expression on his face.

Emerging from the second vehicle was Yangjam Satori, the leader of the *Makai Warriors of Neoasia*, the well-known political and religious group.

It was rare that Yangjam made a trip to Raicema, for the journey was long and the reception was mixed. This time, however, Yangjam knew that he would be visiting the nation much more often. In light of the growing public support for Makaism, an alliance between the two sects was imminent.

The remaining vehicles were loaded with solidly built warriors, all there for the protection of their leader. Many sported thick beards or bushy sideburns and every man had the longest of hair, tightly tied back into a pristine ponytail.

With Yangjam at the helm, the forty men entered the casino through its tall doors. It was empty, cleared in expectancy of Yangjam's arrival. The tall ceiling bore the shining lights of a dozen chandeliers and every table was immaculately stacked, ready for the gamblers eager to start their next game. The floor was carpeted with a thick pile, comforting and inviting.

The men marched forward through some double doors to the left and down a long tall hallway, lined with portraits of serious-looking businessmen.

At the end of the hallway were two tall and heavy panelled doors with intricate handles. Yangjam pushed them open and was greeted by the sight of Sadana Siger, sitting behind a long decorated desk with two bulky men in grey suits standing either side of him.

"Welcome, Master Satori," Sadana said in a booming voice, standing up from his wide padded chair. "I see you have brought many friends with you."

"Master Siger," Yangjam greeted him in a slow melodic voice, bowing his head slightly.

Sadana walked around the desk swiftly, his long suit flapping behind him like a cape. He shook the hand of his counterpart.

"Your men must be hungry. Why don't you let Hector and Rene take them to the dining room where they will eat the finest cuisine our chefs have to offer?"

After a moment of apprehension, Yangjam agreed and the two stout bodyguards led the large group of men out through another set of doors, though several had to be told more than once to leave their leader alone.

"Now we can talk!" Sadana said with authority, a glint in his eye, walking over to a set of filigree sofas that overlooked a well-kept courtyard. As they sank into the cushions, waiters immediately appeared carrying trays of fresh tea and platters of food.

Light streamed in through the tall glass windows, and feeling somewhat apprehensive, Yangjam allowed Sadana to speak first.

"I presume that you have been informed of the death of Jeth Tyrone?" he began. "To say the least, confidence is at an all-time low in the government of this nation."

Sadana's cleanly shaven face and unusually combed haircut mesmerised Yangjam somewhat. The chief of the Raiceman Makai smiled in a frightening way. His piercing eyes looked intently at Yangjam.

"I was not surprised at his death," Yangjam responded after a few moments.

"And what of the new premier?"

"Seth can be reckless. Not that Jeth was any more capable of restraint, but at least he could reach his people. It is clearly an under-valued skill in this *interim* government."

Sadana was happy to hear that Yangjam considered Seth Tyrone's presidency as a temporary matter.

"I am aware that you previously reached an agreement with the Tyrones," Sadana acknowledged. "They supplied you with weaponry and you used your political influence to prevent a full Neoasian alliance with Lengard."

Yangjam did not speak and his silence was confirmation of Sadana's summary.

"My position is one of responsibility," Sadana continued. "We differ in our approach as leaders, yet I believe we have a common goal. The Makai has been fragmented for many years now, not helped by the approach of our counterpart in Lizrab."

Sadana paused. The sunlight streaming through the tall windows lit up his eyes like two balls of molten silver.

"I am eager now more than ever to have global unity in the Makai. It will be a whole new way of government."

Yangjam hummed to himself, reviewing the assertion.

"In Neoasia, we are on the verge of a breakthrough," he told Sadana. "*Makai* is no longer a way of rebellion, not just a religious ideal, but a way of life that has been absorbed by the nation."

"I want the same here," Sadana said in a conniving manner, leaning in closer to his guest. "And it has begun to happen. I have members of the Raiceman elite knocking on my door, all wanting to help to make it a reality. They want Makaism across the nation. It seems the time of overt control is over. We need something more subtle."

Sadana spread his arms wide, like an eagle.

Yangjam thought to himself for a while, falling back into the large golden cushions behind him.

"My only problem..." Sadana said at a whisper, moving over to the sofa that Yangjam was sitting on, "...is Raicema's new leader. Whilst his brother had the support of the people, Seth Tyrone has something more powerful."

Outside, a large bird flew down to the ground from a tree high above.

"He has control of the people through the technology that is in place. Even here, it has taken much planning to ensure we are off the mainframe, to ensure our funding is not infiltrated," Sadana elaborated. "And with half a million men at his disposal, I need some support."

"I hope you are not suggesting a full-scale war," Yangjam said defensively.

"Come on," Sadana toyed, amused by Yangjam's trepidation. "I know you are no stranger to getting your hands dirty. But no, I merely need help in chopping off the head of the beast. If that happens, the body will surely die."

"Why would you need help with that? I know that you gave the order for the death of the previous president, so why not this one as well?"

"It's not as easy as that," Sadana argued. "I am trying to prevent a civil war in this great nation. We are in a delicate place right now. As I said before, I want what you have achieved in Neoasia – acceptance of the Makai by the masses. At the moment there is a polarisation. Some hate the Makai and some follow. I need to act carefully to swing the balance in my favour. There are many that already place blame on the Makai for the death of their leader."

Sadana paused.

"This is a very patriotic nation. It has been indoctrinated into them from conception."

"So what do you propose?" Yangjam asked reservedly.

"That we use your 'supposed' attack on Lengard to our advantage."

Yangjam was surprised at Sadana's sarcastic tone when referring to the recent affair. "But that must already be helping you. Lengard stopped trading with Raicema the day after. That must have greatly weakened Seth's military capabilities."

"That does not help me. I want his capabilities strong, so that when I take over they are prime."

Yangjam listened carefully as Sadana whispered his detailed plan into his ear. By then end, Yangjam was slightly disturbed at the picture he was painting. It was a plan quite devastating to so many people. Yangjam couldn't quite help but feel a little scared of how ruthless Sadana's blueprint was and he began to realise how connected he must be for such a plan to work.

"It's possible," Yangjam agreed after Sadana had finished his whispering. "But I fail to see how this can help the Makai of Neoasia."

Sadana smiled creepily at Yangjam's own pursuits for power.

"The two Makai factions will be the closest of allies afterwards," Sadana declared passionately. "And let us not forget that the Tyrones have already rediscovered a way to harvest the power of the Omniad they have been trying to mine. They already have scores of aircraft ready for use once a plentiful supply of the crystal is found."

Yangjam instinctively reacted with an expression of concern at the notion but it was quickly replaced by intrigue.

"You have seen such an extraction in use in these machines?"

"Not personally but I have confirmation that it has been achieved. The energy emitted from the rocks is like no other, so powerful that a piece the size of my thumb can power a great ship or an aircraft."

Once again, a feeling of apprehension passed through Yangjam.

"With the Tyrones and their followers gone, we will have the ability to achieve that which has been long overdue. We can unify this planet and take full control. We can claim our birthright."

"What about Kirichi?"

"Don't worry about him," Sadana said unconcerned. "He is weak. I have an arrangement to make sure that he does not interfere with our plans, nor will any successor."

After several moments of contemplation, Yangjam simply nodded indicating he would support Sadana in his plans. An expression of satisfaction came across the flat face of the Raiceman leader.

"Good. Now, let me show you around."

The two men got to their feet and Sadana proceeded to give Yangjam a guided tour of the forty-story casino, showing him the roof terraces, plush hotel suites and grand dining rooms where his men were eating roasted meats, drinking large vessels of rich wine and talking merrily. They both sat amongst them, and the bigger-bellied Sadana began to tuck into the feast himself.

"There was something else I wanted to talk to you about," he said after a while, wiping the goose grease from his mouth with a cloth.

"Let's go to the vault," Sadana said, slamming down his knife with authority.

Yangjam agreed and the two men walked along a long corridor from the dining room to an elevator that needed DNA authorisation to enter. Sadana put his hand in the slot.

"DNA accepted. Restricted Access. Provide access codes," the panel outside the elevator echoed.

Sadana entered an eleven-digit code into a pad that slid out of the panel. The elevator doors glided open.

The two men stepped into the lift and it sped downwards for a few minutes.

"We are going three suns underground," Sadana told Yangjam.

When the lift opened, before them was an untouched series of caves and catacombs, and round polished vault doors in the distance.

"I want to ask you something," Sadana said as they walked along the rough rock floor toward the vault.

"Yes?" Yangjam prompted.

"Have you heard of a Raiceman soldier called Jen King?"

"No. Why?"

Sadana paused.

"For several years now I have been trying to track down the location of the four stones of power."

A look a sheer terror appeared on Yangjam's face.

"Why, Sadana? Those are things that should not be tampered

with."

"I have no fear of such things," he dismissed. "Anyway, I believe that this soldier, Jen King, is carrying one of the stones."

"But how do you know?"

"This soldier has a well-deserved reputation of being undefeatable in battle. His strength is that of ten men. He is also not of Raiceman decent and I found out that old man Tyrone brought him to Raicema as a child. I am sure it is because of the stone he holds that he has such strength."

The vault was getting closer and Yangjam could see that huge amounts of metal had been melted into a great cave opening ahead. There was an array of digital panels along one side of the vault.

"If you happen to come across this man, it may be in both our interests to acquire him," Sadana continued.

"I disagree, Sadana. It is better to leave *that* past in the past. And the stones of power are not to be trifled with. They are not of this world."

Sadana let out a great laugh at Yangjam's warning.

"Why, you sound just like my grandfather!" he balked sarcastically. "Let me tell you something about those stones."

Sadana paused.

"Those stones are the key to the future!" he said dramatically. "Whoever bears those stones can yield unlimited power on this planet and beyond. I have been learning many things recently, Master Satori. I have been making many new friends."

Yangjam listened with interest as they approached the vault doors.

"*Those* who put the Tyrone family in power hundreds of years ago have now chosen me, not just as the leader of Raicema, but as the leader of this planet!"

Yangjam had an inkling about whom Sadana was referring to, however, he was quite afraid to voice this hunch. Sadana was entering several codes and electronic keys into the long panel on the vault doors. They slid open majestically revealing great stockpiles of gold bullion and Omniadd crystals beyond.

"I did not realise until recently that I have been chosen by *the gods*. What you see here is just the beginning."

He leaned in close to Yangjam, sending a chill down his spine. His presence now seemed gloomy and ominous.

"They have made contact with me," he said portentously. "And they will soon make contact with you."

It only took Yangjam a few moments to decide that it was time to leave. Sadana seemed amused at the Neoasian leader's visible fear of talking of such matters and being so deep underground. It almost seemed to inflate him.

"Thank you for your hospitality, Master Siger," Yangjam said formally. "However, it is time for me to leave. I will support your vision as best I can."

"Before you go, let me ask you something. If you hate someone, and I mean truly hate someone, how do you feel?"

The question threw Yangjam off guard and he could do nothing but answer truthfully.

"I feel powerful, like I am capable of things I wasn't aware off."

"Exactly!" silver-eyed Sadana said, now looking more like a toad.

"You are drawing that power towards you. It will soon be time for us to draw on the greatest power anyone has ever seen!"

Now Yangjam felt primordially scared and he physically turned to leave the underworld to which Sadana had drawn him.

"In fact, it is now unstoppable, already happening."

Yangjam quickened his pace.

"I will be in touch regarding what we discussed," Sadana said loudly as he turned into the vault with his back to Yangjam.

As Yangjam turned back with a last glance, he was certain that he saw the wings of a creature standing behind Sadana. It looked like a woman. He got out of the casino as soon as he could.

Chapter 36 – The Lion of Giza

On the northeast tip of Ciafra, the Giza plateau had descended into a fever-struck security operation.

King Rufi of Anca Casa was due to arrive any second. The hundreds of security men and military soldiers surrounding the Great Pyramid and other plateau megaliths were all on high alert.

In the distance, six heavily armoured tank-like vehicles spewed up a cloud of dust as they drove along. They were allowed through a metal barricade that surrounded the plateau and pulled up in a circle with one of the vehicles in the centre.

Scores of men poured out of the giant vehicles as King Rufi emerged from the tank in the centre. He was accompanied by three other men, one of whom wore a ceremonial gown and carried a large, key-like object. The men all made their way into an entrance to the Great Pyramid that was usually sealed. At least twenty men guarded the entrance as Rufi stepped into the ancient structure.

Not far away, in the Pyramid of Menkaure, Professor Sorentius was under surveillance as he cleared out his archives from his past thirty years of research. Several men were checking each of the notebooks and paper files that he emptied from the cupboards and trunks in his office. Some were thrown away, whilst others were placed into a closely guarded metal container.

Everyone else who had previously worked in the observatory had now been relocated to other research facilities in Ciafra. Sorentius had been allowed to remain as he was the only person who knew the whereabouts of certain records that were now in high demand.

"Have you found the shaft map yet?" a voice resounded out of a speaker on one of the guard's round helmets.

"Negative," the guard reported back in robotic fashion. "We are only halfway through clearing his office but have only found twenty percent of the target documentation."

The diagram being referred to was an internal map of the Great

Pyramid's shaft system and charted its correlation to the alignment of the stars. Sorentius had spent years compiling the document and secretly knew its whereabouts. He had, however, convinced his captors that it was buried somewhere in the mass of paperwork that flooded his office.

"You know, it might be that some of the maps and blueprints were misplaced during an expedition into the Chephren pyramid a few months ago," Sorentius convincingly proposed to the guards who had now started to empty out stacks of paper themselves.

"Where would these misplaced papers be?" one guard asked, his ears pricking up.

"There is a hidden chamber near to the main burial chamber we were excavating. Some of the paperwork could have been left there."

There was silence for a moment.

"We will go there now," the main guard said with authority.

Sorentius complied and got to his feet, leaving the mass of paperwork stacked up around him. He was then marched out of the observatory into the hot sunshine.

To his left, Sorentius could see the Chephren pyramid and the Great Pyramid behind it. Straight ahead was the giant black metal box that completely covered the giant statue of the *Great Lion*.

"Have you ever seen the Great Lion?" Sorentius asked one of the guards who was standing behind him, trying to find out more about the plans for the ancient statue.

"Just take us to the chamber," the guard said coldly, avoiding the question.

Sorentius marched ahead to the narrow entrance in the base of the central pyramid of the plateau's trinity. The gun-carrying guards at the entrance allowed Sorentius and the six guards behind him to enter. It was dark and musty inside.

"We need to descend for a while," Sorentius told the men, who were all slightly anxious at going into the archaic structure. They followed him downwards into the darkness, with only a few electric torches lighting the way. They walked along, crouching down as they went. The professor moved with agility ahead. Then suddenly, as if by magic, Sorentius disappeared from view.

"Hey, where did he go?!" the guard at the front said loudly, his voice echoing down the stuffy shaft.

"What do you mean? You can't have lost him down here!" another said.

"Quickly! After him!" the commanding guard at the back said. They all sped up down the rough passageway, which was quickly becoming narrower.

"Hold on," one guard said as he was pushed by another behind him. But it was too late, as the guards began to topple down the shaft like dominos falling over.

"Whooaa!" they cried collectively, collapsing into a tangled mess, stuck in the limited space.

Sorentius was actually further up the shaft, hidden in a small tunnel that very few people knew about. He had managed to slip into the tunnel unnoticed and was shimmying his way along as it was only wide enough to strafe across sideways. Eventually he came out in a small chamber with a staircase descending down into the depths of the plateau's underground complex.

Sorentius navigated his way through several passageways and shafts by a dim electric light until he eventually came out at a small, perfectly preserved chamber still containing many artefacts and precious objects.

He walked over to a stone door at the back and pushed it with effort. It creaked open. Beyond was another series of stairways and narrow shafts.

After a while he reached a solid stone wall with two carved handles. He held them both for some time closing his eyes, and then heard a minor rumbling above him. The wall groaned before starting to rise up. Beyond was another shaft.

He was now close to the control chamber of the Great Pyramid, in a shaft that ran beneath it.

I'm almost there, he thought to himself as he reached another wall which also had two handles carved into it.

Ingenious how these use one's own energy to power the wall's movement, he contemplated as he held on tightly to the handles, focusing on transferring his power. The wall slid up silently revealing a magical sight beyond.

Sorentius stepped into a chamber directly beneath the central control chamber in the Great Pyramid. There was a gigantic crystal embedded into a huge slab in the centre and the chamber was made of great blocks of a smoothly cut crystalline rock. The entire space glistened with an overwhelming energy. It was almost as if a vortex could form at any moment, dispersing everything in existence.

Above, in the centre of the cuboid room, was a shallow shaft, one that ran directly into the control chamber overhead. Sorentius could hear light scraping coming from above and he knew Rufi and his entourage were inside the chamber.

He waited for a while, before hearing a buzzing noise. The slab, with the crystal embedded, began to levitate and emit a strange resonance, as if alive with electricity. Sorentius quickly jumped onto the edge of the slab as it rose up. As it came to stillness just below the roof, there was a narrow space for Sorentius to lie in.

He heard a voice above.

"You see this crystal," the voice was saying, referring to the giant gem that had emerged in the control chamber. "This crystal connects directly to *Orion* through the shaft above us."

Sorentius could hear several people shuffling around.

"There are two other crystals behind this wall," the voice continued.

Sorentius desperately wanted to see what the man was talking about and he struggled to turn his head towards the root of the crystal. As he did, he noticed that he could see a miniature image of the control chamber on one of the more rounded faces of the crystal. Rufi was following the man who had been speaking and the professor could now see that this man had an *ankh* in his hand and wore a decorative robe. He was inserting it like a key into a hidden slot on a wall adjacent to the wall that held fifty-four stones.

The stones all lit up like lights on a computer screen. Then the wall slowly faded until it disappeared as if an apparition, leaving Rufi and the other two men astounded.

"It's gone!" one man said in a high-pitched voice.

Beyond were two more giant crystals, positioned at different angles.

"This one connects to *Sirius* and this one here connects to *Regulus*," the man explained further.

Sorentius' ears felt super sensitive and he was hanging on every word said.

"When *the day* comes, Rufi, you should get every man you have in your command here," the man in the robe said with authority. "When the stars of the lion align, it will take more than that black box you have built to hold *Revereo* back."

"And what about Ignis?" Rufi asked.

"That won't affect you," he was told coldly. "You should focus on making the cage stronger."

The robed man removed the ankh from the wall. The wall faded back in. Rufi had to touch it to believe that it had returned. They all left the chamber and Sorentius could feel to slab he was lying on slowly descending back down to the floor. He sat up with a mixture of excitement and fear. One thing was clear to him. He would have to be carried out dead before he would leave the Giza plateau.

Chapter 37 – Isis

There was only one question.

"What *is* real?"

"Follow me." The words resonated into form.

Javu was walking down an empty hallway in the Turian monastery. The smell of rose and sandalwood incense was in the air, yet Javu could not pinpoint its origin.

He stepped into a large empty room at the end of the hallway. It contained only a single chair and three tall windows through which light was streaming. Javu noticed something wooden lying on the chair so he went over to get a closer look at it. It was a Qina – a traditional bamboo flute with six finger holes and one thumbhole.

He picked up the smooth instrument in his hand and felt compelled to blow into the mouthpiece. An airy, mellow sound resonated from the Qina and Javu immediately began to feel light and happy. A euphoric sense of belonging and purpose came over him.

Light poured in blindingly through the window, in perfect synchronicity with the sound of the flute. Then out of nowhere, hovering before him was the great serpent that he had grown to both love and fear.

Respiro's body curled and swayed as he floated in the air, feathers frayed and puffing outwards from what seemed like an inner and constant wind being emitted from the serpent's body. His feathers shimmered with a hundred shades of creamy blues and yellows.

"You were there in Ixon, weren't you?" Javu felt himself ask. "I felt your presence whilst I was there."

"Ixon is what you could describe as my first earthly home. It is a place where you will always find me."

Javu's mind was already stacked with questions.

"Why did the spirits cross over?"

"It was a time when the physical world almost disappeared for good. It was important for you and your friends to see this event because it proves just how important your world is. If the spirits had not crossed over, the fatums would have obliterated everything. If the physical world didn't exist, then Ambitio would rule everything."

"But I thought Ambitio created the physical world?"

"No, Sinidev. It is clear to see for yourself. Look in the mirror behind you."

Javu turned around and was surprised to find a full-length mirror had appeared in the room. He walked up to it and looked at his reflection.

"What do you see?" Respiro asked him.

"I see myself," Javu said straight away.

"And everything looks real to you?"

"Yes. I can see my beard and my clothes. It looks like me, though I look a bit younger than I thought I did."

"What Ambitio created is nothing more than a mirror like the one that you are looking into. Though it seems real, it is merely a reflection, an illusion. Nobody who is born in the physical world has a clear view of what it is really like, because we only see it in the mirror that Ambitio created. However, the fatums have no intention of destroying this mirror. They wish to destroy all of us looking in the mirror, while we are there powerless to do anything."

Javu was beginning to understand.

"Are you saying we are being blinded from the real world so that Ambitio can consume it?"

"Yes, Sinidev."

"And the spirits helped to stop this in the past. How?"

"Unlike those who live in the physical, the spirits are not looking at the illusion. They can see us all for what we really are. Their help was vital as one cannot protect what one cannot see."

"Can you see the real world? What is it like?"

The question was not answered, as the next thing that Javu experienced was a cloud of total darkness. It flew through him like a great storm. Then he opened his eyes.

He had woken up and was lying on a stern mattress with a heavy blanket on top of him. The floor seemed to be moving and Javu quickly remembered where he was and realised that he must have been dreaming.

He sat up woozily from his bed. He was aboard a ship, heading northwards towards the continent of Isis. After a moment or two he got to his feet, wrapped himself in a thick coat and navigated his way up a narrow staircase towards the deck. The first thing he saw was dull, murky clouds above and he felt the gentle dripping of drizzle upon his face. It seemed like a surreal continuation from his dream.

Rekesh was steering the ship from the helm and looked like he was struggling somewhat.

"Hey, have you seen Teltu?" Rekesh shouted over at Javu.

"I only just woke," Javu replied. "I'll go and look for him."

"I think he was on the upper deck before. I really need him to reef the sails. They're puffing like panicked birds!"

Javu continued to climb upwards to the upper deck where he found Reo, Bene and Rama all trying to tie down everything in sight. The winds were strong, rocking the ship and easily causing one to lose their balance.

"Have you seen Teltu?" he asked them.

Reo pointed upwards and Javu spotted Teltu climbing high up on one of the main masts, trying to tie back some of the top sails. A large gust swept over the deck and water sprayed high into the air from below, raining down on them all.

"Ughh," Rama yelped, being soaked by most of the freezing water. Javu had to hold onto a rail to prevent himself from slipping overboard. He decided to climb back below decks where it was safer. On the way down he informed Rekesh that Teltu was already undertaking the difficult task of tightening all the sails.

Down in the cabins below, Elera and Sita were sitting looking at the map Kirichi had given them after their recent time in Turo.

After the long trek back from Ixon, they had spent several days with Kirichi and the Turian monks regrouping and discussing all that they had discovered.

"It's blowing a gale up there," Javu mentioned, sitting down beside them.

"Tell me about it," Elera agreed, rolling her eyes. "It's been like this for a while now. We must be in the heart of this ocean by now."

Javu leant over to take a look at the map.

"I think we are here," Elera said, pointing to open ocean to the northeast of Lizrab. "It will be a few days yet before we reach Isis."

The cabin tilted as the force of a wave crashed against the side of the ship.

"Hopefully this storm will subside soon," Javu said, gripping the seat.

"It's a good thing we have so many experienced sailors aboard," Elera mused, bringing a smile to Javu's face. He decided to tell them both about what he had dreamt.

"I was dreaming just now. I have been trying come up with a clear way to differentiate between regular dreams and the dreaming that Kirichi spoke of."

"Doesn't one actually visit the dream world when dreaming, whilst one simply imagines when having a dream?" Elera tried to clarify.

"Well, yes but I think I now know how to identify when you are in the dream world."

"How?"

"Whilst dreaming, I met Respiro. I was in a room that could have easily existed in the monastery in Turo. He showed me a mirror and told me that looking into it at my reflection was just like what we do every day. We don't really see each other and this planet as we really are. We only see a reflection of it, like an image of sorts, an image that is only the partial truth.

"That's the difference between having a dream and dreaming. When we have a dream, we do the same thing – create images of things. Whereas when we are dreaming, we are looking at things with different eyes. We can see things as they really are!"

"What's the difference?"

"That's the question I was asking at first. But then I realised! Looking at reality is looking at a shared view, whilst what normally happens is we only look at our own view. Ambitio has deliberately made it this way so we all feel alone and isolated. It is the nature of power to segregate and disconnect from the whole."

"So what does the shared view look like?"

"Well, whilst I was dreaming, the room and monastery all looked like I would have expected them to but when Respiro and the mirror appeared, there was something that wasn't quite right, according to my own view. I looked younger in the mirror than I knew I should, so this must have been both mine and Respiro's shared view of what I looked like."

"That means it must be much easier to understand others in the dream world," Elera said, enthused. Javu nodded in agreement. "And he told you that the way we perceive everything around us is like a reflection?"

"Yes. A distorted one. I suppose the best example of that is that we all consider ourselves to be separate entities. But as we have seen, we are all connected in ways we can't really perceive or understand. Maybe if we could see things clearly, we would appreciate those connections more."

The boat was still rocking but it was now a soothing motion, similar to sitting on a rocking chair as a small child.

"Well I know for sure that there is more to life than what we think," Elera said. "I mean, look at what you are capable of, Javu. Nobody would believe it if I told them. They'd think I was crazy. And who knows what the Lemurians were able to do when they existed on this planet."

"Hopefully we'll find out," Javu said with equal enthusiasm.

The three of them chatted about it for a while, before the ship seemed to become steadier, no longer rocking from side to side.

"The storm is subsiding," Javu stated, getting to his feet.

The three of them headed above decks to find that the clouds had broken and rays of sunlight were shining through. Rekesh had tied the rudder and the ship was sailing smoothly in straight line. Everyone else was sitting exhausted on the upper deck, trying to dry out.

"Whoo! That was fierce!" Reo stated with zest, wringing out one of his sleeves.

Looking out in the distance, Javu could see only ocean, though clearer skies seemed to be ahead. He brushed the water off a small wooden stool that had been tied to the deck and sat upon it.

"Do you think we'll find another giant wall on this island we're looking for, Elera?" Reo asked her as he sprung to his feet.

"Not sure. But we definitely need to find a gate of some sort. This last pyramid will no doubt be harder to reach that the others, seeing as though no one has ever found or heard of it."

Rekesh was busy trying to re-tilt one of the two rowing boats attached to the side of the ship, which had become dislodged after the storm.

"Bene, Teltu, can you help me with this?" Rekesh called out to them, straining under the weight of it. They quickly went to his aid.

"So, how long before we get there?" Reo probed.

"A few days yet."

Indeed, it was four days later before the silhouette of jagged icebergs and frozen landscapes came into view. By that time, almost everyone was wearing every piece of clothing they owned in a bid to stay warm, with the temperature having dropped below freezing point. The only sign of life were tall birds with huge, fluffy feathers perched on the ice, occasionally diving down to catch the odd fish that would come close to the surface of the ocean. Nobody had ever seen such pure blue waters, as if they were a mirror image of the clear sky. Some of the peaks in the distance looked like they could easily rival the tallest mountains in Cibola or Neoasia.

"It's fr-fr-freezing," Teltu said, teeth chattering as he looked out at the glaciers and still deep-sea all around them.

"You're telling me!" Elera joked back, wrapped in a thick woollen shawl and several scarves that covered her head and face.

"So how do we start looking for this island?" he asked.

"Well, Kirichi told me to follow my intuition, so that's what I'm going to do."

She turned to Rekesh who was steering the ship.

"Rekesh, head over there," she shouted over to him, pointing to a range of glaciers in a northeasterly direction.

The ship travelled past a number of small ice islands and icebergs, often narrowly avoiding the hidden masses lurking beneath. Two long wedges of ice appeared as they navigated further inwards, running like a tunnel deeper into the continent.

"Go down there," Elera instructed, a pang of nostalgia rising within.

The wall-like icebergs ran for several suns, widening more and more as they got further along. Eventually, they reached an estuary with no more ice in sight ahead.

"Are you sure this is the right way?" Rekesh shouted from the helm. "Seems like we're heading away from the continent."

"No, keep going," Elera yelled back, looking at the map. "Isis is absolutely huge so this must just be an open stretch, though I can't seem to find it on the map."

They sailed along for several hours, until everything solid behind them was well out of view. Once again, there was only endless ocean ahead.

"I think we've gone in the wrong direction," Rekesh stated. "We should have headed more westerly and followed the land around."

Elera was almost inclined to agree, before she noticed something strange in the distance.

"Wait!" she said, running below decks to borrow Bene's telescope. She returned quickly, looking through it at what she had spotted.

"Over there! It's an island!"

Rekesh navigated in the direction that Elera was pointing and as they got nearer, she could see more detail on the island through the scope.

"Trees..."

"No way," Rekesh said defiantly. "Trees don't grow in Isis."

"Have a look for yourself."

Teltu took the rudder whilst Rekesh had a look through the telescope at the island. It did indeed have the outline of trees on its shores.

"I could be mistaken..." he said with surprise. "...but I think it's got a beach too!"

The comment made Teltu rub his hands with delight. Elera called everyone up to the deck and all eight of them stood side by side looking at the island as the ship approached it. It was immense and hosted a tall mountain range. As the trees and coastline came into clear view, the temperature suddenly seemed to dramatically rise. The sun had been shining before but now it seemed to radiate a warming heat that cut through the cold fronts of the sea.

"Hey, it's getting warmer," Reo said.

"A lot warmer!" Bene added, removing his thick, fur-lined coat.

The sun was beating down as if they were in southern Lizrab and before long everyone had to remove most of their clothing.

The ship began to judder as it glided through the water and all of a sudden, it stopped with a fierce jolt, causing both Teltu and Rama to almost topple overboard.

"Whoa! What was that?" Reo said, trying to look over the edge. Rekesh climbed down the ship's ladder to investigate and was soon wading around in the water below.

"The water here is too shallow for the ship. It's stuck!"

"Is it deep enough for the rowing boats?" Elera said, eyeing them as a way to get on the island.

"Should be," Rekesh shouted up as he climbed back up the ladder. Soon after, Teltu, Rama, Reo and Bene all began to help Rekesh untie and lower the boats into the shallow sea. Whilst this was happening, Elera posed a question to Javu that had been bothering her.

"Before, you said that everything we perceive is like a distorted reflection, one that is created in Ambitio's 'mirror'? Well, I just don't know how that can be true. I mean, I can touch this banister and it's solid. Or I can touch you and you will agree with me that I just touched you. So how can we be perceiving an illusion?"

"I'm sorry, Elera, but I don't know how to explain it to you. I guess it is not something that is easy to communicate. I only know what Respiro showed me and when I was dreaming it made perfect sense, but now, I am even starting to doubt it myself."

"Well hopefully we'll understand more when we find the Temple of Earth."

Javu nodded as he spotted Sita and Rama climbing down the ship's ladder to one of the boats that were now in the water.

"I'll go with them," Javu said with energy, following them down.

"The boat down there can hold five," Rekesh said, coming over to the ladder. "Bene, Reo, you go in that one. Teltu and I will get the other one down and go with Elera."

After the second boat had been lowered and everyone was aboard, the two rowing boats set off in the direction of the island, which was still a sun or more away. A great cave became visible just beyond the shoreline and Elera was immediately intrigued by it.

"I can't believe it's so hot," Teltu said. "We can't be in Isis anymore."

Rekesh's boat was the first to arrive on the island's shore and Elera was eager to explore the cave ahead, just beyond the beach.

Rekesh and Teltu found it difficult to keep up with Elera as she sprinted through a sparse beach forest up towards the cave. As they approached it, the three of them were all a little intimidated as they stared into the initial darkness. The rock face rose high, casting a shadow over half of the beach.

Rekesh, Elera and Teltu entered the cave and the shadows were banished by the daylight cascading in through holes in the roof. It was the largest cave any of them had ever seen, as high as a multi-story building. Flowers were growing in their thousands out of the floor and walls.

"I have never seen flowers grow so plentifully out of rock," Teltu remarked.

"This rock is blessed," Elera said, touching some gently.

Rekesh was looking out of the entrance of the cave, waiting for the others. Javu, Sita, Rama, Bene and Reo were only just travelling from the second boat along the beach forest path.

"Where are we, Javu?" Reo asked, mesmerised by the lush, green vegetation growing on the beach. "I never thought places like this existed, only in my imagination."

Javu smiled at the young man's fascination. "We are somewhere in Isis, Reo. It is quite amazing that such a tropical environment exists here in the middle of the ice continent."

"Do you think Elera is right? Is this the entrance to Lemuria?" Reo asked.

"We shall soon find out."

The five entered the cave and all gasped at the beauty of the flowers in such abundance. Elera was walking through the flowers carefully, trying to feel for something with her feet.

"What are you looking for?" Bene asked Elera, walking up to her.

"An inscription of some sort," she answered. "In the pyramid at Ixon there were many inscriptions in the chambers. Those led us here. I am sure this is the island we have been looking for."

Javu walked slowly to the back of the cave, carefully observing the roof and walls. As he reached the back, he looked up at large vertical back wall. He could feel the flow of energy in the cave, rising from the floor and circulating around the walls and roof. There was an affinity about the place and Elera could feel it too. She was soon drawn to the place where Javu was standing. She closed her eyes.

"I can feel the energy of this place," she said, feeling a sensation quite unlike any other. It was almost like an excitement washing over and through her, like a highly charged air everywhere in her body.

She opened her eyes and instinctively saw the energy as an orange mist-like glow, swirling and dancing, the flowers emitting and absorbing the energy in harmony. Everything in sight was radiating the vibrations in different patterns and she could see how one pattern was affecting the next. She noticed a beam of energy flowing from about halfway up the back wall, the source hidden by a mass of purple, yellow and red flowers.

"I can *see* it," she said mesmerised, almost in a trance-like state.

"See what?" Javu asked.

Then she heard it too. It was like a buzzing vibration that passed through her head and mind, resonating through every cell.

"The energy. I can *see* it. I can *hear* it."

Her attention was directed again to a beam being emitted from high above.

"There is something powerful up there," she said pointing to the area. Every member of the party looked up.

"That must be close to a hundred feet up," Reo remarked, straining to see what Elera was pointing at.

"I can't see anything," Rekesh said, also having difficulty seeing anything but flowers in the area.

"I need to get up there," Elera declared.

"What are we supposed to do? Fly up there?" Bene joked.

Javu breathed out a sigh, realising that they had reached a point where unconditional trust was needed amongst the group. Then he turned to face everyone.

"Everyone sit down in a circle. I need to show you something."

Everyone obliged and sat upon the sweet-smelling flowers in a ring of eight.

Javu closed his eyes and began to breathe very deeply, the sound coming in and out of his mouth like gusts of wind. All fell silent for a moment and then everyone gasped in amazement as Javu began to levitate slightly above the ground. He rose to about two feet before gradually lowering back down. It was a sight beyond control.

"How did you do that?" Reo asked, exasperatedly.

"We are all born of an element and this ability I possess is a gift from my elemental protector. I am showing you now because I trust you all with my life and the time has come when we will progress no further unless we all embrace the abilities we have."

Javu's foresight rang true under the incredible cover of the flower cave.

"You mean, something gave you the ability to levitate like that?" Teltu asked, quite amazed that the man he knew so well had such ability.

"Respiro, my guardian, is an elemental protector. They exist. However, it is most rare that one would have an encounter with one."

It was all very hard to take in and everybody felt the uncontrollable feeling of doubt creep in.

"You have a guardian? A spirit?" Reo asked. "Is it here now?" He looked around with a little fright.

"When I was a boy, Respiro – the protector of the air – appeared before me. Ever since, I have been able to float at will."

Everyone seemed to be in complete awe that Javu's life could possibly be like this. It seemed like a made-up fairy tale.

"Now, it seems as though Elera has discovered a hidden ability. She has *seen* something we all cannot see. So we all need to work together to get her up there so she can have a closer look at what she has seen."

"Can't we climb it?" Bene asked, looking up.

"You can try," Elera said with gusto. "But I doubt you would survive if you fell. Javu is right. It is a test of unity."

"Can't you just float up there with her?" Reo asked naively.

"I am not strong enough to do so by myself. As some of you may know, I come from a long line of summoners. When one summons or conjures energy, it is usually from another source like the wind or an animal, however, in the case of the gifts that are granted by the protectors, the energy comes from within. I do not know how to give my gift to Elera, but together, we may be able to conjure enough energy to lift her up."

All but Rekesh took Javu at his word and agreed to be taught by Javu how to summon the energy needed to raise Elera up.

"What if she falls?" Rekesh asked with concern in his voice.

"She won't," Javu said sternly. "And it is important that we all know that."

Rekesh lowered his head. Elera touched him on his shoulder and smiled at him.

"Do not worry, Rekesh. There is no need to fear the worst," she said.

Rekesh smiled weakly and eventually sat up for instruction. Javu closed his eyes.

"Everybody here should try to visualise Elera up there discovering what we need to progress on our journey. Do not focus on *how* she is to get there, only on the end result. Clear your mind of all fear and concern. Feel light, feel positive, feel the unity amongst us."

The others closed their eyes and followed Javu's words.

Elera breathed calmly and quietly. Javu repeated his words over and over. Time passed and Elera suddenly felt a feeling of jubilation and lightness, as if she were in a bubble of water, suspended.

Some time passed in which the group were lost in silence and a strange dream-like state fell on them all.

Javu opened his eyes slowly and looked up. He saw Elera floating high in the air. She was holding some flowers on the wall, but was clearly levitating firmly in one position. Javu did not alert the others in case it distracted them.

As Elera got higher, what she saw was unlike anything she could have imagined. Looking at the point that she had spotted from the ground level, she could see it again in terms of its energy. A beam of hazy light was projected directly outwards to Elera's face, though the light did not hinder her vision in any way. In fact, she could see strange objects made of light moving within the beam. She could also feel the same intense vibrations and hear them pulsating through her head and body.

The objects of light seemed to come close but she couldn't focus on them directly, almost as if it wasn't her eyes looking at them. She did get the sense, however, that the objects were full of an intense ancient energy.

Suddenly, one of them rushed up to her and seemed to jump inside her head. The next thing she knew, she saw only a hazy cream light, similar to what she had seen when she rubbed her head on the Intihuatana stone. She also felt the same weightlessness but this time, there were no beings in sight. She did, however, hear an echoic voice speaking.

"Only the still can reach the gate. The big tree sleeps and can only be awoken by the still. The candle, the breeze, the mountain and the ocean must come together and offer their chosen gifts for the big tree to awaken."

Then as quickly as Elera had been transported to that hazy world of light, she was transported right back to the cave, floating high in the air. The sudden change made her feel woozy and she let out a loud gasp.

Immediately each person opened their eyes and looked up, mouths dropping in awe at Elera floating above their heads. She had lost her energetic view of the world and she saw that behind the flowers was actually a giant crystal. As everyone's awareness came back to the physicality of the cave, Elera felt herself dropping. She slowly drifted back down to the ground from the great height as their focus waned.

There was silence for a moment, the group feeling jubilant and dazed by what they had seen as Elera came to rest on her back, cushioned by the vibrant flowers on the cave floor.

"This is incredible," Teltu said. "We humans are truly more remarkable than we believe!"

"What was up there?" Reo asked impatiently as Elera sat up unsteadily.

"Some sort of energy source," she replied. "I think it could have been a wisdom rock – it was a large crystal. I heard a voice. It spoke of the gate."

Everyone leaned closer as Elera was silent whilst she came around from her experience, her state of haziness causing an expression of unease on Rekesh's face. He leaned over and put his arm around her.

"The voice spoke of the big tree. It said the tree would be awoken if the candle, the breeze, the mountain and the ocean offer their chosen gifts to awaken it." She paused. "Only *the still* can open the gate."

Javu stroked his beard, deep in thought.

"What does it mean?" Reo asked, his eyes wide with bafflement.

"Quite a riddle, Reo," Bene said in a brotherly fashion. "Very cryptic."

"I think it is simpler than it sounds," Javu enlightened everyone. "It is no coincidence that Elera has begun to see things differently when we arrived here. In fact, it is necessary for us to solve this puzzle and advance in our journey. Do you all remember what Kirichi said about our different energy types? He said that he could *'see'* them. Well, I think that Elera is now able to do this as well."

"But what has that got to do with awakening the big tree?" she asked him.

"The candle, the breeze, the mountain and the ocean are all energy types!" he said. "It must be what certain types look like, probably four of us here right now!"

"Are you saying that four of us need to offer something to awaken this big tree?" Bene tried to clarify.

"Exactly!" Javu said with gusto. "And it is down to Elera to tell us which four out of the eight of us it will be as she can *see* what our energy looks like."

Everyone stared at Elera with anticipation.

"I'm not sure," she said after a while. "Didn't Kirichi say that the types were like elements? Remember, he said that Reo was like fire and Bene was like the earth."

"But there are many possibilities as to what an element could be like," Javu concluded. "Fire can be like many things after all – a roaring blaze, a small flame or lightning for example. Kirichi has given us a place to start, however. He said both Reo and Rama were like *fire*, so why don't you two sit side by side and let Elera try to observe you. She can try to work out which one of you is the most like a *candle*."

Both men obliged and everyone else moved aside so Elera could try to see the two fiery men in terms of their energy.

"I don't know how to see energy at will," she said apprehensively to Javu.

"Just ease into it, Elera. Trust that you have always had such an ability, but it has only just been unlocked."

She sat in a comfortable cross-legged position, facing the two men.

Looking at them, it took a while for the strange, blurred misty view to come into sight. She had to almost blur her normal vision to invoke it but when she did, she could almost feel the patterns being emitted from both of them. She realised that *seeing* wasn't just a visual experience but a wholly connective one with her being. She could feel the subtle vibration patterns.

Reo looked and felt like a blazing campfire, constantly burning with a vibrant energy. Rama, on the other hand, looked and felt like a small flame and Elera could relate his calmer energy to the analogy of a candle straight away.

"It's Rama," she said excitedly. "Reo's energy burns much more ferociously."

Everyone could relate to the descriptions, given what they knew about the two individuals.

"Good," Javu said. "Now let's move on to earth. Kirichi said that both Bene and Rekesh were like the *earth*, so you two sit next to each other and let Elera observe you. Hopefully she can see which of you is most like a *mountain*."

The two men did as instructed and Elera began to look at them in the same fascinating way. Bene's energy was very still, almost unmoving. At times she could not even feel the vibration of it. But focusing on Rekesh, she felt something very powerful. It was like jagged bursts of energy, followed by smaller tremors. She was used to his more fiery energy and it felt familiar. After observing him in this way for a few moments, she was jolted back into normal vision by a lightning-like jolt of energy shooting randomly outwards. She closed her eyes, breathing heavily.

"Are you okay?" Teltu asked her.

"Fine," she said, deciding not to mention it. "I think that Bene's energy was more like a mountain as it was quite still."

Rekesh seemed disappointed by the conclusion.

"Okay, let's move on," Javu said quickly, sensing Elera was feeling uncomfortable. "Now Teltu and I will sit together as we are both of the *air* and you can tell which of us is like a *breeze*."

After a moment of composure, Elera once again invoked her ability to see the energy patterns around her. She observed Javu firstly, whose energy seemed to constantly be building momentum and she felt like it was constantly rising and falling, like gusts of wind. When she observed Teltu, she felt a very gentle vibration, like the softest of summer breezes calmly floating all around.

"Teltu is more like a breeze," she said definitively.

Javu did not ask about his own energy and what it felt like. Instead, he moved on to the final element.

"Great. Now all that is left is for you to compare yourself with Sita, though I can hazard a guess as to who is more like an *ocean*."

As he said this he glanced over to the ever quiet and reflective Sita. Nevertheless, Elera attempted to look at Sita's energy, which felt similar to Bene's, very still and sometimes hard to detect.

"I do not know how to observe my own energy," she said to everyone. "But I agree with Javu. Sita does seem like a still ocean."

Everyone felt comfortable with the observations. It felt almost natural even though they all knew that such a group activity would be misunderstood or ridiculed in most of the great cities of the world.

"Okay, so to awaken this big tree, wherever that is, Sita, Rama,

Teltu and I need to offer something together?" Bene tried to simplify with Javu and Elera.

"Yes, you need to offer your *gifts* to it," Elera clarified.

"What gifts?" Teltu asked, confused.

"I'm not sure but I think we should have a look around this island for clues," Javu replied aloofly. "And bear in mind what Elera has learned."

"Maybe we will find a big tree somewhere on the island," Reo suggested.

"But there are so many large trees on the island," Bene noted. "How do we know which *big tree* we are looking for?"

The conundrum was puzzling. They took time out to think.

"Let me tell you a story I was once told," Javu said eventually, adjusting his seated position and readying himself for the tale. "A friend of mine once told me of her misfortune of losing her mother when she was young, due to war in her homeland."

There was something familiar about the account to Elera.

"Her mother had been completely lost during the war, presumed dead. Some years later, my friend was lost in a desert in Ciafra," Javu continued. "There was no river, no forest and no village in sight. She travelled for three days and three nights without food or water, only following the sun during the day and the moon at night. Indeed, my friend strongly related that these two celestial bodies were her only companions during this isolated time.

"On the fourth day, her journey came to an end and she arrived at a village that seemed familiar, yet she could not recall being there before. When she entered the village, she was greeted by an elderly man who instantly recognised her. She had never seen the man before but felt that he was very friendly."

The interest and zest in Javu's voice was yet again captivating his listeners.

"She rested at the village that night and when she awoke the next morning, she was amazed to discover that her mother was sitting by her bed! At first, she believed that she was hallucinating from lack of nourishment or that she was having a vision of some sort. But then the man that she had met the day before entered the hut and explained that he had noticed my friend had a strong resemblance to a woman he knew in a nearby village. He had travelled during the night to ask the woman if she had a lost relative."

Javu paused, smiling at the thought of the incident.

"It turns out that my friend's mother had been living in a remote village all those years, also thinking that she had lost her entire family during the war. Certainly, my friend was forever joyful that she had lost her way on a simple expedition those four days earlier."

"What does this story mean?" Reo asked curiously.

"It simply expresses that you should not underestimate where you find yourself, for it can lead you to what you are searching for."

"So let's all take a look around the island and see what we come across," Elera added, riding on the moral of the story.

The group all agreed and rose to their feet. As they were leaving the cave, Rama noticed something in the far distance on the roof of the cave, again covered by flowers. It looked to be a door or hatch. He pointed it out to Javu, who nodded and ushered the group out of the cave.

"I suggest that we spit into our elemental pairs and explore different parts of the island," Javu recommended, whilst they all stood in the entrance. Most agreed.

The group split into four pairs. Rekesh and Bene headed to the east of the island where the forest was at its thickest. Elera and Sita headed north, past the cave towards a rocky area at the base of the island's vast mountain range. Javu and Teltu headed south back towards the beach shore whilst and Reo and Rama went to explore the more open beach forest than ran around the west coastline. They all agreed to meet back at the cave before darkness fell on the island.

"Remember, our unity is being tested," Javu said ominously to everyone as they went in their different cardinal directions.

Chapter 38 – Gifts of the Cardinals

Earth

○

Rekesh and Bene were wandering aimlessly through the southern undergrowth of the strange island in the midst of the icy continent of Isis. The tall bushy trees caused almost complete darkness with their mass of leaves and vines.

The thicket ahead seemed so crowded that Bene wondered how they would find their way back.

As they headed eastwards, the two men had been talking about the nature of reality for some time as they navigated their way through the surreal setting.

"Even if *other* parallel worlds *do* exist, I don't see what it has to do with us?" Rekesh was saying. "I mean, even if a million other things are happening in the space I am walking through at this moment, why should I concern myself with that? I think that there are some things we are just *not* supposed to know or think about."

There was a long pause.

"Some people don't have the choice, Rekesh," Bene said with conviction. "I think that what Javu was saying about summoning is the key to the matter. We can choose what to summon into our lives but most of the time we are not even aware of it. We often let others decide our world for us."

They stopped at a large bushy plant covered in orange flowers. Their vividness was almost hallucinogenic.

"It is strange, Rekesh. I almost wish to eat one of these bright flowers. Never before have I seen a flower look so fresh and soft," Bene remarked whilst staring at the plant intently.

A flock of birds could be heard overhead flying from the trees and in the distance, the rustling of a bush brought the two men to attention.

"What was that?" Rekesh said, fully alert upon hearing the sound.

"Not sure," Bene replied, trying to look around for signs of movement.

"We do not know what lurks on this island," Rekesh said. "I do not feel at ease here."

"It is strange how such a tropical place exists in the centre of all the ice we saw," Bene correlated. "Who knows what kind of creatures live here?"

"Which way should we go?" Rekesh asked, changing the subject. "These flowers are everywhere. I see more in the distance over there." Rekesh pointed to an array of plants deeper in the forest.

The men walked for another ten minutes before reaching a mass of vibrant, stunning orange flowers. Bene felt compelled to pick one and he put it in his satchel.

They heard water and headed towards the sound, finding a single colossal tree growing by a lagoon. A raging waterfall engulfed and replenished the water from a cavern in the rock face behind. Small streams ran from the lagoon in many directions. The two men stared up at the tree for some time, the sweltering heat gluing them in place.

"Could this be *the* tree we are looking for?"

Rekesh gazed up at the cavern and noticed thick vines growing up the side of the rock. The tree below reached as high as the entrance, with lush, finger-like leaves on large twisted branches. The tree's bark was reddish-brown and had faint scratches at the base of the trunk. They sat down on the bank of the lagoon.

"So you originally met Elera in Raicema?" Bene asked Rekesh.

"I met her once before in Seho but yes, that's where we became close. I used to teach defence arts there. That's how I got to know her. She is a strong woman."

Rekesh seemed anxious and edgy speaking about the past.

"It's strange because I never got to meet her until we embarked on this journey together," Bene said, "but I have heard a lot about her.

My grandfather sees her like a daughter."

"Yes. She always speaks fondly of Kirichi."

"I realised just how much he thinks of her when I found out about his intention for her to be his successor in Turo," Bene revealed. "She doesn't know that I am aware of it. To tell you the truth, I think she's scared to tell me because she thinks that I expect to be his successor. Well, I could never be like my father or my grandfather and I don't want to succeed either of them."

Bene's sentiment went unnoticed, as Rekesh's face had turned to thunder. He had been completely oblivious to Elera's intended role and he felt betrayed and heated because she hadn't told him.

"How long have you lived in Raicema?" Bene asked, not noticing Rekesh's change in mood.

"About ten years," Rekesh said somewhat coldly.

"Do you know my father, Juhi Mattero?"

Rekesh wasn't expecting the question and it made him forget his agitation.

"I know him," Rekesh said without any emotion in his voice.

There was silence between the two as they both thought of what to say next.

"You know that my father is no longer with us?" Bene asked finally.

Rekesh just nodded solemnly.

"So how did you know him?"

"I used to attend a lot of the colloquiums that used to take place, especially when your father was leader. I met him a couple of times."

Bene hung his head, the grief still hanging over him.

"He was a very friendly person," Rekesh said with more warmth. "Everyone liked and respected him."

"Everyone except that lowlife Sadana," Bene said, a hint of anger in his voice. "The first chance he got...he planned it..."

Rekesh did not know what to say so he stayed silent.

Bene said nothing more, and the two sat in silence just staring at the tree in front of them, a melancholic mood falling on the lagoon.

Air

Meanwhile, to the south of the island, Javu was perusing through some spiky shrubs growing on large rocks in the sand of another beach. He was astonished at the diversity of life on the island. The sun in the lower west of the sky cast a warm and bright glow on the rocks and sand, lighting them up in a spectacle of intricacy and grandeur.

Teltu walked over to him carrying some sort of spiky, light green plant in his hand.

"I found this over there on one of the rocks," he said, presenting Javu with the unusual-looking shrub. "It smells really nice, like sweet almonds."

Javu sniffed what Teltu had found but was unable to identify it. "It looks like some sort of air plant."

"Maybe it is the gift that I am supposed to offer."

"If you feel like it is, then it *is*."

"I still don't understand," Teltu admitted. "How could gifts 'awaken' a tree?"

"It is sometimes difficult to imagine how simple things could be involved in something so complex, however, it is all part of the same system of energy. Most of the time it is simply down to intention."

Teltu thought to himself for a while.

"I was surprised before when you said that you come from a long line of summoners," he said finally. "I did not know you practiced sorcery."

"Be careful, Teltu," Javu warned him. "It is easy to assume that the two terms are interchangeable, however, they are not. *Summoners* are concerned with the conjuring of energy for an intended purpose. *Sorcerers* on the other hand, are concerned with the pursuit of *power*, of which summoning may be one of their many tools."

"Well, I did not know you knew how to summon," Teltu corrected himself.

"Why would you? I have hidden it from almost everyone," Javu declared. "And for good reason. You see, summoning is not really anything unique. We all do it every day. The only difference between the average person and myself is that I am aware that I do it and have therefore been able to increase my knowledge and ability to control it. Unfortunately, many on this planet do not understand this and would seek to harm those who speak of it as a normal human quality."

"Can you teach me?" Teltu asked the man he had looked up to for many years.

Javu contemplated his response for only a few moments. "Of course, my dear Teltu."

They walked along the beach, listening to the calming sound of the waves falling in the sea and the rustling of the leaves in the trees around them.

"As far as I know, there are three ways that one can conjure energy. The first is to use special words to create the right kind of atmosphere. Many summoners have done this throughout time, including my own parents and my uncle, Actesh."

The sun seemed to be swimming in the ocean as it dipped into the sea.

"The second way is to use special combinations of existing energy, usually from special items that can store energy themselves. This is what I think the message that Elera received was actually telling us to do. The gifts that you and the others are supposed to bring together could in fact invoke a type of summoning."

"So you think that this plant I picked could be part of that summoning? To awaken the big tree?"

"Most definitely. Plants have the most incredible amount of energy stored within them. We shall have to wait and see how that energy will be harnessed."

Teltu looked at the small, almost translucent plant in his hand.

"And what is the third way?"

"The third way? Oh, that is quite difficult to achieve. It is when you *will* energy. This is what we all did collectively to lift Elera up in the cave."

"And what about the gifts that you said you have received, like being able to float?"

"In effect, the gifts that I have received from Respiro are abilities based on the *third way*. They come from within, where the possibilities are endless."

Teltu had mixed feelings about what he was being told. He felt a combination of pure excitement at the incessant possibilities, tied together with an untold fear that he was learning something he should not be.

"I will teach you a simple summon based on the first way," Javu declared. "To conjure a gentle breeze, speak the words *Gusto Rasparian Venteshuri Mollis*."

"Gusto Rasparian Venteshuri Mollis," Teltu said, quite plainly.

"No, no, no," Javu said, shaking his head. "You have to say it like you want a breeze to come. The words themselves mean nothing. It is *how* you say them that is important. You are trying to create a particular vibration."

Teltu tried again, this time whispering. Again, nothing happened.

"Try speaking more slowly and pronouncing each word carefully, so the full vibration comes out of your mouth."

Once again Teltu tried to speak the words but to no effect.

"Okay, listen to me."

Javu spoke the words softly and with clarity, yet it sounded like the strength of the wind was riding on each word. The moment he had finished the phrase, a gentle breeze wafted through their hair, lasting for a few moments. Teltu was speechless.

"Now practice," Javu told him.

Water

°

Over to the north of the island, Sita and Elera were walking carefully over some jagged rocks at the base of a high-toothed mountain range that ran northwards.

The light of dusk seemed to elevate the peaks higher and higher, shades of black and grey streaking upwards into the sky. Elera breathed in the warm evening air, infused with a pungent sweet tropical smell. The island seemed rather surreal, its diversity and atmosphere like nothing that either of them had seen before.

"It is wonderful that there is a place on the earth that is so unspoilt," Elera said, more to herself than Sita.

They hopped from rock to rock, holding hands at times to keep their balance.

Ahead, Sita spotted a small pond that had formed in a shallow dip in the floor. It was surrounded by a number of carefully positioned stones that looked like they were there to protect it.

"Someone has tried to look after this," Elera said, observing a number of water lilies and species of insects living on the pond. She was astounded that the harsh rocky environment could be home to something so delicate.

Sita was staring at something in the water and she kept moving her head from side to side as if trying to catch a glimpse of it. Then she put her hand in and pulled out something metal from the bottom of the shallow pond. It was an archaic-looking key that was still shiny in some places, but mainly covered with thick, dark green algae.

"A key?!" Elera exclaimed. "I wonder what it's for?"

Sita handed the key to Elera and sat at the edge of the pond. She cleaned it as much as she could in the water, revealing an emblem on the head. It sort of looked like a picture of a horse, but it was so worn it could have easily been any other four-legged animal, possibly a lion or a dragon.

"Mmm, we should keep this," Elera said to Sita.

"Yes..." Sita said, attempting to speak Elera's language. Then her eyes came to rest on a small water lily at the far edge of the pond. She got up and carefully walked around the edge, looking down at the small lily.

"This..." she said. Then she bent down and scooped it up in her hands before walking back around.

"You want to take this?" Elera said, pointing to the beautiful flower with its delicate white petals. "As your gift?"

Sita did not answer as she couldn't understand what Elera was asking but she carefully placed the flower in a cloth and placed it in her round duffle bag.

"You have been together with Rama for a long time, haven't you, Sita?" Elera asked, a range of thoughts spilling into her mind. Sita did not understand so she just smiled back in response.

"I can't imagine what it must be like to be with someone for so long and do everything together. Don't get me wrong, I love Rekesh but sometimes I feel that we are so different."

She paused for thought, drifting into a daze.

"I sometimes think that we are treading two separate paths in life that just happen to be side by side at this moment."

Sita giggled at the sense of confusion Elera was giving off. She rubbed her arm endearingly, causing Elera to giggle as well.

"How do you say 'love' in Hindi?" she asked.

"Many ways..." Sita said after a while.

"Love is a strange thing isn't it?" Elera continued her ponderings. "I mean it's sort of uncontrollable. I've known so many women who have given up everything in the name of love. Some even say it's the only thing that is important in life. I think love is important, but I think having understanding and care for others is equally as vital."

They sat for a while, watching the mountains around get darker and darker, both lost in their own thoughts. It was only when they realised they were both sitting in the complete darkness of a mountain's shadow that they got up and began to make their way back to the cave.

Fire

○

To the west, a small creature the size of a rabbit clambered down a beach tree as the sound of loud talking radiated through the tall dry trees. The creature stopped, scratching its head. The sound was indeed strange.

It was Reo, trying to communicate with Rama, speaking in his usual loud and enthused manner.

Rama had begun to understand a few Raiceman words but still didn't understand most of what was being said to him. Reo compensated for this by speaking louder. It was already dusk and starting to get dark. The beach had stretched for miles.

Rama was trying to listen to the banter of Reo when he suddenly stopped. He was looking very carefully at one particular tree.

"What is it?" Reo asked him.

Rama attempted to speak. "...we...here...before..."

"You have been to this island before?"

Rama shook his head, touched the tree and said the same words again.

"This tree? You have seen this tree before?" Reo boomed.

Rama nodded and patted the tree.

"You mean we are going around in circles?" Reo asked him, motioning a circle with his arm. He attempted to speak.

"...we look...we not see..."

Reo scratched his head in bewilderment.

"What don't we see?" he persisted.

Rama shook his head to indicate he didn't know how to describe it. He picked up a reed from the floor and drew something in the sand. It looked like a spiral, leading to a centre point. Reo was now even more confused. Rama pointed back to where they had come from. Reo inferred that he wanted to turn back and agreed. It would soon be dark. The orange glow of the sunset cast a warming light on the trees and ground, giving the beach forest a rustic, ancient look.

The creature from the tree slowly approached the two of them, shuffling and using all four limbs to walk. It had reddish-brown fur that looked orange with the light of the sunset. The creature looked like a combination of a monkey and rabbit.

Rama approached gently and stroked the creature. It showed signs of affection and started to make a strange cooing sound. Reo was surprised at how tame the creature was.

"Shouldn't we be going back?" Reo urged, slightly unnerved by the impending darkness.

Just then more creatures from the same species scrambled down from the high tops of the beach trees. Some carried small fruits in their hands, which they deposited in a pile in front of Rama. He tasted one and a wide smile spread across his face.

"Mmm...good..." he said.

Reo and Rama ate of the fruit and as they did, some of the creatures started cooing loudly and jumping around. Then suddenly, Reo slumped into a seated position, docile and feeling heavily intoxicated by something. He stared into the forest in a complete daze, his mind swimming.

"Whaaaaa...." he droned uncontrollably.

A vision of people came to him. They looked like peaceful humans, walking slowly and respectfully all around him. The beach forest had transformed into a giant field, full of flowers and lush tall grasses. A woman held up a small stone and it began to levitate from her hand. The others were all praying and reciting in an ancient language. Each person was standing in a circle and the stone rose high above their heads. There was an aura of light surrounding the entire event. It was a spherical bubble of glowing white.

Reo could see a look of calm on each person's face, a completely undisturbed expression. Energy seemed to be flooding into the stone, making it glow intensely white. Then one man raised his arms in the air and began to chant something. The stone dropped to the floor and the spectacle was over. The man walked calmly over and picked up the stone in a cloth and placed it in a wooden box. At this sight, Reo's vision faded.

He awoke to find Rama seemingly asleep on the floor of the forest. It was dark and the creatures had all disappeared. Gradually, Rama started to stir and he sat up.

"Head back..." he said cheerfully to Reo, who nodded in agreement.

As they tried to retrace their initial path back to the cave in a westerly direction, they both realised how wobbly-legged they were. It took some time for them to regain their coordination in the sweeping darkness but eventually they found their way back to the great cave where they were supposed to reconvene.

The others had been waiting for a while at the entrance to the cave when Reo and Rama arrived back. Bene immediately walked to meet them.

"It has been hours since dusk. We went out looking for you, shouting your names but there was not reply," he stated to Reo.

As they approached the entrance, Rekesh and Teltu emerged from the cave.

"All done. We've propped some logs and branches against the walls and placed some on the floor for beds," Teltu reported to the group. He noticed the late arrivals and explained what he was doing. "We have decided to camp the night in the cave and continue with any explorations tomorrow. We have collected some berries, nuts and roots to make a broth with."

Some of the others had already started to enter the cave and Javu was attempting to create a small fire.

"Let's go inside," Bene urged the two late men, both still lost in their experience at the beach forest.

That night, the group ate well from the food that had been gathered and discussed what the individual parties had seen on their travels around the island.

"The diversity of life on this island is quite astounding," Javu said. "Both Teltu and I were quite surprised at the large number of plants that survive from the nutrients in the air. They were growing in the beach areas."

He stopped speaking and sat silently for a while, sipping a small bowl of vegetable broth. His long moustache twitched as he drank and his eyes glistened in the light of the campfire.

The group were sitting around the fire in a circle. Sita and Rama holding each other's arms affectionately.

"This island is a unique place, very diverse," he continued. "It is almost like it doesn't really belong here in the middle of Isis."

"There are strange creatures here too," Reo blurted out. "Rama and I ate some fruit that these monkey-rabbits brought us and then I almost passed out and saw some kind of vision from the past."

"Monkey-rabbits?" Teltu repeated, finding the concept amusing.

"What did you see?" Javu asked, leaning in closer.

"I saw people dressed in strange clothing, praying to a small stone. It floated in the air and it was glowing. In fact, everything was glowing with a hazy white light. It was in a large field but I felt like it was still on the island here. Then the man put the stone in a wooden box. That's all I saw, but when I woke, it was dark. Seemed like only a few minutes..." He trailed off pondering his experience to himself.

Javu stroked his beard and turned to Rama. He asked him what he had seen in Hindi. He translated their responses.

"He saw the same thing as Reo."

"Reminds me of when we were trapped in that pyramid," Bene said to Javu and Elera, referring to the collective vision they had experienced. "Well, Rekesh and I found a big tree in the forest so that could be what we are looking for."

"Mmm, I'm not sure," Elera said, trusting her instincts. "Sita and

I found a really old key in a pond near the mountains. I think we will need it for something."

"We still don't know what we are supposed to do though, do we?" Rekesh asked everyone after being silent for quite a while.

"I mean what does it mean – *the still must come together*. Maybe there is no *'big tree'*. Maybe it's just some sort of weird message left by the people who used to live on this island."

Rekesh's newfound pessimism upset Elera a little and silence fell amongst everyone.

"It has been a long day for all," Javu remarked quietly but with enthusiasm. "I think we should all get some sleep."

At this Reo was already making himself comfortable on a bed of leaves.

Rekesh gazed at Elera, her golden skin lashed with the whips of firelight flickering in the huge dark cave. The flowers seemed alive with movement as if each was an eye watching them all.

"I am tired," Rekesh said, quietly backing into a comfortable position. Before long, everyone had done the same and they went to sleep as the fire turned into a mass of glowing embers.

Chapter 39 – The Genesis Tree

The sun rose like an orange dipped in water, the warm radiance spreading across the sea with every moment of its accent.

At full view, kissing the calm blue water, a ray struck the entrance of the cave, turning the walls inside into a spectacle of bright colours. Each of the flowers opened a little, basking in the enchanting sunlight.

Rekesh was the first to stir. He had in fact, been awake for hours, his mind churning over the past. He rose to his feet and made his way out of the cave, down towards the beach where the two rowboats were securely anchored. He scanned the horizon. There was no sign of movement, only a calm, tranquil stillness in the ocean.

Rekesh gazed out for a few moments, sitting with his legs outstretched on the beach, his belly resonating with a deeply anxious feeling, like he was being closely watched.

In a frightening moment, he thought someone was standing behind him and he flinched as he looked backwards, but no one was there.

He stared out at the sea for some time, smelling the salt in the air. After a while, Elera made her way down to the beach from the cave and walked up quietly behind him. She sat down next to him. He turned around quickly, relieved to see her.

"Why so jumpy, Rekesh?" she asked softly, rubbing his shoulder.

"I didn't sleep so well last night," he said, seeking affection.

Elera stroked his long hair, letting it run through her fingers. He reached out and held her hand tightly.

"I am so scared of losing you," he said sincerely, looking deep into her eyes.

Elera had felt Rekesh's fear of loss before. She knew that it had driven him into dangerous situations in the past. She didn't want that to happen anymore.

"We cannot cling to each other, Rekesh," she said reassuringly, kissing his rough cheek. "We love each other, yes, but nothing stands still. What would you do if I died? We all die someday."

The words created dreadful thoughts in Rekesh's mind and he relinquished his hold of Elera's hand. She immediately took hold of his hand again, softly stroking it.

"I feel that it is important to look after everything on this planet. It makes me feel good focusing on the whole."

"Sometimes it's okay just to focus on yourself and those who are close to you," Rekesh said, a hint of yearning in his voice.

"That is true," Elera agreed. "However, now, we are here together. What more could we want? We are not here in this beautiful place by coincidence. We didn't meet all those people who have guided us this far for nothing. We are here because we can help this planet and all that live upon it to be free."

The words invoked no emotion in Rekesh. He glanced out at the sea once more, the sun now hovering above the horizon, a perfect reflection shining out of the water.

"Some people are beyond help," Rekesh said coldly, pausing for thought. "You know, one of the first things you hear when you reach a Raiceman train station is the word *destroy*."

Elera was surprised by Rekesh's sudden recollection.

"It's true," he said, looking at her. "*Keep to the walkways. Any left luggage will be destroyed. Keep moving.* It's funny, I heard that every day and I thought – this is so symbolic."

Rekesh paused.

"If you don't fit in with the system, you'll be destroyed," he said quite gloomily. "Everything is designed to make you part of the machine."

"It is not like that everywhere, Rekesh. People *can* choose to leave. They just think they can't."

"People cannot leave," Rekesh protested. "Debts keep people in chains. From the time someone is born in Raicema, they are burdened with thousands in debt. There is no physical form to their money so people are powerless. They have nothing."

Elera was going to say something but changed her mind. After some time she spoke. "I remember my father once showed me an old Raicema coin. But even that had the head of one of the Tyrones on it."

Rekesh felt a jolt of guilt whilst Elera was oblivious to the irony.

"So maybe things have always be like that, Rekesh. In some ways we are all powerless. But that doesn't mean we can't be free."

Silence fell for a moment and they heard talking from inside the cave. The waves crashed ahead. Then, the tireless energy of Reo burst onto the scene.

"Hey, you two!" Reo shouted from the cave entrance. "Come in here. We've got to solve this puzzle. What are you waiting for?"

Rekesh and Elera couldn't help but chuckle at Reo's raw energy.

They walked back into the cave, startled by the brightness of the flowers seemingly dancing in the bright light streaming in through the grand opening.

Everyone was awake.

"Let us all focus at this time when we are at our most intuitive and awake," Javu began to say.

"So there is a big tree and *the still* can awaken it?" Reo said loudly to himself, waving his arms and raising his bushy eyebrows. "But there are so many big trees on this island. And what does *awaken* mean?"

"Wait a minute," Elera said, ignoring the question and trying to slow Reo's pace. "Something about *a gate* was said to me when I was up there yesterday. *Only the still can reach the gate. The big tree sleeps and can only be awoken by the still.*"

Now, Reo was intensely confused, however, Javu was smiling.

"I think the gate is here in this cave," he said.

He pointed upwards, directly above where he was standing.

Everyone looked up at the distant flower-covered cave roof.

"I don't see anything," Bene said.

Javu asked Rama to point out the hatch he had spotted the day before. As everyone noticed the small wooden trapdoor covered in reds and purples, some let out a sigh of powerlessness.

"Listen, I know by some kind of miracle Elera floated halfway up this cave yesterday," Reo said with a hint of sarcasm in his voice, "but do you expect us all to believe that we can all do that? And that just looks like an old wooden hatch?"

"Calm yourself, Reo," Elera said softly. "Let Javu finish what he was saying."

"Indeed, I am not expecting you to perform such a feat, Reo," Javu chuckled.

Reo blushed and then smiled dryly.

"Why do you think that little hatch is the gate?" Elera asked Javu.

"Isn't it strange that there's a door in the roof of this giant cave?" Javu asked back. "Also, as a general rule, I find that what one searches for is usually right under one's nose. Or above it in this case."

At this, Javu let out a hearty laugh.

"What about the tree?"

"I have a hunch," Javu said, walking towards the centre of the cave.

"Elera, I want you to try and see the energy of this cave again and this time place your focus on the floor. Try to look for something unusual."

Elera invoked her new ability and was soon seeing the now familiar swirling patterns of misty energy emanating from all objects. She scanned the floor. Not far from where Javu was standing was an intense flow of energy, which seemed to vibrate outwards in all directions in a highly charged fashion. It almost felt like something was pulsating, and the feeling reminded her of when she was trapped in the Bimini pyramid.

"There is something with a lot of energy just over there."

"Someone clear the flowers where she is pointing to," Javu instructed.

Teltu and Bene obliged and before long, a space had been cleared where Elera was pointing. Soft dark brown earth was now exposed.

"Dig there."

Teltu picked up a long stick and started to dig in the soil with it. Rekesh, Bene and Reo joined in and after a while they had made their way down by about a foot, using their hands to scoop out the fresh dirt. Then as Teltu began to dig again, the sound of wood striking wood was heard as he dug the stick in.

"Hey, you've hit something!" Reo said.

They all cleared the dirt around and as Teltu reached down, everyone hovered over the hole, peering down with anticipation.

"Whoa, it's heavy!" Teltu perspired.

Teltu strained and then emerged carrying a large old wooden chest. He placed it on the floor in front of everyone. The lid opened with a creak.

Inside the chest was a smaller polished box.

"What's inside?" Reo asked impatiently.

The box was in a centre chamber of the chest and four other empty chambers surrounded the smaller centre chamber, arranged in a circle. Each of the outer chambers had a small golden handle attached to it.

As Teltu opened the small box, Reo and Rama both let out a gasp of disbelief.

"That's the stone I saw in the vision!" Reo exclaimed loudly, peering down at the oval-shaped stone that seemed to glisten from within.

"Is it a wisdom rock?" Elera questioned. "It has an incredible amount of energy stored inside it. It's quite blinding actually."

"Look, there is a symbol inscribed on it," Bene noticed.

He picked up the stone and handed it to Elera. It was heavy and had a small carving of a tree on it.

"What are those other chambers for?" Reo asked, looking into the old chest. "Are those handles made of gold?"

Javu, who now was quite sure what had to be done, raised his hand indicating everyone to be quiet.

"As I mentioned before, I have learnt the ways of the summoner since a young age. I think I understand how this chest works. Each of the chambers is for the gifts that each member of *the still* has chosen. Each member must hold these gold handles at the same time. Gold is very good for transferring energy."

"Where are the gifts?" Elera asked, impulsively agreeing with Javu's theory and placing the stone back in the box in the centre chamber of the chest.

"I chose this air plant," Teltu said, taking it out of his satchel and placing it in one of the chambers. Sita shuffled around for something in her duffle bag and produced the water lily from the cloth and placed it in a chamber.

"I picked a flower from the forest," Bene said, taking out the orange blossom from his bag and placing it in a spare chamber.

"Did you pick anything, Rama?" Reo asked him, unsure if he had after their strange experience in the beach forest.

Rama took a piece of fruit out of his pocket, the very same that the unusual monkey-rabbits had brought them. He placed it in the final chamber.

"Okay, now each of you hold your respective handles," Javu instructed.

The four of them knelt down and took hold of the gold handles in the box. Almost immediately, Elera's view of the world shifted to her energy view. What she saw was astounding.

Ethereal energy was flowing out of the bodies of Rama, Sita, Bene and Teltu directly into the four respective chambers through the golden handles.

Though each of the energy patterns were slightly different, they were all flowing with intensity and were being absorbed by the gifts that each of them had provided.

Rama's piece of fruit seemed to be glowing with a bright orange energy, feeding off the flow that Rama was providing.

Sita's water lily seemed to be floating in a sea of bluish energy, flooding in from her body.

An almost solid block of energy had formed around Bene's

energy flow, it was glowing and pulsating in a misty green way. Teltu's air plant seemed to be swirling around, rising and dipping in a yellowish zephyr.

The energy seemed to be getting stronger and stronger and suddenly, energy from each of the outer chambers spilled into the centre chamber, like a bathtub overflowing. This caused the stone in the box to glow uncontrollably.

The light became so bright that Elera had to look away. As she did, an incredible force resonated outwards almost like an explosion. It resounded through her ears and then through her entire body, as if a thousand hands had struck the largest of gongs.

At that moment, the world seemed to fade away. She saw only light and she heard only silence as the vibration resonated to a close.

The next thing she knew, she was staring up at the roof of the cave, lying on her back. Something floated down next to her head. Her vision faded in and out. She saw green. A leaf floated down onto her face.

It took several moments for Elera to come around. As she sat up, she almost had to lie down again from the astonishment of what towered above her.

A gigantic tree had appeared in the centre of the cave, lush and green, with a thick knobbly trunk and giant branches. It reached up high, almost touching the roof. Leaves fluttered down like butter-flies.

The walls of the cave glistened from a combination of water and bright light. The flowers still remained, but seemed even more vivid and colourful.

Every other person had been thrown from the force of the energy, all scattered around the cave in a groggy state. Bene and Reo sat up at the same time.

"What the...?" asked Bene, rubbing his eyes in disbelief.

As they sat up, for a while there was silence, each person trying to logically comprehend what had happened, but no one coming up with an explanation.

Reo, constipated with bewilderment, could not contain himself any longer. "A tree! A magic tree!" he raved wildly, directing his words to Elera and Javu. "Is any of this real? You floating around, a tree growing from a box, visions in the forest. I feel like I am in a dream."

"But you are not, Reo," Javu said firmly, getting to his feet and gripping his shoulder. "What most of the planet has been living for millennia has been the dream. Humans have never collectively realised what they are, nor have they ever realised what they are capable of. If they had, the planet would not suffer as it does. Many have tried to discover and teach the truth, but the truth is always clouded by fear and suppressed by the fearful. The time has come for us all to change the way that we view life on this planet, just as Elera has envisioned since she was a young child."

Elera was beaming with glee and she too stood up.

"This is just the start," she said. "Love every moment, Reo, for we are rediscovering something innate and natural in us all."

She looked up at the magnificent tree, which appeared to be several hundred years old.

"How did they do this, Javu?" Elera asked him.

"It is an incredible feat," Javu said with admiration. "The summoner that can store this sort of energy in a stone is the summoner that can do anything. It is beyond what I know."

"I am sure it was the Leiruyi," she said convincingly.

Elera looked around and swiftly noticed that Rekesh was missing.

"Where's Rekesh?" she asked.

Rekesh was not in the cave. He was standing on the beach, watching in horror as three Raiceman ships appeared on the horizon. Their black metallic sheen distinctive even at this far distance. He quickly turned and ran up the beach, back into the cave.

"Quickly," he ordered everyone, as he reached the foot of the tree. "Start climbing. The Raicemans have found us!"

"Found us?" Elera said, shocked by what he was saying. "Why are they looking for us?"

"It doesn't matter," Rekesh barked. "Climb!"

Everyone hastily began to climb the vast tree, Javu going first, followed closely by Sita and Rama and then Elera.

Rekesh held all other men back.

"They plan to kill us all," Rekesh told them, striking fear into their hearts. "You must be ready to fight to the death!"

Teltu's face changed from alertness to concern at hearing these words. Then they all joined the others in climbing the gigantic tree.

Chapter 40 – Vengeance Looming

Seth Tyrone was deep in thought aboard one of Raicema's remaining war vessels. He was in his brother's naval office, surrounded by complicated machines and specialised gadgets. Looking out through a giant porthole at the vast ice-cold ocean, the new president of Raicema felt deflated and uneasy.

How did I end up here? Seth thought to himself, looking around the room in which Jeth had spent many days of his life scheming and planning. *I am now nothing but the shadow of my brother.*

Seth contemplated his early life. His father had been a firm and ruthless leader. He had encouraged competition between his two sons from an early age. Seth remembered the two boys being forced to face each other in bare-knuckle fist fights and being unable to concede until one of them was unable to stand.

Their father would often host such bouts in front of scores of his followers, saying it would bring out the better of the two boys.

Seth had always been physically stronger than Jeth and the result of the fight was always the same, with Jeth lying unconscious with a bloodied face. The praise Seth got for his physical superiority was the only commendation he ever received from his father, however.

Jeth had quickly proved himself to be a strategic genius. At the age of thirteen, he had been instrumental in the Raiceman occupation of southern Ciafra, advising his father on a phased approach by creating strongholds in nearby territories and islands. Their father had made his intentions clear that Jeth would succeed him when he was gone.

Now, in an office that his father and brother had both occupied, Seth felt out of place and unprepared.

"President Tyrone?" a voice resounded through the speaker on desk in front of him.

"Yes," Seth replied reluctantly.

"The watch guard is on his way to report to you personally, sir."

"Very good," Seth said, getting to his feet from the polished ship's chair.

Thoughts of Jeth came to mind again and with them a conversation that the two brothers had when they were young teens.

"When father is gone, together we can create the biggest empire that this planet has ever seen," Jeth had told his brother when they were hunting deer in the Tyrona forest one day.

"Isn't it already the biggest empire?" Seth had asked, quite naively.

"No, Lengard is bigger than us and Neoasia will soon be too," Jeth had said knowingly. *"There is something much bigger than them too. Eventually, we could rule them all. You will be the commander of vast armies."*

"And what would you do?"

"I will take father's place."

Seth walked over to a dressing area in the office. Looking at his reflection in a round mirror embedded in a tall wardrobe, he stared at his own face for several minutes.

Then, in a surreal moment, he saw his brother's face staring back at him.

"Jeth?" he said with surprise.

"Avenge me, brother!" the face said coldly.

He shook his head and the face had disappeared, his own once again looking back at him. He was about sit back down when there was a knock at the door.

"Enter!"

A young guard came in. He had been high up in the vessel's watchtower.

"I came down here personally to tell you that we have spotted something very unusual due northeast of our current location."

"Well, what is it?" Seth urged, sitting down in his chair.

"An island, with trees and sand. It is very strange as everywhere else in this region is covered in ice. We have tracked the perpetrators. Their ship is stationed three suns from here."

At this news, Seth punched a round button on his chair and the captain of the *Stryder* resonated through the deck.

"Yes, President Seth? What are your orders?"

"Head due northeast to the island."

"Yes, sir," the voice echoed.

There was a crackle and then silence.

Seth rose to his feet again, walked out of the office and across the hallway to the ship's elevator. The elevator spoke as Seth entered.

"Location…?"

"Jen King," Seth said sternly.

Jen King was pacing his locked quarters. His mind was confused, thoughts of the past whirling around and crashing in his head.

The visions of the killings in Lizrab haunted him more than usual, so much that he felt like he wanted to jump off the ship into the ocean and swim forever. He reflected on all the orders he had carried out at a whim of a command, at anger and hate of the enemies that he had been told about. He was realising that he was no different to what the Raiceman government had made those enemies out to be.

Cold-blooded murderers, ruthless and heartless, with no vision, no future, he thought painfully. *So much violence, so much hate.*

He was sick of it all now. Blocking it out did not work. The thoughts kept coming. The hypocrisy was infuriating.

Jen could feel the force of the vessel turning and he had to hold on to a metal storage unit to prevent himself from being thrown. He looked out of a thick glass triangular window and noticed from the position of the sun that the ship was heading northwards.

He heard a beep and the quarters' door slid vertically downwards as Seth swaggered in.

"King, we have located a potential hideout of the perpetrators. We shall arrive there soon," Seth said in an authoritative tone. "I need you to wipe these vermin out personally."

Jen's reaction to the order was edgy and instinctive.

"Why?" Jen asked defiantly, looking Seth directly in the eyes.

"Why what?" Seth retorted, taken aback slightly.

"Why should I kill them?" Jen elaborated very seriously.

Seth was now shocked at the continued doubt in Jen's mind, which he thought he had cleared already.

"You are a role model to the young soldiers on this vessel. They will learn from you what it means to defend the honour of Raicema!"

"What honour? All that Raicema does is invade other lands like locusts. Do you think killing those people is going to bring your brother back?"

Seth was shaken by Jen's lack of patriotism. It angered him.

"You speak like a traitor!" he barked.

Jen contemplated for a moment whether to discuss the matter of his origin. He quickly decided that he wanted to, if at least to gain some clarity.

"I met a man who claims to have raised me as a child. He knows me. He knows my mind," Jen began. "He claims I was taken by your father and brainwashed, all because I have some kind of abnormal strength."

Seth just stared in horror. He thought carefully for a moment, realising the day had come that he had often dreaded.

"The man you talked to is a liar. He is a terrorist who wishes to cause friction within the Raiceman government. He must know you are a valuable asset to our ambitions."

"But I actually remember him as a child," Jen insisted. "So you must be lying, Seth. I see you like my brother, yet you lie to me."

At this statement, a look of anger spread across Seth's face, but he held it back and moved closer to the rebellious soldier.

"What does any of this matter?" he hissed into Jen's ear. "You are part of a great and supreme empire. We are the definitive ruling empire. What do you strive for? You have let the enemy corrupt your mind. You are weak, King."

At this statement, Jen was overcome with fury and he lunged at Seth, grasping him by the throat. He picked him up and choked him. It only took a moment, however, for Jen to repent and he released Seth in shame.

"I am sorry," he said, bowing his head and wishing to be free of all aggression.

Seth shook of the attack and then smiled slyly.

"It is only the mind games and corruption of the enemy. Do not be fooled."

There was silence for many moments, both men contemplating. Jen now sat on a stool, head in hands and legs twitching rapidly. He looked up with submission.

"How many are there?" he asked weakly.

"Eight, including the man who murdered my brother," Seth responded, sternly. "We have been tracking them from the Lizrabian region of Turo, where you described your encounter, to an island close by. These terrorists must be dealt with swiftly."

Jen just nodded, feeling deflated and empty.

"Remember, King, you are my right hand," Seth said unconvincingly.

Seth swiftly left Jen's quarters and the door slid up with a thud. Jen glanced out of the window again and could see the coastline of an island directly ahead. He walked over to a large metal cabinet and opened its doors. Inside were many sharp blades and firearms. He picked up an old, used leather shoulder belt and loaded it with a variety of weapons. He put the belt on, over his head and resting on his right shoulder, diagonally down to his waist.

He walked over to the sink in the corner. He turned on the tap and let the water run down his wrist and through his fingers. He always did this before the time for bloodshed came. It made him feel dead already. He imagined blood running down his wrists.

Then he waited in silence.

Chapter 41 – A Land unknown

The great tree had been a feat to climb. The branches were few and far between, extending in winding formations from the thick main trunk, which was as wide as a long boat.

This is truly a tree of friendship, Javu thought, recalling the many times each of them had to combine efforts to climb higher up.

Now, they all sat on two great sturdy branches far above the ground at the treetop. The flower-coated cave ceiling and the mysterious hatch were just out of reach.

Elera was attempting to shimmy along to a point where she could touch the wooden slats. She hopped to another branch, which creaked a little but felt strong enough to bear her weight.

Directly above her, in arm's reach, was the old wooden hatch. It had a gold lock, with intricate swirling patterns running outwards across the slats. There was a small symbol of a horse etched into the metalwork and Elera quickly realised that the key Sita had found the day before could be the perfect match.

She took out the old key from her small bag and had a quick look at the eroded emblem on the head. She held it up to the clear engraving of the horse and besides a few details missing, the images looked like they were the same proportion and shape.

Elera couldn't help but think of Aova as she inserted the key and turned it gently. A loud clicking sound resonated out of the lock and then the hatch creaked a little.

It swung open, almost knocking her off the branch.

Water burst out of the hole, flooding down the tree trunk like a waterfall.

"Whoa!" she said, fighting to keep her balance.

Everyone clambered to a stand in shock at the rapid flow of water cascading downwards at high pressure.

"Hey!" Reo yelped as he almost fell of the branch.

The waterfall did not stop for several minutes and water could be seen running out of the cave's entrance from high above. All the flowers on the roof were soon dripping heavily with large drops of water.

Everyone just stared at each other in disbelief and shock as the fallen water below formed a pool in the cave.

"Well, the key fitted in the lock!" Elera said jovially, trying to look into the darkness that the open hatch now revealed.

"There's a cavity up here," she said, lifting herself up with agility. "It's very wet."

She dropped back down onto a branch close by.

Javu was the first to make his way over to where Elera was carefully balanced.

"I will go first," Javu said in a protective manner.

He shimmied across to the hatch and was surprised to find two hand grips on the inside of the short vertical tunnel, which helped him get inside even though they were smooth and slippery. There was a wide rocky space inside with a surrounding ledge, too short to stand in.

Horizontally ahead was a tunnel that was only a crawl space.

Bene was next to lift himself into the strange space. He handed Javu a small torch.

"You can light the way."

The dark tunnel felt damp and slimy.

Javu led slowly but safely, using the small electronic light. Everyone else slowly lifted themselves into the cavity and followed.

"Now watch out, there's a bumpy part coming up," Javu said in a jovial way as they made their way along.

Rekesh was the last in line and every minute he would glance back, half expecting to see an array of lights from the Raiceman troops.

Some time passed and they crawled along in silence, the humidity making it quite difficult to speak. Javu began to see light at the end of the tunnel and reciprocated this to the others.

"Not far to go. I see light up ahead," he encouraged.

As he reached the opening, he noticed footholds that led vertically upwards, about the height of a human.

As he climbed the natural steps, his head popped out at the basin of a huge lake that was now empty. Surrounding the lake was a beautiful forest with animals roaming freely. A deer-like creature stopped and stared at Javu's large head poking out covered with long grey hair.

The forest was vivid with rich greens and yellows plentifully manifested as luscious leaves on trees, bushes and shrubs.

The sun shone brightly through the treetops, casting a stippled light on the fresh brown floor.

Javu made light footprints in the lake's silky sediment as he walked across the basin.

"Well, this must be where the water came from!"

The others followed, dazzled by the vivacious fullness of the forest.

"I have never seen a forest so rich with life!" Teltu remarked, brushing off some silt from his trousers.

Some of the trees reached high into the sky and their tops could not be seen from the ground.

"Where are we?" Reo asked as he emerged from the hole. "Is this another part of the island?"

Rekesh was the last out and the silt splashed up into his face as he got to his feet. The exhilaration of emerging from the tunnel left everyone in silence for a few moments.

All was very quiet and Javu could hear the sound of running water close by.

"This way!" he said, leading the group into the forest.

Before long, they had reached a small brook, crackling as the fresh water rippled over twigs and dry leaves that fell from the sky. The aroma of the water was sweet and they all took a cupped handful to drink.

Sita, Rama and Teltu all sat down on the bank, the heat beginning to invade their bodies.

"Are we in Lemuria?" Reo asked Elera, eyes wide open.

"I am not sure, Reo," Elera said smiling, beginning to look around. The place was indeed reinvigorating, however, the heat was strange and made it difficult to think. Some time passed without anyone saying anything. It was almost like everyone had entered a state of meditation by just being in the environment. There was an enveloping light in the air.

"Elera, I meant to ask you something," Teltu began to say slowly after a while, looking up at her from his seated position.

"Yes, Teltu?"

"How did you ever find out about the underwater Bimini pyramid? I mean, nobody ever found it before, right?"

Two small creatures jumped across a branch overhead, making a cooing sound.

"Monkey-rabbit!" Reo exclaimed, recognising the creatures and looking at Rama.

Elera smiled and turned to Teltu to explain how she ended up in the Bimini pyramid.

"For a long time, I had a lot of dreams about Bimini," she told him. "It was almost as if something wanted me to find it. Also, I started meeting lots of people who seemed to be there to guide me. I had one specific dream about a cave near to Turo and when I went to visit Kirichi, he told me that such a cave existed!"

Elera's narrative was interrupted by a chorus of birdsong joyous to the ear.

"Kirichi and I travelled out to the cave that I had dreamt of and we went as far as we could into it. Inside, there was an enormous stone slab guarding some sort of underground chamber."

She paused for a moment, her eyes lighting up at the memory.

"Kirichi told me that he owned a very special crystal, one that shines from within. He asked me to hold this crystal against the slab and to my amazement, it began to crumble away into rubble before my eyes!"

Everyone was now listening to Elera's story, most seated on the soft grass.

"Inside the chamber were some ancient writings and tunnels leading deep down into the earth." Elera sat down on the grassy ground, the humidity causing a small drop of water to run down her brow. "One of the tablets I found talked of a *path to Lemuria*, which described the location of the Bimini pyramid as the first step of the path. There was also something else written."

She paused.

"One tablet spoke of the *Lemurian secret* and its importance to the survival of this planet."

"Is this the secret that you think can help everyone?" Bene asked, a little mordantly.

"Yes," she replied, still smiling. "The text written had a very special meaning to me. Maybe if somebody else had translated the text, it wouldn't have been as powerful to them, but for me, it meant so much."

"What did it say?" Reo asked curiously.

"It said that the secret is a key, a *key to remembering*."

"Remembering what?" Reo asked.

"That life is endless. It has no beginning and it has no end. Death is the great illusion that has divided us all."

Reo thought for a moment and Rekesh shuffled his feet.

"To me, knowing that alleviates so much of the sorrow I have felt in my life."

"And is that the secret?" Reo asked.

"No, Reo," she said softly. "That is only part of the secret. My interpretation of what was written about the Lemurian secret was *'That which can instantly wash away the illusion that is blinding human beings from the truth.'* When I read the inscription, I was filled with peace and hope."

Teltu was intrigued by Elera's account.

"What illusion? What is blinding us from the truth? Death?" Reo asked after a while.

"The illusion is that we are contained, that we are prisoners, that we are finite. The truth is, we are already free. We are boundless and infinite, Reo."

Reo wanted to believe it. He wanted to believe that all the suffering he had seen was only a dream and that life continued. He wanted to believe life couldn't be killed, that it was invincible. However, Reo couldn't see it as more than a beautiful fantasy.

Javu, who had been listening to Elera intently, realised something about the brook they were standing next to.

"This brook has been artificially channelled," Javu announced, motioning his arm along its length. "You see how it runs around the trees in quite a purposeful way. Somebody has created it for the creatures here to drink out of."

"Maybe we should follow this brook to its source?" Rekesh suggested.

The others agreed and the party set off, following the winding brook through an array of giant trees and encountering many types of unusual creatures along the way including a rat that walked like a duck with a bushy tail and ponies with thick bushy mains. There were reptilian-looking birds with no feathers except for a few large ones on their wings.

"I don't know where we are," Bene said to Rekesh as they walked along. "But I have never heard of any place like this."

After a while, the group noticed the brook becoming thicker and deeper and many types of fish swimming in its waters.

Ahead in the distance, through the range of tree trunks, a construct of some sort could be seen. As they got closer, they saw a substantial and beautifully crafted building, made entirely of logs, with the brook running under its foundation.

The building was wide but only as tall as the shortest tree, with a dome above made from flexed branches and stems. There were no windows in the building and it appeared as though there was no entrance either.

"Can we swim into it?" Reo questioned, tilting his neck to try to see how the brook flowed underneath the structure.

Rama, without hesitation, lowered himself into the deep water and swam under the building. After a while, he reappeared and motioned the others to follow.

Each person lowered themselves into the water, taking a deep breath and diving down. They all swam into the building.

As they surfaced, they were greeted by the smiling face of a golden statue, sitting cross-legged with palms outstretched. There were two large wooden platforms on either side of the water, both scattered with fresh petals.

"Somebody must come here," Elera said, picking up one of the petals. "And look over there."

She pointed to a hidden stairway, made from branches and rope on the same side as the statue. Everybody congregated on that side, and Elera climbed the steps.

At the top she found another platform, the dome directly above her. Light streamed in through the gaps between the dome branches. Tied to one, was a small piece of tree bark inscribed with a symbol. There was nothing else in sight. Elera descended the stairway, shaking her head.

"There is a symbol up there that I have never seen before. It looks like the *Olma* language but is more obscure. Javu, can you translate it?" she asked, hoping his lingual ability could be transferred to written language as well.

"Unfortunately not," he told her.

Everyone else had gathered around the statue.

"That statue looks like it is giving us something," Teltu remarked, gazing at the golden statue.

The comment gave Elera a shot of insight.

"Wait a minute. That symbol up there could mean *giving*," she inferred, not sure how she was drawing the conclusion.

"So the statue wants to give us something?" Reo asked.

"Or, expecting us to offer something?" Javu suggested, drawing on past experience.

Everyone rummaged around in their satchels and pouches for suggestions of an offering. Elera held up her hand.

"I know."

She reached down and picked up a single rose petal from the floor, instinctively knowing that that was all that was required.

"I don't know why but I know that all it wants is one of these petals."

She placed the petal in the golden statue's hands. A click emanated from the back of the golden monk.

Elera looked behind and saw there was now an opening in its back, with a small wooden box inside. She opened the box and saw a shiny, polished stone with crystalline channels running through a purple and red marbled amalgam.

The stone had an unusual diagram inscribed into it. It was a circle surrounded in totality by eight smaller circles. It had been wrapped in a soft cloth and there was a small inscription etched in the inside of the box. She held the stone up for everyone to see.

"The inscription in the box is again in a language I don't know," Elera said starting to feel a little doubt. "This building seems to house this statue and this stone for safekeeping. Maybe we shouldn't take it."

"I think we should take it," Javu reassured her. "We are not here by coincidence."

Elera put it in her satchel and the group left the building, diving under the brook again one by one and emerging back in the forest.

The group pressed on through the forest, continuing to follow the brook. Elera dropped back with Javu.

"Javu, why can't you understand written languages, yet you can understand and speak every spoken language?" Elera asked him as they walked along.

"With spoken languages, it is like I can understand the direct meaning of what someone is trying to say when they speak, almost like every language is automatically translated into some sort of primal, universal language. It almost feels like music."

"But how come you can speak the languages as well?"

"It is the same. When I want to say something, I just know how to say it."

"So when you met Respiro, you were then able to do that?"

"Yes and I think any person who encounters their elemental protector will receive two gifts of ability."

"What makes you think that?"

"There are only three people I know who have encountered their protectors directly. You are one, Kirichi is another and I am the third. We have each received two gifts from our protector."

"Kirichi told you he'd encountered Aova?" Elera asked with surprise.

"Yes. For a long time we could only speak between ourselves about such matters."

"So what two gifts have I received?" Elera asked, quite unsure herself.

"You have received the gift of *energy seeing* and the gift of *psychic knowing*. Your abilities have begun to show themselves when they were needed, as they always do."

"Do you really think I could be psychic?"

"Before in the hut, you just knew to offer that petal. You didn't try to deduce it did you, you just knew it? So, yes, I think that is one of your gifts."

"What about Kirichi?" Elera asked excitedly.

"Kirichi has received the same gift of *energy seeing* but he has also received the gift of *water shaping*. He is able to make water hold a particular shape."

"Yes, I saw him walk on water," Elera said, still not quite believing it.

"Exactly! And whilst both of your gifts are internal to yourself, one of his is external as he can change things outside of himself."

"And your gifts are being able to float and understand every language?"

"I have given much deliberation to the actual abilities that I have received. My conclusion is that Respiro gave me the gift of *levitation* and the gift of *telepathy*. Both are internal gifts."

"Telepathy? You mean you can hear people's thoughts?"

"Sort of. To me it is just like the purest form of understanding what someone is trying to communicate. It's not like I can tell what you are thinking unless you are trying to communicate with me."

"Amazing!" Elera said after a while. "Can you imagine what this world would be like if everyone opened up to such capabilities?"

"That is both the hope and the fear of our cause," Javu told her quite seriously.

After several hours of walking, they noticed the forest was thinning and mountains could be seen in the distance.

Several more hours passed and the party emerged in an open space with lush fields. Small rodents ate shrubs growing from the ground and a few birds of prey hovered above.

The forest was now just a few copses here and there.

"The Raicemans must have searched the island by now," Rekesh stated to Elera, now walking besides her.

"I doubt they will notice the gateway," Elera reassured Rekesh. "The big tree hides its presence from the ground."

Rekesh just nodded, though deep down in the pit of his stomach, a seed of anxiety was beginning to sprout into a smouldering mass of unknown fear. A terrible vision flashed before his eyes, one of Elera lying lifeless on the floor. He held her close as they headed into the unknown.

Chapter 42 – Pursuit of a Traitor

Jen King stood at the foot of the colossal cave tree, in true wonder of its presence.

Raiceman troops had scoured the island, finding nothing in the east or south forests or in the rocky land to the west.

"Commander King!" shouted a young soldier, running into the cave.

"We are facing many dangers in the southern jungle. Giant lizards seem to dwell there. One of the men's arms was bitten clean off by such a monster!"

"Return to the vessels," King ordered, falling right back into his robot-like way of commanding people. "I will take one last look around and then join you."

The soldier nodded and ran off to repeat the orders. What Jen King had not revealed, was that he had spotted a human hair in one of the branches of the big tree.

After the remainder of the men had left the island, King began to climb the massive tree, half expecting to find people hiding higher up. The bark on the tree felt as hard as rock and it was jagged too, providing difficult hand and foot holds.

A shining, silky moss grew all over the bark, however, somewhat easing the pain of the climb. As King climbed higher, he started to feel drops of water dripping on his nose and forehead.

Looking up only gave a view of green mass and everlasting trunk. He breathed slowly and deeply as he climbed hand after hand at a steady pace. He felt the strength return to his arms as his muscles tightened.

As he placed his foot on a branch, he slipped on the slippery moss and dropped his weapon-laden shoulder belt to the floor. He dangled with one hand from a small branch and powered his way into a seated position, breathing heavily.

He decided to continue and leave the weapons behind, climbing for a good while before becoming enveloped in thick, green leaves, swarms of tiny greenfly living amongst them as though it were the world's biggest city. His arms ached from the effort but the burn felt good, like it was renewing his body.

The leaves were all speckled with water drops, and before long, King reached the roof of the cave and was met with a barrage of vividly colourful flowers. He explored the treetop for a while, walking along the thick branches like bridges, until he noticed a particular bunch of leaves were dripping quite heavily.

He pushed them back to reveal the entrance to the tunnel. He contemplated for a moment whether to climb back down and fetch some men to accompany him, but he swiftly decided to press on alone, uncaring about the consequences.

Whilst King was crawling in complete darkness through the damp tunnel, he began to think once again of his childhood. Another memory came to him. It played out before him like a vision in the darkness.

He was playing outside on a beach with another child, throwing and catching a small rock to each other. The other child had challenged the young Jen to a competition, to see who could throw a rock the furthest into the ocean.

The child went first and threw a rock quite a way, so it made a splash that the two could see in the distance. When Jen threw his rock, no splash could be seen.

"Well, I guess you threw it further," the child had said, "but we can't tell how far this way. Let's do it again over by the Rocky Ridges. That way we'll hear it fall in the distance."

The Rocky Ridges were jagged stone mountains on the outskirts of the village where Jen lived, very crumbly and difficult to climb. The boys had approached the pathway that led into the ridges.

"From here, let's throw in between those two ridges," Jen's young friend had said, picking up a stone and hurling it deep into the small canyon. A crack could be heard where the stone had fallen, a few crumbling rocks heard tinkling down the distant ridge.

The young Jen King had picked up a medium-sized rock and he

had thrown with all his might. Somewhere very far away, an echoed crack could be heard and then a huge rumbling, the sound of rubble falling.

The boys heard screams and had stared at each other in horror. They ran into the canyon, to find huge boulders tumbling down, crashing around some people who had been mining in the ridges.

Later that day, Javu had sat with Jen outside, telling him that he had been given a gift.

"You must be skilful and wise with how you use it. We were very lucky nobody was hurt in your escapade today."

King's memory flashed back to the present, a dim light brightly flowing through the long tunnel ahead.

How can I have wasted this gift of strength on bloodshed since that time? he thought, his head swelling with tension.

As he approached the footholds, he looked up and saw sunshine. He climbed to the basin of the drained lake.

The forest was radiant and its leaves whispered with a soft breeze.

I shall rest here for a while, King thought to himself, feeling exhausted both physically and mentally.

He found a grassy mound at the edge of the lake and lay his head down and within seconds his agitated mind had switched off and he fell into a deep sleep whilst being bathed in sunlight.

When King awoke, the sun was much less bright. He looked up and saw the face of Seth Tyrone and twenty Raiceman troops staring down at him.

Seth threw his shoulder belt, full of weapons, upon him with aggression.

"Well done for locating this place, King," Seth barked arrogantly and with a hint of sarcasm in his voice. King swiftly got to his feet. The sun was dipping in the sky and the wild forest seemed desolate.

"When you didn't return, we thought we'd better look for you!" Seth said sardonically. "It seems as though you need some help in tracking down these terrorist vermin."

"I do not need help," King said defensively and with a little desperation, putting his shoulder belt on. "You may as well return to your vessel. There may be many dangers within these forests."

Seth smiled coyly and suspiciously.

"I think not. We shall accompany you and make sure you do your job properly," Seth regimented.

King knew that Seth had lost all traces of trust in him.

"Incredible how this tunnel was built," Seth announced to his men. "It must have taken much ingenuity. I intend to explore this land fully. I expect that there are many treasures to be discovered."

The other men licked their lips with anticipation.

"These lands may hold many useful materials that we can harvest."

The convoy set off through the forest in the heat, the heavy equipment and armour being carried only slowing their progress. Before long a crackled radio transmission came through every soldier's headset.

"Please confirm location…" the broadcaster said over and over.

"We have ventured further into the island," one of the soldiers eventually replied back.

"Negative," the broadcaster announced. *"The tracking radar indicates you have moved location and it is having difficulty triangulating your positions. Please confirm your location…"*

The narrative quickly annoyed Seth, who had also been listening to the transmission.

"We are still on the island!" Seth barked into his microphone, which was attached to a discreet earpiece.

"Negative, sir," the broadcaster responded once again. *"Initial readings indicate your location has moved at least five thousand suns in a south-westerly direction."*

"The equipment is wrong!" Seth said, dismissing the incomprehensible claim. "We have only travelled through a short tunnel within the island."

"According to current readings, your position is somewhere in the middle of the Pacific Ocean."

"Impossible!" Seth said in a final manner. "Now get off this damn radio!"

There was nothing but silence from the radio for the next ten minutes whilst the men plodded along in the heat.

Then, a different, more frantic voice came over the transmission.

"President Tyrone, President Tyrone, please respond, sir."

"What is it?" Seth said irritably into his microphone.

"A matter of urgency has arisen and you must return immediately to the *Stryder*, sir."

"What matter of urgency?"

"We have received a declaration of war from Lengard, President Tyrone."

"What?!" Seth shouted aghast at the news. "They have made their demands and we are going to fulfil them. This is completely preposterous!"

Everyone stood in silence for several moments whilst the president thought carefully, the heat causing each soldier to shuffle with irritation.

"There is no choice. We must return to the vessels and proceed forthwith to Neoasia," Seth said finally to the men and into his radio. "Give us an hour and we shall all be back aboard the *Stryder*. Do not reply to Lengard. I will appeal to the Emperor of Neoasia personally to help resolve this matter."

For a moment Seth was going to instruct Jen King and a few men to continue on the quest for vengeance, however, he quickly repented, realising King was no longer driven by the same ambitions as he was.

"Reiko, Bill, Jake," Seth addressed three of his men. "Arrest Jen King."

After an initial moment of shock at the orders, the men quickly pointed their guns at the stunned soldier.

"Seth, what are you doing?" King asked, as one of the men

removed his shoulder belt.

"I cannot trust you anymore, King. I believe you have deliberately thwarted our attempts to bringing justice to those responsible for my brother's death."

Though Jen disagreed, at that moment every ounce of fight had left his body and he could not speak, remaining totally silent.

"Bind his hands," Seth ordered as he marched back in the direction of the tunnel that would take them back to the island. As Jen King was marched off with new disdain, there was a part of him that had surprisingly become intensely happy, the origin of which seemed to be the fact that he had somehow found freedom in being imprisoned.

Just before they reached the empty lake, ready to climb back down the strange tunnel, Jen spotted something in the forest that he had seen before. It was a woman, walking with grace and a presence of love that he couldn't completely fathom. As he was pushed down into the basin, he glanced back, but the woman was gone.

Chapter 43 – Road to Lemuria

"*A sorcerer* may not know how powerful they are at first. They may not realise how they affect the world around them. They may not realise the enormity of the forces that they are attracting into their lives."

Javu was describing his view of a sorcerer as he walked along a forest path with Teltu.

"A sorcerer is an observer, a master of disguise and a philosopher. The average person is a prisoner of their own view, staring at the shadow of themselves on the wall, unable to look at their real-self casting that shadow."

He paused. The others were walking up ahead towards what looked like a series of cliffs.

"The sorcerer, however, is not only looking at himself casting the shadow, but he is searching for the light that projects this silhouette in the first place."

Teltu understood Javu's metaphor, however, he was unsure of how one came to be a sorcerer in the first place. Before he could ask, Javu immediately explained, as if reading his mind.

"To become a sorcerer, one must first realise the first fundamental concept about the world we are living in."

Once again, he paused, in time with an unheard music.

"The first thing that the sorcerer finds out is that the world around him seems wrong. It has been interfered with deliberately, intended to incite the belief that we are prisoners, staring at our shadows on the wall as if it were reality. Then, when the sorcerer begins to look carefully, he finds that there are *entities* that exist only to ensure we keep looking at that wall."

"The governments?" Teltu asked.

"Well, they are actually part of this constructed world too, not the actual designer of it."

"Who is the designer?" Teltu asked instinctively.

"It is both ourselves and the source of light that is casting the shadows," he said simply. "We design our worlds without knowing it. But as we are designing, something is interfering."

"What?"

"Another shadow has been added to our own, by something that is standing right besides us."

Teltu flinched, looking around nervously as they walked. There was nothing there.

"You are looking at your shadow," Javu told him, slightly ominously.

The floor ahead was drying and the forest was beginning to open up.

"Even though we feel like we cannot turn away from the wall, we have always been capable of getting up and looking into a mirror at what we really look like."

Their footsteps sounded melodic as they walked, crunching as they stepped over a thick surface of natural grit that had emerged.

"Then, we look for the light source that projects the shadow. We look for it because we believe it will not only reveal our true selves but also illuminate that which has stayed hidden, secretly interfering in our lives."

Ahead, the screeching of a bird startled Teltu into a sharp and focused attentive state.

"We find that the source is a blazing fire that we cannot get too close to," Javu declared. "And then, we discover the truth."

"And what is that?" Teltu asked, gulping a bit.

Javu looked at him directly in the eyes.

"That we lit this fire in the first place. And without that, nothing could have been projected on the wall anyway."

Ahead, there were tall mountainous cliffs with a narrow inlet running through them. The creek was emitting a frightening high-pitched sound. Both cliff faces were jagged and staggered white rock and only a few hardy plants grew upon them.

"How can we change things? How can we stop people looking at the 'wall'?" Teltu asked, now understanding that Elera must also see the world in a similar way. "Elera thinks there is a way."

He realised that Javu would probably define her as a sorcerer.

Before Javu could answer, another question came to mind.

"Before, you said that a sorcerer is only interested in the pursuit of power. Surely those who seek to control us have the same motive?"

"Not quite, Teltu. The pursuit of power is not necessarily good or bad. The pursuit of power is equivalent to the pursuit of knowledge. The control you speak comes from the past. We cannot undo the past. It is a side effect of the fires we have created."

"But if we 'lit the fire' as you said, why can't we just put it out?"

Javu smiled at the childlike suggestion.

"The fire is not the problem. It is the illusion that the shadow on the wall *is* the real us that is the problem. It is the same thing that makes people think they are alone, when really they are surrounded."

"But what is stopping people from looking at the real them?" Teltu exasperated.

"These *entities* that I was speaking of. They are the whisperers. They keep us looking at the wall out of fear of seeing their hideousness, their treacherousness."

Teltu was now truly frightened, but Javu did not seem to care, speaking with raw honesty as though it was something everybody knew.

"They create the *shackles* in this physical dream world that we find ourselves in. Here it *seems* as though there are limitations."

"Well, who made these shackles? Who are these *entities*?" Teltu asked, getting a little frustrated as the questions rolled through his mind.

"Many say they are the children of Ambitio, the force of pure consuming power in the universe. But I think there is more to the story. I believe that there are good and bad entities."

Teltu was satisfied for the time being with Javu's descriptions of how a sorcerer sees the world. He still had plenty of unanswered questions that he wanted to ask though.

The prominent wind blowing through the creek now made the sound of a shrieking animal.

Elera was ahead, making headway through the narrow space in between the two cliffs. She was being blasted with cool air. The sun was obscured from view.

"What beautiful natural place," Bene remarked to Elera, as he walked through the grand, dusty terrain. "It is as if a giant sword has cut this cliff in two."

"We are fortunate in this heat," Elera said. "The rocks guard us from the sun. It wasn't as hot as this when we landed on the island. It is as if we are somewhere else completely."

A wild cat could be seen roaming above on one of the vertical cliff faces in the distance, walking carefully along its ridges. The shadows cast a hazy look on the path they travelled along. Further on the trail spilt into a fork.

"We should be wary," Rekesh warned, catching up with Elera and Bene. "I see that cat descending towards our path. It may be dangerous."

"Let's not jump to conclusions, Rekesh," Elera said. "It is the same as us, is it not? Wandering through this strange land?"

As they approached the fork, the cat jumped down on to the ground and stared intently at the group.

It had bushy and wild light brown fur covered in dark brown spots. It had long whiskers and brilliant yellow and green wide eyes.

The cat walked down the left branch of the fork.

"I think we should follow it," Elera said. "I feel that no danger will come from this animal."

"I agree," Javu said cheerfully as everyone gathered together for a moment.

The group followed the cat's lead down the fork until the cliffs widened and they reached an open marshland, still completely surrounded by tall, rocky mountains that ran either side of the marsh. The dampness of the land caused a foggy mist to spread, greatly reducing visibility.

The cat had now disappeared into the mist.

"Should we follow it?" Teltu asked, scratching his head.

Elera smiled and began to tread carefully onto the wetland, following the paw prints of the cat. Everyone followed, carefully placing each foot on more bushy mounds of dirt, reeds growing out of the boggy parts.

Sita and Rama walked whilst holding each other by around the waist, stepping in time with a unified happiness. Javu and Teltu walked more cautiously. Both men from Seho dropped back again letting the others walk on ahead.

"So, these children of Ambitio?" Teltu began to ask Javu, not knowing if he truly wanted to know. "What do they look like?"

Javu smiled with fondness at his newfound apprentice.

"I will tell you the old story of *Murdrak and Revereo*," Javu said as they walked carefully through the bog. "It is a Makai story that is no longer spoken of."

Javu took a breath, as if readying himself for the tale.

"*Murdrak* once lived on this earth, maybe four or five million years ago. He is a man, but not like any man that you or I have ever encountered. He has the head of a dragon and his skin is like armour, thick and with scales like a snake. Murdrak lived in a time when there was much water on the planet, much more than today."

Teltu was both captivated and slightly terrified by the setting.

"This man, he lived only to bring suffering to others. Many followed him but he never helped anyone. He lived only to rule and conquer everything that came into his path. Many said he was born directly from the eye of Ambitio. It is safe to say that Murdrak was a very powerful being. It was said that one look from this dragon man could kill."

Javu paused.

"Murdrak bore many children. These children were seen as royalty and were taught to be as ruthless as their father."

Teltu felt his heart rate increase slightly.

"A million or so years passed. At that time, the planet was very hot with wild jungles all over the earth. The sun shone brighter than we could possibly imagine. At that time, there was another man, a different type of being. This man's name was *Revereo*."

The mist enveloped them and Teltu could see nothing but grey haziness.

"Revereo too, was a being unlike any that you or I have ever known. He looked like a lion, with large piecing golden eyes and thick golden fur all over his body. He was a loved and merciful leader and was known for being loyal and compassionate. He would often put his life at risk to protect his people."

"Against who?" Teltu asked with fascination.

"Murdrak's descendants. They ruled and they *interfered*. They waged war. Murdrak was kept alive through his followers. They worshipped him and believed they could bring him back into the physical world through sacrifices. Revereo did everything he could to stop this malevolent practice."

"What happened?" Teltu prompted, sensing the story was not going to end well.

"Murdrak's bloodline succeeded. He returned physically. Revereo, knowing that his death was inevitable, battled Murdrak to the bitter end in many wars. He allowed Murdrak to kill him, but in doing so, by sacrificing himself, Revereo was able to rid the planet of Murdrak's influence. You see, Revereo was a powerful sorcerer too, something that Murdrak did not anticipate."

"So Murdrak is gone?" Teltu asked, looking around shiftily like he expected something hideous to emerge from the mist.

"Yes. However, to this day there are those who try to revive the powerful spirit of Murdrak. And some have succeeded in contacting him, in whatever dreadful world he now resides in."

The story was quite overwhelming.

"Do not fear such beings, Teltu," Javu reassured him. "Those beings are staring at the wall harder than anyone."

Javu and Teltu were now lost in the mist. They could see nor hear any of their party, but they plodded on with trust that they would emerge unharmed from the marsh.

Not far ahead, Reo was walking alone, thinking carefully about his life and all the different things he'd experienced recently.

He suddenly felt a strange sensation, as if something close by was trying to tell him something. He looked around but nobody was there. He could make out the silhouette of Elera and Rekesh ahead, engrossed in the challenge of walking on such infirm terrain.

Reo noticed some small bulbous-looking plants growing near the reeds. They seemed oddly luminous, lit up like the moon. Nobody else had seen them and he walked up to a group that grew in abundance. They glowed with an eerie yet appealing green radiance and had hard, round caps covering each sprouting bulb.

Uncontrollably, Reo felt compelled to pick one of the caps and place it in his mouth. It tasted bitter and chewy, and he almost choked as he swallowed it. Immediately, a strange sensation spread throughout his body. He began to feel incredibly hot and sweaty and his vision became blurred from the perspiration. The feeling passed, and after a while he was left with an overwhelming fondness of the marshland before him, which now seemed so familiar and nostalgic. His face drooped disobediently and he couldn't control any of his facial muscles.

He suddenly became aware of the deep roots of the reeds in the ground and could almost feel their strong grip into the earth beneath the marsh. In his awe of the discovery and not watching where he was going, Reo placed his foot in a giant sinking puddle and quickly plummeted down into it. Within a second he was up to his waist in a watery slush.

"Help!" he tried to yelp out to the others who had now surpassed him trying to keep up with the wild cat.

Rapidly, he was consumed from neck to foot in the musty liquid, the suction of the deep bog preventing him from even lifting his arms. The next thing he knew, he felt like he was swirling down into the sludge at lightning speed, twisting and spinning in every direction possible. He felt the breath being obstructed from his lungs and darkness enveloped him.

Then, out of nowhere, a yellow mist seemed to surround him and all of a sudden, he found himself in a very strange location with a floor covered completely in the same translucent plants and the yellow mist all around for as far as he could see.

As he looked around with an unfounded acceptance of his new environment, Reo noticed the mountain cat strolling slowly towards him across the bulbous plants. He noticed that each one was endowed with the same caps that he had eaten and the cat had stopped and was sitting on its hind legs, simply staring at Reo.

At that moment, the strange sensation that he had felt before sinking into the marsh returned and his body began to feel extremely hot.

Then, his skin began to feel like it was melting, causing his eyes and stomach to ache. Before long, he was sure that he had dissolved completely but then, he felt like he was taking a form that was familiar and a little uncomfortable.

The cat was now walking towards him and he could not move. Slowly, as the cat was close enough that he could smell its breath, he felt that he could move something. It wasn't a hand or a foot. It was a paw.

He realised that the cat in front of him was now at an equal height and mass. He looked down and saw fur, yet his vision had changed and he could only see things in brown tones.

The cat seemed to be unusually affectionate, brushing up against him. He quickly became conscious that he had taken the form of a cat and he began to take steps on each of his four paws.

The two cats walked around each other in the mist, the plants beneath their feet feeling like swollen sponges. What seemed like hours passed and Reo developed a strange affection for his feline friend, as if he could instinctively feel where the cat was going and what it was feeling.

Then, Reo suddenly felt tired and he closed his eyes and felt his furry body curl up over the globular plants.

The next thing he knew, he was waking up as if from a strange dream. He was lying somewhere in the marshland and totally naked. All of his clothes had gone as if by magic. He realised that what he had just experienced could not have been a dream.

He heard footsteps squelching in the boggy ground and as they approached slowly, he braced himself for the others to see him in his raw state. Flinching, he was surprised to see the wild cat coming towards him.

The cat looked at him, appearing almost amused, before sitting on its hind legs to rest. The cat did not move, just sat peacefully and blinked slowly. In the distance, he could hear the others talking to each other, yet it was so far away he could not understand what was being said. The cat got up and began to walk in a westerly direction.

"I should find some clothes," Reo said to himself after a moment of composure. He followed the cat sheepishly, covering his genitals with his hand.

Within a few moments, they had arrived at a lone tree growing in the marsh. It had long sweeping branches with vine-like leaves. Reo quickly took some long leaves and weaved them around his lower body using strips of bark and tight knots. After a short time it looked like he was wearing a pair of long shorts made out of the shrubbery. Then, the cat suddenly ran off into the fog of the marsh as the footsteps of the others approached.

"I think it went this way," Bene was saying as his face came into sight. He spotted Reo with surprise. "Reo? How did you get here?"

"And what happened to your clothes?" Teltu added, appearing with Javu behind.

Reo wasn't sure that they would believe him if he said what had happened, but the next person he saw was Elera and he felt compelled to tell her of his experience. "I somehow transformed into a cat, just like the one that we are following."

Rekesh, Rama and Sita who had now caught up, were astounded to see Reo standing there in his foliage-fashioned garment.

"But how?" Elera asked him. His narrow chiselled arms looked ripped as he crossed them in a protective manner.

"I ate a cap from a strange plant over there."

"You probably hallucinated it," Rekesh said, dismissing the claim.

Reo was going to argue back, but was quite confused himself and decided not to. Instead, he hurried everyone after the cat in the direction he had seen it go. He was now sure in the least that it was guiding them somewhere.

The group continued in the hazed visibility for some time until the fog suddenly cleared and a dense jungle appeared in the distance, illuminated by the unsheltered sun.

The temperature quickly rose as they made their way out of the marshland. The jungle ahead was like no other. The trees were so tall they looked like they had been growing since time began.

"Did it go in there?" Reo asked out loud, looking around and not seeing the spotted cat anywhere.

"It must have gone back to its home," Elera told him, a sense of familiarity coming over her. "It seems that it has led us to where we need to be."

"I'm not sure I want to go in there, Elera," Reo said warily, still feeling unhinged from his strange experience.

"It will be fine. It seems a little daunting because it's so overgrown, but I am sure there is no danger inside."

"I don't know, Elera," Reo mulled, stroking his face. "I don't feel right."

"Okay, Reo, it's up to you, but I've come too far to stop now," she said, walking directly ahead. "You can set up a camp here." She smiled at him, realising the enormity of the expeditions that they had been on together. "Maybe our cat friend will come and visit you."

Sita, Rama, Bene and Rekesh followed Elera without hesitation, whilst Teltu and Javu attempted to talk Reo around. He was confused and felt like he needed time to think about everything that had happened. As everyone set off at the edge of the forest, a great feeling of loyalty overcame Reo and his thoughts cleared.

"Wait for me!" he shouted as he ran towards everyone. Elera dropped back with smile and waited for him, giving him a big hug.

As Teltu and Javu walked into the depths of the humid jungle, they began to discuss the concept of the four elements, which Teltu had been unclear about since he had first heard the theory.

"A sorcerer is aware of the elements and how they relate to his own nature," Javu told him.

"I understand that each element has a different pattern of energy, but I still don't see how that changes how a person is or how they behave," Teltu deliberated, twiddling one of his sleeves. "I mean, isn't every person different and unique?"

"Indeed they are," Javu agreed. "The element that one has an affinity with only *influences* how a person is and knowing about it can help that person. Let us take for example the scenario of one becoming upset at the actions of another person. How would you deal with such an emotion, Teltu?"

Teltu thought for a while as they walked, trying to remember the last time he had felt upset and how he had gotten past it. "Well, I usually need to spend some time alone to think it through and then my upset passes."

"Exactly!" Javu said. "You need to think to yourself. I too am best suited to thinking about my problems internally and I often go quite crazy if I do not have adequate time to ponder." Javu chuckled to himself at the notion. "However, this technique is not the best way for everyone to deal with negative emotions. Someone of the *fire* also likes to *think* about his or her problems, but they are better suited to doing it externally, to talk about them. This is just like the energy of fire, spreading itself out externally. You see Reo, he never stops talking!"

This time both of them burst out laughing, especially as Reo looked quite funny ahead in his makeshift clothes.

"What about water and earth?" Teltu asked.

"Someone of the water, like Elera, also needs time for themselves just like you and I to deal with their problems, however *thinking* about one's emotions tends not to be as effective as *feeling* them to get to the bottom of a problem. Someone of the earth also has a preference to feel, but they show it externally."

He paused, as the path ahead got darker.

"Of course as you said, everyone is unique, but those techniques are generally best suited to those energy types. All of us can think and feel and all of us can be an extrovert or an introvert. However, by being aware of one's energy type, one can more easily learn to tame one's emotions. And that, Teltu, is one of the great challenges of a sorcerer."

"But didn't you just say that people with earth-type energy are best suited to showing their feeling externally? That's not exactly taming one's emotions, is it?"

Javu was amused at Teltu's savvy and had to chuckle to himself before replying.

"But it is, Teltu. If someone like Bene or Rekesh showed their emotions more often, then it would be better for them. The pulsing nature of earth energy can cause great build-ups so if one doesn't vent their feelings, there can be explosions later on down the line. Of course, this is probably true of all of us, but even more so for earth energy."

They walked on silently for a while as the cover of the organic surroundings became more and more apparent, demanding the attention of everyone who passed through.

"It is like we are covered by a great roof of leaves," Bene commented to Elera, Rekesh and Reo whilst he looked up. "The branches are so thick, like great pillars."

"I feel that this may be one of the oldest forests on the planet," Elera said.

They walked along an open pathway where the trees were spaced quite widely apart. There were giant pieces of ruby-coloured fruit hanging from some of the trees high above, the likes of which nobody could identify.

The bark of many of the trees seemed to shimmer with a golden glow and the ground was covered with so many species of flowers and grass that it was mesmerising to glance down.

Above, the thick branches that Bene had alluded to crisscrossed like the purest form of grand architecture anyone had ever seen. Birds and other animals could be heard above.

"Do you think there is anything dangerous up there?" Reo asked Rekesh.

"Probably, but it would take them a while to reach the ground."

Light filtered down through wide gaps between trees, which looked like spotlights on certain parts of the forest floor. As they walked further and further in, Elera began to automatically see things in terms of their energy.

She came to the largest group of toadstools that she could have possibly imagined, some of them twice as tall as she was. "You could sleep under these," she mused, looking at them. "Their energy seems so dormant, only now and again giving off a slow vibe."

Looking around, the entirety of the jungle seemed similar, emitting a slow pulsing and sizzling energy, which felt like every inch was slowly cooking.

She sensed something above and spotted a soaring blob of energy gliding within the treetops, burning brightly and ferociously. She wanted to see what she had seen in normal vision and her energy view instantly faded away revealing a large bird flying high above. It had pure black feathers and an orange beak with yellow and red feathers coming out of its head.

"Look up there," she said to everyone, pointing at the bird. "Its energy is like the strongest of fires."

The bird came to rest on a branch high up in the distance.

Bene got out his spotting scope, looked at the bird through it and then passed it around for everyone else to see.

"There have been many myths of a bird that is enshrouded in fire, such as the phoenix," Javu noted. "I wonder if those myths originated from people who could see such a bird's fiery energy."

The group continued on, led only by Elera's intuition. She could feel an incredible excitement about the place and instinctively knew that the entire forest had a great affinity to the essence, probably growing on top of a bed of wisdom rocks. She began to think about the fourth and final pyramid temple and was sure it was in the region.

"It seems to be getting more humid," Teltu said, noticing that his shirt was damp. Indeed, many more large and exotic flowers were growing in abundance all around, a common sign of increasing moisture.

"It was just like this when we disguised ourselves as Raiceman soldiers in Lizrab, huh, Bene?" Reo said with fondness, to which Bene nodded with a smile. How far they had all come since then, he thought to himself.

Whilst everyone began to peel off their sticky clothes, except Reo who seemed to be perfectly dressed for the environment, Elera suddenly had a strong sense that something important was close by. She stopped and closed her eyes, trying to feel what it was she had detected. She turned to the left, knowing they should head that way.

"This way!" she said, breaking into a jog at the anticipation of her discovery. She quickly left the others behind and became entangled in the thick, hot moist undergrowth with great drops of water running onto her face and body from the waxy leaves above.

After quite a struggle, she suddenly broke through into an open space and tripped forward to her knees. As she looked up, she was astounded at what she saw.

In front of her was a circular stone platform, with eight solid stone chairs arranged perfectly on top of it. The chairs had all been carved out of the same giant piece of stone, which also seemed to be deeply embedded into the earth.

"What is this?" she whispered to herself.

She slowly rose to her feet and walked over to the structure, gently placing her hand on one of the seats. She could feel a constant and encircling energy flowing through the cool smooth stone. She climbed onto the platform and started to examine it, noticing there was a straight groove running from each chair into the centre of the circular platform. There was also a small disc-shaped groove perfectly positioned in the centre, the culmination of the lines running from the chairs. As she traced the lines with her finger, she heard the others emerge from the bushes.

"Hey, stop pushing me!" Reo was saying as he tumbled out into the clearing. Rama, Sita and everyone else appeared shortly after.

"Wow!" Reo said as he laid eyes on the seated platform.

Everyone approached it with intrigue and gathered around. Reo jumped up onto it and sat in one of the seats, breathing out a huge sigh.

"This is great. This jungle actually has somewhere to sit besides the floor."

"Get up off there, Reo," Elera scolded him, still examining the structure. He withdrew to the forest floor with a little disappointment. "I am trying to find out why this is here," she said.

The platform reminded Javu of something and he rummaged around in his bag for the stone that they had taken from the statue earlier. "Elera, I think this stone has something to do with it. There are eight circles inscribed here. Maybe they represent each of the eight seats."

She took the stone from Javu and had a look at it again.

"I think you're right," she said placing the stone in the slot in the centre of the platform. It fitted perfectly but nothing happened. "Where's the box it was in?"

Javu handed it to her and she opened it, looking at the inscription inside. She still could not understand what it said, though the symbols looked more familiar. She got down from the platform and walked around it, looking at the backs of the stone seats. She noticed that a small symbol had been etched into each one.

"I think each of us is supposed to sit in a seat," Elera said after a while.

"Oh, now I can sit in a seat!" Reo said sarcastically, getting back to his feet.

"Not just any seat," she told him, putting her hand up. "I have to work out what these symbols mean."

She walked around the platform again, looking at each of the symbols. "I think this one means *mountain*," she said, stopping at one of them.

"Is that like before?" Teltu asked. "When you had to tell us what our energy looked like?"

"Bene, why don't you come and sit here?" Elera asked him. She continued to read the symbols whilst he sat in the chair. She stopped at another. "I have seen this symbol before. It means a *flurry*."

"A flurry like a gust of wind?" Javu prompted her.

"I think so."

"Then that must be me!" he said, walking over to the chair and sitting in it.

The next symbol reminded her of something, but she could not put her finger on what. It almost made her feel homesick, so she quickly moved on to the next chair.

"This one means *candle*," she said, growing in insight. "Rama, can you sit here?"

She also understood the symbol of the next chair almost immediately. "And this one is *ocean* so this is your chair, Sita," she said, moving onto the next and also understanding it straight away. She was almost in a trance-like state, working on instinct. "And this one means *breeze* so this is your chair, Teltu."

Only Reo and Rekesh were left standing at the edge of the platform. Elera had never seen the symbol on the next seat, yet its meaning quickly came to her.

"I think this one means *blaze*."

"So that would be Reo then," Javu said jovially.

Reo quickly took his seat. Now all that remained were two seats.

"Only our seats left, Rekesh," she said to him with a smile, but he did not smile back. A look of worry spread across his face as she began to examine the only chair she hadn't looked at.

"This means *volcano*," she said, sure that Rekesh's energy matched that denotation.

Rekesh said nothing but slowly walked over to his chair. Elera got back onto the platform and before she sat in the one remaining seat, she suddenly realised what the nostalgic symbol on the back of the chair meant.

"What did your chair say, Elera?" Bene asked her.

"It says *waterfall*."

With everyone sat in their respective seats, they began to wonder what the purpose of the platform was and how it could be possible that the eight of them had come together to be a perfect fit for the strange podium.

"I guess grandfather was right, huh?" Bene said. "He said we would create a balance. Maybe this is it. It seems like we're all supposed to be here."

"Remember he said that the planet would change?" Reo said, surprising everyone with his sharp memory.

"I think he was right, Reo," Javu said. "It's inevitable that a change will occur and the balance that we all represent is desperately needed by this planet. Things are extremely polarised at the moment and they have been for a long time. With empires like Raicema and Lengard bewitched with power, we have seen much destruction and poverty. A change has to happen. The world is not right."

"Do you think that the change will have something to do with the entities?" Teltu asked Elera, who wasn't quite sure what he was talking about. "Will we stop looking at our shadows on the wall?"

Javu chuckled a little and explained.

"He means will people become free?"

"I am sure of it," she said knowingly.

"So are we supposed to do here?" Reo asked, looking at the stone in the middle of the platform. "Will another tree grow out of this thing?"

"I doubt it," Javu alleged. "But I presume that our energies will flow into that stone in the middle."

"So why is nothing happening?" Bene wondered.

"There must be a way to summon the energy. Elera, what did the inscription in the box say?"

"I don't know," she said truthfully.

"Maybe the stone is not in the slot properly."

Elera knelt down next to it and noticed that the eight circles engraved into the stone were not lined up with the lines coming from the chairs. She twisted it slightly in its slot and as the circles all lined up, she felt an overwhelming pressure build up beneath her. Looking down, she could see what looked like a well of greenish energy through the platform on which she stood. It was gentle, swirling and rising like a great bubbling fountain.

"It's started," she said, looking up at everyone. Her vision had completely changed and she could see the energy of everything around her – every person that was sitting down, the trees and sky and even the stone platform, which looked like a great sizzling chalice.

Each person looked bigger, like their energy had projected itself upwards and outwards. As she sat back in her chair, she saw the energies of everyone flowing down the channels towards the stone in the centre.

In a surreal moment as the stone began to glow intensely white from the combination of flows it was absorbing, a great beam of energy shot directly upwards into the sky, creating a ring in the atmosphere where it penetrated.

The beam was so bright that it almost blinded everyone and nobody could move.

At that moment, Elera impulsively knew what the inscription said on the box the stone had come in. The meaning seemed to come to her out of nowhere. She looked at each of her friends and tears welled in her eyes.

"The meaning is *home*."

Everything she had searched for had come to this point and she had only just realised it. She slowly and weakly got to her feet, trembling as she took a few steps towards the beam.

"Remember me," she said softly to everyone. "I love you all."

Then she walked into the beam and vanished.

Chapter 44 – The Moon Goddess

"I had this recurring dream as a child. I was asleep in bed but as I woke up to look out of the curtains, there was a giant eye looking in at me, a giant dragon standing and looking in through the window at me asleep. I have never forgotten the dream."

Javu was telling someone this, when he heard a strange sound coming from the sky. He looked up and saw stars. They looked unnatural. Some were gigantic, a distant belt of them filling half of the sky, which looked like a thick line of silver dust.

It was a world both familiar and alien.

"I also have this other dream," Javu felt himself say without emotion. "It is of the skies filled with machines, watching over us. Creation gone blind."

"The first dream is of the past, the second is of the future," the someone who was standing next to him said. Javu could not turn to see the figure, but he didn't feel the need to either.

"Does it have to be that way?"

"It has been that way many times before."

"Will it be that way forever?"

"Are you asking how to end the cycle?"

"The cycle of what?"

"The wheel of power and freedom. It is timeless, the place of the third dream."

"The third dream?"

"I will show you."

The world faded and was instantly replaced with another.

The sky was black and this time, the stars looked much more familiar.

Javu felt something beneath him.

The surface Javu was standing on was very hard. It was so hard, that it actually hurt his feet. He looked down to see grey dust. He tried to look out into the distance, but couldn't focus his vision properly.

He could feel an intense vibration, sharp and continuous. It resonated through his feet all the way up to his teeth. He quickly realised there was something underneath the surface he was standing on.

He heard a faint whisper.

A slight fear wavered through him and he looked to the left uncontrollably. He saw the most beautiful sight, the blue and greens of the earth, a sharp sphere so perfect. The fear was blown away instantly.

"What you are about to see will change you." The familiar voice spoke again. It was the voice of the thoughts in his head, the voice of a guardian.

Javu turned around to the right to see a pyramid. It was so shiny that it reflected the stars perfectly, almost hiding it. As Javu moved his eyes, he saw that the pyramid was coated in perfectly smooth silvery material. He looked at it from a distance for a while. The next thing he knew, he was standing at the foot of the great structure.

"The agents of power are close. We are approaching a culmination."

He looked up and saw the greatest mirrored slope he could possibly comprehend. It did not seem to end, a diagonal road into the cosmos. He dropped his head, looking straight ahead.

In the shadows, there was an open door. He walked towards it slowly. Inside, two people were talking. They did not seem to see or hear Javu.

One person was tall and wore a grey robe with a large hood. The other person was a man who seemed familiar. The man didn't seem to be wearing any clothes, but Javu could not look at his body directly. He was finding it hard enough to focus on his face.

"Everything is in place," the man was saying. "When *they* appear, I want to be by your side?"

There was a pleading in the man's voice, a submissive cry for a warped affection and protection.

"You will be here when it happens."

The robed person had a penetrating voice; a sharp echoing voice;

a mesmerising voice. Javu quickly detected a female presence beneath the robe.

The man seemed infatuated with her and Javu himself felt captivated by the piercing tones that still seemed to linger in the air.

"You will join with us."

The woman dropped her robe revealing a strong yet slender body and a strikingly beautiful face. Javu could not focus clearly on either person in front of him but the woman seemed much taller and her body seemed more solid. The man seemed to be in a state of passionate obsession.

"Open your eyes." The same reassuring voice spoke to Javu.

Javu blinked and then the two people in front of him became crystal clear.

The man was Sadana Siger, the tyrant leader that Javu knew well. As Javu looked at the woman, he was horrified to see that his previous perception of a beautiful young woman had now transformed into a hideous giant crone of a woman with a bony spine protruding out like a bow.

Sadana was still mesmerised but Javu had been jolted into a state of pure terror.

"She is Morbis, goddess of the moon, queen and ruler of the air. She is an adept illusionist. Look carefully."

This time when Javu looked at the strange being in front of him, she looked larger and had silvery wings. He glimpsed her face from the side and noticed she had a sharp, curved beak and translucent skin. Her feet and hands had turned to claws.

"She is the owl woman, known by many names throughout time; Morbis, Isis, Luna, Selene, Diana. A thousand names exist for this woman."

Javu was now highly aware of his environment.

He realised that he was standing in a regal chamber and he noticed scores of circular tunnels running out of the strange pyramidal hall.

"This woman is responsible for manipulating many wars on your

planet..." the voice told him, "*...but she is not the only one.*"

Javu realised at that moment with certainty that the earth had served as a battleground to many different beings in the universe.

"I have chosen the one to be sacrificed," Sadana said to Morbis.

"*It must suffer like never before. Only then can they reach your world.*"

There was an eerie back-tone that almost screeched to life.

Who are they? Javu thought.

The guiding voice told him instantly.

"*She speaks of the children of power, Diabolus, the earth reaper, Murdrak, the water dragon and Ignis, the fire dragon. Only with them can her ambitions be realised.*"

Javu just looked out at the being. He could see her eye. It did not shine. There was no light.

"*I saw him. I followed him.*"

Javu now got the strong sensation that Morbis was talking about somebody he knew, somebody he greatly cared about.

"*He will fight. I know it. He must die. You must kill him and retrieve the stone.*"

Javu now became aware of his own being. He remembered the air stone around his neck. He looked down and it was glowing. It was shining. He looked back up at Morbis and Sadana. They had noticed something. Morbis was now looking directly at him and Javu froze with raw fear.

The face of Morbis was bony and round like an owl. Her eyes were two spheres of darkness. Her silver beak looked razor sharp.

"*The stone penetrates her world. She sees you. We must go.*"

The next thing Javu knew, he was suspended in the air, the black vacuum of space surrounding him. He looked right. He saw the earth with a halo of light perfectly surrounding it. It was the sun, wholly behind the beautiful planet.

Then he looked left. He saw the moon. He realised that he had just been there, standing on its surface, watching another realm of existence.

"*The moon is in opposition to the sun.*"

Javu could see that in regards to the earth, the sun and moon were at 180 degrees in angle.

"Today, we move from earth to air. It is an emotional time for many. It is the hunter's moon."

Javu was in a state of suspension, listening to his guardian with affection.

"You saw the true form of Morbis because of this day. When you awake, you must not forget what you have seen and heard."

Javu looked at the moon once more, its light so cooling and hypnotising. He saw the surface clearly, with specific points all connected like a great web of electricity. It was beautiful.

He suddenly felt very emotional, like he might cry at any moment.

"It reminds you of a child. A child that never lived."

Then he blinked and he was awake.

Chapter 45 – A Union of Power

Jen King was locked in the brig of the *Stryder* war vessel.

He was down in the lower deck and the roar of the engines close by vibrated the thick metal bars he was sitting against.

Jen kept gripping the bars, almost believing he was in a bad dream from which he would soon awake. He pinched himself hard but did not wake up.

This is my reality, he thought.

A single guard was his only company, sitting on a solid metal bench just outside of his cell. Jen knew the guard. In fact, he had lived in an encampment with him several years earlier when they were on a mission together.

"Why'd you have to cause trouble, King?" Billy, the guard, said to him after a while. "None of the boys can believe how much you've changed."

Jen sat silently on the hard concrete floor, not sure what to say. On one hand he felt a loyalty to the men that he had spent so many years with, but on the other hand he couldn't wait to be away from them all, almost feeling pity for their lack of independence.

The flicker of a dim electric light in the brig created a gloomy and barren atmosphere. Only the smell of the wrought iron was mellow and soothing.

"I've had enough, Billy," Jen said after a while. "I won't do what they tell me to anymore."

Billy seemed surprised at Jen's rebellious attitude. "And it's better to be locked in a cell for treason?"

Once again, Jen said nothing.

They both sat in silence for a while.

"Besides," Billy said. "What would you do if you didn't work for the force? You're good at it, respected by everyone. Why'd you want to throw that away?"

"What good is being respected by those around you if you can't even respect yourself?"

After several more moments of silence, the sound of someone coming down the stairway to the brig could be heard, a resonant drum of heavy boots against solid metal.

Seth appeared in the doorway, the shadows of the prison giving prominence to the deep-set wrinkles in his forehead. He was wearing a traditional naval uniform encrusted with jewels with a shiny breastplate.

"It pains me greatly to see you in there," Seth said indifferently, making it hard to tell whether he was being genuine or not.

Jen looked up, his black tangled hair hanging in his eyes and his thick stubble rubbing against his shoulder. He got the sudden feeling that he was like a caged animal, on display for public amusement. The notion angered him and he sprung to his feet, grabbing the bars ahead and pressing his forehead up against them.

"If you think I'm going to go back to my 'old self' then you've got another thing coming!" Jen barked, shocking Seth.

Seth's face screwed up with disappointment and disbelief before turning into a vicious frown. "You will have no more chances," he declared with authority. "Once we have concluded our business in Neoasia, we will return to Tyrona where you will be tried."

Seth turned and promptly climbed the stairs. He looked back at Jen with pity. "My brother was right about you." Then he continued upwards, his short cape whipping against the side of the door as he left.

"Are you crazy?" Billy said to him once Seth had disappeared above decks. "You just gave yourself a death sentence!"

Jen slumped back down along the cold metal bars and closed his eyes. He did not know what the future held for him nor did he care. He felt a raw instinctive urge to survive.

"Billy?" Jen said quietly.

"What?" he replied with annoyance.

"What is the name of the city that we are going to?"

"It's called Yinkoto. It's the capital of Neoasia."

"Have you been there before?"

"No, but I heard that it's a pretty huge city, almost the same size as Raicema City. I heard one of the boys say that almost a third of the population of Neoasia lives there."

Once again, the same awareness of being trapped came over him and he felt a sudden desire to try and break out of his prison. His newfound ambition to escape got stronger and stronger as the sound of the droning engines seemed to get louder and louder.

He imagined overpowering Billy and hiding out on the ship until they reached Yinkoto, but the idea of resorting to violence left a feeling of dread in his stomach. After some deliberation, he decided to cooperate with his captors and he prayed that he would be able to get off the ship later.

After what seemed like hours of thought, his mind swirled into a troubled sleep.

That night, Jen had a strange dream. He seemed to awake in what looked like the Reik Institute of Raicema City. He began searching the hallways for someone yet he couldn't remember who he was looking for. Whilst he was looking, he heard something echoing along the corridors. It was the sound of a baby crying.

He followed the sound, but every room he came to was empty, only filled with books and maps. After a while of searching, he came to a round atrium where he found a small, helpless infant who was lying on a straw mat and crying inconsolably.

Jen looked at the child, its eyes wide and watery. He picked her up in his arms and the noise stopped, great warmth flowing from the tiny being.

Walking back down one of the institute's corridors with the child in his arms, he came across an unusual-looking creature wandering around the hallways. It looked like a miniature gorilla, about the height of Jen's ankle. It turned to face him as he walked towards it and its face was human-like and had an expression of patience.

"So you have found her?" the creature said to Jen.

"Yes," Jen found himself saying back.

"Take good care of her."

"I will," Jen said with the utmost sincerity.

Then, the creature and his surroundings faded away and he awoke from his slumber with a hazy head and an aching jaw from where he had been leaning against the cold iron bars of his cell. He looked down into his arms but the baby was gone. He felt quite upset.

"Get up, King!" somebody was saying to him aggressively as he came round to his harsh reality.

As his vision came into focus, he saw that another soldier had replaced Billy. He had a shaved head and a bulging neck. Jen had never seen him before.

"You have been ordered to the top deck. Stand up so I can bind your hands."

Jen noticed that the soldier had a pistol in his hand and he was pointing it belligerently at his stomach. He slowly got to his feet and remembering his conclusion from the night before, he allowed the soldier to forcefully tie his hands behind him with a metal chain, which was then locked tightly. His cell door was opened and as Jen walked through it, he was pushed violently against one of the metal walls, the end of the pistol shoved into the small of his back.

"Now march!"

Jen was directed upstairs and along the narrow passageways of the lower decks until they reached one of the ship's elevators. It sped upwards through ten decks, opening at another passageway that led to the top deck's landing area, where troops were usually arranged into battalions.

As he walked through one of the heavy iron doors and was bathed in bright daylight, a feeling of relief came over him.

There were several hundred men lined up on the huge spotless deck and several commanders were directing many more.

Jen was pushed forward towards a group of ten or so men by his captor.

The brigadier instantly noticed his arrival and quickly walked over to him. "Look at you, King. You're pitiful!" he said slyly, looking him up and down with disgust. "I never understood what President Seth Tyrone saw in you in the first place. The old president knew you were an untrustworthy piece of garbage!"

Jen said nothing, though a rage was building in his chest.

His silence only provoked the brigadier more, who was known to be a ruthless and unrelenting leader of the troops he commanded. "Do you know what is going to happen to you, King? Do you?" he snarled, his oversized top lip quivering with excitement. "You are to be paraded as the traitor that you are in front of the emperor, as an example of how we do not tolerate weakness. Then you will be executed! Gone forever!"

The brigadier looked like he might burst at the notion, his eyes bulging out with the ferocity of what he was saying.

Jen, however, was not listening anymore to the continuing rant. The news that he would be travelling into Yinkoto had given him the chance he had hoped for.

As the brigadier continued to shout abuse at Jen and began to prod him painfully in the shoulder, Seth arrived on the scene and called for everyone to stand to attention. "Only twenty of us will leave this ship when we dock in Yinkoto," he announced. "It is imperative that the Neoasian's feel no threat from us."

The announcement came as positive news to Jen.

The coast of Neoasia could be seen in the far distance, the skyline of Yinkoto looking like a million jagged little peaks tightly packed together. Jen realised that everyone on the ship was at a pivotal point in their lives. The reality that they were appealing to an equally developed and powerful nation for their own survival was becoming more and more apparent.

Jen thought about just how much the world was changing. He remembered when he was a boy in Tyrona, thinking how it was so one-sided that Raicema dominated everything on the planet and that nobody would ever be able to stand up against them. Now he realised just how much of a small fish Raicema was.

It was becoming more and more apparent that Raicema had

always relied on bigger and older nations like Lengard to fulfil their ambitions and now they had lost their benefactor, they quickly needed a new one for protection.

The desperation of the appeal made Jen feel anxious and forget about his own situation. Part of him wanted to warn Seth that it could all go horribly wrong, though deep inside, he knew it was too late to change the direction that Raicema was heading in.

It took several hours for the great Raiceman war vessel to dock in the technology-laden port of Yinkoto. Robots adorned every surface, recording everything and issuing commands constantly.

After a total of fourteen checkpoints that Seth and his entourage had to pass through, Jen finally laid his eyes on a pinnacle of modern construction.

The city was a marvel. The buildings rose so high into the sky and were so close together that they made Jen feel nauseous. The walking space was one-way single file and while Seth led with his guide, Jen contemplated his escape.

Behind him were twenty men, at one time his comrades and now in the space of only a few days, his aggressors. The thought of resorting to combat as part of his escape only added to his nausea. He decided to bide his time, somehow sure that an opportunity would present itself to flee.

At the ground level of Yinkoto, row after row of machines were embedded in the building walls, like lines of soldiers. Each stood in a small alcove just big enough to stand away from the two single lines of commuters, following each other methodically like ants around a maze.

Jen counted ten different types of machine as he plodded along. There was one for money, several for food, an odd-shaped machine used for tooth repairs, several other health-oriented machines and a body-shaped machine that Jen could only fathom was for enter-tainment purposes. The world at this level seemed superficial and empty, a stopgap to the city dweller's life above.

Jen had believed Raicema City to be the most advanced city on the planet, but Yinkoto was beginning to surpass it on every level. The guide who was leading mumbled something about the complicated lift system and how they had to use the correct entrance. They soon arrived in a more open space, with queue after queue for different giant lifts, all arranged in a circular pattern. The ends of the queues all met in the centre of the circus, to which Jen envisaged must look like a star of people from above.

They joined one queue and Jen quickly contemplated switching to another at the last moment. However, his idea was swiftly quashed when he felt a gun pointing in the middle of his back. His wrists hurt from the tight metal chains.

The lifts were rapid, the people within a blur as they sped upwards to varying levels. Looking up, a small circle of light could be seen in between the distant tops of the buildings. The lift they were waiting for quickly returned. Made of a glasslike substance and projecting a virtual image of the building plan, the entourage entered one of the lifts, big enough for a hundred people.

The lift shot towards the sky without any instruction. It stopped at three other floors before speeding up to what felt like the top of the building. It came to a halt and the doors opened. The guide took Seth to one side as the guards urged Jen out of the lift.

"I cannot pass through the next tunnel, but follow it and you will reach Emperor Gueken's international office," the guide was saying. "You will be greeted there and will be taken to see the emperor."

Seth signalled to the guards to follow him, completely ignoring Jen's presence. They all began walking down a long white oval-shaped tunnel, the sound of the men's heavy boots sounding like rolling thunder. Before long, they had reached a metallic door and it slid open as they approached. Jen noticed an array of cameras and firearms mounted around the door, reminding him of Raicema City.

They walked into a palatial office, decorated in entirety in a marble-like blue stone. The high roof had multiple skylights, with a plethora of information displayed on giant holographic screens from top to bottom of the back wall.

There was layer upon layer of video footage of the streets and entrances in Yinkoto, coming out of the wall like floating stacks of paper. There were also holographic statues coming out of the walls, which looked like effigies of old leaders of Neoasia.

There were many intricately carved stone desks with stern-looking figures sitting behind them, monitoring embedded circular screens.

An aide dressed in a formal uniform approached and greeted Seth only, ushering him towards some large doors to the left of the great atrium. As Seth signalled to his security to follow his steps, the aide quickly explained that only he could continue from this point on and that his men would have to wait in another atrium until he returned.

Then Jen overheard the aid say something very strange. "Please bring your prisoner with you," he told Seth, looking towards Jen.

The president of Raicema was visibly surprised.

"This man is a traitor and I will make an example out of him," Seth told the aide. "But my men must pass through too."

"No, just you and the prisoner."

"Why?" Seth replied quite aggressively. "This man is a criminal. He should be under the guard of my finest men at all times."

"I ensure you that any false move on his part will result in instant death," the aide reassured Seth calmly. "Emperor Gueken wishes to see Mr King."

Seth was distressed at this request, as he had not informed anyone in Yinkoto that Jen was coming. He had no choice but to agree.

Seth signalled to the guards to release Jen from their watchful eyes. Jen moved forward to where Seth and the aide were standing, holding his breath with the uncertainty of his future. He felt anxious and for the first time, he actually cared about his own welfare.

"Very few pass through these doors," the aide commented as he placed his entire face into a head-shaped electronic scanner. A fast whooshing sound was heard followed by a reassuring mellow beep.

Seth was next, yet after his reading a more high-pitched sound could be heard, surely a warning.

Finally, Jen placed his face in the carved slot and was greeted with the same reassuring beep the aide had heard. Seth was unnerved, acknowledging for the first time that he was completely at the mercy of forces greater than he had acknowledged, a place he never thought he'd be.

They passed through the door of limited access into a hallway beyond. A wonderful thought suddenly came into Jen's head. It was a memory of his mother. It presented itself as a wonderful vision of loving dedication.

The scene was of a truly beautiful woman wandering aimlessly through barren woodland and carrying a young baby. She stopped regularly to gather nourishment from the hardy bushes and hidden roots.

She kissed her son often and Jen saw a depiction of pure strength and love that she sent him with every move she made. It appeared to him as a wispy yet airy light aura, surrounding the cheerful baby.

Jen realised he had noticed something then, though so new to the planet, that which he had forgotten now.

The scene shifted to a bed of fluffy leaves, a gift of dedicated gathering, which both he and his mother lay upon in peace until the purity of daybreak soothed their eyes open. The memory caused tears to form in Jen's eyes, yet fortune had granted him a reprieve from the watchful glare of Seth or the aide and they did not see him become emotional.

Within a short moment, the vision had ended.

Jen felt different, like he'd just woken up to something. A sharp sensation that death may be near jolted him into resolute awareness.

"We have arrived," the aide said as they reached the end of the hallway. "Say nothing nor look at nothing but the ground. To do otherwise is a great insult."

They walked through the tallest solid wood doors that Jen had ever seen, opened by two overly dressed doormen.

Beyond was the epitome of human craftsmanship.

A river was running through the most lavish of hallways, the entirety of it made of green jade, purple amethyst and a variety of other sparking crystal slabs.

The place shone in a powerful, overwhelming way and even the flowing water seemed to be charged with energy. The roof was completely transparent and Jen struggled to see what it was made of, as only the tranquil blue sky could be seen.

"The emperor is outside," the aide said to Seth, guiding them both over a small bridge in the hall towards a large open archway that led outside. Nothing could prepare Jen for the sight that he was about to witness.

Outside, Seth and Jen walked out into a spacious and exotic roof garden, stretching wide and long across the entirety of the building. It was the largest garden Jen had ever seen.

Every other roof in the Neoasian capital also had a cultivated roof garden. In some cases they looked like thick forests.

From the top of Yinkoto, the world looked perfectly natural, as if this were the ground that once existed. Jen almost forgot that beneath this fragmented dale of foliage was a beehive of modern technology and architecture. In the distance, an elaborate terrace housed a magnificent pergola, in which a man in a jewelled robe was sitting quietly.

"Bow your head as we approach the emperor," the aide warned as they walked in the direction of the pergola. Jen could not believe the different species growing in the gardens. Some of the flowers were as large as his head.

The structure was painted with black oily paint. It glistened in the sunlight. The aide signalled for them to bow.

They both followed the instructions, Jen noting that the emperor's shoes were made of gold thread and rested on the fur of a dead mountain leopard.

Jen stole a glance up at Gueken's face as they stood before him. It was stern and home to a hundred wrinkles and a heavily oiled black beard. There was no hair on his head and his eyes were so dark that it looked like they were black marbles, snaked with fine red blood vessels.

"Sit," he commanded rudely.

The aide quickly gestured for them to copy him, sitting on their heels, hands lying flat on their knees.

"You have come from the other side of the globe and with few men, Mr Tyrone. You surely cannot be attempting an invasion?"

He laughed strangely, almost cackling in a high-pitched manner.

"No, Emperor," Seth replied, looking up at the perched, regal man, much to the dismay of the aide who tried to indicate frantically to him to look at the floor.

"I come to seek reconciliation with you and your government over recent events in Lengard," Seth continued, completely dismissing the aide's warning. "It has come to my attention that sects of the Makai operating within your nation launched an attack on the Lengardian palace with the help of Raiceman soldiers and equipment. These men were not authorised by Raicema for such attacks and I have word that Lengard are to enter into a conflict with both Neoasia and Raicema imminently."

The emperor listened, almost smiling.

"I appeal to you to create a union with us against any oppression from the Makai. If we unite, I am sure Lengard will withdraw their declaration of war."

There was silence for a few moments before the emperor slowly rose to his feet. He walked towards a terraced area, laden with colourful flower patches, twirling his moustache in an influential and calculated manner.

"What benefit could an alliance with Raicema possibly have for Neoasia?" Gueken said, more to himself than to his visitors.

"Lengard's king is dead. The country wants vengeance. Your nation will be ravaged if they launch an assault on the Makai here. We can stop them from attacking by ridding Neoasia of the Makai here and in Lizrab."

This statement made Gueken laugh hysterically, echoing and frightening in his tone.

"You wish us to save you from your failures, and your brother's failures."

"N-no." Seth began to stutter, sensing Gueken's pity.

"You have failed in Lizrab and you have failed in Raicema," Gueken continued coldly. "You come here asking me to start a war."

The emperor paused and glanced at Seth with eyes that seemed to be devoid of any emotion.

"You ask me to start a war when there is no need for one. And as for the King of Lengard, he is very much alive..."

Gueken signalled to the aide and he ran off, leaving Seth and Jen watching in anticipation. Seth couldn't believe his eyes as the aide quickly returned followed by a very healthy-looking King Constynce of Lengard. He looked smug, like a child who had successfully pulled off a naughty prank.

"But... They told me you were dead," Seth stammered realising the wool had been pulled far over his clouded eyes. "Everyone thinks you are dead."

"Constynce and I decided a long time ago that to succeed in this changing world you must embrace those that are strong," Gueken said. "Raicema became weak a long time ago, untrustworthy, backstabbers that have forgotten their place, forgotten who made them. Your own brother supplied weapons and men to the Makai in this great nation behind our backs!"

Gueken now seemed angry and Jen suddenly became aware of the number of armed soldiers in surround. "He supplied weapons and men that were used to attack your closest benefactor. Those responsible for giving you power in the first place were disregarded in your plans. Your brother made a secret pact with the Raiceman and Neoasian Makai to overthrow Lengard and Neoasia. He actually believed he could rule it all."

Emperor Gueken laughed like a crazed bird at this notion. "Unfortunately for him, we already had the same plan hundreds of years ago."

In total shock, Seth's jaw dropped when he saw who was walking out from beneath a shaded pavilion only a few paces away. It was Yangjam, leader of the Neoasian Makai. He had aged skin lassoed around his frame as he walked towards them in a slow, calm manner. Jen had never seen any of these men before, yet he sensed that both he and Seth were in a very tricky situation.

"But why?" Seth yelped at Yangjam, delirious in his imminent downfall.

"It is quite simple," Yangjam said, stopping Seth in his tracks. "It is an illusion that you ever held power over anything. There are forces at work deciding your fate."

Jen felt distressed and prayed that he would walk away from this situation alive. He knew little about the politics of the nations, but he was certain that a great change had occurred that had spelled the end for Raicema. He knew he had to speak up if there was any chance of escaping the hideous situation.

"Emperor Gueken, I was brought here as a prisoner, a once-loyal soldier to Raicema," Jen began, surprised that all heads turned as he spoke. "I appeal to you to free me. I wish no harm on any of your nations. I simply wish to be set free."

Yangjam walked up to Jen and observed him shrewdly.

"You are the soldier that everyone fears!" he declared finally after many moments of inspection.

"I am not a soldier anymore," Jen replied firmly. "Why did you bring me here? Where are the others?"

"The others have been executed," Gueken said coldly, sending a condemned shiver down Seth Tyrone's spine. "Your ship is burning as we speak."

Anger welled in Jen's chest at this news. Their blinded leader had led his comrades and friends to their death.

"You were brought here to answer one question only. Where do your loyalties lie? Are you loyal to *him*?"

Jen did not know what Gueken was talking about and he could

not think. His mind had gone blank. He was sick from the news that those we once spent so much time with were now gone, their lives disregarded. He began to feel faint.

"Are you loyal to *him*?" Gueken repeated. "Is that why you have revoked your life as a soldier? We know you have seen *him*."

"I am loyal to nobody," Jen said dejectedly with a weight around his heart. "And I don't know who you are talking about."

Gueken's shifty eyes gleamed with an unnatural amusement.

"We have all heard of your capabilities and we think you can be of help to us," Constynce suddenly said. "You have something we want."

"Hah!" Seth sneered, his resentment getting the better of him. "This man is spent. He can no longer give you what you want. He cannot summon *the demon*."

"You are a fool, Tyrone! Just like your brother," Yangjam said snidely, infuriating Seth who almost got to his feet before noticing that armed militants surrounded the walls of the roof garden. "You make it sound so simple."

Jen did not know what the two men were talking about, yet before he could contemplate another thought, Gueken had signalled to a militant and a gun was pointed at Seth.

The sound of the hammer clicked back.

"Every nation on earth has suffered because of Raicema's actions," Yangjam said in a condemning way. "This world has become polarised because of Raicema. Well soon, Raicema as you know it will cease to exist."

Yangjam turned back towards Jen.

"I have heard about you," he said. "I know that the Tyrone's took you when you were a child just like they have taken everything else. You are not a Raiceman. You owe them nothing. So, what do you say? Come and work for me. Neoasia will be unified for the first time in its challenge of ridding the planet of the plagued way of life that Raicema has encouraged. And with the Tyrone's gone, Raicema will to be free to be unified in Makaism."

THE WORLD WALKER

"It will never happen!" Seth snarled.

"It is already happening you fool!" Yangjam declared. "It has been planned before you or your father or your grandfather ever stepped on the earth!"

"Sadana and Yangjam will make sure of it," Constynce added, looking Seth directly in the eyes. "Sadana has been running your country behind the scenes for years. You and your brother lost control and let's face it, he was an unpredictable maniac. I knew a long time ago that he had to go. We used your pointless war in Lizrab to our advantage. Our deal with Sadana is now concluded."

"What deal?!" Seth blurted out, the true horror of his life now staring him in the face.

"Who do you think put your brother out of his misery? It was one of Sadana's men! I agreed to fully support his rulership if he got rid of your brother."

The statement took control of Seth and he rose to his feet as Gueken was grinning sadistically at the fallen leader. Jen tried to stop him but Seth leapt forward at Constynce, pure hatred painted on his face.

In a moment that seemed to transcend time, Jen saw Gueken glance at one of his soldiers, giving him a signal. Instantly, the soldier pulled his trigger.

Within a surreal flash, a shot rang out and Jen lunged forward as the bullet hit Seth directly in his chest.

Seth slumped into his arms, his expression fading to one of shock and then indifference. Jen saw that his hand was covered in Seth's blood, pouring out of the gunshot wound.

As he lay dying looking up at Jen, he opened his mouth a couple of times with difficulty, trying to say something.

Finally, in a whisper of a voice, he managed to get a few last words out. "I...I always saw you...as a brother."

Then his eyes closed and Jen felt the last breath leave his body. A pool of emotion gathered in his stomach, quickly replaced by disbelief and then an inferno of wrath rose up from his feet.

He stood up, eyes burning towards the cowardly Gueken and the scheming Constynce.

The next moments were a blur.

He felt himself running with arms outstretched, fully intent on wrapping his large hands around both of their throats. But then, without warning, he felt a sharp blow on the top of his head. Then darkness came.

Chapter 46 – Money

The *National Reserve of Raicema* stood directly to the west of the Tyrona Presidential Palace. The reserve was a giant archaic building made of limestone, its walls and roof adorned with cameras and automatic weaponry. It had fifty-four giant columns supporting its architrave and pyramidal roof.

The building securely held most of Raicema's real wealth. Contained within secure vaults deep underground were gold and silver bullion, precious stones and valuable papers.

Sadana Siger was sitting inside the large regal office of the reserve's former chief treasurer, whom he had recently dismissed.

"Today, I want to talk about money," he was saying with authority to three professionally dressed men who were listening carefully to the instruction of their new boss.

"I want to make sure you know what money is."

The men all looked surprised, convinced that they were educated about their nation's financial system.

"The *creds* you have in your accounts? Are these numbers money?"

There was silence as the men thought about the question.

"Well, yes," one of the men answered nervously.

"Wrong," Sadana said with authority. "Yesterday those numbers may have been money, but today they are not."

The men were now all quite confused.

"So what is money? Well, the answer is simple."

There was a long uncomfortable pause as Sadana leaned towards the three men, the finest professionals employed by the reserve.

"Money is whatever I say it is," he said so assuredly that it chilled all three of them to the bone. After a moment of astonishment at the claim, one of the men had to disagree, clearly not accepting Sadana's claim to overruling power.

"But the people all agree on what money is and our laws state creds are legal tender. If we disregard the law, tomorrow, the people could start trading matchsticks as money if they really wanted."

"Wrong again!" Sadana said more aggressively. "Matchsticks will not keep a roof over their heads or food in their bellies, for *we* own those roofs and *we* own their food. They need the cred system for the vital things. As for the law, it is whatever the government says it is. I am your new government."

Sadana composed himself as he prepared to continue with his dictation about the current state of money in Raicema. "Creds are a derivative only. Even that small minority that still have original *minted promise notes* will soon have no more of an advantage. To trade those notes legally they need to be in the system. Very soon, they will have to exchange them for creds.

"The only thing of any true value is the *gold*, the *silver* and these original promise notes issued before the cred system was introduced."

"But the promise notes are the basis of the cred system," one of the men protested. "Theoretically, someone could trade their creds for notes, and then trade their notes for gold or silver."

"The law will soon be changed to make such trading illegal."

The men were shocked at the claim and were almost about to object that the people wouldn't stand for it, but something stopped them, possibly the realisation that the people didn't really have a choice.

"It will be your primary goal in the first phase to procure all gold, silver, jewels and minted promise notes in exchange for creds. That is phase one."

He paused as the men all fidgeted at the daunting task they had just been set.

"You know, at one time it was so easy. The people did what they were told because they were afraid."

He paused.

"Now, the people are supposed to trust their government and see them as their saviours. We use computers to keep the people quiet. We cannot just take without giving something in return. The people are not afraid to rebel so we must be smarter."

He glanced up quite frighteningly as he tapped the side of his head. "You may not know, but the technology systems you see here in Raicema are nothing compared to those of the past. Things have become too segregated and that is causing distrust. It is a new day."

The men had no doubt about the statement.

"Soon, every dwelling in this nation will be connected, compulsory, no exceptions to the new *Global Money System*."

One of the men looked confused.

"Global Money System, Lord Siger?"

"Well, let me put it this way," Sadana began. "Here in Raicema, people differentiate themselves from the Lengardians, from the Neoasians, from every other civilised nation of this planet. That is down to not being connected to the rest of the world. At one time having people segregated was useful, but now *we* need them to be unified in what they value."

He looked at the men with a stern face.

"The Global Money System is not just a computer network. It is a control network. It is all of our responsibility to keep control."

He paused.

"So, after you exchange all tangible wealth from the people of Raicema..." Once again he paused as the three men all listened tentatively. "...the promise notes can be destroyed. Then, I want all gold, jewels and silver in Raicema transferred to the *Royal Reserve* in Lengard by this time next year, including all we store here in this reserve. The transfers should be strictly confidential. It is imperative that the people believe we still store gold and silver here for a while. That is phase two."

The men all seemed aghast at the instruction.

"It's not possible..." one of the men said. "There is no way to locate all gold and silver. We do not have the manpower."

"But I do!" Sadana declared loudly. "Besides, people will hand it over themselves."

"But how?" the man asked. "Sixty-three percent of the

population is off grid."

"Not for long," Sadana informed him. "We are rolling out some major legal changes. It will be against the law not to be connected to the mainframe. Those that do not comply will be exiled from the cities and threatened with prison, or worse if necessary."

Sadana looked deadly serious.

"We must have centralised control!" he declared ferociously. "And phase three, is once everyone in Raicema only uses creds, we will make it mandatory to exchange them for global money. That law change will prohibit gold and silver trading and connect everyone to the other nations of the planet."

The men were overwhelmed by the ambitious and controlling blueprint.

"You three have been chosen to drive this project top down. Now go and plan. I will ensure you have as many staff as needed to carry out all the necessary tasks."

The men left the office and walked down one of the spacious hallways in the reserve, towards their respective offices.

"I don't get it," one said to the other two. "I thought Lord Siger was a Makai priest? Don't they believe in equality? Seems like he's trying to lock things down even more than the Tyrones. And I'm not sure a world currency system is going to work..."

"He was the leader of the *Order of the Raiceman Makai*," one of the others informed him. "Haven't you ever head of the *ORM*? It's a bit different."

"Yeah. Don't you know that the *Order* are also known as the secret bankers of the world?" said the third man, twiddling his tie. "Whatever they say goes!"

The first man adjusted his suit and contemplated for a moment. "Well, I guess things are changing around here," he said with a glint in his eye. "Big challenge..." He paused, accepting his position. "...But who cares? As long as we're getting paid, right? One thing is for sure. I want mine in gold."

The other two nodded in agreement.

Chapter 47 – Escape from Yinkoto

Jen King opened his eyes and realised somebody must have hit him heavily from behind. He sat up feeling drowsy with a throbbing pain at the back of his head.

He was in a sealed white room.

Light shone in brightly from a solid glass skylight above and Jen felt woozy as he tried to stand up.

He scanned his surroundings.

The room was empty. The floor was stone cold concrete and the walls were whitewashed. There was a metal door, tightly sealed.

He looked around anxiously in hope of finding a way out.

At the base of the back wall was a small air vent, about the size of a hand. He went over to it and frantically began to pull at the metal grid. He felt a slight breeze waft through. After a short while of effort it came free, but this left only the smallest of holes with a tiny view of another building opposite.

Jen slumped down into a seated position against the back wall.

Contemplating his fate, likely a planned execution, Jen began to reflect on his life. He remembered being trained to kill with just his hands, how to lead men with courage and how to be as observant as a hawk in the heat of battle.

As these deluded and glorified thoughts enter my mind, they are quickly swept with other thoughts, the reality of people suffering, dying in pain. I see women crying at the death and destruction.

Jen's thoughts were racing. He felt like he had betrayed something most sacred and that he desperately needed to make amends.

As his emotions deepened, they were brought to light by the sight of a swift movement beneath his bent knees. A large insect, shiny and black in appearance with large feathery antennas, darted rapidly about the area that Jen was slumped. It stopped, sensing its surroundings before searching quickly for something.

A clanking sound came from beyond the steel door and within a moment, the door had opened, a stern booted guard entering the white cell to check on his prisoner. He began to walk towards Jen menacingly. However, upon seeing the large insect before him, the guard lost all courage and in a frantic hurry to escape his miniature fear, dropped his metal baton with a clank to the floor. He rushed out, slamming the door shut with a panicked fury.

Jen was bewildered and amazed that such fortune had fallen upon him. Without hesitation, he quickly picked up the baton, a heavy long piece of iron, and using his height to his advantage, jumped up at the glass skylight, hitting it along its edge with a ferocity that came from the depths of his entire being.

He had to strike it several times with quick jumps, every strike releasing the anger he had against the oppressors of people and life.

With a mighty quake, the glass above shattered and rained down with tremendous luminosity. Jen closed his eyes as a shard bounced off his body and scratched his face.

The emergence of the pure blue sky sent surges of relief and hope through Jen's body. He jumped harder than ever before, clasping the edge of the wall, strewn with broken glass.

With his hands bleeding, he pulled himself up with a supernatural strength, the light breeze hitting his face and washing away all his fears. He rolled over the edge of the skylight, broken glass crunching beneath him.

He was on the rooftop of a building, yet there was no tranquil garden here, only concrete and glass. Pushing himself to his feet, he heard the guard re-entering below and he quickly ran to the edge of the building.

Several leaps away, there was another building, with large flower patches scattered on its roof. *To reach it will be a feat,* Jen thought, yet was sure he could do it. Realising there was not a moment to waste, he strode back several paces and then ran for his life towards the edge. He felt the ball of his right foot pushing off the edge of the building and his chest and arms crashed onto the wall of the adjacent building. He pushed up with his arms and clambered over the side.

As he got to his feet, he heard a shot ring out and felt a warm sensation at the top of his right ear. A bullet had just grazed it and blood began to pour out quite heavily. It was warm.

He turned to see the guard in the distance aiming directly at him from the top of the skylight. He was ready to take another shot. Jen turned, expecting the fatal blow, but when he heard a faint click, all life was restored to him and he quickly ran ahead. He looked back to see the guard frantically searching for more ammunition.

He ran like the wind, across the long building, past flowers that almost leapt out at him encouraging his escape with a sweet aroma. He found a stairwell that looked old and derelict. He went down it quietly, peeking around every corner for imminent dangers.

After what seemed like five hundred steps downwards, he came to a small square window. The sight of clouds close by told him that he was a long way from the ground.

A few more flights down and he came to a doorway. He opened it slightly to see an empty hallway. At the end was a door and he heard voices behind it. He slowly pushed it ajar to see an enormous hall.

There were people around, tending to the sick and injured. The staff kept passing through another door to bring supplies and remove waste from the hundreds of beds that were present in the hall. He realised that the building was a giant hospital.

It was only at this point that Jen became fully conscious of what he was wearing, a dirty ripped Raiceman uniform. *If I am to get any further, I will have to find something to wear,* he thought.

Observing the staff for a while, he noticed their patterns of movement. Patients would also go through another door now and again, all dressed in white outfits.

He waited for the right moment.

Then, he crawled through the door, ducking in between beds to evade the patrolling staff. He crawled into a free bed when there were only two staff members present.

With as little movement as possible, he got undressed under the white sheet and carefully rolled up his clothes into a bundle and placed them under the bed. He covered as much of his face as possible with the sheet and every time an attendant walked past he would be still as stone, praying nobody noticed anything unusual.

He waited for an opportunity. After a while, the hall was fairly clear and then he wrapped the bed sheet around himself, tying it in several places. He rolled off the bed quietly and made his way evasively to the door where the patients came in and out.

Pretending he was picking up something from the floor, he stood upright and walked through the patient door, finding a long corridor beyond. As he made his way down it, he heard a voice from behind. One of the staff had followed him. The man was speaking loudly in a language Jen could not understand.

Panicked, Jen turned to the man and grabbed him by his collar. The man froze in terror and Jen covered his mouth before he could call out for help. He carefully dragged him down the corridor to a washroom at the end. The man was really struggling and Jen slapped him across the face, intending only to make him calm down. However, the man crumpled to the floor in an unconscious heap.

A pang of guilt ran through Jen's body but was quickly replaced by the urgent need to escape. The washroom had many large sinks and showers. He looked around quickly for an exit but saw only a cupboard door. He opened it, finding cleaning supplies and a variety of clean linen.

Then he heard a lot of clanking from the other side and jumped back with surprise as the back wall of the cupboard started to move. It was actually a door.

Jen hid from view until one of the staff members had retrieved what they needed from the two-way cupboard. He then waited until he heard little noise from the other side and opened the back door, crawling through two shelves to reach the staff room. It was empty for the moment and Jen darted through another door adjacent to reach yet another corridor.

A leap of joy went through Jen's heart when he saw a lift at the end of the enclosed pathway. He ran towards it and the doors opened automatically, revealing a rundown interior with simple buttons to the floors, much less advanced than the sophisticated technology he'd seen when he arrived in Neoasia. He pressed a blue button towards the bottom of the array, hoping it went to the ground level. The lift chugged for a moment and then began to descend.

A million thoughts whirred inside Jen's head, of his need to escape, of what he was escaping from. The light from different levels in the building sped past the crack in the lift door every second or so and Jen counted sixty-six levels before the lift finally came to a halt.

The doors opened and Jen was relieved that before him was another empty corridor. He walked down it quickly, this one much more decorated, with paintings of different animals on the walls. Then he came to some large white doors that slid open electronically. He was so fascinated by what was in the room beyond that he couldn't help but venture in.

The room was large, home to hundreds of preserved animals, birds and insects kept in jars and larger casings. It looked like a laboratory.

There were creatures that Jen had never comprehended before, some looking quite fearsome. As he walked around slowly observing, forgetting his urge to run for a moment, he heard a voice approach him from behind. It was a woman's voice, speaking in the same unfamiliar language that he had heard before. He turned around, startled to see a tallish, dark-haired woman of middle age, dressed in a long pale green overcoat.

She smiled at Jen, immediately putting him at ease.

Bewildered, he mumbled a few incoherent words. "I... Err... I was just looking..." he stuttered away, shuffling his feet and feeling vulnerable in his sheet outfit.

"You are from Raicema?" she asked, holding back giggles from the sight of this unusually dressed large man.

"Yes," he said, contemplating whether to risk taking this woman into his confidence. He would certainly need some help in getting out of the building and the city. He instinctively felt a warm, safe sensation when he looked at her, as if it was someone who he knew and could trust.

"I am trying to get out of the city," he admitted, attempting to gauge her reaction. It was quite unobjectionable. "I was brought here as a prisoner. They are going to kill me if I stay here."

The woman seemed concerned at what Jen was telling her. She smiled with compassion. "We are all prisoners," she said in a soft voice. Her words soothed him.

There was silence for a while and Jen felt selfish for a moment, at being willing to burden this woman with his dangerous situation. He was sure that the guards were searching for him.

They could be in the same building by now, he thought with a jolt of panic.

"Do you have any other clothes I could wear?" he asked her.

The woman turned around and Jen started to worry that she might be going to alert somebody. He stood on the same spot frozen as she disappeared into a little room. Sweating, he imagined forcing the woman to tell him a way out, yet he felt totally ashamed at this thought when she returned carrying a swab and some warm water, which she proceeded to dab Jen's bleeding ear and hands with.

After tending to his injuries, she disappeared again and came back carrying some folded garments. She handed them to Jen. They were overalls. He put them on, wrapping them around his sheet outfit. They were very snug and he looked like a lab worker.

"Thank you," he said sincerely to the woman.

"I show you how to get to the ground level," she said in a broken Raicema accent, walking towards the back of the hall.

Jen followed, wondering how it was possible that this woman was willing to help him so readily. At the back were huge sliding doors that led to another corridor. This one, however, had many lifts along its length.

"Lift number five," she said, smiling.

Jen took her hand and held it tightly with affection and gratitude. The woman seemed to reciprocate this gesture and kissed Jen lightly on his stubbly cheek. The affection that she showed filled him with energy and emotion.

The lift was much more sophisticated this time, with no buttons but a hand scanner instead. Jen began to worry about how to operate it before the woman stepped in and pressed her hand against it, seemingly willing to accompany Jen on his escape.

"No, it may be dangerous," he tried to stress to the woman, but she just smiled.

The lift sped downwards at a supersonic speed.

In an instant, the doors opened and they were both met with a mass of people flowing in different directions from another circus of lifts. The woman took Jen's hand and led him out of the circus, keeping in file behind a particular line of people.

"Down here, everyone is equal," the woman said to Jen as they plodded along between two monstrous buildings. "We all back to the ground."

Jen sensed a melancholic tone to the woman's voice.

"What is your name?" he asked her. "I am Jen."

"I am Euryli. I live here all my life."

"How can we get out of the city, Euryli?"

"There is a big wall that surrounds the city. There are many gates but only royals and statesmen can pass through."

"What about through the docks? That's how we arrived here."

"There, it is more heavily guarded that any of the gates. I know of one possibility."

There was shouting from behind and Euryli began to pull at Jen's hand as she realised who it was. Three guards had spotted him and were frantically pushing people out of the way in an attempt to catch up.

Euryli began to do the same and soon they were running past people down passageway after passageway. They came to a more open square, a rare sight with a few trees and patches of grass. All around were giant buildings with narrow single file walkways in between. They went down one to the right.

"Duck down," Euryli said. "You are very tall."

Jen did as she said and the heads of those walking behind them soon hid them. They could hear the frustration of the guards shouting aggressively back in the square.

"Why are they looking for you?"

"I refused to join them," Jen replied, emotions beginning to surface at the sights he had witnessed in the world above. He kept crouched down for a good while, before they came to a more village-like area, still with narrow walkways, but now with rows upon rows of small stalls and shops, selling clothing, jewellery and a great assortment of raw and cooked foods.

The smell in the air settled on Jen's stomach as a stroke of contentment. One stall was nothing more than a crude metal table with large leaves placed upon it and to the side, a giant pot of noodle soup steaming away on a pit fire. The proprietor looked worn and dishevelled, yet served her customers with an energetic exuberance.

"You are hungry?" Euryli asked Jen. He nodded.

"I will take you to a less exposed place. They serve very good fish."

Jen then realised that he didn't have any means to pay for such nourishment.

"I can pay for us," Euryli said, as if reading Jen's thoughts.

In that moment, normality had fallen on Jen's life and he forgot for a few seconds that he was in any danger. It was as if the real him had emerged and the past was irrelevant.

They walked through the walkways quickly, faced with a hundred offers of pretty objects and food. The further they went, the more slum-like the stalls became, yet they were more crowded, the goods sold now much cheaper and all second-hand. One small table fascinated Jen, selling a multitude of small electronic and mechanical parts that were all from Raiceman and Neoasian machines.

Within a short time they had reached a small dwelling at the back of some wide stone structures, used for fuel storage. A large cotton canopy sheltered some small wooden tables. There weren't any chairs, only thick woven rugs for customers to sit on, and there was a kitchen area at the back, next to one of the stone structures.

"My friend runs this place. She isn't supposed to be here so only locals will know of it. She gets her fuel from these stores here."

Euryli sat down on one of the rugs and urged Jen to do the same.

A dark-haired young woman appeared from around the corner, carrying a box of fish into the kitchen. Her face lit up when she saw Euryli sitting at one of her tables. She rushed over, conversing passionately in the same unknown language that Jen had heard before.

He sensed that Euryli was talking to her friend about him and started to feel slightly embarrassed and nervous. He observed how hard it was for him to trust people.

"This is my friend, Herma," Euryli said, introducing her. "She cannot speak the Raiceman language. She will make fish like you have never tasted. Her brother is merchant who supply fish to restaurants in the city so fish always fresh."

Euryli's broken speech was endearing.

Jen nodded with appreciation. Herma hurried away to begin preparation of the food.

"So how come you here in Yinkoto?" Euryli asked.

"I was a soldier for Raicema once," he said. "Feels like years ago now, but I was in Lizrab only last month. When they knew I didn't want to be part of it anymore, they brought me here as a prisoner."

"Part of it?"

"All the killing. I suddenly felt repulsed by it, as if I was also killing myself."

A warm smile appeared on Euryli's face.

"Now I just want to disappear. I have never felt this way before, like I've completely wasted my life so far."

"It normal, Jen," Euryli reassured him. "I think every person think the same sometime in their life. Where you want to go?"

The question brought a sense of urgency back into Jen's mind. "Anywhere but a city. They are looking for me here so I shouldn't stay too long. Did you say you knew a way out?"

"The city surrounded by a great wall but there are gates to let those allowed in and out. That is only possible way out. They dug down many suns to stop people escaping."

"Why did they build such a prison?" Jen asked, appalled by the restriction.

"Fifty years ago, the Makai rebel here. So much fighting that the government could not control. The emperor thought that if he could not control, at least he could contain. It worked as Makai here now have very different brain than those before."

She pointed to her head and made a screwing motion.

"Like Yangjam you mean?" Jen asked, feeling slightly angry at the thought of the corrupt leader.

"Yes. He is part of government here."

Jen nodded in agreement. "I saw him with Gueken. Who knows how long they have been working together?"

"He leader of Neoasian Makai for thirty years now and he cause many people to leave. He make a mandatory payment system for Makai citizens to give half of what earn to the regime. This on top of compulsory governmental tax system. This why so many Makai in dire poverty."

"What happens if they don't pay?"

"Renounced from Makaism and deemed traitor. Usually person beaten and ridicule…"

Euryli seemed to be struggling in her descriptions. However, Jen understood perfectly and it made him feel even angrier.

"It is the same in Raicema," he said, trying to vent his frustration. "People are brainwashed into believing that everything around them is built to give them a better life and because of this they should be fully responsible for paying for it all. And most people do it. Unlike here, however, you would be lucky to escape with a beating if you didn't comply. The sad thing is that people don't even get the option of saying if they want it or not. There is no choice."

"That is the way of government. You pay for to be protect. But they create what you need protect from…"

The two sat for a while pondering. Jen couldn't help but notice the smoothness of Euryli's skin, golden and shimmering slightly like silk. It made him feel full of hope knowing that such beautiful skin could exist in the midst of so much oppression.

"There is a way to get out, but not nice. We talk to Herma about it."

As if called when her name was spoken, Herma appeared carrying two plates of freshly steamed fish, sweet and spicy aromas flowing into the immediate surrounding area.

The chef said something that sounded like she was praying and then began to walk off. Euryli stopped her and began to converse about something. Herma seemed agreeable as to what they were talking about but then left them to eat their food.

"After we eat, we talk about getting you out."

Jen ate happily for the next few minutes, feeling elated at the kindness of these people that he hardly knew. Every bite of the fish filled him with a rejuvenated feeling of wellbeing.

The food tasted wonderful. The fragrance drew many an insect from the floor onto the table.

"I have been experiencing strange feelings recently," Jen confessed to Euryli. "As if everything that is happening to me is part of a story that I have somehow forgotten."

She smiled at him warmly, reaching out and touching his heavy hand. "When you came into laboratory, I feel similar. I not afraid of you, even though you look very strange."

They both laughed.

"People here only follow," she continued. "They would be happy if they listen to that which help them."

"What?" Jen asked with interest.

Before she could answer, the sound of a commotion close by abruptly ended the conversation. There was shouting. It sounded like the interrogation of some local people. People were shouting back, yet Jen could not understand anything that was being said.

"They looking for you!" Euryli informed him, taking his hand and leading him to the area where Herma was preparing large amounts of fish from a barrel.

"Quick, inside," she said.

Jen hesitated for a moment but then climbed inside the barrel with the fish. Euryli closed the lid just in time as he heard the voices of several guards come around the corner to the unsophisticated restaurant. The guards were speaking aggressively and Jen held his breath and tried not to move.

With light shining through tiny cracks in the barrel, the shiny eyes of the hundreds of fish surrounding him glistened like stars in the sky. He almost lost his bearings for a moment and for a split second he thought he understood the conversation between the guards and Euryli.

He thought that they were asking why there were two plates on the table and Euryli was replying that they were for her and Herma. They warned her that her friend's restaurant was illegal and that it should be moved. Then the guards left and Jen heard them smash some of the chef's plates, to which Herma shouted angrily at them.

Then, the lid opened from above, spilling light into the container and stirring Jen from an unusual awareness.

"You can come out. It difficult to breathe in there?"

"Actually it wasn't so bad," Jen replied, climbing out with his clothes and skin oily and wet.

"I glad you feel that way, because the only way out is in similar place."

The rest of the day was spent trying to covertly navigate back to where Euryli lived. Jen was touched that the woman whom he had recently met had dropped everything to help him.

It was late in the evening and Euryli and Jen were back in the city area of Yinkoto in a small apartment high up in an oval-shaped building.

"Relax, Jen," Euryli said, sensing his nervousness. "Nobody come here except Herma's brother."

They had talked during the afternoon about what Jen had deemed to be a risky plan of escape. He would hide in a truck used to transport fish whilst Herma's brother made his nightly drive out of the city to a nearby lake.

Jen's main concern was that whilst the truck was usually empty so that it could carry fish from the lake back to the city in the morning, this time there would be some left in the truck that Jen could hide under. Pangs of anxiety that the Yinkoto guards would suspect something ran through his body.

If I am found, Herma's brother will surely be shot on the spot, he thought. His concern ran deep for the man that he had never met. *He is going to risk his life for a complete stranger.*

Looking out of the main window in the apartment, a million lights from the skyscrapers lit up every part of Jen's vision. Above looked prettier, with the large green gardens glowing under subtle lights, trees often hanging over the edge of the buildings they had been planted on.

"I like the roof gardens here," Jen said, starting to relax in Euryli's humble home.

There were many bookshelves all around the living area and warm maroon rugs lining the floor. A small room at the back housed the bedroom and bathroom whilst a small cupboard contained a small stove and sink.

"Do you like living here?" Jen asked, noticing the subtle touches that made the place feel bigger and warmer, such as a multitude of candles and small lanterns ideally placed to illuminate small spaces.

"It better to live in a smaller space in the city than more spacious house near the walls. Many robberies and fights out there."

"I meant in Yinkoto in general?"

"I don't have choice really. As scientist I not allowed to leave and no family on the outside even if I leave. My parents come here when I very young. More people migrating to Yinkoto to escape violence from the rebellion. Now things quieter I know many more who want to leave, but very difficult. You cannot live easily outside."

"What is outside of the wall?" Jen asked, realising he knew little about the geography of Neoasia.

"There are few villages but many mountains cover north and west. One more city far east but that state controlled by Lengard."

A noise could be heard suddenly in the bedroom and Jen quickly stood alert.

"Don't worry," Euryli said, chuckling. "It is my cat, Serese."

A grey and white striped cat emerged from the bedroom, walking slowly and stretching its legs whilst doing so. It suddenly ran to Euryli and jumped onto her lap. She rocked on her chair stroking the feline.

"It difficult for her because she no go out much. Some of the guards cruel and torture or kill stray animals that they find."

Jen walked over and sat on a chair next to Euryli. He too stroked Serese, feeling a calming warmth coming from her body.

The cat's eyes were a deep green colour and within a few moments Jen found that he could move his glare from that of the creature's. She sat perfectly still and gazed right back, un-faltered or irritated.

Then, a strange sensation filled Jen's body starting at his solar plexus and making its way up to his chest and along his arms. He suddenly had the feeling that he was dreaming the entire scene and with every stroke of Serese's soft fur, he felt an intense heat grow in the palm of his hand.

He looked down and saw his hand glowing an ember red, every vein in his hand visible, with his bones looking like tubes of dim light.

A sudden apprehension waved through him when he realised that he wasn't in a dream and that he could actually see a sort of aura surround both his hand and Serese. It was mingling and dancing together like two excited children.

He stood up abruptly and his sight returned to normal.

"I..." Jen stumbled, feeling weak at the knees.

"What is it?" Euryli asked oblivious to what had just happened. Before Jen could answer they heard the sound of a truck horn beeping from below.

"Herma's brother is here!" Euryli said, getting to her feet. "Hurry!"

They made their way out of the apartment and down to a small parking bay on the ground floor.

A scruffy-looking man was sitting in the cab of an old red truck, withered planks making up the holding area, a crude wooden gate at the back.

The man got out of the cab, smoking a long cigar. His hair was long and matted and his face awash with stubble. He smiled at Jen and then spoke to Euryli in his native language.

"He cannot speak the Raiceman language. Only those that go to schools here learn."

The man smiled at Jen and signalled for him to get into the back of the truck as he lowered the back gate. Fish had been piled up at either side and there was a space for Jen to lie.

"Jen, I am happy we met," Euryli said tenderly, embracing him. He gazed briefly into her kind eyes before thanking her, wishing her farewell and climbing into the back of the truck, lying flat on his back.

Herma's brother began to push the fish over Jen's body with his hand until every part was covered except his face. Then he lifted the gate up and got back into his cab.

The smell was pungent so Jen tried to only breathe through his mouth. The horizontal view that Jen had as the truck began to drive away was quite spectacular, the stars and moving clouds in the sky making it look like every skyscraper was wobbling in the wind.

Jen counted eighty-five skyscrapers before the buildings began to shrink in size, and before long he could only see the simple roofs of what he could only imagine was a more poverty-stricken area.

There were more trees and Jen spotted several different species of mammals living in them. After a while, they reached a more open area with only a few trees around and no buildings. Jen tilted his head up to look through one of the gaps in the gate. He saw an enormous concrete wall that stretched for as far as he could see with sharp, thick rolls of barbed wire running along the top.

He resumed his hidden position as the truck started to slow down and Jen knew they were approaching a gate. The breaks creaked as Herma's brother stopped the truck and got out of his cab.

Jen heard the stern voices of three men who seemed to be quizzing the fisherman about where he was going. Then Jen could sense one of the guards approaching the side of the truck and peering through the gaps in the planked holding area. Jen held his breath and did not make even the smallest of movements, the anticipation of his freedom causing him to be as still as a rock.

After what seemed like an eternity, the man finally went back to his guard post and again quizzed Herma's brother. This time Jen was sure it was about why he had fish in his truck. Jen prayed that he would come up with a good excuse and after a few moments, the guards all said something less hostile and an eruption of relief pulsated around Jen's body.

The combined sound of the old truck's engine starting up and the gate opening turned Jen's relief into joy. As they passed through, Jen thought just how much the giant metal gates reminded him of prison doors.

Herma's brother leaned out of his cab window as he was driving and shouted something back at Jen, a signal that it was safe to expose himself. He sat up from the pile of fish, amazed to see thick forests and large plains all around. They drove for several suns before coming to a large lake, a great forest and vast mountain range beyond. The truck came to a stop and the fisherman got out and helped Jen down from the back.

"Thank you," Jen said to him, holding his hand in gratitude. He seemed to understand and smiled at Jen, pointing in the direction of the forest and mountains. Jen understood that the way he was pointing was the safest way forward.

Herma's brother went back to the cab and came back carrying some folded garments: a loose cotton shirt and pair of baggy cotton trousers. Again, Jen thanked the kind man. He then got back into his truck and drove off around the lake, seemingly heading over to the other side.

Now alone, Jen decided to wash in the lake and then change into his new outfit.

Jen stayed in the water for an hour, mesmerised by the gentle heat that it emitted and the smoky steam that came out of it every now and again. He just lay back, staring up at the stars and feeling like he never had before. He felt liberated and free to make his own choices about where he would go and what he would do.

But then, a strange and depressing notion came to him. He wasn't free at all. He had no choice but to head in the direction pointed out to him and this thought led to him thinking about the things that he had done in his life that he was now ashamed of. As he began to sink deeper into the pity and contempt that he had for himself, a strange light appeared from nowhere in the forest ahead. He couldn't quite make out what it was and it disappeared, only to reappear again a few moments later, illuminating a section of the forest in the distance.

Jen got out of the lake and put on the clothes that Herma's brother had given him. Then he walked towards the light.

Chapter 48 – Angelo Orentus

Jen wandered into the woody forest.

The light ahead was about the size of a human. It gave the forest a fluorescent glow. Dry leaves were scattered across the floor like a carpet.

A dry breeze rustled the leaves on the floor and it prompted Jen to look up at the sky. The stars were shining so brightly it seemed as though he was closer to them than before, as if he were elevated to the edge of the cosmos.

He looked down and the human-shaped light had disappeared.

Jen walked cautiously to the area of the forest that had since been illuminated.

He saw a man, naked with long brown wild hair, curled up on the forest floor like a baby. The sight was quite surreal and Jen shuffled his feet in mystification. The crunchy leaves felt springy beneath his worn soles.

The man rose up slowly, in the way a leaf opens to the dawning sun. He looked gradually in Jen's direction.

His eyes shone unnaturally.

A feeling of intense fear gripped Jen in his chest and he suddenly felt paralysed. The man walked slowly over to where Jen was standing and touched him lightly on the shoulder.

The sensation of fear was quickly washed away with one of tranquillity. The man was emitting nothing but love and attention. All the pain in Jen's body evaporated, every mental tension and heartache.

After many moments of silence in the state of peace, Jen finally felt like speaking.

"Who are you?"

"You do not know me?" the man questioned in response. His voice and face were quite androgynous and Jen had to look again to confirm that the person in front of him was indeed a man.

"I am like you, Jen King."

"How do you know my name?" Jen asked, curiosity rising from within.

"Unlock your mind," the man said in reply. "You know me."

Then, Jen realised that there was something innately familiar about the man's kind and slender face. He felt a warm sensation around his chest and he looked down to see the stone around his neck glow with an affectionate heat.

"You are not from this world, are you?" Jen asked without thinking, as if the words were being spoken through him.

"That is true," the man said softly. "Do you know my name?"

Jen thought he did, but no matter how hard he tried to remember, he couldn't. Something was blocking his thoughts.

"My name is Orentus," the man prompted.

The name did not remind Jen of anything.

"You have forgotten a lot, Jen," the man said in an amused way.

"I don't know what you mean," Jen said.

"Everything you have been told, everything you have seen and everything you have done..." Orentus elaborated, "... remove from your mind completely."

He touched Jen on the shoulder again.

Jen instantly felt at peace, his mind clear and empty. He could only sense an inner energy in his head, radiating throughout his body. Then he knew who the man was.

"Angelo..." he felt himself say.

"Yes," Orentus said. "That is also my name."

"You are good. You are my friend," Jen muttered, in a trance-like state.

Then he heard Orentus again.

"Your mind only believes that there are categories of things in life. Planets, countries, friends, enemies, wars, violence, people, the ground, the sky, woman, man, good, evil, light, dark. All are not the true reality."

Jen suddenly found himself floating, the ground beneath him dispersing, the sky opening above him. His mesmerised eyes grew wide and he gasped for air realising none was present. Orentus touched him again and he no longer needed to breathe.

"All around you are constructs that seem out of reach, yet now you can see them."

Jen felt distant stars moving towards him very quickly. Within a moment the violent explosions of a fiery sun happened right in front of his eyes. The next moment he experienced only emptiness.

"Learn to *see*," Orentus said, projecting some kind of energy field into Jen.

In a spark, his entire life flashed before him.

He could see Javu raising him as a young child and Guy Tyrone capturing and training him for war.

A scene of his birth played through his mind, his mother close to death and with her last breath of struggling effort, giving him the energy to survive alone. He could feel how his mother felt, a love of union, a love of eternity.

"Your mother is here. Before you were born, she knew she was you and you were she."

Jen was starting to feel the unexplainable. His mind was clear and only the truth existed. The past was washed away and the future was irrelevant to anything, for both had been sown into the seed of the present. He imagined life and the universe as a great tree.

"This higher dimension of awareness that you are experiencing can be reached every day you live, Jen. The energy in your physical being is a culmination of this planet's cry for balance and for peace. You are part of this planet. Why haven't you been looking after it?"

Suddenly, a vast ocean was beneath them both and in an instant they were travelling through the water, deep down into the depths of the planet. They reached the sea basin and hovered there, looking at hundreds of different strange-looking creatures.

Jen could feel nothing except a radiance and connection to everything around him. He tried to move his arm to let the murky water run through his fingers, but quickly realised his body had gone.

Within another moment they were both floating in the sky once again, surrounded entirely by wispy clouds. Orentus was next to Jen the entire time and even though Jen couldn't feel anything physical, he sensed that Orentus was touching him in some way.

"I wanted to see the star before, and it came."

"It is part of you too."

Jen swiftly realised that he assumed he was speaking to Orentus, but he actually wasn't. Everything he thought, Orentus understood. No words were necessary, only the meaning of what he wanted to convey prevailed.

Angelo Orentus let go of Jen and in a flash both were back in the forest outside the Yinkoto region. Jen gazed up from a seated position.

"Was it a dream?" he asked, looking up at the strange man.

"It was. But it was also reality," Orentus answered. "Your energy is not balanced enough to see this reality alone yet. My energy can balance you."

"Who are you?" Jen asked, looking at the human-like figure.

Orentus smiled, his eyes luminous. "I am you. I am this planet. I am this universe," he replied.

Jen was confused. He had returned to thinking logically with reason. He couldn't make sense of Orentus's answer.

"I am a manifestation, just as you are," Orentus said. "I was not born from another, however, that is our difference." He looked at Jen and smiled.

"You are not human?"

"What is human?" Orentus asked in reply.

Jen couldn't answer after what he had just seen and felt. He had experienced the union of his entire being with the sky and ocean, space and stars. It was as if he as a unique entity didn't exist. He felt like he had dispersed like smoke in the wind. He shook his head indicating he didn't have an answer.

"All physical beings are just energy that takes a shape that you recognise," Orentus explained. Jen realised that he was not uncomfortable in any way with Orentus being naked. "I am another of those shapes. Fundamentally, our essence is the same. This particular planet is coming close to destruction, as it once was before. You are a manifestation of energy that can help this planet, just as I am a manifestation that can help you."

Orentus seemed to hover over him, closer to where Jen was sitting causing small currents of anxiety to run through him.

"Do not be afraid of me," Orentus said with an impression of amusement. "Are you aware that you carry something very valuable on your person?"

"What?" Jen asked, puzzled at what it might be.

"The pendant that is around your neck."

The pendant was not visible, hidden beneath Jen's cotton shirt. He took it out so that it was visible, a shiny black bead sewn into a strong leather band. Jen had been in possession of the pendant for as long as he could remember. To him it was a precious token of a past that he had forgotten.

"The stone around your neck is known as the *Earth Stone of Power*. It enhances the connection that the bearer has to everything that is part of or dwells on this planet."

"I have never noticed anything special about it. It has no special powers."

"I assure you that it does. This stone can reach many worlds."

Orentus paused. Jen sensed he was smiling.

"Your stone is one of four that were created a very long time ago. Whilst there is benefit to be the bearer of such a stone, there is a great danger and burden as well. It is because of this stone and your connection to it that you were taken as a child. It is the reason you were groomed for war."

Though Jen knew it was the truth, he didn't want to accept it. He didn't want to feel any more anger or hatred.

"Let me show you what the earth stone is capable of. Take it off."

Jen removed the necklace and held it out in the palm of his hand. His breath shortened when the pendant floated up and hovered towards Orentus who now outstretched a visible hand. It fell into his palm and radiated, shining a strange green and brown light.

"One capability of the earth stone is to convert the energy of the earth into a very destructive form."

Jen was aghast at the thought of such a weapon. "What form?"

"One that I certainly will not be conjuring," Orentus declared. "Many seek the stone for this reason."

An owl hooted in the distance.

"However, I will show you something positive that this stone can do."

He projected energy into the stone that could be visibly seen. To Jen this looked like a field of white light being sucked into the stone from Orentus's mid-section. The stone's light changed from brown and green to white.

The ground started to tremble a little and then a sprout shot out of the ground, growing at an incredible rate. A stem formed, followed by small branches and then leaves. Within a minute, it was as tall as both of them, the stem solidifying into a trunk and blue flowers forming on the leaf stems. Mouth hanging open, Jen watched as a tall tree formed within a few minutes, as tall as the others that had taken many years to grow.

"I can't believe this!" Jen gasped, rubbing his eyes.

Orentus handed the stone back to Jen. It had stopped glowing and he put it back around his neck, hands shaking at what he had just witnessed.

"It is your responsibility to protect this stone from being used for malevolent purposes, Jen King."

"It can make trees!" Jen said in wonder, looking up at the incredible creation.

"It can make a lot more than that. As I said, whilst there is benefit to be the bearer of such a stone, there is great danger as well."

"Who made it? How?" Jen asked, a million questions sprouting in his head.

"A people of long ago had the capability to create such items, which were mostly used for positive reasons. However, this particular stone, along with its three equivalents, was created out of the pursuit for power. They cannot be destroyed and must be hidden from those who pursue power in this world."

Jen didn't really understand what this strange humanlike man was saying, but he couldn't accept that such a responsibility had been entrusted to him.

I am a man who has spent most of his life doing what others told me to, most of whom are obsessed with holding power over others, he thought. *I have helped many people obtain power over others.*

Orentus heard his thoughts. "They have never been able to harness the stone's power because you have never become fully aware of it," Orentus told him. "And that is because you yourself are not interested in such power, which is a rare quality. In fact, you are a strong believer in freedom, Jen, which is why you are standing here in this forest right now, ready to begin a great journey in your life."

The words filled Jen with hope and promise. "But why do I have this stone, if it is so dangerous and powerful?"

"You chose this path long ago."

"So what am I supposed to do now?" Jen asked Orentus, feeling that a great burden had been placed upon him.

"Begin your journey, Jen."

The sky, though dark, seemed to emit an unnatural blue glow though the tree tops. Crickets chirping loudly and the rustle of the leaves played through the air.

"What journey? I have no plans. I only want to escape from this world of violence."

"That in itself is the very seed needed to begin your journey. It has naturally led you to where you are now. You are unbalanced, yes, but your journey will be the balancing act that you need to break free."

Jen could completely relate to what Orentus was saying.

"You are at the mouth of the river of the past. You will navigate that river and achieve what you have been trying to without knowing it."

"And what is that?"

"To find out who you really are and where you really come from. And when you know that, you *will* help this planet and everything on it."

"But where do I start?" Jen asked, suddenly feeling very lost.

"The mountains ahead are the start of your journey. You will learn much about your past by venturing into the peaks beyond."

Jen contemplated what he was being told for a while, still overwhelmed by the things that Angelo Orentus had shown and told him. As he readied himself to set off, feeling totally unprepared, an important question popped into his head. "I have started to see things differently recently. Is it because of this stone?"

"The things you have been experiencing recently, come from you and nothing else," he reassured him. "In fact, I think you will discover many more things about yourself in the near future."

His mind at ease, Jen looked over at the shadow of the mountains in the distance and as he turned back to thank Orentus for his guidance, he was surprised to find that he had vanished without a trace.

Only the cool light of the moon lit up the lake and leaves. Without further hesitation, he took one step after the other, walking towards the mountains and the certainty of change.

Chapter 49 – Lovers Dream

Time no longer existed.

There was only love, endless love.

Above there was light. Below there was darkness. Somehow the two had merged and in between was only stillness, a tranquillity that transcended existence itself.

All urges had disappeared. But alas, beyond each detachment and every peaceful floating moment, the great struggle still raged on. The only difference now was it could not touch her. It could not provoke her. She was free at last.

My thoughts are not my own. They float in and out, like the wind, like the rain, like the sun's rays and the flowers that surround my feet. When was I so selfish as to believe that they belonged to me?

An affectionate entity was close by, a lost part of herself, a reflection. It approached her and they embraced. The warmth coming from the being was familiar and distinct.

Another being was close by, followed by a large group. She could feel bouncy warmth surrounding her, intense energy of love and gentle kindness. She wanted to embrace them all but she found that there were hundreds of beings in surround before long.

She was connected to them all. She could feel it in her heart and in her belly.

Then, a man was walking towards her.

It was Rekesh but like she had never seen him before. He was peaceful, in awe of the atmosphere, almost childlike. He was being guided by the beings towards her.

An intense love swelled in her heart and she felt it burst out as a bright red beam directly into his heart. He ran to her with raw affection pouring out of his body.

They embraced and the world around them faded away. The beings had disappeared and only she and Rekesh existed. She felt their bodies melt into one and she felt complete.

I am what you were. You are what I was.

Together they both felt whole.

It lasted forever.

Then after eternity had faded, a movement could be felt. It reverberated from the inside out. It was a change she was not expecting. A tunnel formed around her and Rekesh had gone, leaving a hole in her heart. She tumbled down it like a helpless child.

She felt the pain of the fall and the cold earth beneath her. The sadness of it overwhelmed her and she cried, sobbing her life into the ground with erosive emotion. She wanted to go back but it was too late. She had arrived.

Chapter 50 – Inside Lemuria

"I have returned," Elera felt herself say.

An intense heat struck her, a heat both dry and moist. She felt her eyes drying quickly as a parched air patch penetrated her body.

The atmosphere was burning her lungs and the beautiful dream she had experienced was fading from memory. She slowly opened her eyes as if from the lengthiest of slumbers, seeing only green above and feeling the melody of nature playing lucidly to her every sense.

Sitting up unenergetically, she felt the soft hot dirt in the palms of her hands, letting its silkiness run through her fingers. Her head felt like it had been emptied of every thought and that it was about to float away.

She could not think. She was only capable of observing her current pose, sitting with arms loose to the ground and both feet touching upon the hot earth. Then, upon hearing the sound of a bird high above, her thoughts came flooding back like a river that had burst its banks.

"The Earth Temple is close by," a voice whispered to her as she remembered her life.

She suddenly felt quite upset, feeling like she had wasted her time on the planet. Her doubt and loneliness only lasted a moment, however, for she then remembered how she had loved others, and how they had loved her.

She rose to her feet, only realising at that moment that she didn't have a single garment upon her body. Mysteriously, there was a light cotton robe hanging on a tree limb close by. She walked over and slipped it on, the soft and fresh cotton cooling her down in the heat.

Her surroundings were undeniably megalithic, and in a pang of nostalgia, she suddenly realised where she had seen the environment before. It had been in her strange vision in the Bimini pyramid, when she had seen a wild forest with unusual buildings and a magical foal that everyone had been watching.

She looked around but she neither saw nor heard nobody around.

The forest was so overgrown that every tree and stone was carpeted in a thick layer of moist green moss, from which countless vibrant, mesmerising flowers grew in profusion.

Now, she could feel the moisture in the air. It was coming from the plants around her.

Elera walked forward, sensing rare discovery, every smooth step a carefully placed one. Beyond the next few colossal trees, she found the past waiting for her.

There were great buildings interspersed within the forest ahead. An ancient city, each structure covered in the same flourishing moss, giving the impression that each building had grown from a deep mass of living algae. Only at the tops of the tallest temples could the brown stone be seen, peeking out from its blanket of dripping slime.

Above, tall trees shrouded any hope of spotting the forgotten city from the sky. Combined with the bright orange and pink flowers of the trees and bushes, the green clammy environment looked like another world, a lost primordial jungle city of the past.

"This is what you have been searching for," the voice spoke again.

Lemuria, she thought.

Each of the great buildings was equally as big as every megalithic structure she had ever come across. It was hard to see how far the city stretched on for, but she could sense it was equally as large as Raicema City.

Elera felt as if she were lost in the land of giants and she counted five of the gargantuan structures, some in the shape of pyramids, others more square in shape. There were also tall, gigantic pillars scattered around the city, thickly coated with vegetation.

The next thing that reverberated through her body was the overwhelming energy that was present in the colossal city. It was radiating from everywhere with an intensity Elera had never experienced before, as if it was the most concentrated of energy forms.

The thought of *seeing* the energy only gave her the feeling that she might be overpowered by it. She had no time to contemplate further, for she had seen something that she barely believed was real.

About a sun away, between two of the enormous, organic struc-tures in the distance, she saw a glowing being. She instantly knew that it was the same magical foal she had once seen in a vision, its presence emitting a rainbow of energy that seemed to pull every-thing towards it. She was sure that she saw the world bend in its direction, as if everything longed to connect with it.

The urge to follow flooded her body and she found herself running towards the being with raw passion and love, an intense sensation within yearning to touch the creature. She felt like the foal was her child, her lost child that she longed to hug close to her heart.

After running for ten minutes, so hard that her muscles felt like they were alight, she reached the spot where the foal had walked. Its footprints were in the black soil, the image of hope imprinted there like a love note left for reassurance. Breathing heavily, she sat down on the floor next to the prints, allowing the air to reach the very bottom of her lungs. All around her were towering structures. It was a land of giants. Elera began to think about what she was doing there in the incredible location.

Why am I here? she thought.

The atmosphere had now calmed and almost seemed normal to Elera. She began to have strong feelings of a deep-rooted connection to something. She heard a sound behind her. She turned around to see someone standing there.

"Rekesh?!" she said slowly, looking at the figure. He was naked except for what looked like a cotton sheet wrapped around his waist. He was glistening with the sweet humidity in the air.

"I followed you," he said, looking like he might burst into tears at any moment. "When you walked into that beam, I followed you. I don't know what happened after that. I was somewhere for a long time. I think you were there…"

She got up and held him close and kissed his cheek tenderly. Love flowed out of her heart and she felt intensely happy to see him.

"Don't be frightened, Rekesh," she told him, embracing him

close to her. They stayed in one position for a long while, holding each other tightly and softly in their lightweight garments.

"This place is very special. It is where it all began."

He looked around in a confused state.

Elera slowly led him by the hand into the ancient city, the pungent smell of the exotic flowers a little sickly at times. Elera looked at each of the buildings. She could not see past the overgrown moss that had covered each of them and she felt as though the structures were almost alive.

"This way…" Something was calling her.

"Where are we?" Rekesh asked after looking with astonishment at the mammoth environment. "This place can't be real! I must be dreaming."

"We are not dreaming," Elera assured him. "That platform must have been some sort of portal to another part of the planet…" She stopped for a moment. "…I've never seen or heard of anywhere like this before, except in the vision that I had. I don't think anyone has been here for a very long time."

Up ahead, as they walked past several tall pillars, Elera spotted the foal again in the distance.

"Quickly!" she urged, starting to run. "This way."

Rekesh followed Elera blindly, unsure of what they were pursuing.

After a while, she stopped and looked around but once again she only found the footprints of the beautiful creature. Then, almost enshrouded by shadows ahead, she laid eyes on the place that she knew her journey would end.

There was a series of cliffs that scaled higher than any of the trees and in front of the rock face was a magnificent pyramid, almost completely hidden by the tall trees around it.

"What is this place?" Rekesh asked, still in a state of vulnerability and straining to see what Elera was looking at.

"It is the very first one," Elera replied, taking Rekesh's hand again and heading in that direction.

As they got closer, they both saw that the pyramid had a shiny outer casing, very much like what Elera imagined the Great Pyramid of Giza would have originally looked like. She was surprised that the immaculate stone wasn't covered with any algae or moss. Moving closer, she realised that the casing was a layer of vibrant crystal.

At the pinnacle, there seemed to be a shiny translucent spire protruding vertically upwards from the top. At the base of the megalithic building was a narrow entrance, surrounded by intricately carved pillars. There were carvings of humanlike figures with strange dragon-like heads.

"I don't have a good feeling about this, Elera," Rekesh said, starting to feel anxious. "I don't think we should go inside."

"We are safe, Rekesh. We are safe together," she said, walking straight towards the entrance and holding his hand tightly.

The interior of the pyramid was the simplest Elera had ever seen. Before her was the largest single chamber she had ever seen, pyramidal in shape and seemingly taking up the entirety of the inner space. It felt light and airy and must have been a sun wide and almost as tall at its pinnacle.

"Strange," Elera commented to Rekesh, confused and surprised. Her voice echoed throughout the entire space. "This is so different to the other pyramids. It's so spacious."

"It *is* very different," Rekesh agreed, feeling intrigued and a little more relaxed. "The others had such narrow passageways and the rooms were very low in height."

"Let's have a look around."

"It'll probably take us a few hours to walk across it," Rekesh said in a jovial way to which Elera giggled.

Embedded in the stone floor were tablets inscribed with hieroglyphs. They stopped at one and Elera knelt upon it, noticing there was a large polished crystal set in the centre of the great slab of stone.

"Can you understand it?" Rekesh asked her, surprised at how

new the tablet looked, like it had never been walked on or touched.

Silently, Elera let the meaning come to her. The tablet seemed to be projecting knowledge directly from its crystal and what she learnt was most surprising.

"In the beginning, spirit and body were one," she recited, as if in a trance. *"There was no birth, no death. The first children came from the essence and from them all else has been born."*

"What are you saying, Elera?" Rekesh asked, not understanding why she was speaking in such a way.

She stopped speaking for a while.

"I can hear this stone. It is speaking to me."

They came to another tablet a few strides away and it immediately began to communicate with her. It was speaking directly to her mind.

"The *Leiruyi* built this temple in honour of the *goddess of the earth,* the mother of this planet," Elera said as if she were narrating. "It was built during the *epoch of the earth,* a time of utmost harmony on the planet. It was specifically built in this location because of the strong connection this land has to the essence."

"Goddess? Essence?" Rekesh said.

"This is the first temple to have been built by the great sorcerers of the Leiruyi, who created it using the gifts they had received from their meeting with the goddess," Elera continued. "They met her in the dream world, where the physical world and the spirit world meet."

She looked up at Rekesh.

"That's all it told me. The other pyramids must have been built later."

"Who is the goddess?" Rekesh asked.

"She must be a protector of this planet," Elera said, thinking about what she had just inferred from the crystal in the tablet.

"And what is *the essence?*"

"I'm not sure, Rekesh. When I was in Ixon, I was told about it but I didn't really understand. I think it is everything, absolutely everything."

Rekesh didn't know what to say.

"I think I see another tablet in the floor over there," Elera said.

They both walked slowly over to the tablet, sensing the immense energy in the place. Once again, the tablet had a crystal embedded in it.

"Knowledge has somehow been stored in these crystals," Elera told Rekesh. "I can understand what they are trying to tell me."

"What is it saying?" Rekesh asked. Memories of his exploits in the Giza pyramid suddenly came to mind.

"It is a warning," Elera said. "It is telling me that as more and more succumb to the force of power, the ways of the great sorcerers are being lost and warped. Those who try to harness this power are unwelcome in the temple."

Rekesh began to feel quite uneasy at this translation.

"I think this message was recorded more recently. There are some symbols carved here…"

Rekesh began to doubt whether the temple would want him there. Sharp memories of Jeth Tyrone sprung into his mind. He looked down at his hands and an image of them covered in blood shrouded his sight. He gasped as he began to feel conscious that somebody was invading his thoughts. He looked over at Elera. She was trying to read the inscription on the tablet.

"It can't be," she said as she translated some hieroglyphs, which looked like images of star constellations. "According to this, this message was recorded in the *age of the great lion*. That's over ten thousand years ago and this message implies the temple has been around for much longer."

Elera saw another tablet and could hear its message from afar. She walked towards it. "This is an important message."

Rekesh listened carefully to Elera's narrative as he fell into feelings of guilt and loneliness.

"The sacred temples have been warped into tools of power. They are now tombs for those who deem themselves royalty. Within these tombs, the children of power now dwell. Those who have taken the sacred crystals are now only prey to the eye of darkness. Protection forever be on this land and all who dwell on it. As the wheel turns those who hate will fall. And those who love will be free."

Both of them were silent for a while as Elera's recital took shape in their minds.

"The crystals it speaks of are the *stones of power*. They are the burden that we all have to bear," Elera said after a while. It was the first time she had ever mentioned such a concept to Rekesh.

"Stones of power?"

"Yes, Rekesh," Elera said, instinctively feeling as though he was hiding something from her. "What do you know about them?"

"Nothing," Rekesh lied anxiously. "Why? What can they do?"

"They can end this world," Elera said chillingly.

Overcome with guilt, Rekesh was about to tell Elera what he knew but she had already walked towards the back of the pyramid.

She had noticed another tablet further into the great chamber and began to walk over to it. The crystal inside immediately spoke to her, before she had even reached the tablet.

"This world is protected by those who love. Without love, it would not be possible for the worlds to be connected, nor could we ever truly be alive."

Elera felt like someone was standing right beside her, conveying the message.

"Many embrace the force of freedom, many embrace the force of power, yet, the third force is the one true force, the one connection that binds us all essentially. If you are to embrace any force, embrace love. It is the essence of existence."

The inference struck a deep harmonious chord in Elera's being and she got a most certain feeling the message was as old as time itself. All the concepts she had come across over the past several months, came together in her being as a heartfelt understanding.

The essence was love. Everything was love.

At that moment, she understood entirely why she had undertaken such a tremendous journey across the globe to reach this point. She wanted so desperately to spread love amongst the beings of the planet that she had searched and searched for a way to prove to people that it was the only thing that mattered.

The message of this tablet is the message of my life, she thought.

"What are you thinking about?" Rekesh asked her as he reached where she was standing.

"I am thinking about this planet and why I am here," she told him softly.

He too began to think about the meaning of his own life.

Thoughts of his early childhood sprung to mind.

"What do you *see* when you walk the earth, Rekesh?" Elera asked him after a while.

"I see a lot of greed," he said. "It seems that almost everybody I have met just wants more and more."

"I see that too," Elera agreed. "It stems from apartness. But you know what I see the most?"

She paused.

"I see fear and segregation. I see people so afraid, people driven to hate each other. And what is everyone so afraid of?"

Rekesh couldn't answer.

"They are afraid of being alone, so they follow blindly. Everyone is afraid of losing that which they love, those who they love. Everyone is afraid of losing their lives. And that fear prevents them from living in the present, it prevents them from loving with a heart full of love. It stops the beings of this world and beyond connecting."

Rekesh completely felt what Elera was saying.

"But beings *need* to love and the result of not giving and receiving love is suffering. The reason I have come this far is to prove that there is nothing to be afraid of. I want to show everyone that love is the *only* true way of life. One can never truly lose another. One is never alone."

Rekesh did not disagree, but he felt a lack of the understanding that Elera clearly had about how love could prevent the suffering caused by loss and the fear of it. For him, love would not stop empires from murdering people.

"What about all those people that are killed in wars? Maybe there is another plane of existence where beings live on, but to those left behind, the loss is all too real. It is something real to be feared."

There was silence as the serenity of the environment made both of them reflect on their lives. Then, Elera heard the same voice again.

"Elera," it whispered to her.

At the very back of the giant chamber in the distance, Elera spotted something. It looked like some sort of cave. They both walked for a while until they reached the entrance.

Her view of the world began to change and she could see the energy flowing around her. Then in a surreal moment, Elera saw an image of Aova shining through the darkness of the cave. She had the beautiful foal standing next to her. She felt that she was being called. She felt that a long lost part of herself was now staring her in the face.

She looked back at Rekesh, knowing deep down that this time, he could not follow her.

"Elera?" Rekesh said as she leaned in closer towards the cave, which seemed to descend deep into the earth.

Surges of emotion flowed through Elera's body. Intuitions flooded her mind. She could see the cave as a vacuum, a passageway to somewhere.

The walls were alive, emitting everlasting energy, breathing with pain at what they had witnessed. She suddenly had the overwhelming sensation that she could not go back, that she could never return to who she was. This was where she belonged. Her journey across the earth had ended and she knew what she had to do.

She looked at Rekesh. He looked so vulnerable that Elera's heart began to ache.

"I will always love you, Rekesh."

Then he watched stunned as she ran over to the cave and jumped into it, disappearing into the void.

Chapter 51 – Path of the World Walker

Elera was descending.

She was falling through the air, darkness overshadowing her. She fell for an aeon, through times past and times present, soaring and gliding with an unfathomed lightness.

A glow emerged beneath her. It rose to her side, muffled and hazy. The glow seemed to be slowing her down. She felt like she was floating and an overwhelming feeling of wellbeing flooded her body. Her mind became quiet, free from anxiety and worry, free from thought. She had complete trust in whatever was going happen, utmost contention.

Elera's eyes closed and when she opened them again she felt as if she had woken up from a long dream.

She was standing on a large patch of ground, covered with a grass both familiar and unknown. It felt alive beneath her bare feet. Everything was vividly rich in colour and density.

In front of her was a vast majestic forest, completely domed by an almost perfect semi-sphere of a cavern. There were four giant pyramids placed at the edges and a fifth at the centre of the enormous cave. The two furthest pyramids looking like small huts in the distance.

Elera was surprised to find that light was so abundant in the globular labyrinth. Looking closely at things was difficult. She had to shift her focus to zoom in on the detail of the cave in surround. The roof seemed to have giant crystals infused into the stone, allowing light to refract into the entire space.

Plants grew in wealth around her feet. Elera didn't recognise any of the trees ahead. Everything seemed hazier, almost translucent at times.

The trees were larger and more magnificent as they got closer to the main pyramid in the centre, and it looked like they were trying to climb it. The pyramid was smooth and it shone like a mirror, also reflecting a vast amount of light onto the rest of the natural dome.

She looked at the four corner pyramids. They all had the same glorious shine.

Elera saw smoke rising from close by and then she saw three figures coming from the forest in the distance.

How have people survived down here? she thought, feeling no fear at all.

She decided to walk and meet them. As she approached, she noticed the people wore indigenous clothes similar to those she had seen throughout Cibola, yet they looked older, made in an archaic way.

These people could have been down here for thousands of years, she thought to herself.

Two women and a man greeted Elera by offering her a large green nut. She ate it instinctively. It was delicious, rich and nutritious. However, it somehow changed her perception. The forest, people and structures beyond all seemed much more solid than before.

"You *see* better..." the man said, pointing to his eyes.

Elera smiled in appreciation and followed their gestures to accompany them. The entire experience felt like a dream. She still had an overpowering feeling of contentment and trust flowing through her. As she walked closer to the structures ahead, she noticed that the three people did not talk. However, they seemed to be fully interacting with each other from their expressions.

Many creatures inhabited the strange forest, which seemed to radiate an ethereal energy. Elera saw many kinds of rodents and birds living in the forest, some of which she could not recollect having seen before. A few deer and horses could be seen further into the dense greenery. They were tame and approached curiously as the group walked through.

Many of the trees had giant bluish fruit, the size of watermelons, and vivid green leaves in the shape of large fans. There were also masses of flowers growing on the ground. One of the women turned to Elera and made a gesture towards a break of light at the end of the forest path. She said something in a language Elera could not under-stand.

As the walk through the forest came to an end, Elera was faced immediately with a group of small stone houses. They were simple and square, with a single opening for a door.

Each house was comprised of a number of large stone slabs, which were seamlessly smooth and almost looked like marble. Elera could see a partial reflection of herself in the stone. They walked past the houses, some people making welcoming gestures as they went.

The city ahead was truly grand. From her current standpoint, the centre pyramid still looked far away and overshadowed everything else, its pinnacle close to the ceiling of the monumental cavern. The ground was covered with soft, dense grass and everyone walked barefoot. The woman who had tried to communicate turned to Elera again and pointed to the pyramid.

They walked for what seemed like an hour, passing grander temples and houses, all made of the same marble-like stone that shone ethereally. Most people wore indigenous attire similar to some traditional dress she had seen in Cibola and were either sitting or lying down, all looking peaceful and in a meditative state.

The city was a very quiet place. Only now and again, the sound of a bird singing or faint footsteps could be heard. It felt like a holy site to Elera.

Eventually, they approached the centre pyramid and Elera saw that it was stouter than other pyramids she had seen, with giant blocks of stone the size of regular houses constituting its imposing structure. Elera had never seen such enormous single blocks of stone. There was a large open entrance leading into a giant chamber.

Light seemed to be radiating from everywhere, illuminating the inside. The light was glorious, it bathed everything and the people inside also radiated and reflected light. The two women and the man that had led Elera to the pyramid stopped and one of the women pointed to another entrance, directing Elera to go inside.

Elera passed through the simple doorway and she was greeted by an elderly woman who looked frail yet full of vitality. She immediately noticed that this woman was luminous, with yellowish rings of energy similar in colour to a warm flame, whirling uniformly around her. Some of the rings seemed to extend out with her every movement. As she gestured for Elera to follow her, she saw one of the rings extend very closely to where she was standing.

Immediately after witnessing this phenomenon, she glanced back at the people that had brought her there and noticed they too were luminous. They were all glowing, their bodies surrounded by what looked like giant luminous eggs. Elera could faintly see an egg-shaped aura surrounding her own body, hazily white. Her aura brightened and became clearer around her. She saw a thousand colours in its soft shimmer.

"This glowing egg that I can see surrounding me. What is it?" Elera asked, the resonance of her voice swaying the air. "I can see filaments of light shooting in from over there."

She pointed to a place towards the back of the egg that encompassed her. She could feel an aching sensation in the back of her right shoulder blade as she had become aware of the strings of light.

"It is your energy egg." A voice seemed to be projected into her mind. *"Those filaments shooting in are feeding you with energy from the universe. The type of energy that you are being fed right now through that particular spot on the egg is specific to the dream world"*

"Am I in the dream world?"

"Yes," the elderly woman told her telepathically.

"Then none of this is real?"

"It is no less real that anything else you have ever experienced. You make it real. We all do collectively."

"But how did I get here? I wasn't asleep. I actually walked into a real cave," Elera insisted, not wanting to doubt her sanity.

"It is true," the woman confirmed, looking more luminous, her energy rings extending further outwards and merging with Elera's energy egg. *"The connection to the essence in the earth pyramid has created a gateway, an energy hole. Many of these gateways exist on the*

earth. You have now been through more than one."

"Is this my body?" Elera asked, pinching herself to validate that what she was saying was reality. "I can feel my skin and how solid my arm is."

"What you are perceiving now is your energy body. It can take any form that you wish it to."

"Energy body?"

"Yes. One's energy body exists, regardless of the world one is living in. It can take different forms and in the physical world a physical body enshrouds it. Here in the dream world, it is easy for you to shape your energy body or even make it disappear," the woman told her. *"Watch. I will show you."*

Then, the woman disappeared before Elera's eyes, only to return again an instant later.

"You have experienced this already."

Thoughts of her experience with Aova and the jade statue in Bimini came to mind.

"In the spirit world, the energy body looks like glowing light. It can be shaped, but there is no real need to do so there."

"Why?" Elera asked.

"Because the beings who dwell in the spirit world serve their purpose better by existing as light. Light penetrates everything. Light is riding on the wings of the essence."

Elera thought for a while about what she already knew about the spirit world. She remembered glimpsing it when she had touched her head to the Intihuatana stone and how all the beings looked like they were moving through endless string-like filaments of light.

"Our shared origin, the one original world is the spirit world," the woman told Elera before the question even came to mind.

Elera began to remember the vision that she, Bene and Javu had collectively experienced in the Ixonian temple. She could visualise the spirits existing in the physical world, all hovering over that vast, murky ocean. Before she could even ask the woman about it, she was already telling Elera the story.

"You know of the fatums and the stones of power that can be used to summon them into the physical world. Indeed, tragedy occurred in what is known as the age of the great lion, when the sorcerer Voro, who had become poisoned with power, summoned the fatum of fire, Ignis, to the physical world. This dragon of death systematically went on a mission to destroy everything in its path. It was at that time that many lands of the earth were lost, destroyed by Ignis, destroyed by fire."

"When did this happen?" Elera asked, feeling as though she was finally discovering the truth she had search so long to uncover.

"In your units of time, this equates to twelve thousand, three hundred and forty-one years ago."

Elera was speechless.

"What you and your friends saw in Ixon was an incredible event that occurred because of the actions of the Leiruyi sorcerers that remained on the earth at that time. They ventured into the dream world and somehow managed to summon beings from the spirit world into the physical world."

"But how could they help?"

"They did this because only the spirits know how to harness the full force of freedom and light, which you know as Affero. This was used to drive Ignis away."

Elera could only listen.

"Affero is, after all, the opposite of Ambitio, which as you know is the driving force behind each of the fatums."

The incredible story seemed unreal, like the farfetched tale of a child.

"This event was the culmination of a great power struggle between two of the original peoples of the earth. That is all I can tell you about that event."

"How do you know all this?" Elera asked. "Who are you?"

At this question, the three people who had met Elera at the cave entrance returned and the wise woman's energy rings seemed to come together into an energy egg. Elera felt a wave of what felt like nausea in her solar plexus from a sudden imbalance that occurred in the immediate environment.

"What's happening?" she asked them all.

"Whenever beings connect into the dream world a change in perception can occur," the woman assured her.

"You asked who we are?" a taller woman said, speaking the words to Elera in a familiar language. "We practiced the ways of the Leiruyi and learnt how to dwell in the dream world indefinitely. In a sense, we are no longer human, though our last physical incarnation was such. We live in this city, known to our people as *Xibalba*. This city and the surrounding forest are constructed completely from our collective imagination."

Elera couldn't believe that nothing around her was physically real. It looked just as solid and genuine as any other place she had seen.

"But where am I now? I mean, where is my body?" she asked. "I must have fallen, deep underground..."

"Yes..." was all the woman said in response. "Physical places share the same space as other worlds. You are somewhere physical on the earth right now, but your energy body is not. It has transcended the physical world. You are in Xibalba."

The tall woman then gestured to the elderly woman at her side who had previously been communicating with Elera.

"Tlaloc, with whom you have been conversing, is actually just a visitor to Xibalba too."

"Yes," Tlaloc, the wise woman projected into Elera's mind. *"The last time I dwelled in the physical world was forty-seven thousand years ago, at a time when the stones of power were originally forged."*

"And you have lived in the dream world ever since?"

"I mostly exist in the spirit world. I only dwell here when there is a purpose."

"Are you saying that you are here because of me?"

Elera knew the answer to the question before Tlaloc could respond.

"Yes. History seems to be repeating itself," Tlaloc said, with what could only be described as sorrow. *"Voro once again walks the earth as*

a new incarnation. He is a most loyal servant of the eye of darkness. This time he not only wishes for the fatums to roam the earth, but he intends for Ambitio itself to appear and incarnate."

The words sent a chill down Elera's spine and she wasn't sure that she wanted to hear any more. However, she got an overwhelming feeling that she knew Voro, the legendary figure that Tlaloc had described. Her mind seemed to freeze as she tried to think of who it could be.

"Voro is now known as...."

The answer was projected into her mind. It was the man who had caused her mentor so much pain, the man who had manipulated so many.

"Sadana Siger."

Elera now felt like she was deeply ingrained in the disturbing story that Tlaloc had been imparting to her. She felt an immense responsibility within.

"Since the Leiruyi dwelled on the earth, humans have gradually sought more and more power in their lives. This has come to a point now when most embrace Ambitio instead of Affero. Most choose to seek power instead of free will, most take instead of give. This has made the force of power and the fatums very strong."

"You said history is repeating itself. How?"

"Ignis has once again been summoned to the earth."

There was silence for many moments.

"But how?" Elera felt herself cry with dread.

"To understand how such a travesty could have come to pass, one must first understand what the fatums actually are." Tlaloc was imparting, though Elera was finding it hard to concentrate, like she couldn't hold onto any awareness. She felt as if the world around her might disappear at any moment.

"The fatums represent everything powerful about the elements that are so fundamental to our existence. Whenever one acts out of power, it only empowers those worlds where the fatums dwell and ultimately the force of Ambitio too."

Elera was in a trance-like state, unable to think or talk. She could only perceive, only observe.

"And, if one possesses a way to enhance such power, one can ultimately control such entities. These creatures are the embodiment of ultimate dark power and their sole purpose is destruction."

Tlaloc seemed to pause for a while.

"And as such, the way in which they are summoned is with just that...destruction. The truth lies with the one who is closest to you."

With a sweep of her hand, Tlaloc seemed to invoke a strange vision, which seemed like it was being projected into a mini-world in front of her.

The holographic scene showed Rekesh in a dingy alley somewhere in Raicema City meeting with a stranger who was wearing a long brown cloak and a large hat to disguise his appearance.

"I have discovered the location," the stranger told Rekesh. The cloaked figure then thrust a rounded stone into Rekesh's hand. "This is the *counterpart*. For you to navigate such a place will require the expertise of someone who knows much about ancient structures. Do you know such a person?"

"In fact, I just met someone like that when I visited an old friend of mine in Ciafra. She seemed to know a lot about that kind of thing."

"Good. Keep this stone safe. Without it, you will be buried."

The scene shifted back in time, to the atrium of an old building and the same stranger standing silently, arm outstretched and holding a gun, lying in wait for someone. The stranger's face could now been seen and Elera knew it straight away. It was Sadana Siger. A man approached, walking calmly and un-expecting of the attack that was about to happen. As he walked past, he was hit heavily with a blow to the head with the heavy gun. He fell to the floor looking up at his attacker.

"Sadana?!" the man expired in shock. "What are you doing?"

"Where is it?" Sadana barked angrily.

"What?"

"The stone! Where is it?"

There was silence between the two men.

"It is not in my possession," the man said sincerely.

"Don't lie!" Sadana spewed. "I know that the stones have been entrusted to the Mattero family."

Elera quickly realised who was laying on the floor in such a helpless and victimised manner. It was Juhi Mattero, Kirichi's son and Bene's father.

"I returned the stone to where it belongs," Juhi told Sadana.

The words seemed to outrage the twisted man and he leaned in close to Juhi, pressing the gun against his stomach. "Where?" he hissed. "If you don't tell me, I will hunt down your entire family until I find out, including your son."

Sadana was staring at Juhi, crazed with anger, intoxicated with power.

"I will burn Lizrab to the ground!"

After a few moments of contemplation, Juhi relented.

"It is in the Great Pyramid of Giza, in the chamber of stones."

"Give me the counterpart! You must have the counterpart?!"

Juhi relented and at that moment Elera realised that he had resigned himself to death. A rounded stone could be seen in Juhi's hand.

A sadistic grin formed on Sadana's face and the scene faded away as he pulled the trigger without another thought.

Time forwarded to the next scene, which was atop one of the skyscraper casinos in Raicema city. It was summer and Rekesh was approaching Sadana as he sat at a large table filled with a great assortment of exotic and rare foods.

"So, did you get into the pyramid?" Sadana asked Rekesh quite bluntly. "You have been gone for many months now."

"It's not so easy. Many of the chambers are sealed and I'm

starting to think that this stone you speak of is just a myth."

Sadana seemed secretly angry with Rekesh but he hid his emotion, speaking softly and with faked affection to him. "Did I not tell you that this is the only way to rid Raicema of those vermin in government? That stone can single-handedly help the people of the Makai be free from the oppression that we have all suffered. That stone is worth ten thousand Raiceman armies."

Rekesh seemed to be taken in by Sadana's lies.

"People have died for that stone," Sadana was saying, hiding his smugness. "I thought you knew someone who could help you navigate the pyramid?"

"I do. But she seemed so reluctant to explore it. She didn't seem to have a good feeling about it. Besides, we have been spending more time together talking about other ways to help the people."

"Oh, so that's it!" Sadana said quite sarcastically and vindictively. "You are falling for this girl?"

Rekesh was silent. Naively, he told Sadana of his future plans. "She is considering moving here to Raicema City to stay with me."

"What good is that?!" Sadana suddenly exploded banging the table and clashing a cascade of clanging. An expression of anger quickly formed on Rekesh's face.

"The pyramid is over in Ciafra, not here!"

"So what?" Rekesh shouted back. "Find someone else to find your precious stone!"

And with that Rekesh flung the rounded counterpart stone onto the table in front of Sadana and promptly left.

The scene ended.

Elera couldn't help but feel proud of how he had stood up for himself. Memories of their time together in Ciafra came back where she had first gotten to know him. She remembered how he had expressed an interest many a time to explore the Great Pyramid and she also remembered how she had never been able to do so herself. It was the one place where she felt completely uncomfortable, like there was immense danger around every corner.

"You were right to avoid that place," Tlaloc was communicating, reading Elera's thoughts. *"You could sense that the stone of fire was there."*

Tlaloc invoked another scene, this time of Rekesh's apartment in Raicema City. He was packing his things, ready to leave Raicema for good. Elera knew that this was shortly before they began to travel the globe together. There was a knock at the door. Rekesh opened it and standing before him was the same calculating man, Sadana Siger, now the chosen leader of the secretive and elitist Order of the Raiceman Makai.

"I heard you were leaving," he said, a flake of sentiment in his voice.

Rekesh just nodded silently.

"You have been missed at many of our gatherings and meetings."

"I no longer want to mix in such circles," Rekesh said quite firmly, referring to the society of wealth that existed in the Order. "I am a warrior, true to my origins. I need little."

"You're starting to sound like those fools in Lizrab," Sadana said sarcastically. "I agree that those that are weak fall, but I don't believe in their primitive and simple ways. Things progress. It is the way it has always been."

There was silence as Rekesh continued to pack.

"I came to bid you farewell. Also, I thought you might like to know a secret that I recently discovered."

Again Rekesh was silent, not wanting to be taken in my Sadana's mastery of manipulation.

"I heard that Raicema plan to invade Lizrab in the near future. I know you may be heading there so it would do you good to be careful. I also heard that Jeth Tyrone himself will be travelling there. Needless to say, you remember the pact that we made and as a *warrior*, I am sure you would do your duty if the opportunity arose."

Rekesh just nodded, not wanting to think about what Sadana was referring to. Then the powerful leader turned to leave.

"Also, if you do happen to venture into Giza again, I heard that the number *twenty-seven* is particularly important."

After Sadana had gone, Rekesh looked down at the bed to see that the rounded counterpart stone had been left there. He picked it up and threw it into his bag.

The vision faded and another emerged in its place – a murky underworld. The scene had moved forward in time. Elera could see Rekesh, Javu and the others deep in the depths of the Giza pyramid. They had found the central chamber and Rekesh was looking at fifty-four stones that were stored like eyes within one of the walls. He was drawn to them and Elera could almost feel the excitement of his dangerous discovery.

He removed the twenty-seventh stone and the chamber began to shake, shocking everyone in the room. Elera could see Sita and Rama clutching each other as they fell backwards. Her professor, Sorentius was frozen still, staring intently at what was occurring. Rekesh then quickly put the counterpart stone in place of the one that he had taken and the pyramid's tremors started to subside.

The stone in Rekesh's hand began to glow red and then the entire chamber filled with light. The scene zoomed out and a great beam of light shot out of the pyramid, seen by many of the locals who all stood, mouths opened in awe. Back inside, the stone in Rekesh's hand was emitting the light.

Then the scene faded out.

Silence had fallen on Xiabala, as if every person who dwelled there had been watching the story unfold.

"Rekesh summoned Ignis?" Elera asked Tlaloc in disbelief.

"*Yes,*" The words were projected into her thoughts harmoniously, "*In removing the stone of fire from its safe holding place, the connection between Ignis and Rekesh was fortified. The beam of light you saw was an awakening for Ignis. That beam actually travelled far across the universe to the place where Ignis, if anyone were foolish enough to look for her, can be found.*"

Elera was speechless, in disbelief. She didn't understand how such a reality could exist, nor could she comprehend how Rekesh could have possibly been involved in creating such a reality.

"You have to understand that Voro is a master of deception and manipulation. Rekesh stood little chance against him given his fiery nature."

"Are you saying that Ignis is on her way to the earth now?" Elera asked, not sure that she wanted to hear the answer.

"When Rekesh took the life of Jeth Tyrone, the summoning was completed and Ignis began her journey, drawn by the destruction of death, through the connection that Rekesh had created with her."

The truth horrified Elera, though for some reason, she did not feel shock or anger at the revelation like she was expecting. Instead, she felt an incredible surge of compassion and love for him, knowing that he had succumbed to the temptations of power, which he had tried so hard to repel throughout his life. She knew he was a good person who loved her wholeheartedly and it began to make her question her own motives in seeking out the ancient pyramids.

Have I been driven by some dormant desire for power? she questioned herself. After what seemed like an age of silence, Tlaloc said something profound.

"You are driven only by love."

Elera knew it was the truth.

"It has been prophesised that there would be at one time, a pure human incarnation of Affero, one who has overcome all challenges to be truly free as a human being. This person will be a being of pure light. This person will be capable of incredible feats, of whatever they will.

"Conversely, it is said that at the same time, there will be a pure human incarnation of Ambitio, one who is powerful, and can command whomever they wish. The clash between these two incarnations is said to bring about the end of the universe as we know it."

Elera felt overwhelmed at the prediction, mixed feelings of responsibility and fear clouding her awareness.

"Voro and others who consider themselves elite have planned for a human form of Ambitio for a long time, longer than you can possibly

comprehend."

"Why do they want such a human form?"

"*Why would anyone want this?*" Tlaloc was asking in response. "*Nobody really wants it, but they have no choice. These people have made themselves into little more than machines, machines that operate automatically without consciousness and at most times to their own detriment. These agents of Ambitio perpetuate the things that end up killing themselves. Ambitio will be summoned not because anyone wants it, but simply because it is inevitable.*"

"But you said we create our own reality?"

"*The beings that are making this happen do not know that, Elera.*"

Elera was now frustrated by the situation.

"*The conundrum, it is rooted in our own creation,*" Tlaoc was relaying, almost answering Elera's thoughts. "*When the physical universe as we know it began, Ambitio was very weak, indeed, only a seed of its current existence. Affero, the giving force of freedom and light, was at the height of its strength then. That is how our universe grew to be so vast and indeed, it is still expanding. However, those of us who have seen it in its totality can tell you that the universe will soon stop expanding.*"

Elera was silent.

"*It is because Ambitio has become so strong that it has created an imbalance. Not only will the universe stop expanding, but it will also start to contract, and when that begins, nothing can stop it. The ultimate consumption will begin and the universe will vanish into the most infinitesimal of spaces!*"

Elera was finding it all hard to comprehend. She had a lot of questions, but decided to allow Tlaloc to continue in hope she might answer some of them.

"*The two forces are everywhere, empowered by the actions of beings, strengthened by belief. Since you have been young, you have known that the world in which you live is not as it should be,*" Tlaloc imparted to Elera. "*You have felt that there needs to be a change, that there is an inequality that is proving harmful to your existence and the existence of others. This inequality, this imbalance has manifested itself throughout all facets of life.*"

"In the physical, you see the great divide between those who consider themselves rulers and those who are effectively born into slavery."

"I have known that many are selfish. They think only of themselves."

"Such is the way of power," Tlaloc coincided. *"And you have sought to change this. You have been seeking a secret, something that will set everyone free."*

"Yes," Elera said in a voice that transcended the space in which she occupied. "I have been searching…"

"What have you been searching for?"

Elera thought about how she imagined things changing. The key lay with making all the selfish rulers realise that they are connected to everyone else. Elera thought about what this meant.

"I want to show everyone that they are the same. They are not alone. They have never been alone. I have been seeking an end to the loneliness we all feel."

"The loneliness stems from the imbalance that has occurred. It began when I was a child, when the stones of power were created. That signified the path in which we were all going to tread."

"What happened when you were a child?"

"At that time, a great tragedy occurred. A child was stolen from its mother, and in this vile act, enough dark power was created to forge the first stone, the power stone of fire, the most powerful of all the stones."

"What child?"

"The child of Ignis of course. It was the first child to be stolen from its mother. The dragon of death exists for a cause. She will be ever vengeful. She is the fire of damnation, a reminder of the misery of unthinkable loss. It began with Ignis, and as it currently stands, it will end with her."

Elera felt an immense empathy at what had occurred. She suddenly had the innate feeling that she was able to soothe the raw pain Tlaloc was describing, that she had the antidote to the poison that had been projected onto the world.

"Who am I?" Elera asked herself out loud, a question that reverberated throughout the entirety of Xibalba.

Then, the answer came to her in the form of an image, clear as blue skies before her eyes. She could see the same wondrous foal that she had seen before, standing in front of her, a young female. She was so real and so close to her that she could smell her sweet breath and hear her rhythmic heartbeat. She was giving out love, only love. Love was the only reality for that being.

The silky foal had eyes that sparkled like the brightest of stars. Negativity could not touch her. She was perfect.

"Do you know who this is?" Tlaloc seemed to be probing Elera.

Elera was almost afraid to answer.

"... This is Kajana, the first world walker. She exists to spread love, to connect the beings of this world in unity."

It was at that moment that Elera felt whole. She could not have imagined how it felt to be whole until it happened. Everything that she had experienced up until that point seemed farcical, as if she had played an over-elaborate joke on herself. Nothing else mattered except the purest of love that existed between her and the being that stood in front of her.

"This is what you have been searching for. She represents what you will be."

Elera was in bliss and absolute elation. Her crown was wavering. Her heart was flowing with a peaceful stream of love that infused the universe. The foal in front of her represented an untainted love like no other, a force so powerful it could cleanse anything that it touched.

"Kajana was born when I walked the earth. It was the same time as the power stone of fire was created. She is the balancing force, the bearer of love, clear to see before us."

Elera was beyond thinking. She could only perceive whole-heartedly. Kajana, the delicate foal, was a vision of purity and beauty. Another image was forming by Kajana's side.

Aova appeared next to her, a magnificent equine form of peace and freedom, her muscular, poetic white body arching with the strain of existence.

It was like looking into an invisible mirror.

"Aova is Kajana's mother."

Elera could not reason what was being told to her, but she knew it was the wholehearted truth and she suddenly felt incredibly powerful, fully of concentrated energy. She felt lighter, as if invisible chains had been removed from her being.

*"You are a world walker, Elera, one capable of bridg*ing the worlds that are currently so hidden from each other."

Elera was looking at Aova and Kajana, separate beings yet the very same as herself. The love she felt had taken her to another place, to her true home. She felt people calling her name. She heard her father.

The words of the spirits filled her head.

"Do not worry, Elera. One can never truly lose another."

"If I enter the spirit world, I will die in the physical world, won't I?"

There was silence for many moments.

"It is true," Tlaloc admitted. *"The only way to live in the physical world with enough energy is to dwell there from birth to death and not pursue the path of the world walker. Restraint will cement the spot on your energy egg to that of the physical world. That is needed to survive in there long term. In the spirit world, instead of awareness coming in from the back of the egg, it comes in directly from the top, filling up the egg. Once one has experienced that, one cannot adjust back to the limited perception of the physical, unless one is born again."*

Elera spent a while searching her thoughts and feelings for agreement that this was indeed what her life had been about. Though it seemed right, something was holding her back, a feeling of loss that seemed so terrifying.

"If this was not meant for you, you would not be here," Tlaloc said after a while. *"For one to walk across worlds is almost impossible. We knew this would happen, indeed, we have been waiting for it to happen. The energy hole that you walked through is almost always closed. It opened for*

you."

"How do I enter the spirit world?" Elera felt herself say. She had the sensation that she was surrendering to something.

"We will help you. All you have to do is wish for that point on your energy egg where light is coming in to move to the top of your egg."

In complete detachment, Elera willed the spot to move. As it began to slowly shift, she felt the energy of the people around her being projected onto her and her perception changing, like the world around was melting away.

Her life flashed before her. She saw her childhood, she saw her friends, she saw Rekesh. Then she saw Aova, standing beside her, the warmth of her body melting into hers. As light began to enter from the top of the egg, everything started to fade away, until there was only light remaining.

All feelings stopped and the wheel of time stood still.

Only an endless, all-pervasive love remained.

Chapter 52 – The Fall of Rekesh

Rekesh awoke in darkness, his body and head throbbing. He had followed Elera into the cave of darkness and the last thing he remembered was falling until he lost consciousness.

Trying to sit up in the darkness with pain, he began to feel a deep-rooted anxiousness when the steady pace of tremors began to penetrate his immediate awareness.

The ground pulsed like a convulsing body, gaining strength with every paroxysm. The entire surroundings seemed to convex and concave in a wave fashion making him feel dizzy and nauseous. For a split second he thought he may be dreaming but the overwhelming fear for Elera's safety brought him sharply into the realm of physicality. Then, with a delayed and lingered convection a sudden burst of all-encompassing waving energy pushed out in every direction, overpowering Rekesh into darkness again.

He awoke to find himself in a large hall, light permeating from the walls and ceiling. His head woozy, he stood up uneasily until he regained his balance. Then, before him, he saw her.

She was lying in stillness, unmoving, like a child asleep. He walked over to her slowly, half expecting her to awake with her usual vibrancy. Instead, she remained, perfectly still, her body like a statue.

"Elera? Are you okay?" He heard the words cascade out of his mouth. Kneeling beside her, he placed his hand on her stomach with affection, expecting a reaction of warmth and reciprocation. Instead, she was as still as stone.

It was then that a well of pain swelled in his midriff until he felt so sick that he could think of nothing else. He shook her, gently at first and then more forcefully with raw panic. She did not move and the pain spread everywhere, so consuming that it was not possible to think, only possible to feel. A black hole was forming.

The pain rose into relief and his tears fell like rain, the splat of each drop like a plunge into the unknown. He died at that moment and the reality he knew was wiped away, replaced by uncertainty, vanquished by nothingness. Then the pain returned like a throbbing thorn in his life. It was unrelenting, unrepentant.

"Elera!" he cried with primal emotion, hugging her body close to his heart.

He kissed her cheek, kissed her lips. He loved her more than anything in the world. He could not live without her.

Then, in a strange moment of sudden awareness, he looked up in horror to witness the sight before him. Not more than a few strides away, the head and body of a hideous, giant snake began to appear.

It writhed in apparent agony, before materialising, its thick dark blue scales forming the most hypnotising pattern. It seemed confused for a moment, before coming to its senses and noticing Rekesh standing before it. It rose up aggressively as if automatically reacting and before Rekesh could contemplate another thought it had attacked, its head like a giant bullet heading straight towards his eyes. He allowed himself to drop and saw the long body of the snake fly above him. He rolled over and drew a giban instinctively.

It dove at him again, this time sinking its long, sharp fangs into his shoulder.

"Arrghhh!" he bawled, dropping his short sword to the floor with a clank. The pain pulsated like a swelling infection in his shoulder, quickly spreading down his arm. The snake's jaws were locked tightly and looking into its round, black eyes, Rekesh could see the pure essence of death radiating outwards. At that moment, Rekesh lost all will to fight.

The snake wrapped itself around him and pulled him to the floor. He lay there with the snake's heavy body on him, waiting to die. But then, looking up he saw a light.

It was in the shape of a woman yet Rekesh couldn't quite see her face. A fire alit in his chest and with a sudden surge of strength he rolled over onto the snake and reached over with his other hand, picking up his giban.

He rose it up and plunged it down it down the snake's neck. Its grip on his shoulder was released and it bounced backwards, coiling up in pain. Then it rose up aggressively, thick blood seeping from its wound.

It jumped high, jaws open with viciousness. As it approached him, it felt like time had slowed down and every saddened beat of Rekesh's heart was in time with that of the snake's. He lifted his sword horizontally and closed his eyes. He jumped up and swiftly swung his sword diagonally upwards. He felt the connection of steel to tough scaled skin and the snake's head was cut cleanly off.

Rekesh fell back to the floor and saw the head and body disperse into a red mist. Then the ground started to shake violently. A giant crack appeared in the stone ceiling above and it quickly ran down the wall to the floor.

Wincing with pain, he sat up and dragged himself over to Elera's body, the tears flooding back. He put her arm around his neck and lifted them both up. Seeing an open door in the distance, he hobbled towards it, all the time looking at Elera's beautiful golden skin. Rubble started to fall from above, crashing around him like meteorites. Passing through, he reached another chamber with a doorway to the outside.

At that moment, the ground rose up, throwing him and Elera to the floor. Looking on in horror, a giant fissure appeared, Elera's body hanging on the edge of it. He tried to reach her, but the poison in his body somehow stopped him.

She fell downwards and then she was gone.

Rekesh was ready to let the earth take him, but in a raw moment of instinctive survival he ran to the entrance just as the walls crashed around him. He ran until his leg muscles felt like they would burst out of his skin.

He flung himself at the small opening as debris cascaded and felt himself being thrown down a staircase as the crash of the door resonated in his right ear. He looked back whilst he was falling seeing the great stone blocks of the ancient pyramid crumbling into a giant pile of rubble, the sky dark above him.

He lay there, the poison pulsating around his body and the sky above stained with ancient dust. He wanted to cry a river and drown in it. The poison was starting to take over, seeping through his veins and forcing him to stare with serenity into the vacuum that his life had now become.

Chapter 53 – River of the Past

Jen King had been walking for days through the *Nicha Mountains*. He had walked through hardy forests and along mountainous pathways. At night he had slept under fallen logs and in the morning he would watch the sun rise like a friendly old clock turning its hand. He hadn't seen a single soul since his journey began and Jen was beginning to wonder if he might be the only man alive on earth.

The mountains stretched on for as far as he could see and Jen had noticed recently that the odd snow shower would fall as the altitude gradually rose higher. He had experienced difficulty in finding food so high up in the barren environment, only gathering a small group of berries now and again.

Jen was presently walking along an open pathway with a few trees scattered around in the distance. The ground was relatively flat and Jen was glad of that after the steep inclines he had recently climbed.

Ahead, he caught sight of something moving in the distance. He began to run to find out what it was, weak from lack of nourishment and drained from lack of direction.

It was a farmer, ploughing a small patch of land with a rake. He was meticulously turning the earth and then raking it in perfectly straight lines.

"Hello," Jen said as he approached him. The podgy farmer smiled at Jen in response but when he spoke, it was in a language Jen did not understand.

Looking around, Jen could not see any dwelling in which the farmer would live. In the distance was the towering presence of snow-capped mountains and little else. The farmer started to point at something over by a tree stump. It was a pan of thick stew bubbling away on a small fire. Jen realised that the farmer was inviting him to eat with him. He smiled with grateful reciprocation at the man.

The farmer placed his rake to the floor carefully and led the way to his small encampment. Jen noticed a number of thick blankets wrapped up in a bundle under a nearby tree, which Jen presumed was the farmer's sleeping arrangement.

The farmer produced two small clay bowls from a bag next to the fire and they both sat on the floor as he scooped a bowl full of stew into the simple vessels. He handed one to Jen. He nodded at the farmer in appreciation.

The hot concoction was the tastiest food Jen had every savoured. Soft and juicy lentils burst with flavour on his tongue with every mouthful. The herbs and spices infused into the thick soup were fragrant and warming and Jen wondered how someone who was clearly in poverty could produce such nutritious food. The farmer ate slowly, his ragged clothes stained with the colours of the earth.

"I am lost," Jen said after a while, knowing the farmer probably wouldn't understand. "I mean, I'm not even sure what I'm doing out here."

There was a light breeze skimming across the flat land, a flock of birds above riding it like a wave. The air was crisp and clean and Jen found breathing deeply left him light-headed. After a while of silence, the farmer looked at Jen directly in his eyes.

"Bahi," he said with enthusiasm, making a movement from his head to the sky. Jen didn't understand what the farmer was trying to say and so silence fell between them again.

After the farmer had finished eating, he rose to his feet and headed back to his patch of land to continue ploughing it. Jen decided to continue onwards into the mountains and he signalled to the farmer in the direction he was going, also shaking his hand in thanks for the meal. He smiled back at Jen and once again made the same movement with his hand.

"Bahi!" he said again. Then he waved, wishing Jen farewell.

The trail ahead was less defined, the well-trodden pathways starting to merge with grasses before eventually disappearing completely.

Before long, Jen found himself at another steep incline heading into a more rocky mountainous area, with a grassier route to the east. Feeling reinvigorated from the farmer's food, Jen pushed on upwards. Several hours into his trek, he began to wonder if he had made a tremendous mistake venturing in his current direction.

For as far as he could see there were dark grey rocks, with no sign of plant or animal life anywhere. He sat down for a while on a large boulder, contemplating whether he should head back down towards where he had met the farmer. Before long, he was thinking once again about the reason why he was wandering aimlessly through the mountains, which tired him greatly. He decided to sleep for a while, and found a small enclosure in the rock face where he promptly fell asleep.

Jen awoke in darkness. He felt strange, light and anxiety free, as if he was floating. He suddenly had a rush of enthusiasm to explore the rocky area and he looked ahead at the mountains in the distance. Then, instantaneously and without limit, he was suddenly there.

The instant movement seemed natural and from his new position on top of a mountain he could see a sparse forest beyond. Then in another instant, he had moved there, standing at the edge of it.

The forest was hilly and the terrain had changed to be much earthier. He tried to focus on some of the trees in the forest and his vision starred to waver, until the entire environment completely faded away.

He awoke under the rocky enclosure as dawn was breaking, realising he must have been dreaming. He got to his feet, his back and hips aching from sleeping on the hard stone.

Jen set off in the same direction that he had imagined whilst asleep and he began to wonder if there could be any truth to what he had dreamt. After some time of walking, he reached a familiar-looking area and was astounded to see the sparse forest in the distance between two mountains. A feeling of mysticism and excitement fluttered through his body.

It took Jen until the late evening to reach the forest. He had navigated through creeks and mountain paths to finally reach the foliage.

The sun was beginning to sink, peeking out from above the treetops. He felt incredibly hungry, having not eaten since the day before. After taking a few paces into the open forestland, he came across a tall, bushy evergreen tree with pinnate leaves. Hanging on some of the higher branches were bunches of reddish, strawberry-shaped fruit, though the outer rind looked spiky.

Jen picked up a branch from the floor and threw it up, felling scores of the eye-sized fruit to the floor. He picked some up and took off the roughly textured rind. Inside was a translucent, white flesh. It tasted like juicy sweet roses. Jen sat on the floor, eating many of the small fruits and making a small pile of glossy brown nut-like seeds that came from the centre of each one.

Whilst he was eating, he noticed something in the forest ahead. It looked like some sort of creature lying on the floor. He got to his feet and slowly walked over to the area, finding a middle-aged woman, wearing a thick woven robe of yellow and orange patchwork. She was covered with a blanket of foliage and her eyes were closed.

"Hello?" Jen said, unsure if the woman was asleep.

Her eyelids opened revealing the deepest brown eyes he had ever seen. They slowly fell upon Jen's face yet she did not move.

There was silence for a while.

"You are from Raicema?" she suddenly asked.

Jen was surprised that the woman could speak the Raiceman language. "Yes," he replied. "Well, not originally, but that is where I lived for most of my life."

The woman said nothing to this and almost looked like she was bored and wanted to go back to sleep. Jen felt a gush of urgency to engage with the woman.

"What are you doing out here?" Jen asked her.

"What are you doing out here?" she mimicked with a hint of haughtiness. "This place is my home."

The woman did not move from her position.

"What is your name?" Jen asked.

"I do not have a name," the woman replied. "I am what you would call...a hermit. You cannot *see* me."

Jen was confused by the hermit's words. She looked very peaceful lying on the ground, covered by the thick bushes. She had a rugged appearance, her robe looked old and worn and she was quite muscular. Her face was defined and lean, her eyes relaxed.

Jen got the feeling that this woman had a great amount of wisdom and again he felt quite anxious to befriend her.

The word and gesture that the farmer had yesterday made to him came to mind for some reason.

"What does 'Bahi' mean?"

The hermit sat up from her position. In the evening light, her complexion was that of golden silk and Jen could only feel an immense sense of beauty.

"You have come here to ask me to be your teacher?" she almost stated.

Jen was taken aback, not thinking that at all, but nodded in any case.

"Very well. I shall teach you what has been taught to me."

She rose to her feet and dusted her clothes of clinging dry leaves. She began to walk deeper into the forest and Jen followed. They soon came to a low-lying valley ahead, the trees spreading out even more.

"You have come here because you thought that you were a warrior. You used to have that description of yourself. But you are not aware of what a warrior is. Well, I will tell you." The hermit bent over slightly when she walked, her eyes focused downwards, as if scanning the ground that she trod upon. "A warrior is flawless in his actions. I say 'his' because I am talking to you, and you are a man. A warrior could just as easily be a woman."

Jen could say nothing and followed the woman sheepishly.

"The *warrior's way* is to clear his mind of all internal thinking. This is to give clarity to his actions."

They walked down into the valley. In the distance, many peaks rose high into the sky, the long grasses of the vale swaying with the glide of the wind sweeping through.

"Once this clarity has been obtained, the *warrior's will* shines through. This is the first step," she continued. "Now, you asked about *Bahi*. But do you know about *Antah*?"

"I have not heard of either word until recently," Jen said honestly. "I only heard a farmer who gave me food say the word *Bahi* and I wondered what it meant."

"These terms are very old descriptions passed down from teacher to apprentice. The person you met was not a farmer."

"He wasn't?" Jen said confused. "But he was ploughing the land."

"He was a guide for you. A guide will also plough the land from time to time."

Jen said nothing to this and they walked on.

"So what does it mean?" Jen asked after several moments of silent walking.

"From the moment we are born, we are within a bubble. Now, everything in that bubble is your *Antah* and everything outside that bubble is the *Bahi*. The Antah is like a place of storage for your thoughts. It stores your reason and descriptions, somewhat like an island. Everything that you perceive now is based on your island of the Antah, where effectively, you are a prisoner."

The hermit stopped talking for a while, observing the floor again in the same blurry-eyed fashion. Her hands were slightly curled and the wind in the valley blew her hair wildly up and down. They walked silently for hours, until darkness fell. By that time, Jen and the hermit were almost at the other end of the valley.

"You are seeking to escape your prison and reach the Bahi for answers." She suddenly broke her silence. "You want to know where you come from. You want to know who you *are*."

Jen could not disagree with the woman's words.

"It is good to conserve energy. In seeking Bahi, the unknown, one often encounters things that challenge one's energy levels. Let us find a good place to rest."

Jen simply followed the woman's instructions, feeling both safe and intrigued by her.

"Try to lose focus on specific things and have a general vision of all that is in front of you. That way you can get a feeling of the energy related to a specific spot."

Jen followed the hermit's instructions and soon after she had found a comfortable spot, so had Jen, basing his choice on the feeling he got about the patch of ground. The darkness of twilight almost made him itch inside.

"Now, where were we?" the hermit said out loud to herself. "Oh, yes, the island of the Antah. This is the place where your perception lies. You base all that you see and know on the concepts, descriptions and feelings that live on this island. The world you know is completely confined to this island."

Jen could see that the dark blue sky above was ever moving and with it rode an excitement like no other. There were streaks of dark grey and the stars were starting to appear like polished crystals. He felt quite comfortable in the way he was resting, legs outstretched and leaning back against a mound of soft earth.

"Yet," she continued, "there is a way to get off this self-constructed island. When we are born, the bubble we are in is slightly open, a path to the Bahi you seek present, a way onto the island, the way that we got there in the first place. As time goes on and we learn from physical experience and from the descriptions others teach us, this opening closes, confining us in our bubble."

The hermit picked some berries off of a bush that was in reach, eating each one slowly.

"The first task for the warrior is to clean up his island, so that there is room for something else in the bubble, so that there is room for his *warrior's will*."

Jen had heard the hermit mention this concept earlier.

"It is with this will that you can open the bubble and reach the Bahi. The will is like light, magical and able to reach anywhere, but it needs focusing!"

The hermit smiled and closed her eyes, instantly falling into a deep sleep. The way that she had described his mind made perfect sense to him, though he still had no idea of what the Bahi was nor how one could reach it with their will.

Thoughts of Orentus came to mind, the strange luminous being that Jen had encountered several days earlier.

"You are at the mouth of the river of the past. You will navigate that river and achieve what you have been trying to without knowing it." The words echoed through Jen's mind.

He began to think about the stone that rested peacefully against his chest and about where he had come from. Questions sprouted in his mind like eager shoots searching for the sun. He thought about Javu, about his life in Raicema and about how quickly his life had changed.

Mystified, his mind gradually let go of these questions as he focused on how fortunate he'd been to be guided through an unfamiliar land by the individuals he had met so far – Euryli, Herma and her brother, Orentus, the solitary farmer and now the hermit woman who was asleep in front of him.

His mind slowly became clear and content, Jen fell into a deep sleep.

That night, Jen experienced a dream that felt more real than he had ever experienced before. He was simply observing a tree, sitting upright against a rock. He couldn't see the tree clearly, but white light began to emanate from it, a faint glow at first. The light got brighter and brighter until it was blinding. Jen looked away and saw himself lying in a slumber near the foliage. He perceived the hermit sleeping close. Jen felt at peace and decided to walk a little over a small hill that was nearby. He came to a pond where fish were swimming and a few birds were floating. The pond looked clear and unsullied.

In the distance were snow-topped mountains and Jen saw a man walking in the distance at the base of the closest one. He wanted to see the man and the next thing he knew, he was at the base of the mountain, the man walking away from him within arm's reach. He saw the man's face. It was as familiar as looking in a mirror at his own reflection. Then there was a noise that sounded like an explosion and Jen felt himself being sucked forcefully into waking up.

A thunder storm was happening just over the horizon and every couple of minutes, there was a flash of lighting followed by an echoing crack. Dawn was breaking and the hermit was still asleep, her hands resting gently just below her navel. She awoke suddenly and laughed at Jen.

"So you were wandering too?" she said knowingly, as the storm started to subside.

"I...uh..." Jen said, sitting up, not sure what had just happened.

"You have just had an insight into time. You travelled around in your dream for what may have only seemed like a moment. Yet six or so hours have passed here." She laughed again. "Tell me, where did you go? What did you see?"

"I saw a man at the base of the mountains. I felt like I knew him. His face was so familiar"

"In which direction were the mountains?"

"I think over there," Jen replied, pointing past a hill. "I came to a pond first and then saw the mountains from there."

"I know of this pond," the hermit told him. "We shall go there now."

"But why?" Jen asked.

"To find this man!" the hermit replied, springing to her feet and confusing Jen with the statement. They quickly set off in the direction of the hill and as they were walking, Jen began to think about the island of the Antah that his new teacher had told him about.

"The island in my mind," Jen began. "How can I clean it up? I have so many bad memories."

"A good question!" she replied enthusiastically. "A good way to clean your island is to face your past. Once you do that, things naturally get cleaned up."

Once again, Orentus's words came to mind.

"You are at the mouth of the river of the past…"

"And how can I do that?" he asked.

"There is a temporary way or a permanent way. Which are you interested in?"

"What's the difference?"

"The temporary way doesn't take long and can be achieved with little practice. The permanent way may take a lifetime to achieve."

"Well, I want to change for good," Jen said after several moments of contemplation.

"I shall teach you both ways," the hermit said, making the choice redundant. The hill ahead almost looked like it was alive, like it was the belly of a green giant. Jen was sure he could see it moving up and down like it was breathing. The morning air was cold and sharp, a faint mist rising up from the dewy earth around.

"The temporary way to clean up your Antah is through dreaming. You will have no doubt noticed that last night, whilst you were wandering around as you slept, your perception changed. You may have seen things differently. This is a result of your island being temporarily cleared. It is a direct result of escaping the physical for a while. There, in the *dream world*, there is no such thing as an Antah."

"You mean, when I had that dream about walking to the pond and then seeing that man at the mountain, I went somewhere else? To another world?"

"It is a world based on what you know."

"But I didn't know there was a pond beyond this hill," Jen protested, finding it hard to believe. "In fact, I still don't know that. I am only assuming that based on what you have told me."

"The truth is, that you actually know a lot more than you realise. In fact, what you know stems from countless experiences that you cannot remember. That is one of humanity's biggest problems – that they can remember everything they know in the dream world and forget it so easily in the physical world. That is why I tell you that this method is only a temporary one to clean up your Antah. It is cheating really, because the Antah doesn't even exist in the dream world."

Jen was finding it all very difficult to take in.

"The Antah is rooted in emotions," the hermit continued as she began to climb a steeper part of the hill. "That is why the only way to permanently clean up the Antah is to face every emotional memory, and the only way to do that is to pass through the six realms of consuming human emotion."

"Six realms?"

"Anger, Greed, Aloofness, Fear, Desire and Pride. They are a cycle, a star formed by the gods of power. And then you may ask, how is that I have been given this burden? Why is it a part of me? I am sure this is not right. Well, by navigating the realms, one learns of why."

"Why?" Jen asked instinctively,

"So you want to jump directly to the conclusion?" the hermit woman asked back in an amused fashion. She looked like she might burst out laughing at any minute. Then she said nothing.

They walked silently for several hours until they had walked over the hill, Jen thinking carefully about everything he had been told. He was baffled at how he had found himself in the company of this woman and her strange philosophies, yet something important was starting to dawn on him. For the first time that he could remember, he felt deeply passionate about learning new things.

In my life, I have always felt so controlled and unmotivated, almost like there was never any point to learn because I would be told what to do and what to believe anyway, he thought. *Now, not only do I feel freer but I feel driven, though I still did not know by what.*

They walked in silence for a good while.

"If one could permanently clear their island, the Antah, what would happen then? You still haven't really told me what the Bahi is?" Jen asked after thinking carefully about what he wanted to ask his teacher.

"It is quite simple. The Bahi is the ultimate truth. It is everything. Whilst dwelling in the dream world one can remember everything they know, by dwelling in the Bahi, one can remember everything there *is to know*. It is the pathway to everywhere, beyond the forces that drive us. It is the essence of existence."

Jen was listening with vigour.

"But it is better to learn to open your eyes before looking at everything around," the hermit said figuratively. "I think you should improve your ability to hold awareness in the dream world. The storm last night easily distracted you."

"How can I do that?"

"Tonight, when you dream of walking around, try to look for your hands. Look at both of them carefully."

After several more hours of walking, they indeed reached a pond that looked incredibly similar to the one Jen had seen in his dreams. It affirmed everything that he had been told and he grew excited about going to sleep that night.

Jen and the hermit prepared a simple meal from leaves, berries and a root that she directed him to gather. His stomach had begun to hurt from the much-reduced food intake since he ventured into the mountains. After they had eaten, Jen found himself a comfortable spot and then fell promptly to sleep.

That night King travelled back to the same knoll in which he and the hermit had stayed a few nights before. The image of the man he saw walking up the mountain was stuck in his mind.

Suddenly, he found himself at a waterfall.

I must be dreaming, Jen thought.

Then he remembered to look at his hands, but even though he could feel them, he couldn't see them. He looked up and saw the man from the mountain, silently approaching the waterfall area, looking around carefully and then taking a drink from a nearby pool. He looked down and he could now see his hands, though they looked different, like an intimate web of whirls and spirals that were

creating glowing hand silhouettes. As Jen observed them more, he felt more calm and in control of his vision.

This dream feels so real, he thought to himself. *I know I am not really here. I am sleeping far away.*

His hands were now getting fuzzier, like a mist of light was merging them into the surroundings. He could see fast patterns of glowing lights swirling and dancing around. The air looked like electricity. He looked up into the sky, and that's when he felt like a vacuum of energy swooped down from the sky straight into his eyes.

Jen could see swirls of light and the wavy nature of the world consuming him. He felt like the sky had expanded just like when he had met Angelo Orentus in the first forest of the Nicha Mountains.

The air was aglow with the web of energy flows that made up everything. His entire body was a giant interplay of flows from the combined network of his veins and nerves all the way down to the light-speed flows of the atoms that made up everything. Jen found he could zoom in and out of his body, observing his organs and travelling down his veins, then zooming in further to see intricate cells and spectacular atoms, electric balls of ether. Even one atom that was a trillionth of the size of one of his blood cells had super-speed energy streaming around and around, so fast it actually looked and felt solid. Jen zoomed in further until he was inside the atom. He was amazed at how looking around was like observing the vastest of motorways, different coloured lights speeding around so quickly that it was impossible to focus on anything.

It is inconceivable just how much of my body is made of empty space, he heard himself think when he observed it at this intra-atomic level.

Besides the speeding energy, all that remained was a universe of space. He drifted there for what seemed like hours, before being sucked into waking up in a pulling-like sensation, bright sunlight and cold air bathing his face. He looked up with surprise to see the hermit bent over observing him.

"Getting good at this, are we?" she said smiling at him and

revealing a few crooked teeth.

Jen felt dazed and his stomach felt cramped with intense hunger.

"You have been asleep for a week!"

"What!" Jen exclaimed, sitting up, his stomach pain fading to a dull ache. "But it only seemed like a few hours."

"Such is the way of dreaming. It is quite remarkable what you have achieved despite being such a novice."

The sky above looked crystal clear.

"What did you *see*?"

"I saw my entire body as a network of energy flows and I could zoom in and out as much as I wanted."

"You *saw* things as they really are. And as we discussed, this type of perception is only possible if you have cleaned up your island inside. What you are searching for, is to obtain such different perceptions here in the physical world, but there is great value in continuing to venture into the dream world for it can guide you, just as I am guiding you."

"What about facing my past?" Jen asked, remembering the hermit's words from before. "How can I do that? I have many painful memories – ones that make me hate myself."

"It is important to remember that the past should be learned from but not dwelled upon. If you begin to dwell on the past, it shall do you no good in cleaning up your Antah. It will only create more clutter. Instead, try to seek understanding. Be compassionate to yourself."

Jen was not convinced. The idea of contemplating or analysing his past terrified him; the fear of regressing to what he once was smouldering in his chest like a bomb ready to explode. He never wanted to return to that way, the way of not caring, of promoting destruction around him.

"The time has come for you to journey on alone," his mentor told him suddenly, shocking him. He felt upset, like he was lost.

"Remember, try to open your eyes to the six realms and keep dreaming."

With that the hermit lay down on her back and closed her eyes. The fact that she had not walked away consoled him.

The sun was bright, much too light for sleep. Jen got to his feet and decided to take a stroll away from the pond area to find some food. As he walked towards some lightly coloured mountains in the distance, he realised that he had forgotten to ask the hermit about the man he had seen in his dreams again. Jen was sure he had met the man before somewhere, maybe when he was younger.

Up ahead, there was a giant plain with a camel-like animal grazing on the tough, long grass. Its eyes like giant marbles, it glared at Jen without expression for a while before going back to crunching the grass with its wide teeth, gaining little juice for its effort.

What a fascinating creature, Jen thought, observing the animal's bushy mushroom coat and its long neck. As he paced on towards the mountains, he came across herds of the same creature, some with their young. Each of the creatures had two humps and they were drinking iced slush that had formed on the ground from the previously fallen snow.

Whilst the air was chilly in this region, the sun was still shining brightly and Jen didn't feel particularly cold. He pressed on across the plain towards the mountains in the distance. He felt so hungry that the thought of hunting something came to mind, but as soon as he had reflected over it, the notion quickly sickened him.

After several hours of walking, he was almost at the base of the mountain and he came across some hardy-looking trees bearing what looked like apricots. He weakly gathered an armful before resting against the tree to eat them. He began to wonder why he had travelled so far, away from the only person that he knew in the mountains.

A slight feeling of panic came over him as he noticed that the sun was setting behind one of the colossal mountains in front. There was no way he could make it back to the pond in the darkness. The steep incline of the mountain base ahead seem like an enormous challenge that Jen did not have the energy to undertake. He just sat there, watching darkness fall all around him and feeling the air become colder and colder. Before he knew it, he had drifted into a strange sleep.

He was still resting against the apricot tree, though he knew he was dreaming for the mountains ahead looked different, glowing with a sizzling energy. He saw the same man he had before climbing up the mountain, and then, instantly, he was there in front of him. He wanted to speak to the man, but the man didn't seem to realise Jen was there. The man looked middle-aged and seemed to be of Neoasian descent, wearing thickly woven indigenous clothing and carrying a beautifully crafted walking stick.

"Hello," Jen felt himself say, but the man continued walking without acknowledgement.

Then Jen noticed something about the man that was profoundly puzzling. Around his neck was a woven ribbon and attached to the end of it was a stone that looked exactly like the one Jen had around his own neck. The strange thing was that Jen had forgotten about the stone until that moment, yet seeing what looked like the exact same stone around the man's neck brought back many forgotten memories.

A memory of the familiar man came to him, somewhere in the mountains, surrounded by hundreds of soldiers that Jen could not place. Every man was dressed in loose yellow clothing consisting of a long shirt and baggy trousers and each wore a decorative headdress, some of which had jewels and sequins sewn in. The man was speaking to the soldiers in their native language and Jen could understand what was being said.

"Death will only bring more death," the man was telling one of the leaders.

"What are we supposed to do?" one tall leader said in response. "Are we to allow the invaders to kill us all? Are we to just sit here and let it happen?"

"That is the seeds that they sow," the man was trying to explain. "You should not plant such seeds in your own futures."

"We cannot just stand by and watch them kill everyone!" another leader said fierily.

"Instead of fighting, run away," the man said.

The leaders all looked appalled and ashamed at even considering such an idea.

"They are the ones who are in the wrong! They are invading us. Why should we run?"

The vision ended and an implausible nostalgia radiated throughout Jen's body and mind. The scene was so familiar that it felt as though he had just personally lived it. In fact, somehow he knew who was invading those people the man had been speaking to.

It was when the Raiceman army invaded Vassini, Jen thought, finding himself in front of the man on the mountain path again. *But that happened fifty years ago. How could I know about it?*

This time the man looked directly at him, just stopping still on the icy slope.

"Hello. Can you see me?"

"Yes," the man replied, sitting down on a rock as a light snow shower fell upon them both. He placed his walking stick on the floor.

"Who are you?" Jen asked. "I see you in my dreams. I must be dreaming now."

The man's prominent features were becoming clearer.

"My name is Zaigan."

Whilst the name seemed vaguely familiar, the nostalgia he had felt now had passed and he couldn't find any deeper meaning to it other than the name seemed correct for the man.

"Does that name mean anything to you?"

"Not especially. Should it?"

"Why, Jen, don't you recognise me?" Zaigan asked playfully.

Jen shook his head, unsure of the familiarity he had felt in the man's presence.

"I am you," he said calmly.

The statement invoked an innate sensation of deja vu in Jen and suddenly even the mountain slope seemed like the most familiar of places.

"We are the same person except we have lived in different times."

Jen was unexpectedly open to the idea.

"How come I can see you and speak to you if you are the previous me?" Jen asked. "Surely we cannot both exist at the same time."

"Your being is getting back to its roots. You are creating this vision of me, your previous self now. I am still you, but in another time, another place."

"So what I just saw, you speaking to those men. That was me?"

"Yes, you actually lived that event, as me."

"But I can't remember anything else about it. I don't know what happened afterwards."

"It is not important to remember such details," Zaigan told him. "It is not even important to remember me or those who came before me. What is important is that you realise *why you are here*."

Jen was in agreement with his former self. He wanted to know why he existed and what he should be doing with his life.

"You have fought hard to break free, Jen King, and you are now in a position where you can help others break free."

"What do you mean?" Jen asked, not understanding what Zaigan was getting at.

"The person you are, the experiences you have lived through, though often traumatising, are all for a reason. They have happened to teach you a lesson, one that I should have learnt when I was alive."

Jen felt soothed listening to the voice of the rugged man, like he was listening to a friendly relative.

"I opposed violence all my life, but could not stop it. I did not understand it, did not understand its roots. But you do!"

Jen felt like he wanted to delve further into the subject but Zaigan was changing the subject quickly, as if the awareness that Jen was holding of him might slip away at any moment.

"We both have the same purpose. We are both *protectors*. We are both one."

"Protectors?"

Jen looked down at the stone around his neck and then at the exact same stone around Zaigan's neck. Before he could muster any questions, Zaigan was telling him something important. "Protect the stone. It holds unimaginable power."

Again, Jen looked down at the shiny formation of motherly black crystal. Jen could feel that it was alive, awaiting something.

"There are two things that you must achieve before you leave these mountains," Zaigan was saying. "You must pass through the six realms to clear your past."

Jen remembered what the hermit woman had told him about the six realms.

"And once you have cleared your past, you must then venture into the Bahi to learn the truth."

"What truth?"

"You are here to change not only this world, but countless others."

The two stones shone in unison, like reflections of each other. Zaigan seemed to be focusing on Jen's stone. "The safety of this stone represents the safety of this planet. This planet is in great danger."

Jen was listening in a trance, unable to move. He began to feel like he was asleep, dreaming the world around him.

"You were a slave to power but you broke free! There are billions of beings that are still slaves, slaves to power, slaves to the most intricate illusion ever created!"

Jen was hearing the words, yet he was drifting away. Zaigan was fading. "You cannot do it alone, Jen. Navigate the realms and enter the Bahi." He heard as he began to lose consciousness: "Find the bearers of truth and love. Find the ones who can cross worlds to help you set everyone free."

Then silence fell and the mountain disappeared. A void came and then an everlasting light filled it. Jen could see creation dawning and he was the artist.

"Set everyone free..." he heard, before his eyes slowly opened.

Chapter 54 – Path of the Snake

Darkness had fallen.

The blurry reality crept in like an unwanted dream followed sharply by the sickening pain of loss. There was no energy, no will to see, no spirit to move. A slight roll was all he could manage, until his head slammed down onto the solid ground, the wet dirt spraying up into his face.

The rain hammered down with cold stabbing ferocity and the skies roared in agony, lightning and thunder dominating the heavens.

He could see a cave in the distance, dark and hollow like his heart. He thought he saw something, a flicker of light, strangely glowing from within. The sight of it gave him a moment of relief and he dragged himself to his feet. A snap of thunder overhead cracked like a giant twig snapping.

Crippling venom trickled through his veins like acid, a curse that he had now submitted to. It was his punishment that every subtle movement burned from within.

Rekesh staggered into the cave and he saw the warm glow again. It travelled down the tunnel inside. He felt totally sapped. Seven days of hell had drained his body and poisoned his mind. He knew he might die soon. He held on to the wall and dragged himself along, his legs starting to bow.

Ahead he could see candles burning, and a subtle light radiating from a being he couldn't quite focus on. With a last burst of energy, he fell forward and collapsed at the feet of someone, slowly rolling onto his back.

The human peered down at Rekesh and then lightly touched his forehead sending a surge of relief through his body. He started to float slightly upwards. His head draped backwards, arms winging with reprieve from his pain and exhaustion. He tried to speak but no words came out. He saw a young human but could not distinguish its gender. The human looked both masculine and feminine from what he could see.

He then heard a voice in his head. "Unlock your mind," the androgynous voice said. "You know me."

Rekesh felt a warm light radiating from the being. It was purifying his body and he suddenly fell back to the cave floor with a bump.

"Feel the light wipe away all that should not be there."

After a moment, Rekesh felt strong enough to stand. The same warm white aura was still vibrant around the person. The wind and rain could be heard howling and splattering outside of the cave and darkness was slowly creeping in, leaving only candlelight to illuminate the cave walls.

"Who are you?" Rekesh asked weakly, leaning against the cave wall with fragility.

"You do not know me? I am like you, Rekesh Satori."

"How do you know my name?" Rekesh questioned him, mystified.

"I can see your thoughts. I see every fear, every dream, every event that goes around and around in your head."

Another crack of thunder reverberated through the tunnel sharply.

"It is important for you to let go of Elera."

The statement sent a wave of pain and then anger through Rekesh, but he quickly pushed it away. The confusion of what he was experiencing was all he could bear the think about.

"She had to make a difficult decision, one that will greatly affect the progress that the people on this planet make."

Again an overwhelming surge of anger passed through Rekesh. He covered his face with his hands wanting to cry, but all he felt was despair and resentment. He felt betrayed by Elera, like she hadn't been careful enough in her life. The result was the resounding pain in his chest that would not go away, a nightmare born in his heart.

"Be strong, Rekesh. Feel love, not fear. Do not hate."

Images of the close times Rekesh had spent with Elera over his lifetime flashed through his mind. The human-like being reached out and touched Rekesh lightly on the shoulder. As he did, Rekesh found himself back in the moment of an earlier time, when Rekesh and Elera were talking about love.

Rekesh was insisting that she stop taking so many risks because he loved her so much.

"Love is not just about two people, Rekesh, it is about everything, the reason why great things happen," she had said. "Love everything."

The memory quickly changed to the time Elera was alone in the underwater pyramid at Bimini, walking through the ruins. Rekesh could now hear every thought going through Elera's head at that time. She felt alone but she felt alive. She was sending out intentions of love to the building itself, even though it had imprisoned her. She was praying, praying for the building, praying for the planet, praying for him, praying for everything.

I pray for Rekesh not to worry about me.

He could hear her voice, as if she were standing beside him.

But I want to worry about you, Elera, he felt himself think.

Another flash and Rekesh was back in the cave, the stranger looking at him with calm eyes.

"It is important that you let go of your fears, Rekesh," the being was saying. "Elera tried to help you with this many times."

The statement infuriated Rekesh and something gripped him. Without thinking he grabbed the being by the throat, pushing him against the wall. The pain of being without Elera had turned into fiery lava erupting through his body.

"Shut up, just shut up!" Rekesh yelled aggressively.

The being closed his eyes calmly. "I am your fork in the road," he said slowly, unaffected by the aggression being projected upon him. "There is no going back after this day."

"What do you mean?" Rekesh barked forcefully.

"It is quite simple, love, not hate. The most dangerous place one can venture is that place where one hates oneself, where one is in fear of oneself."

Rekesh was looking into the eyes of the being and he saw something unearthly, a shine from beyond.

"When that happens, one then becomes a monster, open to the darkness in the universe."

Rekesh jumped back with a fright as the being he was gripping morphed smoothly into a familiar face. It was the stranger that had helped Rekesh navigate the mountains of northern Ciafra when he was anxiously travelling to Giza. Rekesh was now holding a much wider and muscular neck. He released his grip with shock.

"Casar!" he exclaimed, almost toppling backwards.

"Actually, most know me as Mr Orentus. However, from time to time I like to take different forms. Casar is one of my preferred forms as he lives a very simple life."

His voice was exactly the same as Rekesh remembered it.

"Who are you?" Rekesh trembled, sure that he was in a nightmare. He hoped that he would wake up at any moment.

"I am a man who once had to take the same path as the woman you love so dearly. I tried to warn you of what was to come, Rekesh. I tried to warn you when I gave you that chart."

Rekesh tried to think but it was difficult, the throbbing pain in his head, arms and legs growing more intense.

"That chart of something in the sky?" he blurted finally.

"That something was yet to come. You made that chart into a reality when you listened to Sadana Siger, when you chose power over freedom."

Rekesh was horrified at what he was being told.

"For someone like you it is harder to repel the force of power, but many have been there to help you. You have let your ego control you."

"I don't understand," Rekesh said, awash with emotions and confusion. "I never meant any harm, especially not to her."

Orentus didn't speak but just touched Rekesh on the shoulder. He looked different now, like a young rugged man.

Rekesh was transported to an earlier time in Raicema City, a time before he had even met Elera. Sadana had called Rekesh to his private home, a wealth of gardens and grand structures built solely for his exclusive pleasure.

"Rekesh, you are one of the most loyal Makai warriors I have seen," Sadana was saying to him. "And as such I think it is time to initiate you into some of the Makai's most sacred knowledge."

Sadana had been filled with such vigour as he spoke.

"I am about to initiate you into an ancient secret. Only members of the *Order of the Raiceman Makai* are privy to information about such matters."

Sadana had looked proud, like a father watching his son graduate from school.

"The Raicemans resent it greatly, but there was once a much greater force on this planet, one that they are trying to keep secret from their people, a force that ruled for thousands of years and in essence, still rules today."

Rekesh had felt that he deeply wanted to learn more about such power.

"This empire was so great that they built structures like no other empire has been able to recreate. They are the architects of giant pyramids built all over the planet, architects of powerful technology that surpasses anything that exists today." Sadana's eyes had widened with a wild excitement. "Technology that can do whatever the bearer wishes, be it build the tallest of buildings or destroy a city."

Rekesh had been bewitched by the possibilities and had listened to every word Sadana had said in awe of his knowledge.

"The Makai, our way of life, is all that remains of this great force that has now been forgotten. But it is down to us to revive it."

Rekesh had been unsure of such ambitions, yet his lack of knowledge had allowed him to be drawn in to the mystique of Sadana's chronicle.

"What is this technology that you speak of?" Rekesh had asked.

"Special stones that have been endowed with immense power. These stones go back to our earliest ancestors."

Sadana had convinced Rekesh to become a member of the ORM, promising wisdom and greater freedom in society. Rekesh had been apprehensive, yet the elitism had appealed to him, he could feel that now.

"One day I may call upon you to retrieve such a stone," Sadana had said. "The Raicemans do not know of their capabilities and it would be a disaster for us if they did."

Rekesh had felt the sentiment greatly. At that time, he had been completely anti-Raiceman, feeling revulsion and contempt at the views and way of life of the nation.

"With these stones, we can prevent the atrocities that the Raicemans carry out on our people. No child will suffer like you did."

That statement had not only reminded Rekesh of his parents' death, but it had strengthened his belief in Sadana's vision. He suddenly realised what Orentus meant by ego. It was the part of himself that could be manipulated, the part that was afraid and needed constant reassurance. It was the part that he now wished he could cut out of his being.

Reality of his current environment returned, the dark cave surrounding him and the androgynous being standing before him. His anger had subsided and his head was filled with questions, the sickening pain still pulsating in his head.

"Could I have helped?" he questioned himself out loud. "Could I have stopped her?"

"Whilst your own progression is married to Elera's, you are both on different paths. There is no way you could change the direction in which she was walking."

"But is it my fault?" Rekesh cried out, grabbing hold of Orentus again.

"Elera has chosen her path. Your actions, if anything, have only sped up her journey along it."

"So it *is* my fault she's gone. She would still be here if I hadn't taken that stone, if I hadn't taken Jeth Tyrone's life, if I hadn't lied to her." Rekesh bowed his head, letting it hang as the pain rose again, this time stronger than ever before. It throbbed from his chest outwards so even his fingernails, even his hair hurt with a stabbing feeling that sickened him.

Orentus was silent, glowing strangely and chanting something under his breath, praying for forgiveness, wishing for recovery in the tortured man in front of him. Many moments passed, the shriek of the wind fanning the emotions, an irritation that would not cease.

"Life continues," Orentus said finally. "Let go of the past now."

Rekesh suddenly understood that he was firmly in the present and that he could not go back. He abruptly felt a sudden pang of remorse for his actions. But then he felt what he had always feared, total loneliness. It created a vacuum inside his heart and he felt empty. He shook free the vision and the touch of Orentus.

Something flashed in his mind. It was a vision he had seen a lot recently, the face of a terrifying creature, the face of a snake.

The poison in his body returned as if called from the deep.

Anger and hate consumed him through the pain, directed at the world, aimed at life.

The being who had tried to help him now irritated him. Tears streamed from Rekesh's eyes, yet they were hot, like the burning lava of a raging volcano. Orentus was speaking to him but seemed more distant.

"I am your fork in the road. If one hates oneself, then one becomes a monster."

When he looked up, there was nobody there. The candles flickered in the wind and then blew out. Then, there was a man in front of him.

The man was large and physically superior, his muscles like molten sacks of heavy metal. Rekesh could not see the colour of his body but as he focused on the man's face, an intense fright shot him directly in the eyes.

All he could see was the large head of a cobra. Its shiny dark green and silver scales surrounded two bright silver eyes and the cobras fanned headdress was intensely mesmerising. He was glued to the spot, unable to move.

Rekesh felt something sharp in his hand and he looked down to see that the man's arm had turned into another long cobra, its fangs buried deep into his palm. He was bleeding and he could feel the burning venom flowing into his arm.

He closed his eyes.

He felt angry but something was telling him not to be.

He opened his eyes and there was nobody there, not Orentus, not Casar, not the strange cobra man.

Rekesh was alone. He was alone in the darkness of the empty cave.

Chapter 55 – The Panda and the Mountain Fox

Jen King had been dwelling in the dream world, talking to his previous self, Zaigan, for several nights. It was strange looking at the wrinkled face of the old man and every now and again a pang of nostalgia would return, almost like Jen was looking into the mirror of the past.

"I still don't understand about the *world walker*," he said to his reflection. "You have told me about the dream and spirit worlds but I don't understand how such a person can *walk* between them."

"That's just it," Zaigan said. "People can't usually understand. The world walker is special in that they are fully aware of how to transcend worlds. The world walker travels to where they are needed."

"How do you know this?"

"The real question is, how do *you* know this? Whilst you think you are talking to me, you are really talking to yourself."

Jen was silent for a while whilst he tried to make sense of the conundrum.

"What about the six realms?"

"It's time for you to go deeper into the mountains," Zaigan said to Jen. "Only by dwelling there by yourself can you discover the answers to all your questions."

"But there is so much that I wish to ask you about. How did you die? Who were you? I know what you say, I mean... I say, is true. I was once you."

Zaigan smiled at Jen but then got up from his seated position on the rock and started to walk away. As he did, he faded, finally disappearing all together.

Jen was alone. He contemplated travelling back to the lake where the hermit woman could be, but decided instead that he would journey on into the giant mountains ahead. That's when he realised he was still in a dream world and he began to panic, not sure how to wake up.

But am I really dreaming? he questioned. *Everything looks so real.*

No sooner had he asked that question did he wake up with a sore back, leaning against an apricot tree. It was dark but dawn was breaking on the horizon to the east. He just sat there gaining his bearings, staring at the mountains ahead.

They look like gods, he thought, as he gazed at the colossal structures, intricate and complicated, with their grooves and mysterious shadows.

From his current vantage point, Jen could make out six mountains, but the range looked like it stretched on behind them into perpetuity. With a surge of determination, he pushed himself to his feet and set off into the unknown.

The next several months were filled with hardship for Jen King. He crossed paths with not one human or animal. The conditions were cold and wet at times. The higher he climbed into the mountains, the more stark and barren it became. He mainly lived off a type of berry that he found growing on trees in the mountains, red and plump with a bitter taste. He collected them every few days when he would be fortunate to come across yet another tree, as if it were the same one waiting for him. He lost a lot of weight during those months, and he grew a mighty long beard, bushy and wiry.

Then, after three months and seven days of travelling, he came across a small cave, about halfway up the second great mountain. Jen had slept in smaller enclaves than this most nights. It was a blessing to him.

As he entered, he realised that the cave was already inhabited. In the shadows at the back, was a large presence, only round, luminous eyes giving an indication that it was not afraid, not hostile.

Jen decided not to go in, still unsure of what the creature was. Instead, he sat down by the entrance and before long had fallen into a deep sleep, the reassurance of life present in this mountain a great comfort to him.

When he awoke, a giant panda was sitting next to him, meticulously chewing away on sticks of bamboo. Jen was so surprised by its vivid presence that he fell back, almost seeing pools of water everywhere.

The creature was beautiful, with snow white and coal black fur merged like cloud and night sky. Jen watched the panda eat for a while. It seemed out of breath, working hard to get the nutritious innards of the bamboo from its sturdy casing. Every so often, the panda would stop and look up at Jen, almost smiling with its eyes. Then it would go back to work.

When it became dusk, the panda left the cave area, climbing high into what looked like a mountain forest. Several hours later, it returned, carrying numerous bamboo canes in its mouth.

This routine continued for several days and Jen began to enjoy the panda's company. It allowed Jen to sleep in the doorway of its cave, yet at the current altitude the weather was much calmer for some reason, so Jen had little need to.

Jen would sometimes venture up to the forest where the panda often travelled, laden with bamboo and little else. Jen wondered how such a large creature had ever adapted to survive on this hardy plant.

Similar-sized creatures in Raicema survive solely by hunting, he thought.

It seemed like it was against the norm of nature for this giant being to spend most of the day and night extracting what it could from such a plant.

But otherwise, the creature would surely die.

After several days of coexisting together, the panda did a very unusual thing. Whilst Jen was standing, observing the colossal view of Neoasia, it stood on its hind legs, an act it rarely performed, and put its paws on his shoulders.

It looked deep into Jen's eyes, with kindness, with appreciation.

Jen felt touched, like he'd broken a barrier that he'd placed between himself and every other living thing. The panda dropped down back onto all fours and went back to its necessary task.

For weeks, Jen contemplated. He thought about his life carefully, what he had achieved, what he wanted to achieve. Every negative thought made him ask questions, and every question always led back to frustration.

Why are there so many telling me I can change? Out here, alone, there is nobody to harm, but as soon as I am back in Raicema, back in reality, I will be back following the crowd, just like cattle led to slaughter.

He fluctuated in his ambitions, in his desires.

Maybe I won't go back, he thought. *Maybe I can live out here until I die. I have cared for nobody, and nobody cares for me.*

As Jen sank deeper into the wallow of pity, a strange thing happened. The panda, sitting down, resting in a slumped position, looked up at Jen and spoke words to him, clear and resonant like a young child.

"Do not be sad," it said, jaw unmoved but eyes wide and full of gleam. "I have lived here for seventeen years and I feel happy that you have come to visit me."

Jen was taken aback, shaking his head to make sure he wasn't dreaming.

"Did you just speak to me?" Jen asked the panda, quietly and unsurely. There was no answer from the great creature.

I must be going crazy, Jen thought, now concerned that he was hearing things.

"You are not hearing things." The resonant voice spoke again, clear as sweet music. "You are simply *listening* to me".

Jen looked around wildly, searching for another human that could be speaking such words.

"It is I you are listening to, this creature that you have been dwelling with here for many days now."

Now Jen was still and silent, in shock that this non-human could communicate with him. He just stared at the panda for a while. The creature had now stopped eating and was in a slumped position, breathing lightly and looking at him.

Jen's inner ears were throbbing slightly, an unusual but comforting sensation. The strange pools of light returned and with them a bright light above his head, something that felt like the sun but wasn't.

"Why can I understand you?" Jen asked. "Am I dreaming? Are you a figment of my imagination?"

"I am real," the panda replied. "It is clear that we are communicating now. The real question is – why do you have to question everything? Most of the time, things are just the way they are and we can just accept that."

For a while, there was silence, and a strange sort of fear engulfed Jen. It was the sort of fear when one first faces something, a fear of the unknown.

"Why are you afraid of me?" the panda asked. "I shall do you no harm. I choose not to hunt, to leave the mountain creatures alone. We all rely on each other. I am sure things are the same where you come from."

"No, they are not," Jen said, feeling more at ease with what he was experiencing. "People kill each other, one way or another."

"Because they feel fear of each other?" the panda asked.

Jen thought for a while and then smiled slightly. "Yes, I suppose they do."

"But what is there to fear? Why would you be born if not to help each other?"

At that moment Jen realised the sweet nature of the creature before him.

"Once one loves, one's world is changed," the panda was saying. "Then, you cannot imagine anything else."

"Things are different where I come from. People are taught from an early age to want things so much that they are willing to kill for them," Jen explained. "Or at least, support those who would kill."

Jen hung his head in shame.

"I can sense your sorrow. Have you killed?" the panda asked.

"Yes," Jen replied woefully. He glanced out into the distance, a hazy mist now blocking the tremendously vast land that lay before the mountains.

"I too have killed," the panda admitted. The revelation somewhat surprised Jen, after the panda had talked about choosing not to hunt.

"I once killed a mountain fox that was going to eat my child. I had to choose whether to let go and let my child die, or fight back to save my child's life."

"I would not call that killing," Jen said. "I would call that defending."

"And is that what you have done?" the panda asked. "Defended? The ones you care for?"

"Not exactly," Jen said in shame. "I have followed orders to kill."

The panda said nothing for some time and Jen could sense that it was contemplating their conversation.

"I believe there is no difference," the panda said, finally. "You have done what you have done out of fear, the fear of not being accepted. I have done what I have done, too, because of fear. My fear was the fear of loss. But I can see that both of those fears are the same thing."

Jen sat in silence for a while, thinking about what the panda had said, about how unbelievable the entire experience was.

How am I communicating with this animal? Everyone knows animals can't speak? I must be dreaming.

He turned to the panda to ask it another question, but was surprised to find that it had vanished, without a sound.

The panda has probably grown hungry and gone on the search for bamboo, Jen thought to himself.

He waited, but it grew dark and the panda did not return. The mist had enveloped the cave area now and Jen was also growing hungry. He ate the last of the red berries he had gathered and entered the cave to go to sleep. He did not think that the panda would mind as they were now on speaking terms.

Before long, Jen was in a deep sleep.

He awoke to an empty cave, still no sign of the panda. He decided to go in search of the great creature, into the bamboo forest.

The mist had passed and a clear view of a sweeping valley was now present in all its glory. The shadows of the clouds projected on the spacious lands like the silhouettes of strange creatures. The sun streamed down in rays, a majestic and inspiring display of light creating warmth and a glow of prosperity throughout Neoasia.

As Jen climbed the steep rocks that led up to the edge of the forest, he began to wonder if he had been imagining things over the last few weeks. He had been alone for quite a while now.

Has my mind been playing tricks on me? Have I dreamt the entire thing?

The bamboo forest was thick and difficult to navigate. Some areas had tightly-packed groups of bamboo that grew so close together that neither light nor could air get through.

The forest was like a maze, certain pathways clear enough to proceed, whilst others were a dead end of bamboo mass. After a while of stumbling about the maze, Jen began to grow frustrated and slightly dizzy. He came to rest on a round stone, next to a strange-looking plant, orange and blue in colour, with long spikes and purple fruit. The fruit looked juicy and fully ripe.

Jen picked one carefully. He was about to take a bite when he heard a voice speak to him.

"I wouldn't eat that if I was you," the voice said, gruff but a little squeaky.

He looked around and saw a short stout creature on all fours, with bushy light brown fur and sharp teeth.

"Those fruits are poisonous to most that eat them. I almost died once from eating one of those."

Jen didn't even question how he was able to understand this creature. Instead, he decided to ask for the creature's help.

"I am looking for a panda," Jen said, wanting to laugh at how funny the sentence sounded. "It usually comes into this forest to search for bamboo. Have you seen it?"

The words Jen spoke seemed to fill the creature with sadness and for a long while the creature sat on its hind legs staring into the air.

"Are you okay?" Jen asked. "Have I said something to upset you?"

The creature looked at Jen, its eyes lighting up a little.

"No, you didn't," the bushy creature replied. "I was just feeling sad because you reminded me that my mother was killed by a giant panda."

"Are you a mountain fox?" Jen asked, in disbelief, unsure if this was related to the panda's story.

"I don't really know what I am," the creature admitted. "Why are you looking for the panda?"

"I'm not sure," Jen said truthfully "But I feel very different since I came to this mountain. The panda I met can be no ordinary panda, just as you can be no ordinary mountain fox."

The fox seemed amused slightly, its tail waving a little with excitement.

"Are you hungry?" the fox asked.

"I am," Jen said, feeling his belly rumble with emptiness.

"Come with me," the fox said.

It walked away, deeper into the maze of bamboo. Jen followed immediately, still fighting back the doubt that he was living reality. The forest was cool, almost cold from the shade. Only a few rays of light got through the bundles of giant bamboo.

The fox was travelling along an intricate path, very confusing and mostly a blur to Jen, but eventually, the pair emerged in a clearing with a wide path leading out of the forest. In the centre of the clearing was a large bush, laden with juicy fruits.

"These fruits are safe to eat," the fox said. For a while, they both ate, sitting on the soft, moist moss that grew all over the forest floor.

"Why did you come to the mountain?" the fox asked Jen.

"I came here because I needed to escape," Jen said, after some thought.

"Is something hunting you?" the fox asked.

"Maybe," Jen replied. "I am running away from my life as a soldier. I do not want to kill anymore. All I want is to live in peace. Ever since I stepped onto this land, something has been helping me. First, a strange person shows up in the forest and tells me I should travel into the mountain. Since then I have met a hermit woman, dreamt a vision of my previous self and spoken to two animals. I've been in these mountains for months and it still feels like a dream."

The fox was silent, clearly amazed by Jen's account of recent events. It wagged its bushy tail, seemingly amused by his tale.

"The path behind us leads to a special part of the mountain. There are many humans ahead," it said to him slowly. "The panda lives alone, as do I, and in these mountains you should do the same."

With that statement the fox stood on all fours and walked back into the depths of the bamboo forest. Before Jen could utter a word, he was alone again.

Jen sat for a while, gazing at the magnificent bush next to him. It seemed to glow with a wonderful green aura. It reminded him of Angelo Orentus and the unique appearance he had, glowing and vivid. Jen stood to his feet, took one piece of fruit from the bush and headed along the mossy path.

The path ended after a short while, presenting Jen with a wonderful view of another mountain. Jen was about halfway up one side of a huge valley, made of the two mountains.

In the distance, down in the valley, Jen could see smoke rising.

I am home, Jen thought to himself, the picture in front of him as familiar as his own face.

Chapter 56 – Return to the Past

It took Jen King three days to arrive at a small village at the bottom of the great valley. Finding little food during his descent of the mountain, Jen was famished with hunger.

He stumbled towards a simple hut, his simple garment well worn, before collapsing face first in the dirt. As he lost consciousness, he heard voices speaking in a familiar language. He awoke on a comfortable pile of hand-woven rugs and blankets.

An elderly woman was tipping water into his mouth from a silver vessel. He raised his head, his vision slightly blurred. He could see the outline of three figures before him and seemed to be in a large sturdy hut.

"Who are you?" Jen asked weakly, feeling dizzy again.

He placed his heavy head back onto the pile. He could hear the trio speaking amongst themselves in their native language. His mind was swimming, and the words they were speaking seemed blurred and faint. Then the elderly woman put something in Jen's mouth, a small piece of root. It was the foulest thing Jen had ever tasted and the other two figures held Jen down whilst she made sure that Jen swallowed it. He felt like vomiting and his head began to spin.

A moment or two passed, his stomach knotted in excruciating pain. Then, all of a sudden, he began to feel better, his stomach completely relaxing. He felt lighter and more peaceful. He no longer felt dizzy and his vision came into focus.

The elderly woman looked about seventy years old and had long, droopy earlobes, pierced with gold rings. Standing behind her were two younger men, dressed in loose cotton clothing and with shaved heads. They were both smiling and the woman began to smile too as she saw Jen propping himself up onto his forearms.

The woman turned to one of the men and said something in her native language. To Jen's astonishment, he realised that he had understood exactly what the woman had said. She had told the man that *"he reminds me of my father with the way he moves."* Jen was confused about how he had understood the language as he had no recollection of learning it. One of the men said something else to the woman and Jen understood what he said as well. He said that he thought Jen *"can understand what we are saying."* Jen immediately got nervous, as he had no idea how to speak in their language.

The woman knelt down close to Jen and asked him something. Jen instinctively knew that she had asked him what his name was.

"Jen King," he replied. "I think I can understand what you are saying, but I don't know how to speak in your language."

The woman turned to the men and said that she could not understand Jen but thought that *"he said his name was Jen."*

Jen repeated the word "Jen" whilst pointing at himself.

The woman smiled, acknowledging his primitive communication. Then, another younger woman entered the hut from outside and Jen could easily translate what she said to the elderly woman.

"Rua," she had said, which Jen assumed was the elderly woman's name. *"Come quickly, Rinpoche's condition has worsened. We do not think there is long left."*

Everybody left the hut and Jen began to wonder with frustration at how he was able to understand these people.

The name Rinpoche *seems very familiar to me.*

Jen attempted to get to his feet, but at first he began to swoon with dizziness. He held on to a small wooden box used for storing blankets and within minutes he was standing, breathing deeply to get his strength back. He was very weak.

Jen took a step and although shaky, he walked through the door to the outside, where the area was surrounded by large woodland. There were only three huts made of wood in the village, but Jen could see a number of tent-like dwellings further down. He slowly walked towards them. As he got closer, he could see that one was large and was filled with people. He could hear an elderly man's voice speaking slowly from inside.

The man's voice is Rinpoche, he thought, suddenly realising who he was, a leader and healer.

"I am a shaman, a man whom others turn to for advice and blessing."

The entire scene before him seemed familiar. The entire village seemed to be congregated inside the tent before him. Though he could not see him, he knew Rinpoche was dying.

Everyone is focusing their awareness on this man who will soon leave this world. The thoughts sprung into his mind.

Jen didn't have time to contemplate how he knew what was happening for he could understand the words that were coming out of Rinpoche's mouth and he wanted to listen to them. The words soothed him.

"Remember that fear is the instrument of power," Rinpoche was saying to the villagers. *"When you face it, do not try to control it. It can only be dispersed with kindness and love."*

Then all went silent for a long while. A young man came out of the tent and was shocked to see Jen standing outside.

"You should be asleep," the man was said in his language. *"You are not well."*

And then, spontaneously, Jen opened his mouth and spoke in the man's native language. *"I am feeling better,"* Jen replied, as if he'd spoken the words a thousand times before.

The man exhaled sharply in disbelief and promptly went back into the tent. Jen followed him and saw many villagers all praying for Rinpoche, who had passed away whilst lying on his side, with one hand supporting his head. His eyes were not closed and yet were as still as stone. Some people were sobbing with grief at the sight of the lifeless man in his unique pose.

The younger man was whispering to Rua, who was listening with a sorrowful smile. Everyone stood there for a long while, sending kind wishes to the man and his passing.

Then, a miraculous thing happened. Rinpoche moved slightly and rested his eyes on Jen.

"My old friend," he said to Jen with love in his voice. *"You came back to see me."*

Then his eyes closed fully and he passed away, slumping down slightly.

Everyone was silent and shocked. One woman fainted. Rua rushed to help her as did two others. She looked back at the deceased Rinpoche, lying there in the same position, happiness spread across his face. The younger man from before came over and gently led Jen away from the place. He took him to another, smaller tent with cushions on the floor and urged him to sit.

Jen waited alone in the tent for a while, until Rua entered, a smile on her face. She knelt beside Jen slowly and then spoke softly and slowly.

"*Can you understand me?*" she asked Jen.

"*Yes,*" he replied in the native language.

The simple word threw her aback slightly, but she quickly pressed on.

"*What is your name? Jen?*" she asked.

"*Yes. My name is Jen King.*"

"*How long have you been speaking our language? Not many speak it.*"

"*I have only been speaking it since I arrived here,*" Jen said mystified himself at how it was possible. "*Just before Rinpoche died.*"

Rua looked at him carefully, with wonderment in her eyes.

"*You know him,*" she stated. "*And he knows you. How?*"

"*I don't know,*" Jen said. "*He seems familiar. The language just came to me.*"

"*Why did you come here?*" she asked.

"*I am looking for the world walker and the six realms,*" he replied. "*I have been guided here by a man who claims he was me in another time.*"

These words made Rua's eyes widen with excitement and suddenly a young girl who had been listening in outside, came in.

"*Is it him?*" she asked excitedly. Rua told the girl to go back outside and then apologised to Jen for the intrusion.

"*What was the name of the man who told you to go on this journey?*" Rua asked.

"*His name was Zaigan,*" Jen replied, to which Rua gasped in disbelief.

After a short silence, Rua looked up at Jen carefully, almost gazing past him.

"*Yes!*" she said. "*I feel that you have the same energy. How remarkable that you should arrive today!*"

Rua gazed at him in awe for several moments and Jen could tell that she truly believe Jen was the re-embodiment of Zaigan.

"*We call it linking when you remember something from a past life. Some remember their favourite possessions, some their dear friends but you, you remember your entire previous language!*"

She let out a mighty piercing laugh, resonant and joyful, yet it startled Jen, who was still in some disbelief about the entire concept.

"*Who was Zaigan?*" Jen asked.

"*Zaigan was Master Rinpoche's teacher and mentor throughout his childhood,*" Rua stated, somewhat amused that Jen did not know.

"*And you really believe that I am him?*" Jen questioned. "*It could be a coincidence I arrived today.*"

"*There are no coincidences,*" Rua said firmly in reply, a twinkle in her eye. "*Now come with me. There is a way we can be sure before you continue your journey.*"

The statement surprised Jen as he didn't know where he was going himself, just blindly following random advice as he saw it. *But there are just too many concurrences for this journey to be leading nowhere,* he thought.

He got to his feet and followed Rua outside, where many villagers were waiting, all eager to get a good look at the reincarnation of their old master. One villager approached and lowered his head slightly with respect, offering a tightly bound vegetable pastry to Jen. He took it and thanked the man. It was delicious and instantly re-energized him.

Rua was already walking away from the village, followed by the same two young men as earlier. Jen quickly caught up and ahead was the path to a small mountain. They walked slowly for an hour before reaching a clearing at the summit.

"Now what is so special about this place to you?" Rua asked Jen, as they reached the top. He took a look around, seeing only a few rocks and one lone wolfberry tree. The mountain was low enough to be able to see the village down below, even though there were large misty clouds looming.

"I don't know," Jen said, not recognising anything.

Rua looked disappointed and walked over to the tree. She stroked its smooth bark and looked at Jen, seemingly trying to jog his memory. After many moments of silence, she tried a different approach.

"Where do you live? What is your occupation?" she asked.

"I am..." Jen was about to say, before realising his statement would be wrong. *"I was a soldier. I used to live in Raicema, but I don't live anywhere now."*

At first Rua frowned slightly, looking confused, but then she smiled. *"You have realised killing is wrong?"* she asked.

"Yes," Jen replied hanging his head in shame at the reminder of his past.

"Zaigan was a very peaceful man. He always encouraged non-violence and promoted love between all humans. But towards the end of his life, he became distressed at the level of violence on the planet. The land you came from was at war with this area, murdering and fighting over the land," Rua said, thinking back. *"He found it hard to communicate with the foreigners, found it hard to encourage peace."*

The clouds were travelling quickly and they formed vibrant and mesmerising swirls above.

"Rinpoche was the only one present when Zaigan died. And his master told him that he was allowing violence to consume him, and by doing so, he would be reborn in the heart of violence, where he could help the most."

Jen was amazed at this account but suddenly felt very low and unworthy of such acclaim.

"I have helped nobody in my life," he said coldly, dismissing the explanation for his violent past. *"I have killed many, without feeling, without compassion."*

Rua once again frowned at this but then spoke seriously to Jen.

"Your journey is just beginning. Your life is just beginning."

The words filled Jen with hope and he felt at peace again, glancing out on the beautiful unspoilt view. He felt like he had completely recovered from his previous weakness.

Rua took a seated position on a raised patch of land and the two young villagers sat beside her. They all closed their eyes and began to meditate, as if trying to clear the air. Rua was chanting some words slowly and softly, the young men just listening silently still.

As Jen looked out upon nature, his mind at ease, he drifted into a vision. A woman was giving birth upon the small mountain, next to the tree Rua had been touching. A man was crouching next to her, stroking her hair and trying to calm her with soft words. The vision sped to a tent in the village where a young boy sat with his parents, humming and chanting together.

The vision quickly faded. Jen fell to a seated position.

"What did you see?" Rua asked, witnessing the moment.

"I was born here," he said in disbelief. *"I mean, Zaigan was born here."*

A large smile spread across everyone who was sitting on that mountain, including Jen and for the first time he truly and whole-heartedly knew that he had not arrived at the village because of coincidence.

"Why am I here?" he asked Rua.

Rua looked at Jen carefully for a while, before getting to her feet and walking up to him. Jen dwarfed Rua, the top of her head only just reaching the middle of his chest. Despite this, she reached upwards and held his face in her hands.

"Do you know that Zaigan was my father?" she asked quite calmly. *"I feel his presence in you, yet you are very different."*

She looked up carefully at Jen's face, taking in every detail. She observed the consistency of his hair, his sharp bone structure and the deepness of his dark skin.

"Each is born for a reason, though as you go on you will find all reasons

are really the same," she said softly. "For now, Jen King, learn from your past, for it shows you truth and the way to the future."

She paused for a while.

"You asked about the six realms, but you are yet to walk through them. Navigating them is the best way to learn from your past. Remember though, no matter how much the past fascinates or disturbs us, it is not as important as what we are living now."

"And what of the world walker?"

"The world walker is an ideal that my father believed in," she said, smiling. "It is when a person breaks free of not only their past but also of the limitations of this universe in which we find ourselves living."

"I got the impression that the world walker was a real person who exists and whom I should try to find."

Rua let go of Jen and signalled to the young villagers that it was time to go.

She turned back to him with a smile. "It may be possible that such a being exists and if so, that is a great hope," she said, turning him to face the other side of the small mountain. "If you travel down this mountain, you will reach a tunnel that leads to the monastery where we have all learnt many things. It may be a good idea for you to become reacquainted with your past, so you can start living in the present."

With those words, Rua began to walk away in the opposite direction towards the village. Jen began to feel desperate, like he was losing the only people who really knew him.

"But shouldn't I stay with all of you?" he cried out as they walked away.

Rua and the others paid no attention and once again, he was alone, feeling anxious and unsure of what he should do. He looked down the opposite side of the pinnacle and saw a windy path down a rocky incline. His mind was awash with thoughts of the village and the people he had met.

His life seemed surreal and he no longer felt like he was floating along, letting the currents of power control him. Now rather, he felt like he was part of a flowing story, with an endless supply of guiding waterways coming to meet him. He decided to press on, for the first time feeling excitement about whom or what he might meet.

The path was a challenge, with sharp rocks protruding out of the soft soil in an awkward fashion, as if they had been placed there intentionally. Hardy shrubs grew along the path edge, barely moving in the strong breezes. Down below was the entrance to a cave. It was a narrow entrance, yet inviting in its open luminosity.

As Jen arrived before it, he was intrigued to find a small statue of androgynous nature, carefully placed on a small ledge at the side. The statue had a peaceful face with large eyes and open hands. He ventured into the cave, surprised at how light and airy it was, brightly coloured mosses growing artistically up the walls.

Despite its narrowness, the passageway felt quite open and before long Jen could see a bright light at the end. The cave tunnel opened at a sheer vertical drop, another beautiful and glowing valley encompassing Jen's vision. He looked around for a way down, but could see no feasible route. The opening was high up, and below there was nothing but rocks and trees.

He scanned the face above the opening and noticed a small ledge. He clambered up using a few cracks as footholds and immediately noticed there was another ledge above. He climbed higher, each ledge revealing another above it, like giant rungs of a mountain ladder. He stopped for breath, looking up to estimate the distance to the top. It was nowhere in sight.

After multiple gargantuan feats of strength pulling himself upwards, ledge by ledge, Jen finally began to see the top of the cliff. With a final pull, his fingers straining to grip onto the crumbly surface, he shook as he brought his chest onto the edge, his legs still dangling over the mammoth drop.

As he looked up from his difficult position, the incredible sight of a monastery drew his breath. Ahead, integrated fully into a great rocky mound, was a castle-like structure, with giant glassless rectangular windows and a progressively towering architecture.

Behind the monastery was the greatest of mountains, topped

refreshingly with pure white snow. In front was desert-like land. Jen
dragged himself to his feet to take a better look. He walked forward
slowly, amazed at how light and airy the atmosphere was. Jen's head
felt spacious and free of thought and he felt twinges of joy and
delight at his surroundings. He knew that he now would, as he once
had before, become most acquainted with the magical place before
him.

Chapter 57 – The Cycle of Seduction

Jen walked slowly towards the monastery, drawing in the atmosphere around him. There was a patchwork carpet of irrigated terraced fields in the distance, immediately before the incline of a rocky mound, into which the giant stone building had been integrated.

As Jen got closer, he noticed there was a river running down from the imposing mountain behind, winding down around the steep rocky hill and through the patchwork fields. He could hear the tumbling of melted slow falling into the river from above, somewhere deep in the high distance. Other than that, there were peaceful periods of silence. As he continued to walk forward, the faint tinkling of something made of metal could be heard every now coming from the direction of the monastery.

It took Jen an hour to walk down to the fields. They were all farmed immaculately and hundreds of types of dark green vegetables grew in them.

He walked up to some crumbly steps that looked like they had existed since the beginning of time. They wove upwards into a long dark corridor, where huge pillars seemingly carved from the mountain rock held up the patchy roof terraces.

Shafts of light infiltrated the inner spaces in the same way in which rays of sunlight beam through clouds. Jen could hear deep rhythmic sounds of chanting and because the experience felt so vivid and surreal, for a moment he actually thought that he was dreaming.

Along the corridor, small staircases and worn thresholds branched off every so often. Some of the walls were intricately painted with scenes of forests and mountains. Jen saw old wooden doors with elaborate locks that looked like only ancient keys would fit. Peering through one such lock, Jen saw an old kitchen, bowls of grainy flour and jars illuminated by the bright beams from above.

At the end of the corridor was a giant window, the cool mountain breeze drifting through calmly. The window opened out onto a magnificent view of the mountain, and goats could be seen outside climbing easily amongst the rocks. Ahead was an open hall, with tall, carved pillars and life-sized statues. Light was streaming in from above through holes in the roof, creating a celestial interplay of illumination.

One statue ahead looked particularly lifelike, a man sitting in a yogic position, light shrouding all colour. As Jen approached the statue, he was taken aback when its eyes suddenly opened and he realised it wasn't a statue at all. The man smiled. He was dressed in a light brown robe with a shaved head and of plump appearance.

"Oh!" Jen said, surprised to see life in action. "I am sorry to disturb you."

The way the light had been cast on the figure had made him look like stone. The man did not speak but Jen could hear the metallic sound again from behind him. As he looked back in the direction of the corridor, he saw another monk walking towards him, of similar appearance and carrying a small tin chime. The monk approached Jen and placed his hand on his shoulder.

"Welcome," he said softly, as they looked forward at the statue-like man.

"Hello," Jen greeted back. "A woman called Rua told me to come here. Do you know her?"

The monk smiled, amused and touched by Jen's words.

"Of course," he laughed as if it were the silliest question in the world. "Everyone knows each other here. My name is Quan."

The man held Jen's hand in a gesture of warmth.

"I see that you have met Yangji. I am sure that you mistook him for a statue."

Quan laughed and so did Yangji, who began to rise to his feet. He too placed his hand on Jen's shoulder affectionately.

"I have come here to learn about my past and the six realms," Jen said after a while, feeling quite open. "I want to be able to help people, to be free."

Yangji smiled at the monk in such a way as to tell him to leave Jen and him alone. The monk smiled back and then left the hall, walking back down the corridor with his tin chime echoing lightly.

"I can see that you have many questions," Yangji said slowly and melodically. "Knowledge can be learnt from others or can be learnt from observing. Here, we tend to observe more."

There was a silence.

"Let us go for a walk," Yangji said. "Please tell me about your long journey."

They walked in silence for a while.

"I used to be a soldier," Jen began, as they started to walk back towards the corridor. "But I just couldn't do it anymore. One day, it must be many months ago now, I started walking into this forest on the outskirts of Yinkoto. I had escaped from a prison there and some people helped me get to the forest."

Jen paused.

"I met this person there. His name was Orentus. He told me to walk into the mountain to discover my past. I have been doing so ever since. I have been alone mostly."

They walked to the outside of the monastery, along lengthy old pathways and towards some pretty gardens. The mountains in surround were breathtaking.

Jen told Yangji about everyone that he had met, including the wandering hermit, Zaigan, the great panda and the mountain fox, Rua and Rinpoche. He told him about his dreams and how he could control where he went in them and how he had met Zaigan in his dreams. Yangji said nothing, just listening with interest.

"Zaigan, my previous self," Jen continued, "told me about someone that he referred to as the *world walker*. He said that the world walker can cross different worlds, like from the physical to the spirit world. I think the same thing may be happening to me. I don't feel like I truly know where I am."

"What do you think the spirit world is?" Yangji asked, Jen's words finally stirring him to speak.

"I am not sure," Jen said. "Maybe a place that we go when we die."

"I never met Zaigan," Yangji said, detouring from the subject. "I was born after he died, yet I have heard the story of his life. He was a *bodhisattva*, wanting to help as many people as possible to be free from suffering, yet I am told he found this difficult towards the end, as is always the case when you are surrounded by suffering."

Yangji sat down on a stone bench, which looked out onto some more patchwork fields, where a herd of Qiang horses and several goats grazed freely.

"The spirit world, as you and Zaigan call it, is in effect, separate from the physical world, but in essence is exactly the same. What I mean by this is that it is only an illusion that the two are separate."

"So really there is only one world?" Jen tried to confirm.

"There are countless worlds!" Yangji said confusingly.

Jen was surprised by this and remained silent, waiting for Yangji to continue. Instead, the large man burst out laughing.

"Every world is born of the same essence. The one in which we are speaking right now may be different from another like the spirit world, but we are all capable of dwelling in either. It is only from our own point of view that the worlds are separate. If we could see things as a whole, we would see the worlds are connected as one."

Jen was silent, trying to understand Yangji's philosophy.

"That is what the world walker, as you call him or her, is capable of doing. The world walker can see every world as one and thus is able to cross into such worlds at will. An average person is not even aware of other worlds until death, but that is just the start."

"And what of the six realms?" Jen asked. "Zaigan told me I must pass through them to face my past."

Yangji was silent for a while as a light breeze fanned their faces. Jen was amazed at how quickly he had struck a rapport with Yangji and that the intricate local language he was speaking seemed more clear and understandable to him than anything he had experienced before. It was like he had finally got his lost memory back.

"There are six realms of *power*," Yangji began. "The six realms are born out of impurity, the impurity of grasping. There are six negative emotions that correspond to each of these impure realms and your past is locked in these realms, keeping you from seeing who you really are. Those that dwell in such realms have little or no awareness that there is anything else in this universe, that they are connected to so much."

Once again, Yangji paused, this time to hear more snow tumbling down from the mountains in the distance.

"The first is the *realm of humans*, born out of a strong attachment to *fear* or *doubt*. Most creatures that live a physical life are not here because of choice, yet there is the opportunity to understand more through experience, just like you are doing now."

"So we are in one of the realms right now."

"Well this world, the physical world, has elements of all the realms as you will see. However, the *realm of humans* is very similar to the physical world, but it is not here."

"What is it like to be in a realm?" Jen asked.

"They are very much like the dream world that you talk about, so you can think of them as being part of that. The dream world is the bridge between the physical and the spirit world so when we die or are born, we pass through the dream world. This is where one usually encounters the *realms of power*."

Yangji sat silently for many moments, breathing calmly with his eyes half open, seemingly staring at a tree down in the field.

"The second realm is the *realm of the gods*, born out of a strong attachment to *pride*. There, egos have taken over and one wishes control and power over others. Many who repress others are drawn into this realm."

Jen still didn't really understand what a realm was or how one was drawn into one.

"What are the realms like?" Jen asked. "You are telling me what they lead to in physical life, but not what they are like."

Yangji was amused by Jen's impatience and let out a deep

chuckle.

"The realms are the same as what they lead to," he said, tapping the side of his head. "They are here, yet that is all that exists within the realm. For example, the realm of humans is filled with terrifying manifestations whilst the realm of the gods is filled with ruthless egos, all competing to be a god."

"And then after you have been in a realm when you die, what then?" Jen tried to confirm.

"Eventually the urge will come to want to escape and that is when you are physically born. However, you should remember that I am only describing what I believe. You must find out for yourself and not cling to these ideas."

But by now, Jen was already deeply interested and wanted to hear more. The breeze wafted across the landscape and peppered their faces with a sweet aroma.

"Tell me about the other realms," he said, pressing Yangji on.

"The third is the *realm the demigods*, born out of a strong attachment to *jealousy* or *desire*. One drawn into this realm would easily give in to desires and be likely to be addicted to pleasures."

Yangji paused.

"And what would this realm be like? Well, it would be filled with an endless indulgence of pleasures. Doesn't sound so bad eh? Well not all of us share the same pleasures do we?"

Jen thought for a while, starting to understand Yangji's explanations and metaphors. In the distance Jen could hear the faint sound of harmonic singing, delicately carried on the thin air.

"The fourth is the *realm of animals*, born out of an attachment to *ignorance*. Those drawn into this realm are lazy and ignore opportunities to learn or progress in their lifetime. At least we know you weren't drawn into that one, huh?"

Yangji laughed out loud, causing some of the animals to look over to the stone bench where they were both sitting. He suddenly rose to his feet with a boisterous burst of energy. "Let us walk back to the monastery," he said to Jen. "There is something I want to show you."

They walked back to the main entrance of the monastery. It was cool inside yet it felt warming and relaxing.

Yangji continued with his account of the impure realms. "The fifth is the *realm of ghosts* or *avarice*, born out of a strong attachment to *greed* for material wealth. One drawn into this realm would find it hard to accept that all material things are a manifestation only, an illusion, and cling to them greedily. This realm is usually very similar to some cities that empires build, filled with the exploitation of people to produce more and more, filled with an everlasting greed for more and more things!"

The description reminded Jen of several places he had lived and visited including Raicema City and Yinkoto. Thoughts of the thousands of people that worked underground in the city reactors came to mind, civilisation gone insane.

They walked to a small winding staircase and Yangji began to climb the old stairs. Jen followed. The stairs seemed to go up a long way.

"The sixth and final impure realm is the *realm of demons*, born out of an attachment to *anger*," Yangji continued. They climbed the ancient stairwell, step by step. "One drawn into this realm would have a tendency to instinctively react violently to any fear that they have. They create a world of suffering around them, which becomes their own personal hell. I am sure there is no need to describe this realm any further."

Yangji looked back and smiled at Jen as they reached the top.

"The six realms are also known as the *cycle of seduction*," Yangi said as they came to an archaic looking door. "As all of the emotions that they represent are what keep us in chains throughout physical life."

There was a glint of mischievousness in Yangji's eyes and then he smiled at Jen, as if he were about to say his entire explanation of the realms was an elaborate joke.

"And that brings us to the *seventh realm*, which in fact is not based on emotion at all," Yangji said as he fumbled in his robe pocket for a key to the arched wooden door at the top of the stairs.

"The only realm free of attachment, the *realm of pure light*. This is not light that casts a shadow, but the light that *is* everything. This realm can only be reached by those that free themselves of attachment to emotions, release themselves from the grasping and clinging in life that is so easy to give in to."

He pulled a shiny metal key from his pocket, the grip shaped like a lotus flower. He turned the lock slowly with the key, making a scraping sound. As he pushed the door open, there was a creek and then a dazzling flicker of light shining through the opening. As Yangji and Jen walked through the door, Jen was amazed to witness a room with no roof, light penetrating every crevice, so bright that Jen covered his eyes. The light was warming and invoked a sense of calm.

"Why is it so bright in here?" Jen asked, still instinctively covering his eyes. "It wasn't this bright outside."

Yangji let out another laugh from deep within his belly.

"You can open your eyes fully. The light in here will not hurt you. If you open them, you may see where the light is coming from."

Jen tried to open his eyes but found that his instinct was to protect them by closing them again. After a few attempts however, he opened them fully and adjusted to this strange brilliance. He looked around the room and saw nothing but luminosity at first, but then he saw something moving.

It was almost as if another world were fading into the room, a world of intense everlasting light.

All around him were thousands of minute luminous entities, swirling around in a joyous dance. They looked like little sparks of fire that were white hot, whirling about as if they had just sprung to life. The light penetrated everything. Even when Jen closed his eyes again, he could still see the light.

"Now, what I want to show you is what happens when one is attached to a negative emotion, and thus a powerful realm," Yangji said slowly and melodically. He paused for a second as if thinking hard about something. Then he said something that Jen was not expecting. "So, Jen King, how many beings have you killed throughout your lifetime?"

The question instantly filled Jen with a well of dread. His stomach felt heavy and sickly. He began to think about the people he had killed and his heart too started to become heavy, a lump of solid stone in his chest. He closed his eyes, enshrouded in darkness, wallowing in sadness at his thoughts.

Then he felt Yangji place his warm hand on his shoulder and he opened his eyes. The room was now much darker and Jen could not see even one of the entities he had seen before.

"At that moment, you began to cling to your emotions," Yangji said.

Jen was overwhelmed by the experience and for a moment he almost though he was going to cry, tears naturally forming in his eyes.

"I want you to stay here with us, Jen King," Yangji said. "Every day, I want you to come to this room. And on the day when you cannot make the light go away, that is the day that you will have escaped your past, and you will truly be free."

Chapter 58 – The Six Realms of Power

It was late in the evening.

The low resonant sound of a monk's bamboo flute saturated the air like a timeless story of hardship and longing.

Jen, Yangji and two other monks were eating a light dinner of fresh steamed vegetables. Jen had reflected on what Yangji had taught him and had decided that he was going to stay at the monastery for the foreseeable future. He still had many questions to ask and his mind often felt like it was recoiling from the constant line of thoughts in his head.

"Yangji, I want to ask you about the world walker," Jen said after a while of silence. "From what you have told me, I still do not understand how such a person can exist?"

Yangji was silent until he finished eating. Then he looked up from his wooden plate and smiled at Jen.

"The *world walker*, as you have called such a manifestation, could only relate to a kind, compassionate spirit that has the ability to willingly travel into other worlds, including the realms of power that I told you about today."

He paused with a glint in his eye.

"Why would a being do this? How can they do this? The answer is simple. They *wish* to help other beings that are trapped in such realms."

Jen listened very carefully as he crunched on a cucumber-like vegetable. It was crisp, refreshing and healing.

"When I met Zaigan in my dreams, he told me that I am looking for the world walker. What did he mean?"

"I think that Zaigan was trying to tell you that you should aspire to be like the world walker in order to reach the realms of power," Yangji said.

"But I'm not dead," Jen protested, unsure of what Yangji was getting at. "How can I leave this world otherwise?"

"You do not need to be dead to visit the realms," the friendly

690

monk replied calmly.

"But you said that you are naturally drawn to a realm when you die?" Jen argued. The other monks were surprised at his feistiness.

"Yes," Yangji agreed. "However, you have already told me that you visit the dream world when you sleep. If you can consciously do that, then you are also able to navigate the six realms. After all, the dream world is the gateway to other worlds. Even the dead dwell in the dream world."

"Then how do you know the world walker is not also in the physical world with us?" Jen questioned.

"I do not know," Yangji validated. "The world walker could be anywhere. However, the realms of power are not physical in the sense that you can walk through a door to reach them."

"So how *do I* reach them?" Jen asked.

Yangji just smiled, getting up from his seated position and not willing to talk about the subject any further.

The next day, after a night of pondering and little sleep, Jen walked alone around the monastery's gardens, trying to understand about the realms and how they related to the world walker. He had the strongest feeling inside that Zaigan was right and that he needed to find such a being, though he did not know what for.

He sat quietly on the floor, staring at some pretty purple flowers with vivid green leaves, letting his vision fade out into a blur and back into focus whilst he let his thoughts carry him.

He reviewed his life in his mind. He thought about his early years of adhering to strict regimes at the hands of the Tyrone family, his life as a soldier and his recent journey that had taught him so much.

As he thought, a young monk, no older than thirteen years old, walked over and sat beside him.

"Hello," said the boy. "My name is Zopa".

Jen smiled at Zopa and offered his hand.

"Hello, I'm Jen," he said surprised at how striking the young monk's yellow-brown eyes were.

"I have heard you will be staying with us for a while."

"I'm not sure," Jen admitted. "Sometimes I don't really know what I'm doing here in the mountains. But I can't think of anywhere else I'd rather be."

Zopa thought for a moment, crossing his legs and sitting up straighter. "We are all here because we wish to be," he said to Jen. "Though we all may have different paths. What is your *path*?"

"I don't really know," Jen said honestly, surprised at how mature the young man was. "All I know is I was definitely on the wrong one before I came to Neoasia."

He paused, trying to clear his mind of negative memories.

"Since I came here, I've been finding out lots of things about myself. I hate to fight. I don't like living in Raicema. And apparently, I lived as somebody called Zaigan in a previous life who came from this region. Maybe that's why I'm here."

Zopa was fascinated by Jen's account, his eyes widening with interest.

"It is very good that you know about your previous self," Zopa said. "It is a good step to understanding your path."

"All I know is that Zaigan was a monk and he was looking for somebody who is a *world walker*. I think I'm supposed to be doing the same."

"Not necessarily," Zopa cautioned gently. "Your path could be very different from your previous self, but how you got to this point is because of your previous self."

Zopa started laughing a little at his line of thought.

"Even though really you are just the same," he said, amused at the contradiction.

"There is so much I don't understand," Jen said dejectedly. "I have so many questions that need answering."

"You think too much," Zopa said, giggling to himself. "It is good *not* to think as well."

Up ahead, Jen saw several monks tending to the fields, turning over seeds and looking at the crops. Many animals gathered around the monks, who fed them seeds and nuts. One goat playfully chewed on a monk's rope belt.

"Have you seen any spirits recently?" Zopa asked inquisitively.

Jen was surprised by his question and unsure of how to reply, as he had met many strange entities over the past few months.

"What do they look like?" Jen asked back.

"They can look like anything," Zopa said. "They can look like an aura of light or like a human or like an animal. They can even look like a rock or a ripple in a pond."

"In that case," Jen said. "I think I have seen quite a few."

Zopa got to his feet and offered his hand to Jen, as if he wanted to guide him somewhere. Jen took his hand and also got up. Zopa led him down into the fields and walked him through them, past the monks and animals and towards the river that ran down from the mountain.

The water looked as clear and bright as a star, the light shimmering on its purity. Tall trees lined the banks, and the melodic whistling of a variety of birds could be heard creating a symphonic atmosphere. Zopa knelt down near the river and wadded his hand in it as if playfully trying to attract something. After a short while a fluttering sound came from upstream, followed by a silhouette swimming towards them beneath the surface, occasionally spraying water. Eventually, the head of a large fish appeared, with dark wide eyes and a humped back.

The fish's scales were both golden and silver. It seemed to hover in the water near to where Zopa had left his hand.

"You called for me?" A strange voice seemed to radiate through the air. At first, Jen though it might be Zopa speaking but then he noticed how the fish seemed to be unnaturally focused on both of them as they stood there at the riverbank.

"Hello, Kun," Zopa greeted the fish. "How is the river?"

"Restless as always," Kun seemed to reply, though the voice felt like it was directly in Jen's head. He turned to Zopa and whispered

to him.

"Is that fish really talking to us?" he asked quietly.

"Kun is not a fish. He is the spirit of this mountain and its rivers. He lives in a form that he chooses."

Jen just stared at the fish in disbelief.

"*Your friend is like the riverbed. He is easily capable of change,*" Kun told Zopa, who seemed amused by the analysis. The great fish's attention then focused on Jen.

"*You should meet our mother.*"

The fish then dove below and in a swift action, sprung out of the river into the air with a graceful and agile movement, arching its body into a crest. Then in a strange twinkle of light, Jen felt like he was waking up from a dream.

The next thing he knew, the fish was gone and in front of his eyes was a great bird, with wide wings, white as the clouds. The creature flapped its great wings once and rose high into the sky with immense power, swiftly returning with a graceful gliding movement.

"He likes to be known as *Peng* when he is in this form," Zopa whispered to Jen as the great bird descended to their eye level.

The bird was staring at Jen intently, almost like a predator stalking its prey.

"*Yes,*" Peng said directly to Jen, who felt quite delirious at what he was witnessing. "*You must meet Gaia. I think you can do much good with the abilities that she can grant you.*"

Zopa seemed surprised at the great bird's suggestion. Then, Peng flapped his long wings and flew high into the sky, soaring above and into the mountains beyond.

"He likes those forms the best," Zopa informed Jen. "He knows the river feeds the mountain forests and he likes to keep his eyes on both."

Jen simply accepted the surreal experience, feeling both excited and fearful of what he had just witnessed. Zopa smiled at him with warmth. They both began to walk back towards the monastery.

As they reached the main stairway, Jen was greeted by one of the monks he had met the day before. The monk informed Jen of his many duties whilst he was to reside in the monastery, including gardening, cleaning and ploughing the fields.

Jen was set to work straight away, yet he had never been so happy to be participating in the wholesome chores.

Whilst he worked, he thought about all the unexplained things he had encountered and within no time the entire day had passed.

As he was finishing scrubbing the kitchen floor, the monk returned to wish him goodnight.

"You have worked very hard today, Jen. Be cautious if you go *walking* tonight."

Jen didn't understand the monk's comment.

That night, Jen fell asleep physically exhausted, but mentally he felt quite vibrant. He immediately drifted into a strange dream-like location, which looked very much like a large hallway, the walls lined with scores of intricate metal doors.

As he stood before one of the doors it opened for him, dispersing before his eyes. He walked forward and entered a small town, with short block-like buildings lining the narrow streets. Jen could see people staring out of their windows with concern and intrigue, trying to work out who he was.

There were no trees anywhere in the town. The pavement seemed to be made of rough stone. As he peered into some of the houses, the people scurried away from their windows like frightened mice, quickly closing rounded shutters to keep him out.

Then, at the end of the street, Jen noticed what looked like a large animal. Walking towards him was a tall beast, which looked very much like a brown bear. The creature had wild ferocity in its eyes.

An intense fear gripped him, so strong that he was unable to move, a feeling that he had experienced before. The creature suddenly let out an ear-bellowing roar. It was terrifying. As it spotted Jen, it began to run towards him.

Panic set in. He ran back up the street but he could only see darkness ahead. He looked back. The giant creature was almost upon him. He looked around for something to fight the petrifying beast with but the streets were empty.

Then he looked left and saw unnatural lights. He quickly ran in that direction, the roar becoming quieter as he left the strange town. Looking back, Jen saw that he had lost the creature. He felt relief and turned to get his bearings.

Jen found himself in an open field and in the distance he could see a tall, wide building, lit up from inside with a spectacle of lights. Just by looking at it, he was drawn in and before he realised it, he was standing right outside the building.

The great structure looked like a large coliseum. He could hear the sound of cheering from inside. He pushed open the tall heavy doors to find a huge crowd watching a fight between two men, who both had chiselled muscular bodies and were standing inside a large square metal cage.

The men were performing death-defying feats, such as jumping high in the air, clinging to the cage and then flying at almost lightning speed towards their opponent in attack. The men never seemed to touch each other, yet raw power seemed to be radiating from their beings.

With swift stabbing movements, they seemed to release beams of power at their opponent, often knocking the other off their feet to the roar of the jeering crowd.

Jen could feel how bloodthirsty the crowd was and every now and again a wave of incredibly powerful energy travelled through the people, often after a big move by one of the magical fighters. One of the men in the cave was now perched on top of it and seemed to be conjuring something between his two open hands, arms stiff and muscles bulging. Jen saw a ball of red mist-like energy form in the space between his open palms.

The god-like man then pelted this ball at his opponent, knocking him off his feet in spectacular fashion, his body spinning like a yoyo in the air. He crashed onto the hard floor and the crowd went wild, screaming and chanting. Then, another man immediately climbed into the cage, another muscular giant ready for the next fight.

Looking around, Jen noticed that every member of the crowd had a similar crazed look of power shining in their eyes, and Jen could feel the blissful adrenaline carrying the people.

Jen himself felt an incredible urge to step into the cage and show off his fighting skills, the raw adrenaline he used to feel in the heat of battle returning like an old friend. Jen had never realised until now just how exhilarating the feeling was and he saw that the heavy doors of the arena were closing.

Jen felt a panicked urge to escape. He quickly decided to leave, knowing that if he didn't he would be trapped in the arena forever. Barging his way past brawny, sweaty men and aggressive cheering, he eventually made his way back outside the building and was surprised to find that the field the coliseum had stood in was now gone.

Instead, he was facing a beautifully crafted city, every building made of marble and gold with elaborate carvings and the sun shining down at the most perfect of temperatures. A light breeze wafted through the spacious streets.

There were groups of people everywhere, some strangely wearing furs over their shoulders and others wearing pristine silks and jewels. Many were lying around on large open sofas, being waited on by Kivili servants carrying large round golden trays, full of exotic fruits and perfectly cooked meats.

The groups of people seemed to be at odds with one another. One group would whisper amongst themselves about another group and Jen could feel an air of jealousy and scheming.

A woman from one group walked over to a man from another and seemed to flirt with him but then shockingly, she withdrew a knife and stabbed the man repeatedly, laughing as she did this.

The other people in his group just looked on unfaltered until the woman returned to her group, all of them smiling at her act. The man who had been stabbed seemed to be fine.

Now the other group were talking quietly, planning something.

Jen thought they were going to retaliate for the woman's attack but instead they all focused their attention on Jen who was silently stood, observing the movements in the city.

The group began to walk towards him with envious stares. Jen could feel that some of the women in the group were trying to seduce him in the way that they moved. He could smell them, sweet and enticing. He struggled to break free of the enchanting glances of the beautiful, sultry women coming towards him. He turned and quickly fled down one of the city streets.

Ahead, he soon came to another part of the city, though it was very different, a slum with vacant-looking people loitering around in rags. There were hostile, scruffy-looking dogs everywhere and rats scurried around the broken-down streets.

Every building was a dangerous ruin, with broken glass and metal wire protruding from the crumbling walls.

Some people were on all fours, trawling the ground for scraps of food and often bloodying their exposed knees on shards of glass.

"You've cut yourself," Jen found the courage to say to one young boy who was scavenging in heaps of rubbish.

The boy looked up at Jen with a wild look in his eyes, like a vicious hunter that had just spotted its prey. The boy picked up a large shard of glass from the floor, cutting his hand in the process and suddenly began to charge at Jen, growling like a wild dog.

"I just want to help you," he said to the boy, holding up his hands. Others had now gathered around the boy like a pack of wolves and they all started barking raucously.

"Can't you understand me?" Jen yelled at them, growing frustrated.

They all looked vacant, like parts of their brains had been removed. The wild people stamped their feet and growled aggressively, so Jen turned and fled once again.

He quickly walked down a long street and came to a very

different part of the city. It reminded him of Raicema City or Yinkoto, with tall skyscrapers reaching high into the sky. He noticed strange-looking planets and stars scattered in the cosmos above.

The buildings were all exactly the same, made of pure crystal glass and cone-like in shape. He entered one and noticed row after row of uniform offices. Peering into one, he saw a strange-looking man sitting at a desk surround by an enormous amount of items, ranging from random metal objects to piles of food and drink.

The man looked deformed, with an unusually long, narrow neck and a round potbelly. His face was ogre-like with sunken, mummified skin and he had fine greasy hair that dangled down onto a shabby-looking suit. He just sat there, eating and drinking and counting the thousands of silver and gold coins stacked on his desk.

The ogre picked each one up with his narrow, bony fingers and placed it onto another stack whilst glugging a dark, thick liquid and devouring odd-looking pieces of meat. He repeated this over and over.

Jen began to feel an overpowering sickness develop in his chest by looking at the vulgar being, but found it difficult to look away. The man's activity seemed to be getting faster and faster, more desperate and greedy by the second. Jen had to fight with all his might to finally look away and get out of the building.

As he walked through the skyscraper's main door, he was surprised to find that the city was gone, replaced by a dense forest with little light and many trees on fire. He could hear gunfire and explosions all around. A feeling of primordial dread filled him as he realised he had just walked into a war zone.

He heard a groan to his left and spotted a man who had been maimed, dying in a pool of blood. He felt the urge to go over and help the man, but the sight of three angry soldiers running towards him petrified him. The men were carrying the biggest guns he had ever seen. Pure terror shot around his being and he ran into the forest past charred patches of ground and smouldering trees. He felt a bullet fly past his head, narrowly missing him and then felt the powerful force of an explosion nearby.

It knocked him off his feet and into a resonant dizziness. As he looked up with blurry vision from the floor, he kept trying to tell himself that he was only dreaming, that he could wake up at any moment.

Jen saw the soldiers running towards him with rage upon their scarred faces and as they were about to open fire on him whilst he lay helplessly on the floor, he spotted something in the distance.

There was a human-sized being enshrouded in light, walking calmly and projecting ethereal energy all around.

A small foal walked by the being's side, with a tail made of gentle fire.

Both beings were radiating a feeling of love and healing. The floor and the air seemed to warp around them as they walked slowly and peacefully through the hellish place. He heard the sound of the guns firing and as he felt the bullets strike and pierce his body, he suddenly woke up in a panicked cold sweat. He was in his room at the monastery.

Jen's head felt dizzy and he also felt a little nauseous. He quickly got out of his simple bed and put his face in his hands, breathing heavily and trying to accept it was just a dream. Visions of the places he had been haunted him and for a long while, he was unable to move, afraid of what might be around him.

Outside, it was still dark, yet the glimmer of the peeking sun was beginning to emerge on the horizon outside his bedroom window. His heart felt anxious, like he had drank ten cups of strong coffee.

It took several minutes for Jen to calm himself enough to stand. He felt the desperate urge to speak to Yangji and so ventured out to find him. Jen's room led straight onto the main hallway and he followed it outside into the monastery's beautiful gardens. He spotted Yangji outside, meditating on a thin rug in the crisp early-morning air.

"I had a dream about horrible places," Jen said to Yangji as he walked towards him.

"Sit for a while," Yangji told him. "Think of nothing except your breathing. Listen to it go in and out like the waves on a shore."

Jen did as he was told and tried to mimic Yangji's agile pose. It was difficult and painful on his joints so he just sat on his heels instead. They sat in silence for almost an hour, just breathing in and out rhythmically.

"So, Jen, tell me about your dream," Yangji said after some time, after slowly coming out of his meditative state.

"I visited many disturbing places that I have never known. It really felt like I was there. It was so realistic. But things kept changing. First I was in a small town and then it changed into this big city which itself kept changing."

"Tell me about each place."

Jen told Yangji about the small town with fearful people, the strange arena full of powerful fighters and the pristine city full of the scheming groups of people. He told him of the slum with children like animals, the strange skyscraper city with the deformed man and the horrible jungle war zone.

"Were they the six realms?"

"Yes, they were manifestations of the six realms of power, I believe," Yangji said. "It is very fortunate and a testament to your strength that you were able to escape each of those places. It is very easy to become trapped in such a realm."

"But I was only dreaming?" Jen said, feeling unnerved at Yangji's word of warning and starting to doubt his own reality again.

"Dreaming is still existing, Jen. It is sometimes just as dangerous to dwell in the dream world, as it is to exist in the physical world. It is especially fascinating that you got away from that terrible jungle where a war was raging. That must have been most difficult for you given your recent past. Beings are totally consumed by anger and hatred in such places."

Jen remembered seeing the blurry being of light and the supernatural foal and realised they may have helped him escape that hellish place.

"I saw a human walking in that place with a strange foal," Jen recalled. "The entire environment sort of warped as they walked through it. I felt so safe when I spotted them. There was light everywhere."

"Where? In that hellish place?" Yangji tried to clarify.

"Yes. I felt like they were there to help. Who were they?"

"They were world walkers, Jen," was all Yangji said.

Later that day, Jen was tending to some of the plants outside after visiting the room of light that Yangji had first shown him on his arrival to the monastery. He hadn't been able to see the all-pervasive light that he had witnessed the first time he had visited the room.

He felt quite anxious, mainly because he was gravely concerned about going to sleep that night in case he ended up in one of those frightening places again. As he clipped back some of the bushy undergrowth using some archaic tools, Zopa came up to him smiling.

"Everyone is very excited about your ventures in the dream world," Zopa told him.

Jen was surprised that everyone in the monastery had been talking about it. "Why?"

"Because it means you are rejecting the pursuit of power and are now seeking freedom. Eventually you will be able to venture into those realms that are so frightening and help the trapped beings that are stuck there, just as the spirits that you saw were trying to do."

"Are you sure they are both spirits?"

"I believe they are very special spirits. Ones that we should all aspire to be like."

Jen was silent as he thought about what Zopa was saying. He did feel like he wanted to help all those people he had seen, but he still didn't understand how he would be able to. "I currently have no intention of trying to reach those atrocious places again."

"Take it one day at a time, Jen," Zopa said very maturely, not appearing at all like a boy anymore. "We are all here to help you."

Jen continued with his chores, allowing his mind to go blank as he worked. Though he felt uncertain about what the future held, he felt as though at long last he had somehow returned to his true self and that he indeed had a *path*, like Zopa had described previously.

The seed of doubt and regret that had dictated his life for so long felt like it had sprouted into a shoot of hope that was reaching for the sky and beyond. He vowed that he would not leave the monastery until that shoot had grown into a strong tree.

Chapter 59 – Three years pass

Jen King had changed.

Life and death had somehow merged. His past fears had dissolved into the unknown.

The wonderful unknown.

It was the awakening of something that had been dormant for most of his life. As he reflected, he felt the widest of smiles spread naturally across his face. He felt true happiness for the first time in the simple fact that he had lost all selfishness. His former life involving bloodshed seemed less important now, as he had forgiven himself by vowing that every moment in the future would be a kind one.

Who knows what the future will bring?

In the three years that had passed, whilst Jen King had been absent from the world, major political and social changes had rippled their way around the major cities and towns of the world. The first time Jen heard of this was aboard the *Green Bottle*, a merchant ship that had allowed him to travel on board from Yinkoto to Raicema City.

"Raicema feels different now," Leften, the ship's first mate told Jen as they stood on the bow looking out at an eternity of ocean. "When word spread that the Tyrones were dead, the Makai stormed all the military bases and within a year they had complete control of the west; Tyrona, Muscpiti and many other provinces."

The wind shook the sails high above.

"The east and Raicema City are also under Makai control, but there is still a resistance against them. The funny thing is, the resistance seems to be spearheaded by people who used to follow the Makai."

Jen was silent and solemn.

"Raicema City is getting really run down because this Satori guy stops any supplies or building materials coming in from overseas to suppress the resistance. Funny how things change, eh?"

"Who is Satori?" Jen asked shocked at the revolution that had happened in such a short period of time.

"Somebody who runs the show in the Makai, though I've never seen him. Doesn't seem to make himself public. From what I've heard, he's pretty twisted. I've heard horror stories about the cities in the west."

"Like what?"

"That they are teeming with looters and criminals. People aren't safe. Not that the way the Tyrones used to control people was a good thing, but now, it's like...there's no order. That's what I heard. Glad I've never been there."

Jen reflected on what he had been told. *So things haven't really changed that much,* Jen thought. *The same lack of care still exists.*

The sails flapped with the continuous gusts of wind and the ship dipped and rose like a cork bobbing along.

"So you've been living in the mountains, huh?"

"Yes, for quite a while. I've almost forgotten what it was like to live in a city."

"You heard about that thing in the sky?" Leften asked Jen, changing the subject.

"No, what is it?"

Leften looked shocked that Jen wasn't aware of what he was speaking about.

"Well at first people thought it might be a comet because of its fiery tail. We all thought it would just pass right by, but now people are getting worried because it seems to get closer every day. You can't see it here, but tomorrow when we get closer to Raicema you'll see what I mean."

Jen had not heard of the entity in the sky and the concept of it immediately captured his curiosity. "How long has it been around?" he asked, not remembering anyone talking about it when he was last in Raicema.

"About two years now. People have sort of gotten used to it but to tell you the truth, it's pretty scary, like a big dragon coming towards us from far away."

Jen could see the concern flare up in Leften's eyes.

"Nobody knows what it is," he continued. "Maybe it is a comet but if it is, then it's closer to us than I'd like it to get!"

Up ahead, the sea was getting choppy, white peaks forming on the jagged waves. Jen could feel the wind was picking up speed and Leften's loose woollen clothing began to flap just like the sails.

"You'll have to excuse me," he said politely, pushing his green hat firmly onto his head. "I'll have to lend a hand. Why don't you go below decks for a while? Seems like a storm's brewing."

Indeed, the sky had quickly been covered in grey streaky clouds and the lighter atmosphere of moments ago started to feel heavy and charged. Jen took Leften's advice and walked down the small wooden steps in the centre of the ship to the galley, where rich teak lined every surface.

Jen sat down on a bench and began to contemplate his return to Raicema.

"Go home. You must take my place."

They were words he had heard often.

What could only be described as a woman of light had appeared in Jen's dreams recursively for almost a year, an aura of a young woman who said nothing except the same statement, the words radiating through his head every time.

"Go home. You must take my place."

He had tried to speak about these visions with Yangji, but the monk had plainly refused to discuss their meaning.

It is most unusual how I began to dream about this woman, Jen thought.

After spending hundreds of nights navigating the different realms of power, Jen had suddenly stopped dreaming for over a year. Instead, he would fall into the deepest of sleeps every night.

Then, one night he was sure that the glowing silhouette of a woman had appeared in his room in the monastery, like a magical phantom. After that he had resumed dreaming, every dream the same, of the glowing woman repeating the same message.

Just by closing his eyes, Jen could visualise the being, the shape of a young woman hazed by an all-encompassing green light. She was truly beautiful.

Jen could hear the eerie creaking of the ship's base as the power of the water made its presence felt upon it. He began to drift into a strange watery dream, to a place that made Jen feel like every cell in his body was floating.

He seemed to spread out until his body had dispersed and when he opened his eyes, all he saw was a familiar faint green haze. He tried to look around but realised his body didn't exist, a feeling he had experienced many times before.

I must be dreaming, Jen thought.

He tried to open his eyes again expecting to see the ship's galley but was surprised to find that he was unable to. He couldn't move physically or feel his eyelids anymore.

"Intend to look, and you shall," a voice spoke in Jen's head.

He visualised turning his head and it happened in an instant. Again he saw nothing but green haze. He felt that he wanted to ask a question.

Who are you? he thought, feeling a presence was listening to him.

"I am here to guide you, Jen."

I feel like I have been here before.

Then, in a wisp of swirling fog-like movement, the same hazed silhouette of a woman appeared in front of him, glowing white and green.

"Go home. You must take my place." The same familiar words were spoken.

Are you a world walker? Jen asked in his thoughts.

The question was not answered but instead, Jen found himself transported to a large open field where a small girl was playing in the crops. It was as if he was standing in the field, yet his body was not there.

The girl was chasing a luminous butterfly, repeatedly stalking and pouncing to try and catch it in her tiny hands. Every time she leapt at the resting creature, it would jump off playfully, causing her to giggle with joy. Jen watched for a few moments before noticing something very unusual.

Every time the girl jumped for the butterfly, she seemed to get a larger distance off the ground and Jen realised that the butterfly was somehow lifting her up higher and higher each time. Before long, the girl was floating as high as the butterfly. It was flapping its blue and yellow spotted wings and her feet were brushing the tops of the crops.

"The world of the butterfly is full of laughter. This is one of my favourite worlds," the voice said, softly and with a musical tone.

Is this young girl you? Jen felt himself ask in his mind.

Once again the question was not answered and the vision changed to one of a small island that Jen had never seen before. The island was tropical and covered in bright sunlight but suddenly an all-encompassing darkness began to shroud the island.

The ground began to break apart and chunks of earth flew upwards, steam pouring out of the giant fissures that were forming. Jen heard screams, yet he saw no people. Trees were uprooted violently and huge waves formed around the island, crashing onto the shores ferociously.

Jen tried to look up but found that he could not. The scene faded away to the same green haze Jen had experienced earlier. The woman of light appeared again before him and Jen could sense an urgent feeling radiating from her, so strong that Jen felt it vibrate through his entire being.

"It is coming. I need your help."

Suddenly the green haze and woman of light disappeared as if being pulled into a vacuum. Jen thought he was going with it for a moment, but then he felt his heavy eyes opening.

He was lying on a hard mattress below decks on the *Green Bottle.* Nobody else was around. He sat up and his head felt drowsy. Light was pouring in from an open trap door and the storm seemed to have subsided.

Jen rose to his feet with a little dizziness and confusion. He walked slowly up the narrow stairway, greeted by dazzling morning light and a blast of cold sea air.

"Hey!" Leften shouted out, spotting Jen from across the deck. "Finally you're awake!"

He hurried over, mystified by Jen's appearance.

"What did you take? You've been out cold for two days now."

"Two days?" Jen gasped unbelievably, contemplating on what only seemed like a few minutes in the strange dream world.

"Yep. You went below decks the other night when the storm hit and then not one of us could wake you up. We shook you pretty hard last night. Had me damn worried for a while."

Jen felt a little weak and sat down on a wooden crate. Though it seemed amazing, he had learnt to accept such unexplainable events in recent times and so he decided not to dwell on it.

"Are we close to Raicema?"

"A couple of hours away. You'll be able to see the shoreline soon."

A few other members of the crew spotted Jen and they all rushed over to check he was okay. He explained away his long slumber as extreme exhaustion, yet he could sense that most thought something strange had happened.

"I've never seen anybody sleep for two days solid. The captain would throw me overboard if I even got a quarter of the shut eye you get," one short ship-hand joked, winking at groggy Jen. Despite the fuss, Jen had his mind on one thing only and that was finding out about the entity in the sky. The woman of light had shown him the devastating future to come should the entity continue on its path, yet Jen still did not know what it was or how to prevent such devastation.

He got to his feet, still wearing the lose clothes he had worn two days before and headed to the stern, where Captain Aglin, a tall, stern trunk of a man stood, gazing out at the white frothy trail left by the sturdy ship as it cut through the water.

"Mr King," he greeted Jen somewhat jovially. "I thought that you had left us for another world."

His comment rang true without him knowing it. Jen smiled affectionately at the kind man who had been good enough to allow him to travel with his crew for only a few items: a small sculpture Jen had crafted out of bamboo and an old Raiceman scarf that Aglin now had wrapped around his muscular neck.

"What will you do when you get back?" Aglin asked, his deep voice permeating the air. "Join the resistance? I am sure many of your old soldier friends will have done the same."

"I have no interest in any sort of conflict," Jen clarified calmly. "My life exists for a reason as does yours and everybody else's. All those who seek to fight are seeking something that can never be a positive reason for living."

"Oh, and what is that?"

"Power. What I have learnt about power is that it is not something you gain, but something that gains you. It has a life of its own."

"Maybe so, but I can't bear to think of it as a monster that tries to enslave us. Just look at Leften. Who'd want to enslave him?" Aglin said, causing Jen to laugh.

"I feel happier not pursuing it none the less."

Aglin agreed. "So tell me of your time in the Neoasian mountains? I suppose you met many men of knowledge?"

"I met many men of knowledge and many women of knowledge. Actually, I met many creatures of knowledge as well."

Aglin seemed amused.

"My time there has changed my life," Jen continued. "When I arrived in Neoasia I had lost the will to live, yet I began to find it so quickly when I reached the mountains. Now I want to embrace life, not destroy it."

"You wanted to destroy life before?" Aglin questioned him in surprise.

"Well I did destroy many things, no matter what my intention was."

There was silence between the two for a few moments.

"And you think having nothing to live for can cause such destruction?"

"It depends on whether you are *searching* or not."

"What do you mean?" Aglin asked him.

"What I mean is that if you are searching for something to live for you cannot be destroying anything because you are creating something just by looking. But you need to have the will to look in the first place. I didn't have that so all I did was destroy in my aimlessness."

Aglin thought deeply about what Jen was saying.

The two philosophised for another hour before the familiar coastline of eastern Raicema could be clearly seen with the distinctive skyline of the giant buildings of Raicema City.

Jen, however, could pay no attention to the familiar shapes of the land on which he had lived for most of his life. His full awareness was fixated on the now-visible comet-like entity in the sky. It glowed in a meld of yellows and greens and had a long orange tail. It did look like a dragon or serpent floating in the sky, just as Leften has described.

"How close is it?" Jen asked Aglin, his attention too drawn to the threatening sight.

"Rumour is that it's only a year away. Can you imagine if that thing actually hit the earth? Everything would be wiped out."

The chilling vision Jen had seen earlier came to mind. "I don't even want to imagine it."

The ship drew closer to the dockland area of Raicema City, which still looked exactly as Jen remembered it, an array of long wooden jetties dwarfed by their massive concrete counterparts, which were used for the larger military vessels.

The *Green Bottle* landed beside an older wooden jetty, one of the oldest structures still remaining in the city. All around were a range of different-sized vessels, from small merchant ships carrying a dozen people to colossal carriers and tankers capable of carrying thousands of people.

As Jen placed his foot on the strong wooden planks, he felt both warmness and an emptiness collide in his chest. Being back felt like a return home. However, he quickly realised that it never felt like home in the first place. A pang of loneliness and homesickness struck him.

"Okay?" Aglin asked Jen, carrying a leather duffle bag. "I suppose you'll be wanting to catch up with a few people. One word of warning – the city, though it looks similar, is quite different now." Aglin was deadly serious. "Watch your back. There are a lot of people who have vengeance in mind against those who used to work for the old government. Try not to say too much."

Jen nodded in appreciation at Aglin's concern and bid the crew farewell, wishing them thanks for their kindness and friendship. Then he walked forward, back to a place to which he thought he would never return.

Chapter 60 – Return to Raicema

Jen walked towards the *Garad Central Station*, one of the main public transport hubs in Raicema City.

Along the way, he noticed subtle differences in the people he observed. In the past the overall atmosphere had been one of rushed conformism, with most people totally focused on their tight schedules with not a moment to spare.

Now, everyone seemed much slower, many loitering around or simply bored. Others were watchfully eyeing every person who passed them by. There was an overwhelming feeling of suspicion and distrust in the air and Jen noticed the state of disrepair that the station had fallen into.

Its walls were no longer white but a faded grey and every window was cracked, some even shattered. The large round building with its spiral roof looked more like an old oddly shaped factory now. There were hundreds of people sat around aimlessly on its main stairway.

Jen walked past several people and some held out their hands for money. Others seemed intoxicated, barely able to open their eyes. He quickly made his way towards the west hub, wanting to head straight into the city.

When he reached the range of platforms bound towards the central areas of Raicema City, he was astounded to see the state of the hover trains that stopped there. The trains had been totally decorated in graffiti, ranging from ugly scribbles to beautiful depictions of meadows and forests.

Jen stood still for several minutes, watching train after train zip by, each one unique in decoration. The train Jen boarded had the most intricate painting of a mountainous backdrop on it, reminding him of where he had been over the past three years.

The inside of the train was dilapidated. The top mechanical units that once housed automated weaponry had all been ripped out, with loose wires hanging down above the heads of the seated passengers.

It did not take long to reach the city and Jen looked out at many of the giant buildings he had become familiar with in the past. He almost felt the same familiar urge to run away. He shrugged it off, knowing his life was now his own no matter what happened. He was confident.

I know this city. I almost feel like it's an old dance partner.

The train pulled up outside of *Hub Central*, which to Jen's surprise still looked similar to how he remembered it. There was a long hallway with a glass dome, teeming with platforms and lifts. People seemed much busier here, though the previous black-suited types were no longer present, replaced by many in colourful robes and loose clothing.

The first person that Jen thought about was Toji, the young boy who was always so genuine. Though he was unsure if he would be there, Jen switched to another train in the direction of the Reik Institute.

Within a few moments he had arrived at the familiar stop. To his surprise, he found that the building had been renamed to the *MCS*, the *Makai City School.*

I wonder if Toji still comes here, he pondered as he walked under the tall archway.

Inside, though it looked similar, the subject matter being taught had changed dramatically. The same holodome that Jen had seen over three years ago now depicted a different battle in the conquest of Raicema.

"...The blood of the brave Makai warriors, who battled their Raiceman invaders for nine days to defend their homes, stained the red plains of Calegra..."

It continued in the same resonant voice.

"...Over seventy thousand men and women perished in the battle, yet this battle spelled the beginning of the downfall of the Raiceman Empire."

Ahead, there were scores of computer terminals with holographic screens that people were interacting with. As Jen walked past the ghostly digital projections, he noticed that various subjects that had been banned previously were now being taught, such as Astrology and other religious teachings.

Jen looked around the different chambers for Toji, spotting many changes all around. Old and dusted books were now present in their thousands, a mass of hidden knowledge now readily available.

Jen was tempted to stop and read some of the books on the history of Ciafra, a topic completely banned from the Raiceman learning centres in the past, but he decided to press on in his search for his young friend.

Whilst in awe at the raw energy of the children in the centre, dashing around like worker bees, someone tapped Jen on the shoulder. He turned around to see the dark brown eyes and flowing black hair of a young man who looked vaguely familiar.

"Jen, right?" the man said to him.

Jen nodded in reply.

"I met you once before on the borders of Lizrab."

At first Jen thought the man could have been an ex-Raiceman soldier but then he remembered where he had seen him.

"You were with Javu that time I caught up with him in Lizrab," Jen exclaimed, noticing how the man looked much more confident than the boy who had stood in the background three years earlier.

"We were never formally introduced," the golden-skinned man said jovially. "My name is Reo Fernandez."

Jen shook Reo's hand with an assured warmness.

"I see you have left the military," Reo commented, observing Jen's simple clothing. "You look very different than before. It's unbelievable how quickly things can change isn't it?"

Jen nodded in agreement and the two walked out of the former institute towards an outdoor terrace area where many children and adults were reading books or looking out on a panoramic view of the city.

"Do you know what happened to Javu?" Jen asked Reo as they sat upon a stone bench with the view of the great metropolis in front of them.

"He went back to Seho with Teltu. He said that was where he belonged after..." Reo paused, "... Well, I haven't seen him since."

Jen could sense an emotional twang in Reo's prominent voice. There was silence for a while.

"I was raised by him as a child," Jen told Reo, who looked surprised by the statement. "It would be nice to see him again."

"He never mentioned it. But then Javu had lots of secrets he never told anyone," Reo said in a mysterious way.

He leaned close to Jen as if he was going to whisper something. "I think that he was capable of magic. Like this one time, he made Elera float up a giant wall. He made us all believe we were helping, but secretly, I think it was just him."

"Where were you all going that time in Lizrab?" Jen asked, gaining more and more curiosity about his former guardian.

"We were heading to Cibola to find a lost pyramid. Apparently, it was one of four pyramids that had been built by an ancient civilisation called the Lemurians. Elera and Javu seemed to think that Lemuria still existed somewhere and for months we travelled all over the world searching for it."

"So that's what you were looking for in Lizrab?"

"Yes, in the north. I never saw it but Javu, Bene and Elera found a pyramid in a place called Ixon. After that we went to Isis."

"I know," Jen remembered. "The Raicemans were following you."

"That's when things started getting truly unbelievable."

Reo's eyes were alight with enthusiasm as he told the tale like he'd known Jen all his life. "We reached a cave in Isis and if by magic, this giant tree appeared out of nowhere," he continued. "And when we climbed it and followed where it led, we found ourselves in this hot place that was just incredible! Sometimes I still think it was all a dream."

Again, Reo seemed slightly saddened, as if he had remembered something upsetting.

"I was there," Jen said, remembering the colossal tree and the sweltering land that it led to. "I was supposed to capture you all, but I never managed to catch up. I was a very different person then."

"Then it was real?" Reo asked himself, slightly morose.

Silence fell for a moment as they both looked out on the vast city.

"There was no going back after climbing that tree."

Jen was staggered at how true Reo's statement was. His life had never been the same after following Javu and the others into that mystical paradox.

"So, did you find what you were looking for? Lemuria?"

"I think we all did in some way," Reo replied enigmatically.

They sat silently together for a while, looking out at the skyline of skyscrapers and the sea in the distance.

"I am looking for a young boy by the name of Toji," Jen said after some time. "Do you know him?"

"Sorry, I don't," Reo replied. "It's likely he left the city to be honest. It's about ninety-five percent Makai here now. Anyone who doesn't follow is forced out eventually."

"Do you follow?"

"I let them think I do," Reo said roguishly, with a wry smile. "I remember when I first came to this city, there were these old warehouses where you could stay as long as you agreed to work for them. Now those warehouses are empty and you get a nice apartment in one of those skyscrapers over there instead."

"What do you have to do for it?" Jen asked warily.

"Attend their meetings and recruit more people, basically spread the *word* of Makaism. Of course you have to give them most of anything you earn if you work. That's why most people don't even bother. You can get it all for free if you know what to say."

Jen though about how this was a stark contrast to how the Tyrones had run Raicema City. If you didn't work in a commercial sector, you were automatically conscripted into one of the military units dotted around the nation.

"Well, I guess it's better than living your life by fear," Jen commented out loud, thinking of how hard people used to work in the city because of being afraid of the alternative.

"I'm not so sure," Reo said in response. "At least that gave people some motivation. Now there isn't any. A lot of people don't know what they are supposed to be doing. If you got the option to work hard but not get much back or not work at all and get the same what would you do? It's easy to take the second option and do nothing."

"Maybe that's what people need," Jen suggested. "It must be better than not having any choice at all."

"Maybe," Reo admitted. "But there's a lot more crime because of it. People are bored."

He looked out at the endless procession of buildings creating a staggered silhouette against the brilliant blue backdrop of the sky.

"Don't get me wrong. I'm not talking about everyone. There are many people who now have the opportunity to learn about all sorts of things that they couldn't before. When I first came to this city, I didn't know anything about history or astronomy or about the different places and cultures that exist on the planet. Now that sort of information is freely available to everyone in places like this. That's the one good change that's happened since the Makai took power."

"So who is actually in charge now?" Jen asked Reo. "I heard someone mention the name Satori?"

The question seemed to agitate Reo, like it had prompted some sort of longstanding concern inside him. He shuffled his feet and looked at the floor with intensity. "Rekesh Satori is..." he began before changing his words. "...was a friend of mine."

Reo looked gravely upset at the thought.

"He is the main figurehead for the Makai leadership in Tyrona but he is never seen in person. His name and image are used but there are others who are really running things in Raicema like Sadana Siger and this old king from Lengard. To be honest, I'm not sure if Rekesh is even alive anymore. One thing's for sure, they are giving him a bad name with everything that's going on over there."

Reo now seemed to be angry.

Memories of that fateful day in Yinkoto came to Jen's mind when the conspiracy against the Tyrones had been revealed. The name Rekesh also seemed familiar.

"They are in collusion with Neoasia?" Jen tried to confirm.

"Well, that's not really a secret. Both nations need a sustainable energy source," Reo said knowledgably. "The Neoasian government knew that Sadana and his followers would eventually overthrow the government here so they knew that they had to share power with the Makai leaders over here. Otherwise, they wouldn't have access to Raicema's power supply."

"What power supply?" Jen asked with intrigue.

"Wisdom rocks. The reason why Raicema were always waging war against Lizrab was so they could mine the wisdom rocks there."

"Wisdom rocks?"

"Well, the Raicemans called the processed fuel *Oricalc* but Javu always referred to the rocks as that. Basically it is a type of crystal mineral that is incredible good at storing energy. But what the Raicemans found out is that when a wisdom rock reaches its capacity it then gives off energy at a million fold of what it has stored. So they built all these reactors in Raicema to harness this energy. Don't you know about them? They built them over ten years ago apparently."

Jen shook his head. "I never knew why we were going to war. I guess I didn't really care back then. But I never saw or heard of these reactors. I only know about the ones under the city."

"They are the same thing," Reo explained. "They are well hidden and built underground. The Tyrones never managed to get their hands on enough wisdom rock for them to generate energy in the reactors. That's all changed now."

"Why?"

Again, the same look of agitation and disappointment spread across Reo's face. "Because they have found a place where there is loads of it. Shipments of it began arriving in the west. It won't be long before the entirety of Raicema is powered by it."

Jen was both fascinated and troubled by what he was being told. "And Neoasia want to do the same thing?"

"Definitely, but they don't have access to the source. I've heard people say that within a year the techniques to extract the energy will be so good that they can be used in all sorts of machinery. They even say it won't be long before the sky is full of flying machines again."

Jen was astounded at the level of progression that the nations of the earth were in the midst of. The reasons behind all of the wars that had been waged were now becoming apparent.

Then, an intuition came to him. He began to think about the stone hanging around his neck and how it could be made of the same mineral that Reo was describing. He began to think about the entity in the sky and made the overwhelming feeling that its presence was strongly related to the same mineral.

"Do you know anything about that thing in the sky?" Jen asked Reo, eager to learn as much as he could about it. Reo seemed to be thinking about his response, almost as if he were trying to decide whether to divulge all he knew or not.

"It's Ignis."

"Ignis?"

Reo looked around nervously to see if anyone was listening in. He got to his feet. "Let's go over there," he said pointing to a less populated part of the roof terrace where nobody would be able to hear their conversation. They walked over and took a seat on a wooden bench under a bushy tree.

"Ignis is a *fatum*. Do you know what that is?" Reo asked, lowering his voice as he spoke. Jen shook his head not hearing the term before. "Okay, this might seem hard to believe but there is a force out there that is trying to control us all, encouraging the pursuit of power and consumption."

"I know of this force of power," Jen disclosed.

"How?" Reo asked intrigued, having not spoken to anyone for three years about such a matter.

"I have spent the past three years living with people who spend their entire life trying to understand such forces. I myself have encountered this force."

Reo was shocked by Jen's revelation.

"Much of my time in the mountains of Neoasia was spent learning about the different *realms of power*. When I first started learning about them, mainly through dreaming, I didn't realise that the force of power existed," Jen said.

Reo was gleaming that he had found somebody he could talk to about such concepts.

"But after navigating the realms over and over," Jen continued, "I started to notice something. Even though each of the realms is very different in the way one behaves and feels, there is a common trait in each of them and that is the fact that the ultimate driving force behind each of realms is the pursuit of power. Even fear which is a common human trait is driven by power, by the urge to try and conserve oneself."

Reo was fascinated by what Jen was telling him.

"But what does this force have to do with that thing in the sky?" Jen asked.

"Well, apparently there are these things called fatums which are completely driven by *Ambitio*, the force of power. I don't know where they come from but there a four of them, each corresponding to one of the elements; fire, water, earth and air. The Lemurians discovered these fatums and tried to harness their pure power, creating four special stones that were capable of summoning them."

The story was coming back to Jen like an old song.

"That entity in the sky is Ignis, the fatum of fire, also known as the dragon of death. Most people think it's some sort of comet but some know the real truth."

"Why is it coming here?" Jen asked, somewhat in disbelief.

The same look of disappointment and upset appeared on Reo's face. "Because she was summoned to the planet by Rekesh," Reo said finally, almost cringing at the words he was speaking. "Though

I am sure he was manipulated into doing so."

"Is anything being done to stop it?"

"What can be done?" Reo asked in response, genuinely unsure of any remedy to the problem. "Sometimes I pray that I will wake up and the entire thing will be a bad dream."

"Mmm," Jen murmured, knowing the feeling well.

"It's seems that Rekesh has been completely enslaved by power," Reo declared. "I think Elera left us because she knew that and she tried to do something about it."

Reo seemed to be getting more agitated talking about it. "But in the end, I don't really know…"

Jen nodded, knowing all too well how easy it was to be drawn into one of those realms of power. Suddenly, he realised where he had heard the name *Rekesh*. It was the same name as the man who had killed Jeth Tyrone, the same name as the man Jen had once fought in the jungles of Lizrab, the man who would not let him pass.

He decided not to mention these things to Reo, knowing that he was already distressed about the negative actions that Rekesh had been responsible for. Instead, he decided that he wanted to visit the old Raiceman HQ and see if he could track down some of his old friends.

"Is the Raiceman HQ still around? Has that been taken over as well?"

"The building is still there but I'm not sure what it's used for now. There are still a few ex-Raiceman soldiers that live here but they keep themselves to themselves. The whole Makai thing has a tendency to make people feel like they have a duty to expose anyone anti-Makai. I've seen mobs form against anyone who speaks out about it."

"Maybe this city *is* the same as before," Jen pondered out loud.

Reo let out a long sigh but then perked himself up and stood to his feet. "Come on. I'll go with you to the old HQ. I'm heading that way anyway."

They began to walk out of the learning centre and towards the train hub. As they walked, Jen became curious about the journey that Reo had taken with Javu and how it had seemed to change his life, just like Jen's journey in the Neoasian mountains had changed him.

"You said you went on a journey with Javu and some others to find some ancient pyramids? How did you end up on such a fantastic expedition?"

"It all started in this city," Reo told him as they boarded a train and took a seat. "I met a man called Bene Mattero who turned out to be the grandson of the Makai leader down in Lizrab, Kirichi."

"I have met Kirichi," Jen said, astounded at the constantly emerging connections between the two men. "He helped me a lot."

"Well, Bene and I ended up travelling down there to see him and that's where I met Javu and Elera. They were already searching for Lemuria. Anyway, Kirichi thought that the eight of us all had a part to play in protecting the planet and that Elera was the one to lead the way."

"Eight?"

"Yes. Me, Bene, Javu, Elera, Teltu, Sita, Rama and Rekesh. I didn't meet Rekesh until a bit later."

Reo was thinking about the fateful journey with glazed-over eyes. "We reached this strange place with eight seats and there was one for each of us, like it was waiting for us to arrive. And that's when I realised that there is so much about this life that we don't know."

"What do you mean?"

"Well for starters, Rekesh and Elera disappeared in front of our eyes. That was the last I ever saw of her."

"Why? What happened?" Jen asked him, sensing the immense grief that was resurfacing.

"We waited by those eight seats for weeks until finally, Rekesh appeared out of nowhere. He told us Elera was dead, that he'd seen her be consumed by the earth. We couldn't believe it but when we asked him to explain what happened he wouldn't. All he said was that Elera had died because of him. That's all he said over and over."

"What happened to everyone?" Jen asked with emotion, aghast at the events that had occurred. The two of them got off the train as it stopped outside the old central military zone of the city.

"Rekesh just disappeared and I didn't hear anything about him until about a year later when I found out he was living in Tyrona and involved in the government here. Bene went back to Lizrab. I still see him now and again."

Reo looked up in the sky as he walked. "And as I mentioned before, Javu and Teltu went back to Seho. I think Sita and Rama went back with them." Reo paused. "I haven't seen any of them since it happened."

Jen was truly astounded by the account and could not think of anything to say to Reo. He racked his brain for some words of comfort but instead opted for silence, feeling it was more appropriate. They walked along until the familiar outline of the square building came into sight, though the outside was completely decorated in graffiti and many of the windows were smashed.

"Well, this is it," Reo said. "Bet it's not how you remember it, huh?"

"That's for sure," Jen agreed.

"Calegra, where I'm from, has changed a lot too. Everything is changing."

There were only a few people walking about in the run-down area. Small piles of rubble were scattered around.

"I'm sorry to hear about Elera," Jen said after several moments of silence.

"That's life, I guess," Reo said in a melancholic fashion. "I sometimes feel like she's still around." He smiled weakly and then said his farewells to Jen. "I live in that building over there," he said, pointing to a tall high-rise block that had over fifty floors. "Apartment six on the thirty-third floor. You're welcome to stay whenever you like."

"Thank you," Jen said with appreciation, feeling touched by Reo's generosity even though they'd practically just met. "I'll bear it in mind."

As Reo walked away along an elevated footpath, Jen couldn't help but feel like he wanted to know more about the journey that he and Elera had taken in their search for Lemuria.

As he was thinking about her, a strange sense of familiarity came over him whilst he walked down a long ramp to the old HQ, but he was sure it wasn't because of the building ahead.

He was sure he had met Elera many times before.

Chapter 61 – Friends and Enemies

Jen had been sitting looking at a building in which he had once spent many years of his life. It was now in ruins. The former headquarters was now a dilapidated wreck, looted and crumbling from the outside. There was debris and junk littered all around and mice darted in and out of the rubble piles nearby.

The main doors of the building had been boarded up, but there was a smaller door at the side that was open with a small sign next to it that read *Defence Centre*.

Inside was one of the large hallways that used to be filled with sophisticated computer machinery. Now it had been turned into a crude gym, with a few hard mats scattered around. There were several men sparring on the mats in a variety of different styles, some boxing, others grappling and a few using some flexible kicking techniques.

One of the men looked vaguely familiar. It took Jen a while to realise that it was Amaru Ramone, one of his old comrades. He looked different because he now had a shaved head instead of long hair.

"Amaru? Is that you?" Jen called out to him causing him to glance over.

"King? It can't be!" Amaru gasped, dropping his defences and receiving a foot in the mouth from his opponent because of it. "Ugghhh!" he groaned, dropping to his knees and raising his hand up in defeat.

"I can't believe you're still here," Jen said, walking over to him.

It took Amaru a while to get to his feet and eye Jen with intrigue. "You've lost so much weight!" he said, looking with disbelief at the man he'd once known. "And look at your hair! When did you get back? I thought you were dead."

Jen told Amaru about the past three years. He told him of being arrested by Seth Tyrone and witnessing his murder at the hands of Gueken and Yangjam. He told him of his time wandering aimlessly

726

though the mountains and his period at the old monastery.

Amaru listened with fascination. "I would never expect you to stay in a monastery for three years." He laughed, remembering Jen as the serious brute of a soldier everyone once knew.

"You were once the most feared man in Raicema. Are you sure that you are Jen King?"

"I am," Jen said with certainty.

"Well it seems like you've had a better time than most of us. It's like being a criminal having any past affiliation with the Tyrones," Amaru revealed. "That's why I just deny it if anyone asks me. Most of the boys in here are in the same boat. Strange, but this is the only place left that still feels like home."

"So what are you doing these days?" Jen asked. "It must be nice to have more freedom?"

"Not really," Amaru said with dissatisfaction. "It's pretty boring. Spend most days here sparring with these guys. At least it feels like I'm keeping active. I was never interested in joining the resistance."

"The resistance? I've heard about it. Who is it, ex-soldiers?"

"It's mostly a group of lower-level commanders that used to *serve* under the Tyrones but also smaller pockets of *radical* Makai who aren't happy with the way the nation is being run from Tyrona. I think a lot of people thought things would change more dramatically if the Tyrones were overthrown, that there would be a more regional approach to the government."

As Jen pondered the new power struggle that had developed in Raicema, a man walked into the building. He looked vaguely familiar and was followed by two other men.

"He's part of the *resistance*," Amaru whispered to Jen, nodding in his direction. The man has an aggressive look on his face and was erratically scanning the simple gym to see who was around. He was puffing out his chest to make himself look bigger.

It was then that Jen remembered who the man was.

It's the brigadier. He thought of the man that had belittled him after his arrest on the ship to Yinkoto.

He could feel an imminent confrontation brewing and it was not long before this feeling turned into reality. The brigadier locked his eyes on Jen and after a few moments of trying to work out who he was, he stormed over like a bull and shoved him violently in the chest.

"Well, if it isn't the traitor!" he sniped, looking around to make sure his two associates were backing him up. "What the hell are you doing back in Raicema?"

"I have as much of a right to be here as you do," Jen said firmly, feeling a little agitated at the man's voice and tone. The brigadier smiled slyly and then without warning, he punched Jen heavily in the stomach, winding him.

"Smart ass!" he snarled.

An old familiar well of aggressive energy began to form in Jen's upper stomach, like a dark swirling cloud of might. He rose back up slowly, unscathed and with fire in his eyes.

"Come on, let's do this!" the brigadier shouted, pushing him on the shoulder and making a fighting stance. "I heard people say you were the best fighter they'd ever seen. Now it's your chance to prove it!"

The image of a cage flashed in Jen's mind.

Amaru and the two men that had accompanied the brigadier both stepped back, clearly expecting a showdown. Everyone else who was sparring stopped and crowded around the two men who were staring intently at each other.

Jen was torn. On one hand, he was aware that violence would not resolve the anger the large man in front of him was displaying. But on the other hand, a strange energy was beginning to flow into his body, one that made him feel intensely alive and powerful.

A tension swelled in the atmosphere and a rush of adrenalin shot through Jen's body from his feet to his head as the brigadier charged at him, swinging heavily for his head. At that moment, Jen lost all guilt for the act that he was about to perform.

He ducked and sidestepped left, avoiding the blow.

The small crowd let out a gasp.

At this moment, time seemed to slow dramatically and Jen thought carefully about what he was involved in. He saw a mix of anger and pride in the expression of his incumbent opponent, the split-second actions and possible reactions playing through his mind. He saw him coming for him again, this time with an uppercut motion. He instinctively ducked, the brigadier's fist just skimming his long hair, a few strands flying up with the swift motion.

The possessed brigadier quickly turned and attacked again, but without avail, for Jen could easily predict what he was going to do, as if every motion had been slowed down.

Every person gathered around was looking on intently with bated breath. A million images streamed through Jen's mind. Again, he dodged several more jabs and heavy swings by the tall aggressor.

People were starting to laugh now at the bully's failure to connect with any of his attacks. This seemed to irritate him further. However, a feeling of wellbeing had come over Jen. He realised that he had already denounced his violent life and could never lose what he had gained.

He decided to quickly end the situation.

As the brigadier swung his heavy fist towards Jen's face, Jen leaned back seeing each of the brigadier's rough knuckles fly past his eyes. He breathed in deeply and then made an open-handed pushing movement towards the brigadier's chin, causing him to soar spectacularly up in the air at the loud gasps and shouts of everyone watching.

The brigadier flew backwards gracefully, eventually landing twenty paces away with a thud on one of the hard mats. "Uuuhghgh!!" he groaned as he crumpled from the impact.

Everyone was stunned, as was Jen, but for very different reasons. Whilst each of the spectators was amazed that the myth of Jen King's incredible strength was true, Jen was shocked at the fact that he hadn't even touched the man.

He had felt no physical contact whatsoever between his open

hand and the brigadier's chin, yet he had flown back like he'd been hit by a train.

As the brigadier's two comrades ran over to attend to their half-conscious friend, Jen felt an implausible urge to escape the situation. He quickly ran out of the building without explanation, whilst Amaru called after him. He headed back up the long ramp and along the elevated walkway that Reo had walked along earlier.

Before long, he found himself in a small park, with a number of trees and benches scattered around. Jen felt confused, almost like he had awoken from a dream and was having difficulty distinguishing reality from fantasy.

He spotted Amaru looking for him but he kept quiet and ducked down. After a while, his old friend went back inside the small refuge.

After walking in a number of obscure directions in the park to avoid being followed by a likely irate brigadier, he found a bench that was enclosed by a semi-circle of tall trees.

I am far from there now.

He sat down and breathed deeply, trying to clear his mind. He rested his hands on his lap, palms up and just stared at them.

How could I have done that? he questioned himself over and over.

Jen sat there staring at his hands in bafflement for several hours until the sun disappeared from sight behind one of the tall skyscrapers. He thought about his life and where he was at the moment. Not a soul had passed by during that time.

Maybe I should visit Reo.

As he readied himself to head over to Reo's apartment block, a woman walked by whom Jen was sure he knew. "Hey," he called out to her. "Don't I know you?"

She turned to look at Jen, her flawless dark skin and curly black lacquered hair shimmering in the late afternoon light. She walked over to him, looking at his face carefully.

"Yes, I think I did meet you once," the woman said to him, her loose cotton dress rippling in the light breeze that was flowing through the park. "You used to work for the Raiceman military didn't you?"

Jen nodded, but he still could not remember where he'd met the woman before.

"I guess you could say I did too in some way. I used to be a researcher for the Tyrone government. Don't you remember?"

Jen still couldn't recall.

"We met about seven years ago on a trip to Ciafra. I was going there to do some surveying of the west coast and I sort of hitched a ride with the ship that you were on. You sure look different now."

The memory of the trip came back to him, one of many that he'd tried to block out. It was a trip to suppress a Makai uprising in the north of the continent. All that he remembered was being stuck in an encampment for several weeks, occasionally invading small towns to fight a number of rebels there.

"What is your name again?" he asked her, feeling a little embarrassed at not remembering.

"It's Sula. Your name is King, right?"

"It's Jen. All those guys used to call me by my last name. I never understood why."

"Probably their way of not getting too attached," Sula said knowledgably with a smile. "After all, soldiers don't last long, do they?"

Jen nodded in agreement.

"So, it doesn't look like you're still following that way of life," she commented, observing Jen's simple attire. "Not interested in fighting anymore?"

"Let's just say that I've seen things over the last few years that have changed me and have allowed me to realise what is important in life."

Sula nodded with sincere understanding. "Something similar happened to me," she said to Jen with honesty. "I met this woman quite a few years ago now whilst I was on a research mission. She was so beautiful and had an incredible outlook on life. She was so positive and hopeful. Anyway, I saw her do things that you wouldn't believe. After that things changed so quickly for me."

Jen raised his eyebrows with intrigue.

"She was looking for these old structures that she thought had been built by an ancient civilisation."

An almost humorous pang of recognition came over him.

"You're not talking about Elera are you?" Jen asked, sure that the topic couldn't be a coincidence.

"Yes!" Sula gasped. "Did you know her?"

"Not really," Jen replied. "But it seems that my life is quite tied to hers. I mean, we seem to have strong connections to a lot of the same people."

"I never saw her again after I left Bimini, but I couldn't get the things I'd seen out of my mind. I even went back to Bimini many times but it was never the same."

Jen wanted to learn more about the woman who had been a recurring theme throughout the day.

"Tell me more about Elera," he said. "Though I never met her, I feel as though I know her."

Sula nodded. "Well, she was looking for this statue in the Bimini islands. She said it would tell her more about these old pyramids she was looking for. There were some other people on the island who she knew. I still don't know how they got there."

Jen was sure one of those people was Javu.

"We dove into this lake and there was a tunnel that led under the island. It was like nothing I've ever seen before. Then we got to this cavern and we found the statue. It was like something out of a fairy tale, made out of this glowing jade stone."

Jen was listening carefully to the account.

"Then, as we were standing there looking at it, it just disappeared. And if that wasn't unbelievable enough, a little while later, Elera disappeared too, right in front of my eyes! I couldn't believe it!"

Her story drew many parallels with the story Jen had heard Reo recall earlier. Sula paused for a few seconds, recalling in her mind those implausible events that she had witnessed.

"Also, it was strange how we met in the first place," Sula continued. "I was driving to the island on a boat and she was just floating in the middle of the sea. I picked her up and took her back to the island and she told me that there was a pyramid under the ocean, where she had been trapped for a week. I thought she was crazy at first. Silly of me, really."

Jen smiled, appreciating the sentiment.

"I think in some strange way, I was supposed to meet her. I'd only gone to the island because of the disappearances, which in itself was strange."

"The disappearances?"

"Well, you yourself must know that Bimini used to house a pretty big military base. A week before I went out to the island nobody could be contacted there, so I was sent out to investigate."

Jen vaguely recalled such an event taking place.

"After I met Elera, I went out to the base and it was empty, completely abandoned. It was a mystery to me what actually happened there for a long time. Then about a year ago, I bumped into a man here in Raicema City. He told me he had been on the island when it was abandoned. And he told me something that I would never have believed if I had not witnessed the things I have."

"What?" Jen asked, enamoured by the story.

"He told me that one day, a strange light came out of the ocean. It was a light that shot upwards into the sky. He said it was one of the most incredible things he had ever seen."

The sound of shouting could be heard in the distance; angry men arguing. Jen was sure it was the brigadier searching for him.

"Then, he told me a strange man appeared on the island, dressed in a black robe. This man never revealed his face and when confronted, he disappeared before everyone's eyes."

Sula paused, looking scared about what she was about to say next. "When he reappeared a few hours later, he was accompanied by what the man described as *giant monsters* that proceeded to attack several of the men. Everyone fled for their lives. Of course, nobody believed their stories."

She paused again, realising how farfetched the story sounded.

"Before I met Elera and saw what I saw, I would have never believed him. Now, I think anything is possible."

Jen smiled at Sula, happy that she was so open-minded. "Not everything can be explained in life," he said, now thinking about the dragon in the sky. He was about to ask Sula about it when she seemed to sense that it was unsafe to loiter in their present location. The sound of shouting nearby followed.

"I don't live far from here," Sula said. "Why don't you come and have something to eat with me?"

Jen nodded with a smile, feeling very comfortable in Sula's company. They set off deeper into the park away from the shouting. Jen began to feel a sensation he had never experienced before. It was one of love for the city around him.

It was a sentiment that he never thought he could feel.

Chapter 62 – The Way Home

It was dusk and the chalky light had created an evening energy that held an unfathomed excitement.

As Jen and Sula walked along a small pathway away from the park, Jen began to think about how he hadn't had much contact with women throughout his life. He realised now that he had missed having friendships with women and that his life had mostly been filled with power-hungry men.

Sula walked elegantly, her dress moving like a gentle wave rising and falling into the ocean. Jen noticed that the buildings up ahead looked a lot older than was typical in Raicema City. Instead of lines of glass-fronted skyscrapers, there was a collection of smaller five-storey buildings made mainly of thin deep red bricks.

The roofs of the buildings were all flat with rails running around the top and there were a number of small trees and plants hanging from the rooftops.

"I've never seen this part of Raicema City before," Jen said to Sula as they got closer to the buildings, which were arranged over several streets.

"This is one of the older parts of the city," Sula told him. "I like living here because it feels more natural. I used to live on the forty-third floor of another building and I felt like I was floating in the air all the time. I'm not sure humans are supposed to live so high up. I was lucky to get a ground-floor apartment in that building just over there."

She pointed out where she lived. It was a beautifully decorated building, each of the windowsills home to a number of plant pots. The edges of the building were clad in smooth white stone.

"I know how you feel," Jen said. "I just got back to Raicema City today but I just spent three years living in the mountains and I've never felt so real. Feeling the earth beneath your feet gives you a lot of strength."

"Which mountains?" Sula asked with surprise as she opened her front door.

Inside was a dimly lit narrow hallway, with a number of paintings of scenic backgrounds on the walls.

"The mountains outside Yinkoto, in Neoasia," said Jen. "I travelled quite a way into them so I'm not completely sure where I was living."

"Sounds wonderful," she commented, opening a heavy, panelled wooden door that had been painted so many times the features looked blunt and rounded.

Beyond the door was a small room with a few studded chairs and a small wooden table. There was an alcove in one corner of the room, packed full of books stacked in all directions. Sula walked over to a small lamp and switched it on, creating an ambient glow. The decor was nostalgic and Jen felt like he had travelled back to another time.

"Sit down for a while whilst I put something in the oven."

Jen complied and sat in one of the chairs. Soon, the clinking of metal pots and the sound of running water could be heard from what Jen presumed was the kitchen.

He noticed a book in the alcove that stood out to him. It was small book, yet it had a unique colour, a mix of orange and green. He reached over and picked it up. The title read *Hidden Abilities: The lost knowledge*. It seemed to be handwritten.

As he opened the book to the first page, Sula came back into the room carrying two tall glass beakers of fruit juice.

"That book was a gift from a woman I met in Ciafra," Sula told him, instantly recognising the book in Jen's hand.

"Sorry, I was just curious," Jen said, feeling like he'd made an imposition.

"Oh, don't worry," Sula said with warmth. "You can look at any book you like. I recommend reading that one. It's the only copy I know of in the Raiceman language. My friend had it translated for me. It's the only book I know that can explain the things I saw on Bimini Island."

"Oh, like what?" Jen asked with interest.

"Let me just finish what I'm doing in the kitchen and we'll talk about it."

Whilst she was gone, Jen had a chance to read the first page, which gave a brief introduction into the human body and its anatomy, followed by a summary about the capabilities of the body. It said that *'over time human beings have trained themselves to only rely on their physical abilities and have lost touch with energetic abilities that were possible beyond the physical.'*

"Everything will be ready soon," Sula said as she came back in the room and sat down in the opposite chair. Jen smiled, touched by Sula's hospitality and friendliness.

"So, did you read the beginning?"

Jen nodded and closed the book. He picked up his drink and took a sip of the tangy, fresh juice. Sula did the same.

"The original author wrote it based on the knowledge of a *shaman* in northern Ciafra. My friend Juliana is originally from here. She used to work as a researcher too but she has lived in Ciafra for a long time now."

She paused.

"Whenever I go over there I stay with her. Juliana met a man whilst she was camping out in the forest one time and he told her about the shaman. He said that he had spent a year writing down everything that the shaman had told him and the book you are holding is a translation of that writing."

Jen was fascinated, the glowing light of the lamp behind him making the story even more thought-provoking.

"The book is mainly about things that we can all do that we have simply forgotten how to."

"Like what?"

"Well, for instance being able to *see* the world differently or move things by just thinking about it. One of the main things it talks about is how one should understand their own energy."

Jen looked out of a quaint window in the room, dressed with candles and several crystals hanging from the clasp.

"I think when one knows their own energy, one can then unlock the hidden abilities that the book describes. It's like being able to tap into some kind of natural magic that exists all around us."

"There were many people at the monastery where I was living that had abilities that were hard to believe," Jen said, sensing a familiarity with the concepts that Sula had mentioned. "And I know what you mean about a *natural magic* that exists. I have seen it many times whilst dreaming. It always felt like a connecting energy that is everywhere."

Sula felt warmed by what Jen was telling her. She had no idea that he knew so much or that he had been around people who had such capabilities.

"You have been to the *dream world*?" she asked him. "It talks about that in the book too."

"Yes. It was quite strange how I began to drift into that world. It wasn't always at night either. Sometimes I'd just rest my eyes and the next thing I knew, I was in a completely different place. I think I learnt more over the past three years dwelling in the dream world, than living here in the real world."

A few people passed by outside. They looked like a small family.

"Well, according to that book, the dream world is just as real as the physical world."

Jen nodded in agreement and took another sip of his juice.

"So what do you plan to do now that you are back in Raicema?" Sula asked him. It was the same recurring question that he didn't know the answer to.

"Actually, at the moment I just like the fact that I don't know what I'm doing," he replied. "How about you? What are you doing now?"

"Well, I'm still doing my own research, mainly into alternative energy sources. I haven't worked for the government for several years now."

She smiled in a half-hearted manner.

"I worked for the new government for a while when they first took power but then they got very secretive and now they don't employ many people from the old government."

"Did you work on anything to do with *Oricalc*?" Jen asked, remembering what Reo had told him earlier.

"Actually, it's funny you should mention that because the last project I worked on was to do with that." She took another sip of her juice. "There is a major research facility over in Tyrona where I used to work and before I left I saw all these shipments of what looked like rough crystals coming in. I heard someone call it that, *Oricalc*."

They talked for a while longer about what Raicema was like now that a Makai government was in power and then Sula got up and pulled out a small table with folding sides. She extended it and placed it in between the two chairs.

"Be back in a minute..."

Sula headed into the kitchen and shortly after came back carrying two plates of steaming hot food. "I hope you like fish," she said, placing the plates on the table.

Jen nodded and they both ate the reddish steaks and green vegetables that Sula had prepared for them.

"It's really tasty," Jen said, chewing the juicy fish.

After they had finished, Jen helped clear the plates and table away and they began to talk about what life used to be like in Raicema for them both. Jen told Sula of his realisation that he had been wasting his life doing something so destructive. "There was a time when I couldn't believe what I had done, what I was capable of. It was like there were two versions of me, one who was capable of good and one capable of bad."

He paused, noticing that it was quite dark outside.

"I remember feeling so low, like my life was worthless, like everything I touched would be destroyed. I cried so much."

Tears formed in the corners of Jen's eyes, mainly from the happiness that he was free of such feelings. Sula was looking at Jen compassionately and listening attentively with empathy.

"I didn't know how to put right all the things that I'd done wrong," Jen confessed. "So I just kept doing wrong, hurting people, killing people blindly. It was like quicksand pulling me down further and further into an abyss of darkness, closing me in."

Sula reached over and touched Jen's hand.

"Then something happened to me. I think I went crazy for a while, so many emotions swirling around me every moment of every day. It seemed to last forever, until one day when I was in the middle of it again and I felt this incredible urge to run away. I had felt it before, but never as strongly as on this particular occasion. So I ran. And everything that happened to me since that point has helped me. Every person I met was guiding me, often in strange ways."

"I have experienced the same thing," Sula said.

"Even the fight I had with a man called Rekesh was a sign. It was a test. A test to see if I could choose walking away over fighting."

"Did you say Rekesh?" Sula asked, making sure she'd heard right.

"Yes. He's the man who is at the head of the new government right?"

"Well, I don't think that's true but one thing I know was that he was Elera's partner."

The revelation surprised Jen and it felt like another piece of a giant jigsaw puzzle had been filled in.

"Though the last time I saw him, he was like an empty shell," Sula said with sorrowed emotion. "Inside, there was nobody there."

"I have heard that from someone else today," Jen said, remembering Reo's words. "How do you know him?"

"I briefly met him a long time ago but then I met him again on Bimini Island after I met Elera. He used to be very active in the alternative defence scene here in Raicema City."

She paused as she recalled those days that now seemed so simple.

"When I heard that Elera had died, I went to see him but he was so different. He was obsessed with the Makai government and Oricalc."

Jen felt concern at what he was being told.

"The last time I saw him was a few years ago. He told me Elera had died. It was then I realised that he had also died in some way."

Suddenly, thoughts of Ignis entered Jen's awareness and he remembered that he wanted to ask Sula about it earlier. "What do you know about that thing in the sky?" he asked her. "Did Rekesh ever say anything about it to you?"

"No," Sula replied. "It had just appeared the last time I saw him but he didn't care at all about it. Everyone else I speak to is quite fearful that it might hit the planet one day. From what I've heard, most comets just pass right by so I'm not so worried."

Jen decided to say no more on the subject, not wanting to alarm Sula to the potentially devastating reality.

"Well, I think I should be going," he said, getting to his feet with a smile.

"Wait," she said standing up to. "Where will you go?"

"I have a friend who said I could stay with him," Jen told her reassuringly.

"But you can stay here," she suggested. "I have a spare room. Besides, it's dark now. Raicema City still isn't safe at night."

"But you hardly know me," Jen heard himself say, realising, however, that the same was true of Reo.

"I trust you," Sula said, touching Jen on the shoulder lightly. "Please, it would be nice to have you stay."

Jen smiled and nodded, thinking how fortunate he was to have come across such a kind woman.

"I'll just go and check the room is ready," she said, disappearing down the hallway.

Jen sat back down in the chair and began to think about Ignis and what he could do to stop it. He still couldn't quite believe that such a being existed, though he was now used to accepting that anything was possible. He wanted to talk to Javu, to discuss the imminent threat and also to find out more about his childhood. He wanted to remember where he had come from.

"Your room is ready," Sula said softly, as she reappeared from upstairs. "You must be tired after your journey back."

She led him along the narrow hallway to a small room that had a folding wooden door and was just big enough for a single bed and a small bedside table. There was an old sash window next to the bed and the floors were all deeply stained oak floorboards.

"It's small but I like this room," Sula said warmly.

"It's great," Jen said, feeling the comfort of the room radiating out. "Thank you for letting me stay."

"Well, goodnight. See you in the morning," she said, closing the door after Jen as he sat upon the bed.

He felt tired and he lay down on the soft blankets with his hands cupped over his chest. He reached over and switched off the bedside lamp and returned to his position. He closed his eyes and within a few moments he felt peaceful, drifting into a light sleep.

Jen awoke in the middle of the night with a strange sensation ringing through his head. It was like the lightest of vibrations in the shape of a wall that was continually passing through him. He heard it buzz in his ears as it passed but he found it difficult to awake.

Then, a vision came to him. It was hazy at first, a blob of grey light fading in and out but gradually, the blob began to take a more defined shape. It started to look like a pear and once again he heard the buzz of the vibrations wave through his head. Then the blob of light began to take the form of a man, yet the face and features were completely out of focus.

"*Jen…*" He heard an otherworldly voice radiate into him.

He tried to focus on the light and after a few moments, he saw the being's face take shape, every feature made out of pure light. It looked like Javu, with a long beard and matured droopy ears. He focused on the nose of the being and it too looked familiar.

"*Jen. It's me, Javu!*" the voice said.

"Javu?" Jen felt himself say, beginning to feel like he was dreaming, though the sensation felt quite different.

"*You are not dreaming. You are awake.*"

As soon as Javu said those words the dark silhouette of Sula's small room came into focus in the background, yet the strange apparition of Javu was still floating there in front of him.

A sharp shot of fear passed through him, the fear of the unknown.

"Take a deep breath. This is the first time I have managed to achieve this."

"What?" Jen croaked, this time feeling the words come out of his mouth. His hands and feet were full of pins and needles and he was developing a cold sweat.

"I have entered your awareness remotely. My physical self is sitting in the hut in Seho. That is where you grew up."

"I can't believe it," Jen heard himself say, his mind still feeling woozy. He began to feel like he was dreaming again.

"Take out your stone."

Feeling half awake and unable to focus, Jen put his hand into his shirt and felt the cool, smooth stone hanging around his neck. He took it out and light spread everywhere, engulfing the apparition of Javu.

"Now think of me!" Javu said before the light swallowed up everything around.

The next thing Jen felt was an incredibly forceful pull on his insides, originating from where his belly button was. It spread all around his body quickly and it felt like he was being pulled apart. He wanted to cry out but he couldn't breathe.

Then, the wall of vibration came back, but this time louder and wavier. The sound of it was painful. It carried him away like the greatest of tidal waves and he felt himself falling at lightning speed.

He felt fear but it passed as he allowed the unknown to consume him. At that moment a different feeling came, like he was being suspended in air. The vibration ceased and then he saw a tunnel of hazy light, which he seemed to be hovering inside.

Then, in a motion so quick that he couldn't fully comprehend, he felt himself being sucked into the tunnel, at which point he could not hear anything but a sizzling vibration. He could not feel anything except the separation of every atom in his body.

At that moment he felt so free that he thought he would disperse into nothingness. The end of the tunnel came almost as soon as he had witnessed the start of it. Time had ceased to exist.

He awoke to the feeling of a hard mattress beneath him. He sat up with dizziness to see Javu's wrinkly face smiling at him and the night-time heat of Ciafra swelling in the air.

"Am I dreaming?" he heard himself say. "Where am I?"

Javu was smiling so purely that Jen instantly felt at ease.

"You are home, my son."

Chapter 63 – Abilities & Power

Jen opened his eyes. The world waved in and out.

He moved his eyes slowly. He saw straw and wood.

His hands were face up and he could feel something soft beneath the backs of them. He realised that he was lying on a bed somewhere.

"Ahh, you are awake?" a familiar voice said.

It was a voice from the past.

For a moment, Jen thought he was a child again.

Then, he realised where he was.

He sat up and saw Javu sitting at the end of the bed.

"How did I...?" Jen began to say.

"You have changed, Jen," Javu said softly and affectionately, "both in appearance and in spirit. How does one change so?"

Jen was in a hut. It invoked a powerful sense of nostalgia in him and he knew straight away that he had grown up there.

"But how...?" Jen said, slightly confused.

Now he felt fully awake, completely immersed in the environment. He could feel the sweltering heat of the land in the air of the hut. A sudden rush of panic shot through him, as he realised he was not sure if anything was real.

"Do not worry, Jen," Javu said, reading his mind. "Your dilemma is common to those who venture into other worlds. Trust me, *clarity* is not far away."

"But if I am really here, that means I travelled a thousand suns in what felt like an instant?"

"Such feats are just the start for you," Javu said with conviction.

Javu stood up from his seated position on the bed. He walked across the oiled wooden floors and then sat upon a rug not far away. He rested his hands on his thighs.

Outside, through the hut's wide window, Jen could see a thousand stars shining brightly in the clear navy sky.

"It's time for me to tell you about a few things that I know. These things would make no sense to someone who hadn't *seen* what you have."

Jen was motionless.

"You are the bearer of special gifts, Jen. They are *abilities* that can help you achieve whatever you wish."

The air was flowing calmly in the hut.

"When I found you as a baby, you were a very happy child but you could be a little temperamental at times. There were occasions when you would get angry quite suddenly but I always knew you meant no harm. It was simply that you were frustrated and a little unbalanced."

Jen was listening with openness to the story of his past.

"Then, you began to display an extraordinary strength," Javu said. "You would carry six Kivilis on your back, and not small ones at that!" Javu chuckled at the memory. "At first I thought that your strength was because of the stone that I found you with. Whenever you got affirmative or energetic that stone would glow like a firefly, but then I realised that the stone wasn't giving *you* such energy, but *you* were giving energy to it."

Jen looked down at the shiny black bead around his neck. He had almost forgotten about it again.

"Do you know where the *earth stone* comes from?" Java asked him.

"When I was in the forest on the outskirts of Yinkoto, a strange being showed me its power and told me it had a connection to the planet. I assumed that you gave it to me as a child."

Javu seemed defensive at the thought.

"I only *bound* it for you. And yes, the earth stone has a very strong connection not only with this planet but to the eye of darkness that secretly influences everything we do." Javu's tone was now serious. "It is your job to protect it and make sure it is not used for destructive purposes. It is a burden placed on very few."

Jen found this hard to believe and began to voice his disbelief but Javu was adamant.

"It is true," he insisted. "When I found you as a child, the stone was not far away, glowing a bizarre green light. When you were old enough, I bound the stone in leather and put it around your neck for safekeeping."

Javu paused for a moment.

"One thing that you may not know about this stone is that it is invisible to many people. When the Tyrones took you as a child, they were looking for the stone but they could never see it. All they saw was a piece of leather around your neck. Only a few people can see this stone."

"Can you see it?"

"Not anymore."

Jen was surprised at this but now he realised how very few people had ever enquired about the stone throughout his lifetime.

"It has evidently protected you over the years."

"Is it because of this stone that I am here right now? I mean, is that how I can be here now when I was just in Sula's apartment in Raicema?"

"No, Jen," Javu informed him. "That was result of you seeing the world as it really is. It *seems* as though you have an unnatural physical strength, but that is not actually what you possess."

The thought of the altercation that Jen had found himself in with the brigadier earlier that day came to mind and before Javu could say another word, Jen felt compelled to tell him about it. "Earlier today, I ran into a man who doesn't like me," Jen told Javu. "And he started a fight with me." The wind outside seemed to be rising. "At first, I refrained from striking him, but then I felt I had no other choice and I did, or I thought that I did. But, I'm sure I never touched him, yet he flew backwards like a bird flying through the sky."

"Exactly!" Javu said excitely. "You didn't touch him! That is what I am trying to tell you. Your strength is not physical."

"Are you trying to say that I can move things with my mind?"

"You just told me you did that today?" Javu asked Jen for the answer. "And you have been doing that subconsciously all your life.

Even carrying those six Kivilis on your back as a child, you were lifting them with your energy, not your physical strength."

"I can't believe it!" Jen said, shaken with the prospect of such power. He gazed out into the darkness of the sky.

The stars seemed to be watching him.

"In the past, such feats were the norm for our ancestors that once dwelled on this planet. In fact, their progression into the *true reality* was a hundredfold of our own progression."

"What true reality?"

"The reality that each of us knows deep down but just cannot see clearly. The reality that the world we live in is not solid in any way."

Javu was wide-eyed and serious.

"It only appears solid to us because we perceive it that way! And we do that more and more when we are bogged down from the pressures that are imposed on us by those who want to control us, those influenced by *power*." A hint of light had struck the sky outside. "But you have broken free! And because of that, you will discover more and more things that you are capable of."

Jen was thinking deeply about what Javu was telling him. It was like a full awakening to what he already knew. He had seen in his dreams how that which appeared solid could so easily disperse. He was sure that was also true of the physical world.

"Now," Javu continued, "though essentially we are not solid and not restrained, we do have differences in how our energy behaves. I, for example have a strong affinity to *energetic air* and you Jen have an overwhelmingly strong affinity to *energetic earth*." Again Jen looked down into the deep black stone. "That is why the abilities that you are beginning to become fully aware of are intrinsic to your type of energy. *Telekinesis* and *teleporting* like you have already demonstrated involve a full awareness and understanding of the energy type that you possess. You are now becoming one with this type."

"Can you perform such abilities?" Jen asked Javu.

"Well, I have different abilities. I can *levitate* and can also project this ability onto other beings. I am also capable of *telepathy*, which has served me very well throughout my life. My most recent ability seems to coincide with your own awakening and that is the ability of *projection* where I can cross the dream world's boundaries to be seen in the physical world. That is how I appeared in your room tonight."

Jen felt as if he had known such feats were possible all along.

"As I said, it is the first time I have performed such an act, so I myself am in a period a great change."

"I have seen people who have such strange abilities when I was living in the mountains in Neoasia," Jen began to tell Javu. Jen described where he had been for some time.

"In fact," Javu said after a while. "The monastery where you resided for several years is located on the borders of Neoasia and Vassini, which is very close to the region of Vassini where I found you as a baby."

"It makes sense," Jen said in response to the news. "As I felt a very strong connection to that area and lots of things confirmed that."

He told Javu about the experience at Zaigan's village and how he had connected to what seemed to be a past life during his time there. Javu did not comment on this, instead pressing forward with something that was clearly on his mind from the beginning.

"Now, one of the most important things I need to tell you about, which like I said would not really seem possible unless you had opened yourself up like you have, is about summoning or conjuring," Javu said with the utmost seriousness. "Whilst the abilities that you and I display are a form of summoning in that we call energies forth for a particular purpose, there are some on this planet and elsewhere that will use similar techniques for negative reasons."

"What, like a *sorcerer*?" Jen asked.

"Yes, such beings have and still do exist. I have myself in my current lifetime faced such a being, a man called Vuktar. He was lost in a realm that one would not even want to glimpse. His mind was full of nothing but destruction and death."

A stroke of terror cut across Jen's heart and visions of war came to his mind.

"Have no fear," Javu said to him calmly, sensing the distress that such a subject could cause. "But you should be aware of such entities. Fortunately, such beings cannot usually perform these negative *conjurings* without the help of powerful objects, such as the stone you have around your neck and the one I have around mine."

At that statement, Javu reached into his cotton top and revealed a small grey stone, also bound in a leather cord. "This is the *air stone*, one of four stones made in the past by the Lemurian people. You have another of the four, the *earth stone*. Elera had the third I believe, the *water stone*, which was given to her by Kirichi. The fourth stone, the *fire stone*, is now lost."

He paused at the enormity of what he was about to say.

"It is through the fire stone that Ignis was summoned to this planet. That is why the bearers of such stones should be incorruptible to the force of ultimate power, the eye of darkness, *Ambitio*."

Jen was trying to take it all into context. Then, a feeling of great responsibility seemed to float down upon him as he realised his protective role on the planet.

"Why would someone create such stones?" Jen asked finally, after many moments of contemplation.

"I have asked myself the same question many times, my son," Javu said sincerely. "But such a question is irrelevant now. The stones themselves are actually balanced and are simply powerful channelling tools to reach into other worlds. Used correctly, I am sure that they can be used for good, but their existence poses a threat to the planet and we are seeing a realisation of such a threat now in the form of Ignis."

"Can't we destroy them?"

"Jen, the same applies to these stones as does to ourselves. We could destroy the physical stones quite easily, but that which has been endowed upon the stones will still exist. The true power of these stones is not in their physical form."

There was silence for a while whilst Jen allowed what he was being told to crystallise in his mind. After a while, a question seemed to pop into his mind. "How can I use this stone for good?"

"That is something you will have to work out yourself, Jen. I only know of the power of the stone but I cannot use it or tell you how it can be used. After all, it was not bequeathed to me."

Jen got to his feet and took the necklace off, holding the stone in his hand. It was of the deepest black imaginable, as if an entire universe of darkness was contained within the small sphere. Just by looking at it, Jen felt drawn, as if he might be sucked into the stone. He looked away, a small pulse of fear throbbing in his stomach.

"What about Ignis?" Jen said, putting the stone away out of sight. "How can such a being be called forth using such a stone?"

"I do not wish to speak so much about such matters," Javu told him in a warning tone. "But I will say that there are certain realms of existence that one does not even want to imagine. It is the epitome of negativity to dwell in such realms. Those who do become trapped in a *pyramid of power*."

"Pyramid of power? I've never heard that expression before," Jen said, interested by the metaphor.

"Well, a pyramid is a representation of power. At the bottom, the strong foundation is made up of the masses, all leading to a single point. This exists in those realms and also in the world today in the societies we live in."

Jen could picture the metaphor.

"At the bottom are all the lost souls living in ignorance and fear and at the top are the few who have all the power. The same is true of the physical pyramids on this planet. They are tools for channelling power."

"You mean that those pyramids that Elera was searching for were all made for power?"

Javu did not ask Jen where he'd heard of Elera.

"I am unsure of the intention behind those pyramids being built.

However, they are *consuming* entities, make no mistake about it."

Jen was slightly confused about what Javu was trying to say but he had another question.

"You just mentioned *the few* at the top? Who are they? People like the Tyrones?"

"They were not at the very top," Javu said, almost laughing at the thought. "The Tyrones were puppets. In our human societies, those at the top are part of a global network that consists of several families that have tried and succeeded in controlling us all, mainly through fear and ignorance. And as you know, fear and ignorance are vehicles for power."

"What families?"

"Well for one, the person who is really pulling the strings in Raicema at the moment. Sadana Siger is from a family that has craved control for as long as anyone can remember and the *Siger* family did this by being part of this worldwide network. In fact, the Siger family heritage goes back over three thousand years, probably to a time when the pyramids that we were just talking about were still in use."

Jen was surprised Javu knew so much.

"That is why Sadana knows things that other people don't and why he never made himself a public figure," Javu continued. "Look at what has happened with Rekesh. Sadana is using his image just as he used the Tyrones."

"Sadana was involved with the Tyrones?"

"The Tyrones were involved with many people in this small network of people who hold the *real power* over human societies including Sadana Siger, Yangjam Satori, Sai Gueken and Archibold Constynce."

"I think those last three men you mentioned were all there when Seth Tyrone was shot," Jen said, remembering that fateful day in the skies of Yinkoto. "Sadana wasn't there though, only the other three."

"Well, he would have been very busy putting an important part of their plan into action. He was at that time systematically rolling out his underground army to take over the key buildings in Raicema at a time when the Tyrones were at their greatest weakness."

Jen was totally unaware of such a plot.

"The Tyrones were starting to know too much, so they needed to be removed in the eyes of this network. That is why there's a new government in power in Raicema now, but ultimately, this *new* Makai Empire won't last long either. It too will be replaced with another puppet when the time is right."

"When would the time be right?"

"Try and think about why the Tyrones were assassinated," Javu said, his clinical language somewhat surprising Jen. "They had failed numerous times to achieve what this network wants, which is to keep control over the people of this planet. They can't fully rely on technology yet. Whilst they have enough to survey us, they do not have enough to truly control us worldwide."

Jen felt like he was being taught an important lesson.

"So, the *network* needs governments to carry out their plans. And if they fail, they just replace them. However, this recent shift of power signifies something else. It is a sign that what this ancient network has been trying to achieve for millennia is starting to become reality."

"What?" Jen asked.

"They want to have a single point of power. Have you heard of the *wisdom rocks*?"

"I have heard all about wisdom rocks from Reo," Jen said declaratively, which pleasantly surprised Javu. The grey-bearded man smiled at the news that Jen was naturally encountering people who could guide him.

"Your time away has truly put you back in oneness with the *essence*. You will continue to meet many that will guide you," Javu proclaimed mystically.

Jen knew it was true. Ever since that first moment that he'd broken free of the control that the Tyrones had placed him under, he had been guided to where he was sitting at that very moment, aided along his path by many helpful beings.

"Now where was I? Oh, yes, wisdom rocks. As the Tyrones began to discover that this mineral could be exploited to produce energy that could drive their technology, they began to become greedy and forgot that they themselves were being controlled by people higher up in the *'pyramid'* than they were." Outside, a plethora of birdsong seemed to erupt in unison at the sun starting to rise. "They tried to play people in the network off against each other, but of course, the network knew this the entire time."

Javu let out a sigh, ready to reach a conclusion. "The irony is that this small global network at the top of the pyramid of society is itself a puppet of Ambitio."

"It's unbelievable," Jen said, all the while instinctively knowing that it had to be true, that it felt right in his gut.

"Indeed. And it has been so for millennia. That is why people like us are here to restore the balance."

They sat as the sun rose, discussing in more detail the different families involved in the network.

"The majority of the power is in Lengard, where there are several families that have a heavy influence in the decisions that are made. Lengard used to take a very active approach to warfare but now it leaves it all to Raicema. Effectively Raicema is Lengard's personal army now."

Jen knew it was true and remembered all the direct communication lines to Lengardian command centres.

"King Constynce as he was once known, is quite a boisterous character and liked being in the public eye. However, he has no problem letting the public think he is dead to achieve the goals of the network. His family hold more power over people than any other group of people on this planet. The Satoris and the Guekens have ruled the east for long periods of history but they approach it with more discipline. If you step out of line, you will quickly be removed."

"What about Lizrab and Ciafra?" Jen asked, not aware of any

major centralised governments in either of those lands.

"Either the raw terrain or lack of resources have prevented the network from fully controlling these lands in recent times," Javu said with a grin, "which is the main reason I live here!"

At that both men let out a great laugh and Jen realised what a dilemma the planet was in, both for humans and everything else that lived on it.

"Now you should get some rest," Javu said. "We can talk more in a few hours."

Jen agreed and Javu went over to another section of the hut which had a partition made from a wooden folding screen with a beautiful picture of a feathered serpent across it.

Within a few moments, Jen drifted into the dream world once again, a familiar realm of hazy whitish light surrounding him. He saw someone walking towards him and before long the familiar silhouette of the woman of light was standing in front of him.

"The truth will be free," she was saying, her voice the most beautiful ethereal melody Jen had ever heard. *"You must take my place."*

Jen then fell into the deepest sleep he had done for a long time with the same words playing through his mind over and over.

"Followed by its past.
Pride is rooted in desire. Pride is followed by desire.
Desire is rooted in fear. Desire is followed by fear.
Fear is rooted in ignorance. Fear is followed by ignorance.
Ignorance is rooted in greed. Ignorance is followed by greed.
Greed is rooted in anger. Greed is followed by anger.
Anger is rooted in pride. Anger is followed by pride.
This cycle forms the dark eye."

Chapter 64 – The Eye of Hope

Jen awoke and it was bright.

He felt a hard mattress underneath him and he stared up at a web-like structure of tree limbs. The criss-cross pattern was firmly holding in place tightly-packed bundles of straw.

Jen jumped up excitedly as he realised he was still in Seho and his conversations with Javu the previous night had not been a dream. He immediately went outside, filled with intense inner warmth from the outer heat of the Ciafran sun. He shielded his eyes from the brightness and saw that Javu was awake and adjusting a small table outside.

"Did you sleep well?" Javu asked Jen cheerfully, placing a tray full of banana and coconut sections on a small wooden table. He went back in the hut and emerged with several different coloured rounds of bread.

"Yes," he replied. "I still can't believe that this isn't a dream. I am really here?"

"Well, yes," Javu said jovially. "Except that we are never really anywhere, but also everywhere."

Then he burst out laughing at his conundrum, especially at the bewildered expression that it caused Jen to exhibit. Jen walked over and sat upon one of the old chairs, the legs of it warped by time. The sun was shining so brightly that even the wooden shutters could not prevent the brilliance of light from illuminating the inside of the hut.

"Wow, it's so bright."

"It is *Affero*, the *eye of everlasting light*."

"Affero?"

"Affero is the complete opposite of Ambitio," Javu said as he pointed up to the sun. "She is shining brightly for you."

"The sun?"

"Not the sun itself but the *spirit of the sun*, which manifests itself as all suns and bright stars in the universe. Can you see that light? It is everywhere."

Jen realised that he was most familiar with the light. He sat silently contemplating Javu's words as the heat relaxed every cell in his body.

"*Will* you be experimenting with your new ability today?" Javu asked enthusiastically after a while, propping up a large umbrella made of bound straw to shield them from the intense light.

"You mean I can do it again. I can travel wherever I want in an instant?"

"It is possible because of the light," Javu said. "It is not so much wherever you want but wherever your *will* takes you."

Javu sat on the opposing chair. He signalled for Jen to begin eating the fruit and bread.

"When you say my *will*, what do you mean?" Jen asked, scooping out the soft, sweet coconut with a spoon.

"Your *will* is like your wishing power," he said simply. "It is the ultimate freedom we have in changing our lives."

The two ate quietly for a while whilst Jen pondered over Javu's concept of freedom.

"So, would I be able to get back to Raicema now in the same way?"

"It depends on whether or not that is what your *will* desires. I assume for the time being at least, that that is not what you really want."

"Why do you say that?" Jen asked.

"Because I know that you are looking for someone, and that person cannot be found in Raicema."

"Are you talking about the world walker?"

"If that is what you choose to call this being, then yes, I am."

Jen suddenly felt a little apprehensive, as if he was unwillingly walking towards his own death.

"If you wish to find this being, then you must go to one of the spiritual openings on this planet."

"Spiritual openings?"

"Yes, there are several of them on the earth."

Jen felt like he had already visited such places during his time away.

"People of long ago built great structures at many of these locations."

"Where?"

"Well, the sites of the *four pyramids of power* are the locations that I know. Giza, Bimini, Cibola and..." Javu paused as if he were about to let out a trusted secret. "...and Lemuria."

"Lemuria?"

"It is only a fragment of what once existed. But it is like no other place on earth. It is the past incarnate."

Jen felt an incredible urge to seek out this mystical land. Javu seemed to read his thoughts.

"You want to go there?"

Jen was silent.

"Lemuria is hard to locate. I know now that Lemuria belongs in the past," he said solemnly. "We can learn a lot from knowing our history, but that is where our interest in the past should end."

Jen was surprised at Javu's shrewdness about the subject. They both continued to eat the fruit and bread.

"However," Javu began again, "the spiritual openings at such locations exist as a way to cross worlds. These can be the worlds of Ambitio or the worlds of Affero."

The image of the woman of light seemed to spring into Jen's head and it was even more vivid in the bright sunlight. He decided to ask Javu about it. "I keep having these recursive dreams about a woman who is made entirely of light. Through I cannot see her clearly, I can hear her and I can feel that she is a woman. I think she is trying to contact me. She always says the same thing over and over."

"What?"

"*You must take my place.*"

"When did you start having such visions?"

"They started about a year ago."

"And can you remember how you feel around this being?

Frightened? Excited? At peace?"

"I feel very calm. Like I can trust her and that I already know her in some way."

Javu leant back in his chair, allowing the sun's rays to catch the left side of his face. He stroked his beard as he thought. Then he tapped the wooden table with his fingers in a rhythmic motion. "What do you know about Elera Advaya?"

"Not much," Jen admitted. "I have heard about her from Sula and Reo."

There was silence for a moment.

"I also know that she died."

Javu seemed uncomfortable at this statement.

"Elera achieved that which each of us on this planet should aim to achieve," Javu said with much affection in his voice. "That is to see ourselves for who we really are." Javu paused. "We are not just a physical form like so many on this planet believe and Elera knew that from an early age."

The heat seemed to be singing.

"And not only did she know that, but she wanted everyone else to know it too. She believed that by uncovering our past for all to see, our real past, that it would open people up to reality."

"What reality?"

"The reality that existence is endless. We are all part of the same infinite truth. We are all part of an *essence*, one *unlimited* consciousness."

They ate again for a while, until the sun was so hot and bright that they had to retreat into the shade of the hut.

"How did Elera die?" Jen asked as they sat at another table inside, a little afraid of the response.

"I only know that she did not succumb to Ambitio, that she was incapable of that. And to me, that means that she died physically with full awareness of why that was supposed to happen at that time. She has moved on to another level of existence."

It was warm in the hut and sharp streams of sunlight shot in through the gaps in wood and straw. Jen's thoughts went back to the woman of light. "Do you think that the woman of light is Elera?"

"What does your heart tell you?"

Jen fell silent for a while as he allowed the answer to come to him. The he felt an overwhelming surety that the two beings were indeed the same.

"I believe so. But what does she mean, *I must take her place*?"

"Elera, like yourself, went through some incredible changes in her life. She began to develop abilities that most would consider incomprehensible."

"Like what?"

"She began to see all physical things in terms of their energy vibrations and she became increasingly psychic, like the future and present had merged for her. Indeed we could never have located those ancient places which were lost for so long without her abilities." Javu paused as he removed a few dying leaves from a large plant on the windowsill. "She believed that all people could also perform such abilities and her intent was to make as many people aware that they have unlimited potential. She wanted to open them up to the truth of who they are. I think this *intent* is what she wants you to continue with."

Jen felt as if he was starting to develop that intention naturally. He felt as if he had escaped a prison and that he wanted as many people as possible to also escape.

"Her place in creating a global awareness that we are being controlled is vital to the people of this world. Who better than someone who has been through what you have to relay that message."

"And what of the world walker? How do they fit into this? Do they have the same purpose?"

"All of those who open themselves up to Affero, the force of will, the force of freedom, the eye of everlasting light will have this same intent. A *world walker* is fully immersed in Affero, just as Elera was."

"So is Elera the world walker?"

"One of many," Javu said, slightly puzzlingly. "But I know that the being that you are seeking is not Elera."

"Then who is the world walker I am looking for?"

"First, you should ask *what* a world walker is?" Javu said to Jen, twiddling his long beard into a twist of coarse grey hair. "A world walker is one who *willingly* transcends worlds to ease the suffering that other beings are experiencing."

"What worlds?" Jen asked, slightly confused. "Are you talking about those places I have seen in my dreams, those realms of power? I have visited them many times. I have seen many extremes in *those* places."

Javu was surprised at Jen's in-depth experience of such places. It slightly concerned him.

"Yes, the realms you are describing are the six realms of Ambitio, the realms of control. If you dwell in such places when you dream, you must be careful, because such worlds are so powerful that they can draw you in permanently, even when you are asleep!"

Jen was now taking the issue seriously.

"So you have visited the *world of the gods*?" Javu probed.

"I have visited a place where the inhabitants are all giants, battling each other in epic fights," Jen described, thinking how much that particular place felt like everyone was a god, struggling for ultimate power. "That world was quite mesmerising. I was immersed in energy, I could feel the euphoria there."

"Indeed," Javu agreed "But what you should understand is that such a world is only a collective consciousness of a group of beings."

"You mean that place wouldn't exist without its inhabitants? Even in my dreams?"

"Exactly!"

The two sat in silence for a while. Cattle could be heard mooing close by. The sound of a farmer shouting followed.

"That's what this physical world is too," Javu said suddenly, pushing a window open and looking outside. "Every world is the same. It is simply our collective experience. And a world walker is trying to help beings realise that they are actually creating such worlds as we live them."

Javu stood up and went outside again.

Jen followed as Javu began to eat several slices of fresh watermelon that had been left on the table outside. The lightest of breezes passed through the hot dry air.

Jen suddenly remembered something and looked up into the sky. It was too bright to see anything. "Have you heard about this creature in the sky?" he asked quite reservedly. "A dragon? Are we all creating that too?"

"Exactly, Jen!" Javu said with joy bouncing in his heart. "*Ignis* is simply a culmination of concentrated negative energy, formed by those who worship Ambitio."

Even the light coming up from the ground was hot and a smoky cloud of dust could be seen in the distance where the farmer had recently herded his cattle.

"It is the longstanding projection of such negativity upon the masses that has caused this manifestation to approach the planet."

"So is it real?"

"It is very real."

It was news Jen did not want to hear.

"So how can we stop it?"

"The one you are looking for can help you," Javu said mystically. "It will take the opposite to restore the balance so that Ignis will cease to exist. You are part of that opposite, Jen, just as Elera is."

As the sun heated the dry ground all around, Jen thought about what he was being told. He had experienced himself how existence could change when you truly wished it too and he could see no reason why Javu would be telling him false information. However, a feeling of great apathy had come over him, the feeling that the task ahead was so enormous that it was almost impossible to attain.

"Remember that you are not alone, Jen," Javu said soothingly after a while, almost reading his mind. "Just as there are those who embody the power that exists, there are those who embody the freedom." He paused. "And that brings us to who you are looking for…"

"Who?" Jen asked, knowing the truth was imminent.

"Gaia."

"Who?" Jen repeated.

"She is our mother. She is the *aether* of this planet, the spirit of the earth."

At that moment, Jen felt a strong tug around his belly button, like something was feeding him, the breath of a mother giving life to her child.

"She is there to protect you. She is with you every step you make."

The conversation had suddenly become overwhelming for Jen and he had to excuse himself and go into the hut. He felt hot and inundated with emotion. A strange homesickness had come over him. Javu did not follow, simply sitting outside in the sun whilst Jen lay down inside. Eventually, he came back outside, more composed and ready to resume the conversation.

"When I was in living in the mountains, I saw a fish turn into a bird and this bird spoke to me," Jen said, remembering the experience. "This creature told me to seek out its queen, which it said was the spirit of the earth. I have struggled to accept that what I saw was real."

"Indeed," Javu said, unsurprised by the story. "Witnessing such miracles is most troubling. It will certainly make one question their entire belief system!"

Then Javu burst out laughing which made Jen feel at ease. He breathed out heavily as he reaffirmed that anything was possible.

"Gaia has in the past, been seen to manifest herself in the form of a human woman. After all, the earth's collective energy is definitely more female than male and a good thing too!"

This time, Javu and Jen both laughed together.

"You are seeking Gaia," Javu said strongly after a while. "Find her."

"How?"

"You should use the *earth stone* to channel your energy to reach her world. Go to a spot in the planes that you feel comfortable with and if you *will it*, she will come to you."

Jen felt a little uncomfortable at the idea.

"Javu, I need to ask you something first," Jen said, and Javu could see that he was anxious. "Why me?"

"Why you what?"

"Why is this happening to me?"

"It is happening to you because you want it to happen to you."

The words resonated out and Jen knew there was no more to say. It was time for him and Javu to say goodbye again. As he stood up and was about to say the words, Javu said them for him.

"Ignis is close, Jen. Next time we will spend more time together. When it is all done, we shall laugh."

A great smile formed on Javu's face, genuine and warm. Jen turned away with a tear in his eye and for the first time, he reached with lack of fear for the stone around his neck.

"If I do not see you later today, I will assume all has gone well," Javu said after him.

Jen nodded to himself as he headed out into the warm air of Seho. As he was walking he began to think about what the black stone around his neck represented. It was a crystal, but Jen knew it was more than that. He had felt energy permeating from it in the past but he had ignored it then.

Now he had the reassurance that he no longer wanted anything negative in his life, he was sure only good things would come to him through the stone.

Thoughts of Orentus came into his mind, the strange being of light that had approached him in the forest of Yinkoto. He drew a parallel between that being and the woman of light he now knew was Elera.

So life continues. The insight came to him, giving him a lasting inner confidence.

Chapter 65 – To the Earth

Jen walked out into the heat.

He walked until he looked back and saw Seho in the far distance. He sat upon a round mound and closed his eyes. After several moments of listening to his breathing and the gentle wind rustling the dry grasses, he opened his eyes and slowly looked down at the shiny bead in his hand.

It had turned a vivid whitish green, like the inside of ripe asparagus. He felt drawn to it, almost lost in a mesmerised state. Then, as if waking up from a dream without ever being asleep, everything changed.

The ground and shrubs around him still existed, yet they seemed alive in a way Jen could not fully comprehend. The surfaces of the plants appeared to be wavering, the rich greens and browns continually merging into each other with a pulsating motion.

Looking at the ground, Jen saw that it was emitting a sizzling energy. It looked like a gassy effervescence. He found that he could zoom his vision into this energy and observe the most minuscule of detail, such as tiny insects and grains of sand. They were living in the breathing soil.

He had the sensation of going deeper and deeper into the earth, through an endless amount of soil and rubble, past countless species of tiny creatures and buried items. No matter how much he wanted to stop and return to his seated position, he could not. He was being taken by something.

For what seemed like hours, Jen travelled down into the depths of the planet. Though he felt no physical sensation, he knew he was intact and that something was pulling him.

Eventually, he arrived in a strange cavity, lava flowing like a river through a cave full of catacombs. Strange vapours poured upwards and great blue and green crystals grew from the roof.

Jen had landed on an elevated ledge with lava all around and before him sat a very strange-looking creature.

The being had orange and brown skin with little hair. The creature was thin and frail with a face similar to a Kivili. It was silent and a sense of calm could be felt emanating from its body.

"Is Gaia here?" Jen asked the creature.

It looked at him with its deep-set sullen eyes.

"She is everywhere," the creature seemed to say, but its lips did not move. "Why are you here?"

"I am here to learn," Jen said quite instinctively

"Before you can see her, you must pass *three trials*," the creature said, its wrinkly skin and protruding brow-bone moving very slightly.

Jen noticed how lean the creature was. Despite its frail structure, it had the most defined and smooth muscles that he had ever seen on any being. Jen felt himself telepathically agree to take the trials and the creature reached down amongst the cracks of the rock on which it was perched. It held up a piece of slate and upon it was an etching of a five-pointed star in the form of a *pentagram*.

"On this *star*, where would *you wish to be*?" the creature asked.

At first, the question was perplexing and Jen did not know how to respond, but then an instinctive feeling came over him that the central point of the star seemed like the most balanced place, which he felt was important.

He pointed to the centre of the star. The creature showed no emotion and turned the slate over. On the back was another etching, this time of a six-pointed star in the form of a *hexagram*.

"On this *star*, where are *you now*?" the creature asked.

Again the centre of the star seemed to speak to Jen yet for an unknown reason. Then, Jen got the overwhelming feeling that he was at a different position on the star. He felt like he was at the top point of the star and so he placed his finger on the slate at that location.

Again the creature said nothing and it placed the slate back amongst the rocky cracks and produced another, smaller slate.

"Now for the last trial."

He held up the new slate and it had a picture of a circle with two interplaying components.

"In this *circle*, where are *we now*?"

To this question, Jen did not know the answer.

He thought about it for a while, but had no intuition towards where to place his finger.

"I don't know," Jen said after some time of contemplation.

"Then, you cannot see our mother."

Desperation engulfed him that the creature was about to disappear. Jen tried to silence his mind and let the answer come to him. The creature kept the image held up for Jen to look at.

Then, in a sudden epiphany, he had the overwhelming feeling that the position was just before the light dot and he placed his finger there.

The creature put down its slate.

"You have passed the trials," it said. "You are with Affero."

Then quite suddenly, the world around him began to disperse and in its place a green haze began to form. The creature had gone in an instant and Jen had the strong sensation that he was dreaming.

The green world was incredibly strange, as if vast oceans and mountains were formed out of fog and mist. They were floating in sky like clouds both large and small. He looked around and a small patch of land had formed beneath him, the earth rich and abundant with shrubbery and bright flowers.

He began to feel much more peaceful and relaxed and he felt an urge to sit down upon his heels, resting his hands on his knees. He watched the joy of creation flourish all around him.

The land expanded as far as his eyes could see; trees and great bushes sprouting all around. A number of creatures started to appear, from insects to birds and small rodents to horses.

A great natural forest formed, teeming with life, the interplay of the different creatures and plant life around him seemingly dancing in unison. He saw the trees grow, he saw the leaves form and the flowers bloom.

Then he saw her. Walking slowly and followed by a thousand creatures, she was so vivid that Jen was completely mesmerised.

She was a beautiful woman.

She had dark skin with freckles, yellow eyes and moss interwoven into her curly black matted hair. Birds and insects lived in her hair like it was a nest, popping in and out energetically.

She had vines and leaves as her jewellery. Her skin shimmered with a green and brown glow. When she walked, the creation around dipped beneath her. An exodus of animals followed her and flowers were constantly growing and withering on her hair and skin.

As her feet melted into the ground, flowers and shrubs began to grow there rapidly.

"You have sought me, and I am here." A voice radiated through the air, deep yet soft and womanly.

Jen was in awe of the being in front of him. The vivacious and vibrant form of a perfect woman interwoven with the plethora of nature was a captivating sight. He felt overwhelmed.

"I am here to learn," Jen felt himself say.

"Then ask me what you will."

"What did those symbols mean that the creature showed me?" Jen asked, feeling like he couldn't formulate any reasoning for how he had passed the three trials.

"The five-pointed star represents the elements and where we come from. The points represent earth, fire, air, water and the essence, which is the top point."

Gaia's voice was like a song and Jen felt quite euphoric listening to her, like he could predict and relate to every note resounding around him.

"You passed this trial because you are aware that balance is the most important thing if one is to lead a physical existence."

Two feisty squirrels jumped up onto their queen's shoulder, chirping away at each other.

"And what of the second symbol?" Jen asked.

"The six-pointed star represents the different realms of energy that

exist."

The words made Jen think of the different worlds that he had visited in his dreams.

"In total there are actually twelve different realms, six on each side of the hexagram. The star is formed from two triangles placed on top of each other, one pointing upwards and one downwards. The upward triangle represents the male realms and the downward triangle the female realms."

Jen was intrigued and wanted to know everything about the symbol.

"The hexagram is two-sided. It has both negative and positive qualities."

Suddenly several fox-like animals appeared and lay down next to the voluptuous woman in front of him.

"If you are looking at the hexagram in a negative sense, the male triangle is comprised of three negative realms. You know these well."

Jen got the feeling that Gaia knew everything about him.

"These are Ignorance, Avarice and Anger. The downwards triangle represents the negative female realms of power: Fear, Desire and Pride."

Jen immediately related these six realms to those that he had visited many times.

"When it comes to the realms of Ambitio, it is important to be honest to where our current weakness lies. You passed this trail because you are aware that you are still in Ignorance and are seeking knowledge."

Jen could relate to this conclusion, though he could not fully understand it.

"What about looking at the six-pointed star in a positive light?" Jen asked, a tree of questions growing in his mind. "What are the other six realms on the other side of the star?"

"The upwards male triangle represents the three positive male realms of Affero: Wisdom, Patience and Joy. The downwards female triangle repre-sents the three positive female realms of Affero: Faith, Contentment and Humility."

It made complete sense to Jen and it was almost like he knew it at the exact moment the message was being communicated to him, like he was remembering something he had long forgotten.

"*As for the third symbol…*" Gaia began.

"It is the endless struggle for balance between Affero and Ambitio," Jen finished the sentence, causing a smile to form on the beautiful face of the queen of nature.

"*And you passed this trial, because you are aware of where we currently are in this struggle,*" Gaia told him. "*The balance is distorted and Ambitio has reached a culmination. This balance must and will be restored.*"

Jen knew it was true and felt an overwhelmingly joyous feeling in the area of his heart, like he had fully connected to something and it was giving him energy. Questions poured into his mind.

"What does Ambitio look like?" he felt compelled to ask, though upon doing so a pang of fear entered his heart. However, he wanted to be brave and fearless.

"*It looks like the greatest of black circles that is twisting the very space and time that it is consuming,*" Gaia said, at which point Jen saw it in his mind's eye.

The spirit of the earth was right. Ambitio looked like a giant eye, its centre a perfect pitch-black circle. Jen held the vision only for a split second for in a panicked moment he thought he might get sucked rapidly into the black hole.

"And Affero?" Jen said, somewhat desperately.

"*It is the ever pervasive light. That is all you will see of Affero, the freedom of pure light.*"

The words calmed Jen and he felt peaceful, as he knew this light. Then more questions came to him. They flashed through his mind like a river and for a second he thought he already knew all the answers but then he realised he wasn't capable of remembering properly. He would need to work through each one.

"Gaia, does Ignis really exist?" he asked, remembering what Javu has said. "Is it just a figment of our imaginations or is a colossal dragon really heading towards the earth?"

"*It all depends on which world you are seeing as your reality,*" the beautiful voice of wisdom told him. "*There are some who dwell on the*" *earth who choose to bring awareness down to the level where the fatums exist. Conversely, there are some like yourself who choose to bring awareness up to the level where we, the protectors, exist."*

"Are you saying you don't really exist?" Jen asked perplexed.

"I exist," Gaia said profoundly. *"But is up to you how you perceive my existence."*

"So, most people on the planet are perceiving that Ignis exists?" Jen tried to confirm, feeling like he was starting to understand. "But does that really make her exist in that form?"

"The more people perceive her that way, the more real she will become."

A fundamental question sprung into Jen's mind, one that immediately frustrated him. "How did this all begin?" he asked, shaking his head. "How can all this be possible?"

"You are asking why there are fatums yet also protectors, why there is negative yet also positive, why there is darkness yet also light, why there is power yet also freedom?"

"Yes!" Jen exclaimed. "If I can understand that, I will be able to help others understand it too and then people will stop believing in Ignis."

"One creates two," was all that Gaia said in response.

The generality of the answer frustrated Jen further.

"Be careful, Jen," Gaia said with affection, sensing his mood. *"I am not trying to hinder you. Annoyance leads to anger, a most dangerous realm. Stay balanced and at peace."*

Jen instantly returned to a state of calm as if Gaia had projected a balancing energy upon him.

Insights came to him.

He began to see that all of the different worlds and realms that he had become aware of were really the same thing, but he still didn't know how all these different worlds had come to be. An intuition came to him that the answers lay with those who perceived the worlds.

"You wish to know about your history? How you came to be?" Gaia said psychically. *"I will tell you."*

Jen could feel gentle insects crawling on his feet. He dare not move for fear of injuring any of them.

"There will and has always been the essence, the one consciousness of which we are all a part. From this consciousness came Affero and Ambitio and everything else comes from these two forces."

Several creatures all climbed up Gaia's arms and hair as if getting ready to hear their favourite story. A hundred birds flocked down and rested on the flowering shrubs that grew all around.

"The world you are perceiving now is at a much higher vibration and we are at the pinnacle of creation here, indeed Affero is all around us."

Jen could sense it.

"For a long time, Affero was the greatest force in existence and creation flourished. Universe after universe was created, so many stars and planets that it would make the human mind boggle. However, the force of power was slowly growing and as the material world began to take shape, Ambitio began to exert its influence over many things. This is especially true of life that formed on the earth."

Several birds chirped in unison, a melody so sharp and pure.

"Ambitio creates illusions to drag beings down to lower vibration levels and what started out balanced on this planet soon became imbalanced."

Gaia's eyes were incredible, glowing an ethereal white light. Her skin was a rich brown and glistened with the light that was coming out of the foliage that was draped all over her and growing out of her, pulsing and throbbing with the heartbeat of the earth.

"The first human forms developed from the earth, of which I myself am a manifestation. They looked very different to you, more slender, translucent and androgynous in nature. These beings helped all life on the earth develop including rocks, plants and sea- and land-dwelling creatures."

Jen could almost picture the beings.

"As Ambitio's grip strengthened on some of these creatures, a different type of being began to form upon the earth of the same type that Ignis is related to. Many of these creatures relied on the realms of power to guide them through existence. These creatures over time became a new root of

human form and despite their hierarchical allegiance to Ambitio, they quickly became a very advanced civilisation. Indeed before long these new human creatures, who became known as the Leiuryi, had found ways to leave our planet and explore the galaxies that surround it."

It was the story of the past that Jen already knew. He felt like he was recovering from amnesia.

"This happened long ago and in the meantime another root of human form was evolving on the earth, that which became known as the Kesarin, which means, those of the fire. Shortly after, yet another root formed and these peoples were known as the Equus, which means, those of the water. These two new roots of human form also progressed quickly and left our planet."

Several large mammals bore their teeth in an unthreatening way, their fur bushy and soft.

"Much time passed and eventually another root formed, which were known as the Terra, which means, the real earth. This was the last human root to form. The Terra were also progressing quickly until something happened that affected every human root that had formed on our planet."

Jen sensed that something destructive had occurred and that he had somehow witnessed such a travesty.

"Because of this event, the Leiuryi, Kesarin and Equus all returned to the earth," Gaia continued. "The human beings that exist on the earth today are now an interwoven mix of these ancient roots and the newer Terra root."

Jen was in awe of what Gaia was telling him and wanted to know more. "When did all this happen?"

"The scale of time is hard to perceive for you. The Leiuryi originally formed approximately four million years ago, the Kesarin three million years ago and the Equus two million years ago. The original Terra evolved a million years ago but the mixing of these four roots is relatively new."

"How new?"

"The first time each of the roots came into contact with one another was approximately seventy thousand years ago. However, time is a limited perception. It is an illusion created by Ambitio."

Jen was shocked. He felt like he had been jolted into reality and that everything he previously knew was only a dream. Intuitions flooded in, like the return of a lost memory. "I sense that something destructive happened? The event you say that brought the roots together? What was it?"

"*Ignis came into our solar system and disrupted the balance that existed. Ignis destroyed another planet that used to be close by. Because of that, the Kesarin and the Equus were forced to return to the earth. The Leiuryi followed shortly after and then the roots began to mix.*"

"And what happened between then and now?" Jen asked with his mind totally open.

"*The Leiuryi were the dominant civilisation on the planet up until thirteen thousand years ago and they created the oldest human structures that still exist today,*" Gaia told him. "*By that time, humans were becoming so mixed that the history of human roots was becoming lost. Since then, more and more have given in to the force of Ambitio, which is why you have seen more and more people controlled and less and less people free. And those who are instigating the control on the masses are the least free of all.*"

Jen suddenly had the feeling that he didn't want to hear anymore. There was so much to take in that he felt like his entire belief system had suddenly crashed around him. Some of the words that Javu had spoken earlier swirled around in his mind. He felt like he needed to know what it all meant and where it was all heading.

"What about the future?" Jen asked the magical being standing before him, the vast forests and herds of animals gathered around all swaying in some mystical trance. "Ignis has returned."

"*Humans must find freedom within,*" she replied melodically. "*And to do that each must awaken to their true purpose in life. It is the true test of physicality, for before a being enters a body, they know exactly what they wish to achieve. It is the challenge to remember by learning from experiences.*"

Jen fully agreed with Gaia. However, he wasn't sure how he could make enough people awaken to make sure that Ignis ceased to exist. Then, he remembered that he wasn't alone and realised his pursuit of the world walker had completely slipped his mind.

"Gaia, can *the world walker* help me make Ignis disappear?"

Jen realised that there were probably many world walkers in existence and that he didn't really know who he was looking for.

"You speak of Azreal, *the spirit of compassion,"* Gaia said with an incredible sense of love in her voice. *"He will not stop until all are free. If you can find him, he will help you free the earth of Ignis. He knows things that I do not. He has seen things that I cannot."*

"Do you know where he is?" Jen asked, feeling like he'd made an incredible breakthrough in his quest.

"Azreal will be wherever there is suffering. And the most suffering occurs in the realms of Ambitio."

It was the news that Jen had did not want to hear.

Just thinking about those realms was horrific enough. A great feeling of apprehension came over him at the thought of entering one of those degraded worlds. Gaia glowed a spirited and effervescent green light.

"It has been the greatest struggle of my existence to protect Azreal," Gaia confessed with apparent emotion. *"He chooses to dwell where Ambitio is at its strongest, spreading the light into the darkness. Whenever he has occupied a physical body, he has been hunted ferociously. If you ask for his help, you must also protect him, just as you must also protect Elera."*

Jen was surprised at the mention of Elera's name. He wanted to ask Gaia about her, but he suddenly got the feeling that the queen of the earth was starting to slip away from his perception.

"How can I reach Azreal?" Jen asked urgently.

Gaia did not answer but seemed to conjure what looked like a miniature globe that appeared and then hovered in front of her. It glowed blues and greens and Jen recognised the shapes of the land on the apparition. He spotted Raicema, Ciafra and Lizrab. Jen could see a light green energy field coming out of Gaia's heart and wrapping itself around the globe.

She closed her eyes slowly, her eyelashes brushing her smooth and supple cheeks. The plant life flourished and gigantic flowers grew all around.

Gaia breathed in and out slowly and the entire atmosphere seemed to vibrate in unison with her breathing. Then she opened her eyes. *"Azreal is currently in the realm of Avarice, where there is much suffering at this moment."*

Then Gaia seemed to be conjuring something else that looked like a bright tube of light. It slowly got denser and denser until it took the shape of a small flute made out of a smoky colourless crystal.

"I wish to give you this flute for protection. The sound that radiates from it will bring light to the darkest of places. Music is the universal language that every being can understand."

The flute floated over to where Jen was knelt and he took it in his hand. The cold crystal was soothing and still.

"But how can I use this in the dream world?" Jen asked, suddenly feeling shaky and unstable. "I mean, whenever I entered the realms of power through dreaming before, I felt like I didn't have anything with me, sometimes not even my body."

"It is because the dream world is merely a window to the other worlds. However, beings in those worlds can still see and hear you and you can conjure objects in the dream world. Before you enter the dream world in search of Azreal, look carefully at the flute and the earth stone that I have given you."

Jen looked down at the two objects, one in each hand. Then he looked up at his mother and realised that she had been there, protecting him throughout his entire life.

"When you arrive in the world of Avarice, look at your hands and remember what those two objects looked like. I promise you they will then appear and you will be able to use them like you can in the physical world."

Jen nodded, believing fully what Gaia was telling him and feeling less and less fearful by the second. Then the earth beneath him started to disperse.

"Now it is time for you to go," she said affectionately. *"But before you*

do, I wish to make you aware of something. I have said already that you must protect Azreal, but I have not told you what from."

A stale energy spread into the atmosphere causing everything to become quite silent. Even the chirpy birds that had been ruffling their feathers now were as still as stone.

"There is one who wishes nothing but harm upon beings. That one is my opposite, the prince of earthly darkness, Diabolus. He is the one who is hunting Azreal."

"But how can I protect him from such a demon?"

"You must be free of the emotions, free of the dark realms of power. Be fearless, be wise, and emit love. Then, both you and Azreal will be safe."

At that statement, the world around him began to disperse fully and Gaia seemed to float backwards at lightning speed, all the animals, plants and ground around vanishing before his eyes.

In a flash he was back sitting on the dry mound on the outskirts of Seho, the earth stone in one hand with its light fading and the crystal flute in his other hand.

An intense excitement filled his body and he wanted to shout at the top of his voice, to let everyone know that existence was so incredible and endless that everyone should wake up and see it for what it truly was. He stayed on the mound for several moments, gaining his composure and trying to achieve the balance that Gaia had conveyed was so important.

Everything that he had learnt now seemed like second nature to him, like he had known it all his life. He stood up, looking up at the bright sky and wondering how much time had passed. As he walked back to Seho, he thought about all the things that he wanted to talk about with Javu.

However, as he walked past some of the outer huts in the village, he began to realise there was nobody there. He ran across to Javu's hut and it was empty inside, everything left there as he remembered it except for a few missing blankets. He walked back outside onto the hot sandy ground.

"Hello?" he called out in the direction of a group of huts. There was no response.

Looking up into the sky, he noticed that Ignis was now closer and more visible. It looked like a round ball of grey and red fire with a greenish tail, and bigger than the sun in the sky. Jen fought back feelings of fear and went back into Javu's hut. After preparing some rice and pulses that he found in clay jars, he sat down and ate slowly.

Then he lay down on the bed and held up the flute and earth stone in his hands. After an hour of staring at the two objects in a strange dreamy trance, he slowly felt his heavy eyelids close.

Chapter 66 – Azreal & The Realm
of Avarice

Ahead was gloom. He could feel it in his heart.

Jen was standing at the gate of an ancient city with colossal and imposing grey buildings beyond. They were all gothic in appearance. The iron gate was tall with spikes at the top and an emblem of a dragon in its centre.

The dragon had its wings fully stretched. Jen looked down at his hands and they looked at like an electric network of bright energy. As he looked at them more they began to solidify and he remembered the flute and the stone. As he did, they appeared instantly in his hands.

Jen felt the smooth crystals and was amazed at how real they felt. It was impossible to tell the difference between what he now perceived and what he believed was physicality. His newfound awareness was somewhat dazzling. Though logic had escaped him, he knew deep down that he was asleep in a hut in Seho.

He looked at the gate and willed it to open. It separated with a creaking sound revealing a stone-lined road with diamond-shaped paving slabs. There were grimy gothic square buildings on either side.

At the end of the road was a narrow tunnelled passageway with security cameras placed at every angle of the curved roof. Jen walked onto a longer wide road with intricately decorated stone buildings. They had large rounded windows and square pillars.

A number of emblems, mainly of dragons and serpents were displayed on the buildings in the forms of coats of arms or plaques.

There were archways that Jen had to walk under and branching off from the long road were numerous streets with rows of shops selling gadgets and uniforms. He could not see any people in the shops.

In the distance, Jen could see a large domed building with a spire and cross upon its top. He walked along the road until he came to the end, where he reached a circus with three buildings all facing each other. One of them was the rounded domed building he had seen before. Another was square with hundreds of round pillars and the final of the trio was gigantic with a great wall around it that seemed like a city in itself.

Walking next to this wall, Jen came to some giant black iron doors, intricate stone pillars at either side and six steps leading up to it. In the iron were two crests with raised emblems of dragons facing each other.

Once again, Jen willed the doors to open and they did with a thunderous resonance. Beyond was a marble walkway, which he navigated slowly. After a few steps, the iron doors closed behind, sending a small wave of fear down what he perceived as his spine. He shrugged it off and pressed on. He soon came to a polished atrium with passageways leading off in twelve different directions.

Going down one passage, he reached a room with its door wide open. Inside, there were two ugly men stuffing their faces with the flesh from piles of dead uncooked animals. Jen could mainly identify goats, deer and cows, all still with their hides on. The sight made him feel sick and he quickly moved past the room, surprised to find that the two scaly-faced men did not notice him.

He came to another room, again with its door wide open.

There was a man counting stacks and stacks of gold coins on a large marble table. He was salivating and had a slightly different face to the two previous men, more like a frog with large boils on his skin, yet he wore the same uniform-like suit that Jen had also seen in all the shops.

Once again, he stood there observing, yet again unnoticed. A great feeling of empathy passed through him at watching the man frantically count his bullion over and over. He decided to move on in pursuit of Azreal.

Jen walked along the passageway a little further until he came to another open room. Peering inside, he found it lined with row upon row of weapons, one wall containing thousands of knives and swords and another opposite wall full of guns and rifles.

The back wall had thousands of mirrors all over it and there were eight strange-looking creatures with arched backs and deformed faces, their eyes round and bulging.

The creatures almost looked human because of the suits that they were wearing but they were devoid of any other human feature.

Each dragon-like man was systematically selecting a weapon from one of the walls and then violently destroying the mirrors one by one. The strangest thing of all was that every time one of the creatures would successfully destroy a mirror by shooting it or throwing a blade at it, they would then all weep uncontrollably. They all let off a high-pitched whining sound at the same time.

Jen felt both frightened and deeply sympathetic for the hideous-looking creatures. He felt the area of his heart pulsating and arching. He could not understand why they were locked in such a strange ritual.

He looked down at the flute in his hand and decided to play it. He put the mouthpiece to his lips and blew hard. A melodic, ethereal sound came out and radiated in every direction. Jen could see the sound as light.

The creatures all stopped what they were doing and looked around, instantly spotting Jen. Their icy stares shocked him so much that he stopped playing.

Soon after, an overwhelming fear shot through his body as each of the creatures aggressively showed their razor-sharp, drooling teeth. Then they started walking towards him quickly, their snakelike eyes sending a shot of icy fear into his being.

Instinct took over and he ran out of the room and back along the passageway towards the atrium. Looking back, he saw scores of the creatures now running after him, all brandishing knives and blades and screeching a terrifying sound.

As he reached the circular atrium, he gasped in horror as he saw that hundreds of the creatures were now emerging from each of the twelve passageways.

Jen could not find the will or the courage to open the tall iron doors from which he had entered the frightening building. He turned around to realise he was now circled by the crazed reptilian beings. He was trapped.

Just as he thought he was about to meet his end, he saw a brilliant light emanating from one of the passageways, which drew the attention of each of the creatures who all looked at it mesmerised. The light calmed him and he heard a voice in his head.

"Play the flute again. There is nothing to fear."

Jen put the crystal flute to his mouth and began to play.

A beautiful melody came out that seemed to be beyond where he was standing. Jen could see the music again, an auric vibration that lightened the atmosphere.

Jen heard the clang of metal on marble as each of the creatures dropped their weapons to the floor. They stood silently still as the melody radiated through their bodies. As Jen was playing, the light in the distance seemed to be floating towards him, coming straight through the crowd of hypnotized beings. He saw the shape of a man, walking elegantly and slowly.

Jen knew it was the world walker, Azreal.

Azreal's features became clearer as he entered the atrium. He had long, thick flowing hair that glowed with a white light. He had a long beard. His face was kind and he smiled in a most natural way as he approached Jen.

"You can stop playing now," Azreal said to Jen softly. *"There is nothing to fear."*

His voice seemed etherised, almost androgynous.

Jen stopped and the creatures around seemed to wake up as if from a daze. Then they all slowly plodded along the passageways back to where they had come from, not a hint of violence or hatred amongst them.

"You have to understand," Azreal began, *"that the world has shrunk considerably for them."*

Jen nodded and just stared at Azreal.

"Are you really a man?" Jen felt compelled to ask. "I mean, you look like one but then again I am dreaming?"

"In the spirit world, we take the form of our last physical body. This realm, Preta as it is known here, is itself a part of the spirit world but its inhabitants do not know that. Many led their last physical lives greedily and materialistically, and so their form has changed. It is a reflection of themselves just as I am a reflection of myself."

"So I am seeing the spirit world now?"

"Yes, however, this is only one face of it. There are countless others," Azreal said jolting Jen's perception a bit. *"However, this is a distinct, real place. From the earth, this place would seem very far indeed."*

"And you are really here?" Jen asked.

"We are both here, Jen," Azreal said. *"Though you have reached this world through dreaming, if you really wanted to, you could fully transfer your existence here like I have."*

A serene energy filled the air.

"It would be difficult for you, as you are still very much attached to your physical form and quite understandably so."

Jen wanted to know more. Azreal knew so.

"It is likely that you would have woken up in your bed should one of these beings have attacked you. For me no such attack nor waking would have occurred, for I am already as awake as I can be."

Though Jen couldn't fully understand what Azreal was telling him, it felt like the truth. He decided not to dwell on the matter and explain his purpose. "I am here because I want to stop Ignis from coming to the earth," Jen said. "I know you can help me. I have spoken to Gaia."

"Ignis is a sign," Azreal revealed. *"The sign that people must choose whether to see themselves alone or as one with the planet on which they dwell. It is a true test of love over vengeance."*

"What do you mean?"

"Ignis wants revenge, and anger and hatred fuel her. Love, on the other hand, is represented by so many."

"But how can such a monster be reality?" Jen asked, lost in the horror of it.

"The stone that was used to summon Ignis was fed with a vast amount of power sucked from the earth. Voro, or Sadana as he is now known, and his servants, have carefully orchestrated this event to happen. They want a war. They thrive on violence. And there is no better way to start a war than to spread fear. The fear of the unknown, twisted into illusions and lies."

Jen was confused at how Ignis could start a war and how the people Azreal was speaking of could create such fear.

"What do you mean they want a war?" he asked, not quite sure at what Azreal was telling him. "With who?"

Azreal did not answer the question. Instead, he opened his hand and in it appeared a shiny, completely symmetrical cross. He held it up for Jen to see.

"What do you see?"

"A cross," Jen replied. "Like the one on top of the building outside."

"This is the sign of war," Azreal said transparently. *"No matter which way you turn this cross, you still have one line pointing up, and one at odds with it across. This is Affero and Ambitio."*

Jen had heard much about the two opposing forces in the universe.

"You asked with whom these pawns want a war," Azreal continued. *"The answer is Affero, freedom, expansion, creation."*

He paused, allowing Jen to absorb what he had been told.

"They only want destruction, but they are lost like these souls here, lost in an illusion."

There was now silence in the atrium and Jen could almost see the light of Affero permeating through the dingy atmosphere.

"Only a very few are at the opposite of love. These people are nothing more than robotic slaves. Most are stuck in one of the realms of power, trapped in ignorance or fear of the truth. But the true instigators are not of the physical, but of the extremes of power. These culminate as one source of power, Ambitio."

The youthful Azreal paused, and closed his eyes. He seemed to be praying, tenderly wishing for protection.

"You are seeing an extreme in the form of Ignis."

"So what can I do to balance these *extremes?*" Jen asked, remembering what Gaia had said.

The question went unanswered. The world around Jen seemed to be emitting a blinding light. It would dim and rise, almost swaying in an unheard rhythm.

"Let me tell you the story of Cecil Constynce," Azreal said, sitting upon the floor of the atrium cross-legged.

Jen did the same. He remembered not long ago being surrounded by thousands of bloodthirsty creatures.

"Cecil spent most of his life in Ciafra, ruling over the mining of precious crystals and stones," Azreal began in a calm and melodic tone. *"He was obsessed with these stones and their capability to channel energy."*

There was a pause.

"Cecil was born into a family that had for many generations been in positions of power in the human societies on the earth. He wasn't actually from Ciafra, but was sent there from Lengard. This was before Raicema even existed in the form it does today, several hundred years ago."

Jen felt more real and solid, like he was listening to an old friend who knew the world like he did.

"Cecil had heard from local shamans in Ciafra, of an ancient statue that had been made long ago. It was a statue made of jade crystal that wore a mask to represent contentment and love. He asked where to find this statue and he was told that it was lost under the sea."

A tranquil sound played in the air that almost sounded like panpipes. It was as natural a sound as the waves of the ocean.

"Cecil spent ten years searching trying to find this statue and eventually he succeeded with the help of his family in Lengard. His obsession for crystals and stones was rooted in the traditions and rituals that he had been indoctrinated with from an early age."

Azreal paused again.

"When he found the statue, he took it to his family. Then, plans for this

statue began to form."

"Plans?"

"Though the statue was created to serve as a beacon of light and freedom, in the wrong hands, it was turned into a prison. It is now a symbol of the darkness that exists."

"I'm not sure I follow?" Jen said honestly, trying to piece it all together. "Is the darkness you speak of *Ambitio*? Power?"

"Affero and Ambitio are opposites but are still one. One pushes, one pulls. One gives, one takes. One creates, one destroys.

The darkness is the extreme, the epitome of pure power. It is where each of the fatums were born, where death is the endless reality and the light cannot be seen."

Jen was awash with emotion. He wanted to weep at the sadness of it.

"This extreme stems from imbalance."

The truth spread through Jen's heart and seemed to travel up his body to his mind. He had the sensation of something opening at the top of his head. He wanted to know more about the statue.

"Azreal, tell me more about the statue. How was it used as a prison?"

"Cecil and a powerful group of families were seeking the jade statue. The ancestors of these families are still running the human societies of the earth as we speak."

Jen was listening attentively.

"When Cecil brought the statue to them, a gathering was called in which six people attended. Cecil was one of them," Azreal said with emotion. *"At this gathering, a most powerful ritual was performed."*

"What happened?" Jen asked.

"The ritual of the dark is intended to summon demons into the physical world. At this ritual, a human sacrifice took place and Murdrak, the ancient dragon warlord, was summoned before the six people. The six people worshipped this demon and considered him to be a god."

Azreal paused once more.

"However, as with everything in this universe, Murdrak has an

opposite, a wondrous being, the spirit of water and light, Aova. When this great horse heard what Murdrak was commanding, to start a global war, Aova appeared and banished Murdrak back to the horrific world from which he had come."

Jen was astounded by the story.

"Unfortunately, Cecil's family knew that such an occurrence might transpire and the purpose of the statue was revealed."

Azreal seemed truly upset at his recollection.

"Aova was imprisoned in the jade statue. The ritual of the dark is about increasing power through sacrifice and the imprisonment of those against power. Part of the ritual involved removing a mask from the statue's face, which symbolised the key to the prison that Aova would be placed into."

"Why did they do this?" Jen asked feeling saddened by the story.

"Aova only spreads love and the light. They are afraid of the light."

"Why?"

"The light, in ultimate Affero, makes one face their choices and actions. Many of those beings had caused so much suffering, that to face their past would be frightening and overwhelming. So instead, they choose illusion and deception. They just cannot bear to face the truth... However, their avoidance is in vain, for the truth is inevitable."

Jen understood completely, but he felt like he had missed the point that Azreal was trying to make. "But what does this have to do with Ignis?" Jen said, returning to his intention of having sought Azreal out.

"Aova is the only one who can balance Ignis. The time has come when the light and the dark shall appear before humanity once again. Your part for now...is to free Aova."

"But how?"

"The jade mask and statue must be reunited," Azreal told him. *"The mask itself is still in the possession of the Constynce family and the statue is on the island of Bimini. Only when these two symbols are reunited, can the water horse be released from her physical prison."*

Azreal paused, a wondrous glow emanating from his eyes. Jen could see a rainbow in them.

"*Then,*" Azreal said softly, "*the water horse will balance the fire dragon. The equilibrium of fire and water will be restored.*"

"Aova looks like a horse?" Jen asked, the words reminding him of the foal that he had seen before. "Was it you I saw in that world of hellishness where war was all around? I saw a foal walking besides you?"

Azreal smiled and love seemed to radiate from his entire body, spreading an ethereal light throughout the air of the atrium.

"*It was not me that you saw there, but I know of the being you speak of. The foal is Aova's child, Kajana, otherwise known as the Lemur spirit.*"

Jen was in awe.

"*She is also known as the last unicorn. She usually walks alone.*"

I thought that unicorns were just a myth, Jen thought.

"*You will find, Jen King, that nothing is a myth. There is truth in everything if you look deep enough,*" Azreal said with a truthful spirit. "*Kajana is the child of the spirit of water, Aova and the spirit of fire, Revereo. The union of fire and water is a representation of love and Kajana spreads love wherever she goes, instantly changing everything around her.*"

Jen could recall how the world had bent around the gentle creature as she had walked.

"*She is the ultimate truth, the one who can set us all free. I have accepted her and I will walk endlessly helping others to accept her too.*"

A sudden passion came over Jen and he eagerly wanted to meet Kajana.

"And what of Affero? What does Affero look like?" Jen asked.

Azreal met the question with a well-humoured laugh. "*It is hard to glimpse a force so true,*" he replied with a great smile. "*But it is possible. The spirit of fire, Revereo can sometime offer a glimpse to you. Revereo is also the spirit of the sun and the lion's eye can sometimes morph into what looks like an eagle of pure light. That is the only way I know to describe Affero, a colossal eagle of light.*"

Jen was inspired and full of an energy that he'd never felt before. He felt a wavering throb in his heart, forehead and stomach. He looked down and saw four misty globes of light had appeared. They were located where his heart, belly button, groin and base of his spine were.

"*They are your openings to Affero and the essence,*" Azreal said, observing the glowing openings. "*There are three more. There is one where your throat is, one where your forehead is and the one that comes out of the top of your head.*"

Jen felt a tremendous energy at the top of his head; it felt like a part of his skull was gone, like he could press his finger down into his mind.

"*When we are born, we are open to Affero and the essence. But as we learn about the physical we become closed off. It is the lesson of life to be like we are when we are born.*"

As Azreal was speaking, the atrium was filling with more and more light and before long, Jen couldn't even see Azreal.

Jen had so many questions. He wanted to know more about Affero and Ambitio. He wanted to know about the *essence* that Azreal was speaking of. There was so much more he wanted to learn. "Azreal?!" he called out, not wanting to leave the enlightened being now.

An overpowering wave vibrated through his body. Before he knew what was happening, all he could see was light.

Then, he woke up in his bed. Light was streaming in through an open window and the heat of the land jolted him back to the physical world.

His throat was dry and he had a cold sweat. He found that his legs ached, like he had run vigorously. He remembered running whilst he had dreamt. He felt the top of his head and his heart, but they were solid and he couldn't sense the openings any more. Sitting up, he looked around but Javu was still nowhere to be seen. He got up and walked outside and as before, the village was completely empty.

Looking up, he saw that Ignis was bigger than before and looked more solid, like a burning ball of molten metal. The effervescing flames glowed phosphorus green.

I don't have much time, Jen thought. *I have to get that mask.*

But at that thought, Jen was stuck.

He didn't want to travel for a week on a boat to reach Lengard, where he was sure security into the country would be stringent. He had only visited Lengard once and had been astounded at how controlled the people were there. He had felt the tremendous power of the place then but he still wasn't sure why.

Jen was sure the mask would be there.

I arrived here in a much better way, he thought to himself.

He couldn't understand how he had gotten from Raicema to Ciafra instantaneously, but he was determined to reach Lengard in the same way now.

Chapter 67 – Journey to Lengard

Jen had spent three days alone in Seho trying to repeat his previous feat of teleportation. His plan was to use the same method to reach Lengard and retrieve the jade mask.

He was sure that freeing Aova was the only way to prevent the destruction that Ignis would surely bring. He could not describe why he felt such surety, but it felt like the strongest of urges within.

My perception of reality has changed, Jen repeatedly thought.

Only a few years earlier, the unearthly concepts of other worlds, magical horses and gigantic dragons would have been laughable to him. But now, Jen perceived such entities with the utmost seriousness.

I have to get that mask and free Aova, he thought passionately, a fire rising within his chest.

He had meditated over the possibility of such an accomplishment ritualistically. He had tried to visualise the places he wanted to go. He had tried several approaches but nothing had worked.

Javu must have summoned me, was the only conclusion he could come to.

Jen had tried to reason how he had travelled from Sula's apartment in Raicema to Javu's hut in Ciafra. It was a distance of several thousand suns but he had perceived the journey to be instantaneous. He remembered Javu's face appearing in a dream beforehand.

Maybe I'm wasting my time trying to understand without Javu here. I'm sure I would have been in Lengard by now if I had gone by boat.

Jen was currently just outside of the village, sitting in a small forested area. There was an incredible freshness in the air and a number of insects and birds could be heard all around. If he closed his eyes he could hear the melody of the forest, the birds singing with an unequalled unity.

What do I remember about that place?

Jen had tried to imagine the buildings and streets that he had seen in Lengard on the one occasion that he had been there before. It was difficult as he remembered feeling little affection for the place.

I am stuck.

Jen had tried to use the earth stone and the crystal flute to conjure some kind of energy to aid his ambition. He had even tried to reach Gaia and Azreal again. All attempts at dreaming those extraordinary worlds had failed.

Focus, Jen, focus… he kept telling himself.

Concentrating on teleporting a short distance had simply left him exhausted. He had grown increasingly baffled at how it was possible for him to be in Ciafra. He was starting to doubt his own awareness of what was real.

Am I dreaming now? I cannot tell…

Seho was still empty and Jen had not seen one person during that time. It was starting to remind him of his first days in those mountains. That seemed like a lifetime ago now.

I need help.

Jen had realised over the past three days that the earth stone was not controlled by anybody or any force. He looked at the stone now.

Nothing, not even a glint.

Looking down at the floor, he began to see a line of red ants carrying little pieces of straw and wooden shards.

The ants were working in unison.

One began to crawl onto Jen's leg and he had the urge to flick it off, but fearing for its welfare, he resisted. It crawled up his side to his arm and along to his hand.

Jen put his hand to his face to look at the ant closely. It was shiny and incredible. It reminded him of a miniature tank. He heard thoughts in his head. *'Live by the energy lines,'* the thoughts were saying to him. *'You cannot see. Go up high to see.'*

Jen carefully placed the ant to the floor and rose to his feet. He decided to follow his thoughts and he saw a hill range in the distance. He decided to go there.

Jen walked throughout the day and late into the night until he was ascending the steep incline of a hillside. He came to rest in a small forest halfway up. He was quite high and he glimpsed the valley and sea beyond in the darkness. He felt tired and the sound of the sea waves sent him into an instant sleep against a tree.

Jen awoke as the sun was breaking. He could see a great line of light travelling down the valley and another crossing from the sea. Seho was situated at the intersection of the two lines. Jen could see a vortex of ambient light shooting upwards from Seho.

Is this real? he thought, doubting his perception.

A sudden realisation came to him. He felt intrinsically that the planet was a vast network of energy lines. He had an intuition that many cities had been built on the lines or one the vortexes.

As he imagined a line travelling from Seho to Lengard, he felt a strong tug on his midsection. His belly button was tingling.

Jen looked down. The earth stone was shining brightly around his neck. He could see ambient streams of light shooting out from Seho towards him. The flute in his pocket was resonating. It was singing by itself.

The tug on his belly was becoming unbearable. He felt sick from the force. Then suddenly, Jen was flung towards Seho, travelling at lightning speed.

He could see nothing but a blur. A cascade of images flooded his mind. They were of the places he had seen in Lengard.

Then he felt wholly overwhelmed. A vibration was shaking his body. He lost consciousness.

Jen opened his eyes to find himself lying on a bed in a strange room. Looking up at the arched stone roof, it invoked a pang of familiarity, but Jen couldn't get his bearings.

Before he had another chance to think, he heard a door handle turning. Sitting up, he saw that there was a door opposite and someone was about to open it. He quickly rolled off of the bed and slid under it just in time.

Two people entered the room and Jen could only see their shoes. A woman was wearing purple suede high heels and a man was wearing polished black pointed shoes.

"Oh, there it is," the woman said, picking up something from the bed – her bag or purse, Jen presumed.

The man opened a cupboard and ruffled around in it for a moment and then the couple swiftly left the room. After waiting a while to make sure the couple didn't return, Jen got out from under the bed and had a better look.

He realised it was the same room he had stayed once before when he had been in Phoenicia. The room looked different now. It had been freshened up with new paint and furniture, not the dull greens and browns that he remembered. He had a quick look in a full-length mirror. He looked unruly.

Jen remembered how well-dressed the Lengardian people were.

His attire was worn and not suitable for walking the old streets of the city. He opened the cupboard next to the mirror and found a long brown raincoat. He took it off its coat hanger and tried it on. It covered almost all of his simple clothing when he fastened up the shiny black buttons.

Looking up at the top of the cupboard, he saw a grey hat. He pushed his long hair back and placed the hat on his head.

I can now easily pass for one of the workers in this city, he thought.

Jen felt ready to venture outside. He had already chosen not to rationalise his arrival in the room. Instead, he wanted to use the opportunity to achieve what he had dwelled on for days.

Jen opened the door and walked out into the thickly carpeted hallway. Darkly stained wooden doors ran along its length. Jen remembered that the building had been a private lodge for military personnel in the past, but now it looked like it was a hotel.

Wealthy-looking people were coming in and out of their rooms as he walked down the hallway towards the double lifts at the end. They were old and as he had remembered them, still working on a shaft mechanism, with golden mirrors inside and space for no more than five people.

As the lift chugged downwards towards the lobby, Jen realised that he had no idea how to locate the jade mask. He had a vague feeling it was somewhere in the royal palace, yet he was sure access would be severely restricted. He remembered the security was very strict in that area of the city.

As the lift opened, Jen was greeted with the sight of many people standing around in the marble-floored foyer, either checking in to the hotel or waiting for help from the staff.

Jen walked straight through the crowd and outside onto a small cobbled street, wanting to avoid interaction with anyone. The sky was grey with thick clouds and there was a slight drizzle in the air. Before long he came to a discreet subway that led down to the city's underground train system.

He walked down some metal-lined steps before coming to a modern-looking tunnel, a stark contrast to the traditional-looking streets above.

The tunnel was lined with a synthetic, smooth plastic and had bright, harsh lighting from its roof, corrugated steel panels on the floor and a giant cavern-like station at the end. Huge stone pipes ran across it in many different directions.

Ahead was a barrier with glass doors and adjacent to them were a range of different machines. Jen saw people going up to the machines and inserting a key-like card into a slot, whilst others simply held up their hand to access the system. In every case, the details of the person came onto the screen in front of them, including a picture and some sort of map, which Jen presumed was their travel history.

The people would press a button or two on the screen and then continue through the barriers without touching anything. There was nobody official around to ask for help so Jen asked a woman who was doing something on one of the machines.

"Excuse me. I'm new to Phoenicia," Jen said to the middle-aged lady. "I want to travel on the trains but I'm not sure what I need."

"Where is your key card?" she asked him, holding out her hand and expecting him to produce it.

"I don't have one," Jen said, suddenly feeling conscious that he should be careful about who he spoke to.

"Impossible!" the woman said in genuine surprise. "How did you even get into the city without one? They should have given it to you during immigration. Where do you come from?"

Jen was silent as he realised he should be covert about his intentions of being in the ancient city.

"Oh, I know," the woman said suddenly. "You must have one of those new international chips that work on any of the transport systems. Put your hand up to that reader over there."

Jen did not have such a chip. In fact, he had opted out of such a voluntary program when he had worked for the military.

He quickly made an excuse to the woman and swiftly left the station via another close-by tunnel. The tunnel was lined with small sphere-like cameras that recorded everything.

At the end of the tunnel, steel floating steps led up to the surface. Jen was sure that the technology, like that in Raicema City and Yinkoto, was based on magnetism. He stepped on one and it bounced slightly as it floated smoothly upwards.

At the surface, Jen found himself at a wide, main road with many vehicles speeding along at high velocity.

A steel barrier ran along the road and Jen spotted what looked like a small station where people were waiting for something. A train-like vehicle stopped and people boarded from the roadside.

Jen ran over and jumped onto the vehicle before it sped off. He wasn't sure where it was heading so he asked a man with a cane who was stood next to him.

"It stops at the old temple and then the financial district."

"I am trying to get to the palace," Jen said.

"Get off at the next stop. You can walk from there. You look like you've got a good pair of legs on you."

Jen thanked the man and looked around the carriage. He counted ten different computer systems including several information terminals and several news broadcasting stations.

The woman's voice was reporting the events of the world, though Jen instantly realised the way the events were being described was biased. It heavily promoted Lengardian, Raiceman and Neoasian dominance over the societies of the earth.

"Ciafran and Lizrabian uprisings against democracy once again force world leaders to hold an emergency meeting to address the threats to the financial sectors..."

Jen observed a virtual map of the train route and a number of terminals to pay for and get snack food. He noticed that everything was paid for with the same small, key-like cards that were simply held up to a panel. People seemed to use the cards for everything.

His stop came and Jen got off the train, thankful there were no barriers present. Walking outside onto the road, Jen instantly noticed there were lion emblems and gargoyles everywhere. They were on the roofs of buildings and along the walls of the narrow lanes. The old walls were chalky and made with large bricks. Sometimes the gargoyles looked like a lion, other times a serpent-like creature. There were also sculptures of a unicorn bound in chains on some of the roofs, which were also decorated in golds and greens.

Ahead was a large temple-like building and surrounding it many well-kept pretty gardens. There were plenty of large old trees anchored into the pathways. Jen got the sense that this vicinity of the city was almost like the inside of a palace, with the outer wall surrounding all of the oldest and largest buildings.

Numerous darkly stained wooden benches ran the length of the walkways. Jen looked up but saw no security cameras anywhere. He spotted courtyards with old paving surrounding them and walked through many decorated arches.

A bell tolled in the distance as Jen walked past little beaded gardens. He noted offices, a giant park and a large palatial white building with archaic round towers before he seemed to reach the opposite side of the vicinity. There was a great arch leading out to another long road beyond. Jen observed a large sculpture above the arch of a unicorn with wings.

The road ahead was lined with tall, block-like buildings, all decorated with fancy stonework, often in the shape of flowers or animals. At the end of the road was a large park and in the distance, Jen could see the tall towers of the Lengardian Palace, the most recognised and central building in the entire nation of Lengard.

He walked through the park slowly, thinking about ways he could get inside. He knew there was a visitors' section of the palace but he was also sure that this area would probably be far from where the jade mask was located. Nevertheless, he reasoned that he would stand more chance of getting inside by posing as a tourist.

Eventually, Jen reached the visitors' entrance to the palace, where scores of armed guards, all wearing black uniforms, were standing either side of a tall iron gate.

Jen noticed a small group of people sitting quite a way from the gate. They were all dressed in ragged clothes and had a number of banners with the words *'freedom of speech'* and *'speak without fear'* written on them.

The guards clearly had their watchful eyes focused on the group. Jen slowly walked up to the gate and addressed a guard sitting on a stool there. "I wish to visit the palace," he said to the guard. "Is this the right entrance?"

"The palace is closed to visitors today," the guard replied sternly and with authority.

The statement took Jen by surprise. He wasn't quite sure what to do next. He stood there for a while, trying to think before the guard suddenly got snappier with him. "Can you please clear this area, sir? I told you that the palace is not opened today!"

"When will it next be opened?"

"It will reopen again from next week."

"Next week?" Jen blurted out.

"Yes! Is that a problem, sir?" the guard asked suspiciously, his tone alerting the other guards around him.

"No, no. I just travelled here to see it and might not be here then."

The guard just grunted and went back to observing the group of protestors. Jen felt like going to speak to them but didn't want to raise any more suspicion from the guards so he headed across the park.

Following the giant metal gating around, Jen tried to look for another way in. After walking for what seemed like hours, he began to realise that the palace was heavily fortified and inaccessible.

It was getting dark and the drizzle was turning to heavy droplets of rain. Street lamps began to come on, emitting a fake, yellowish light. Jen began to feel pangs of panic at being alone in a city that he didn't really know.

He had no money or assets. He would need to find somewhere to stay so he could think more clearly and come up with another plan. Then it dawned on him.

Thinking is making me go around in circles.

Jen hadn't allowed one thought to enter his mind when he had teleported to that hotel room and he was sure the same approach would guide him to where he needed to be now.

He walked along several streets until he came to a river and he spotted a bridge with benches under it. He walked down some steps and sat upon one of the benches, the bridge roof protecting him from the rain. The shelter allowed him to reach a calmer state.

Jen stared into the water watching its wavy ripples spray up like energetic fish. There were thousands of huge pebbles making up a riverbank and he laid his eyes on their smooth round patterns. Then he spotted something glistening in the water.

At first he thought it was an old bottle cap or a piece of broken glass but then an urge came over him to get a closer look. He scrambled over the pebbles to the shallow water and was amazed to look down and find a key-card. It was just like the ones he had seen the citizens of Phoenicia using earlier. It didn't have anything printed on it but looked like it had been in the water a while as a few bubbles of green algae had formed around its edges.

Jen reached down and placed his hand into the water, grasping the slimy card. He cleared the algae off and put it in his pocket, deciding to move on from the bridge.

He walked along the bank to a busier more populated area. He came to a row lined with smaller residential houses with a larger building at the very end. It had a sign *Grimnor's Inn* and another sign stating *Vacancies* next to it.

Jen felt compelled to go inside and was greeted by the warm smile of a stocky, bald man with grey stubble. "'Ello," he said in a strong rural accent.

"I am looking for a room for the night," Jen began to say. "But I don't have very much money."

"Let me 'ave a look?" the man said in a friendly tone, holding out his hand. Jen knew he wanted his key card. He handed it to the man, hoping that it would help him.

"Whooaa!" the man said with surprise as he touched the small device to a computer terminal in front of him. "Not much money, eh? You're too loaded for your own good mate!"

He turned the screen of the computer so Jen could see the details. There was a picture of a man. He was cleanly shaven in the picture but he had the same hair colour. Jen had a beard and the innkeeper seemed to assume that Jen was the same man.

Below the picture was the name 'Corporal Scott Johnstone' and beneath that the sum of money that the person owned, *28'000LE*. Jen realised that the key card's owner must have been in the military.

"You call twenty-eight thousand Legs not *much* dosh?" the man said in surprise. "I guess you must 'ave been on plenty of dangerous missions to earn that little lot. I used to be in the forces meself, but I got sick see. Now I run this place." He smiled at Jen revealing only a few teeth. "Grimnor's me name."

Jen shook hands with Grimnor and reiterated his request for a room for the night.

"You got the pick of the place. I got a nice room on the top floor. It's got its own bathroom. I'll do it for twenty Legs for you soldier."

"I am not a soldier anymore," Jen said defensively, an old feeling of regret coming to him.

"Whatever you say," Grimnor said retreating from his remark. "So, howzat sound to you?"

"Sounds perfect," Jen said.

"It's room ten," Grimnor said, reaching down and producing a key. He handed it along with the key card to Jen.

"Thanks."

As Jen began to walk up the stairs, Grimnor shouted up after him. "Breakfast is at eight."

As soon as he entered the musty room, Jen lay down. There was one small window and the room had wooden beams. He fell asleep instantly.

Jen dreamt of Ignis in the sky and of Aova, imprisoned in a statue. He dreamt of Gaia's world. He dreamt of Raicema and Ciafra and of times past and present. He could see his old life and he could see himself now.

All he could feel was gratitude and the deepest sense of happiness at his existence. That gratitude and happiness had washed away all fears, and only love remained.

"Only love is real. Everything else is an illusion."

Jen could feel that something was watching out for him and the love he had for that something could not be explained. He felt a love that was pure and capable of changing the world in an instant.

Chapter 68 – An Ancient Agenda

Having rested somewhat peacefully on a sturdy bed, Jen awoke to the smell of grease and baked bread. He got up and went down to the tiny dining room of the small inn.

Grimnor greeted him with a gust of energy. "Morning, mate!" he said, plopping a bowl of sliced bread on a laid out table and running back into the kitchen next door.

Jen took a seat and poured himself a glass of water from a jug on the table.

The kitchen door swung open a moment later and thick steam poured out. Grimnor emerged carrying a plate of cooked meats and eggs. Jen wondered how the man stayed so energetic under such a confined environment.

"When did you start running this place?" Jen asked, trying to strike up a conversation.

"About six years ago now," he replied, pulling up an old chair to Jen's breakfast table. "Never looked back. Some of me pals weren't as lucky as me. A few of them are 'omeless so when I don't 'ave customers, I let them stay for a while. Not busy much these days anyway."

"Why aren't you busy?"

"Because it's too damned 'ard to get into this city!" Grimnor almost choked as he ate a vegetable. "I mean, it's not like the people who pass through this way 'aven't already got somewhere to stay, if you know what I mean?"

Jen didn't know what Grimnor meant, but he decided to press on and try and find out some more information about the city.

"I am here to do a bit of sightseeing but I heard the palace is closed. Is that true?"

"Probably got another one of them summits goin' on."

"Summits?"

"Yeah, every so often, all the leaders of the world get together 'ere in the palace, but they're not the leaders that me and you know, if you know what I mean?"

This time Jen did know what Grimnor meant. He realised that the group of protestors he had seen outside must have known it too.

Sadana is here along with all the people that Javu told me about, he thought to himself.

There was silence for a while whilst Jen ate the breakfast Grimnor had prepared for him, though somewhat begrudgingly as it had been a long time since he had eaten meat. It left him feeling very heavy.

"You know, there is another way into the palace," Grimnor said surprisingly after a while. "I 'eard about it from this guy who once stayed 'ere. Got proper trolleyed one night and started going on about 'ow 'e'd been in the palace loads of times and 'ow 'e always got in through a secret passage."

"What passage?" Jen asked, amazed that Grimnor would know such a thing.

"Apparently it's underground, but you can't get to it using a regular train. This guy said 'e 'ad to get on a special train that stopped 'alfway down one of the tunnels and then there was this entrance and that led to the palace."

"Which tunnel?" Jen probed. "Do you know?"

"'Said it was between Palace Station and Temple Station."

Jen formulated the coordinates in his mind and a plan began to take shape. He didn't waste any more time so he thanked Grimnor for his hospitality and quickly set off to the main underground train station near to the palace.

He hoped the key card that he had found would discreetly get him through the glass barriers. Jen walked there in ten minutes, observing the stark contrast between some newly built skyscrapers and more archaic-looking buildings.

The station was very elegant, with giant marble pillars holding up a magnificent hallway. At one end there were scores of machines and ten glass barriers. The station seemed to be more heavily guarded and monitored than the others.

Jen had counted twenty-three video cameras by the time he approached the glass barrier. It opened automatically as he approached it, seemingly detecting the key card that he had in his coat pocket. Beyond there were some floating steps going deep underground.

Travelling down, scores of holographic images projected onto the tunnels round walls. Most of these were for food or entertainment technology.

The most interesting projection was an advert for *RM Sig-Lenses* that *'conveniently carry all the data you need to travel comfortably to other nations.'*

Jen noticed the only locations that were shown by the advert were Raicema City and Yinkoto.

'Royal Military Sig-Lenses. Watching out for you!'

At the end of the tunnel were two platforms going in opposite directions. Jen found the platform towards the temple stop and boarded the next train that came, which arrived swiftly.

As the doors hovered into place with a thud behind him, an idea came to him.

There was a red handle opposite that read *Pull in Emergency.*

Jen looked around the carriage and saw two people, but the carriage beyond was empty. He quickly walked along and hopped into it as the train set off.

Once inside he quickly located another emergency alarm and sat on the seat beneath it. He looked out of the windows into the darkness of the underground tunnel.

A few moments later, Jen noticed a few flashing lights and then he saw a small tunnel ahead, branching off at right angles. He quickly pulled the red handle and the train abruptly came to a stop, a loud screeching sound coming from the track.

Jen got to his feet and opened the back door, which connected to another carriage. There were a few people in the carriage and as Jen slipped down between the gap in the carriages onto the coal-lined track, one man called out at him. Jen knew exactly where he was going and it wasn't long before he'd reached the secret tunnel.

At the end of the tunnel was a round steel door. Jen could not see a way to activate the panel but as he walked up close to the shiny metal, a whirring sound was heard and then the door began to open upwards with a smooth motion.

I wonder if it is this card?

Beyond was another tunnel, but this one was lined with a shiny white metallic material. Jen walked along it, amazed at how minimalist it looked with not a camera or door in sight.

A wide atrium with several passages emerged at the end of the tunnel. They were labelled *Laboratory, Gallery* and *Office*.

Jen instinctively knew that the gallery was where he should go but curiosity got the better of him and he went down the passageway to the laboratory. He cautiously looked around every bend on the way.

When he got to the end of the passageway, the different mammoth laboratories ahead were all empty. They were arranged into sectors, each in the shape of a triangle.

Jen walked into one of the labs and saw steel table after steel table full of Sig-lenses. Each table had a different colour palette for the lenses and Jen realised every blend of colour existed. There were thousands in quantity.

He picked up a bright blue lens and placed it to his eye. Before he knew what was happening, it seemed to suck itself onto his eyeball but his initial alarm was replaced by fascination at what he was now seeing.

It was like a different world interlaced with lab. There were a number of strange-shaped objects that looked highly malleable and a number of virtual screens that ran like a window frame around his field of view. He thought about seeing one of those screens in more detail and it happened, zooming in and startling him a bit.

It was a screen detailing all of Jen's physical attributes.

His height, weight and body condition were displayed as a diagram with colour-coding indicating the status of his muscles and bones. He thought about shrinking the screen and it acted on his thought, shrinking to a small tab.

The other screens all seemed to hold different information about him and his environment. He looked at the virtual malleable objects. They looked so real, and he put his hand out to touch one. To his shock, he felt that he could actually touch the object, feel its supple nature. Jen felt baffled and he quickly took off the Sig-lens.

Jen turned to leave but on his way out he spotted another lens, which he was instantly drawn towards. This one was completely transparent except for a small rainbow-coloured ring in the centre.

When Jen put it to his eye, he was transported to a world that was both familiar and foreign to him. The lab still existed, but now Jen could see it in terms of its energy, which looked like billions of inter-connected filaments of light, some different colours than others.

Metallic objects such as the tables looked like they were fizzing, yet were constant and dense. The air around him was alive with small whizzing shoots of light and it reminded him very much of what he had experienced at the monastery in the Neoasian mountains. Everything was interacting with these magnetic and electric filaments.

Jen saw the Sig-lenses in a new light and he noticed that every one was both sucking in and giving out energy in small yet long filaments of twisting light. He realised that it must be by this mechanism that the previous lens was able to read his thoughts and also make him believe those virtual objects were real.

Jen suddenly became aware that the current lens on his eye was doing the same to him and so he quickly took it off. Fascinated by the device, he placed it in his coat pocket. Moving out of the lab and into another he found a similar layout. Instead of lines and lines of lenses on each metal table, however, now there was only a single micro-scope on each one.

I wonder what these are for?

Jen had a look into the eyepiece of one of the magnifying lenses and noticed it was focused on the bowl of a spoon containing a small amount of liquid. When Jen focused the view to its maximum he saw thousands of little crystalline machines floating in the liquid, impossible to see by the naked eye.

Each microscopic machine was a cube with a number of arms protruding from the main body, some with very intricate pincers and others with miniature containers of different coloured liquid molecules. The nano robots were moving around in the liquid and often interacted with each other. The sight was quite frightening and Jen wondered what the purpose of such miniscule robots could be.

He decided to get out of the laboratory area and head back to atrium that led to the gallery of the palace. On his way out, he felt compelled to look through the window of another of the labs. What he saw was surreal.

On a table in the centre of a lab was a human body, yet it wasn't a whole body. Hundreds of small wires were connected to the table and different parts of the body were simultaneously growing. A large computer screen at the back of the lab showed a long line of sequential codes running and executing.

Jen realised that the human bodies were growing based on some sort of pattern or blueprint. The whole scene seemed like something out of a nightmare and Jen walked quickly back towards the atrium.

The light of Affero, The darkness of Ambitio, played in his head over and over, though he did not know where it was coming from.

Before long he came to the passageway towards the gallery and in a few minutes he arrived at grand, stone steps. At the top was a large hallway, with shiny marble pillars in lines holding up a large domed roof.

The roof had been painted with the most elaborate scene of a battle on horseback, depicting hundreds of soldiers. Ahead were two great wooden doors, with swirled metal decorations attached to them.

One door was slightly ajar and beyond was a treasure trove of shiny objects including golden vases, crockery made of lavish combinations of pure crystals and a number of outfits. The costumes were all laced with hundreds and sometimes thousands of jewels.

Each piece in the gallery was protected by a ten-inch-thick glass enclosure. Jen wandered around the empty place until he came to a wooden carving of a man, depicted as having a strong muscular body. The face of the wooden sculpture was covered with a light green mask. Jen instantly knew that it was the mask he was looking for.

The face of the mask was beautiful, completely androgynous in appearance with smooth, supple features and large, wide eyes. It dawned on Jen that he had no idea how to get the mask out of its secure casing.

After a few moments of contemplation, something that Javu had told him came to mind. After Jen had first teleported to Seho from Sula's apartment, Javu had told him that he had been given gifts from the earth. One gift was the ability to teleport and the other the ability to move things with his mind, often without knowing that he was doing it.

Now, it seemed like the perfect opportunity to attempt such a feat with full awareness. Jen had no clue how to begin. Then he remembered the Sig-lens in his pocket. He took it out and placed it on his right eye, causing everything around him to appear as the same interacting network of light filaments. He looked at his hand and its energy field seemed to spread much farther than the size of his physical hand.

Jen looked at the mask and he could see it was glowing but didn't have any energy filaments surrounding it. In fact, it seemed dormant. The glass barrier was also energy, but this energy was resonating and its filaments seemed to be tightly interwoven, not as free as those coming out of his hand.

Jen imagined the filaments from his hand spreading out towards the glass and they instantly reciprocated. However, as they touch the glass they seemed to be repelled by some sort of magnetic field. Jen only saw this by the way it curved the filaments of light from his hand.

He looked at the floor and it too looked like dense, interwoven energy streams slowly vibrating and glowing. He willed his hand's energy field to expand downwards and as he saw it touch and penetrate the stone floor, he felt a small vibration go through him.

He saw that at the point the filaments of energy from his hand had met the dense energy of the floor, what looked like a small vortex had formed and the filaments were passing through this spiral of energy. He imagined them coming out of the floor inside the glass casing and he quickly saw a vortex opening at the bottom of the enclosure.

The extended filaments from his hand were reaching up like fresh shoots from the earth. They seemed to gain speed as they twirled upwards towards the jade mask and as they interacted with it, it began to glow intensely. It was almost like the energy of the mask had hooked itself onto the extended energy field from his hand.

Jen pulled the mask downwards through the vortex in the enclosure and back through the one in the floor near to where he was standing. He felt a tremendously powerful energy land in his palm and he quickly took of the lens, astounded to find the jade mask in his hand. There were two perfectly round smooth holes in the floor where he had imagined and seen the vortexes. He gasped in disbelief and then got the incredible urge to get out of the palace as soon as possible.

Jen began to head back in the direction of the atrium, surprised to find that a sliding metal door now blocked the passageway. It would not open. He turned back to the museum and spotted a downward staircase that he hoped would lead to an underground tunnel.

It took a long while to navigate the staircase and Jen counted over two hundred steps before he reached the bottom. After the last step, Jen reached an eerie and dimly lit crypt littered with stone rectangular tombs. Dust and the odd cobweb covered a number of strangely shaped archways.

Jen had an overwhelming feeling that he was not alone in the crypt and began to wonder if he had made a mistake venturing down into the depths of the palace. After a while of searching around for a way out and finding none, Jen decided to go back up and have a look for another escape route. It was then that he heard the raspy voice of someone behind him.

"So, soldier, you have come back from the dead!" a well-toned, yet sinister voice said. Jen turned around and immediately recognised the man behind him.

It was Archibold Constynce, the man who had conspired with other leaders to get rid of the Tyrones.

"Yes, I was sure that Corporal Scott Johnstone was at the bottom of the river, yet here he is, inside the royal palace."

There was an overly sarcastic tenor to Constynce's plum yet grating voice. It was clear that the owner of the key card Jen had found had stepped out of line, to the extent where he had been permanently removed.

"I could say the same about you," Jen replied without fear. "You were supposedly assassinated by Makai rebels, but no, here you are in the royal palace."

Constynce seemed to be amused by Jen's courageous reply and he let out a derisive sigh.

"You have my grandfather's mask in your hand," Constynce said more seriously. "Why don't you do yourself a favour and give that back to me?"

"This mask does not belong to you," Jen said with strength.

"Oh, how wrong you are!" Constynce blabbed. "Everything on this planet belongs to those from who I am a descendant. Therefore it does belong to my family and me. Your life and everything you touch is simply rented to you! That mask will not leave here."

Jen saw a horrible glare form in Constynce's eyes, like the darkness of the world was behind them with not a glimmer of light escaping from the hideous void.

"Those from who you are a descendant?" Jen said more to

himself, remembering what Gaia had told him. He felt a fearful urge not to speak to the man but he quickly overcame it. "You mean those humans that left the earth? The Leiuryi and the Kesarin?" He probed the old crooked king. "I know that we are not alone in the universe. I know that there are powerful and wondrous beings that most people know nothing of."

Constynce gave out a distorted cackle of a laugh. "We, of the *order*, have known about our history since time as you can comprehend it began. The Leiuryi and the Kesarin? My, my, we do know quite a bit don't we, Mr King?"

The tone was patronising and Archibold seemed to salivate as he glared at Jen. His form was decrepit and he wore a robe-like garment, with jewels sown all along its rim.

"I know that all you want is power," Jen said back more forcefully. "You and your cohorts want to control everyone! I have seen the kind of thing you are developing in those labs. What are those tiny robots for? A new way of controlling people? A new way of killing people?"

Constynce did not answer but seemed to be moving in an odd fashion, like he was uncomfortable and restless. It made Jen get shivers down his spine and he realised that the only way to get out of the palace would be by unordinary means.

The grim, dingy crypt was filling him with a slow fear and he began to panic, like he was being trapped in an invisible prison. He felt an innate desperation to see something natural and he turned and quickly ran back up the long staircase to the gallery hallway. He did not look back to see if Constynce was following.

Jen was out of breath by the time he had reached the top. As he stopped for deep breaths of air, he noticed another staircase opposite, leading upwards. He quickly took the stairs, which again were lengthy and spiral. They led to a roof terrace.

Seeing the cloudy sky immediately brought a sense of calm to him and he tried to imagine being transported into one of the nearby ley lines of energy. Nothing happened and he realise he was still feeling fearful and panicked.

I need to teleport out of here.

He noticed some sort of domed building on the roof with a great spire protruding out of the top and he headed towards it instinctively. Inside, he was surprised to find it filled with complicated machinery, which seemed active. It was making a soft humming sound.

There were five buttons running along a main control panel labelled *Clear, Cloud, Rain Cloud, Storm* and *Snow*. Jen stood back in revulsion as he realised that the machine was used to control the weather. He peeked outside and saw that there was thick cloud above the skies of Phoenicia.

Mask in hand, he quickly studied the controls and realised that there were various gauges and switches. He pressed the *Clear* button several times but looking outside, nothing happened so he took the Sig-lens out of his pocket and placed it on his eye. He saw the machine as a vast interplay of electrical energy that seemed to be magnetically contained. He imagined the energy from his hand freeing some of that energy and he quickly began to feel heat in his palm. He focused intently for a few moments on this task and then he heard a crackling sound and the smell of burning wafted in the air.

Jen took of the lens and saw the machine was on fire. He quickly fled from the building just as there was a small explosion behind, culminating in a metal spire clanging to the ground next to him.

Then he saw an implausible sight. The sky was beginning to clear, as if the force that had been attracting all the clouds over Phoenicia was now pushing them away instead. Bright sunshine filtered down and soothed Jen's face and body. Then he noticed the distant form of Ignis was now visible.

At that moment, he felt the presence of someone behind him.

"You are intent on causing trouble today, aren't you?" Constynce said raspily.

He seemed different, more genuine in his tone and more life in his eyes. Though Jen was still cautious, he also felt affection for the dilapidated, old man for the first time.

"You are not the only one who has been indoctrinated with *the knowledge*".

"I have not been indoctrinated," Jen replied defensively, not liking the clinical language that Constynce was using. "Much of what I now know has been revealed to me through my own journey of discovery."

Constynce said nothing to the statement. Instead he seemed to want to impart something and so he changed the subject.

"Did you know this planet tilts?"

"No."

"Well now that you do, can you guess why?"

"No."

"The *Leiuryi*, as you call them, were the first root of humans to form on this planet. They lived in the northern lands at a time when this planet did not tilt. They were so knowledgeable that before long they had found ways to travel throughout the entire universe."

Jen had heard the same thing from Gaia.

"The *Kesarin*, as you call them, were the second root of humans to form and were even more intelligent than the Leiuryi. They too left this planet to explore the universe. Whilst these two original roots of human form were on their incredible journeys, another root formed on the earth, yet these humans were simple in nature, not endowed with the knowledge of their predecessors."

Jen did not agree with this last point. He was sure everything that existed in the entire universe was essentially equal and aware unless tampered with. Constynce continued the account of his beliefs unfazed.

"Whilst the Kesarin and the Leiuryi were travelling throughout the universe, they encountered each other for the first time and a great war began between these two roots, a war of great magical powers. The Leiuryi were defeated in a vast battle that took place all over the universe and they fled back to where they had originally come from, this planet on which we are now present. The Kesarin followed and were deceived by the cunning of the Leiuryi. They proved themselves to be of superior power when they created an illusion that they were hiding on a nearby planet, the second sun."

Jen let the old man continue his account.

"The ancient planet Tiam was a world almost completely filled with water. When the sun shone on this planet, it lit up so brightly that it looked like a smaller version of the sun. The Kesarin destroyed it. This caused our planet to tilt and the weather to change dramatically across the lands. Water flooded down from Tiam into the atmosphere and settled into many oceans.

"The Kesarin, believing that they had ended the war, continued their journey throughout the universe. The Leiuryi remained here on this planet. They created a great empire and interbred with the primitive humans that at that time dwelled on the lands. Since then, to keep *order*, the true history and knowledge that these great gods brought has been preserved by a select, chosen few. You are fortunate, Mr King, that you have come into this knowledge within your lifetime."

Jen felt patronised and that the story had been distorted from the truth somehow. He felt parts were missing.

"Originally we used the method of divide and rule to control the masses, but now things are changing," Constynce said calmly, looking up at the distant form of Ignis in the sky. His demeanour was changing, almost like he was allowing a hideous power to possess him. "She has been summoned so the change can begin, the change that we have been preparing for thousands of years." Constynce's face had expression, yet his eyes were empty, like they were void of all compassion and sensation.

"What change?" Jen asked, not sure he wanted to hear the answer. He was sure he could see Constynce's face changing shape slightly, taking on an uglier form.

"The change this planet needs is to go back to the way things were. We must create *order* out of chaos!" Constynce laughed in a frightening and robotic way.

"You want to use Ignis to create order?" Jen said with scepticism and confusion, to which a devilish grin appeared on Constynce's shrivelled face.

"What do you think most people's reaction is going to be to a giant molten dragon coming towards them from the skies?" the crooked old man said sadistically, cackling again in a disconnected manner. "Oh, help me! Do something to stop all this horror, all this destruction! And then, the order will come. It will be order from a single point, *true power* ruling over all. People will be begging for our technology. They will ask us to take care of them, like small children."

"But why?" Jen asked weakly, his heart aching from the vision that Constynce was unveiling and the things that he had seen in the laboratories beneath them. "People just want to live in peace."

"Ha! Humans are mere robots. I was born with the right to be the divine servant of the true powers who will finally rule over the earth."

"Who? The Leiuryi?"

"Ha!" Constynce almost chocked violently. "The Leiuryi are my blood but they are not the true powers that have created all this, the true powers that have the divine vision!"

"What true powers?" Jen asked with a sense of terror.

"Oh you will find out soon enough," Constynce hissed, striking a sickening vibration into Jen's chest and lower belly. "If you are deemed worthy then you will see. Now give me that mask before you condemn yourself to a lifetime of suffering!"

Jen had to quickly shake the horrible, hypnotic words that Constynce was speaking to him. He turned away, staring into the light of the sky and soon after, he felt a warm, ambient light surround him. Constynce did not seem to notice yet the presence instantly relieved Jen of all of his fear and Constynce did notice that. He seemed to become edgy and uncomfortable and looked around shiftily.

"There is no true power except that which is within and that which is one with us all," Jen said, not from himself but from something speaking through him. "You shall experience what you force on others. We shall not be manipulated anymore, only free of all chains."

Then he thought of Seho and Ciafra and something began to tug on his navel area, like there was a string attached to it and something was pulling it.

I know why I am here, Jen thought, feeling a welcome responsibility descend upon him.

The next thing he knew, he was sucked into the nearest energy ley line with a boost that seemed to come from behind. He moved across the city at speeds that his mind could not comprehend. He knew he had temporarily dispersed from physicality and was now without a body.

Within seconds, he was travelling at the speed of light and in a flash, he was back on Javu's bed in Seho, the jade mask firmly in his hand. His ears buzzed and his body tingled intensely.

A wave of joy and relief vibrated through his heart, spreading out into the hut. His memory had gone blank and he couldn't remember the conversation he had just had. He felt glad for that. Then he felt a presence in the room. He sat up to surreally see Javu's smiling face peering down at him.

Chapter 69 – The Rulers of Power

"Javu!" Jen said loudly with a childlike excitement, jumping up and hugging the short man and dropping the jade mask to the bed.

"You have returned, my son!" Javu said, reciprocating his affection. The two held arms and just looked at each other for a while to make sure they were real and solid.

"Come and sit down. I'm sure there is much for you to tell me. It has been four weeks since I last saw you."

He ushered Jen towards a rug on the floor and noticed the jade mask on the bed.

"Well, well, what a beautiful mask. No doubt it is of great importance to this time that we find ourselves in."

Jen couldn't help but feel like Javu was humouring him and that deep down he knew exactly what the mask was needed for. Jen nodded and sat cross-legged upon the pile rug.

Javu did the same, facing him.

Jen began to talk about all his experiences since he had last seen Javu. He spoke of the earth stone and Gaia, his journey into the world of Avarice, his meeting with Azreal and his mission to Lengard.

Javu just sat there listening for an hour as Jen recalled everything he had been told, given and seen. He spoke of his newfound abilities of *teleportation* through the *lines of the world*, and how by invoking such a view of lines of energy, he could actually manipulate that energy which also affected the physical world.

"My hand actually created two holes in a floor," he went on, an inner energy making him expunge his entire mind. "I could see these fibres of light changing and moving how I wanted them to."

Jen talked about the advanced technology that he had seen. Finally, there was nothing left to say and only questions came instead.

"Where were you and everyone else?" Jen said, looking around. "After I came back from Gaia's world there was nobody here."

"Oh, it's that fool Hasu," Javu declared with amusement. "He began to panic as Ignis started getting more solid and the entire village was soon in a tither. I felt compelled to accompany the resulting exodus into the desert to try and instil a sense of calm in everyone."

Javu leaned close like he was going to whisper. "Hasu was never a very good chief, you know?" Then he laughed heartily.

"I can't believe four weeks have past. It only seems like a few days to me."

"Sometimes it feels the other way around," Javu said knowledgeably.

Jen did not feel like entering into a discussion about dreaming, as his mind was flooded with more pressing questions. "Where is everyone now?" he asked, still not hearing much activity in the village.

"Most are still out in a desert camp. A few of us came back – Teltu, Fera, Lentu and Nehne and of course myself. I had a feeling that you would be back soon. In fact, I had only been here an hour before you appeared on the bed over there."

Jen realised that he wasn't wearing the coat that he'd found in Raicema, only the simple cotton suit that he left with. "What did it look like when I started to appear?"

"It was almost like you'd been there the entire time, lying on the bed but I just could not see you. Then suddenly, it was like a light was shone on your shadow, and you appeared."

Jen accepted the perception.

"Javu, I'm a little confused about Ignis," Jen said calmly. "I have learnt so much recently that I'm not sure whether Ignis is real or not. I mean, I have seen worlds where things just appear out of nowhere. What's to say that this great dragon from Ambitio in the sky is not an illusion?"

"Exactly, Jen!" Javu exclaimed. "Everything is an illusion and we can change everything if our will is strong enough. If you remember that and become aware of it, even the most trying of situations become easy to navigate."

The advice did not help Jen's understanding of the matter. He still didn't understand how such an entity could be manifested.

"So, Ignis doesn't really exist?"

"It depends on your perception," Javu said. "We are the interpreters."

Javu paused as the wind blew outside.

"There is a place where Ignis exists and it has taken a tremendous amount of energy to bring Ignis from that place into the perception of those that are here in the physical world. I am talking about years and years of negative energy."

Jen listened carefully.

"If enough people believe that Ignis exists, it will become real in this world. As more and more people are looking up at that thing in the sky, Ignis is becoming more real by the day."

Again, Javu paused as the wind blew.

"It is time to make people realise that they are in control of what they perceive."

Jen slept for a while as Javu went out around Seho. When he returned Jen wanted to resume their conversation. Another baffling topic had come to mind.

"Both Gaia and Archibold Constynce told me about the roots of human beings, stretching back millions of years. Constynce said that the *Kesarin* and the *Leiuryi* were at war with each other."

"There is more to know," Javu interrupted with a serious tone. "Do not listen to those who are consumed by power, for their beliefs are twisted and I mean that quite literally. Only what the *great mother* has told you is accurate."

"So there wasn't a war between the Kesarin and the Leiuryi?"

"Oh, there was a war. But the war was always in the minds of a few, not everyone. Those who carry out wars rarely know the true reason for them. That mirrors what happens in the world today and what has happened for millennia. However, the few people who instigate such agendas and actually create the wars are themselves puppets of the true *bearers of power*."

"What bearers? Constynce said something about that but he wouldn't tell me."

"Well clearly not, for to protect that force is his entire purpose in life or so he perceives it that way. For Constynce, to divulge the true nature and identity of those that control him would mean instant death and his desperation to survive is what keeps him alive."

"But who are these powers?"

"Well, why don't you tell me? You have already ventured into their worlds. You have lived three years in the mountains, learning all about it."

Then Javu let out a joyous laugh that resonated all around as it all began to come together in Jen's mind. It was intended to lighten what Jen was remembering.

"You mean those horrible dream worlds, that hellish jungle, that dismal city of greed. In those places, my emotions reached their limit. I saw true horror. I saw true loss."

Jen instantly wanted to cry. Javu allowed him to compose himself. He had stopped laughing. The blowing wind outside soothed Jen's heart like the air drying wet strings.

"Those places are what are controlling these leaders?"

"Yes! Those realms are constructs of power and remember what I told you about power looking like a pyramid when you see it in terms of its energy. They are the six realms or the *six pyramids* of Ambitio."

Jen could barely recall.

"Even in those distorted and perverse worlds, there is a hierarchy. And at the top of each hierarchy is the connection with the six humans who effectively run everyone's lives here on earth. Each of the *six* here has a connection to the rulers of the realms of power."

"Six leaders? Are there always six?"

"Yes, one to represent each of the realms of power."

"Who are they?"

"Constynce is strongly connected to the ruler of the world of *Pride*. That is why when you look at Archibold Constynce, he sometimes appears to change form. Why? Because the ruler of the world of Pride stays close to him, manipulating him and encouraging him to drag as many spirits as possible towards that horrible world."

"It is the same with Sadana, or Voro as he used to be called, though his allegiance is to a different ruler. That ruler dwells in world of *Avarice*, the place where you went looking for Azreal."

The sun was becoming stronger outside and the hot air wafted in through the open windows.

"But the thing that each of these six rulers of the realms of power have in common is their violent and uncompassionate nature. In the extreme of any form of power, violence and hate manifests itself." He paused. "That is not to say that *Ambitio* should be looked upon negatively. Indeed, power exists as part of a balance with freedom."

"Azreal told me the same thing," Jen told Javu. More questions came to him. He wanted to know more about the roots of humanity that he had heard about. "But how does this relate to the ancient human roots that Gaia told me about? How did we get to where we are now?"

"The *Leiuryi* were a very knowledgeable people and most were at one with the essence and the universe. The same applies to the *Kesarin*, the *Equus* and the *Terra*. All four human roots were given the same balance and were equal. No one root is better than the others."

"So, was there a planet called *Tiam* and *was* it destroyed?"

"Yes that is true in a physical sense," Javu said mystically, his confirmation shocking Jen a little.

Now the sound of the waves was riding on the wind, creating an ethereal melody.

"Constynce said that the Leiuryi created an illusion on Tiam. He said that made the Kesarin destroy it. Is that true?"

"No! That is preposterous!" Javu exclaimed with gusto. "It was not the Leiuryi that created such an illusion but those bearers of power that we have just been talking about. What happened on Tiam is what is happening now on this planet."

Jen was starting to understand.

"There was a time, Jen, when these creatures, the rulers of the realms of power, actually existed in the physical world. That was so long ago we couldn't possibly comprehend it. However, there are those who are desperately trying to make that a reality again.

It is those beings that have the connection to *extreme Ambitio*, or the *eye of darkness* and the fatums that now threaten the earth."

"So the Leiuryi, the Kesarin, the Equus and the Terra roots of humanity had all been manipulated?"

"Yes. And the Leiuryi are an important people in our history because these rulers of power chose the Leiuryi to be their servants and everlasting link with the physical world."

It was starting to make sense.

Jen knew in his heart that every human form that had existed was essentially perfect. He knew that something must have interfered with humanity for there to have been so much continual suffering in life. He had seen those perverse worlds, where all that existed was mind-consuming illusion. He felt determined to prevent such illusion from spreading through the universe.

"That is what it means to be a world walker, Jen," Javu said, reading his mind. "We must do all we can to help this interconnected universe." He paused and smiled. "I think you should rest some more."

Chapter 70 – The Verge of Change

Jen napped for an hour. He awoke with a queue of questions in his mind and the wind echoing in his ear. Javu was sitting peacefully at the table looking at two objects, the jade mask and the crystal flute. They seemed solid and normal and it seemed implausible that the objects could have been manifested in another world.

"Let me make something to eat," Javu said. "Jumping all over the planet must have made you hungry! I will tell the others to eat with us too."

Javu got to his feet and began to chop some vegetables on a piece of smooth teak. He lit a small fire in his wood burner and placed a large pan of water on top. Then he plopped each of the chopped vegetables into the hot water and added a number of herbs and spices. It was getting hotter outside.

Whilst the broth was cooking, Javu opened a cupboard and took out a small bowl that contained a number of charred embers and was lined with ash. He placed it next to the jade mask and crystal flute, which were lying dormant on the table.

"Before we eat, I want to show you something," Javu said, and Jen got to his feet and stood next to the table.

"I still can't believe that Gaia just made that flute appear," Jen commented to Javu.

"Once you know how to manoeuvre energy, such feats are simple, especially to the great mother."

It made Jen think about all the things he had come to know that at one time he did not. Javu began to burn some hardy-looking dried purple leaves in the ash bowl and soon a pungent, medicinal aroma had spread throughout the hut.

"This herb is a close friend of mine," Javu said. "I have known it well for much of my life."

Jen was intrigued and they both stood there, staring at the thick smoke coming out of the bowl. Then, in a surreal moment, a face seemed to form in the smoke. It was humanlike but constantly changed shape and Jen almost thought he saw several faces that were familiar to him in the thick pouring smoke.

Then, the smoke seemed to spread out like a landscape within the hut. Mountains and clouds formed as Jen's mouth opened with awe. Javu was staring intently at the smoke formation. Birds of smoke flew out of the clouds and smoke rivers formed on the mountains, flowing down realistically. Then in an instant the smoke dispersed and after a few moments it had completely disappeared.

"Whaaa?" Jen blundered, stunned by what he had just seen. He realised that Javu had somehow created the entire scene of smoke. "How did you do that?"

"I know this smoke. I know its energy and I can mould it as I please. The same is true of anything. The secret is to connect using the energy that comes out of your belly," he said slowly and simply. "You should practice, Jen, for the time will soon come when your life will depend upon the abilities that you have been given."

Javu left the hut to fetch the others that had returned to the village, leaving Jen to contemplate the abilities that he had recently demonstrated whilst in Lengard. He remembered how everything looked with the special Sig-lens on his eye. He wanted to discuss it with Javu.

A few moments passed and then two men, a woman and a young girl entered the hut, followed by Javu. Every one of them had a smile on their face.

"Jen, this is Teltu and Fera," Javu said, making the introductions to the couple, "and this is their daughter Nehne."

Jen took an instant liking to the trio, who looked a very close family. They all smiled. The man behind them had a sterner face and seemed to be analysing Jen.

"And, this is Lentu," Javu said, to which Lentu nodded in a welcoming fashion. "He is the village educator and loves to talk about similar things to you, such as history, empires and other wonderings."

Javu, Teltu and Fera all laughed but Lentu seemed to be a little offended and just huffed like a goat.

"Well, nobody's laughing now are they?" he said with vexation. "Look at that damn thing in the sky? You think that's here by accident?"

"Yes, yes, Lentu," Javu said in a settling tone. "Now let's eat. There will be time for serious talk later."

Jen was fascinated by Nehne, as she seemed to be paying no attention to the banter of the adults and instead had immediately gone over to the crystal flute resting on the table. She did not touch it but seemed to gaze at it with affection. Jen went up to her and also looked at the flute.

"It has a beautiful sound," he said. "Do you want to play it?"

"I'd better not," Nehne said in a very mature way. "Javu told me that this flute was made for you."

Jen was taken aback by the words and the grown-up approach of the child. Nehne turned her attention to the jade mask. She picked it up and turned it around. She gazed at the smooth jade stone of the inner mask. For a moment, Jen thought she was going to put it on and a stroke of panic touched his heart.

"Nehne," Javu's stern voice suddenly came from nowhere. "Come outside now."

Nehne put the mask down. Jen breathed a sigh of relief, but he did not know why.

The others were carrying plates, bread and the large vegetable stew outside. Jen and Nehne followed and everyone sat around an old wooden table, shaded from the sun by a straw parasol.

The vegetables were delicious. They were soft and full of flavour, bursting with hot juice as they entered the mouth. Everyone ate silently for a while and then Nehne asked a poignant question.

"Why do some animals eat each other?" she asked, taking everyone aback.

"They do it to survive, Nehne," Fera told her daughter. "We too hunt fish to survive."

"But why not just eat vegetables like we are doing now?"

825

Fera didn't know what to say to Nehne and Jen was intrigued by the little girl's viewpoint.

"Let me tell you a story, Nehne," Javu said slowly. "There is a man that I know who lives in the mountains of Vassini, where Jen and I originally come from. This man was quite old when I last saw him, he was maybe eighty years of age, and that was a while ago! Since he was a young man, he has not eaten one thing nor drank one drop of water. He has learnt to take everything he needs from the air that he breathes. He can absorb the energy that surrounds him. Now, it would be very difficult for us to do what this man does, because we are used to getting the energy we need from the food that we eat. Also, for many that live in cities, there is an extra problem that money is needed to trade for food. So you see, Nehne, it is because of what some animals learn that they eat other animals. Humans have learnt that money is needed to buy food and they will do all sorts of things they don't really want to in order to get that money. I am sure if an animal had a plentiful supply of growing vegetables, they would not learn to hunt."

Nehne was quiet as she listened to Javu's narrative.

"We are lucky that Seho has been self-providing for many years now," Lentu added, speaking more to Jen than Nehne. "It is much harder inland. Many villages and towns are reliant on what is brought in by those that have the means to do so."

Everyone ate and talked about Ciafra and the different animals that lived on its diverse land. Then as the sun started to fade, Teltu, Lentu and Fera got to their feet and thanked Javu.

"We will be setting off early in the morning to fish around the southern bays. The fish seem to be moving farther and farther south these days," Fera said.

Nehne jumped up and hugged her mother's leg.

"I'm going too for the first time tomorrow!" she said excitedly.

After everyone had left, in the warm orange sunlight of dusk, Jen sat down next to Javu. "Why aren't they scared of Ignis?" he asked.

"They know it's an illusion," Javu replied.

Jen knew it was the truth, but he could not reason how it was possible. He suddenly felt very tired and he excused himself, ready to go to sleep for the night.

"Sleep well," Javu said, reclining back and looking up at the appearing stars.

Jen fell asleep very quickly. He dreamt of Gaia's world, of Azreal and of the things he had seen in Phoenicia.

He dreamt of the roots of humanity, of a story that he was trying to unravel. Then, the memories that were playing through his mind began to solidify and become much more real and he found himself in a familiar world of ambient, white light, in which he was fully aware of his presence.

A glowing light floated towards him and began to take shape.

It was the woman of light. It seemed like it was only a moment ago that Jen had seen her last.

"Elera," he felt himself say.

"Jen, tomorrow is the day that your life will change forever."

What he was being told invoked a strong sense of progression and attainment.

"Love is the answer. Only love."

Jen felt like he was floating down a slowly swirling tunnel, the presence hovering in front of him.

"Aova?" he felt himself resonate.

"You must take my place. Free Aova. Free them all."

Then peace fell for a while.

Jen awoke to feel like he had slept for ages.

An energy filled him that was so remarkably full of life he felt like he could bench press a few small men. He walked outside into the hot sunshine and it warmed his skin like butter on toast. Javu was reading something quite intently. It was a piece of paper with a number of geometric shapes inscribed into it. It made him forget his dream about Elera.

"What are you reading?" Jen asked with immediate interest.

"It is a foretelling from the past," Javu said, looking up at his longhaired son. "It is the very story that is now being told – of you, of Elera, the forces and their children."

"Elera? The forces and their children?"

Jen now felt dazed.

"The forces of antiquity have many children including the monster that now approaches this planet," Javu explained. "Ignis herself is the child of Ambitio. Aova is the child of Affero. These two beings are essentially the same. That is why, if as predicted by this prophecy, Aova and Ignis were to meet, they would simply act as a mirror to each other."

Jen was listening carefully, yet a strange mood had overcome him, like he couldn't possibly bring himself to believe such fantastical creatures could exist.

"It is your mind trying to talk you out of the truth," Javu warned him, reading his thoughts. "Let me tell you something that will seem much more real to you."

Javu paused patiently as Jen shuffled his position.

"Sadana and the others are trying to reform the *Order of the Dragon*."

"Order of the Dragon?"

"When Lemuria sank beneath the waves after Tiam was destroyed, the order was created to preserve the knowledge that you are now rediscovering yourself. That was only fifteen thousand years ago, Jen."

"Tiam? The planet that the Kesarin destroyed?"

Javu did not need to confirm for it suddenly dawned on Jen that the Kesarin and the Leiuryi could still be around to this day.

"They exist...not just in the past..."

"Fifteen thousand years ago, the order was the supreme rulership on the planet, made up of members from mixtures of the four roots of antiquity. Members of the order mysteriously appeared in the lands that still exist today after Tiam was destroyed."

The sun was healing and made Jen feel no worry or fear.

"These people knew how to manipulate energy, how to conjure and how to summon. They used this to their advantage to manoeuvre their way into positions of power all over the planet."

"Are you talking about people like Sadana and Archibold Constynce?"

"Yes, however, the order was different. At its head were the rulers of other worlds. Those dark places that you have seen could be readily *seen* by the masses back then. People instinctively rebel to outright control so since then everything has quite literally gone underground."

Jen could say nothing, though his dream of Elera was coming back to him and her words were playing in his head.

"Jen, tomorrow is the day that your life will change forever."

Today is tomorrow, he thought.

"The order had to go underground as well," Javu continued. "Now, it will no longer hide and the order will be reformed."

"Can't we stop it?"

"Stop what? It is the cycle, Jen. If you are asking how to break the cycle, then I do not know."

"So why are you telling me this?"

"So that you are aware of who and what you will be dealing with today."

Then Javu smiled but Jen felt a shot of fear.

"The order want to use Ignis to create an illusion of power that can distort everything. Only Aova can dispel such an illusion. Either way, the perception of the world is going to change today. It is a new era!"

Jen spent a few moments reaffirming his main intention in life. It was to restore the balance that he himself had helped distort in the past.

"Let me tell you of the capabilities of this order so that you are prepared, as there is not much time left before you must go and face them."

Now Jen felt a surreal adrenaline surging throughout his body, a nostalgic feeling that he used to get before entering a battle. It almost felt like shoots sprouting in his belly, absorbing the sunlight and trying to break free.

"It was the order of the dragon that built every megalith on this planet, including the *four pyramids of the elements*. I have recently visited two of these four pyramids, the *fire pyramid of Giza* and the *air pyramid of Ixon*."

Javu paused as a giant wave crashed into the sea behind them. It sounded like the roar of a lion.

"Elera visited all four pyramids in her lifetime. Her last physical day on this earth was at the very first megalith that was built, the *earth pyramid of Lemuria*."

The image of the woman of light floated into Jen's vision.

"Every one of the pyramids was built under the capability of the order. Their purpose is to manipulate energy. The giant stones at each of the structures were not physically lifted upon each other but were manifested there. One who does not know would not understand this, but you have experienced such possibility in your retrieval of the mask."

Jen was silent for a while as he thought about it. He knew it was all true yet he had an overwhelming apprehension.

"You will be dealing with skilled sorcerers and summoners, Jen, so watch everything, perceive everything. The time is coming when demons and angels will once again walk the earth."

Jen deep down knew that something pivotal was shortly to occur.

"I dreamt of Elera last night," Jen told Javu. "She said I should take her place. She said I should free everyone. What did she mean?"

Javu smiled. "It is my opinion, that in the past, every single human on this planet was able to perform all the abilities that you have learnt, all the abilities I have learnt throughout my life and essentially any ability that they could possibly think of. Endless possibilities!"

The wind whistled about them.

"Humans could visit any of the worlds that exist at will and conjure energy ways we cannot possibly comprehend today. I even believe that the humans of the past did not die. They simply chose to walk from one world to another when they had finished their experience and were ready to move on. That is freedom, that is who we really are! We are all world walkers. Elera knew that!"

Jen understood, but he had no idea how to unlock such potential from every being that existed on the planet. The feat seemed impossible.

"What has happened in recent history is that humans have been manipulated into forgetting who they really are," Javu continued. "And who are they really? Simply the essence, infinite consciousness, everything that possibly exists, endless possibility. Death is nothing to fear, because it is an illusion, just like everything else in this world."

Jen was filled with an incredible determination to change things. "But how can I possibly make everyone realise this?"

"You are the proof. Elera was the proof," Javu said simply. "And what will happen today, will also be the proof."

Jen rose to his feet almost automatically, as if called by something. He looked up. Ignis was nowhere to be seen. Only the brilliance of the golden sun spread its light through the blue sky.

"Go, Jen. Today is a day of great change and you have your part to play."

Without another word to Javu, Jen walked into the hut and picked up the mask and crystal flute. They felt as cold as ice.

He walked back outside and kissed Javu on his forehead.

Then he walked away.

Chapter 71 – The Great Melee

Jen had drifted.

A world was forming before him.

It was familiar. It was green. It was pure.

Gaia appeared, radiant and surrounded by majestic deer. She was stunningly beautiful, Jen's idea of the perfect woman. He felt nothing but love for her. The deer and other animals surrounding the goddess seemed to feel the same way.

Jen was in a forest in which every blade of grass and every leaf emitted an omnipresent light. He could see the energy. He could feel it in his heart, dancing like an excited child.

"So you are awake, Jen?"

Jen could feel laughter but he could not speak.

"Go to Bimini. They are waiting for you."

Jen felt his presence was slipping. He began to recall something. It was his legs moving. He looked down to see that he was walking over a large hill just outside Seho.

He looked up and Gaia and the forest had vanished, a vision now faded.

The jade mask was in his hand. It was glowing.

Bimini...

Jen was on the hill where he had first observed the lines of light across the earth. It took him a while to climb to the top as the sun was shining down with a surreal heat. Every step he took caused streams of perspiration to flow from his body and brow.

At the summit he sat and breathed deeply, looking out on Seho and the dry landscape. The sight of Gaia had caused shoots of excitement to spring from his being.

Ignis was still nowhere to be seen in the sky.

Bimini... he thought.

Jen had fond memories of Bimini. It was a place that he had been many times during his time in the military. He began to imagine the encampment that he had helped build in the mangrove forest of the south island. He visualised the shape of the trees that he had lay under at night and the smell of the salty sea that lingered in the air.

He felt his forehead throbbing slightly as the bright rays poured down on his face and head. Then he saw the lines of the earth as he had done before.

This time, he also saw smaller channels of energy alongside the two giant energy streams that crossed paths over Seho. Jen perceived that the entire surface of the planet was covered with an intricate web of energy, with the main lines looking like a great grid wrapped around the globe.

Jen felt a pull in his belly and then he felt the familiar sensation of being sucked rapidly into the energy lines. The world blurred past him as he faded in and out of consciousness. He could perceive patterns of light and energy, yet it was not the same as looking directly with his eyes. Instead, it was like he just knew that the lights were there.

What seemed like a few seconds passed and then Jen was jolted into full awareness as his back hit something hard and rough. It was the solid branch of a leafy tree.

He looked around to see that he had been wedged in the middle of two converging branches with leaves and insects thrown all over his body and face.

The jade mask was still in his hand.

The air was warm and humid with a fragrant smell in the air, like that of freshly crushed fruit. He freed himself and climbed down, dropping to the floor with agility. He was standing in a clearing and the arrangement of the trees looked familiar. It was the location where the encampment had been set up all those years ago. Jen spotted an old tent peg in the ground that had been left behind.

I am in Bimini, he thought. He felt a sense of power at having teleported a third time. The ability felt much more familiar to him now.

He heard rustling ahead.

Okay, where to now? he thought to himself.

Before another thought could go through his mind, he heard loud talking coming from nearby.

"Are we safe here?" he heard a man's voice say.

Jen tiptoed over to the area where the voices were coming from. He peered through the branches of a large bush and saw three men. They instantly reminded him of Raiceman soldiers, though their outfits were slightly different.

The men wore rounded helmets that only covered the back of the head and strange glowing filaments arranged in a grid across their chests. Their outfits also looked lighter and more flexible and seemed to be made out of a rubber substance. The men wore Sig-lenses on their eyes and the vibrant colours made their faces look sinister. All three guards were smoking cigarillos and they seemed to be guarding something.

"Master Yangjam said that only the cavern would be affected," one of the guards reassured the other. He had a large busy moustache.

"I don't know..." the other guard said with apprehension. "The impression I got last week was that the entire island would be involved, maybe even all the islands for a hundred suns around."

This news seemed to worry all of the men and they began to smoke intensely, taking large puffs of smoke deep into their lungs.

"What is he doing with those other leaders anyway?" the least knowledgeable of the guards asked.

"It's got something to do with the planets," the moustached guard said. "Master Yangjam is a powerful man. The ritual that he and the other leaders are performing today has something to do with that thing in the sky."

"I heard it was a dragon," the third guard said nervously. "All I know is that he said to expect tremors on this island. Let's hope we survive, eh?"

The guards all laughed anxiously and continued smoking.

Jen wondered what Yangjam was up to and was sure that the other leaders were likely to include those present at Seth Tyrone's death.

Jen slowly sidestepped around the area until he was in the swampy jungle of the mangrove forest, away from the guards. He held the jade mask close to his chest for protection.

Before long he was knee-deep in the warm swamp, using the vines of the trees as leverage to pull himself along. He soon came to a clearing with three round holes of pure blue water. The holes seemed to be very deep. Monkeys screeched above his head.

One monkey scrambled down to the floor and stood looking with intrigue at Jen. It seemed to be startled by something, highly alert to its environment and almost frightened. A tremor came from deep in the earth and the monkey quickly climbed back up the tree to safety.

Jen pressed on through the woodland, heading wherever his instinct told him to. Before long, he had come to a very thick, less moist part of the jungle where the ground seemed steeper. He climbed up the incline for a while before coming to the edge of a steep hill.

All he could see as he looked down was thick jungle. He headed into the undergrowth without another thought. After fighting through tightly bound branches and ripping his shirt a few times, he eventually broke out into openness.

Before him was a most strange sight.

Jen was now standing at the summit of one edge of a large, coliseum-like cavern, the sides sloping steeply downwards into a concave. There were scattered trees positioned at equal distances apart on all sides of the circular cavern.

At the bottom, there were six people and a ritual was taking place. The people were standing in a large circle and in the centre of the circle was a jade statue. He looked down at the mask in his hand and saw that it was glowing brightly with an ethereal green light. The stone around his neck and the flute in his other hand were also alive with energy.

Hiding behind a wide tree, he observed what was happening at the bottom of the cavern. He instantly recognised three men, Yangjam and Gueken from Yinkoto, and Archibold Constynce, whom he had recently seen in Phoenicia.

The remainder of the six was comprised of two other men and a woman and all seemed to be quite aged. One of the men that Jen did not know was speaking loudly in a language that Jen did not understand. It seemed like he was introducing something to the circle of people. Then he picked up an object by his side and placed it over his head. It looked like some sort of large jewelled necklace.

"Gumeba Vutma," the man said loudly to the other members of the group. The man was black with tightly curled hair that emerged from his head in two triangular shapes. He had wide-open eyes and Jen could see them shine unnaturally in the distance.

"Sai Gueken," the familiar viper-like face of Yinkoto's ruler said out loud whilst he picked up a large necklace and placed it over his head. It shone in the sunlight. Jen realised that every person had such a necklace next to them and were all saying their names out loud.

"Archibold Constynce," the deceptive king from Lengard said next, following the ritual with his own jewelled chain.

"Iliza Rothberg," the only woman present now added her own name to the strange scene.

Iliza had a high-pitched voice that sounded sharp and crisp. She was dressed in a highly decorated purple gown and Jen could see the thousands of gemstones sewn into the garment glistening in the rays of the sun. Her necklace was the most elaborate of all. It glimmered with green and blue gemstones.

Yangjam was next to announce himself.

"Yangjam Satori," he said, placing his necklace over his head.

The sky above looked unnatural. Though the sun was shining, strange blankets of clouds were moving around heavily in the atmosphere.

"Sadana Siger," the final man said after a while, placing a heavy necklace of red gemstones and placing it over his head.

Voro... Jen thought instinctively, taking a long look at the man that Javu had told him all about. His thinking seemed to affect Sadana, who looked around suspiciously. Jen began to panic but then something else commanded his attention.

Jen noticed somebody approaching the human circle of six from an area outside his vision. The man looked young and bedraggled with sharply cut black hair but Jen couldn't see his face.

The man walked slowly into the middle of the circle in a strange way, almost like he was being pushed against his will, yet he was not struggling. The man seemed submissive. He reached the centre, and sat down next to the jade statue.

Jen got a look at the man's face. He recognised him instantly.

Rekesh... He thought of the man who had crossed his path in the past and seemed inexplicably linked to his own life. Rekesh seemed completely dazed, as if he were heavily sedated.

The jade statue began to glow in pulsating fashion.

Sadana began to look up into the sky with both arms open and began chanting loudly. Jen noticed he had a large crystal in his hand and that it was glowing with a red misty light.

'The fire stone,' something almost whispered in Jen's ear.

Overhead there was a great rumble, like the closest lightning cracking loudly high above. Jen looked up with shock to see the outline of a dragon. It was penetrating the earth's atmosphere and it looked like there had been an explosion in the sky. A ring of fiery clouds was forming around the giant creature and its body was a swirling interplay of glowing greys, greens and reds. Long forks of lightning shot off in all directions from the surreal entity.

Jen felt intense pangs of fear within. The pain was so sharp that it doubled him over. He almost dropped the mask to the ground. In his crumpled position, Jen looked down at the earth stone around his neck and it was glowing with a gentle green light. He could feel its energy vibrating around his heart, soothing his pain.

The six leaders were all chanting something now. They seemed to be focusing more and more intensely on Rekesh and the statue. Jen began to see energy lines forming between the six figures in the distance below, forming a hexagram of ethereal grey light.

Again, another loud rumbling sound came from above and Jen looked up into the sky to see that the giant dragon had almost doubled in size. The sun was shrouded by the disturbance in the atmosphere. Jen could make out a fiery tail. It was becoming darker.

He had the sudden urge to move.

Jen picked up the mask and slowly began to walk down the bank, going from one tree to another to hide from sight. His mind raced with how he could get the mask onto the statue, an act that he was sure would do some good.

Then, an overwhelming surge of energy shot through his body.

It was almost like being pushed heavily by a giant hand and he began to run down the bank uncontrollably, his legs going faster and faster, burning with heat. As he was running, he realised that the earth stone was giving him a rush of power, as if it was pumping his heart and commanding his legs to move.

The trees coming towards him sped by like city traffic. His legs had a mind of their own, knowing exactly where to step. He had reached halfway down at an incredible speed in what seemed like only a few moments. It was then that the six leaders below noticed him.

Jen felt an incredible fluttering feeling in his chest and he jumped high into the air uncontrollably, as if time had slowed down. He hit the slope below with incredible force and power, closer to the bottom. Those below looked up at the side of the hill.

Jen began to run again, his legs burning with the sheer strain his muscles were under. He gasped as he toppled headfirst down the hill. He rolled and he rolled, miraculously missing the solid trunks that blurred past. The earth stone had released him from its command.

As he tumbled to the bottom, he managed to roll forward. He came to a stop, crouching like a tiger. The mask was still in his hand

and vibrating wildly.

Everyone was looking at him.

Archibold grimaced at seeing the jade mask in Jen's hand.

"Quickly, Sadana! Do it! He has the mask!" Archibold yelled over at his fellow consort.

"Extraho Increndia Ignotus," Sadana began to chant ferociously, giving Jen a feeling of light-headedness as he ran forward.

The red crystal in Sadana's hand began to vibrate and then an intense red light shot out of the stone into the atmosphere. It seemed to strike the dragon above in the belly, though Jen could not see properly as a strange haze was forming.

Then, Jen's stomach suddenly tied itself into a painful knot. He could sense immense danger and it made him freeze to the spot with terror.

Then, he knew that his worst fear was about to be realised.

He looked up to see a fireball hurling down towards the earth from the sky. It shrieked as it fell in the distance, far away from Bimini. There was an almighty explosion and the earth shook.

Through the grey haze, Jen could see smoke rising far away into the sky. There was a sudden vibration. The earth was rising beneath his feet.

The haze was lifting.

At that moment Jen realised with certainty that he was completely in control of his own life and the pain left his stomach.

There is nothing to be afraid of. These people are trapped.

He began to walk forward, fully intent on returning the mask to where it belonged.

Sadana seemed drained of energy and was perspiring.

The other leaders noticed Jen walking towards them and they all frantically tried to get Sadana's attention. Jen noticed that the six leaders were all wearing Sig-lenses.

Jen was suddenly taken aback by an enormous screech overhead and looked up to see the silver eye of the translucent and molten dragon. Its long neck and body took up his entire field of view as he stared upwards with shock.

Jen could see Ignis's body clearly now. It was getting more solid. Its giant scales like sharp leaves, interwoven with dark green ridges that looked like mountain ranges. The creature's eye was giant and mesmerising, an intricate blend of every shade of grey imaginable. Jen thought he could see shining silver stars scattered throughout the reptilian eye. Its narrow pupil seemed to be sucking everything towards it and Jen suddenly felt himself being lifted upwards. He began to feel the shroud of anger wrap itself around his heart and he struggled to free himself from the powerful pull.

He looked down, trying to control his growing fright. He could hear the dragon in his mind, poisoning him with wrath and revenge. Images of all the men he had killed flashed across his eyes, twisting and torturing him. He felt an overpowering rage at the scheming leaders below. The feeling was nostalgic and self-consuming.

He saw the giant creature open its sickening mouth. A ball of red mist was swelling there. Then it combusted in a dramatic build-up of energy and was projected downwards at a supersonic speed. Jen saw it hurtle down towards an island in the distance, and on impact, the island was obliterated. A mushroom of fire and smoke plumed into the air. The waves of the ocean rose up in protest at the violence.

At first Jen felt hatred but then, all emotions left him and he felt powerless, open to death.

At that moment, he felt a presence by his side. Something tickled his fingers. It felt like an animal gently licking his fingertips. The sensation seemed to release him from the consuming pull of the dragon's eye. He began to plummet. Time slowed down as he landed on the earth with a bump. His entire skeleton vibrated as it absorbed the shock of the fall.

'Get up,' Jen heard in his head as he tried to shrug off the impact. 'We are here with you.'

He felt the mask was still in his hand. The stone around his neck was pulsating profusely, jolting him with grounded energy.

Jen sprung to his feet and ran forward, not looking up. He passed

Archibold and Sadana with agility. He saw the green statue ahead. It looked beautiful, the face of an angel smiling with peace. He reached out his arm with the mask and held it up, feeling the pull of the mask to its bearer.

He could see something moving within the statue.

Freedom seemed inevitable.

Then, unexpectedly, he felt the heavy blow of an arm in his face. He hit the ground heavily and with a sharp pain in his cheek. He looked up to see Rekesh staring down at him in a robot-like fashion. His eyes were vacant, like the life had been drained from them.

"Rekesh!" Jen gasped. "What are you doing? We have to stop this!"

The shell of a man before him did not answer. Jen felt so overwhelmed that he could not think. Then he heard the shriek of another fireball. It was so close that Jen could feel the scorching heat as it burnt through the air.

Despair filled him as the fireball landed in the sea close by with a brutal impact. Then, the greatest of waves rose up into the sky. The ocean swelled like a great creature breathing heavily. Water was everywhere, raining down from the sky and visible as tall waves all around.

The earth shook violently and a jagged fissure appeared close by, causing several trees to collapse and fall into the depths of the island. Dust spewed into the air.

At that moment, Jen's perception changed. Time slowed down. He could see things that he previously could not. There were beings everywhere that looked like hazy blobs of light. He could see that the trees looked different. They were magnified by a surrounding aura of pink light. Jen felt the pull of the earth stone around his neck.

He then became aware of something that sent an intense shiver down his spine. He looked with horror at Sadana to see two black wings coming from behind the malevolent leader.

Then, a hideous being stepped from the shadows, its crooked body stretching upwards with caution. It looked like a giant deformed bird with a more human stance and face. The sight was so hideous that Jen instantly froze with primal fear. He knew that the worlds of existence were merging.

'Morbis.' The name of the creature was whispered to him.

Sadana seemed to be in a hypnotic state, unaware of what was happening around him. Morbis took two terrifying steps forward on her giant claws.

The unearthly birdlike being flapped her wings and rose high into the sky, shrieking in a most revolting pitch. The nauseating sound sent tremors through Jen's stomach. A memory came to him, a memory of being chased through the jungles of Aradonas. He remembered those mesmerising black wings, watching him.

The owl woman peered down at Jen from above. The sight of her was magnetic and though Jen wanted to look away, he could not.

The island shook as great waves crashed on its shores. Jen was flung backwards as the ground beneath him trembled aggressively. The presence of Ignis and Morbis, watching the destruction from above, invoked a deep-set sensation of doom within his chest as he lay in the broken ground.

The mask was nowhere to be seen, thrown during the turmoil. He felt dominated and submissive. The destruction continued around him as water and earth sprayed into the sky. He felt the piercing glare of the owl-like humanoid penetrating him from the sky above.

Then, the owl woman was choking him from far away.

Jen could not breathe. Morbis was flapping her wings. The air was leaving his lungs. Her eyes contained the void of death. The monstrous dragon above screeched and Jen saw fire in the sky.

It's the end of the world, he thought as tears flowed from his eyes.

With no air in his lungs, Jen was fading.

Then he heard a voice. It was a most trustful voice, the gentle voice of a woman.

"Jen. These creatures are lost. They have been consumed by darkness. You must spread the light. Spread the light through Aova. Spread the light through water."

The warm tears poured down his cheeks. The sensation somehow sent Jen into a state of awakening. He felt love and all pain left his body.

The atmosphere was lightening and he could see more beings appearing all around him. They look like glowing eggs of light, shimmering with pink and peach shining patterns. He could feel the eggs reaching out to him, tickling him around the navel area. He felt the same sensation of an animal licking his fingertips.

And then all of a sudden, Morbis was no longer strangling him from the sky. She was back behind Sadana, cowering in a pitiful way.

"Now move!" the voice said to him.

Jen looked at the statue. Rekesh was close by. The other five leaders were all sprawled out on the floor in terror. Rekesh had picked up the mask and was holding it tightly in his hand.

Jen got to his feet. He sprung forward like a buck, running quickly towards the statue without thinking. His body had taken over.

Ignis was above, her unearthly presence exerting unbearable pressure.

"I will not fight you, Rekesh," Jen said loudly as he drew near to the vacant man before him. Rekesh was staring forward but at nothing specific, not even Jen.

"Forgive him, Jen," a woman's voice was saying to him. "Love cannot exist without forgiveness. I have forgiven him."

Jen looked down. The stone around his neck was glowing intensely, like the brightest of stars. It was lifting him up, making him stronger.

Rekesh lunged towards him unexpectedly and Jen jumped high into the air. He seemed to be suspended there, watching Rekesh fly by within hand's reach below. Jen landed on his feet with the agility of a cat.

Rekesh rolled and turned around, sadness and despair in his eyes. He lunged forward again but Jen grabbed him and held him close, hugging him so tightly that he could not move. Rekesh struggled to wriggle free but he could not break Jen's strong embrace. Eventually, he stopped struggling.

There was a piercing roar from above. Ignis seemed infuriated.

Fire oozed from her snout.

Jen saw another ghostly ball of intense red energy forming in the great dragon's mouth. It suddenly burst into flames and she seemed to spit it down towards the earth. In that moment, Jen knew he had to act. He felt that he had lost his human form and was now an animal, having to react instinctively to survive his predator's onslaught.

The ethereal fireball was heading straight towards them from the sky above. In that terrifying moment, Jen thought he saw an eye in that fireball. It was an eye lacking any life, an eye of pure annihilation. Jen was sure he had glimpsed death in that very moment.

Jen released his grip from Rekesh and in a swift movement, took the mask out of his hand. The movement was so precise that Rekesh involuntarily opened his hand.

Without hesitation, Jen sprung forward, arm outstretched towards the jade statue. It was floating above the ground, glowing intensely. Millions of filaments of light were energetically flowing throughout the statue's body.

As Jen lunged forward with the heavy presence of Ignis and the fireball above, he felt a magnetic force between the mask and the statue. It suddenly flew out of his hand, majestically wavering itself onto the statue's face.

As it connected, the mask seemed to melt into the same beautiful expression of oneness and love. Jen fell back as a surreal shockwave emanated from the space the statue was occupying.

The statue disappeared in an all-encompassing light and in its place emerged the slender and supple body of a large horse. It was pale blue and white, its long tail swaying like gentle waves in the sea.

Jen saw that Aova's eyes were round pools of pure water. As soon as he gazed into those beautiful eyes, he felt every emotion possible flood through his body. He wanted to weep and laugh at the same time. He wanted to be fearful of the fireball above. He wanted to get angry with the six leaders yet he wanted to love and forgive them as well. He wanted to enjoy all the riches he had encountered and yet be still as a rock. He wanted to take nothing from life and he wanted to love everything.

Tears formed in his eyes as the muscular creature looked upwards gracefully. Water streamed from Aova's eyes as if she were crying for every travesty that had every occurred.

Time had stopped and all fears dissipated.

Aova's eyes reflected Ignis and the fireball in the sky. Then she began to glow with a divine white light.

Jen felt water on his face. It was soon soaking through his clothes. He realised the water was in the air, suspended there with weightlessness. The dragon above seemed stunned now, like it had seen itself in a mirror and was petrified at the sight.

Jen looked around slowly in an overwhelmed state. The six leaders were all soaked and seemed to be in shock. They all looked like a lightning bolt had struck them in their hearts. They were shaking, their expressions blank and vacant.

Water was everywhere, floating through the air in huge droplets. Then, it seemed to form more of a swirling pattern. From Jen's perspective, it looked like he was on the inside of a giant cone whose walls were made of swirling waterfalls.

Great droplets the size of his body splashed around him.

The sight lasted only for a few moments.

Suddenly, it felt like the world had exploded with water and light. Water flooded upwards at an incredible rate. It was everywhere and created an almighty suction. The cone had changed shape and now looked more like a pyramid from the inside, its walls growing straighter with the intensity of the flow of water.

Jen had to hold onto a thick tree root protruding from the broken ground to stop himself from being sucked upwards.

Looking at the six leaders, they were all floating through the air. Each one was terrified, screaming out in fear for their life.

Jen felt no such emotion, only feeling wonder at what was happening. An opening was forming at the top of the water pyramid, revealing the cosmos, so full of stars it was blinding. The fireball and dragon were nothing but stars.

The water was falling now, like the heaviest of tropical rainstorms, hot and cleansing. The suction had stopped and the leaders came hurling back to the ground.

"Uhhghhgg!!" Constynce cried out as he hit the ground with a thud nearby.

It rained profusely, soaking into the earth until it became a swampland. Sludge and globules of mud flew everywhere, covering Jen from head to foot. Looking up only gave witness to a deluge.

Jen felt himself sinking and held onto the strong tree roots that had somehow remained at the surface. His face was covered with water and mud. He could not see anymore. He felt the earth stone lifting him up.

Then, the rain began to stop and the clouds above separated.

Jen wiped the thick mud from his eyes and nose, gasping for breath. He slowly regained his vision. He looked around slowly.

The air was thick with moisture.

Aova was nowhere to be seen. The horse had vanished and the environment felt very different.

Jen had a raw instinct that he was standing on a much bigger landscape than he had been previously. He looked up and Ignis was nowhere to be seen. It was dark with hundreds of stars shining brightly in the sky. It was the clearest night Jen had ever witnessed.

Rekesh lay unconscious on the floor, covered in mud. There was no trace of the statue and the six leaders were sprawled around the cavern. Jen got to his feet. He fought to keep his balance against the sliding mud. He saw Archibold Constynce trying to sit up close by. He looked injured and delirious.

"You meddlesome fool," Archibold croaked as he tried to push his crooked body into an upright position. "It has taken years to summon such a beast."

Then he coughed and laughed in a pathetic and deranged way. Jen felt sorry for him, upset that such a destructive entity was so important to him. Jen quickly realised that all six leaders were the same, lost in the extremes of power.

"Don't you realise how many people you are hurting?" Jen said sternly. "So much destruction has happened... What for?"

"Our father and his children feed off destruction," Archibold replied dejectedly. "We are nothing compared to those above us. If you had known your place, you would now be witnessing true power, the one true power."

Then, an intense look of vulnerability appeared on Archibold's face. He was frightened, staring straight ahead to the left of where Jen was standing.

Jen realised that he was not alone. He looked to his left to see Aova, the beautiful horse of love and water. Its strong supple body was emitting a hazy light. There was someone else standing next to the ethereal equine being.

Jen saw a creature like no other. It was a foal of pure energy.

Its fur was fiery and warming and its presence was changing everything. It was the picture of innocence, a vision of devotion and oneness. In the space in which the foal occupied, it felt to Jen like there were millions of worlds joined together. The sensations he was feeling could only be described as perfectly harmonious.

Archibold was enamoured, staring at the young creature with infatuation. His heart was glowing like an orb and he had begun to look younger. As Jen looked with awe at how the Lengardian King's disposition had changed, he felt another presence above to his left.

He looked at Aova to see that someone was sitting upon her. It was a beautiful woman, glowing with love and light. It was the woman of light.

"Elera..." Jen felt himself say.

The woman of light was looking at Rekesh, who seemed to be stirring from the calamitous events that had just taken place.

Jen turned his attention to Rekesh. He was getting to his feet and looked lost and frustrated. He looked around blindly, like he had just woken up from a nightmare.

Then he saw her.

Jen had never seen such an extreme transformation in someone's appearance. Rekesh's facial expression went from one of suffering and sheer grief to the epithet of joy and love. Seeing Elera had changed him instantly. He smiled beautifully at her and his eyes flooded with tears. He looked like a young man, full of vitality.

At that moment Jen realised the enormity of the loss that Rekesh had suffered. His face was tranquil now, at peace with himself and life. Then Jen perceived a strange occurrence. He realised that Rekesh was actually lying unconscious in the mud. It looked like another copy of Rekesh had stepped out of the lifeless body lying there on the ground. The double began to walk peacefully towards Elera.

She slowly slid down from Aova's supple back and walked towards him. They met not far from where Jen was standing and touched each other with loving affection. They stood silently in a perfect embrace, light emanating from both of them. They looked like one being. An ethereal egg-shaped aura could be seen surrounding them.

Aova and the foal walked towards the couple and touched them on their arms with their soft noses. The energy egg that surrounded Elera and Rekesh expanded to encapsulate Aova and the foal.

Together, they looked like a perfect family.

The aura of the egg expanded, shimmering with the colours of the rainbow. As it touched Jen, he felt unity with everything that existed, a oneness so pure that he felt like his entire being had faded away and love was all that remained.

At Roundfire we publish great stories. We lean towards the spiritual and thought-provoking. But whether it's literary or popular, a gentle tale or a pulsating thriller, the connecting theme in all Roundfire fiction titles is that once you pick them up you won't want to put them down.